QUEST FOR THE KINGDOMS

REY TERCIERO
MEGAN KEARNEY
COLORS BY MEAGHAN CARTER

An Imprint of HarperCollinsPublishers

PART 1

BLOOM

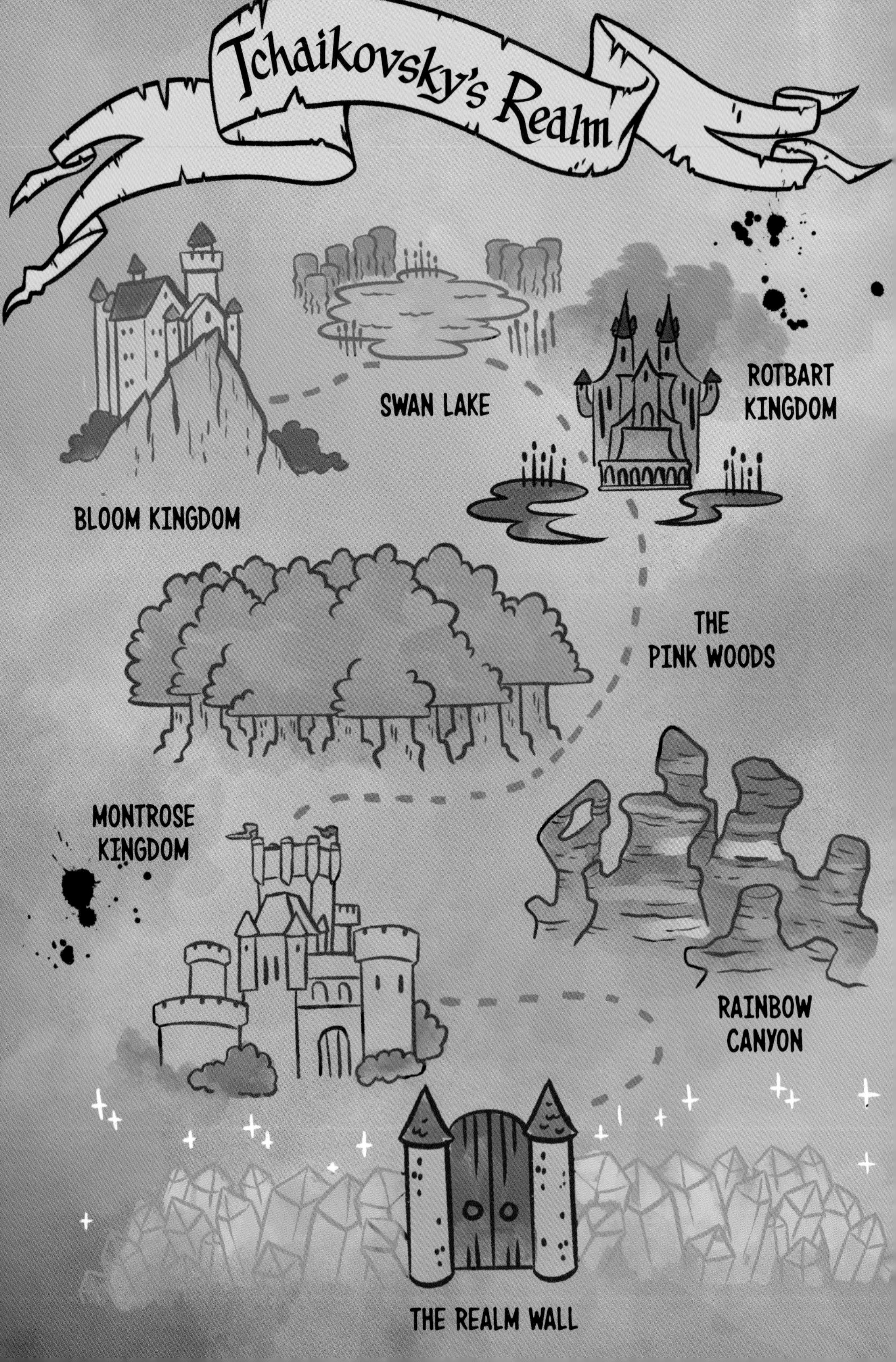
Tchaikovsky's Realm
SWAN LAKE
ROTBART KINGDOM
BLOOM KINGDOM
THE PINK WOODS
MONTROSE KINGDOM
RAINBOW CANYON
THE REALM WALL

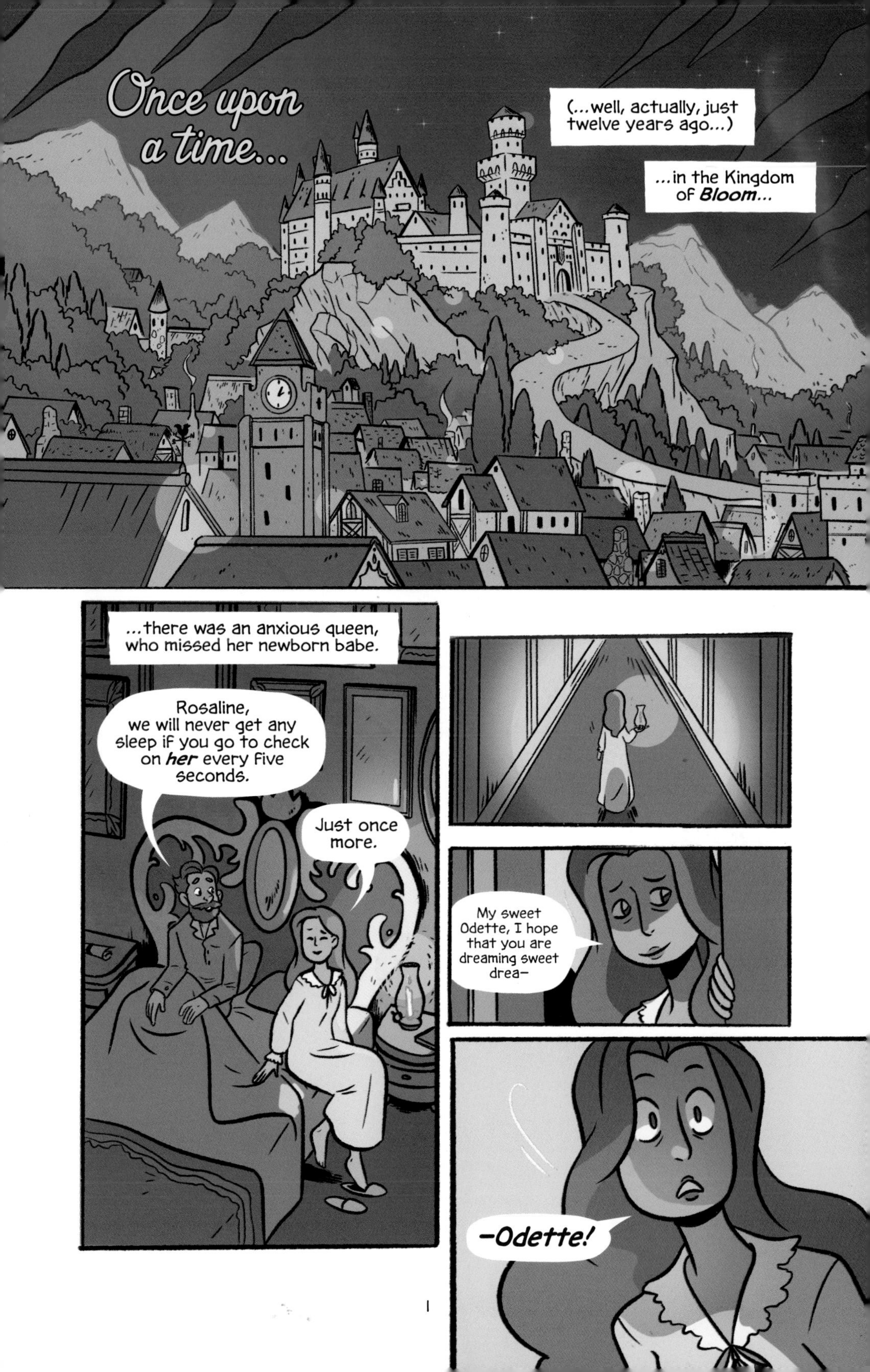
Once upon a time...
(...well, actually, just twelve years ago...)
...in the Kingdom of Bloom...
...there was an anxious queen, who missed her newborn babe.
Rosaline, we will never get any sleep if you go to check on her every five seconds.
Just once more.
My sweet Odette, I hope that you are dreaming sweet drea—
—Odette!

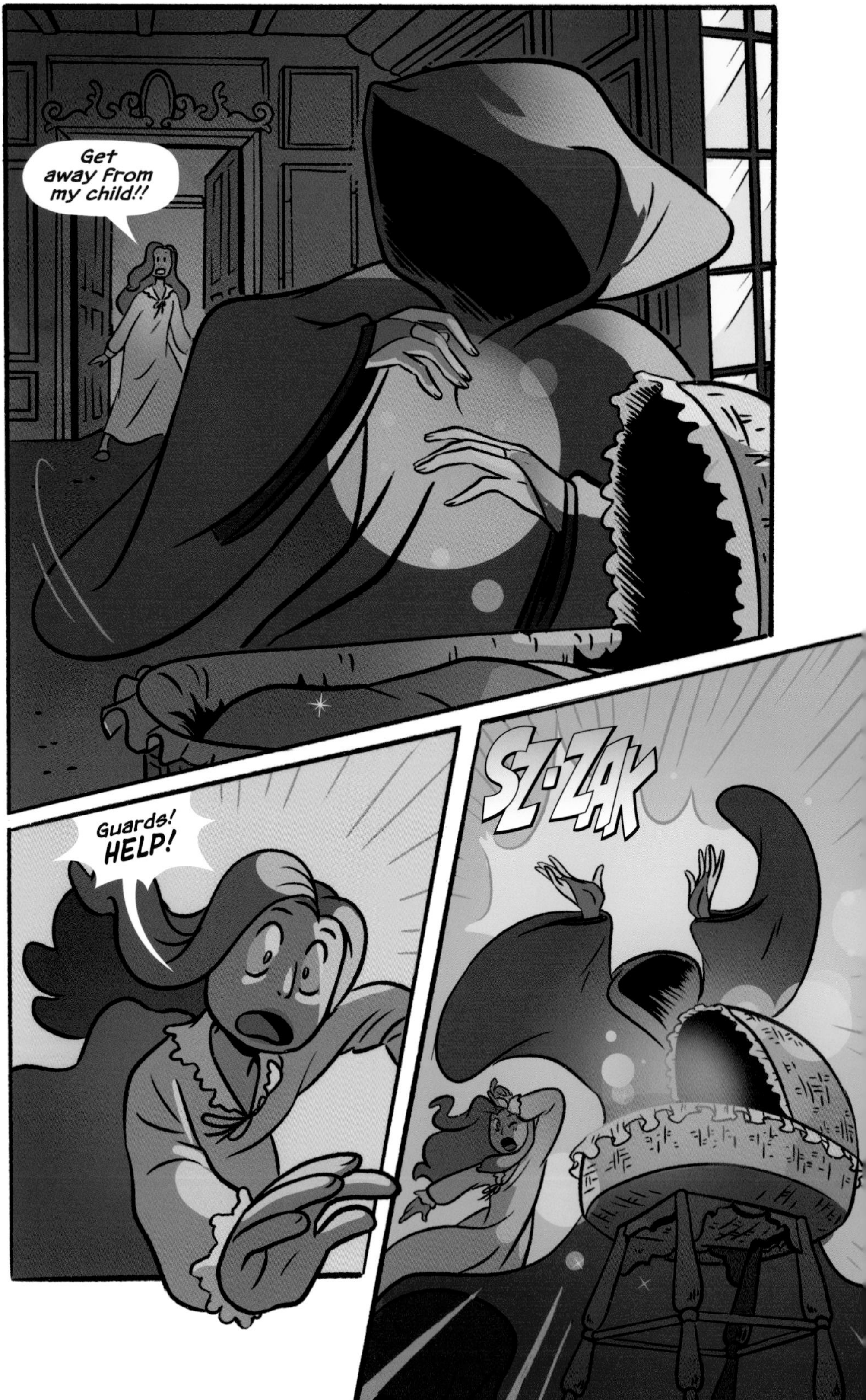
Get away from my child!!
Guards! HELP!
SZ-ZAK

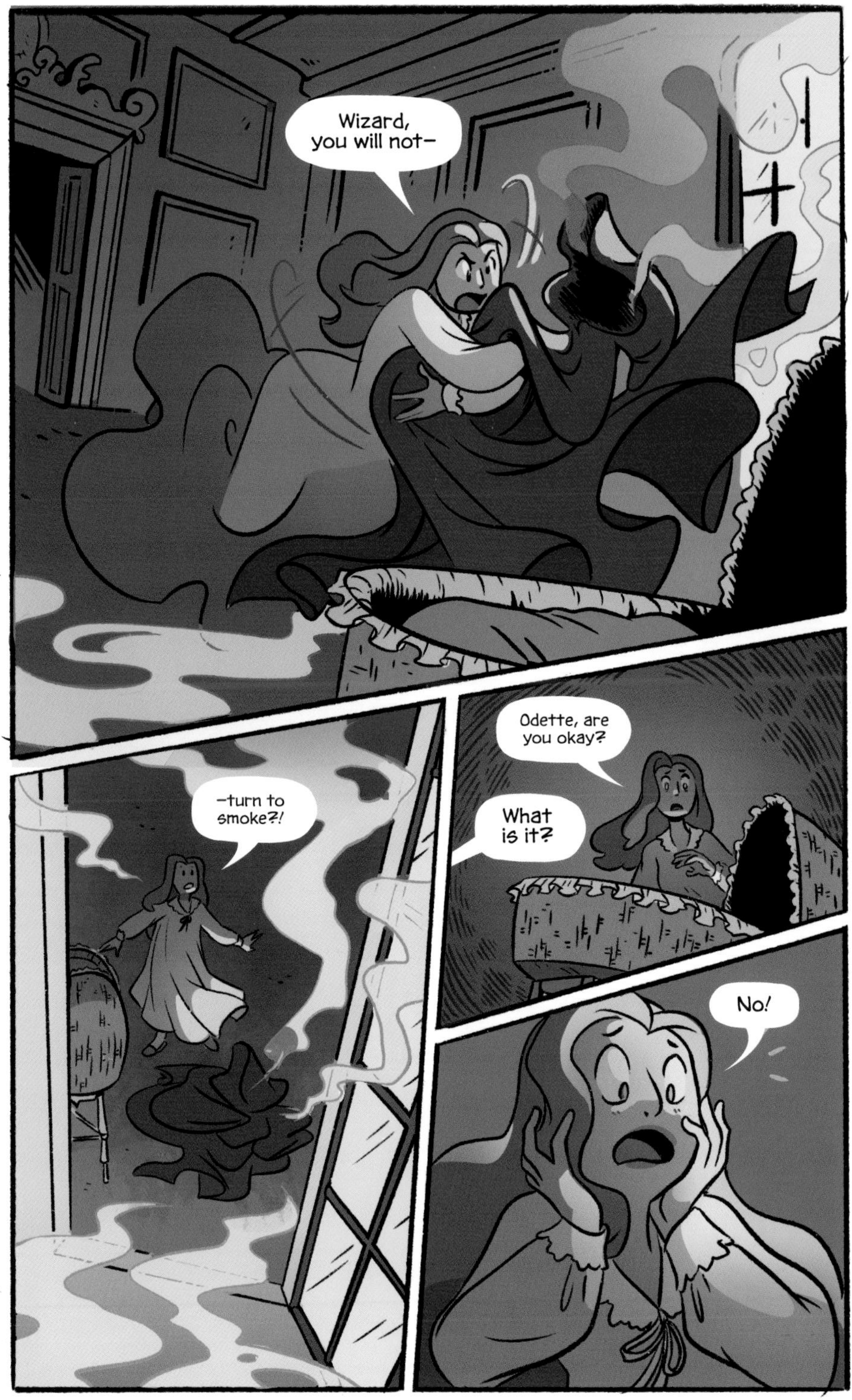

Wizard, you will not–
–turn to smoke?!
Odette, are you okay?
What is it?
No!

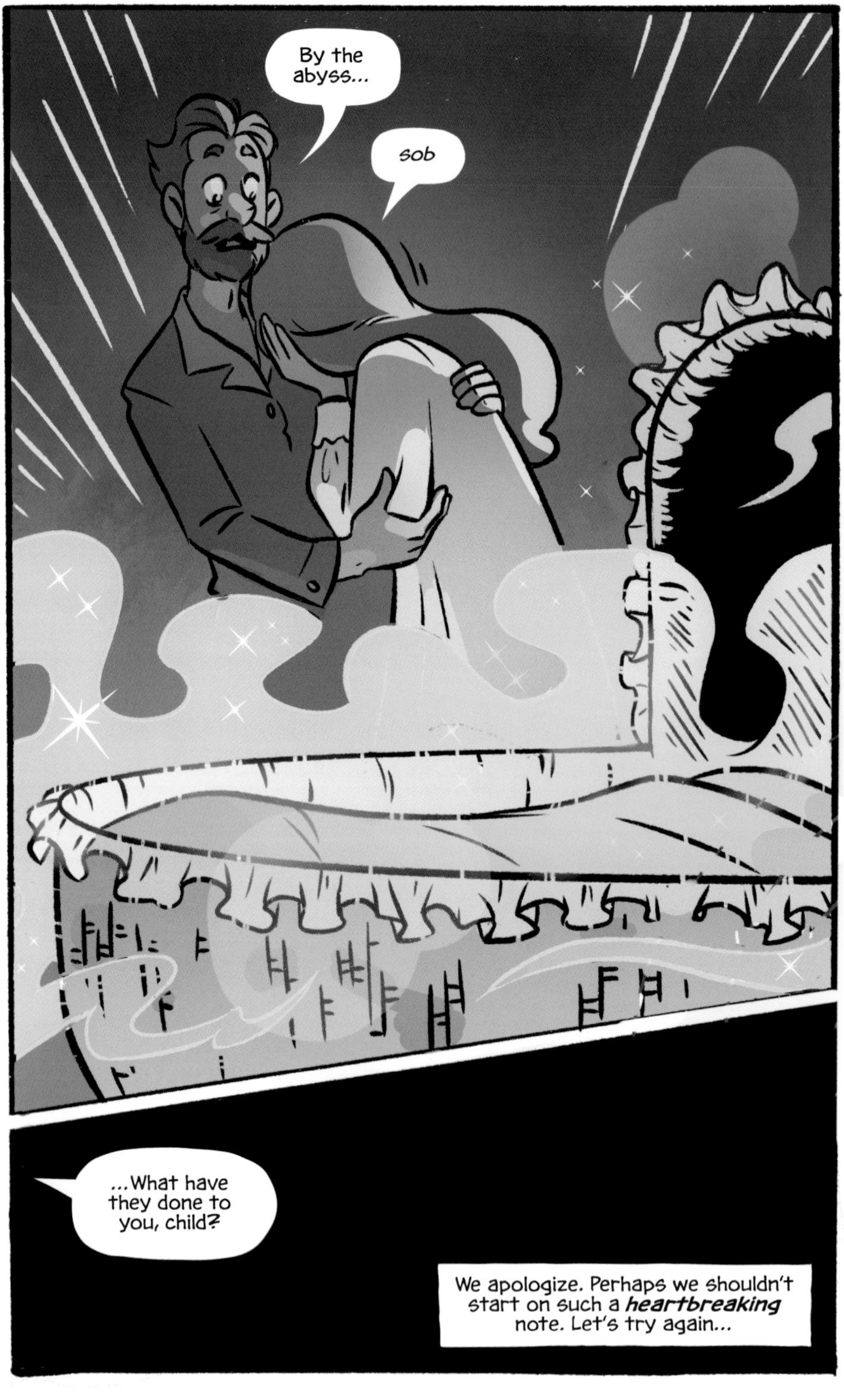
By the abyss...
sob
...What have they done to you, child?
We apologize. Perhaps we shouldn't start on such a ***heartbreaking*** note. Let's try again...

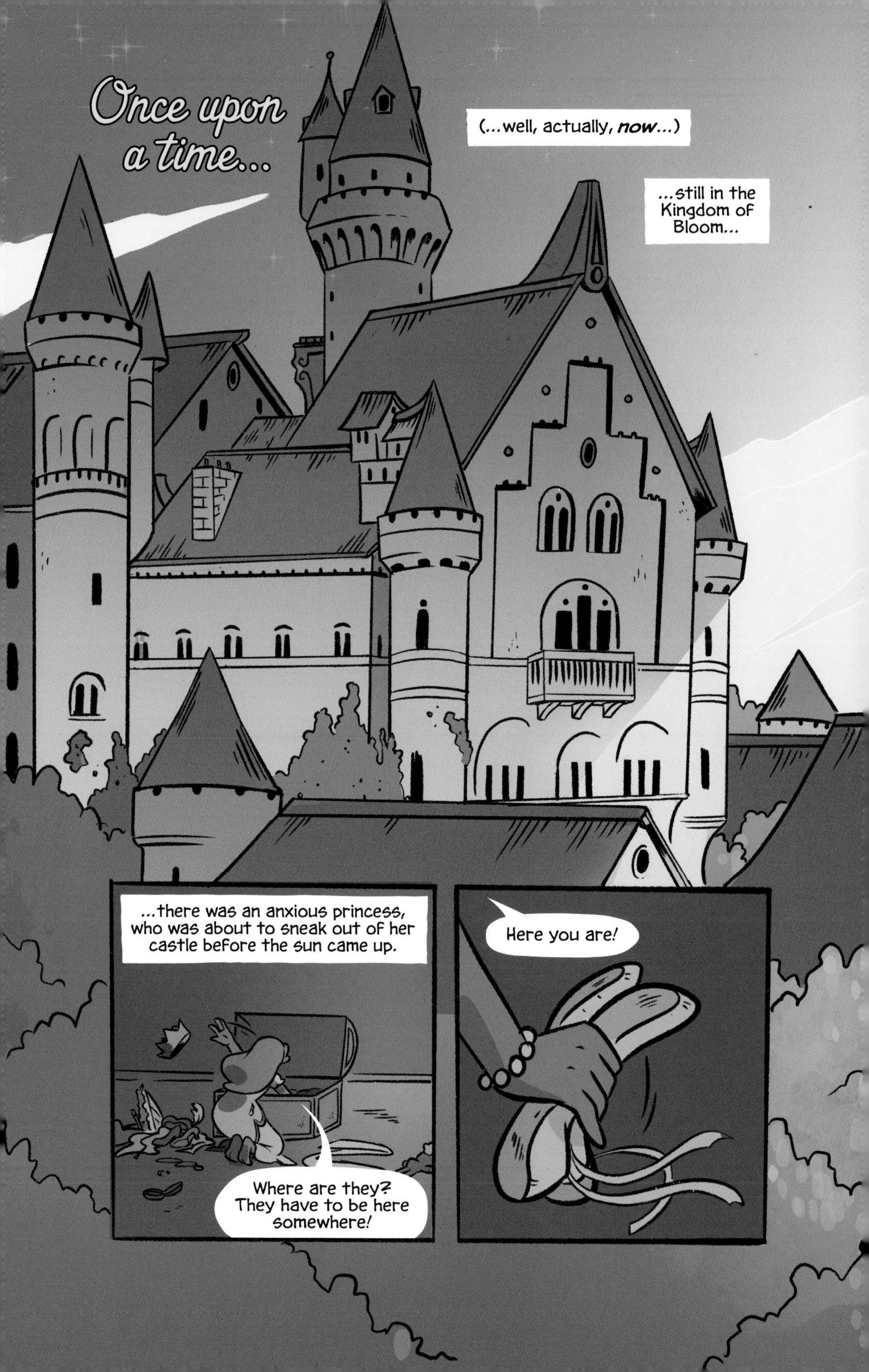
Once upon a time...
(...well, actually, now...)
...still in the Kingdom of Bloom...
...there was an anxious princess, who was about to sneak out of her castle before the sun came up.
Where are they? They have to be here somewhere!
Here you are!

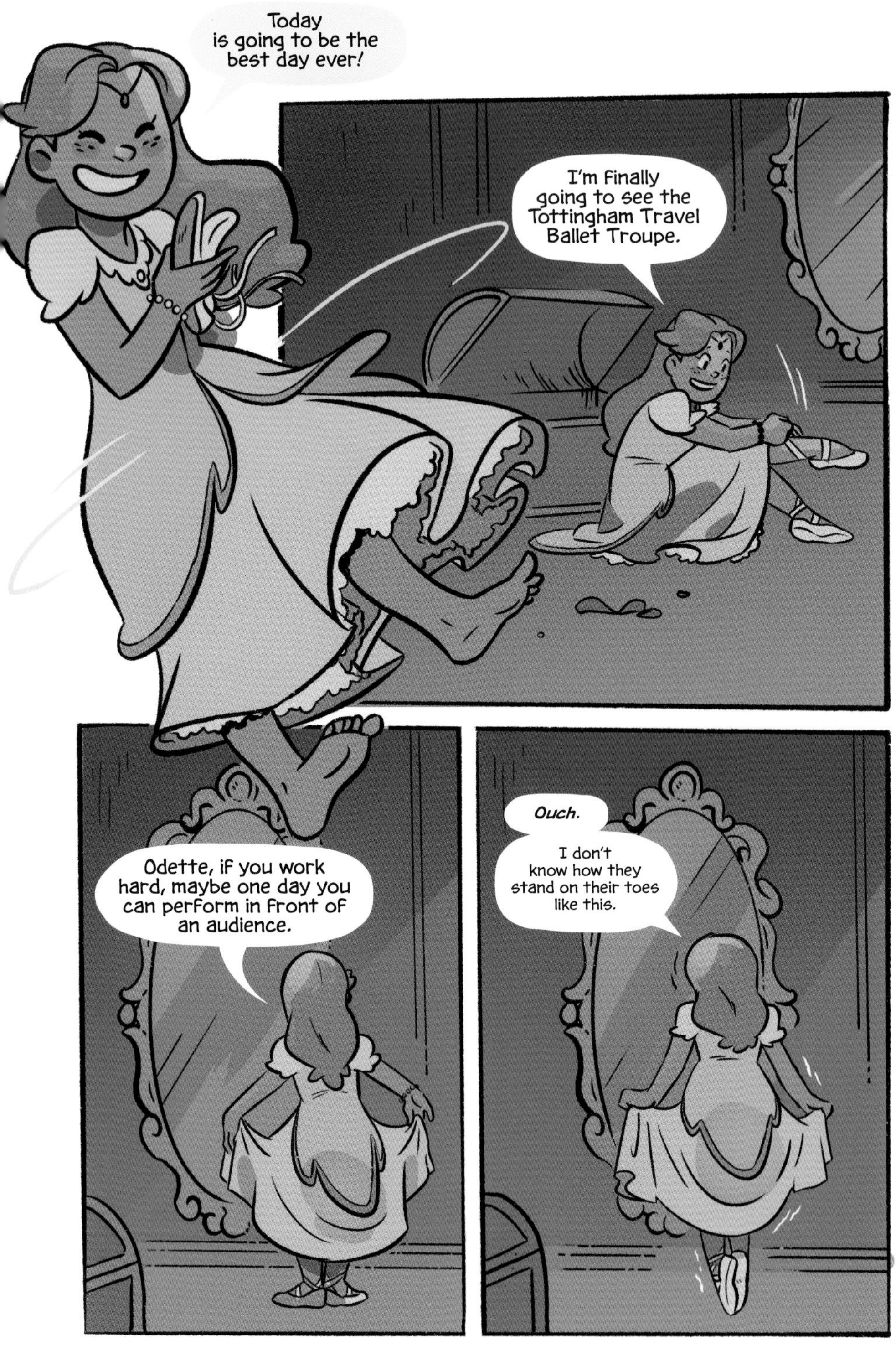
Today is going to be the best day ever!
I'm finally going to see the Tottingham Travel Ballet Troupe.
Odette, if you work hard, maybe one day you can perform in front of an audience.
Ouch.
I don't know how they stand on their toes like this.

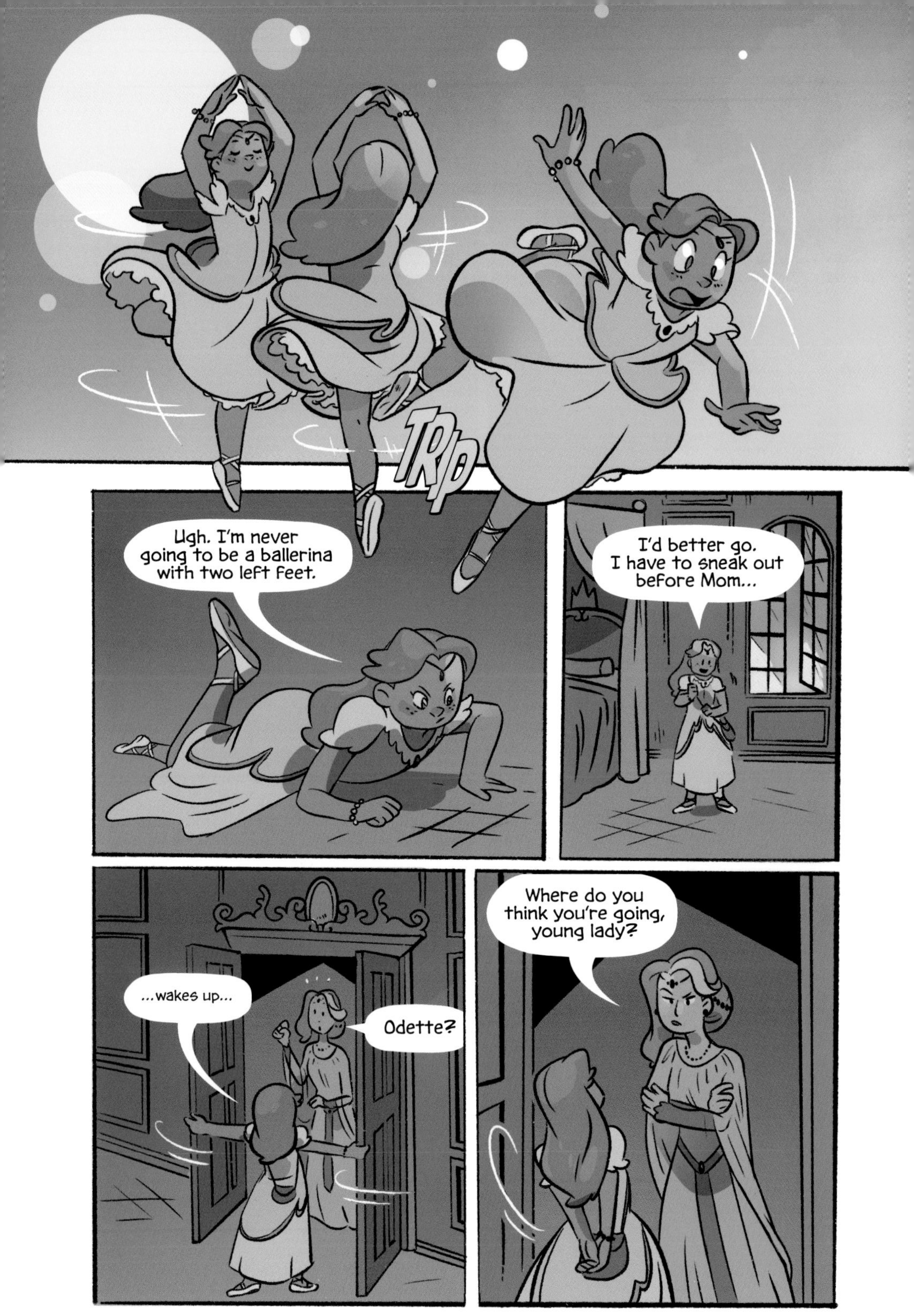
TRIP
Ugh. I'm never going to be a ballerina with two left feet.
I'd better go. I have to sneak out before Mom...
...wakes up...
Odette?
Where do you think you're going, young lady?

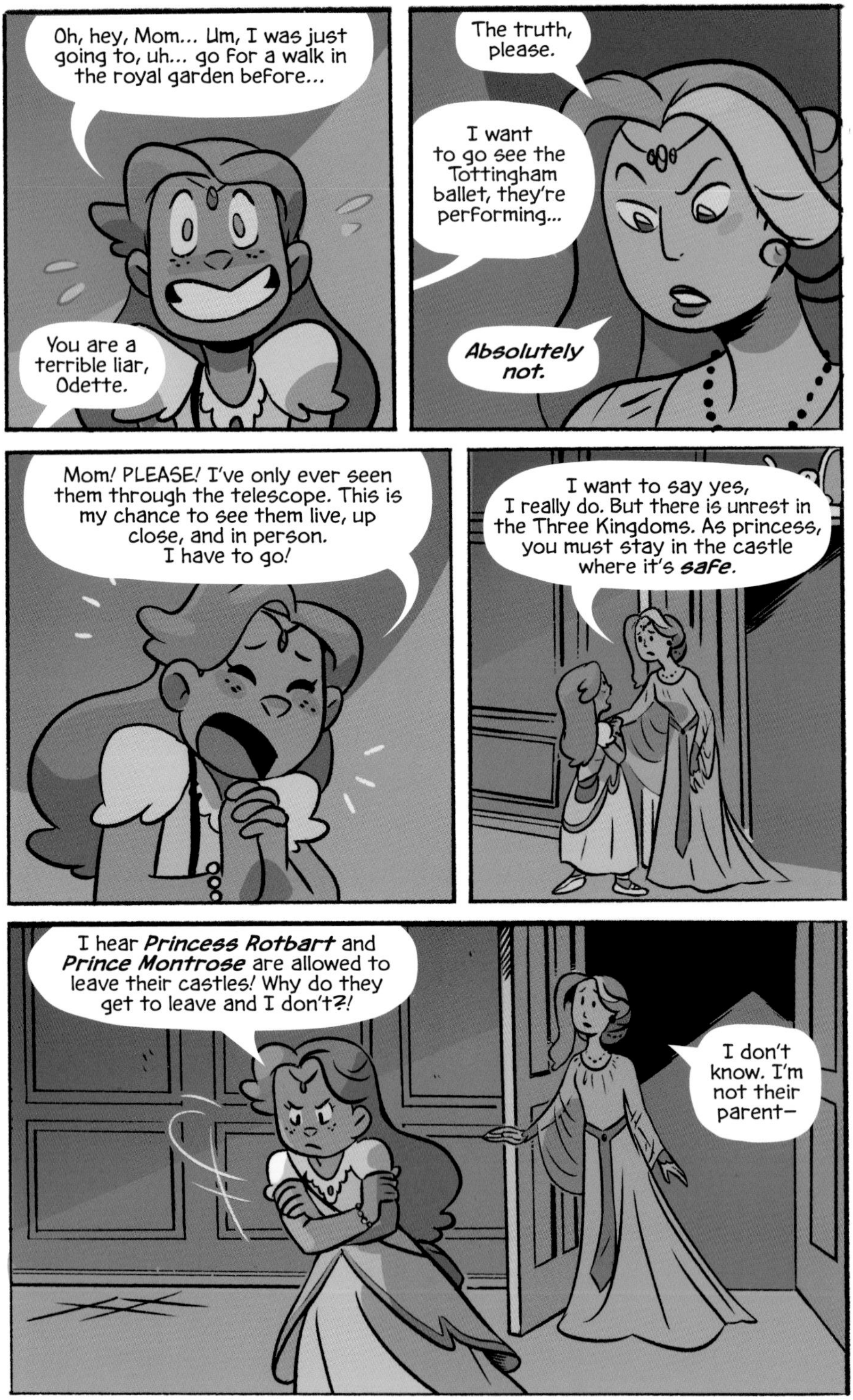
Oh, hey, Mom... Um, I was just going to, uh... go for a walk in the royal garden before...
You are a terrible liar, Odette.
The truth, please.
I want to go see the Tottingham ballet, they're performing...
Absolutely not.
Mom! PLEASE! I've only ever seen them through the telescope. This is my chance to see them live, up close, and in person. I have to go!
I want to say yes, I really do. But there is unrest in the Three Kingdoms. As princess, you must stay in the castle where it's safe.
I hear Princess Rotbart and Prince Montrose are allowed to leave their castles! Why do they get to leave and I don't?!
I don't know. I'm not their parent—

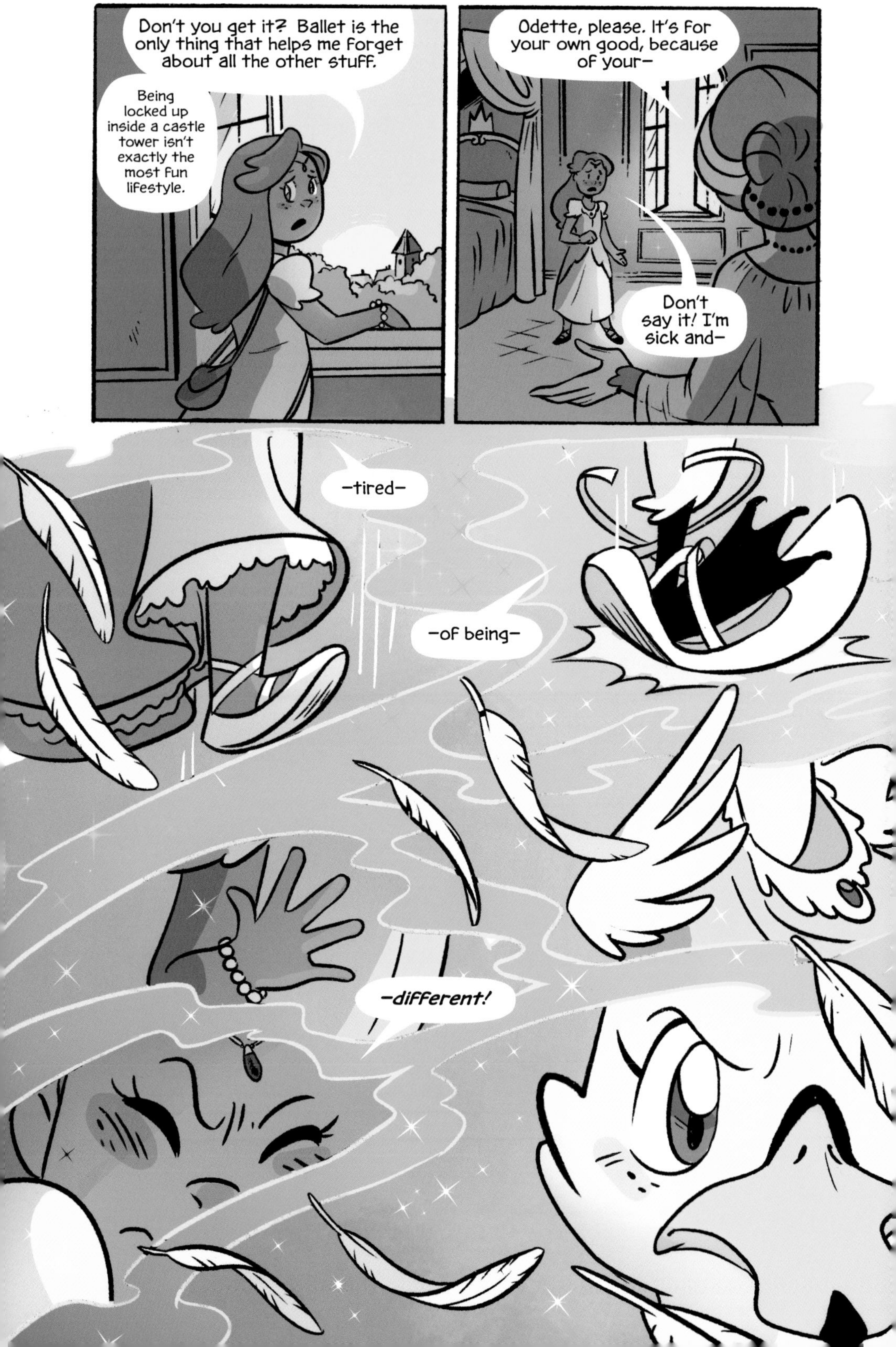
Don't you get it? Ballet is the only thing that helps me forget about all the other stuff.
Being locked up inside a castle tower isn't exactly the most fun lifestyle.
Odette, please. It's for your own good, because of your—
Don't say it! I'm sick and—
—tired—
—of being—
—different!

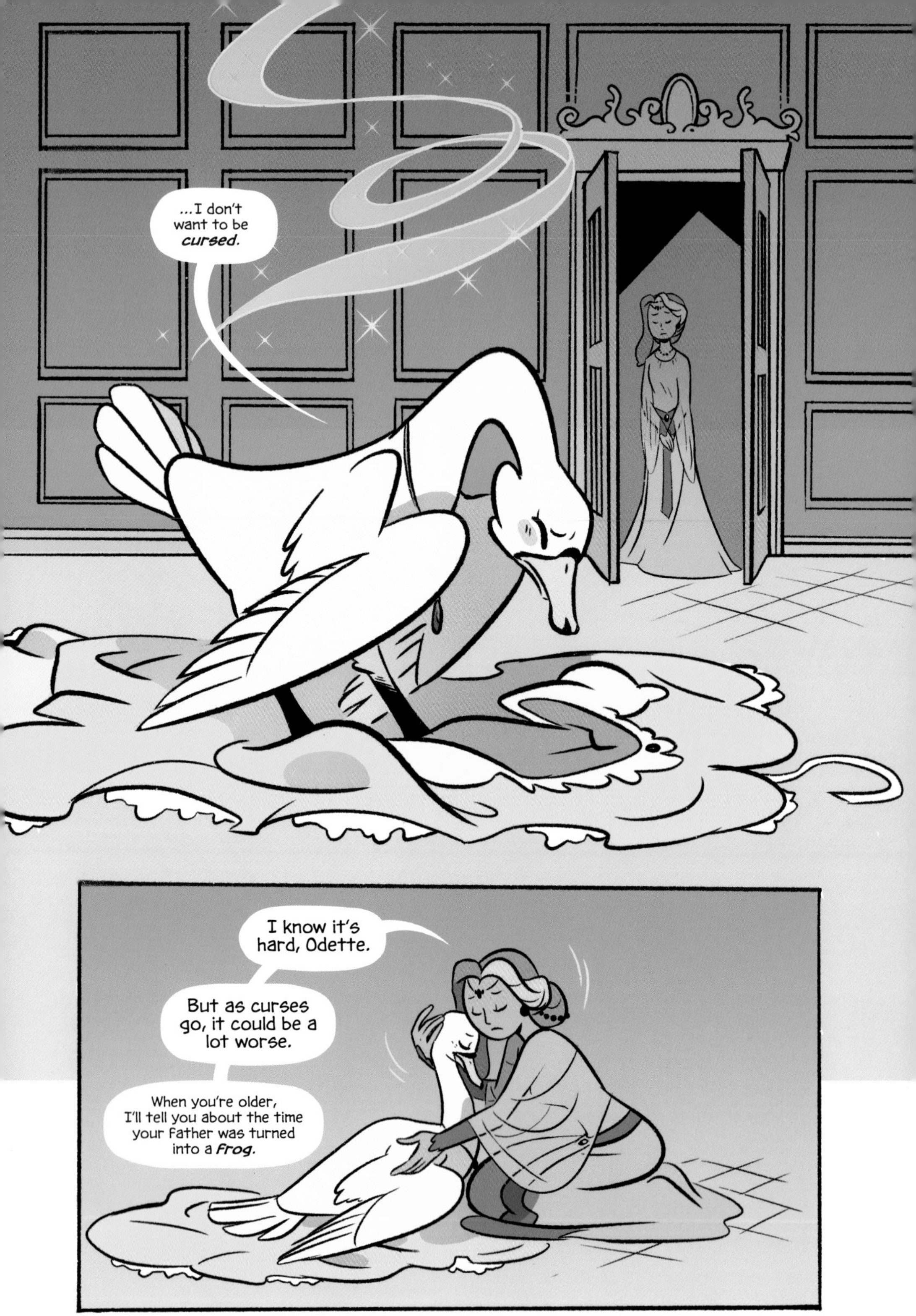
...I don't want to be *cursed*.
I know it's hard, Odette.
But as curses go, it could be a lot worse.
When you're older, I'll tell you about the time your father was turned into a *frog*.

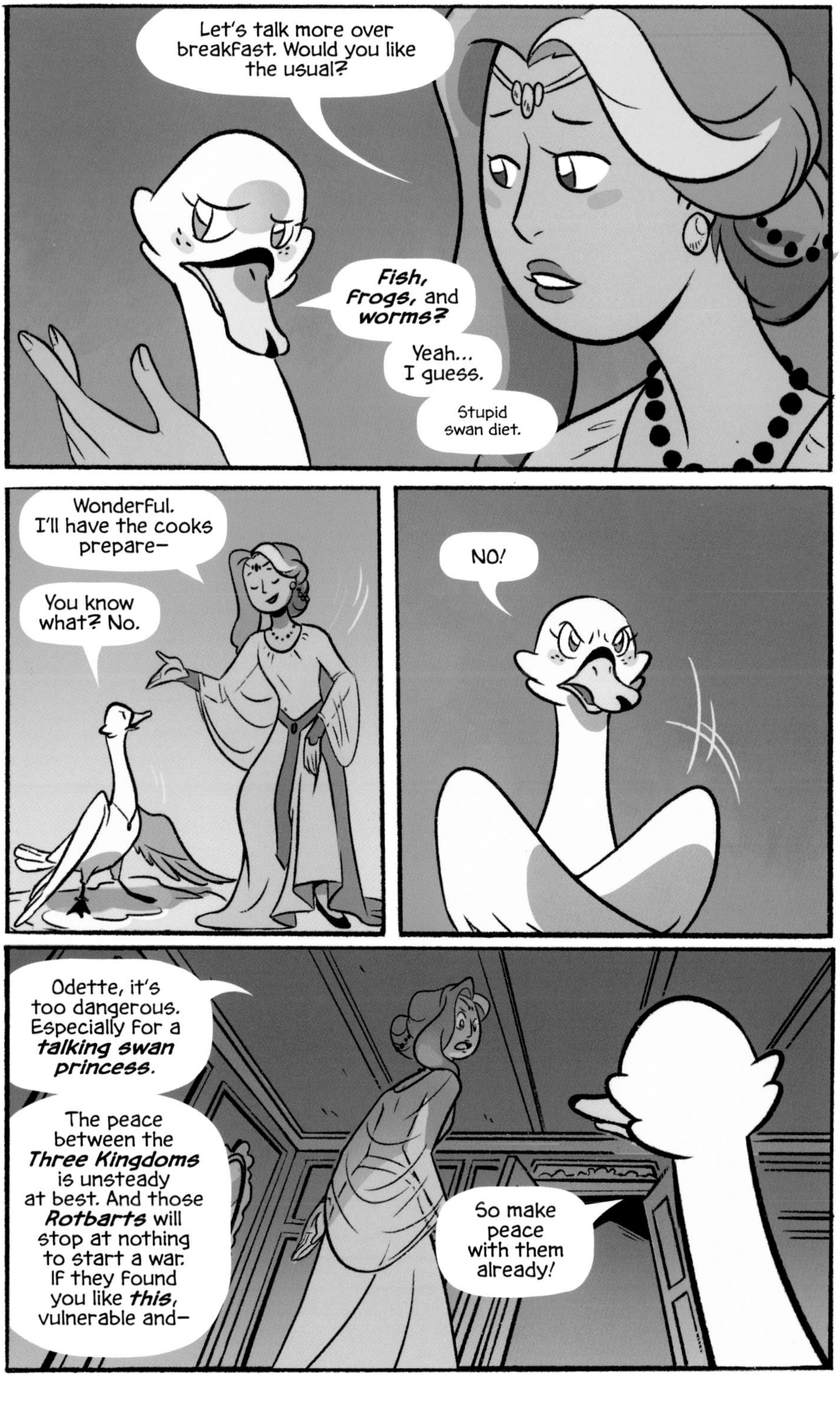
Let's talk more over breakfast. Would you like the usual?
Fish, frogs, and worms?
Yeah... I guess.
Stupid swan diet.
Wonderful. I'll have the cooks prepare–
You know what? No.
NO!
Odette, it's too dangerous. Especially for a talking swan princess.
The peace between the Three Kingdoms is unsteady at best. And those Rotbarts will stop at nothing to start a war. If they found you like this, vulnerable and–
So make peace with them already!

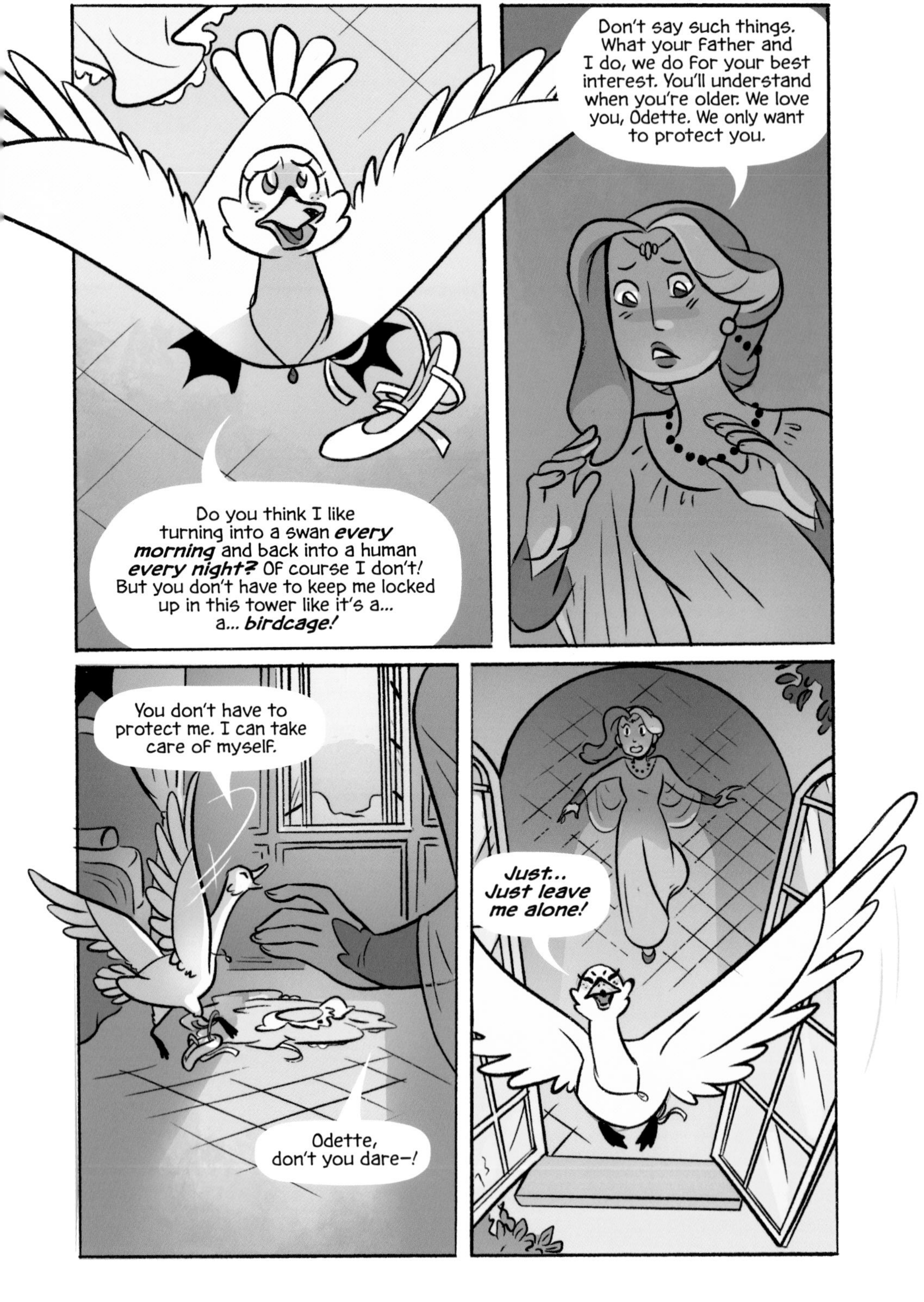
Do you think I like turning into a swan *every morning* and back into a human *every night?* Of course I don't! But you don't have to keep me locked up in this tower like it's a... a... *birdcage!*
Don't say such things. What your father and I do, we do for your best interest. You'll understand when you're older. We love you, Odette. We only want to protect you.
You don't have to protect me. I can take care of myself.
Odette, don't you dare-!
Just... Just leave me alone!

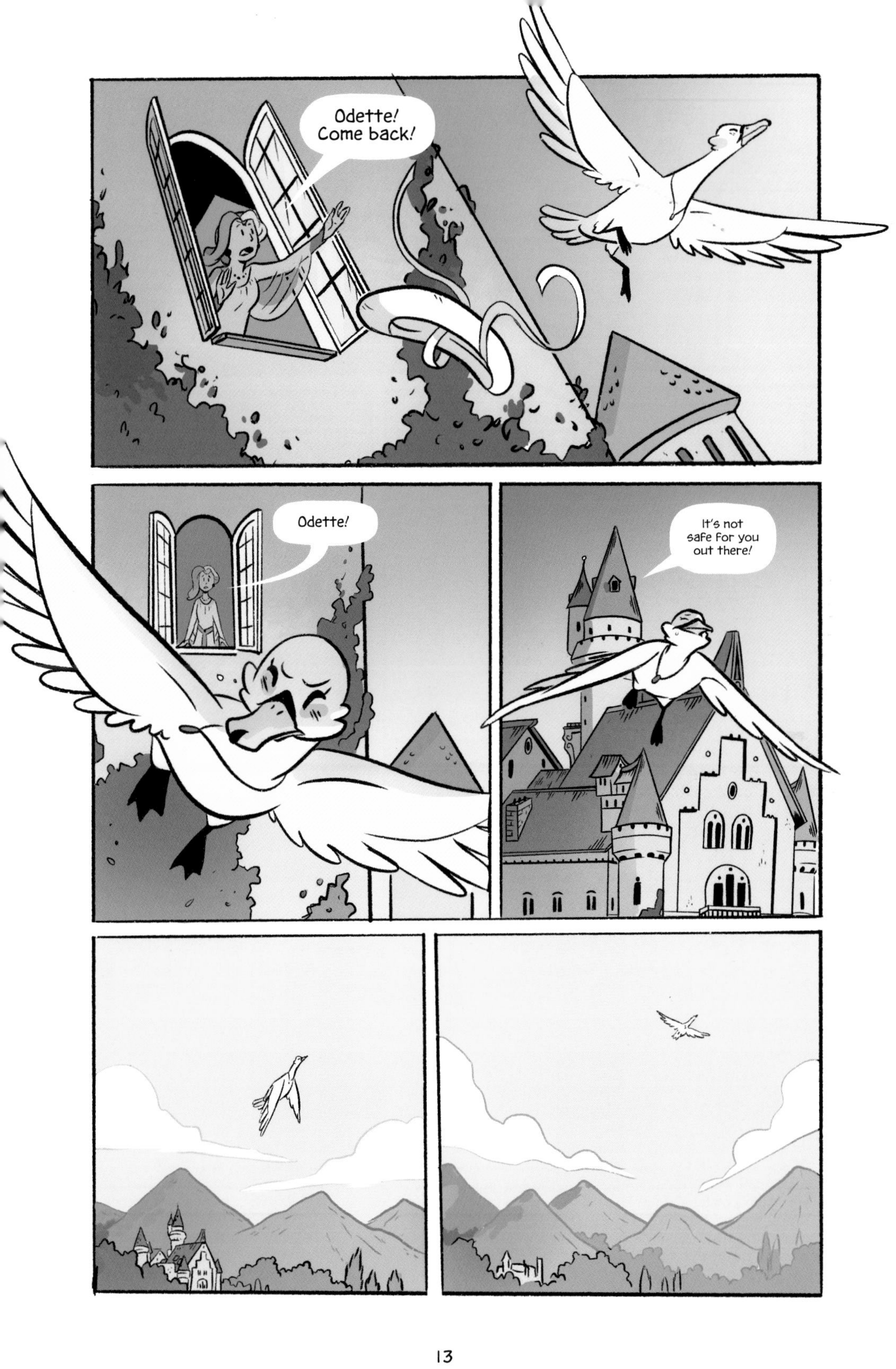
Odette! Come back!
Odette!
It's not safe for you out there!

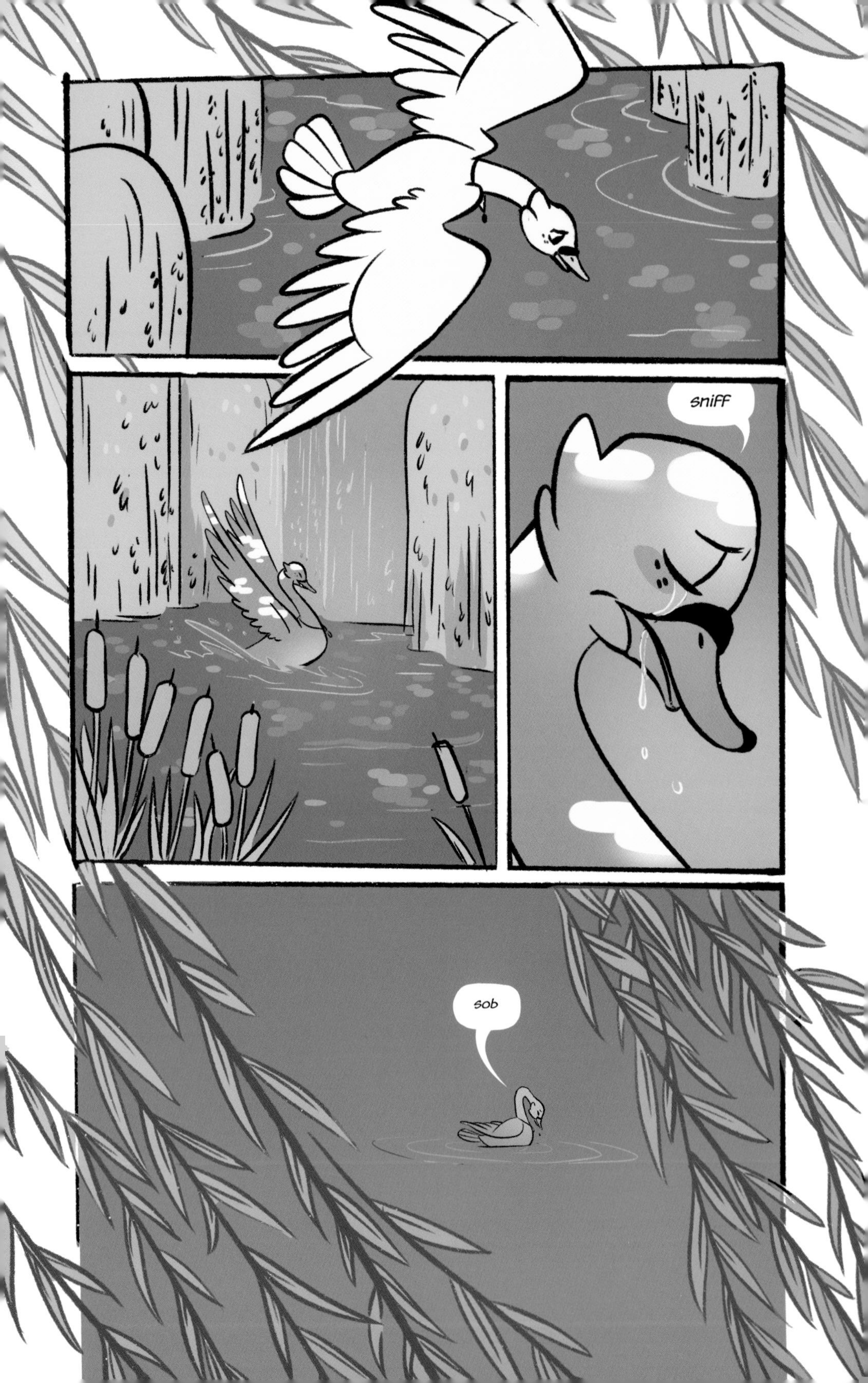
sniff
sob

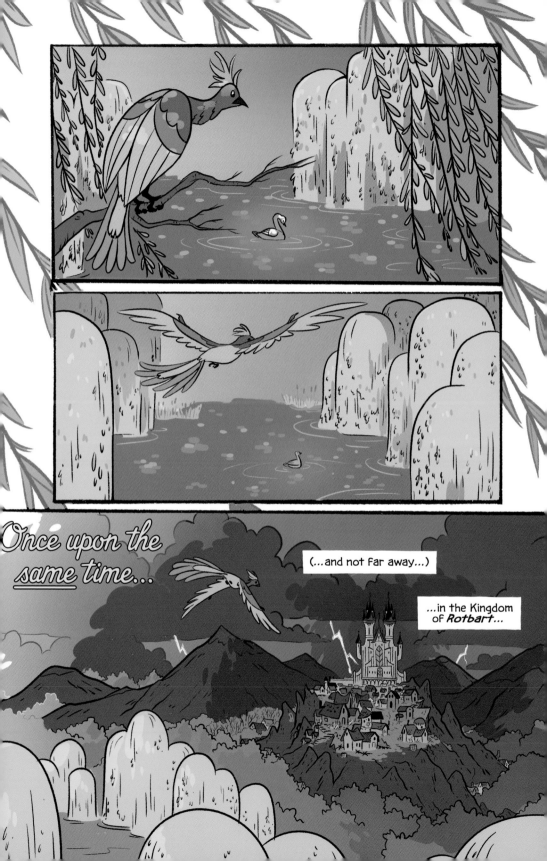

Once upon the same time...

(...and not far away...)

...in the Kingdom of *Rotbart*...

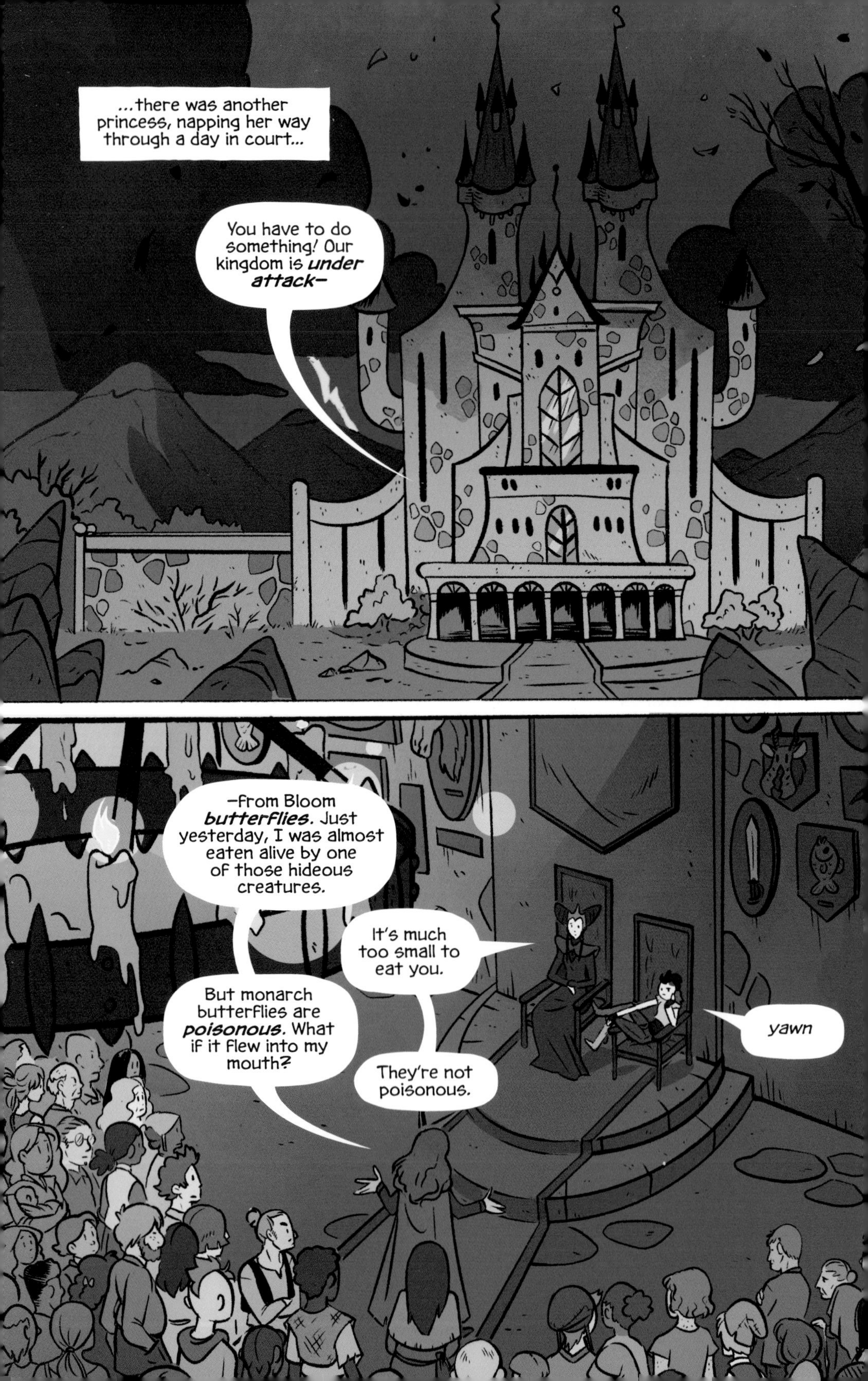

...there was another princess, napping her way through a day in court...
You have to do something! Our kingdom is *under attack*—
—from Bloom *butterflies*. Just yesterday, I was almost eaten alive by one of those hideous creatures.
It's much too small to eat you.
But monarch butterflies are *poisonous*. What if it flew into my mouth?
They're not poisonous.
yawn

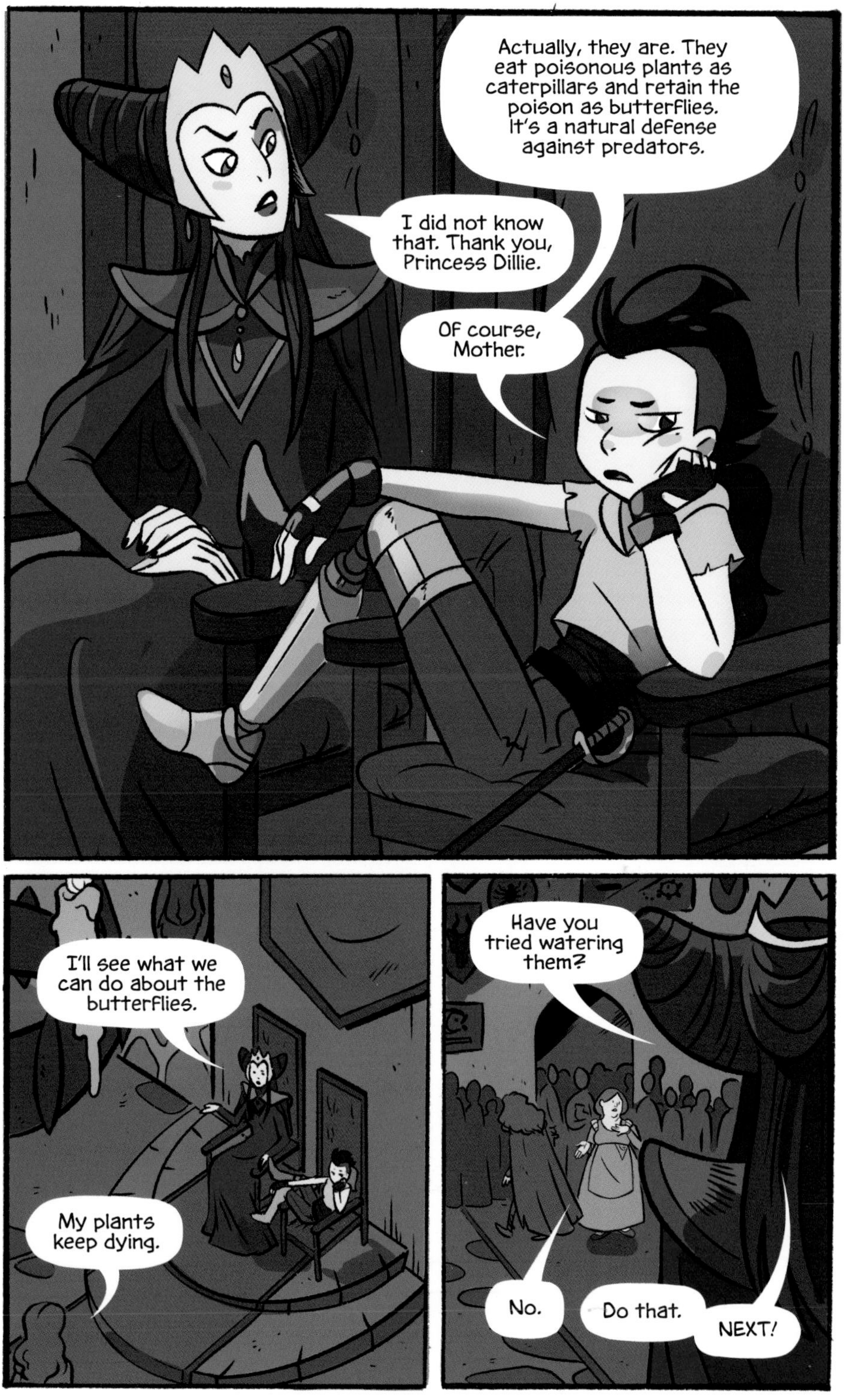
Actually, they are. They eat poisonous plants as caterpillars and retain the poison as butterflies. It's a natural defense against predators.
I did not know that. Thank you, Princess Dillie.
Of course, Mother.
I'll see what we can do about the butterflies.
My plants keep dying.
Have you tried watering them?
No.
Do that.
NEXT!

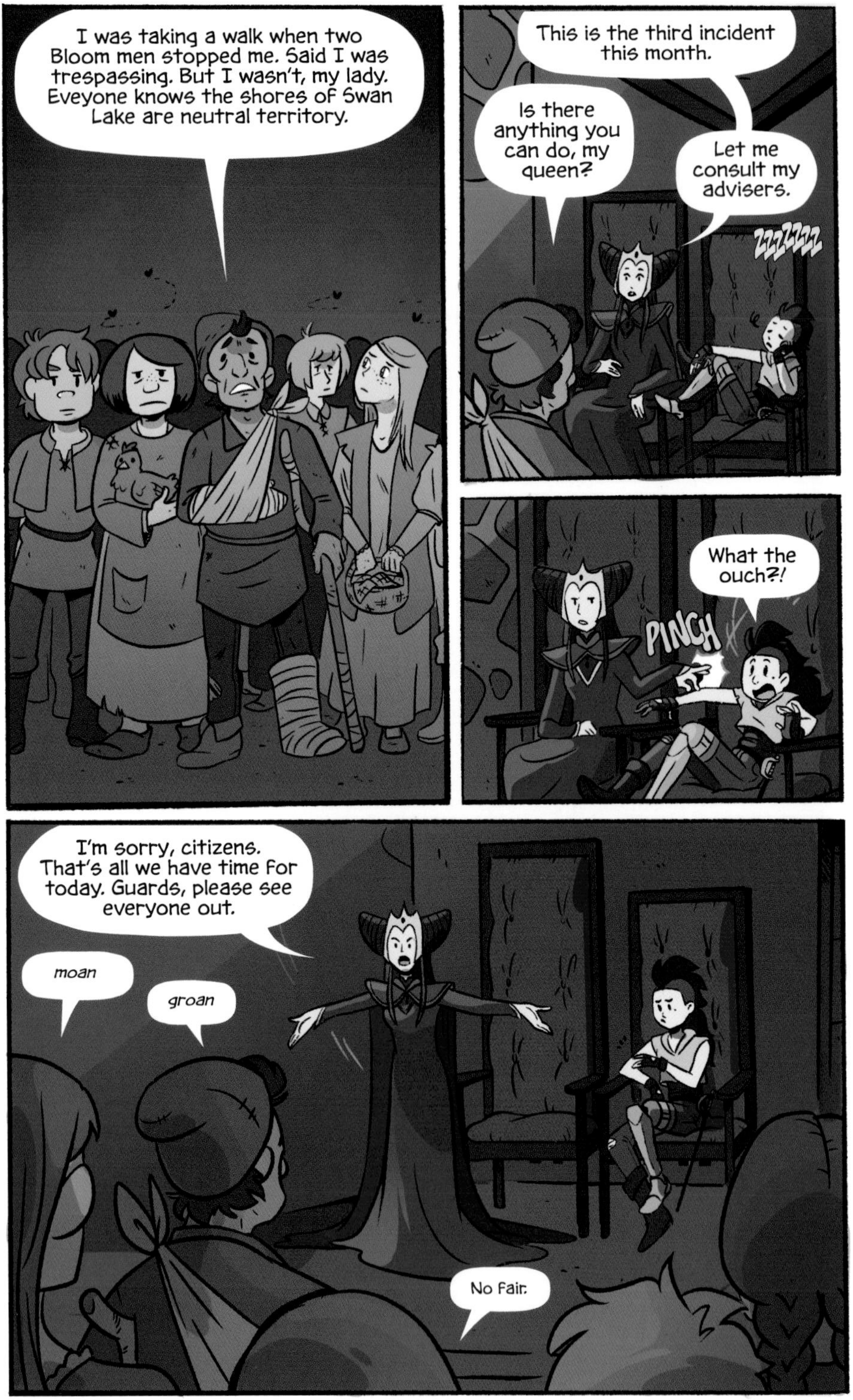

I was taking a walk when two Bloom men stopped me. Said I was trespassing. But I wasn't, my lady. Eveyone knows the shores of Swan Lake are neutral territory.
This is the third incident this month.
Is there anything you can do, my queen?
Let me consult my advisers.
ZZZZZZZ
What the ouch?!
PINCH
I'm sorry, citizens. That's all we have time for today. Guards, please see everyone out.
moan
groan
No fair.

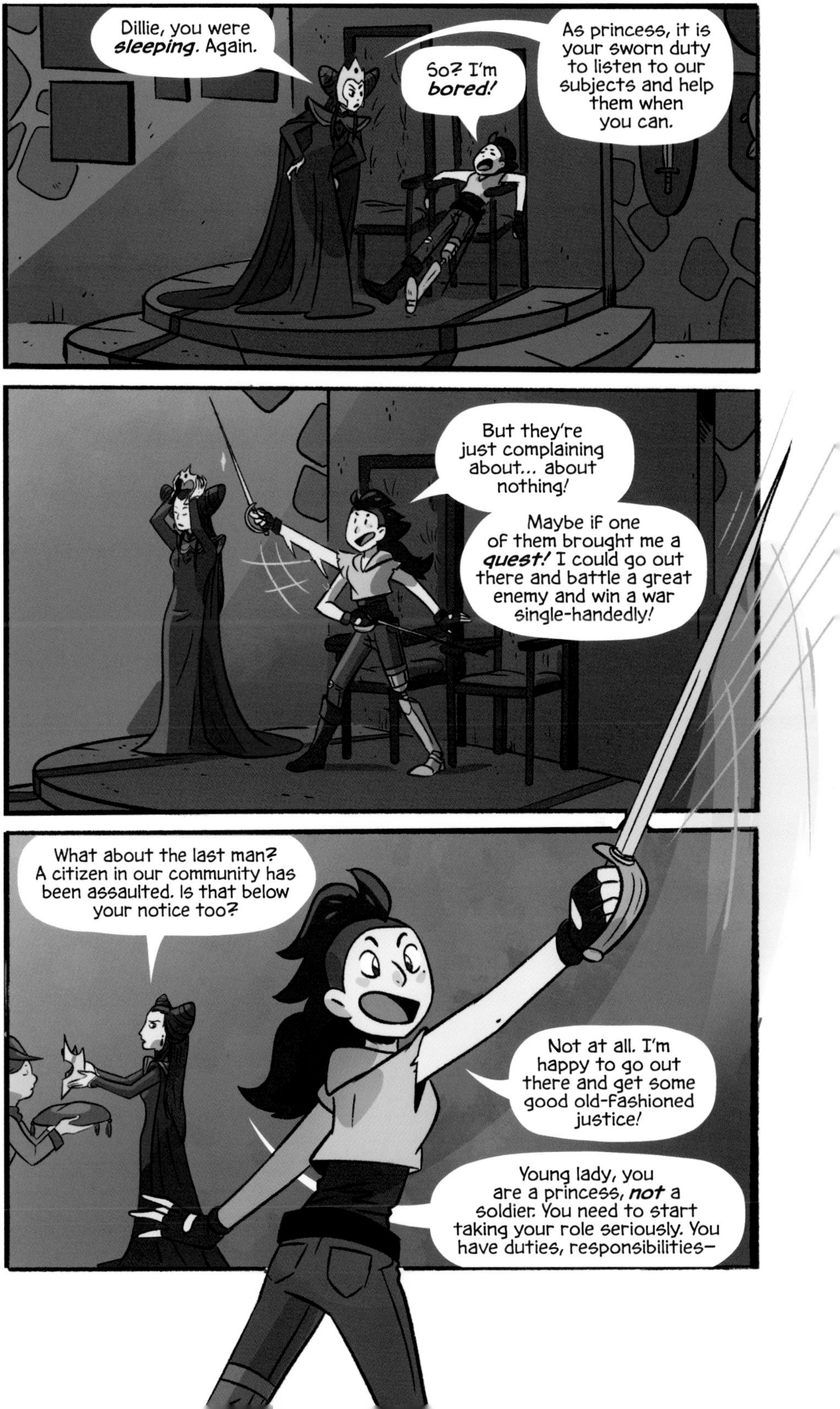
Dillie, you were *sleeping*. Again.
So? I'm *bored!*
As princess, it is your sworn duty to listen to our subjects and help them when you can.
But they're just complaining about... about nothing!
Maybe if one of them brought me a *quest!* I could go out there and battle a great enemy and win a war single-handedly!
What about the last man? A citizen in our community has been assaulted. Is that below your notice too?
Not at all. I'm happy to go out there and get some good old-fashioned justice!
Young lady, you are a princess, *not* a soldier. You need to start taking your role seriously. You have duties, responsibilities—

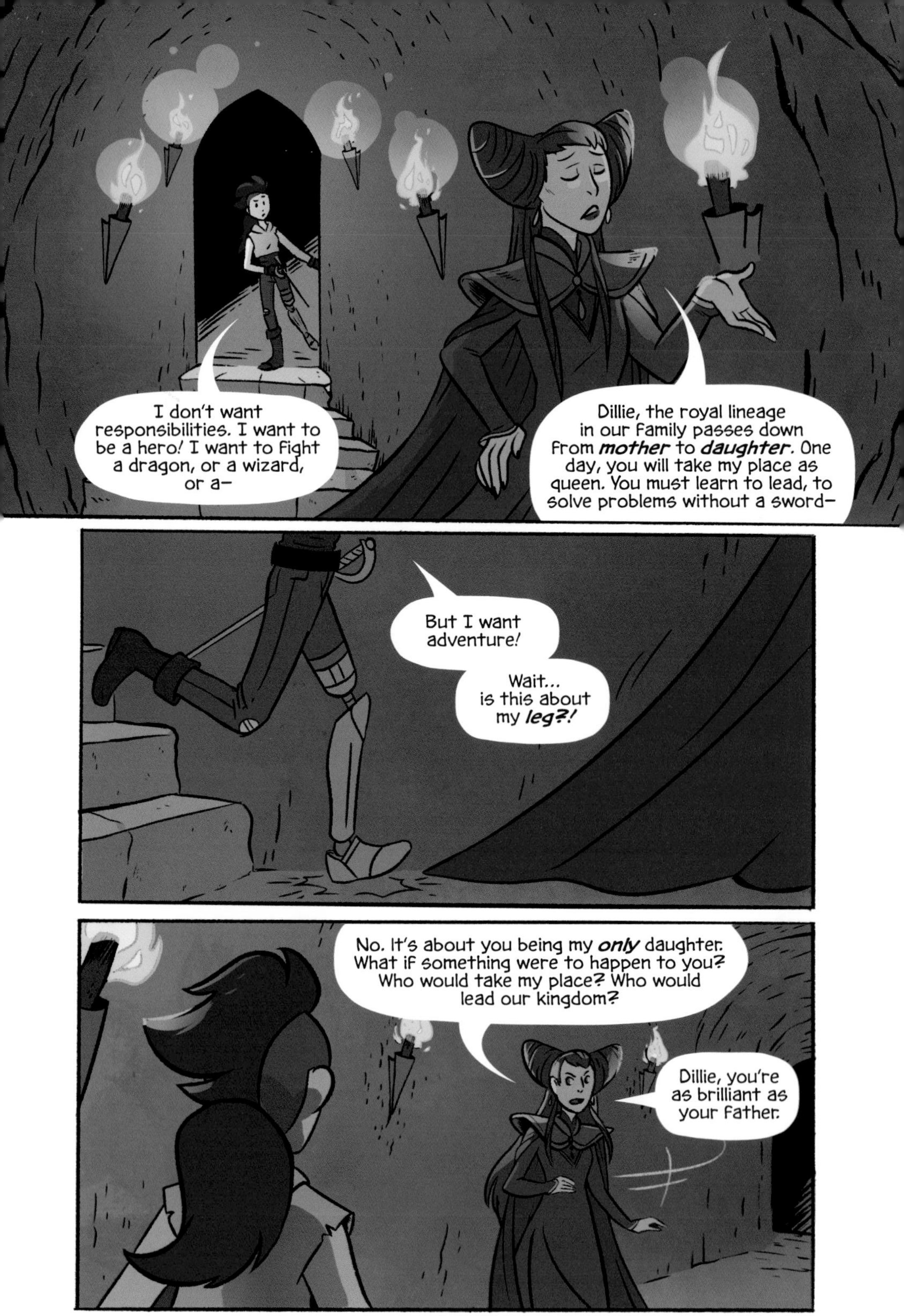
I don't want responsibilities. I want to be a hero! I want to fight a dragon, or a wizard, or a–
Dillie, the royal lineage in our family passes down from **mother** to **daughter**. One day, you will take my place as queen. You must learn to lead, to solve problems without a sword–
But I want adventure!
Wait... is this about my **leg?!**
No. It's about you being my **only** daughter. What if something were to happen to you? Who would take my place? Who would lead our kingdom?
Dillie, you're as brilliant as your father.

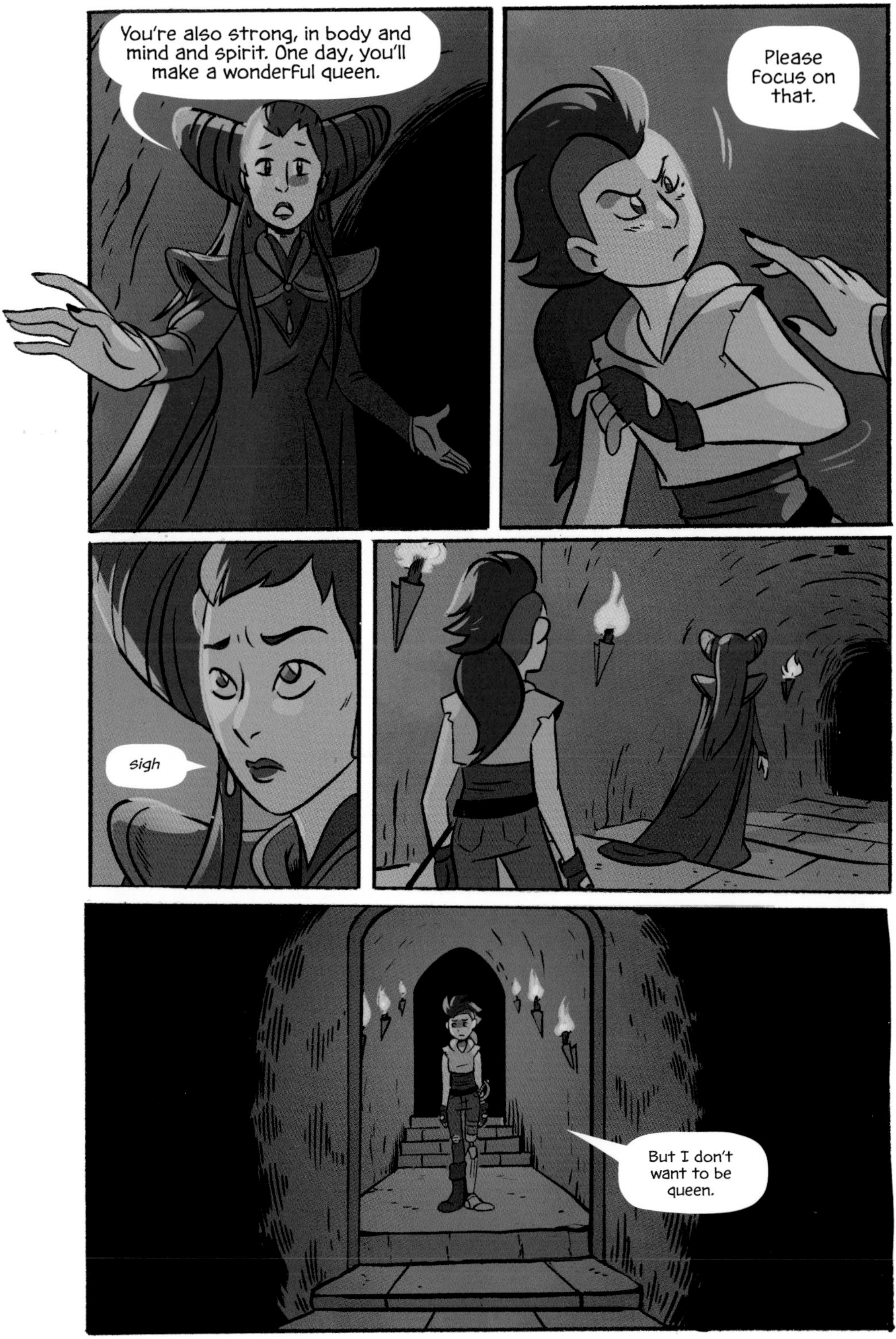
You're also strong, in body and mind and spirit. One day, you'll make a wonderful queen.
Please focus on that.
sigh
But I don't want to be queen.

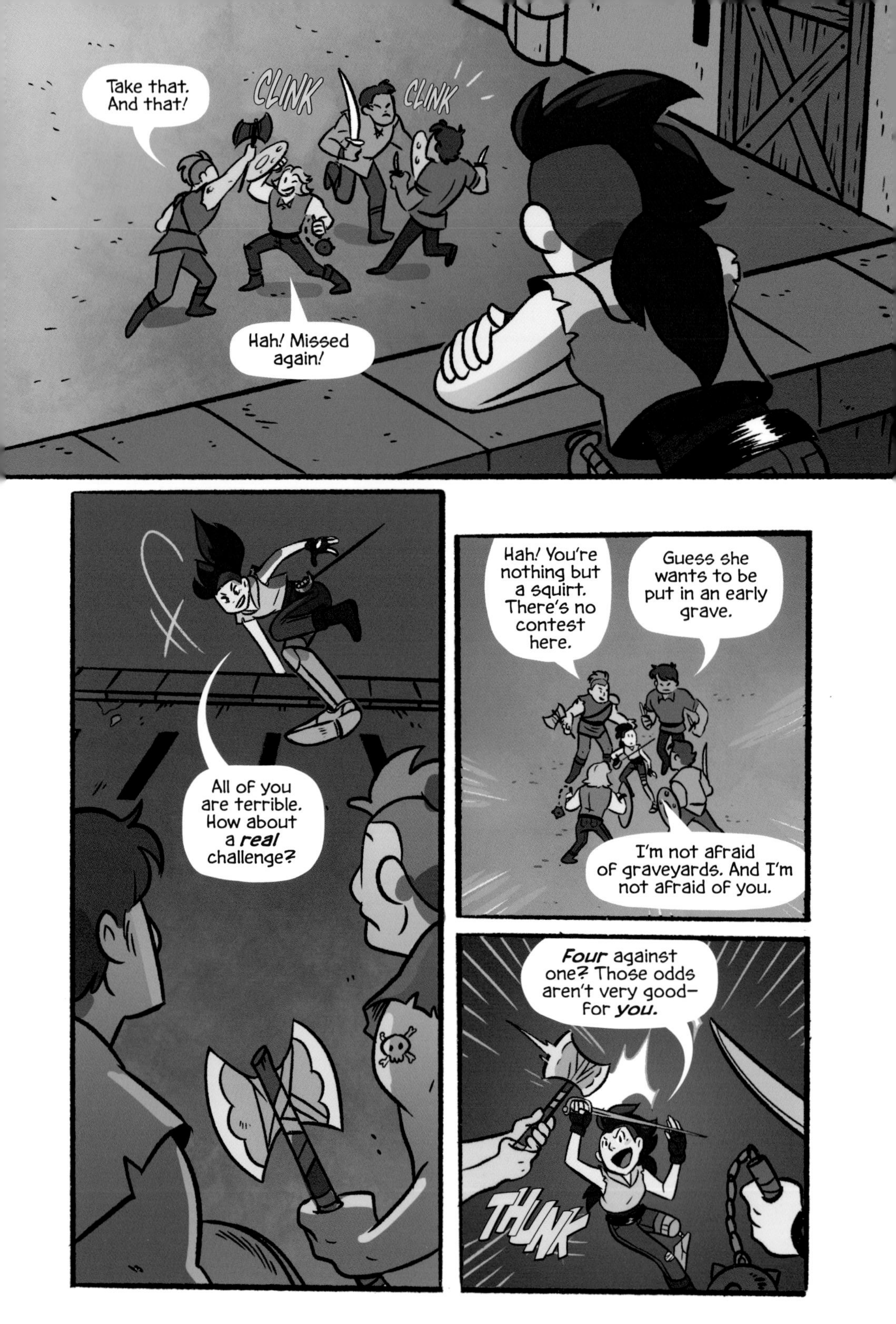
Take that. And that!
CLINK
CLINK
Hah! Missed again!
All of you are terrible. How about a *real* challenge?
Hah! You're nothing but a squirt. There's no contest here.
Guess she wants to be put in an early grave.
I'm not afraid of graveyards. And I'm not afraid of you.
Four against one? Those odds aren't very good— for *you.*
THUNK

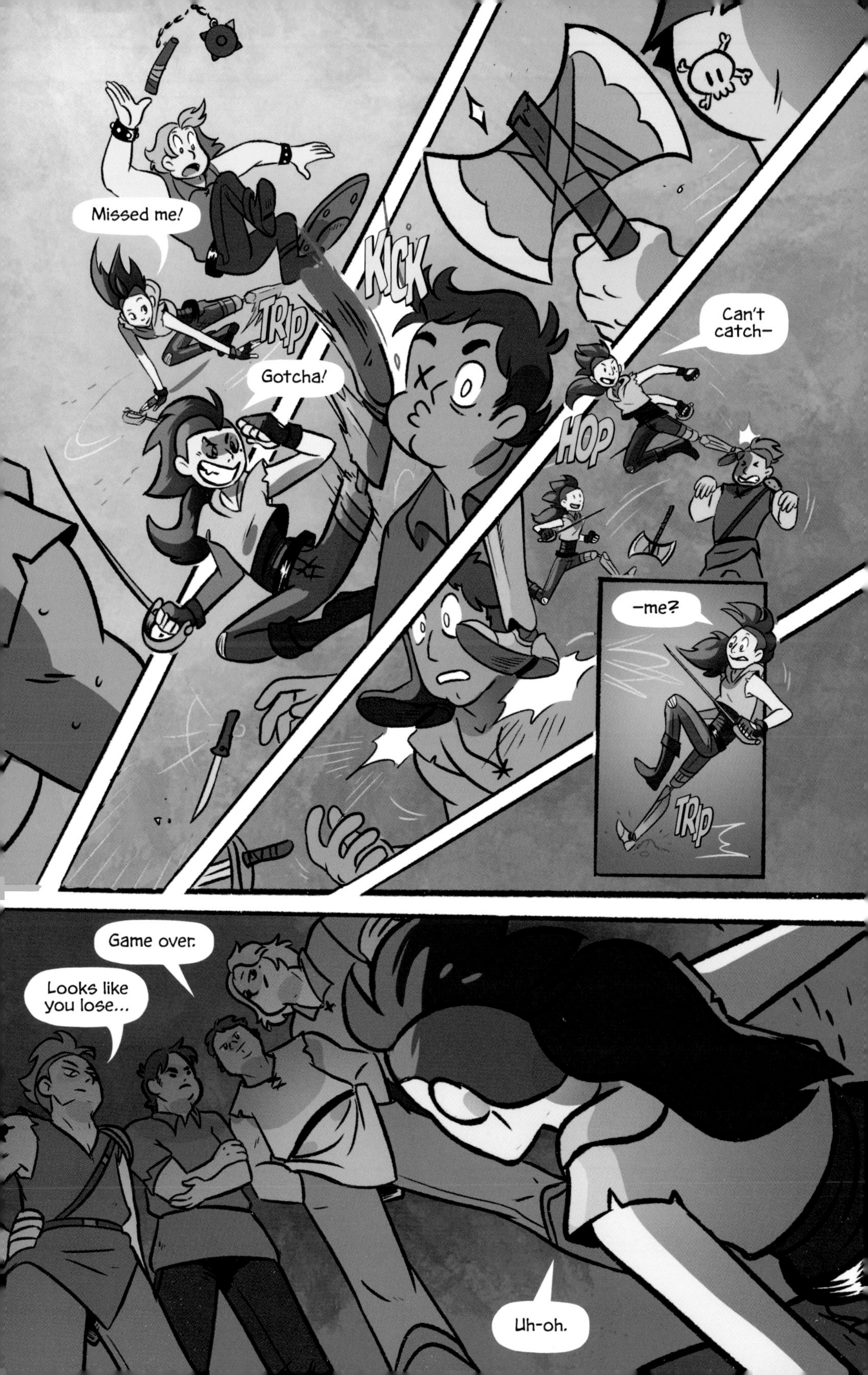
Missed me!
KICK
TRIP
Gotcha!
Can't catch-
HOP
-me?
TRIP
Game over.
Looks like you lose...
Uh-oh.

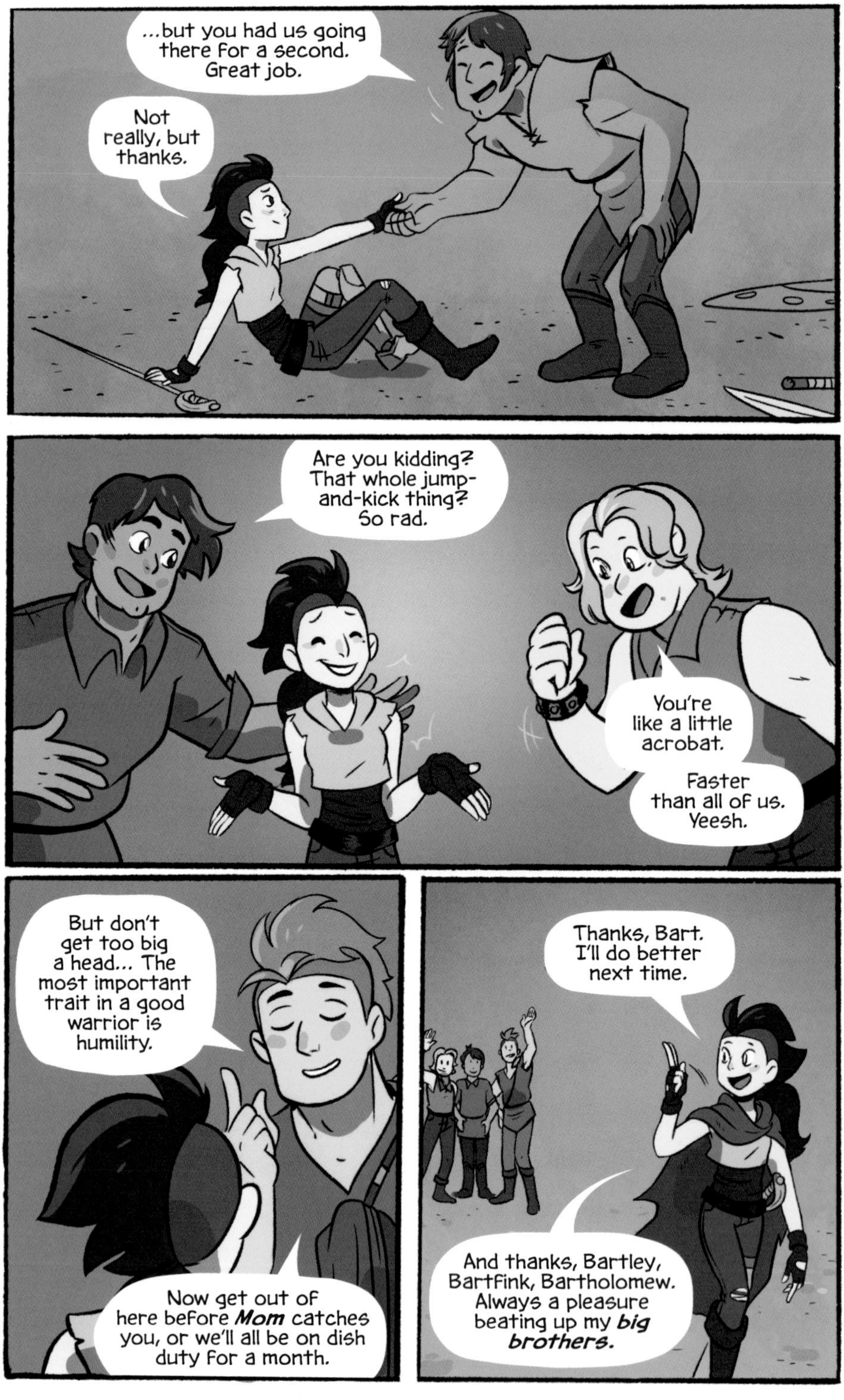
...but you had us going there for a second. Great job.
Not really, but thanks.
Are you kidding? That whole jump-and-kick thing? So rad.
You're like a little acrobat.
Faster than all of us. Yeesh.
But don't get too big a head... The most important trait in a good warrior is humility.
Now get out of here before **Mom** catches you, or we'll all be on dish duty for a month.
Thanks, Bart. I'll do better next time.
And thanks, Bartley, Bartfink, Bartholomew. Always a pleasure beating up my ***big brothers.***

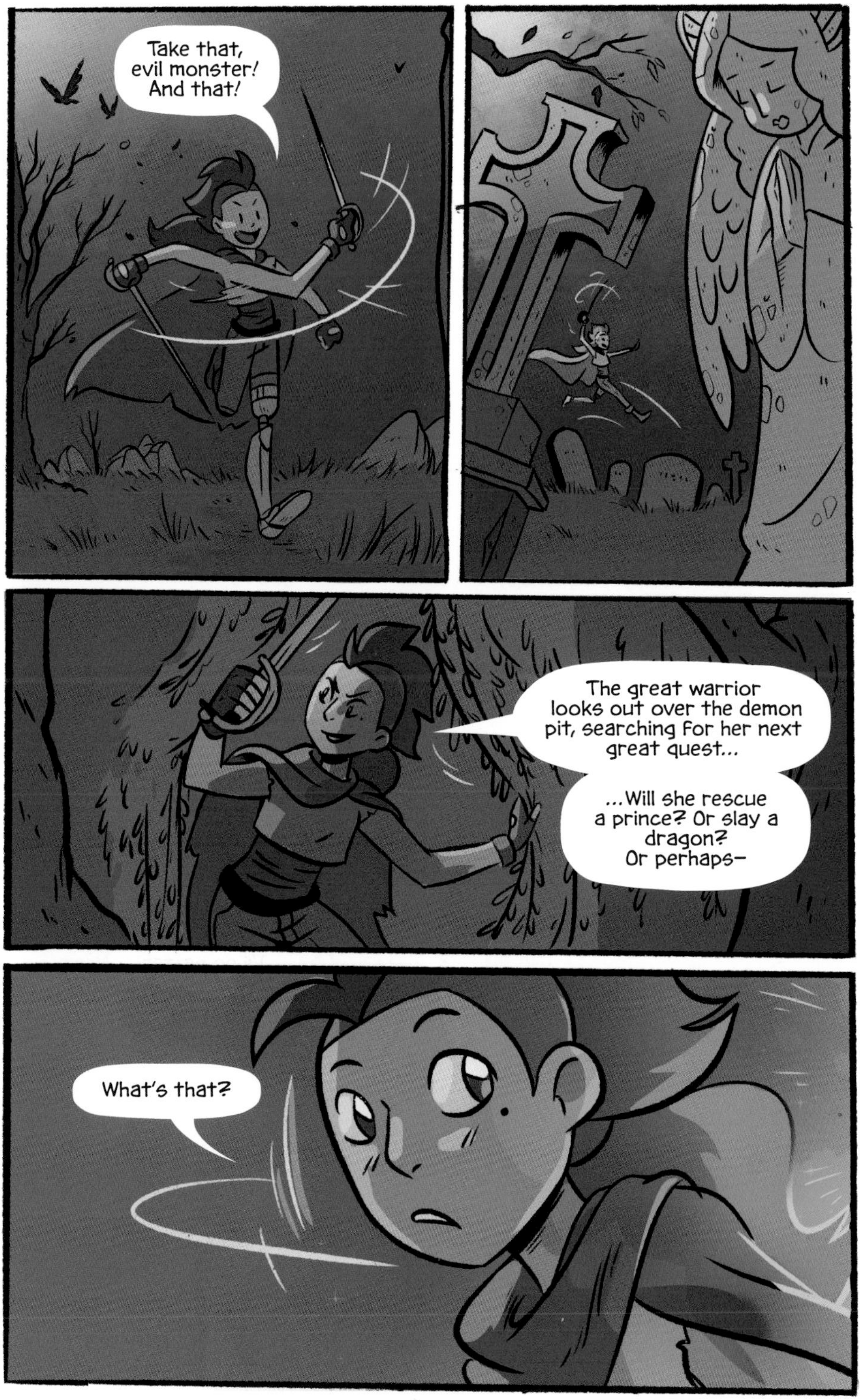

Take that, evil monster! And that!
The great warrior looks out over the demon pit, searching for her next great quest...
...Will she rescue a prince? Or slay a dragon? Or perhaps–
What's that?

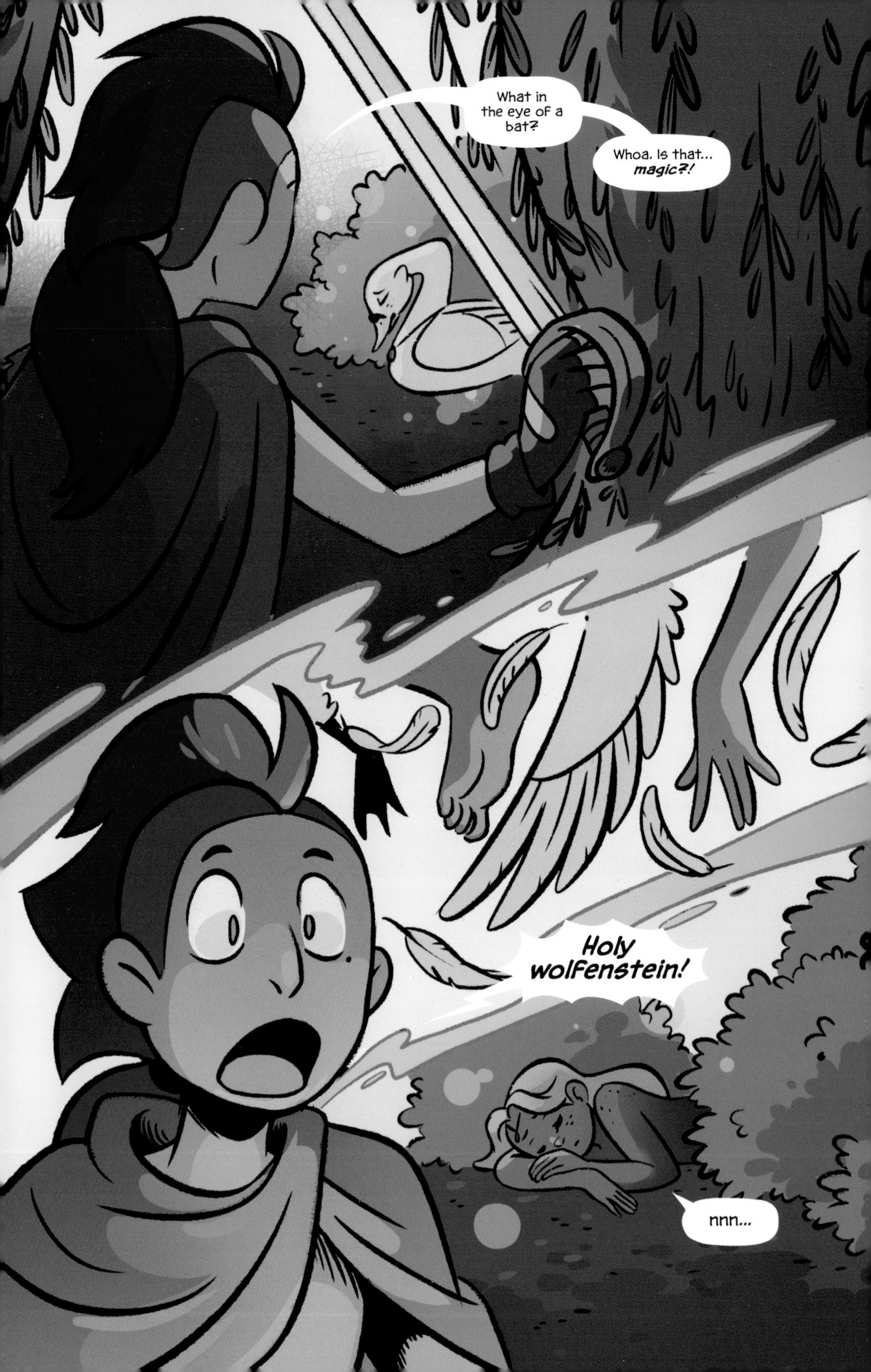
What in the eye of a bat?
Whoa. Is that... *magic?!*
Holy wolfenstein!
nnn...

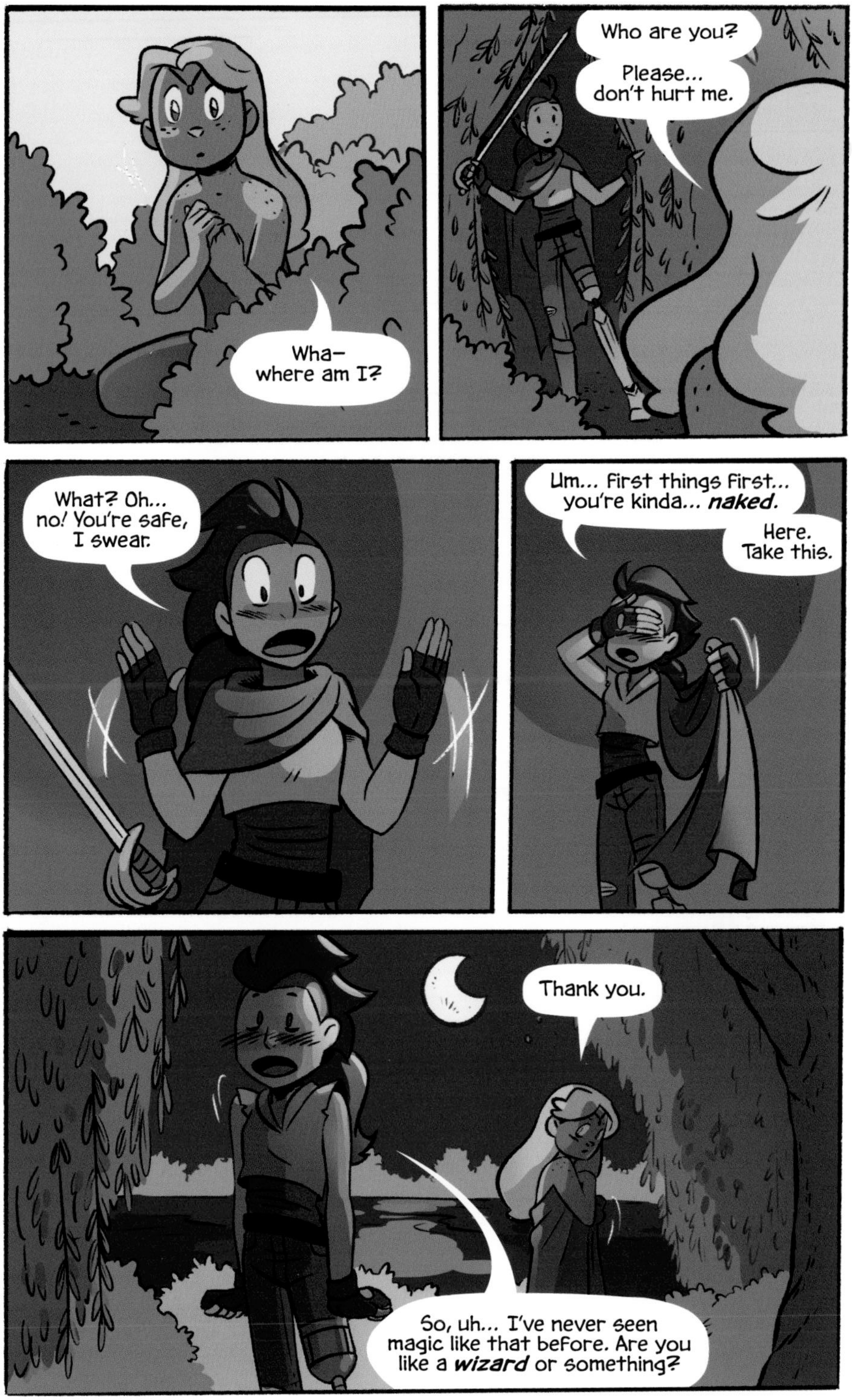

Wha– where am I?
Who are you?
Please... don't hurt me.
What? Oh... no! You're safe, I swear.
Um... First things first... you're kinda... *naked.*
Here. Take this.
Thank you.
So, uh... I've never seen magic like that before. Are you like a *wizard* or something?

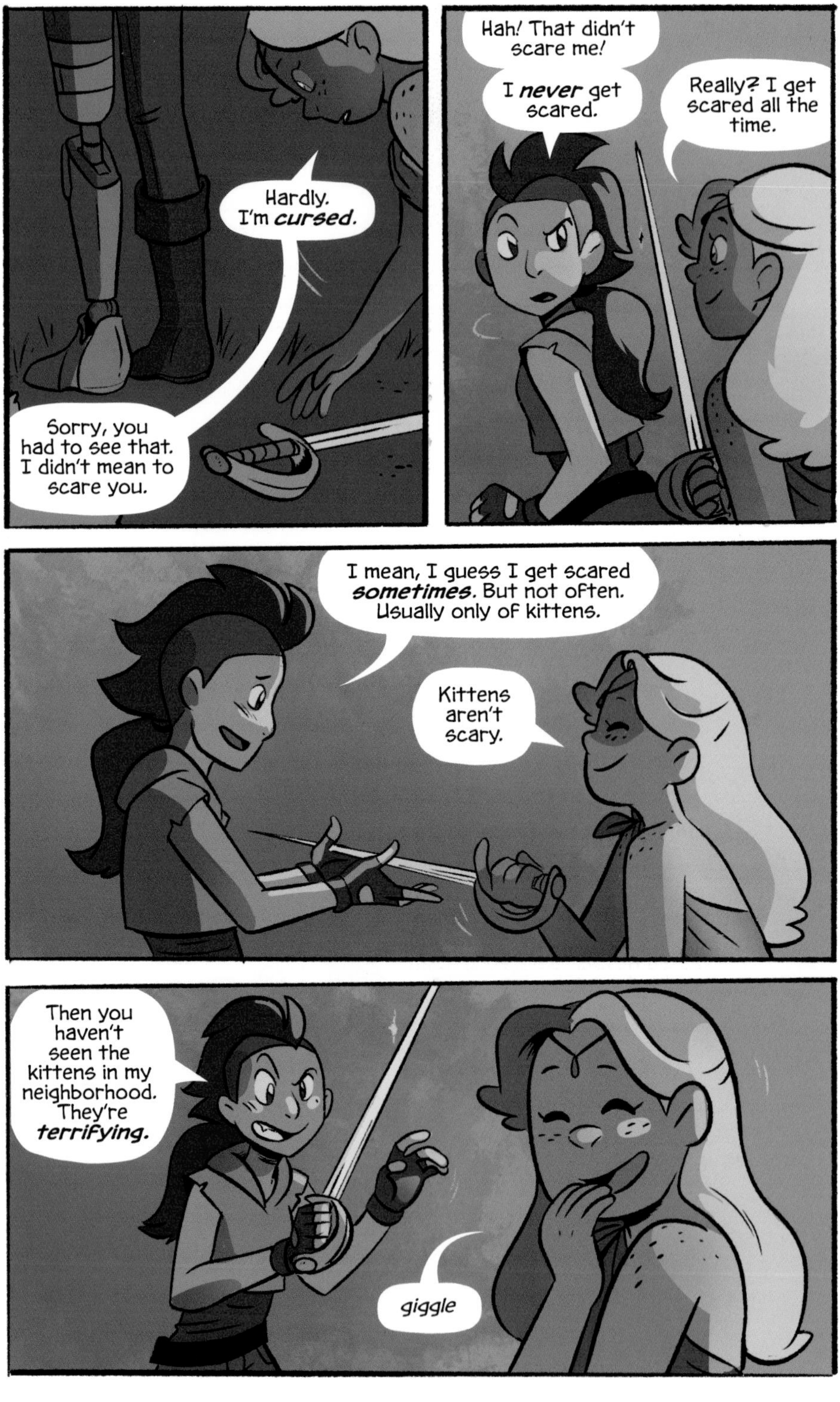
Hardly. I'm *cursed.*
Sorry, you had to see that. I didn't mean to scare you.
Hah! That didn't scare me!
I *never* get scared.
Really? I get scared all the time.
I mean, I guess I get scared *sometimes.* But not often. Usually only of kittens.
Kittens aren't scary.
Then you haven't seen the kittens in my neighborhood. They're *terrifying.*
giggle

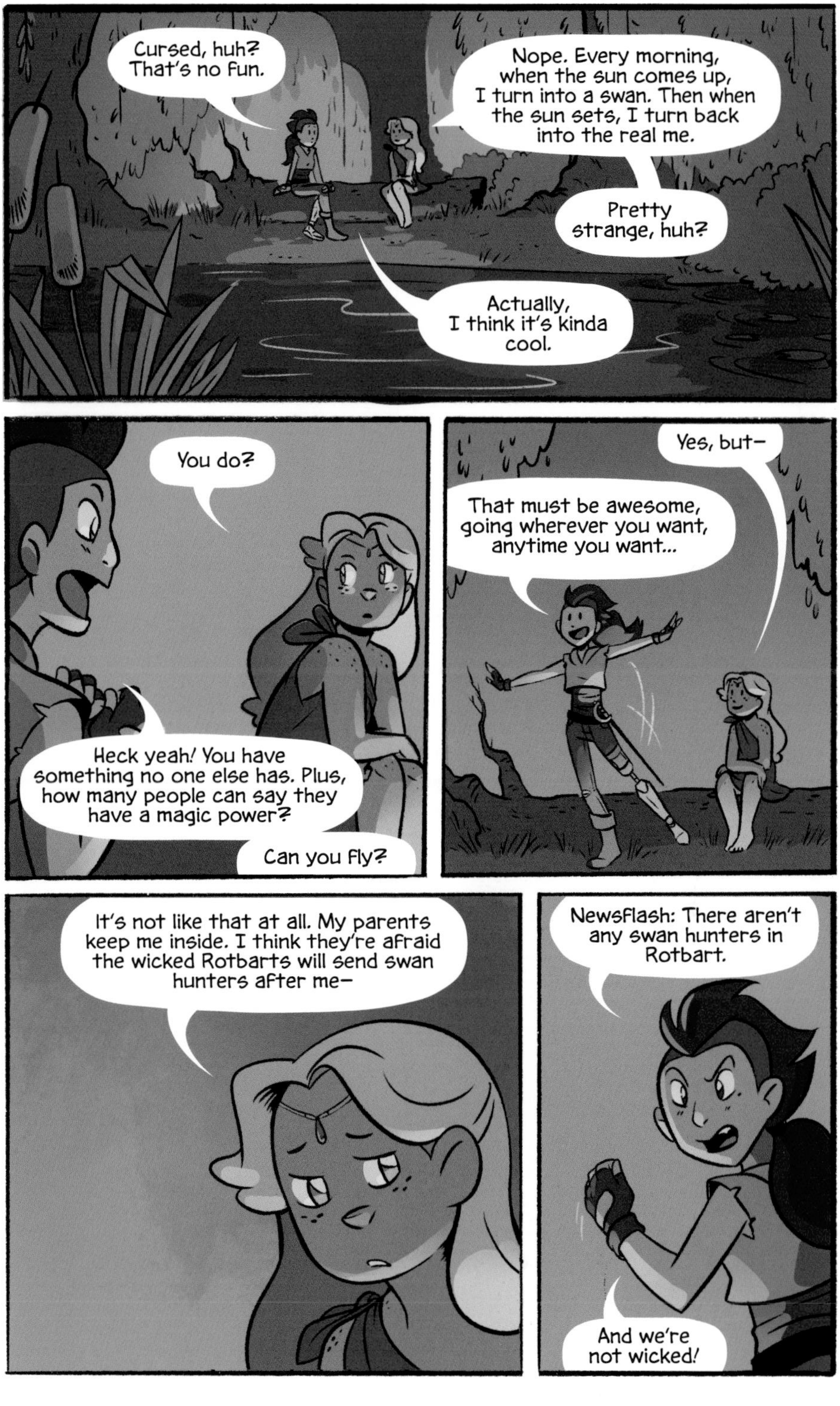
Cursed, huh? That's no fun.
Nope. Every morning, when the sun comes up, I turn into a swan. Then when the sun sets, I turn back into the real me.
Pretty strange, huh?
Actually, I think it's kinda cool.
You do?
Heck yeah! You have something no one else has. Plus, how many people can say they have a magic power?
Can you fly?
Yes, but–
That must be awesome, going wherever you want, anytime you want...
It's not like that at all. My parents keep me inside. I think they're afraid the wicked Rotbarts will send swan hunters after me–
Newsflash: There aren't any swan hunters in Rotbart.
And we're not wicked!

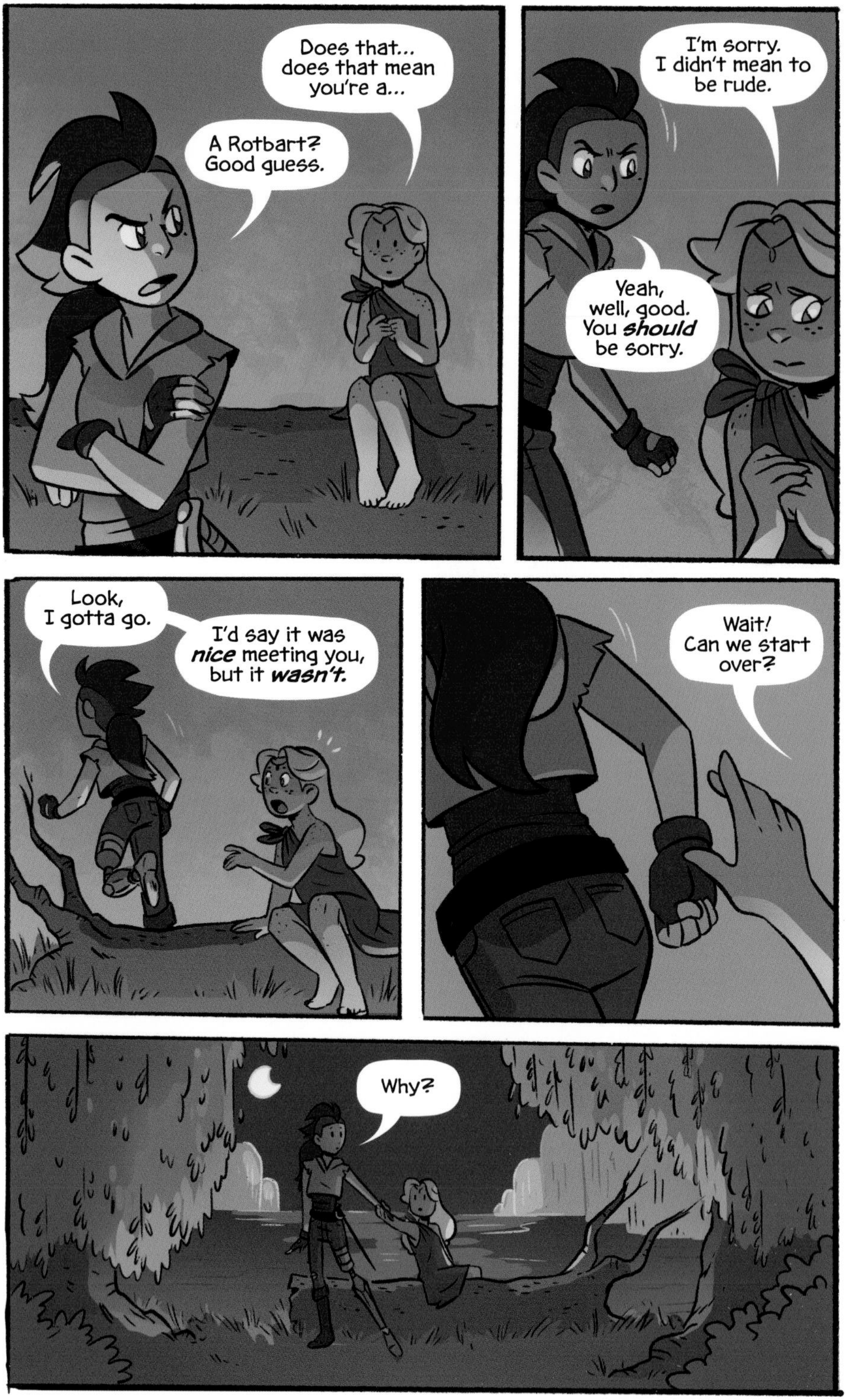
Does that... does that mean you're a...
A Rotbart? Good guess.
I'm sorry. I didn't mean to be rude.
Yeah, well, good. You *should* be sorry.
Look, I gotta go.
I'd say it was *nice* meeting you, but it *wasn't.*
Wait! Can we start over?
Why?

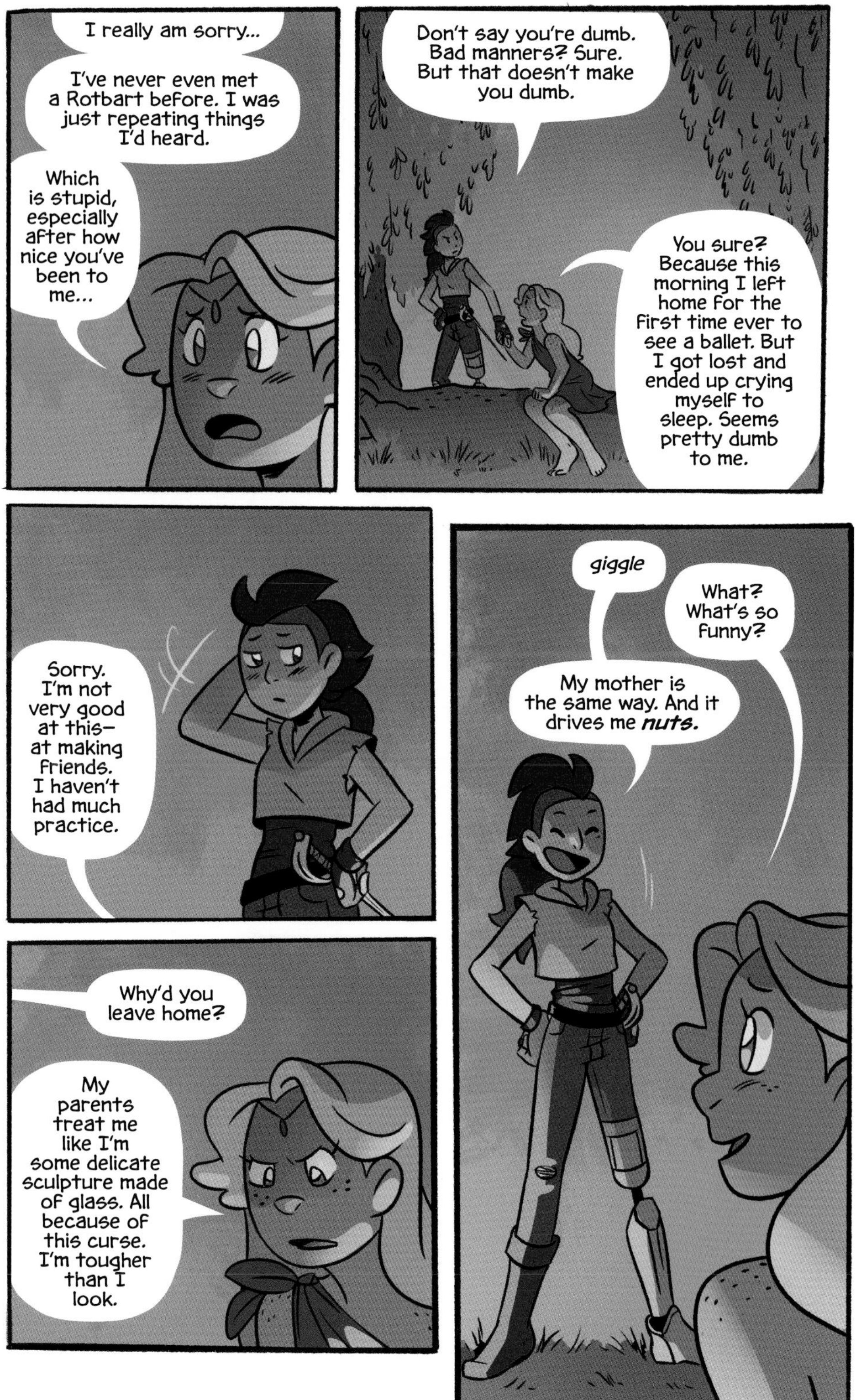
I really am sorry...
I've never even met a Rotbart before. I was just repeating things I'd heard.
Which is stupid, especially after how nice you've been to me...
Don't say you're dumb. Bad manners? Sure. But that doesn't make you dumb.
You sure? Because this morning I left home for the first time ever to see a ballet. But I got lost and ended up crying myself to sleep. Seems pretty dumb to me.
Sorry. I'm not very good at this— at making friends. I haven't had much practice.
Why'd you leave home?
My parents treat me like I'm some delicate sculpture made of glass. All because of this curse. I'm tougher than I look.
giggle
What? What's so funny?
My mother is the same way. And it drives me *nuts.*

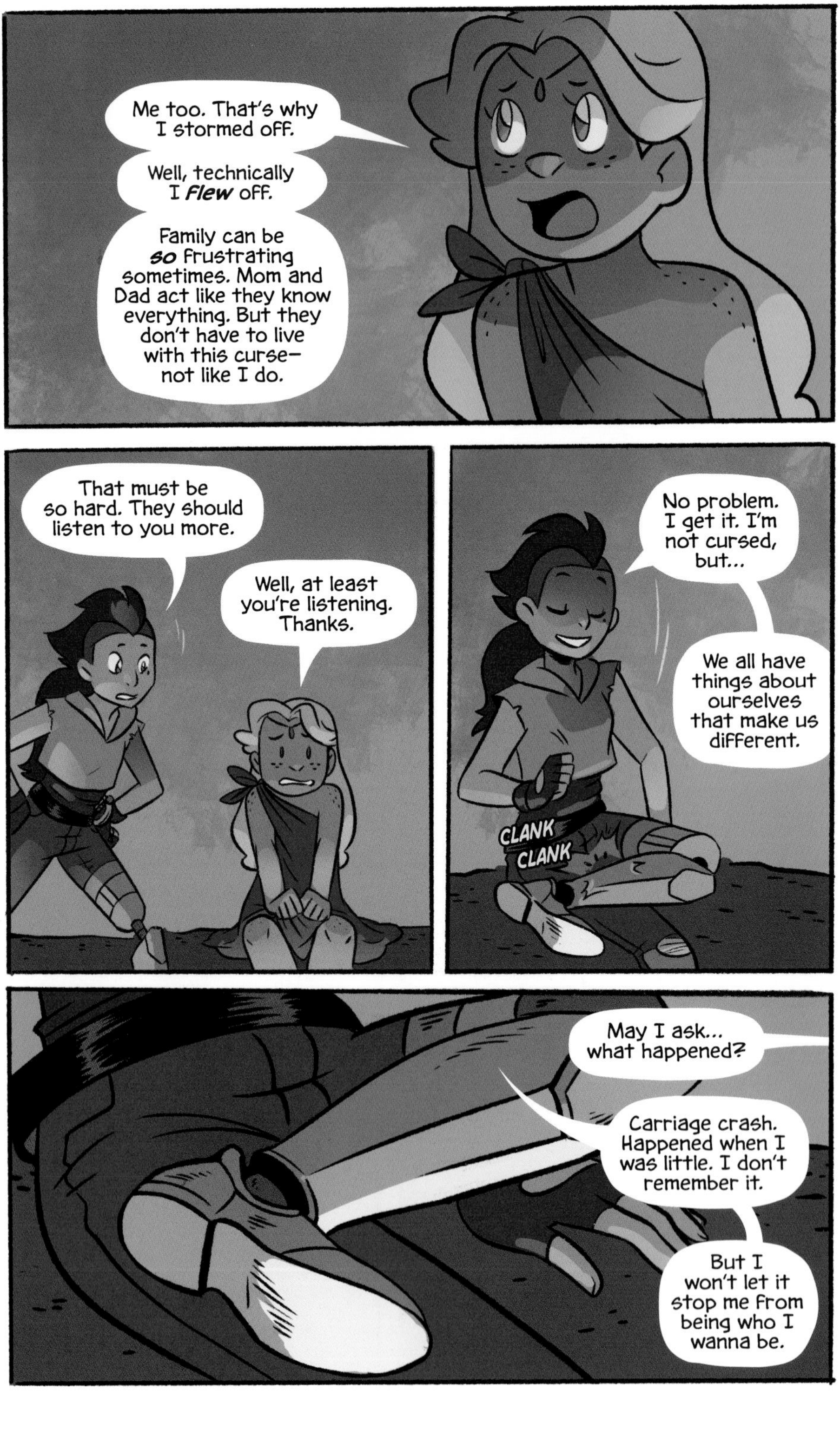
Me too. That's why I stormed off.
Well, technically I *flew* off.
Family can be *so* frustrating sometimes. Mom and Dad act like they know everything. But they don't have to live with this curse— not like I do.
That must be so hard. They should listen to you more.
Well, at least you're listening. Thanks.
No problem. I get it. I'm not cursed, but...
We all have things about ourselves that make us different.
CLANK
CLANK
May I ask... what happened?
Carriage crash. Happened when I was little. I don't remember it.
But I won't let it stop me from being who I wanna be.

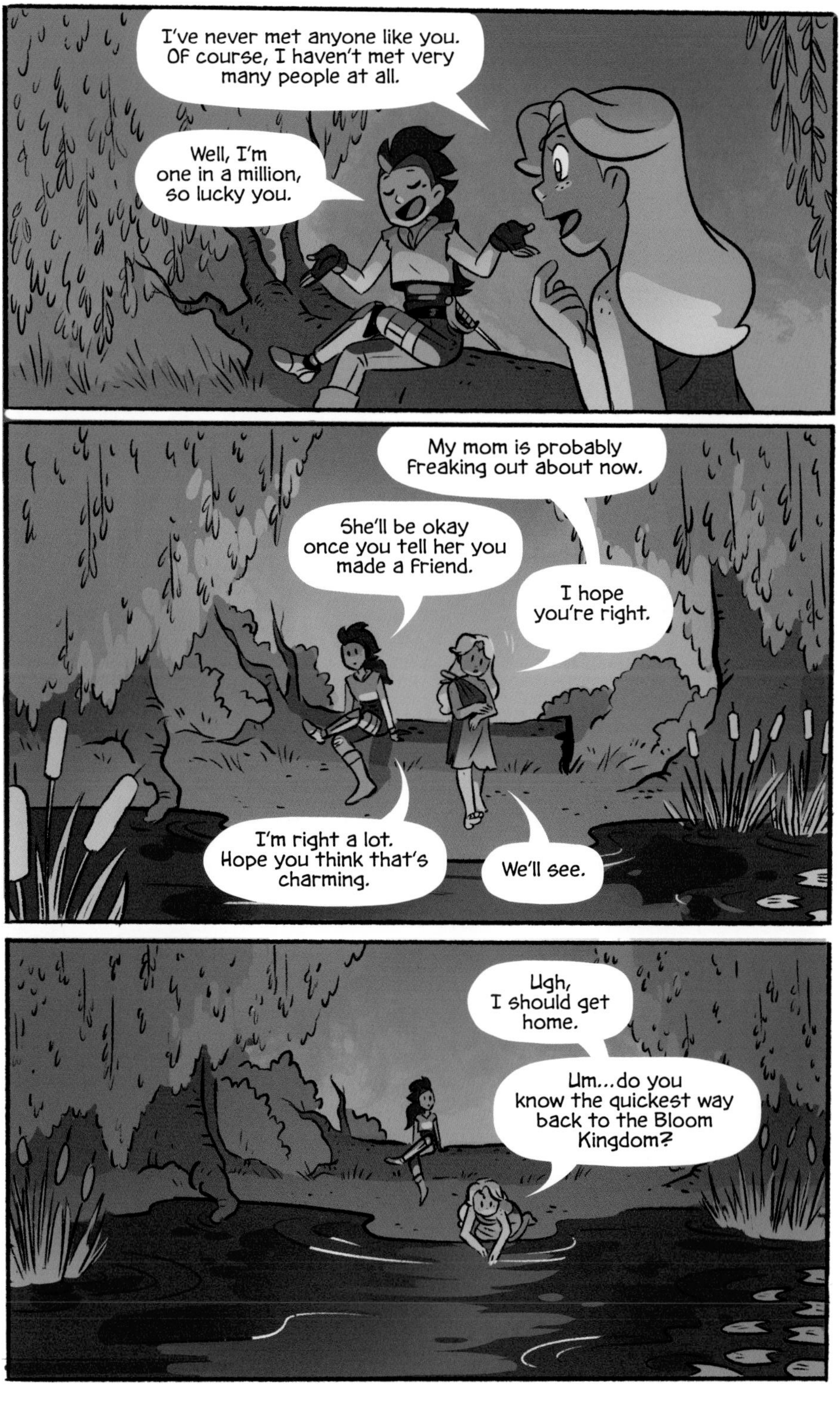
I've never met anyone like you. Of course, I haven't met very many people at all.
Well, I'm one in a million, so lucky you.
My mom is probably freaking out about now.
She'll be okay once you tell her you made a friend.
I hope you're right.
I'm right a lot. Hope you think that's charming.
We'll see.
Ugh, I should get home.
Um...do you know the quickest way back to the Bloom Kingdom?

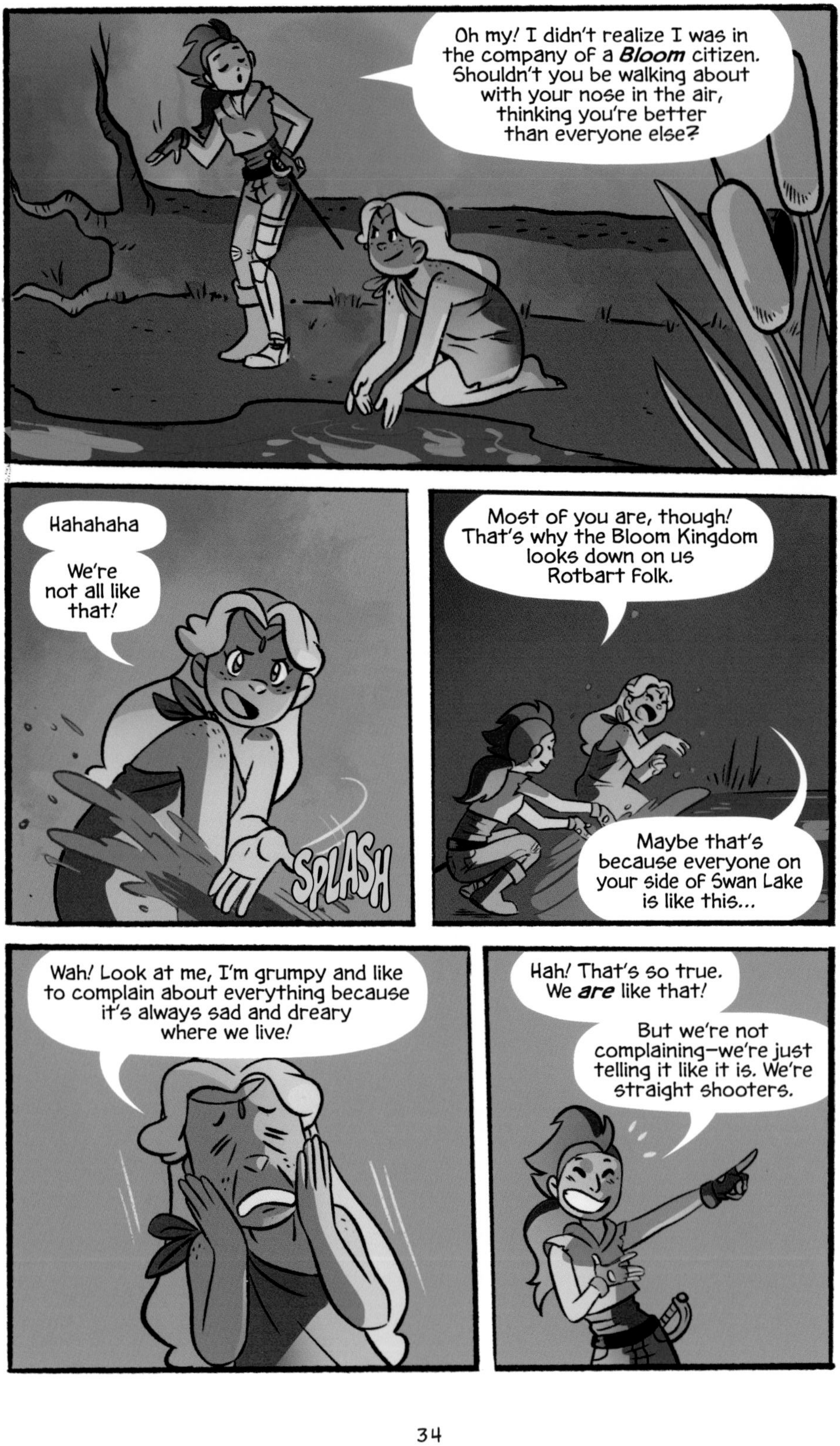
Oh my! I didn't realize I was in the company of a ***Bloom*** citizen. Shouldn't you be walking about with your nose in the air, thinking you're better than everyone else?
Hahahaha
We're not all like that!
SPLASH
Most of you are, though! That's why the Bloom Kingdom looks down on us Rotbart folk.
Maybe that's because everyone on your side of Swan Lake is like this...
Wah! Look at me, I'm grumpy and like to complain about everything because it's always sad and dreary where we live!
Hah! That's so true. We ***are*** like that!
But we're not complaining—we're just telling it like it is. We're straight shooters.

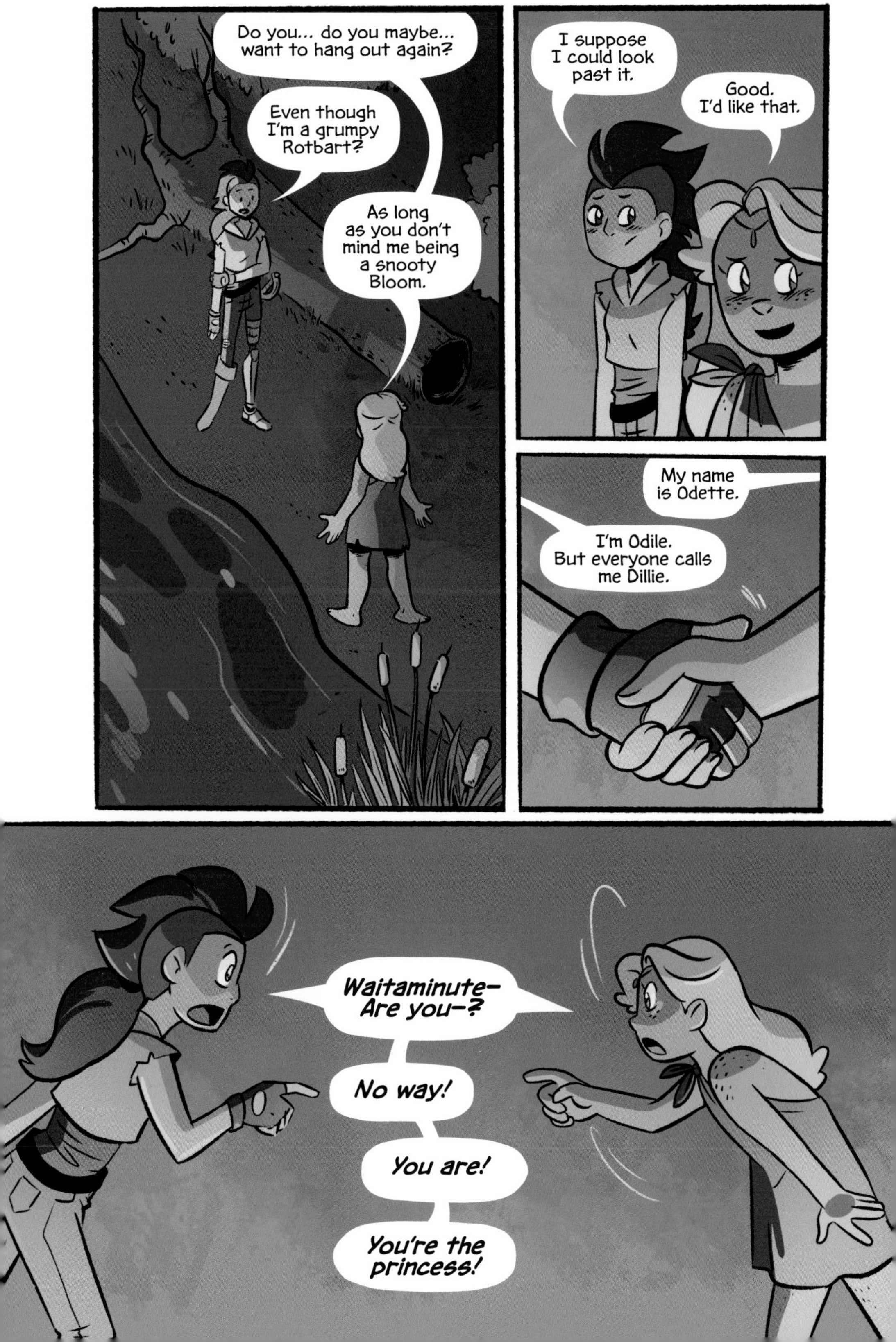
Do you... do you maybe... want to hang out again?
Even though I'm a grumpy Rotbart?
As long as you don't mind me being a snooty Bloom.
I suppose I could look past it.
Good. I'd like that.
My name is Odette.
I'm Odile. But everyone calls me Dillie.
Waitaminute- Are you-?
No way!
You are!
You're the princess!

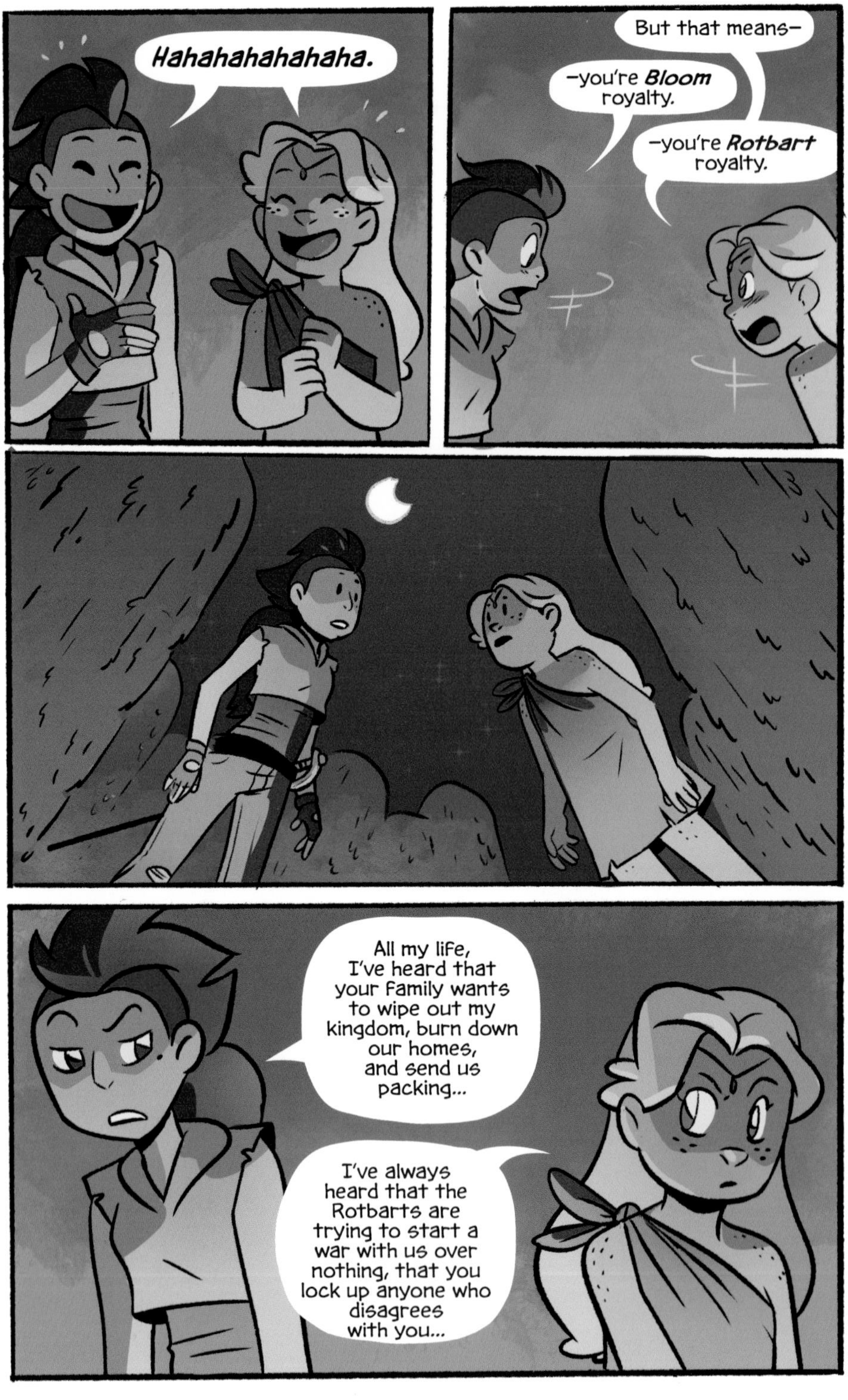
Hahahahahahaha.
But that means—
—you're **Bloom** royalty.
—you're **Rotbart** royalty.
All my life, I've heard that your family wants to wipe out my kingdom, burn down our homes, and send us packing...
I've always heard that the Rotbarts are trying to start a war with us over nothing, that you lock up anyone who disagrees with you...

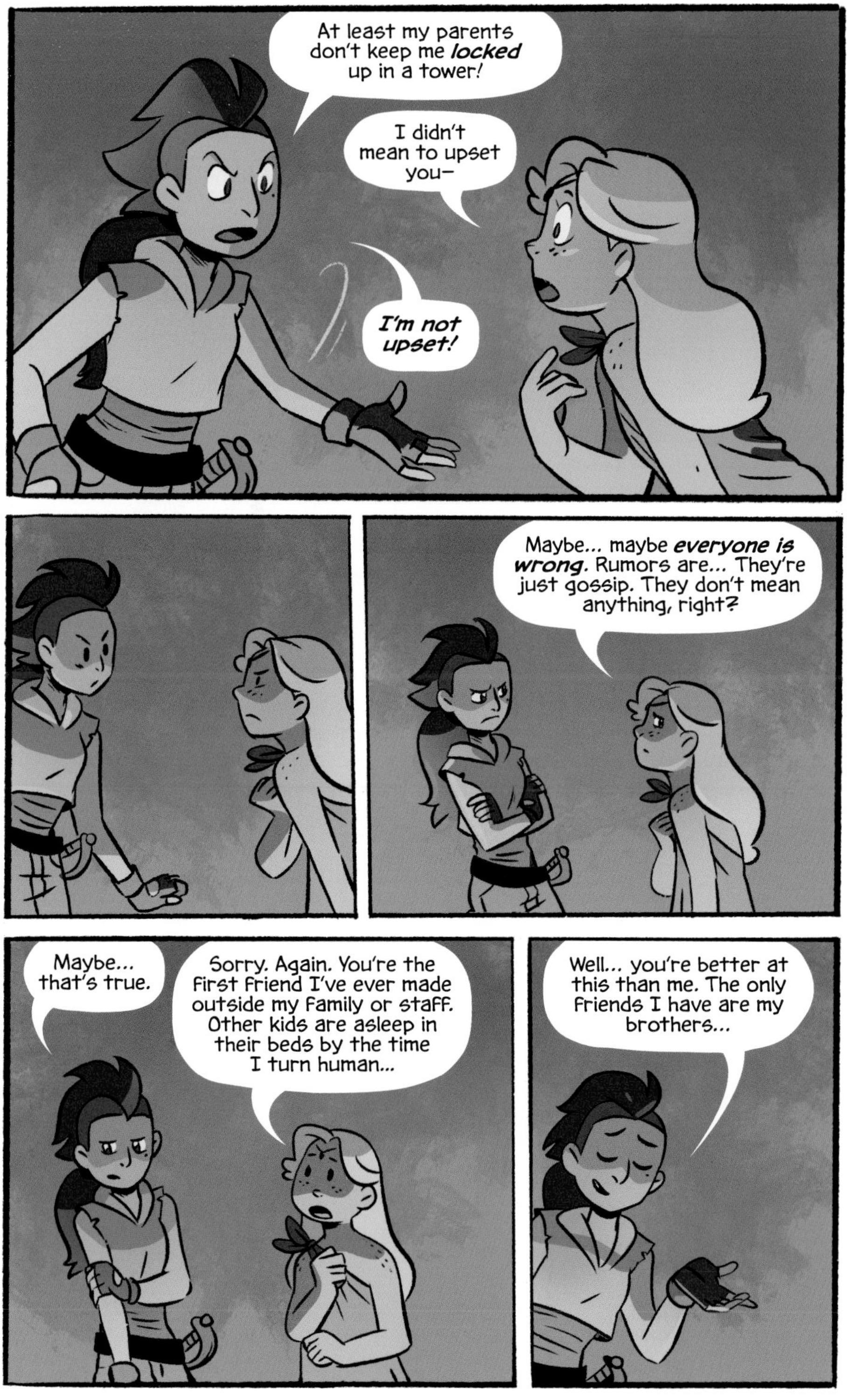
At least my parents don't keep me *locked* up in a tower!
I didn't mean to upset you–
I'm not upset!
Maybe... maybe *everyone is wrong*. Rumors are... They're just gossip. They don't mean anything, right?
Maybe... that's true.
Sorry. Again. You're the first friend I've ever made outside my family or staff. Other kids are asleep in their beds by the time I turn human...
Well... you're better at this than me. The only friends I have are my brothers...

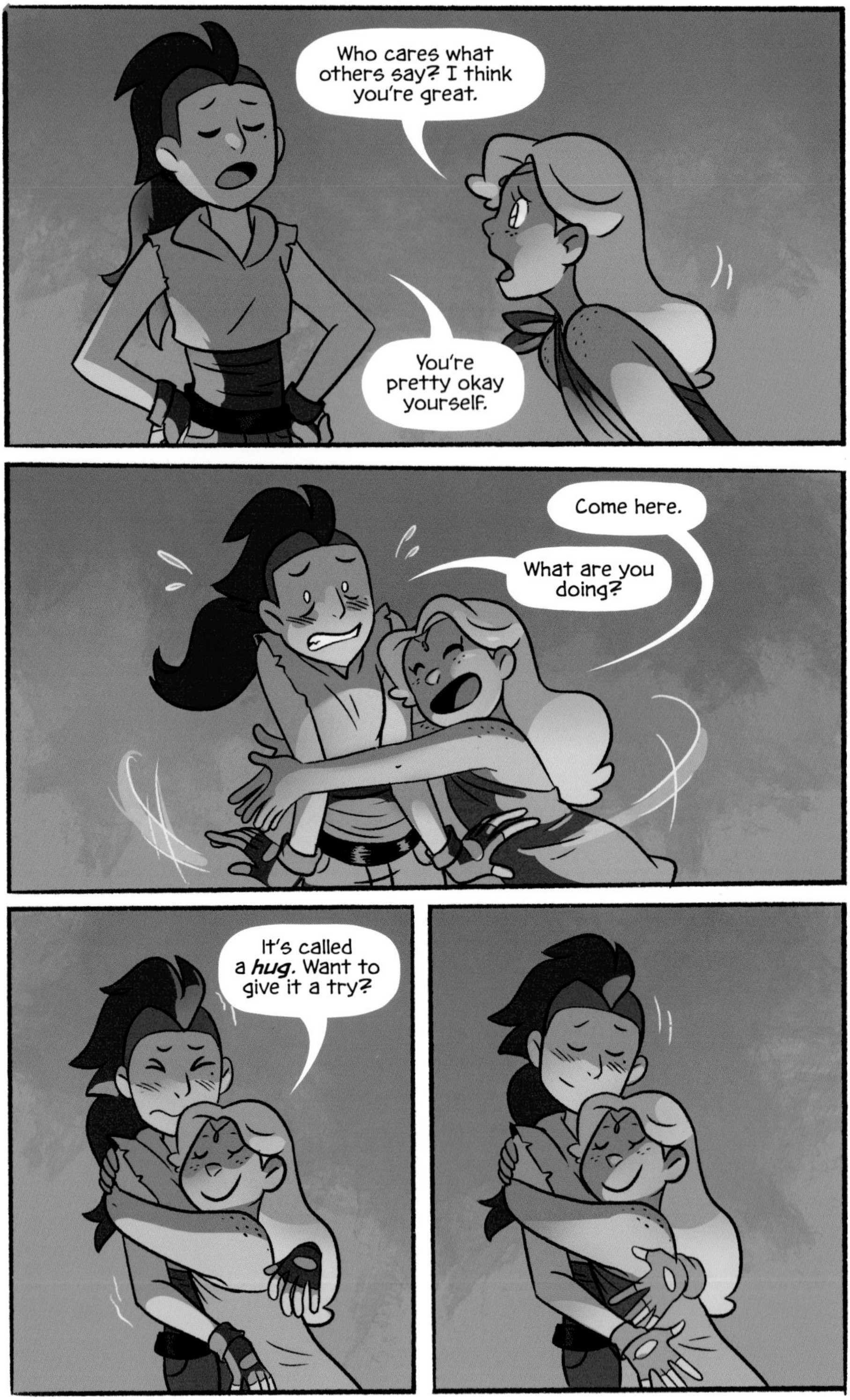
Who cares what others say? I think you're great.
You're pretty okay yourself.
Come here.
What are you doing?
It's called a ***hug.*** Want to give it a try?

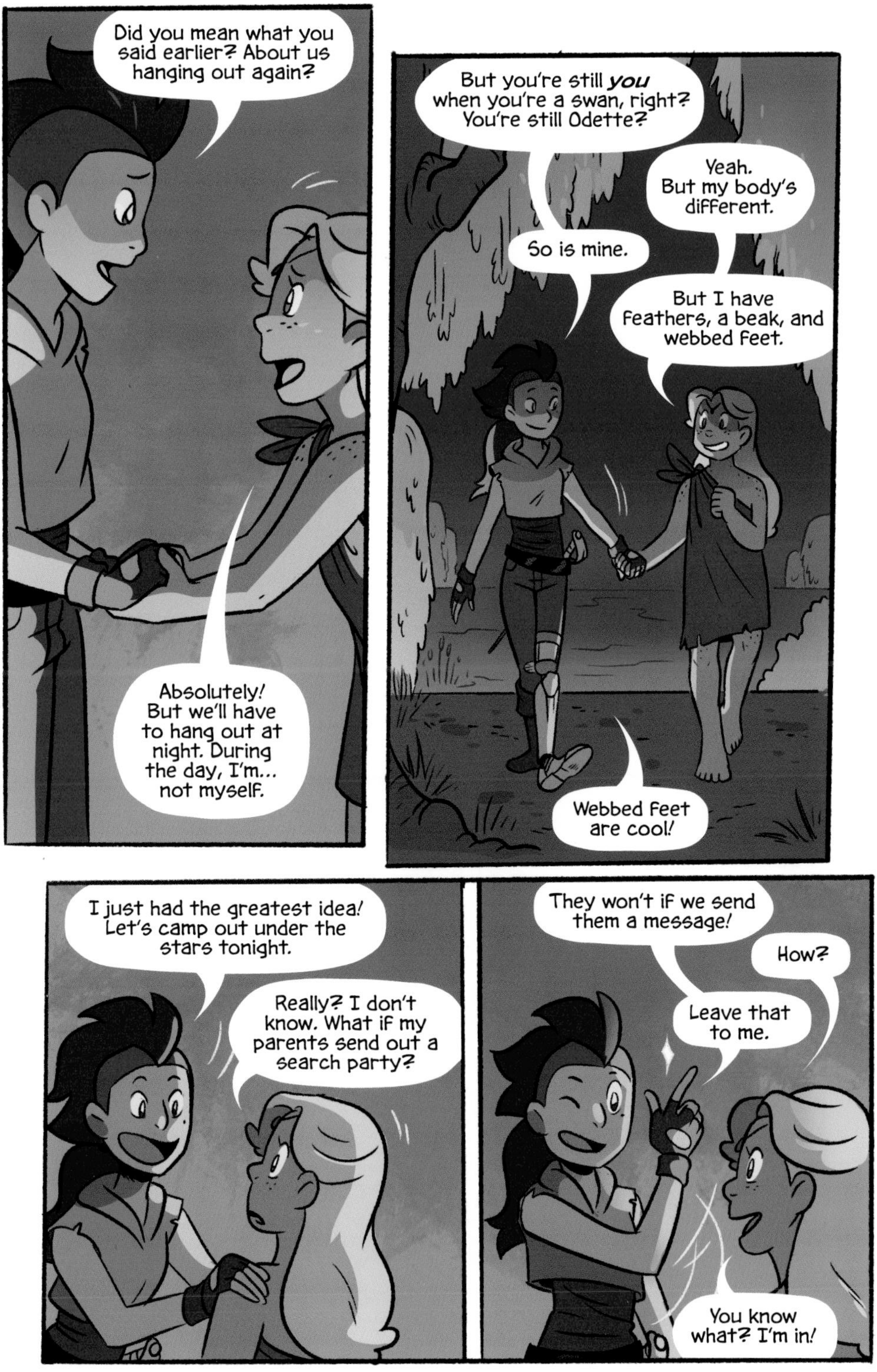
Did you mean what you said earlier? About us hanging out again?
Absolutely! But we'll have to hang out at night. During the day, I'm... not myself.
But you're still *you* when you're a swan, right? You're still Odette?
Yeah. But my body's different.
So is mine.
But I have feathers, a beak, and webbed feet.
Webbed feet are cool!
I just had the greatest idea! Let's camp out under the stars tonight.
Really? I don't know. What if my parents send out a search party?
They won't if we send them a message!
How?
Leave that to me.
You know what? I'm in!

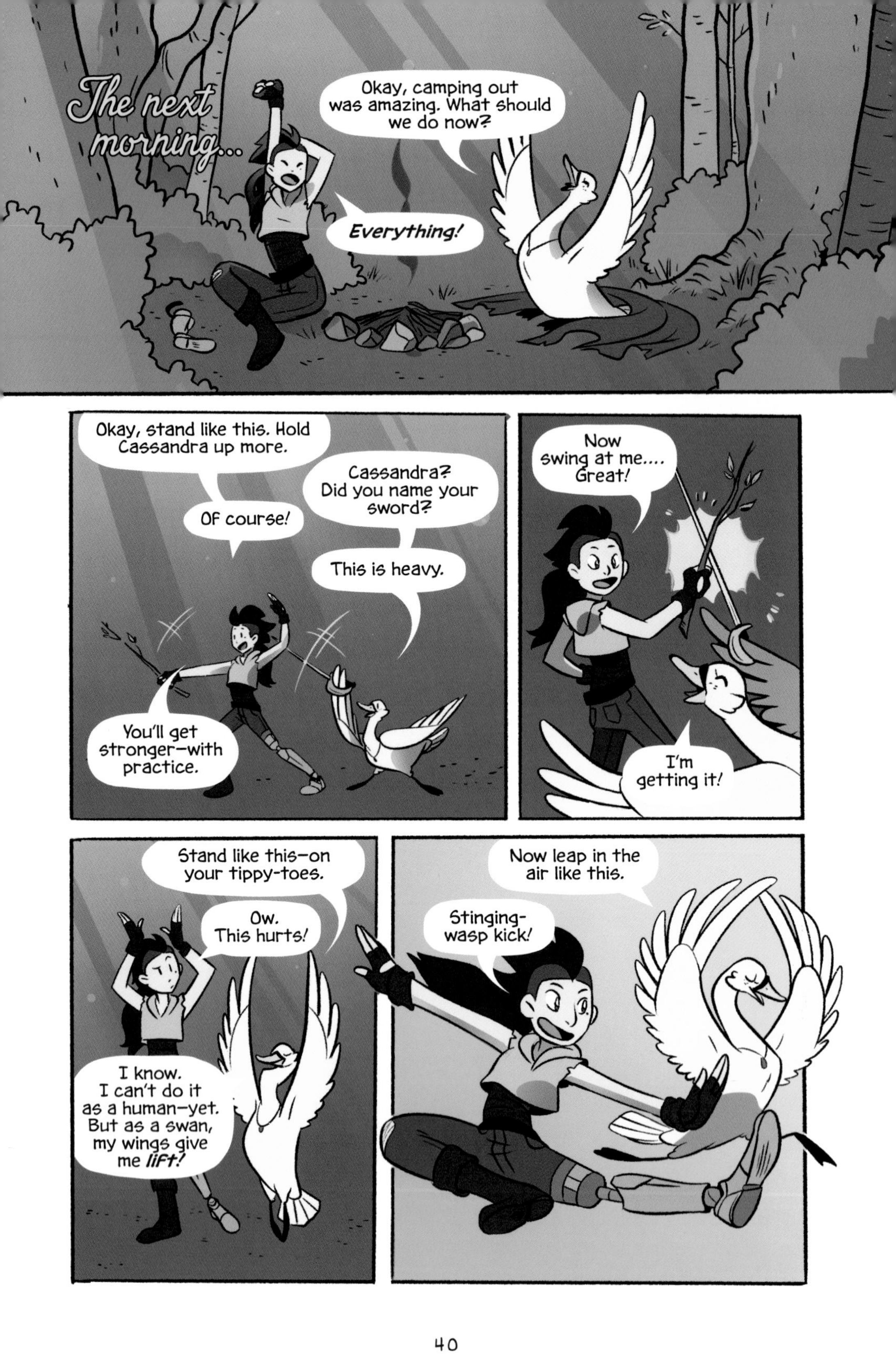
The next morning...
Okay, camping out was amazing. What should we do now?
Everything!
Okay, stand like this. Hold Cassandra up more.
Cassandra? Did you name your sword?
Of course!
This is heavy.
You'll get stronger—with practice.
Now swing at me.... Great!
I'm getting it!
Stand like this—on your tippy-toes.
Ow. This hurts!
I know. I can't do it as a human—yet. But as a swan, my wings give me *lift!*
Now leap in the air like this.
Stinging-wasp kick!

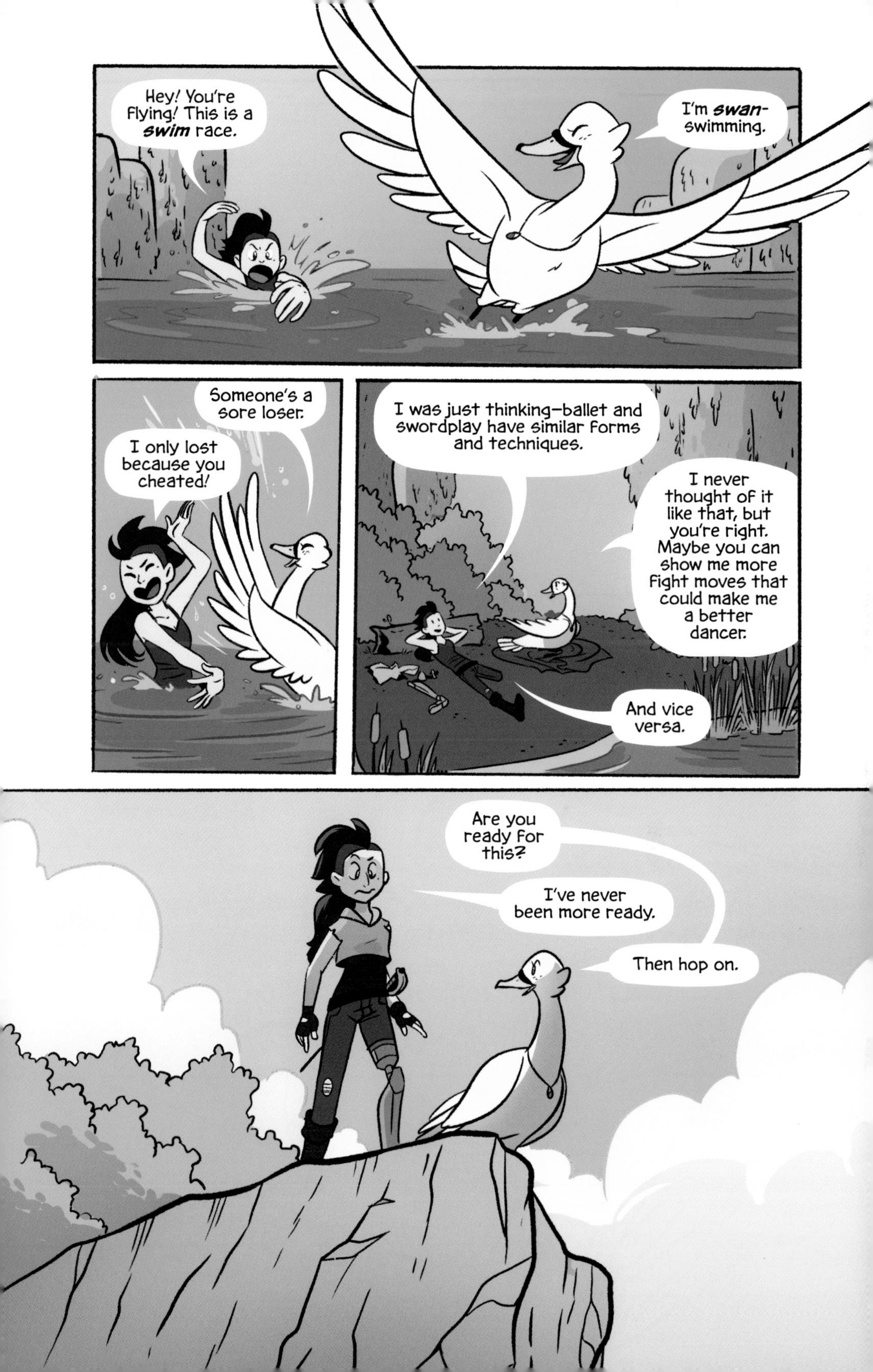
Hey! You're Flying! This is a *swim* race.
I'm *swan*-swimming.
Someone's a sore loser.
I only lost because you cheated!
I was just thinking—ballet and swordplay have similar forms and techniques.
I never thought of it like that, but you're right. Maybe you can show me more fight moves that could make me a better dancer.
And vice versa.
Are you ready for this?
I've never been more ready.
Then hop on.

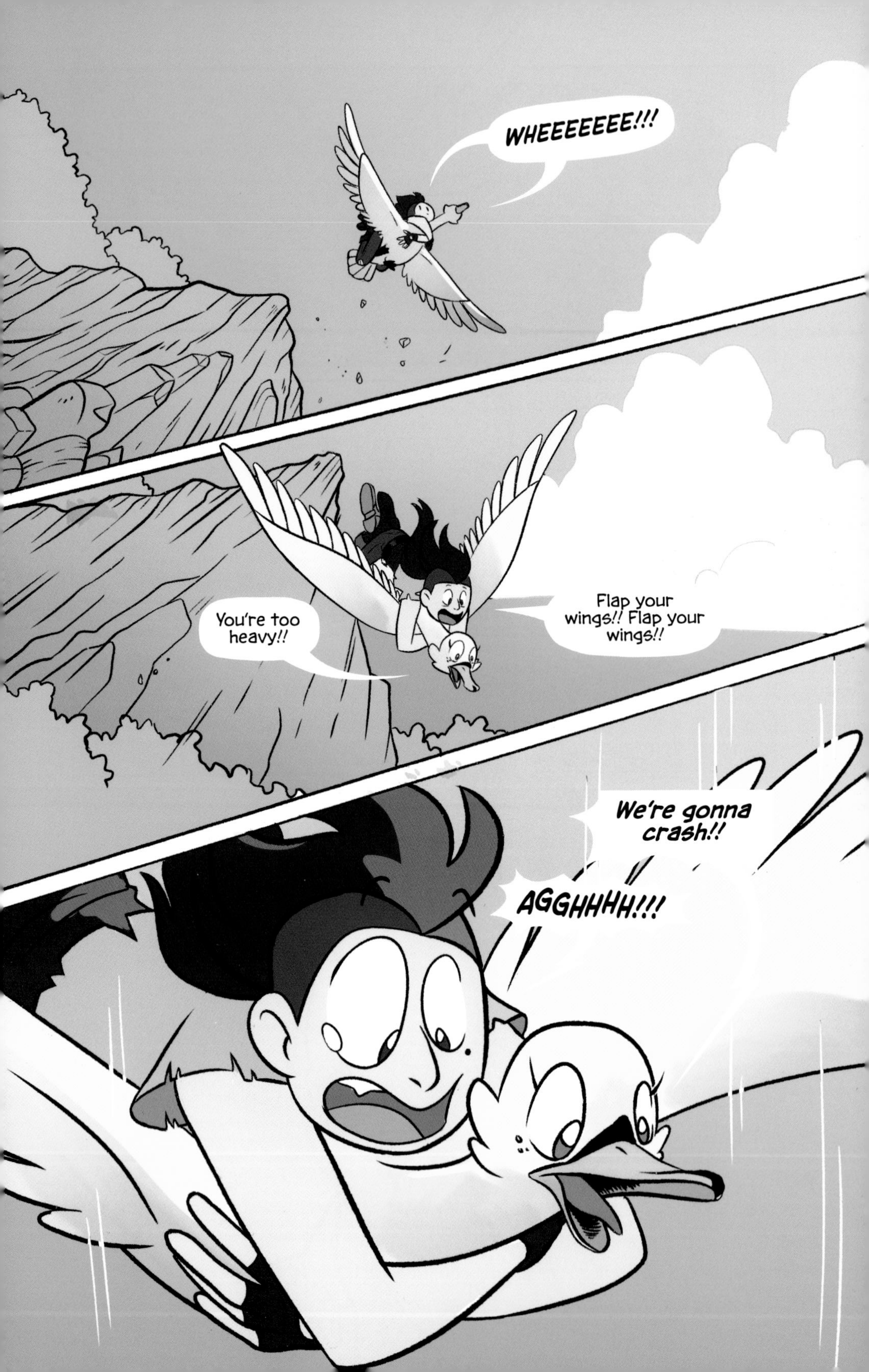
WHEEEEEEE!!!
You're too heavy!!
Flap your wings!! Flap your wings!!
We're gonna crash!!
AGGHHHH!!!

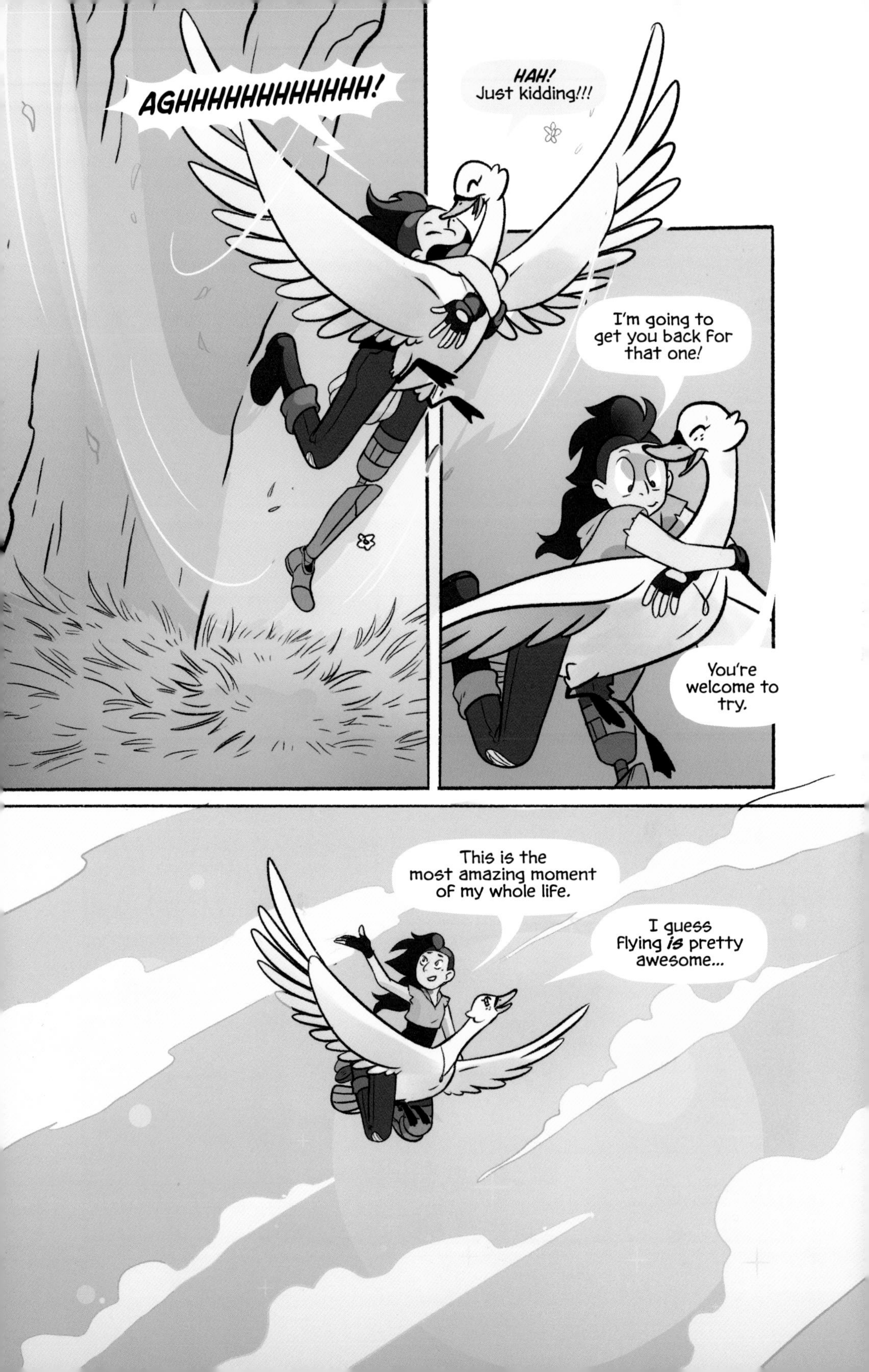
AGHHHHHHHHHHHH!
HAH! Just kidding!!!
I'm going to get you back for that one!
You're welcome to try.
This is the most amazing moment of my whole life.
I guess flying *is* pretty awesome...

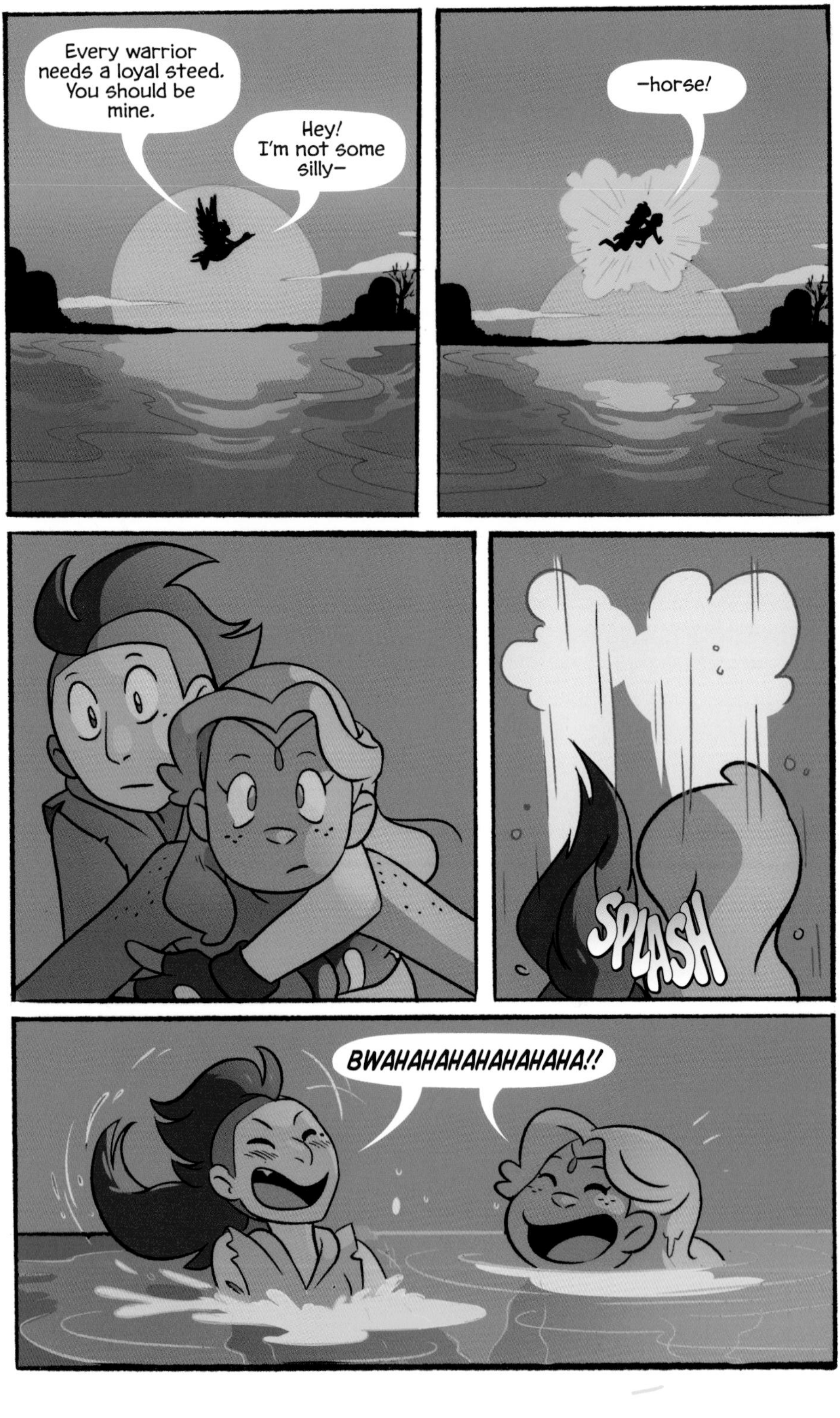
Every warrior needs a loyal steed. You should be mine.
Hey! I'm not some silly—
—horse!
SPLASH
BWAHAHAHAHAHAHAHA!!

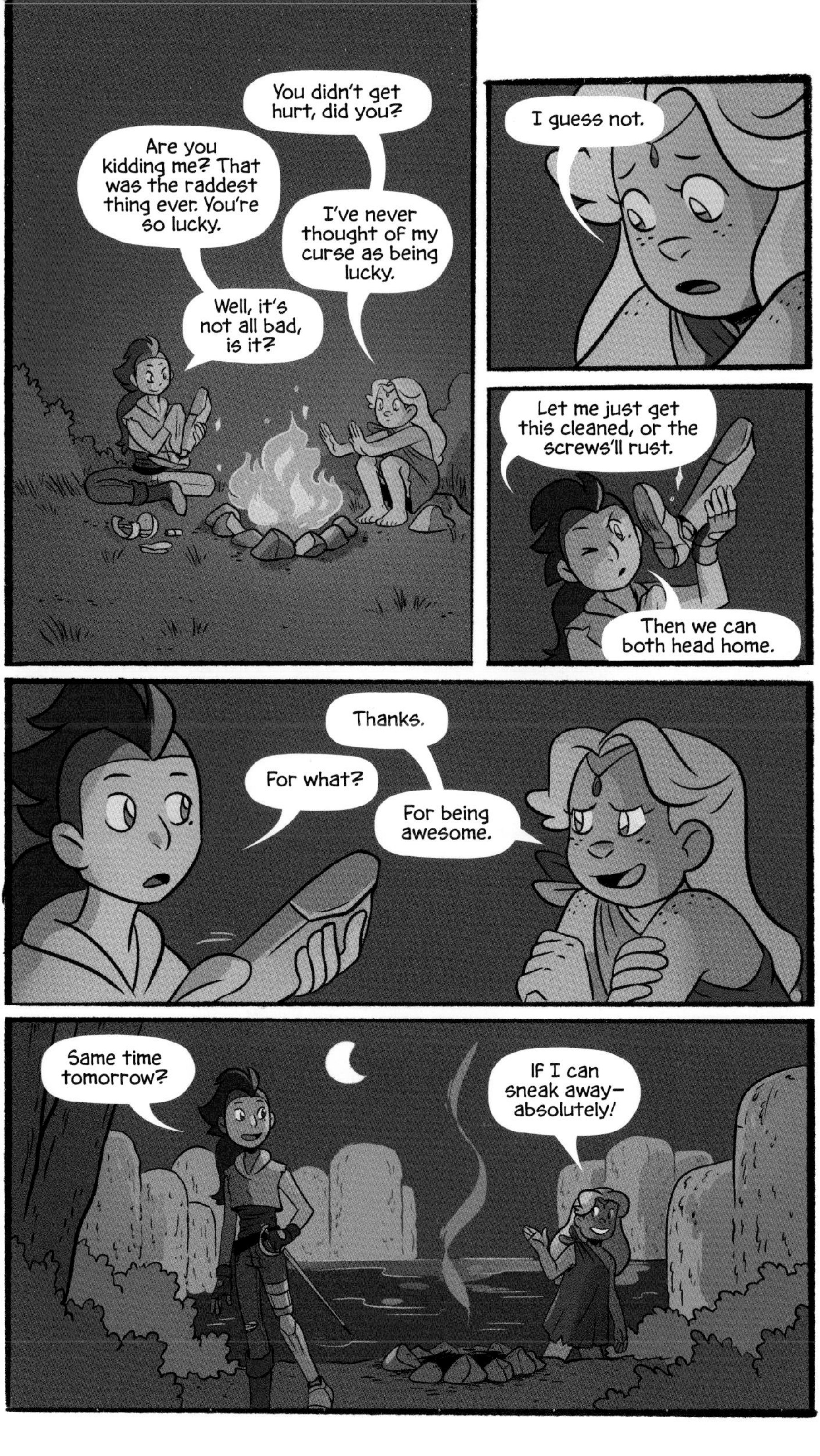
You didn't get hurt, did you?
Are you kidding me? That was the raddest thing ever. You're so lucky.
I've never thought of my curse as being lucky.
Well, it's not all bad, is it?
I guess not.
Let me just get this cleaned, or the screws'll rust.
Then we can both head home.
Thanks.
For what?
For being awesome.
Same time tomorrow?
If I can sneak away—absolutely!

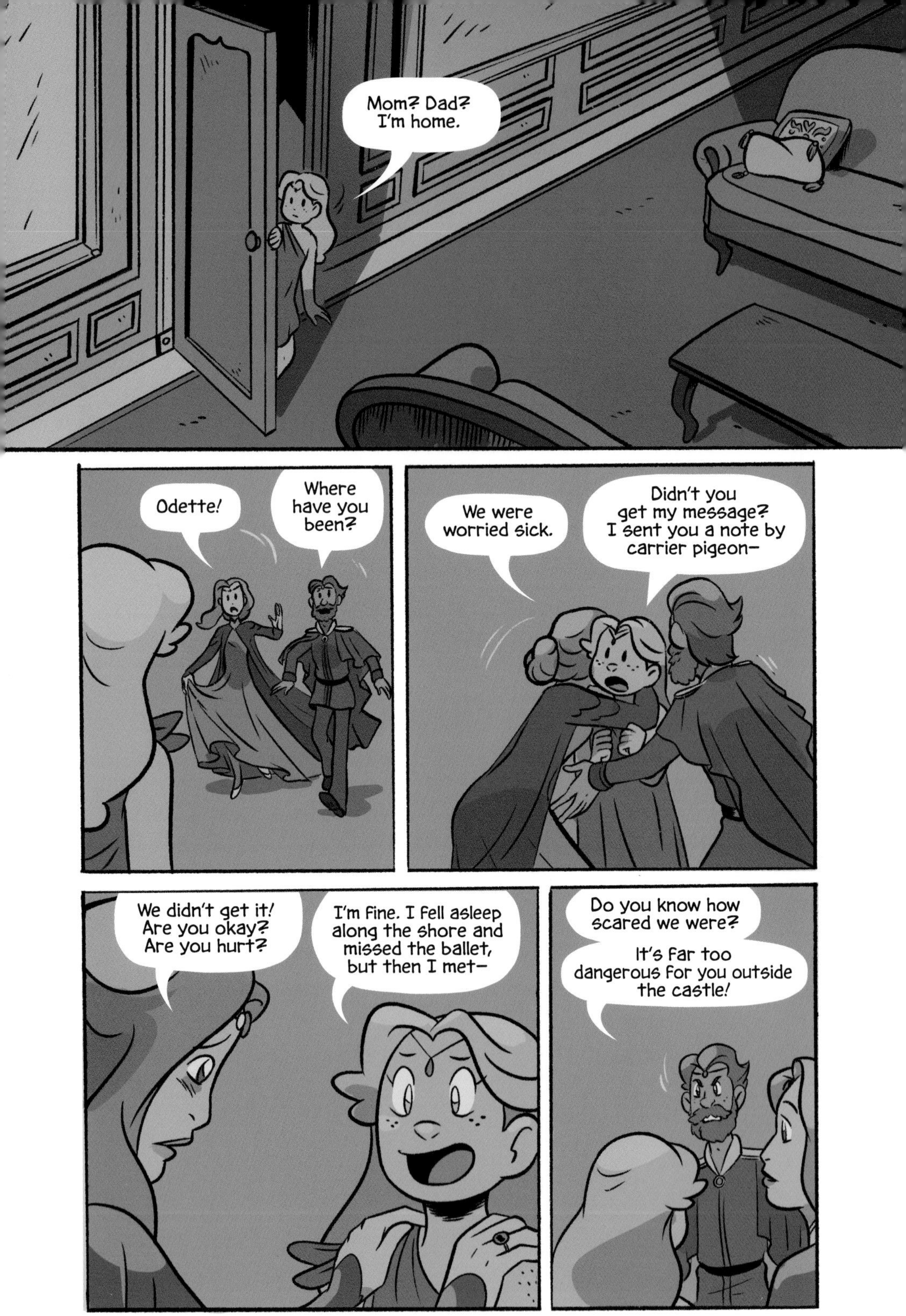
Mom? Dad? I'm home.
Odette!
Where have you been?
We were worried sick.
Didn't you get my message? I sent you a note by carrier pigeon–
We didn't get it! Are you okay? Are you hurt?
I'm fine. I fell asleep along the shore and missed the ballet, but then I met–
Do you know how scared we were?
It's far too dangerous for you outside the castle!

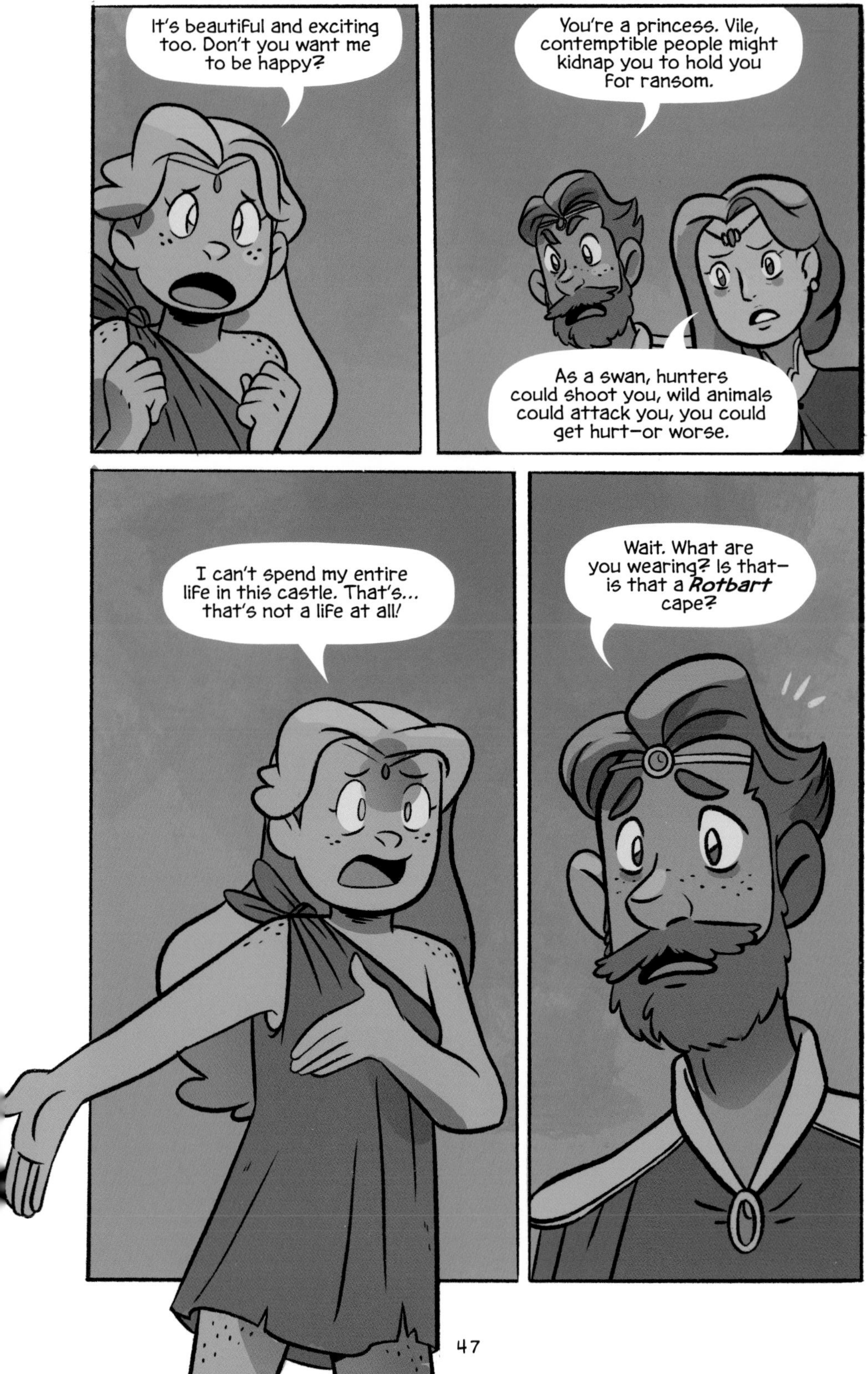
It's beautiful and exciting too. Don't you want me to be happy?
You're a princess. Vile, contemptible people might kidnap you to hold you for ransom.
As a swan, hunters could shoot you, wild animals could attack you, you could get hurt—or worse.
I can't spend my entire life in this castle. That's... that's not a life at all!
Wait. What are you wearing? Is that— is that a *Rotbart* cape?

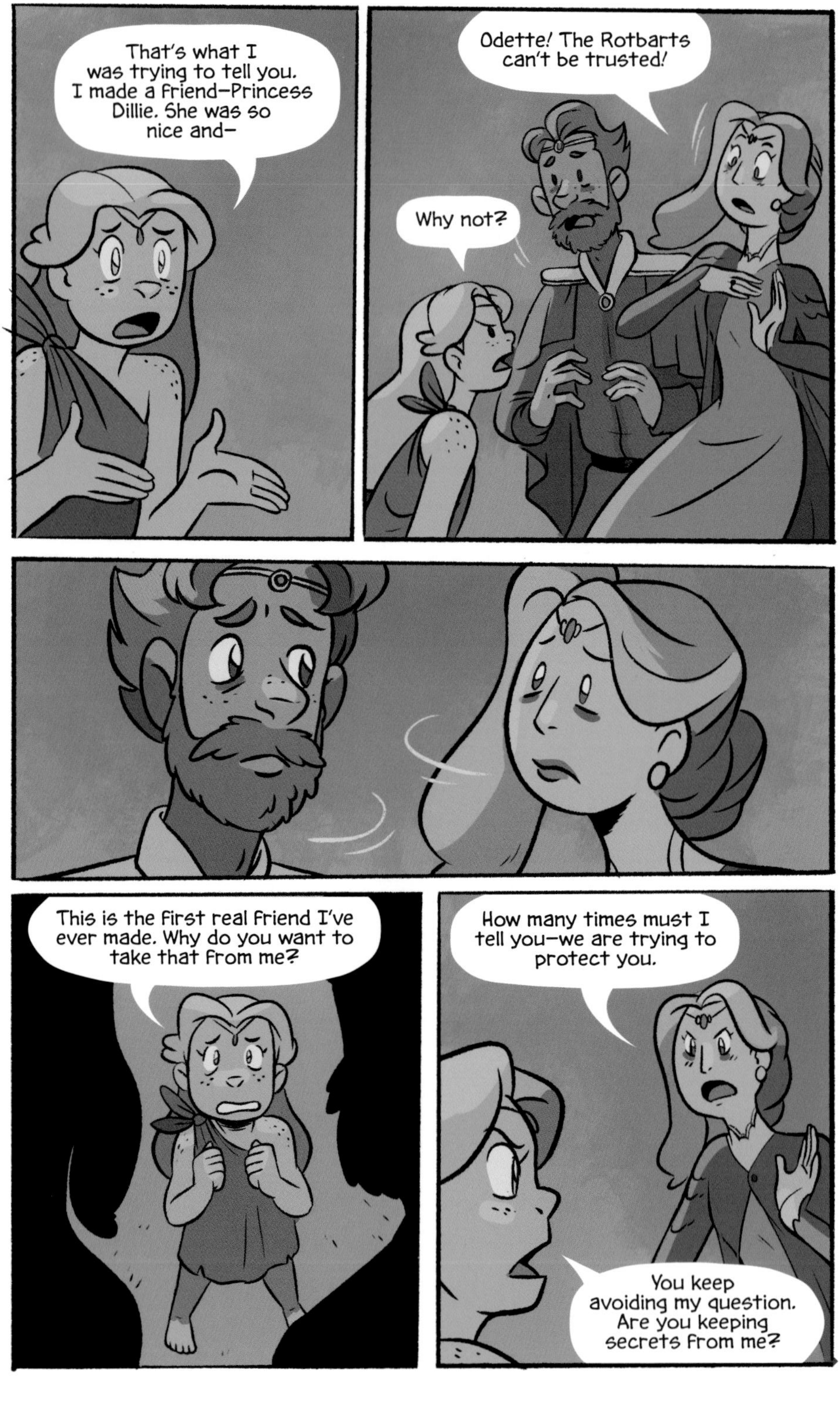
That's what I was trying to tell you. I made a friend—Princess Dillie. She was so nice and—
Odette! The Rotbarts can't be trusted!
Why not?
This is the first real friend I've ever made. Why do you want to take that from me?
How many times must I tell you—we are trying to protect you.
You keep avoiding my question. Are you keeping secrets from me?

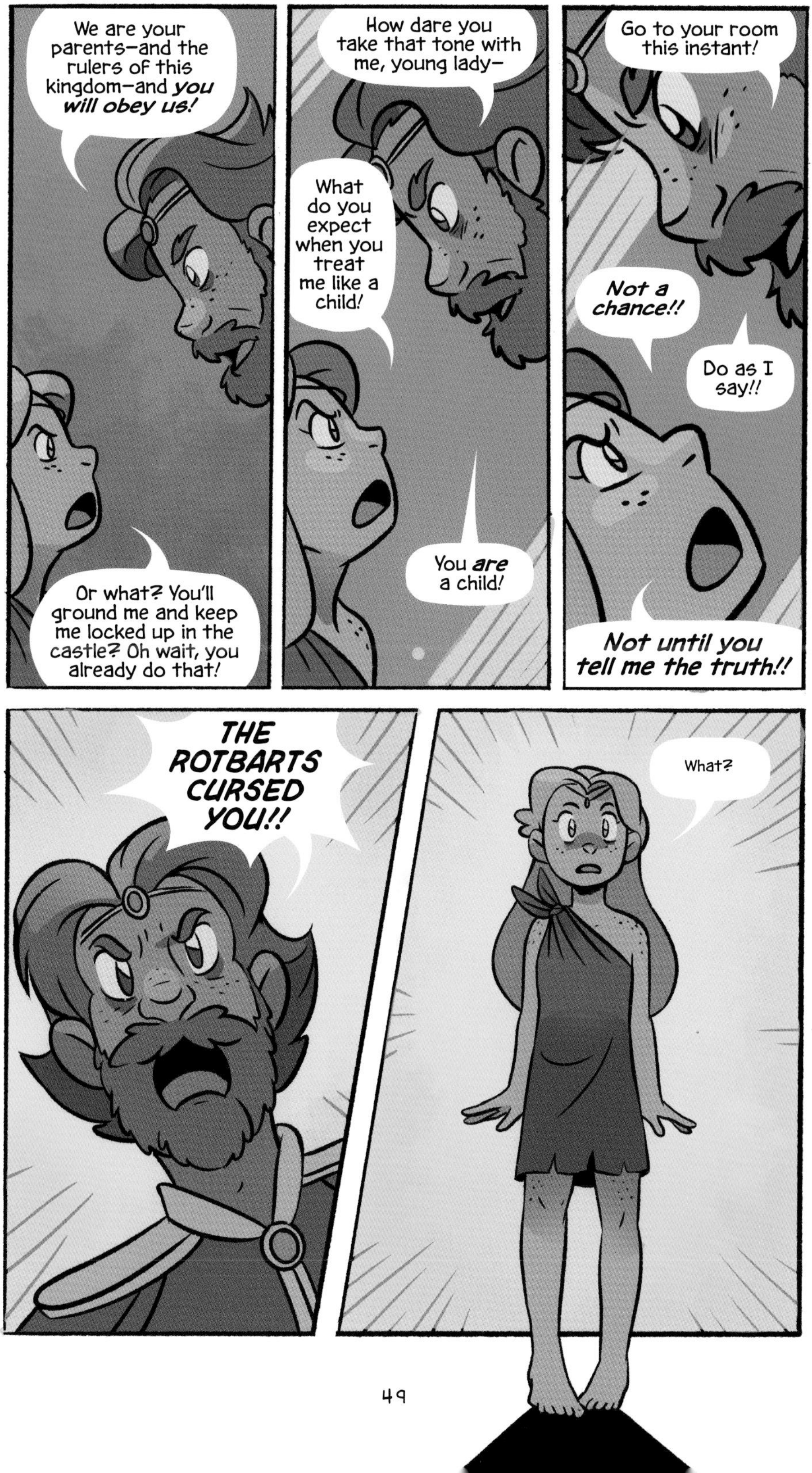
We are your parents—and the rulers of this kingdom—and *you will obey us!*
Or what? You'll ground me and keep me locked up in the castle? Oh wait, you already do that!
How dare you take that tone with me, young lady—
What do you expect when you treat me like a child!
You *are* a child!
Go to your room this instant!
Not a chance!!
Do as I say!!
Not until you tell me the truth!!
THE ROTBARTS CURSED YOU!!
What?

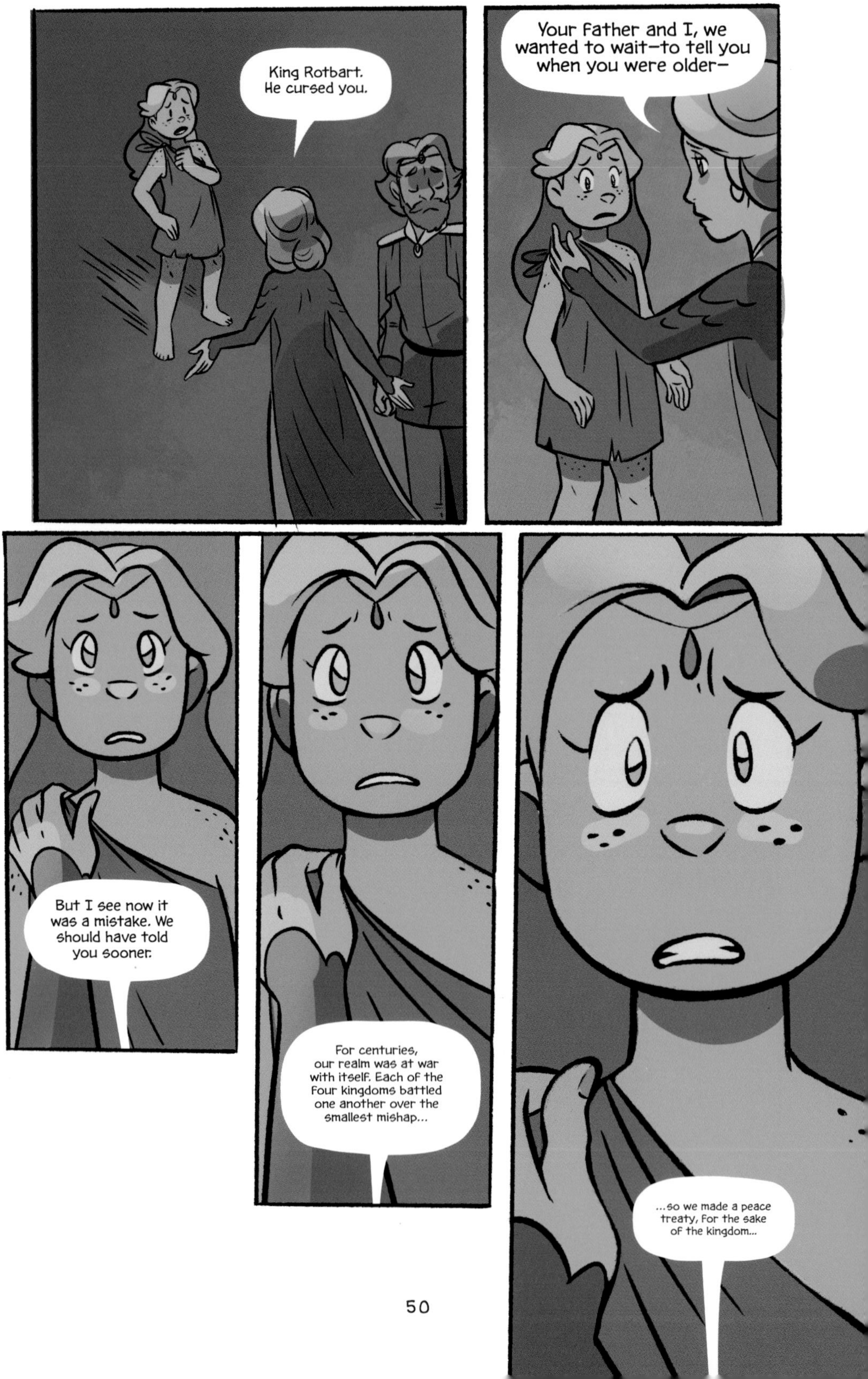
King Rotbart. He cursed you.
Your father and I, we wanted to wait—to tell you when you were older—
But I see now it was a mistake. We should have told you sooner.
For centuries, our realm was at war with itself. Each of the four kingdoms battled one another over the smallest mishap...
...so we made a peace treaty, for the sake of the kingdom...

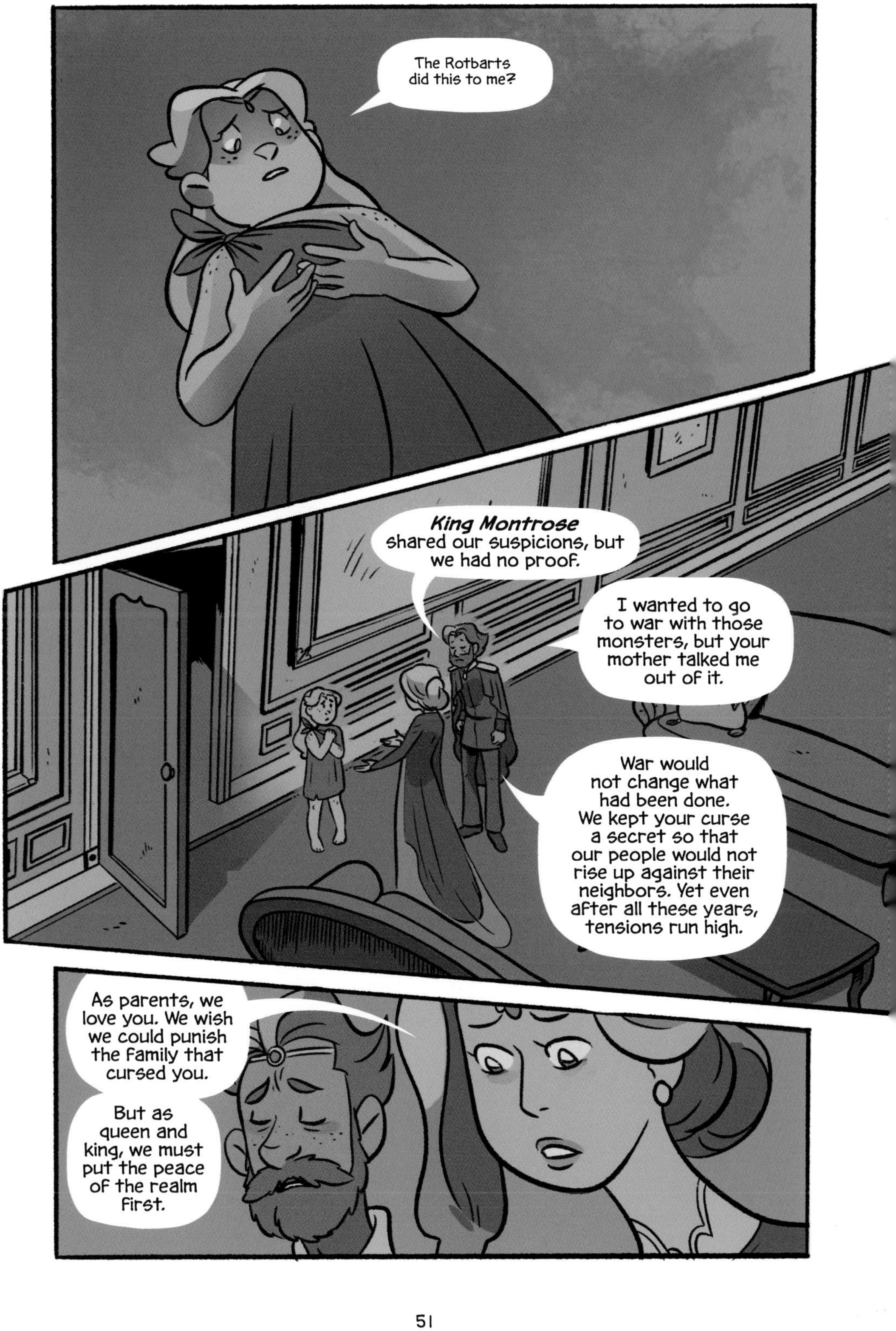
The Rotbarts did this to me?
King Montrose shared our suspicions, but we had no proof.
I wanted to go to war with those monsters, but your mother talked me out of it.
War would not change what had been done. We kept your curse a secret so that our people would not rise up against their neighbors. Yet even after all these years, tensions run high.
As parents, we love you. We wish we could punish the family that cursed you.
But as queen and king, we must put the peace of the realm first.

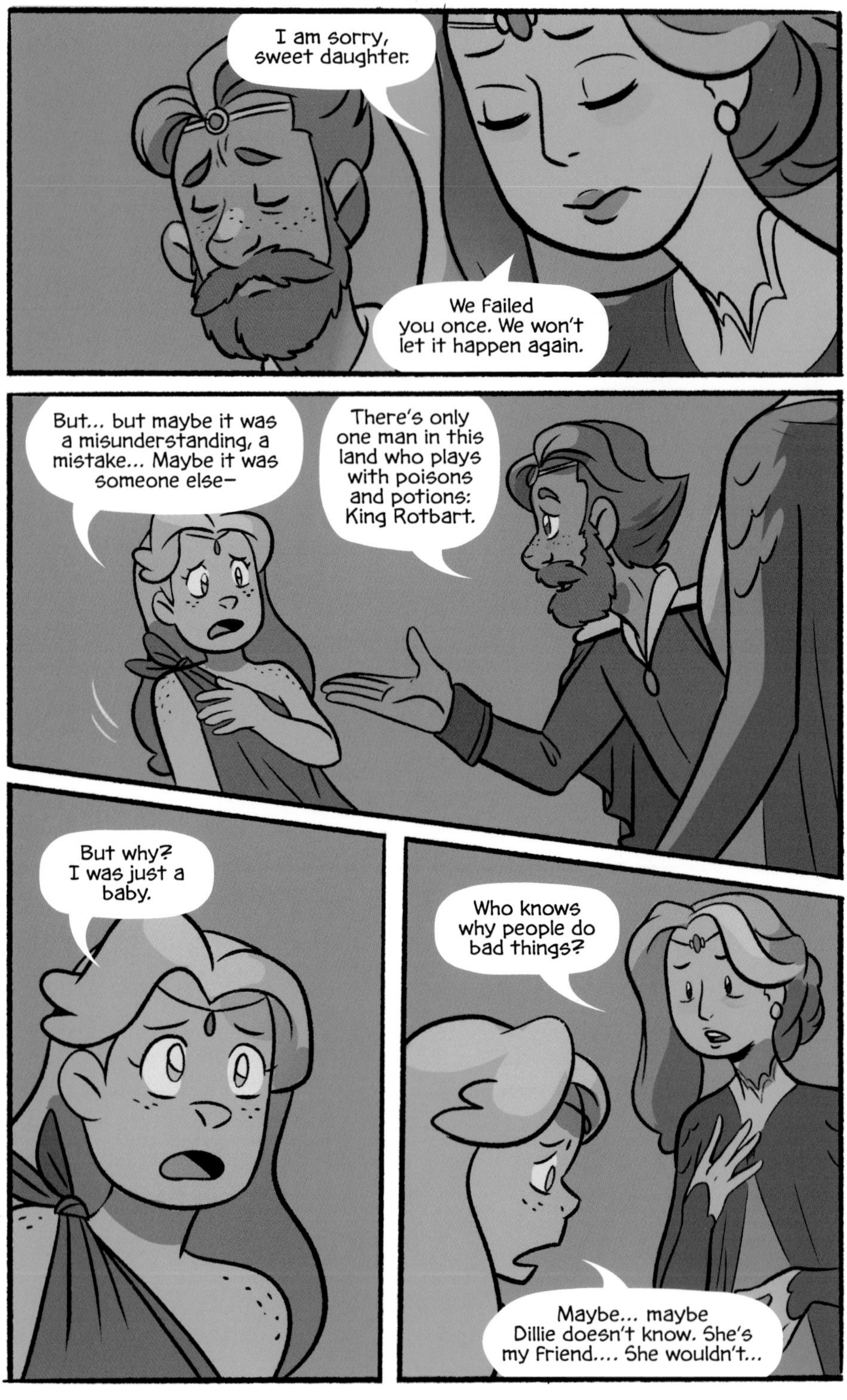
I am sorry, sweet daughter.
We failed you once. We won't let it happen again.
But... but maybe it was a misunderstanding, a mistake... Maybe it was someone else–
There's only one man in this land who plays with poisons and potions: King Rotbart.
But why? I was just a baby.
Who knows why people do bad things?
Maybe... maybe Dillie doesn't know. She's my friend.... She wouldn't...

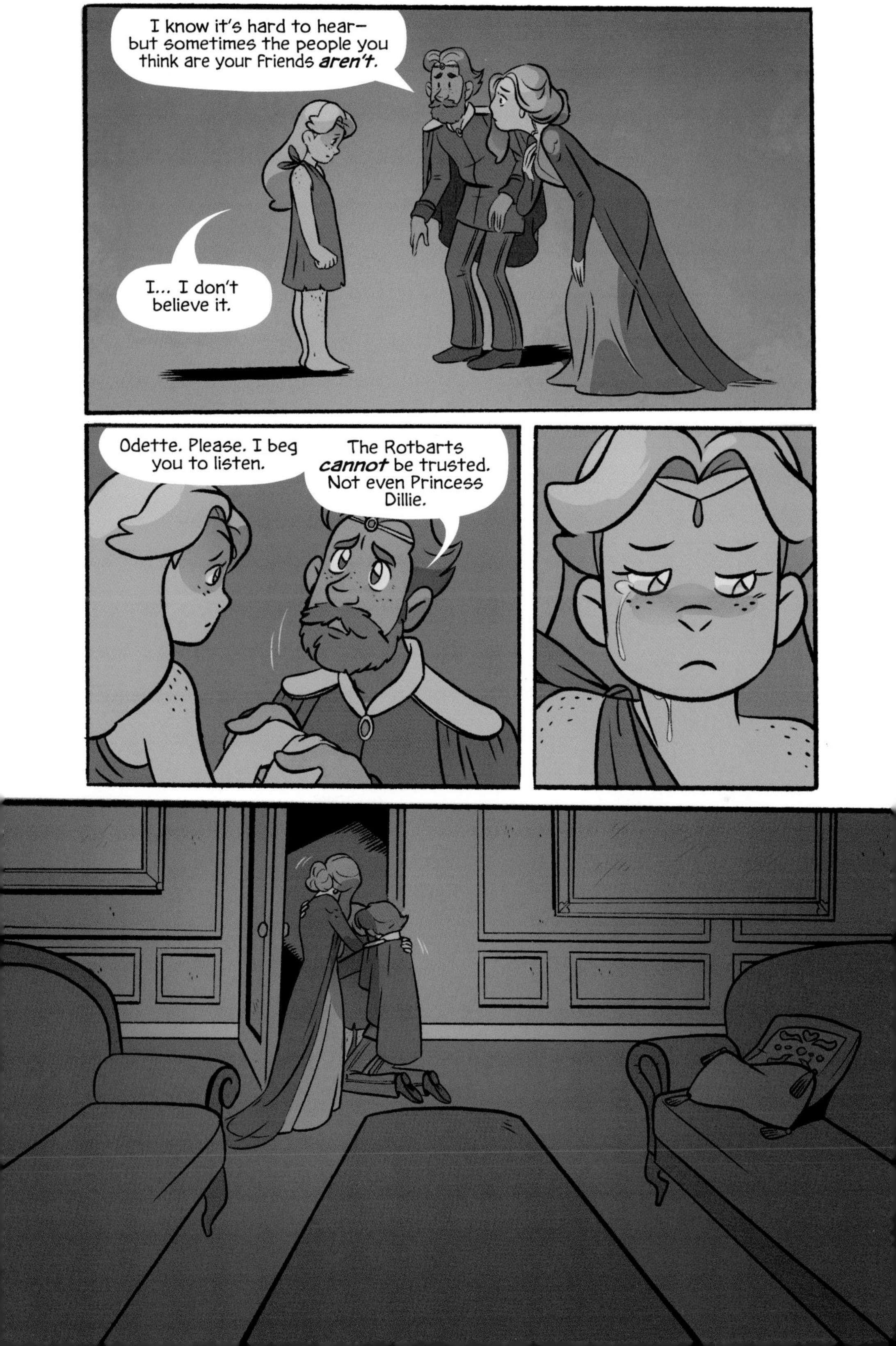
I know it's hard to hear—but sometimes the people you think are your friends *aren't*.
I... I don't believe it.
Odette. Please. I beg you to listen.
The Rotbarts *cannot* be trusted. Not even Princess Dillie.

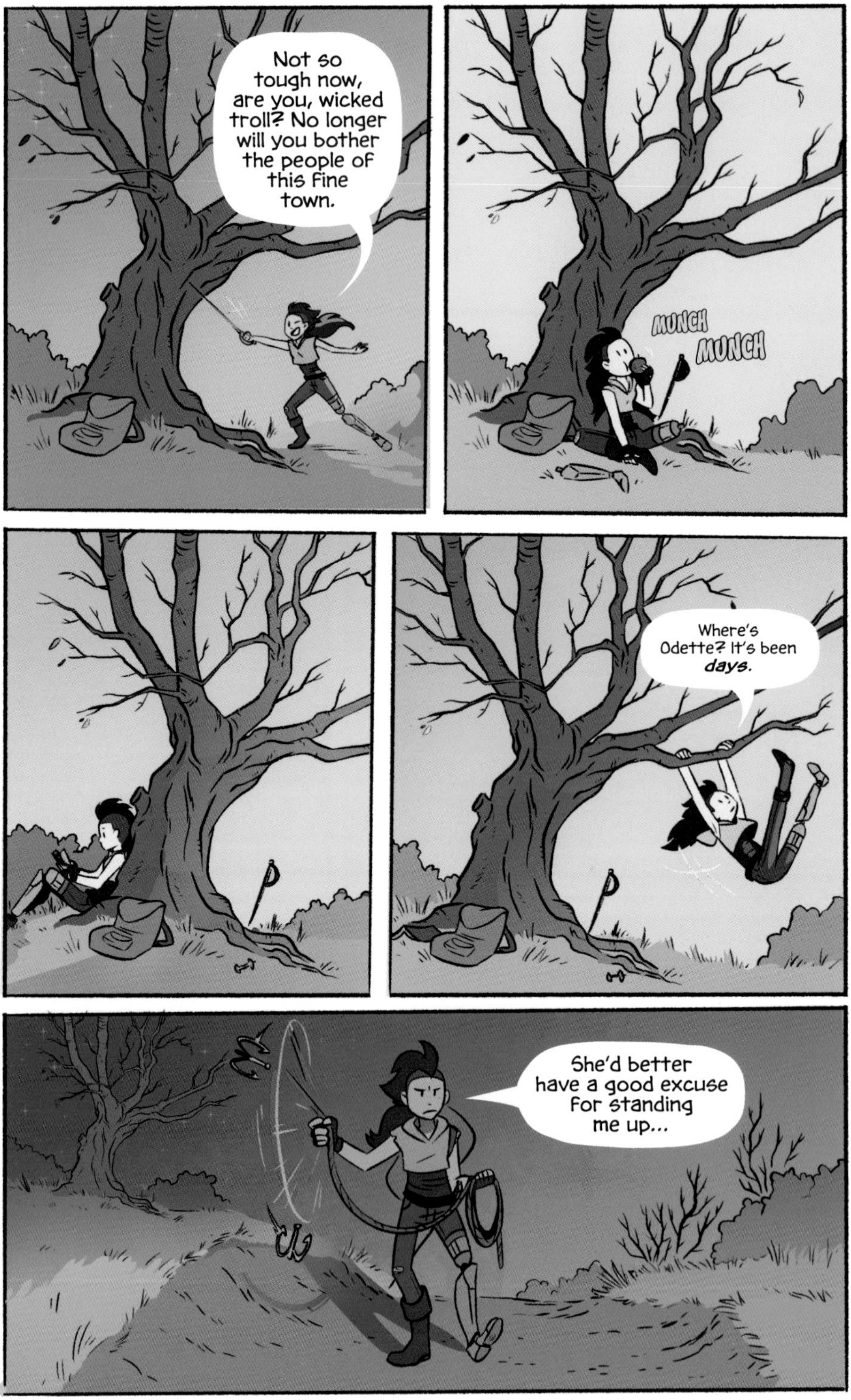
Not so tough now, are you, wicked troll? No longer will you bother the people of this fine town.
MUNCH
MUNCH
Where's Odette? It's been *days.*
She'd better have a good excuse for standing me up...

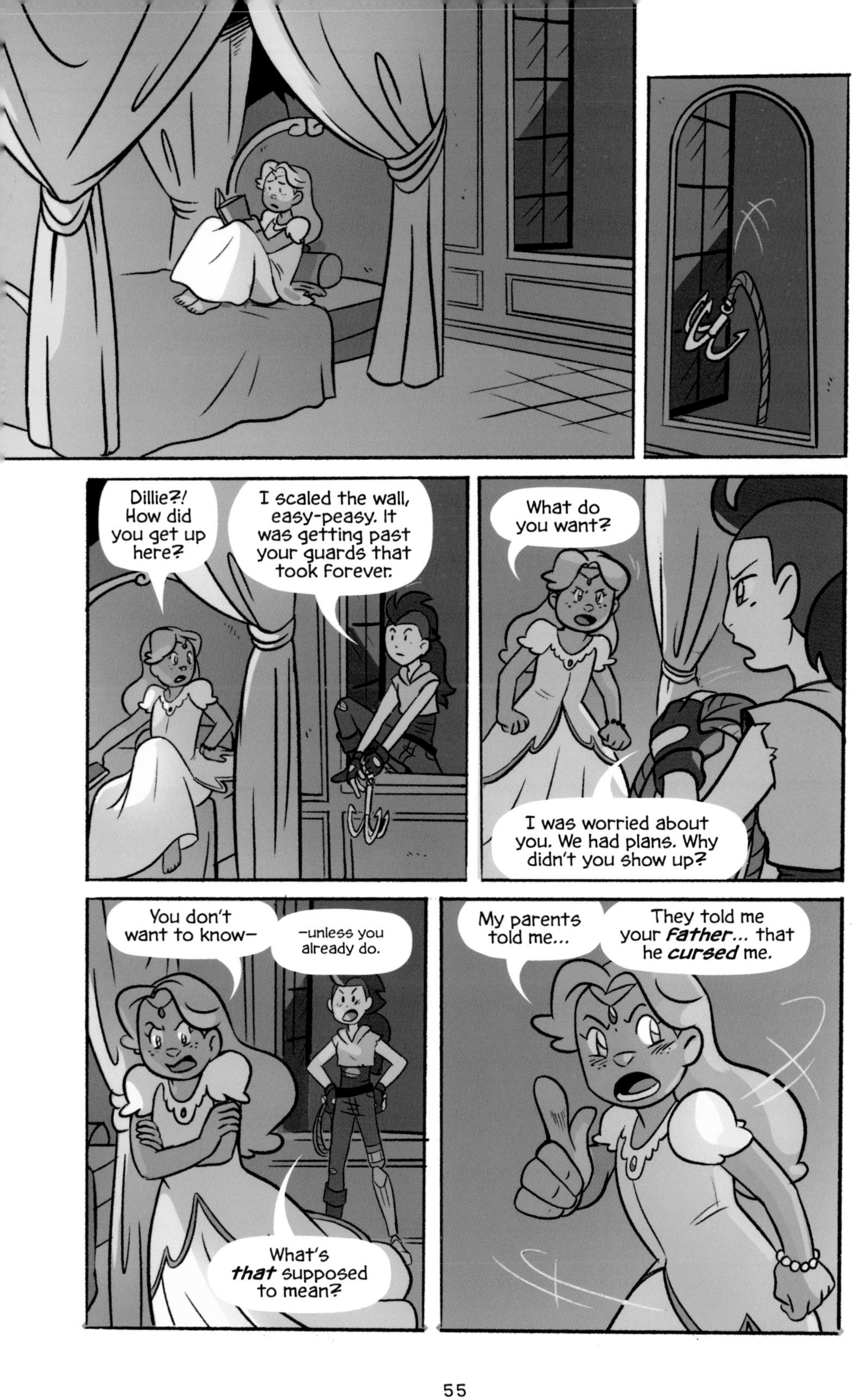

Dillie?! How did you get up here?
I scaled the wall, easy-peasy. It was getting past your guards that took forever.
What do you want?
I was worried about you. We had plans. Why didn't you show up?
You don't want to know—
—unless you already do.
What's *that* supposed to mean?
My parents told me...
They told me your *father*... that he *cursed* me.

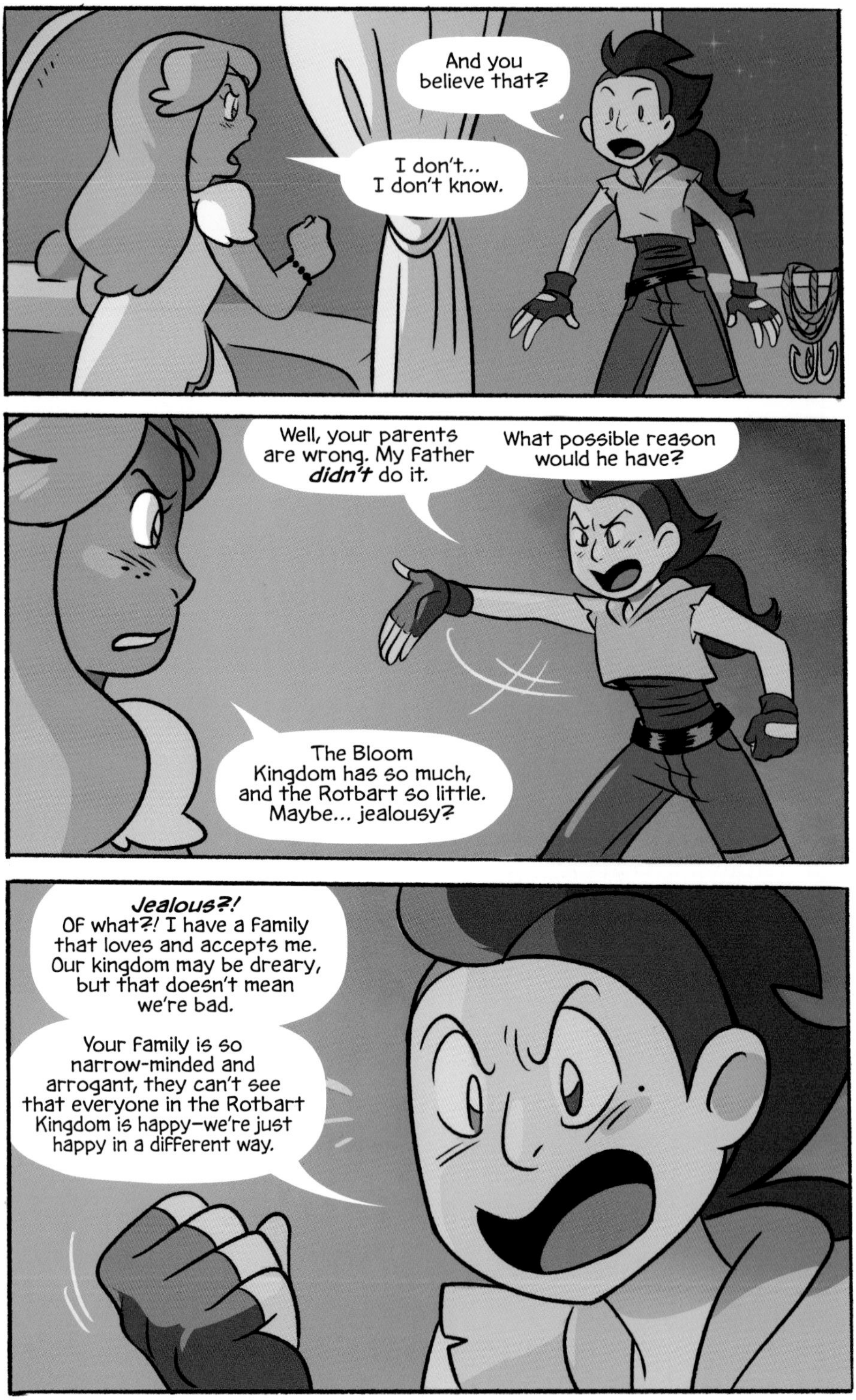
And you believe that?
I don't... I don't know.
Well, your parents are wrong. My father *didn't* do it.
What possible reason would he have?
The Bloom Kingdom has so much, and the Rotbart so little. Maybe... jealousy?
Jealous?! Of what?! I have a family that loves and accepts me. Our kingdom may be dreary, but that doesn't mean we're bad.
Your family is so narrow-minded and arrogant, they can't see that everyone in the Rotbart Kingdom is happy—we're just happy in a different way.

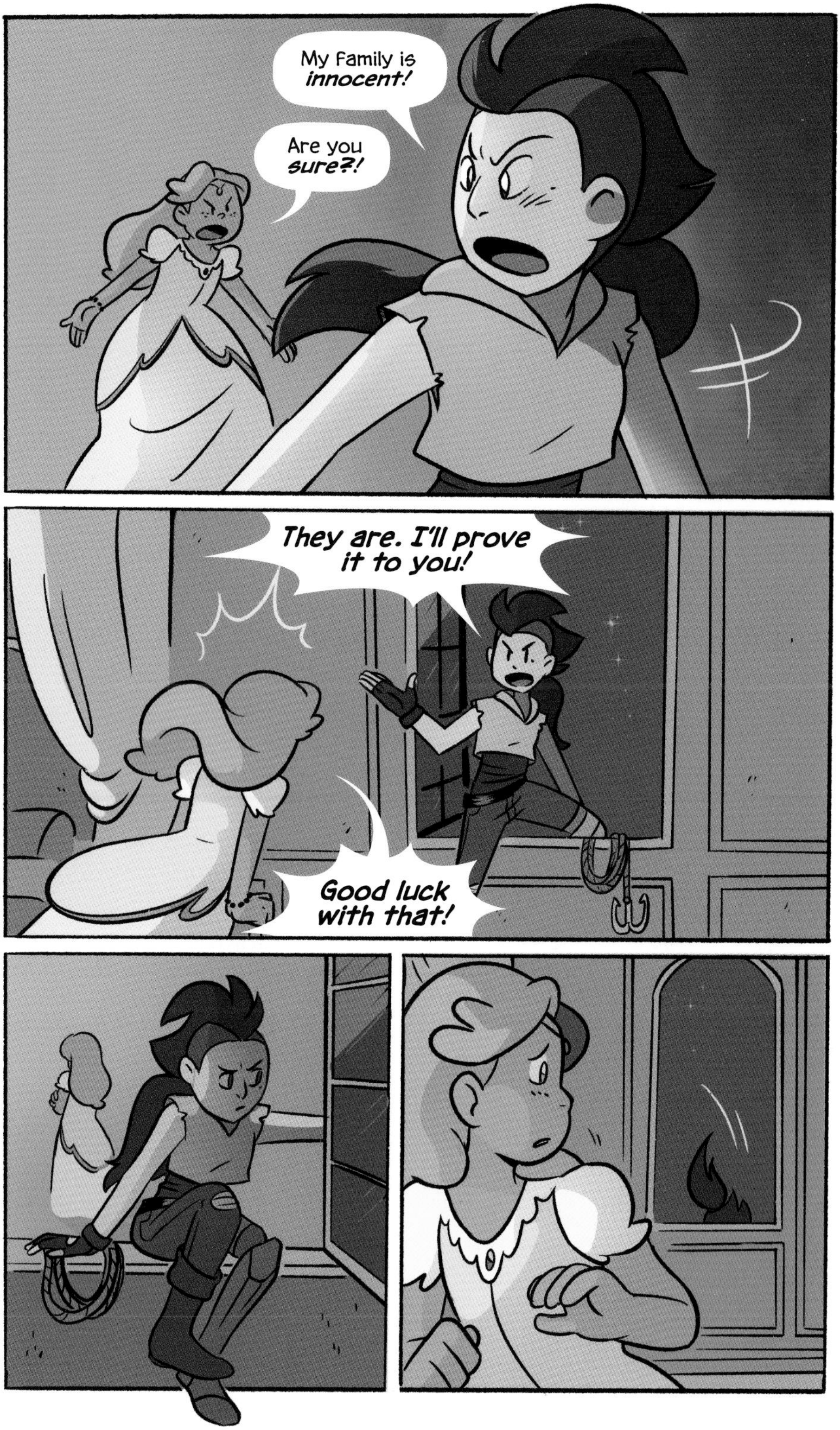
My family is innocent!
Are you sure?!
They are. I'll prove it to you!
Good luck with that!

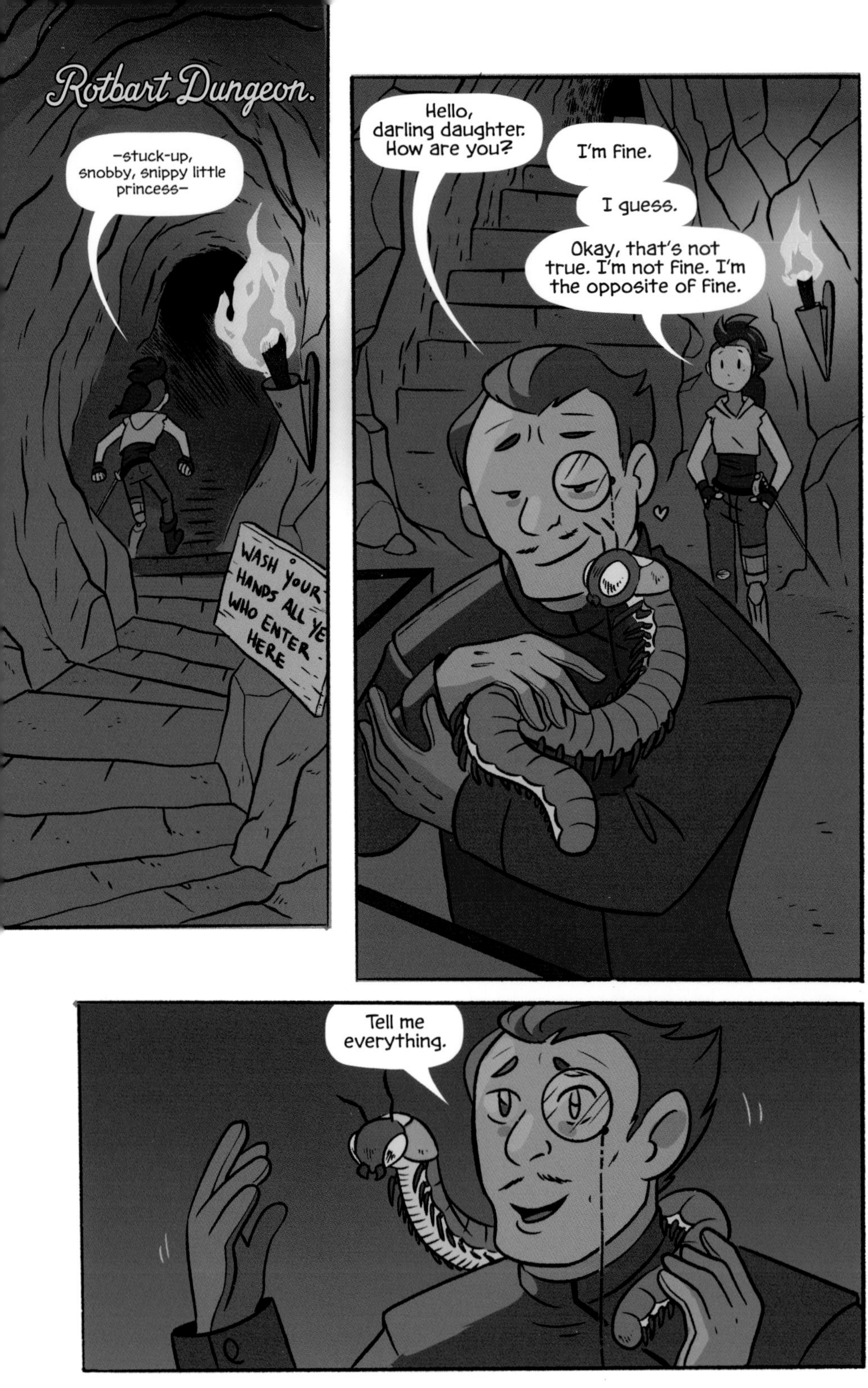
Rotbart Dungeon.
—stuck-up, snobby, snippy little princess—
WASH YOUR HANDS ALL YE WHO ENTER HERE
Hello, darling daughter. How are you?
I'm fine.
I guess.
Okay, that's not true. I'm not fine. I'm the opposite of fine.
Tell me everything.

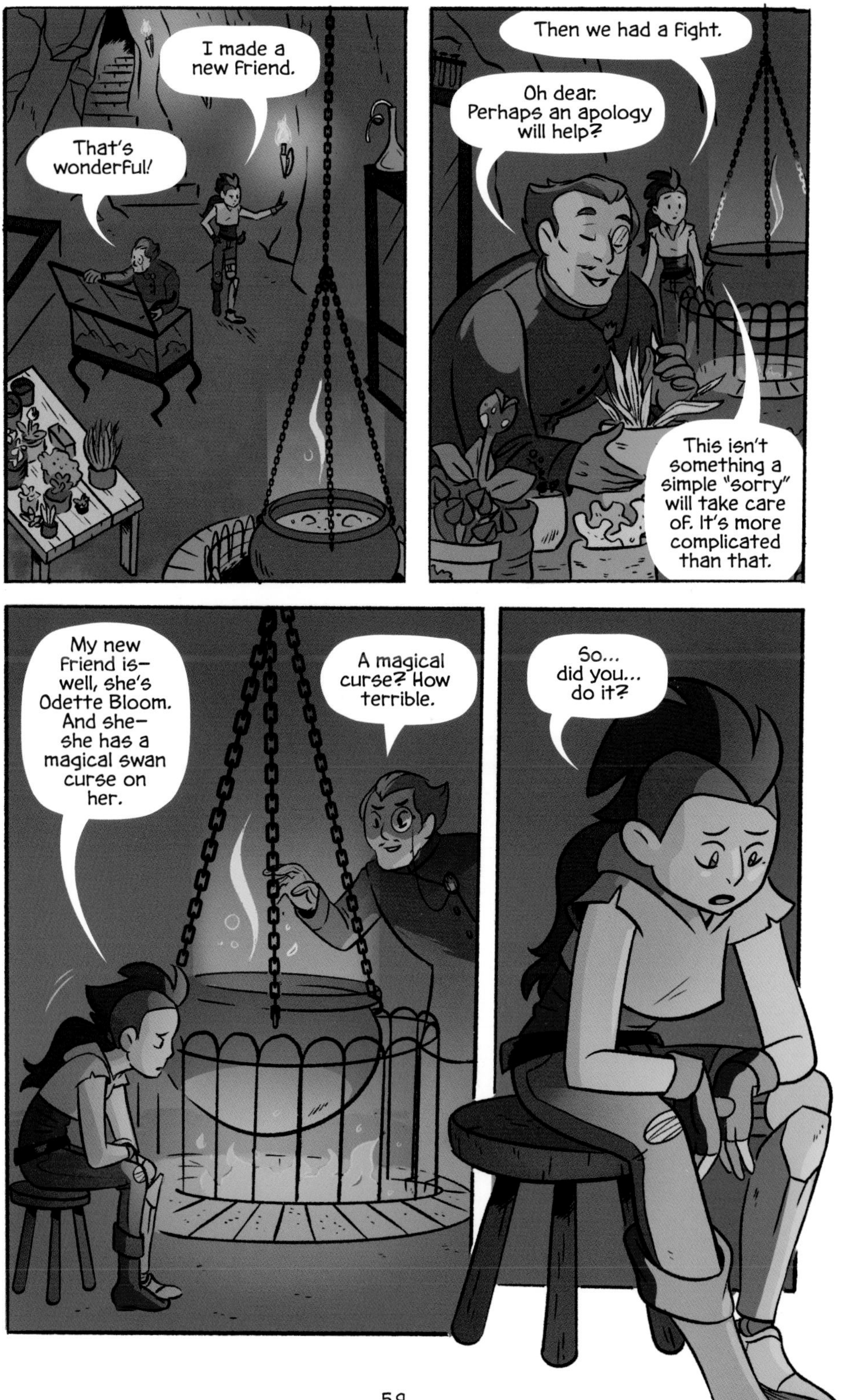
I made a new friend.
That's wonderful!
Then we had a fight.
Oh dear. Perhaps an apology will help?
This isn't something a simple "sorry" will take care of. It's more complicated than that.
My new friend is— well, she's Odette Bloom. And she— she has a magical swan curse on her.
A magical curse? How terrible.
So... did you... do it?

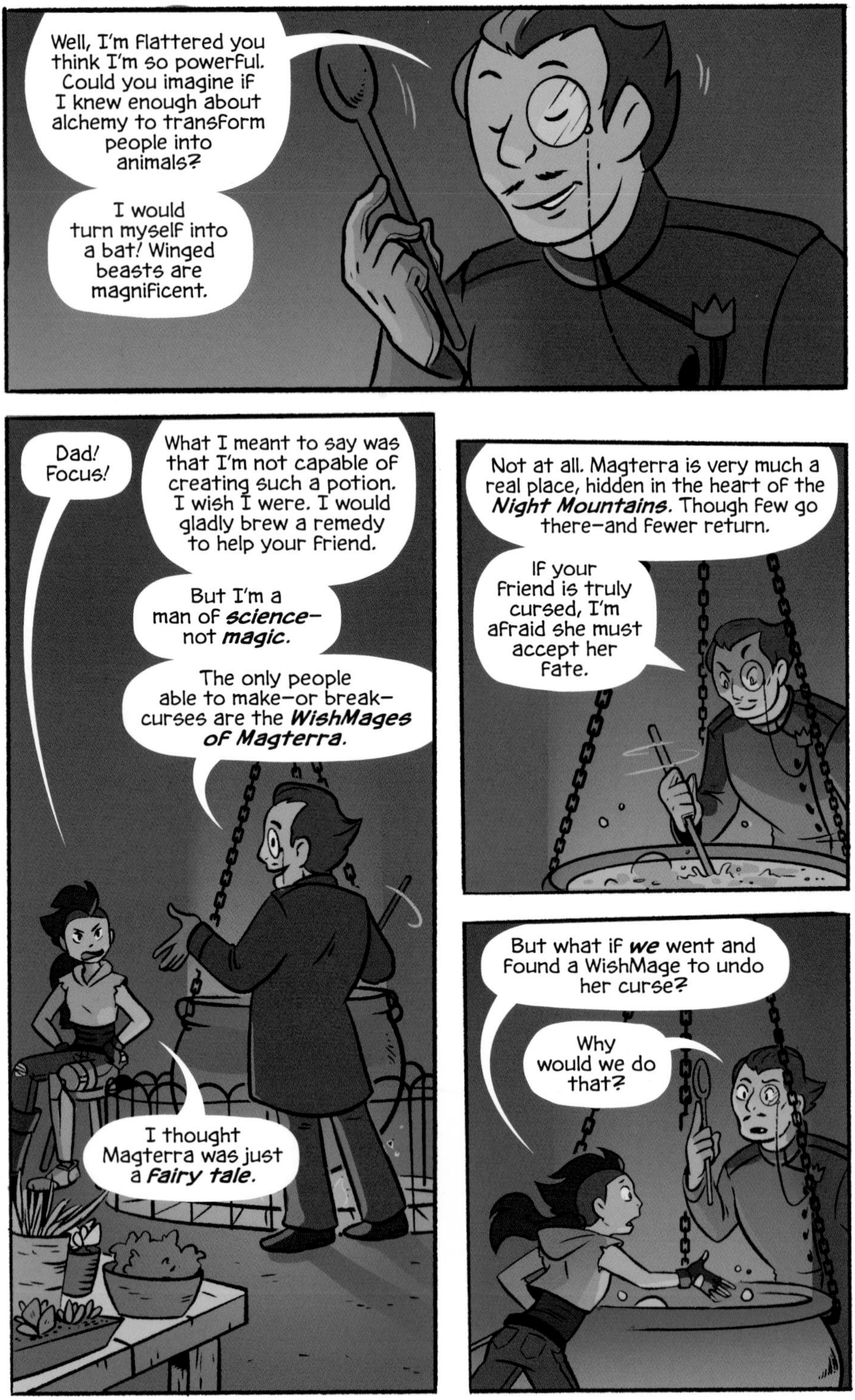
Well, I'm flattered you think I'm so powerful. Could you imagine if I knew enough about alchemy to transform people into animals?
I would turn myself into a bat! Winged beasts are magnificent.
Dad! Focus!
What I meant to say was that I'm not capable of creating such a potion. I wish I were. I would gladly brew a remedy to help your friend.
But I'm a man of *science*—not *magic*.
The only people able to make—or break—curses are the ***WishMages of Magterra.***
I thought Magterra was just a ***fairy tale.***
Not at all. Magterra is very much a real place, hidden in the heart of the ***Night Mountains.*** Though few go there—and fewer return.
If your friend is truly cursed, I'm afraid she must accept her fate.
But what if ***we*** went and found a WishMage to undo her curse?
Why would we do that?

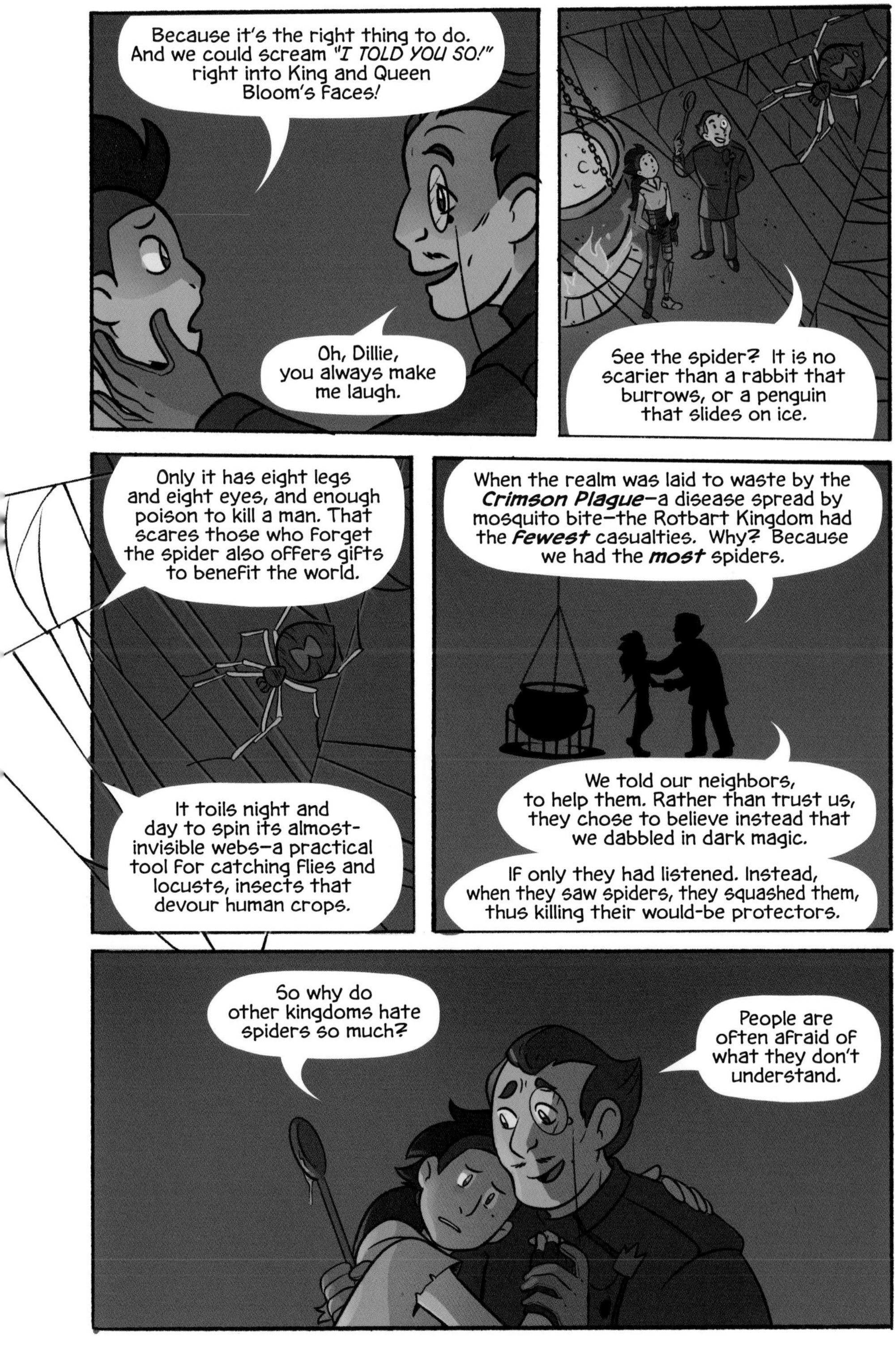

Because it's the right thing to do. And we could scream *"I TOLD YOU SO!"* right into King and Queen Bloom's faces!
Oh, Dillie, you always make me laugh.
See the spider? It is no scarier than a rabbit that burrows, or a penguin that slides on ice.
Only it has eight legs and eight eyes, and enough poison to kill a man. That scares those who forget the spider also offers gifts to benefit the world.
It toils night and day to spin its almost-invisible webs—a practical tool for catching flies and locusts, insects that devour human crops.
When the realm was laid to waste by the ***Crimson Plague***—a disease spread by mosquito bite—the Rotbart Kingdom had the ***fewest*** casualties. Why? Because we had the ***most*** spiders.
We told our neighbors, to help them. Rather than trust us, they chose to believe instead that we dabbled in dark magic.
If only they had listened. Instead, when they saw spiders, they squashed them, thus killing their would-be protectors.
So why do other kingdoms hate spiders so much?
People are often afraid of what they don't understand.

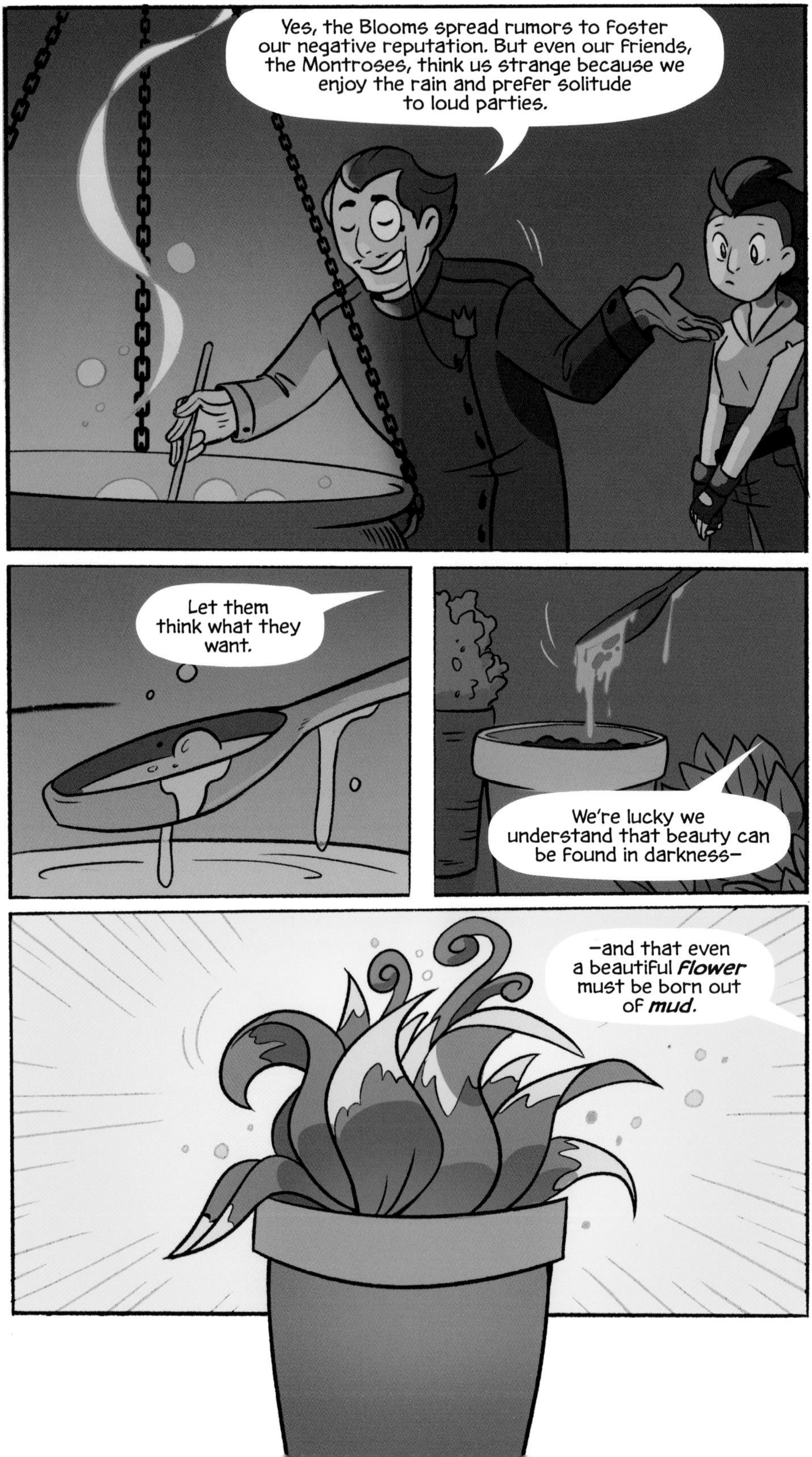
Yes, the Blooms spread rumors to foster our negative reputation. But even our friends, the Montroses, think us strange because we enjoy the rain and prefer solitude to loud parties.
Let them think what they want.
We're lucky we understand that beauty can be found in darkness–
–and that even a beautiful *flower* must be born out of *mud.*

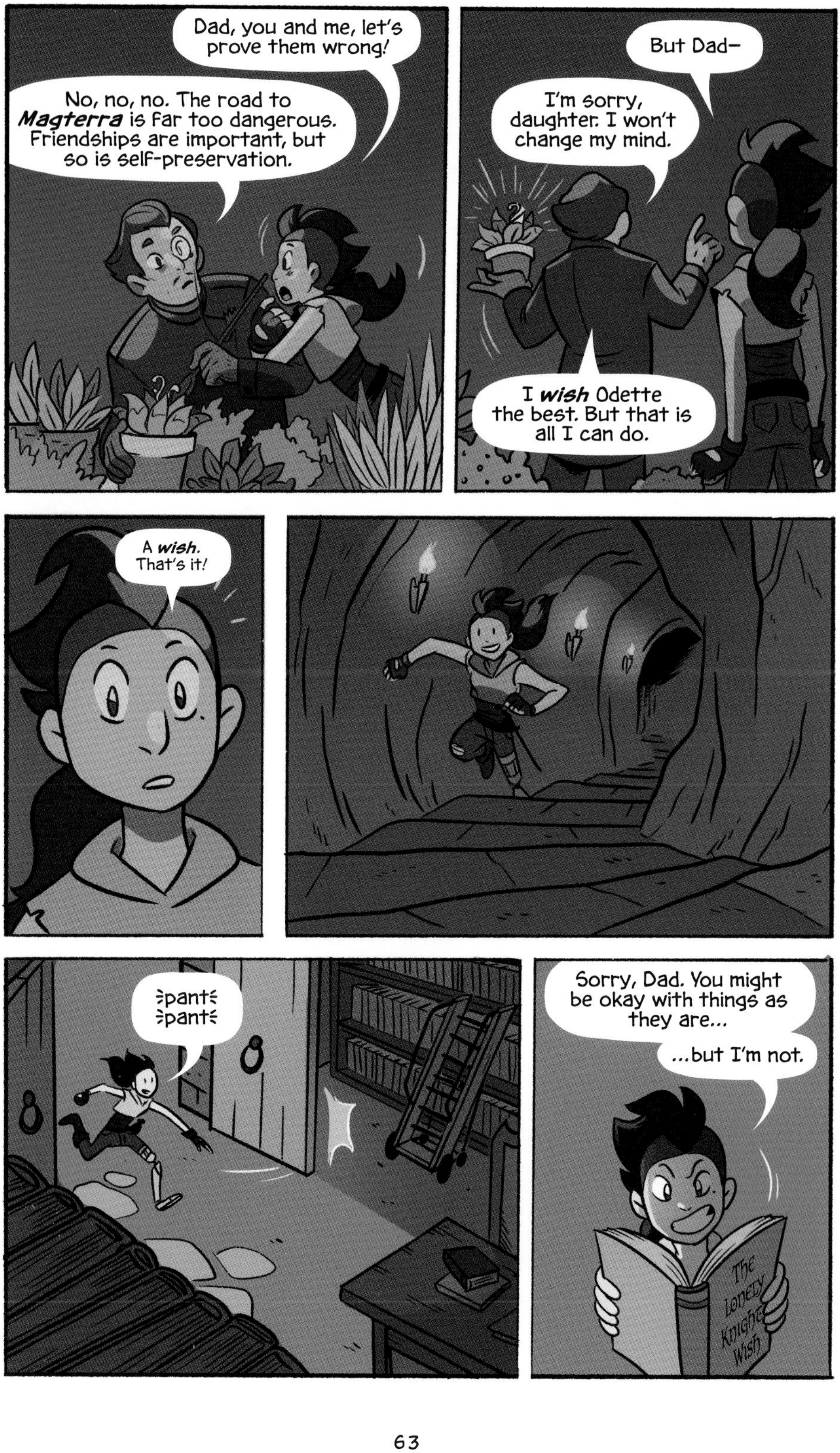
Dad, you and me, let's prove them wrong!
No, no, no. The road to *Magterra* is far too dangerous. Friendships are important, but so is self-preservation.
But Dad—
I'm sorry, daughter. I won't change my mind.
I *wish* Odette the best. But that is all I can do.
A *wish*. That's it!
pant pant
Sorry, Dad. You might be okay with things as they are...
...but I'm not.
The Lonely Knight Wish

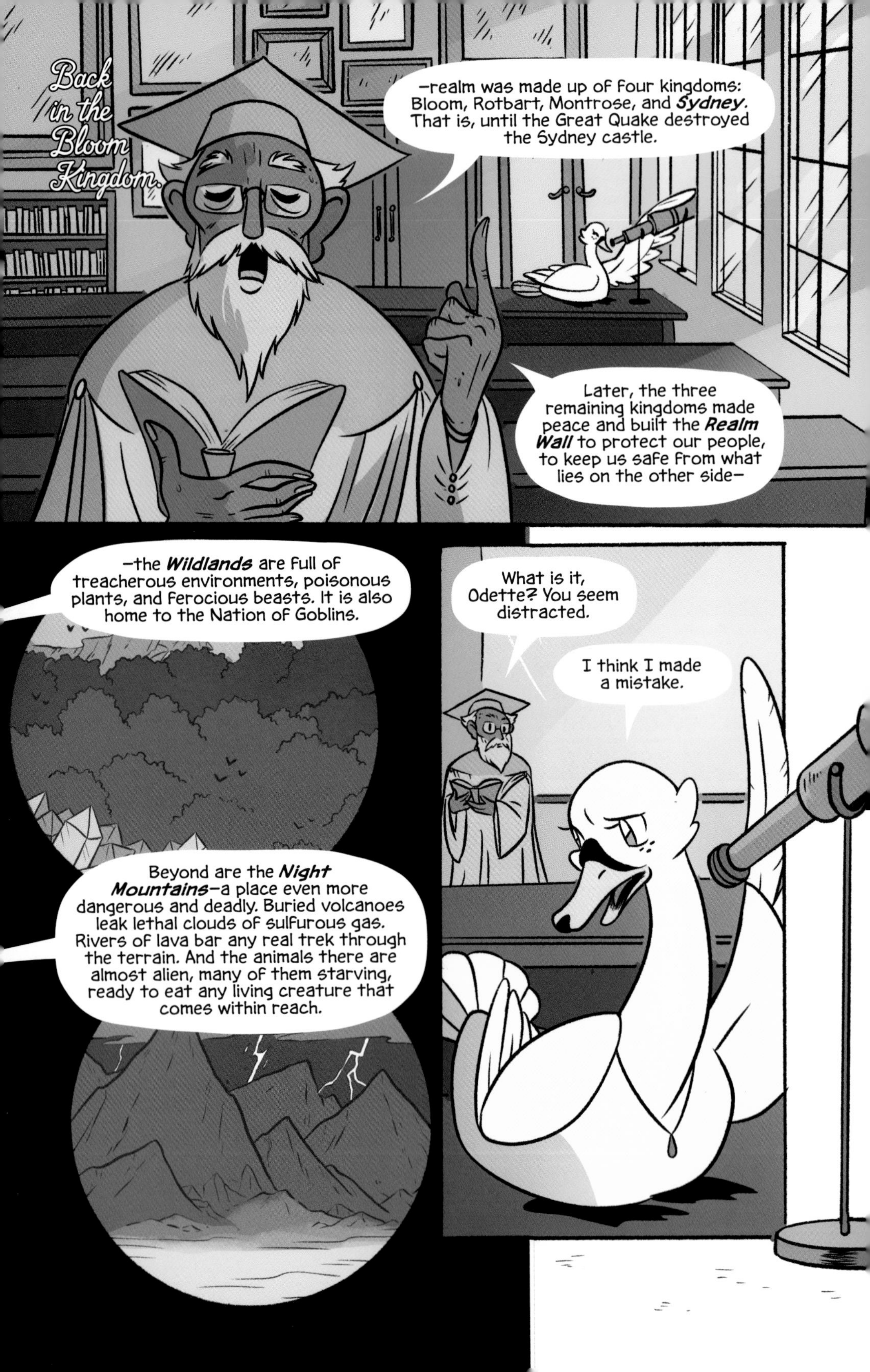
Back in the Bloom Kingdom.
—realm was made up of four kingdoms: Bloom, Rotbart, Montrose, and *Sydney*. That is, until the Great Quake destroyed the Sydney castle.
Later, the three remaining kingdoms made peace and built the *Realm Wall* to protect our people, to keep us safe from what lies on the other side—
—the *Wildlands* are full of treacherous environments, poisonous plants, and ferocious beasts. It is also home to the Nation of Goblins.
Beyond are the *Night Mountains*—a place even more dangerous and deadly. Buried volcanoes leak lethal clouds of sulfurous gas. Rivers of lava bar any real trek through the terrain. And the animals there are almost alien, many of them starving, ready to eat any living creature that comes within reach.
What is it, Odette? You seem distracted.
I think I made a mistake.

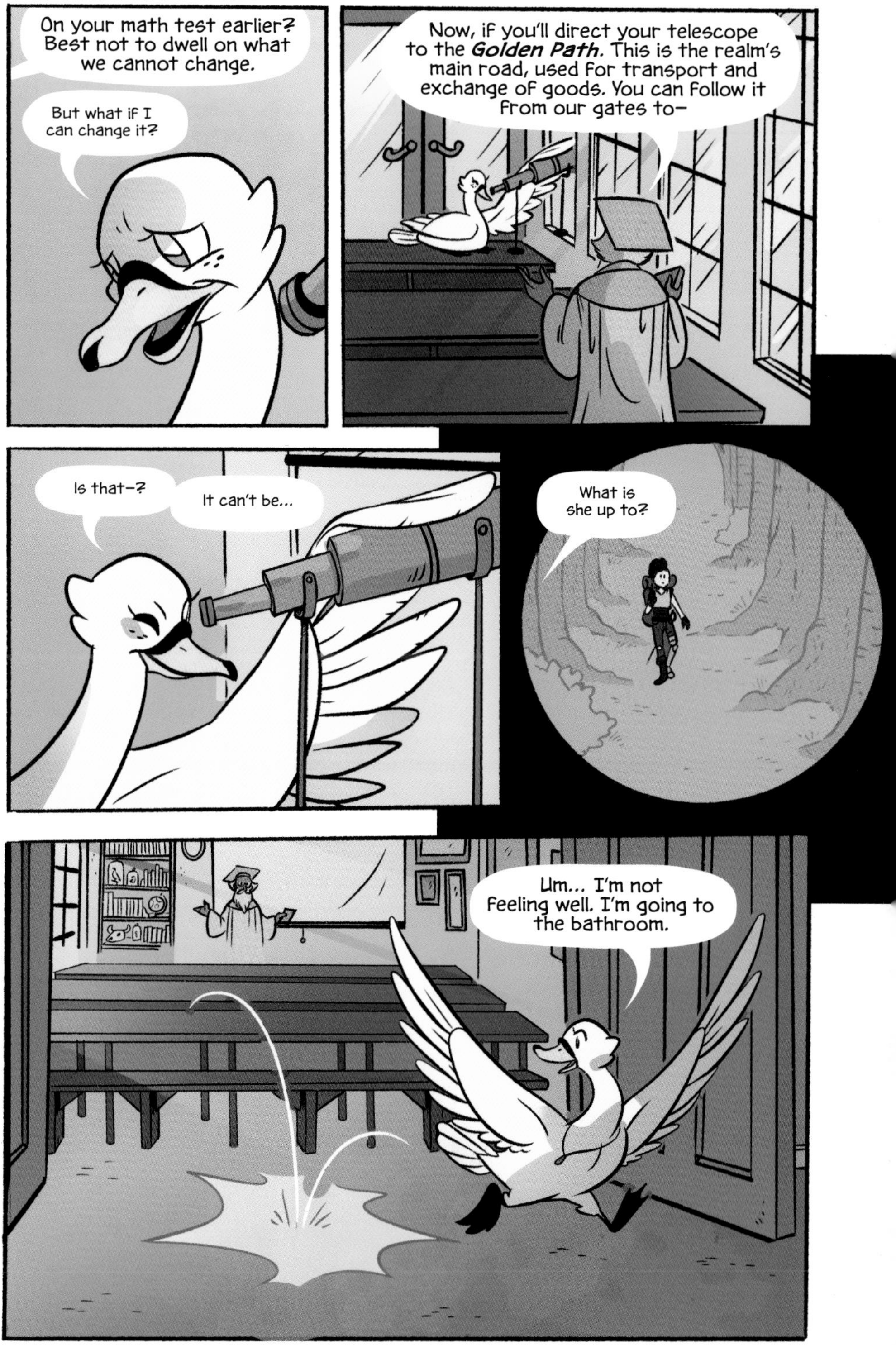
On your math test earlier? Best not to dwell on what we cannot change.
But what if I can change it?
Now, if you'll direct your telescope to the **Golden Path.** This is the realm's main road, used for transport and exchange of goods. You can follow it from our gates to–
Is that–?
It can't be...
What is she up to?
Um... I'm not feeling well. I'm going to the bathroom.

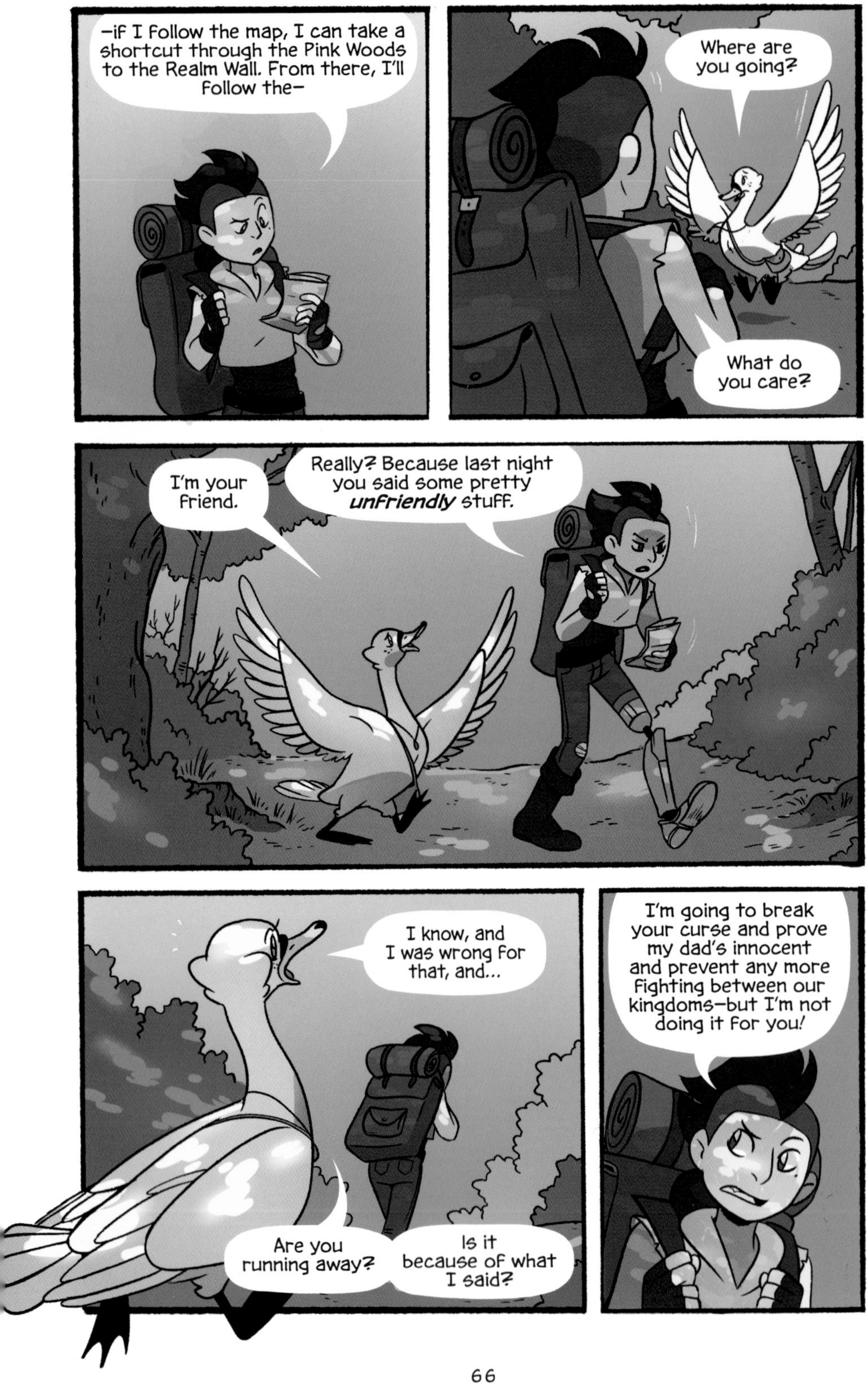
–if I follow the map, I can take a shortcut through the Pink Woods to the Realm Wall. From there, I'll follow the–
Where are you going?
What do you care?
I'm your friend.
Really? Because last night you said some pretty *unfriendly* stuff.
I know, and I was wrong for that, and...
Are you running away?
Is it because of what I said?
I'm going to break your curse and prove my dad's innocent and prevent any more fighting between our kingdoms—but I'm not doing it for you!

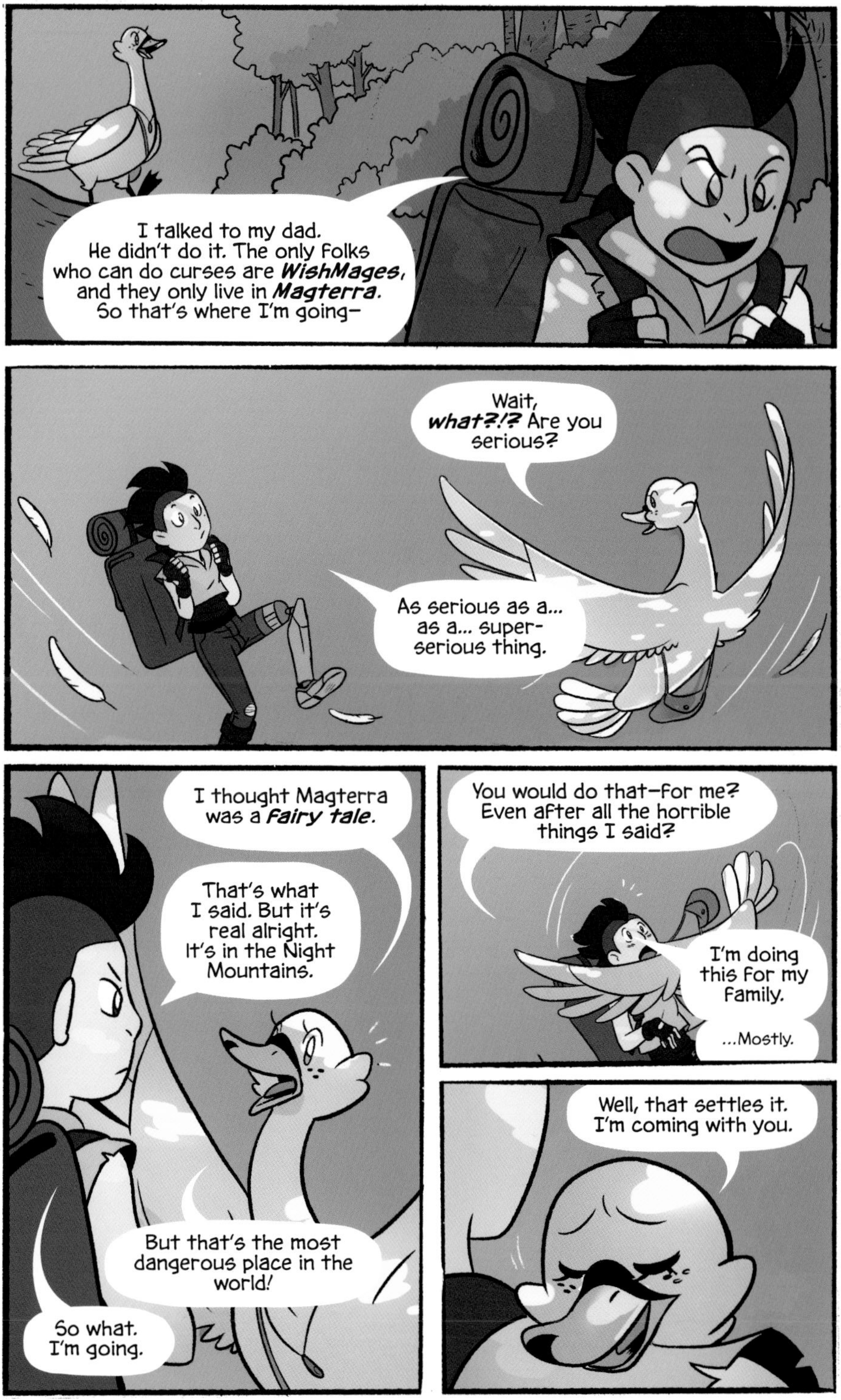
I talked to my dad. He didn't do it. The only folks who can do curses are *WishMages*, and they only live in *Magterra*. So that's where I'm going–
Wait, *what?!?* Are you serious?
As serious as a... as a... super-serious thing.
I thought Magterra was a *fairy tale.*
That's what I said. But it's real alright. It's in the Night Mountains.
But that's the most dangerous place in the world!
So what. I'm going.
You would do that–for me? Even after all the horrible things I said?
I'm doing this for my family.
...Mostly.
Well, that settles it. I'm coming with you.

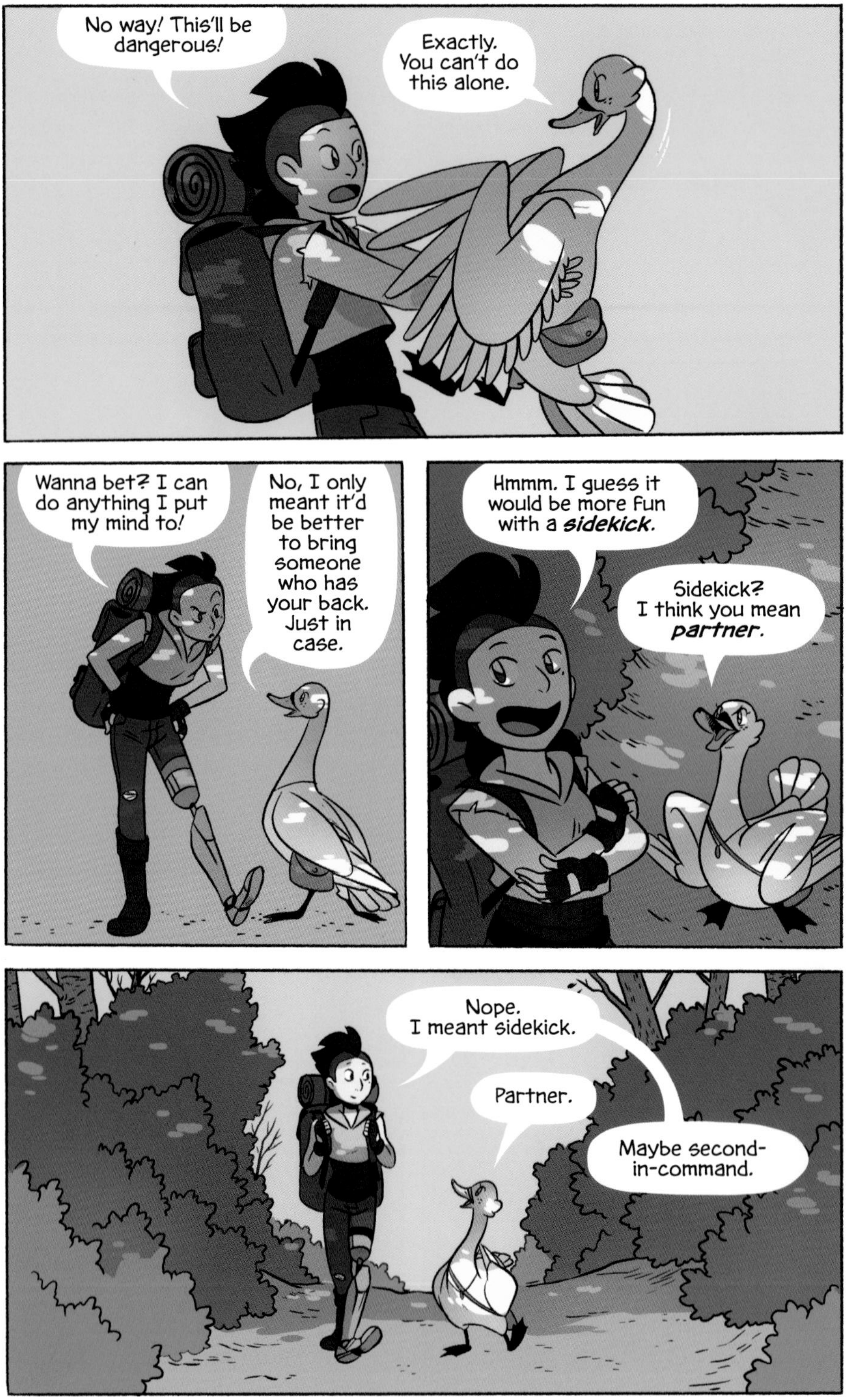
No way! This'll be dangerous!
Exactly. You can't do this alone.
Wanna bet? I can do anything I put my mind to!
No, I only meant it'd be better to bring someone who has your back. Just in case.
Hmmm. I guess it would be more fun with a ***sidekick.***
Sidekick? I think you mean ***partner.***
Nope. I meant sidekick.
Partner.
Maybe second-in-command.

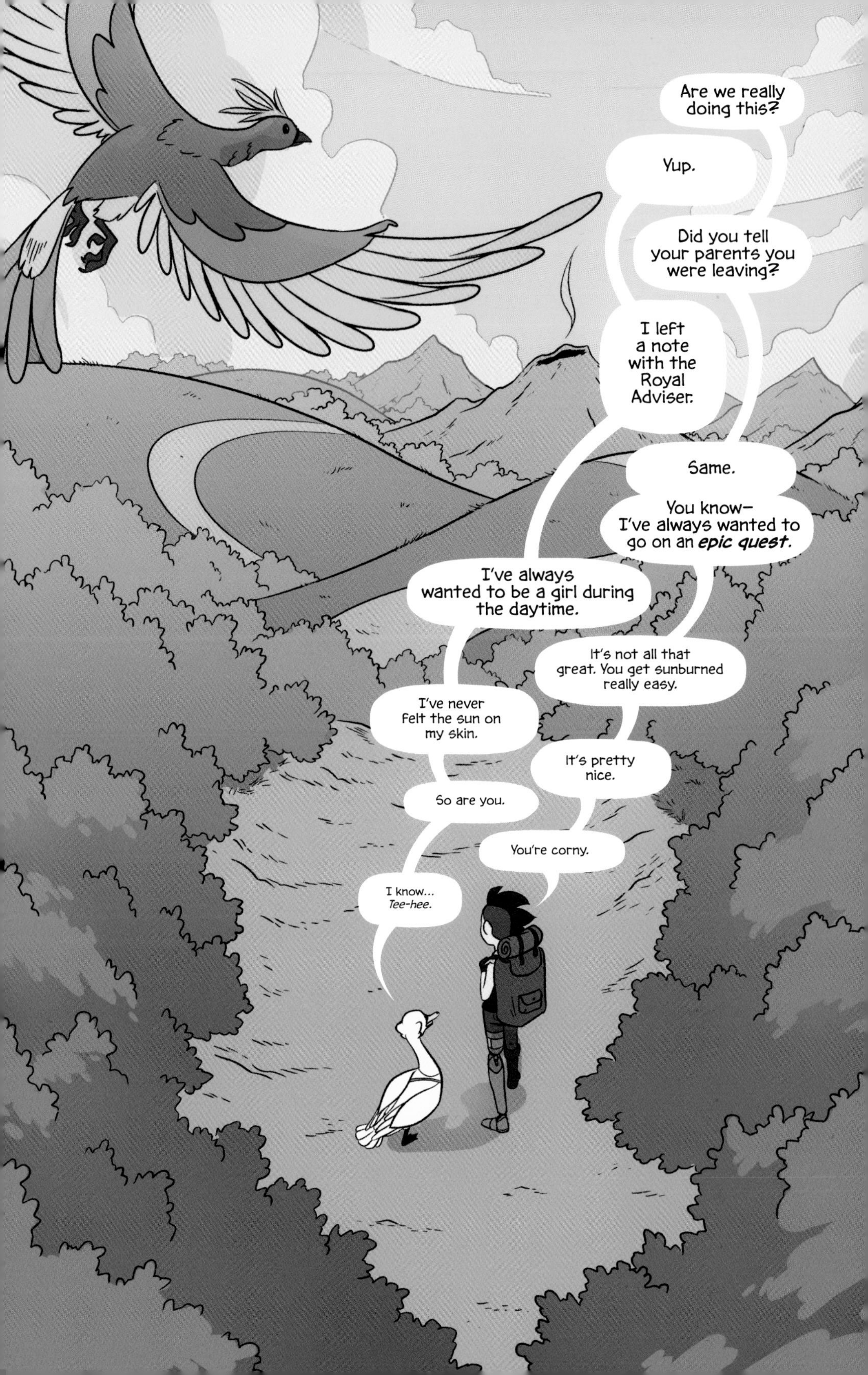
Are we really doing this?
Yup.
Did you tell your parents you were leaving?
I left a note with the Royal Adviser.
Same.
You know– I've always wanted to go on an *epic quest*.
I've always wanted to be a girl during the daytime.
It's not all that great. You get sunburned really easy.
I've never felt the sun on my skin.
It's pretty nice.
So are you.
You're corny.
I know... *Tee-hee.*

PART II

ROTBART

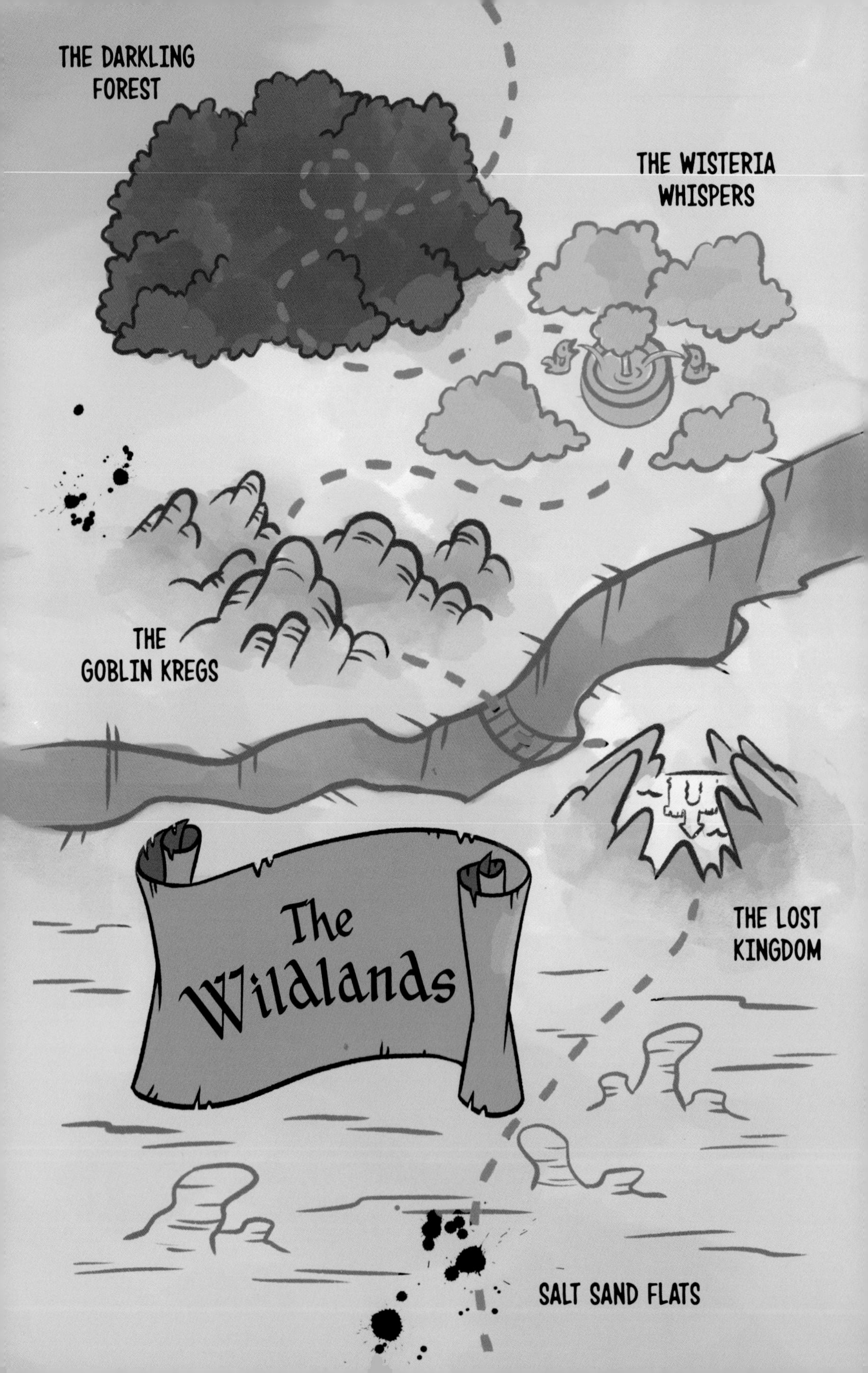
THE DARKLING FOREST
THE WISTERIA WHISPERS
THE GOBLIN KREGS
The Wildlands
THE LOST KINGDOM
SALT SAND FLATS

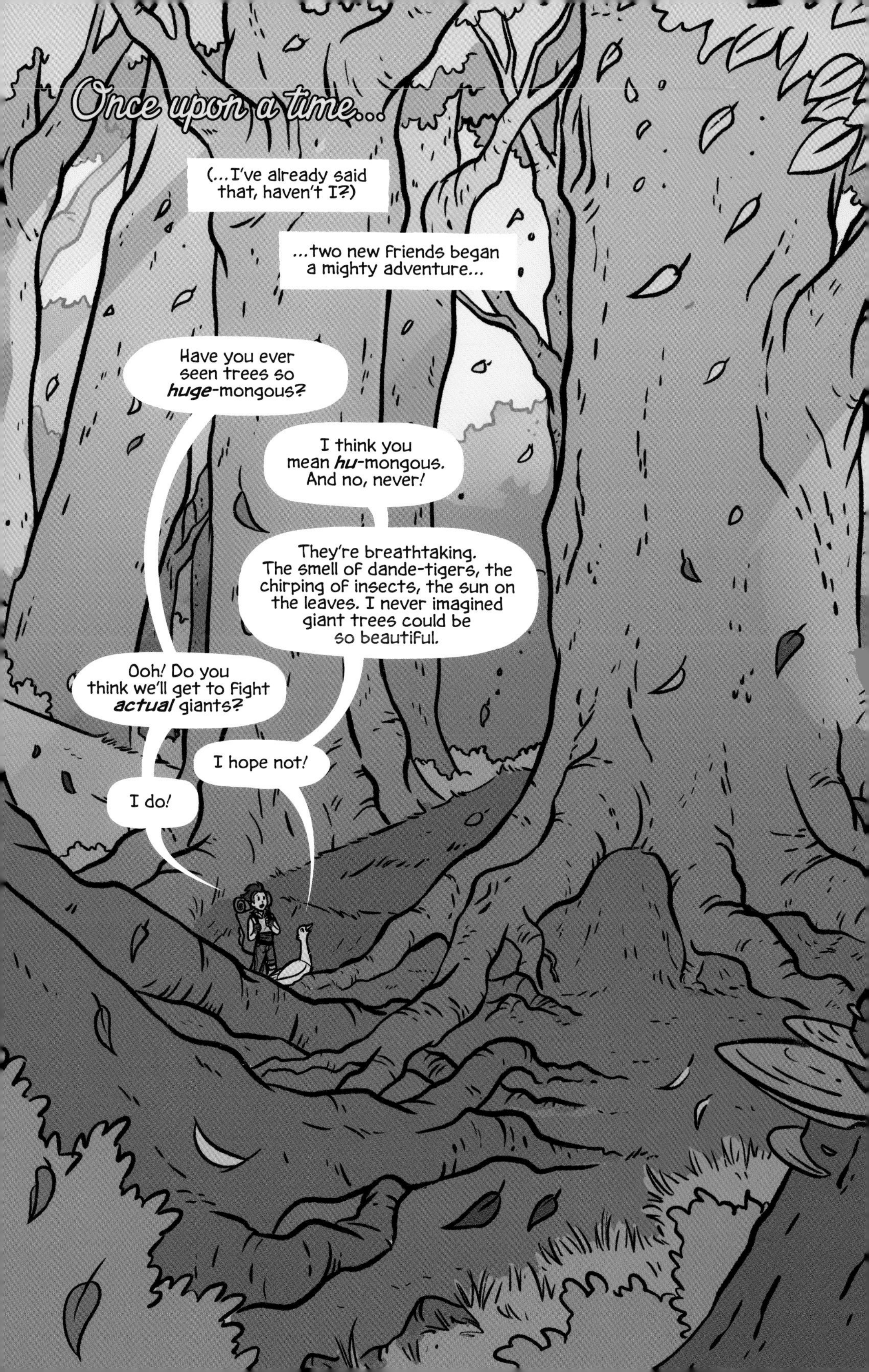
Once upon a time...
(...I've already said that, haven't I?)
...two new friends began a mighty adventure...
Have you ever seen trees so *huge*-mongous?
I think you mean *hu*-mongous. And no, never!
They're breathtaking. The smell of dande-tigers, the chirping of insects, the sun on the leaves. I never imagined giant trees could be so beautiful.
Ooh! Do you think we'll get to fight *actual* giants?
I hope not!
I do!

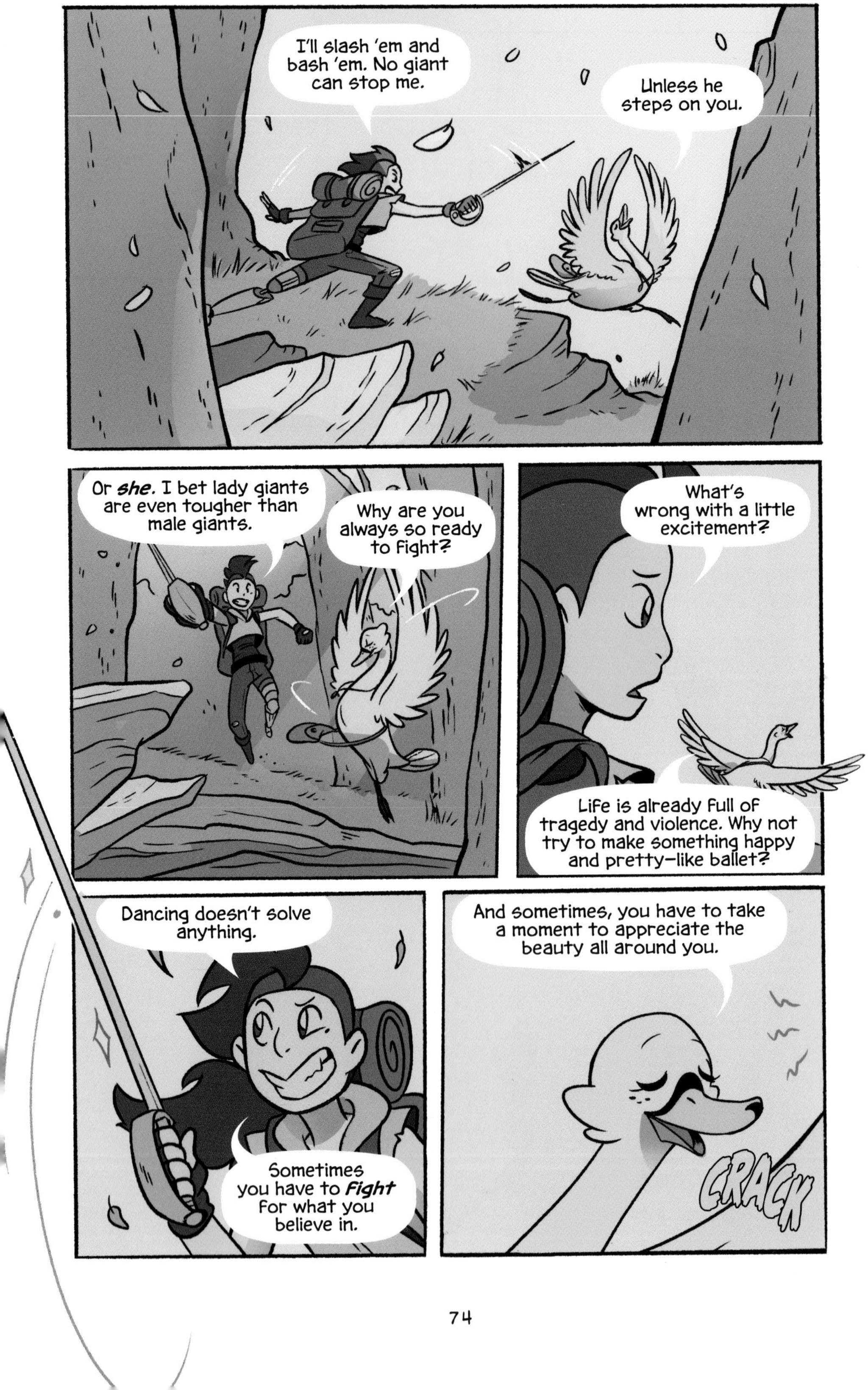
I'll slash 'em and bash 'em. No giant can stop me.
Unless he steps on you.
Or *she.* I bet lady giants are even tougher than male giants.
Why are you always so ready to fight?
What's wrong with a little excitement?
Life is already full of tragedy and violence. Why not try to make something happy and pretty—like ballet?
Dancing doesn't solve anything.
Sometimes you have to ***fight*** for what you believe in.
And sometimes, you have to take a moment to appreciate the beauty all around you.
CRACK

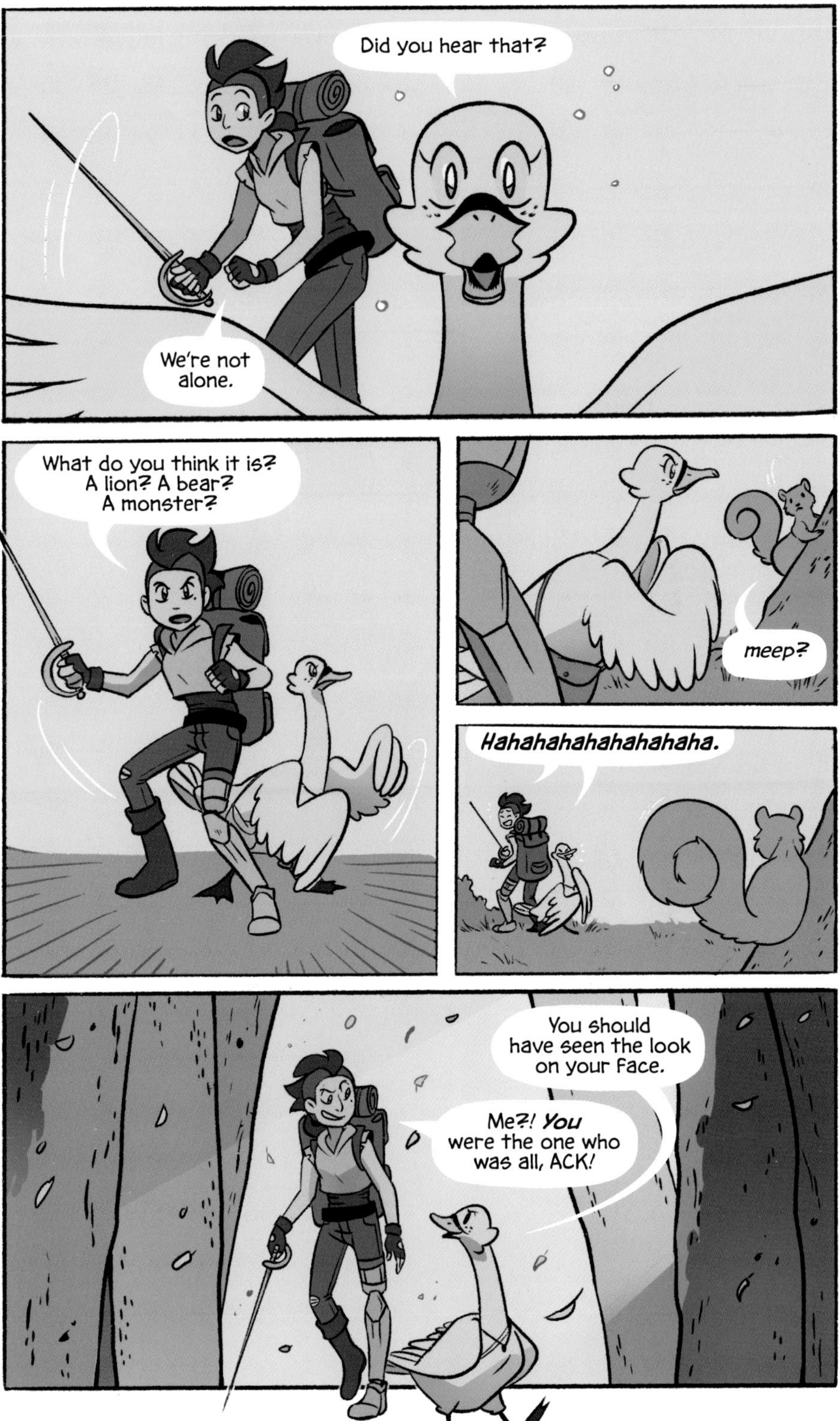
Did you hear that?
We're not alone.
What do you think it is? A lion? A bear? A monster?
meep?
Hahahahahahahahaha.
You should have seen the look on your face.
Me?! *You* were the one who was all, ACK!

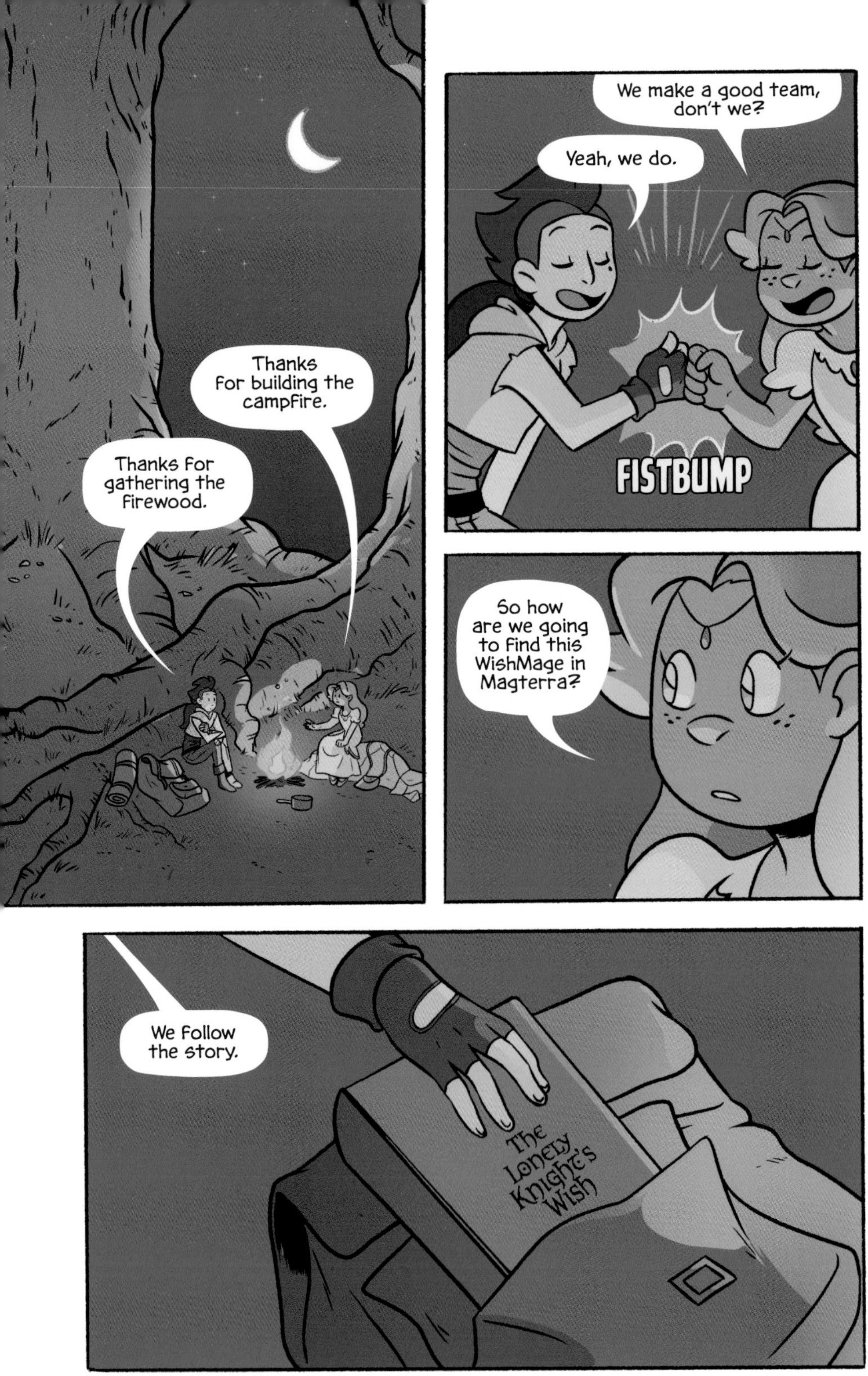
Thanks for building the campfire.
Thanks for gathering the firewood.
We make a good team, don't we?
Yeah, we do.
FISTBUMP
So how are we going to find this WishMage in Magterra?
We follow the story.
The Lonely Knight's Wish

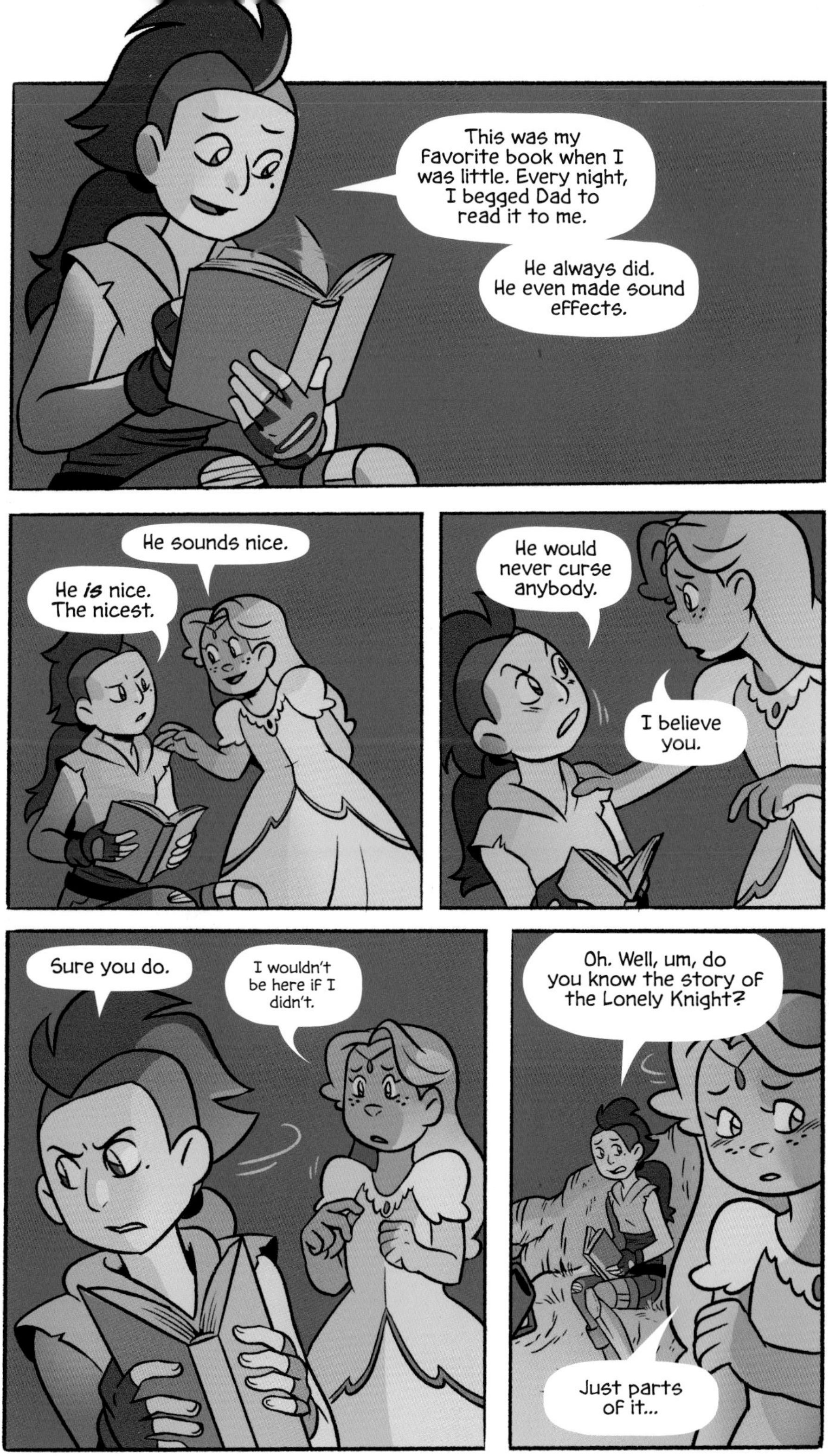
This was my favorite book when I was little. Every night, I begged Dad to read it to me.
He always did. He even made sound effects.
He sounds nice.
He *is* nice. The nicest.
He would never curse anybody.
I believe you.
Sure you do.
I wouldn't be here if I didn't.
Oh. Well, um, do you know the story of the Lonely Knight?
Just parts of it...

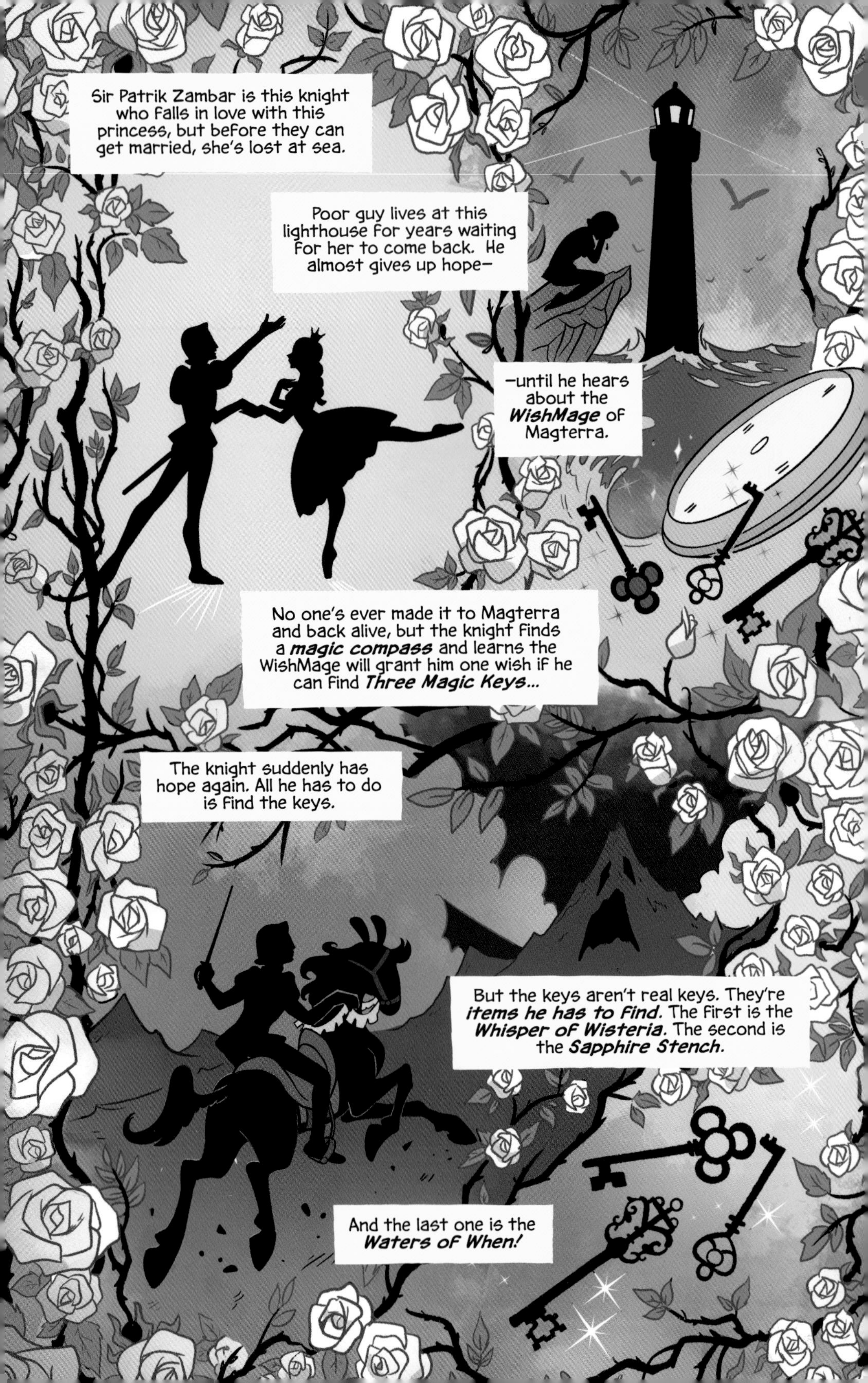
Sir Patrik Zambar is this knight who falls in love with this princess, but before they can get married, she's lost at sea.
Poor guy lives at this lighthouse for years waiting for her to come back. He almost gives up hope—
—until he hears about the *WishMage* of Magterra.
No one's ever made it to Magterra and back alive, but the knight finds a *magic compass* and learns the WishMage will grant him one wish if he can find *Three Magic Keys*...
The knight suddenly has hope again. All he has to do is find the keys.
But the keys aren't real keys. They're *items he has to find*. The first is the *Whisper of Wisteria*. The second is the *Sapphire Stench*.
And the last one is the *Waters of When!*

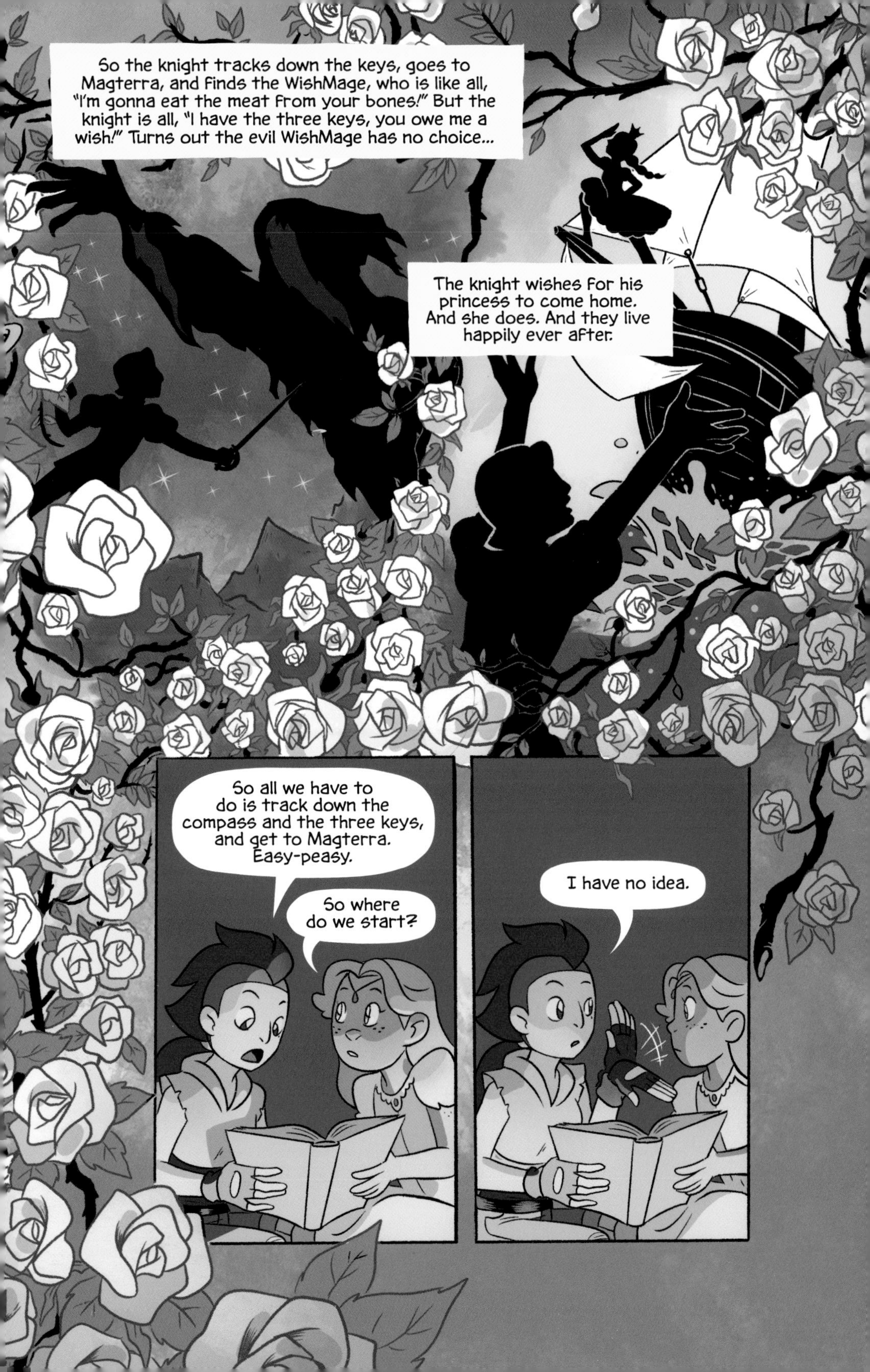

So the knight tracks down the keys, goes to Magterra, and finds the WishMage, who is like all, "I'm gonna eat the meat from your bones!" But the knight is all, "I have the three keys, you owe me a wish!" Turns out the evil WishMage has no choice...
The knight wishes for his princess to come home. And she does. And they live happily ever after.
So all we have to do is track down the compass and the three keys, and get to Magterra. Easy-peasy.
So where do we start?
I have no idea.

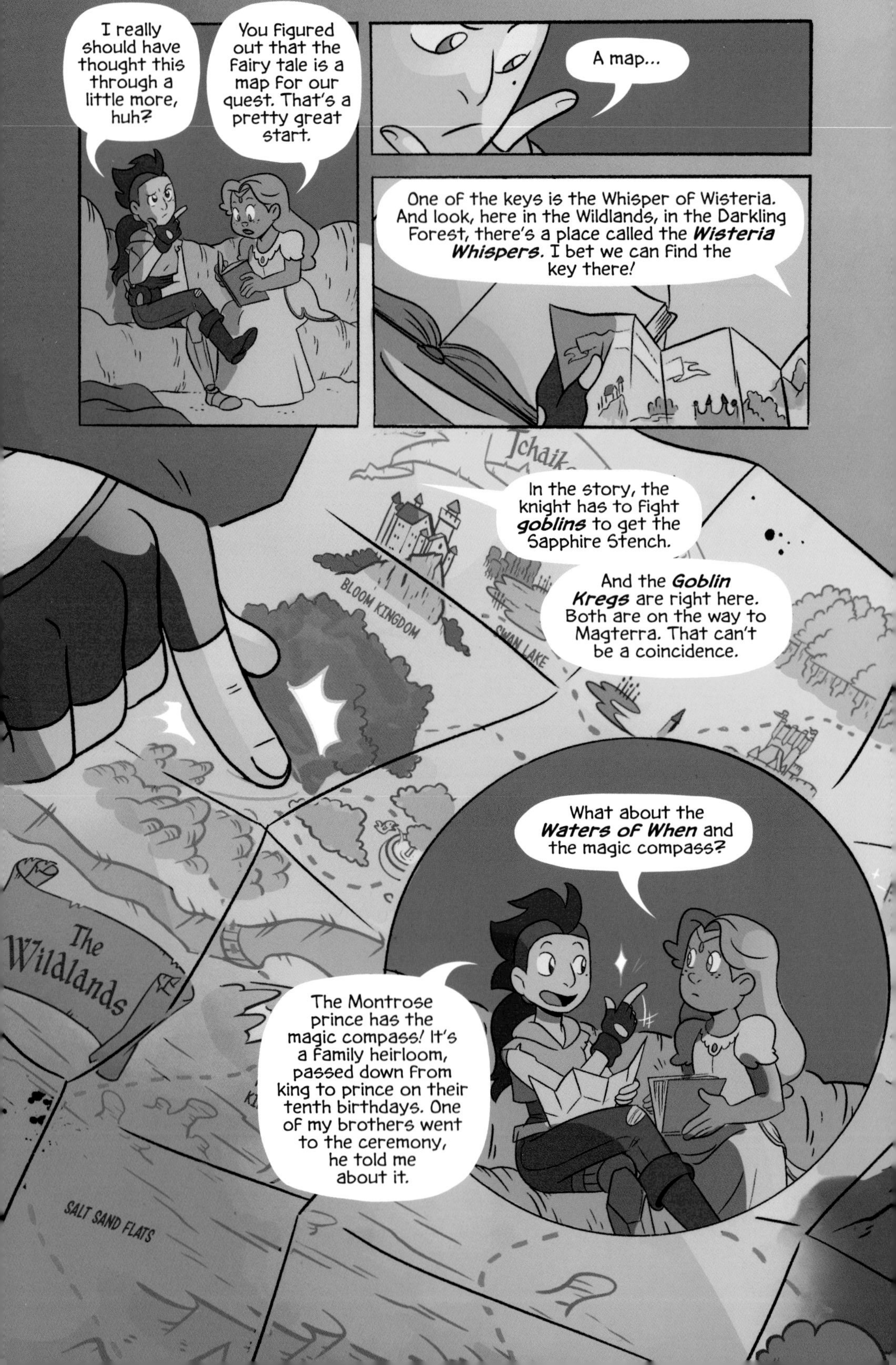
I really should have thought this through a little more, huh?
You figured out that the fairy tale is a map for our quest. That's a pretty great start.
A map...
One of the keys is the Whisper of Wisteria. And look, here in the Wildlands, in the Darkling Forest, there's a place called the *Wisteria Whispers*. I bet we can find the key there!
In the story, the knight has to fight *goblins* to get the Sapphire Stench.
And the *Goblin Kregs* are right here. Both are on the way to Magterra. That can't be a coincidence.
BLOOM KINGDOM
SWAN LAKE
The Wildlands
What about the *Waters of When* and the magic compass?
The Montrose prince has the magic compass! It's a family heirloom, passed down from king to prince on their tenth birthdays. One of my brothers went to the ceremony, he told me about it.
SALT SAND FLATS

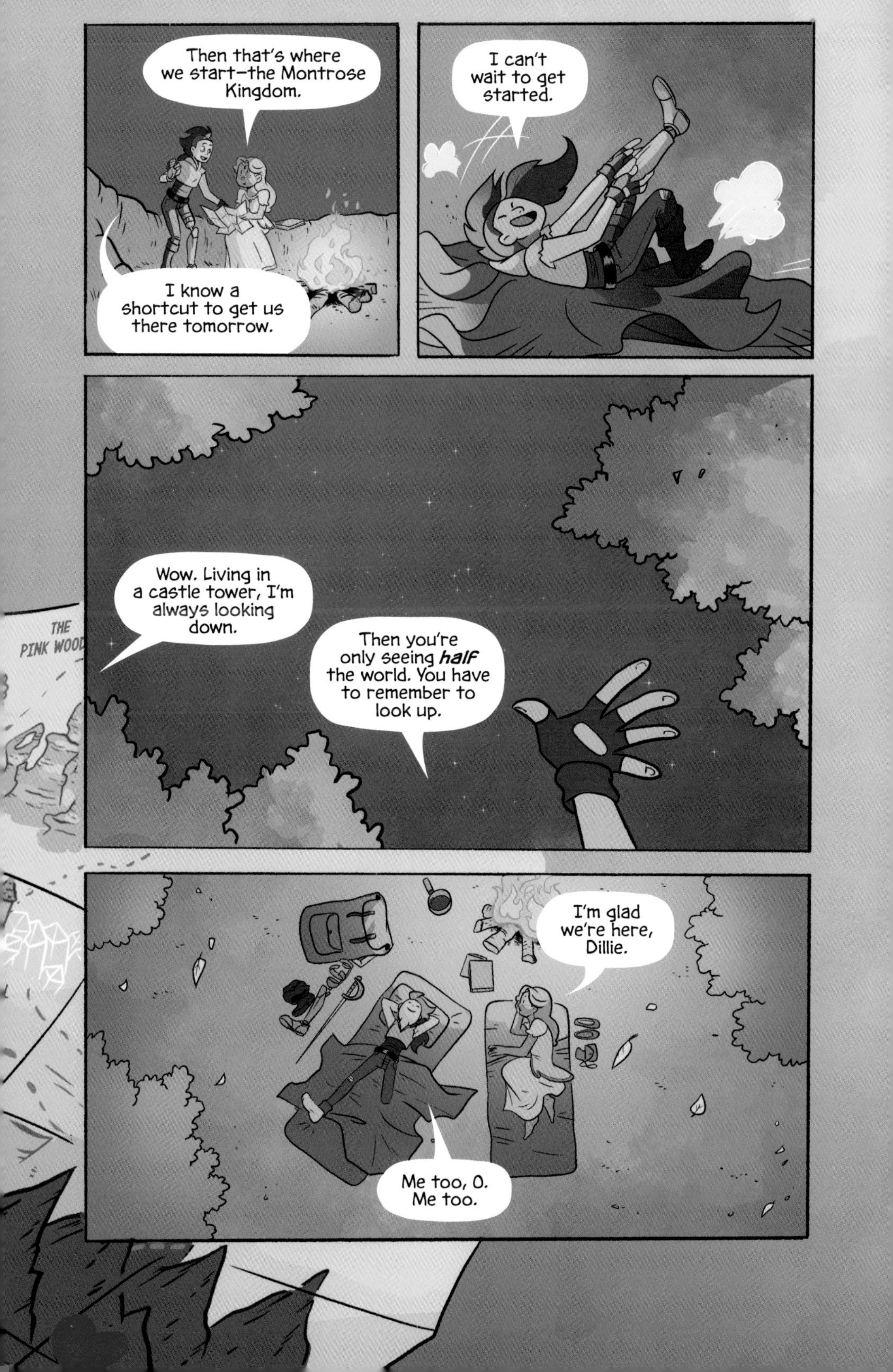
Then that's where we start—the Montrose Kingdom.
I know a shortcut to get us there tomorrow.
I can't wait to get started.
Wow. Living in a castle tower, I'm always looking down.
Then you're only seeing *half* the world. You have to remember to look up.
I'm glad we're here, Dillie.
Me too, O. Me too.
THE
PINK

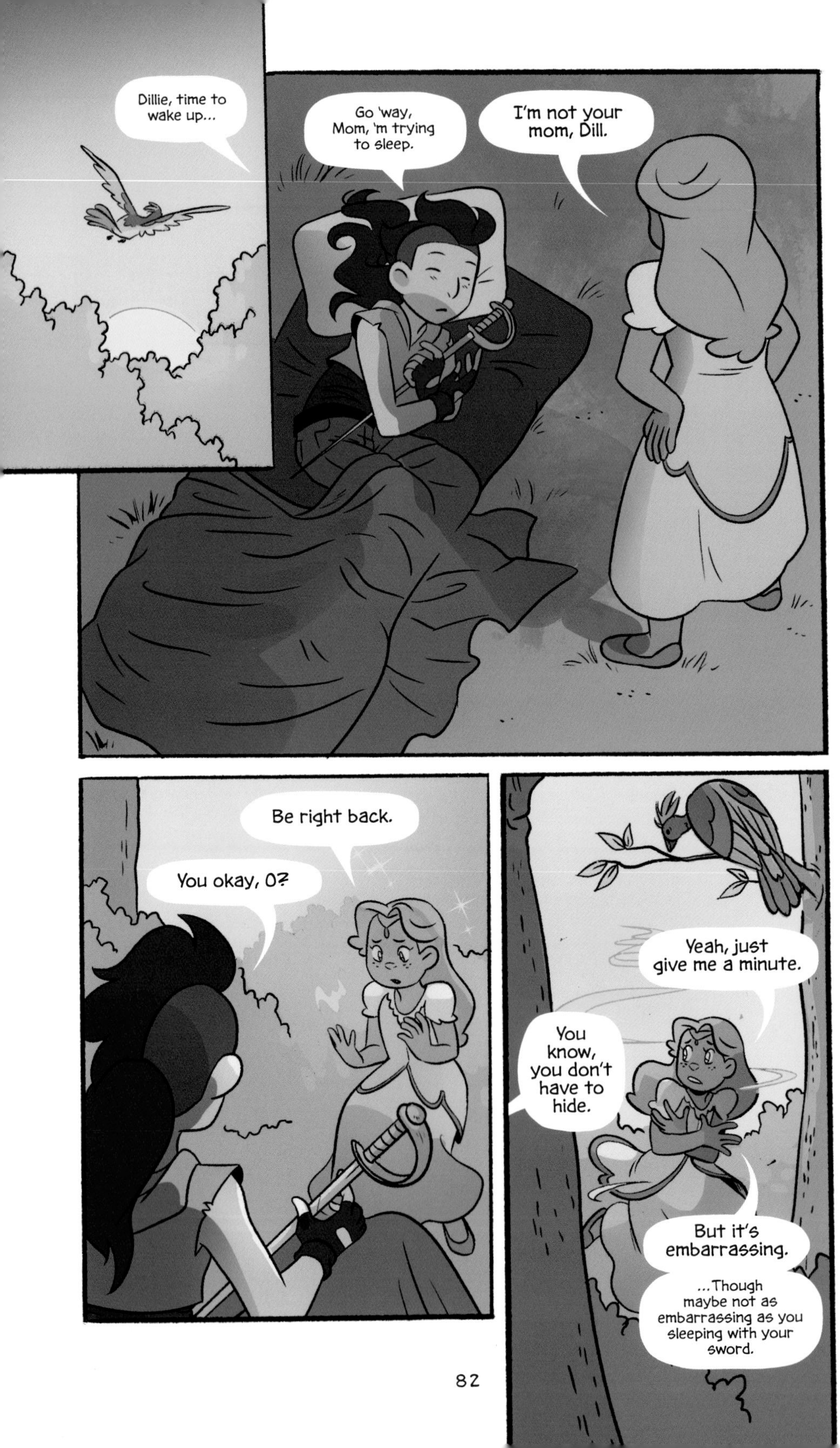
Dillie, time to wake up...
Go 'way, Mom, 'm trying to sleep.
I'm not your mom, Dill.
Be right back.
You okay, O?
Yeah, just give me a minute.
You know, you don't have to hide.
But it's embarrassing.
...Though maybe not as embarrassing as you sleeping with your sword.

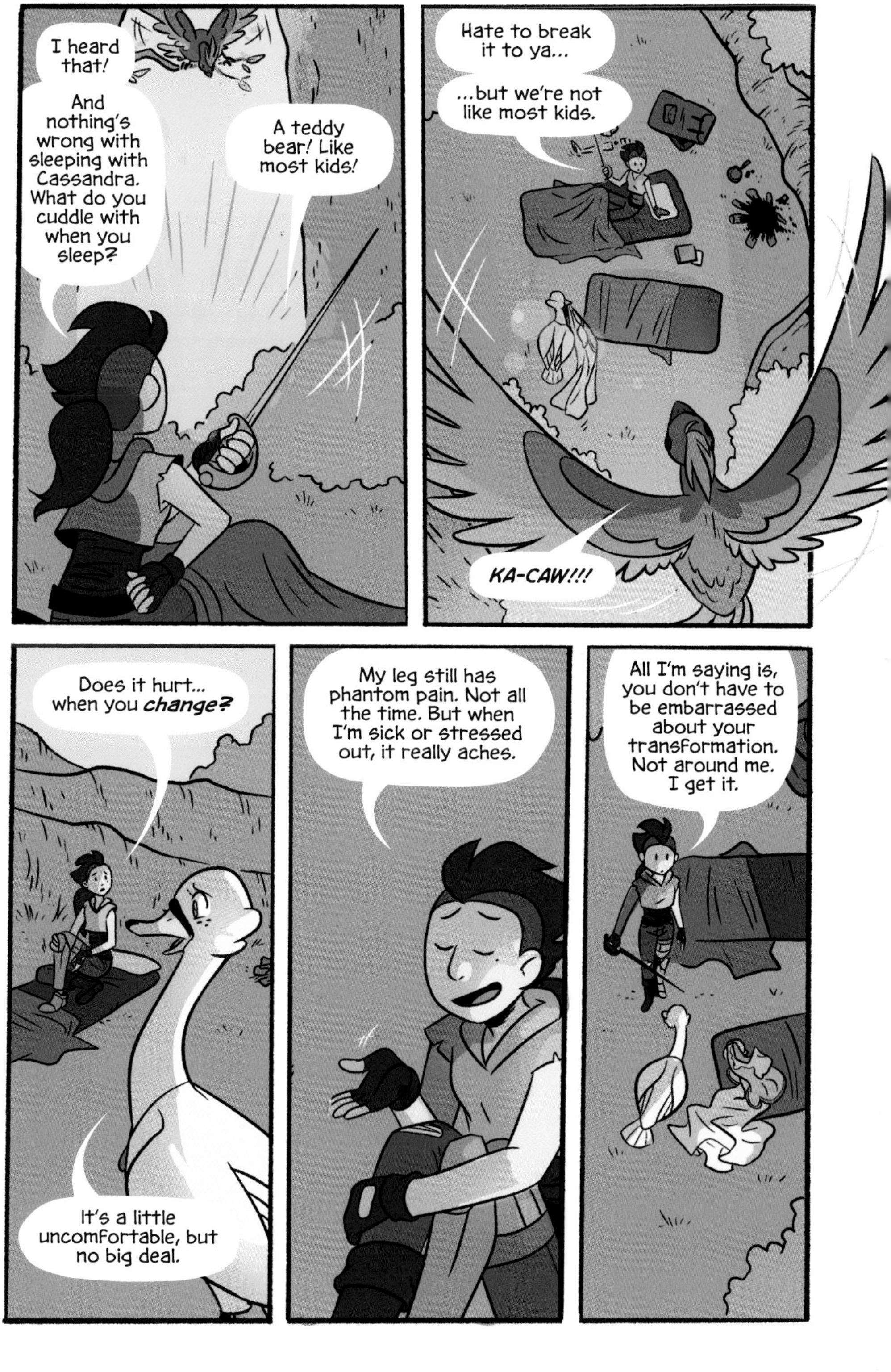
I heard that!
And nothing's wrong with sleeping with Cassandra. What do you cuddle with when you sleep?
A teddy bear! Like most kids!
Hate to break it to ya...
...but we're not like most kids.
KA-CAW!!!
Does it hurt... when you *change?*
It's a little uncomfortable, but no big deal.
My leg still has phantom pain. Not all the time. But when I'm sick or stressed out, it really aches.
All I'm saying is, you don't have to be embarrassed about your transformation. Not around me. I get it.

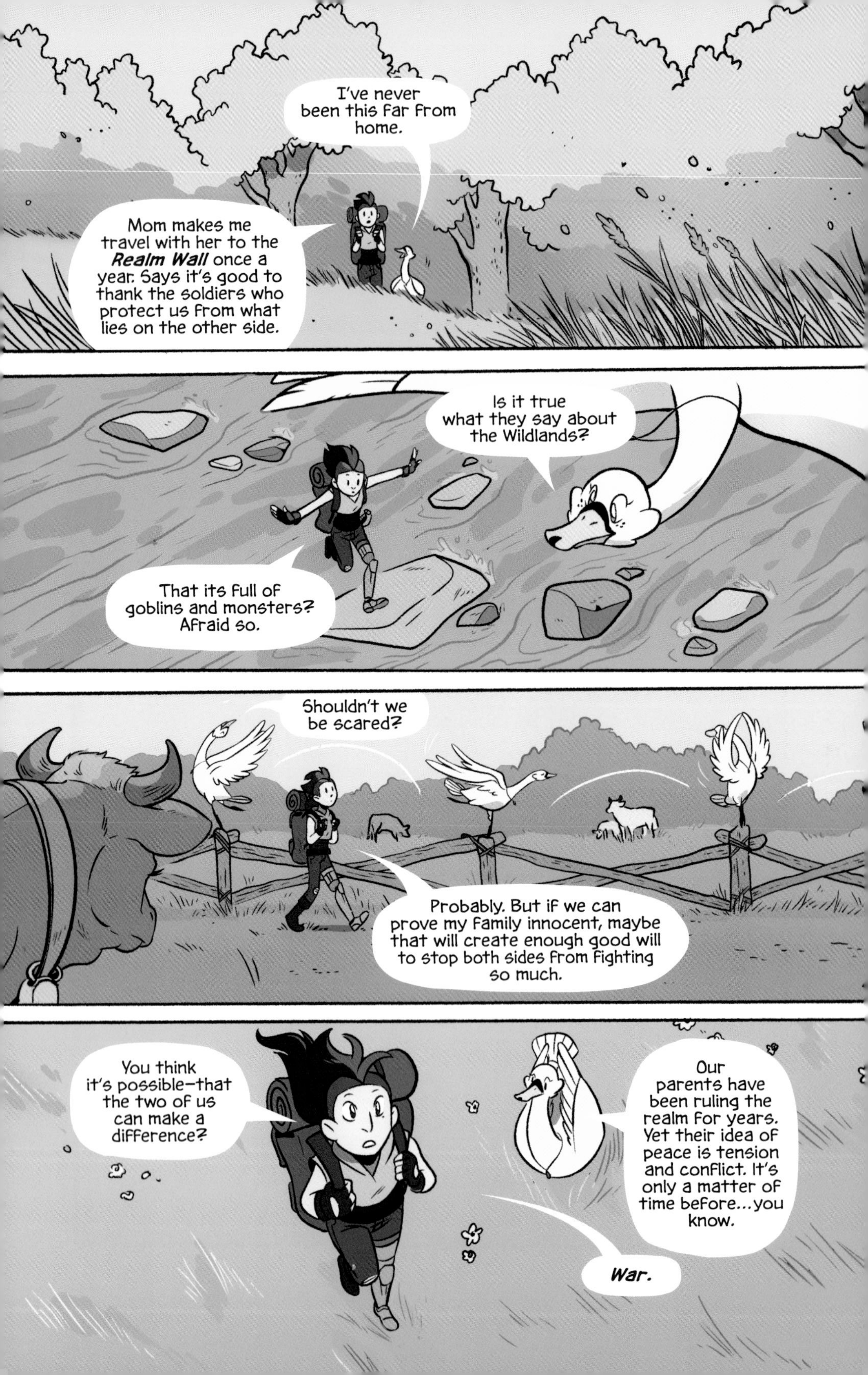
I've never been this far from home.
Mom makes me travel with her to the ***Realm Wall*** once a year. Says it's good to thank the soldiers who protect us from what lies on the other side.
Is it true what they say about the Wildlands?
That its full of goblins and monsters? Afraid so.
Shouldn't we be scared?
Probably. But if we can prove my family innocent, maybe that will create enough good will to stop both sides from fighting so much.
You think it's possible—that the two of us can make a difference?
Our parents have been ruling the realm for years. Yet their idea of peace is tension and conflict. It's only a matter of time before...you know.
War.

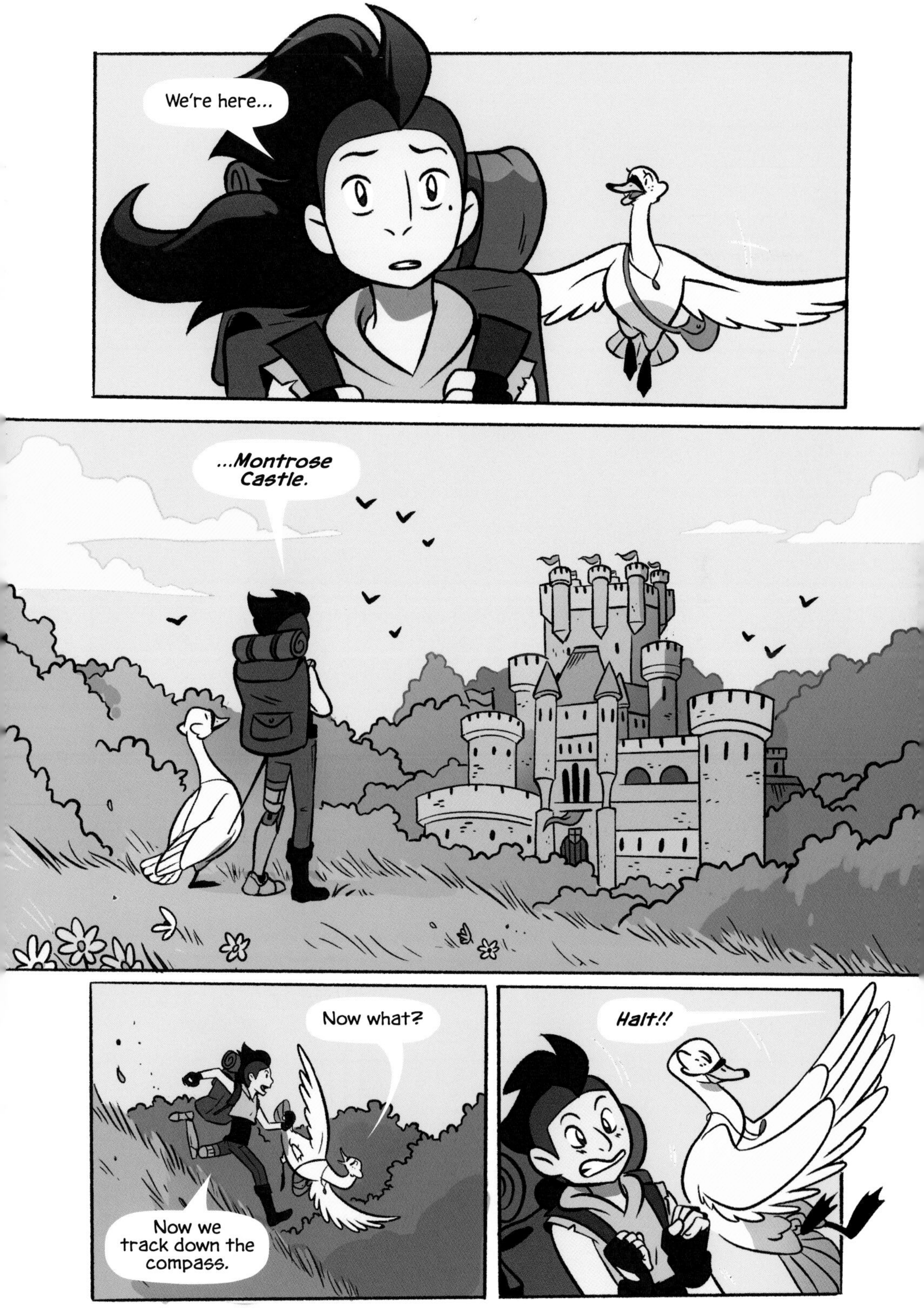
We're here...
...Montrose Castle.
Now what?
Now we track down the compass.
Halt!!

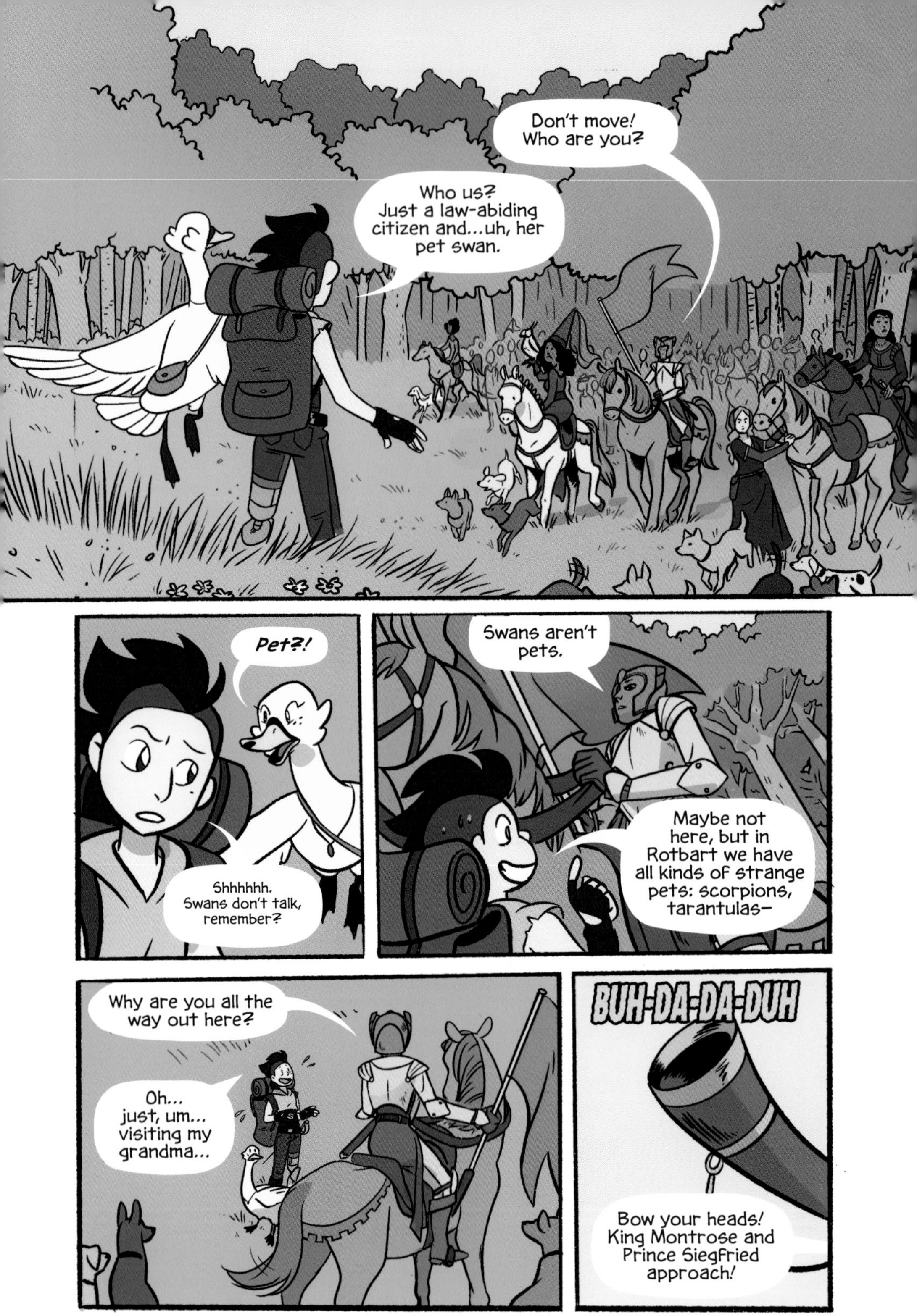
Don't move! Who are you?
Who us? Just a law-abiding citizen and...uh, her pet swan.
Pet?!
Shhhhhh. Swans don't talk, remember?
Swans aren't pets.
Maybe not here, but in Rotbart we have all kinds of strange pets: scorpions, tarantulas—
Why are you all the way out here?
Oh... just, um... visiting my grandma...
BUH-DA-DA-DUH
Bow your heads! King Montrose and Prince Siegfried approach!

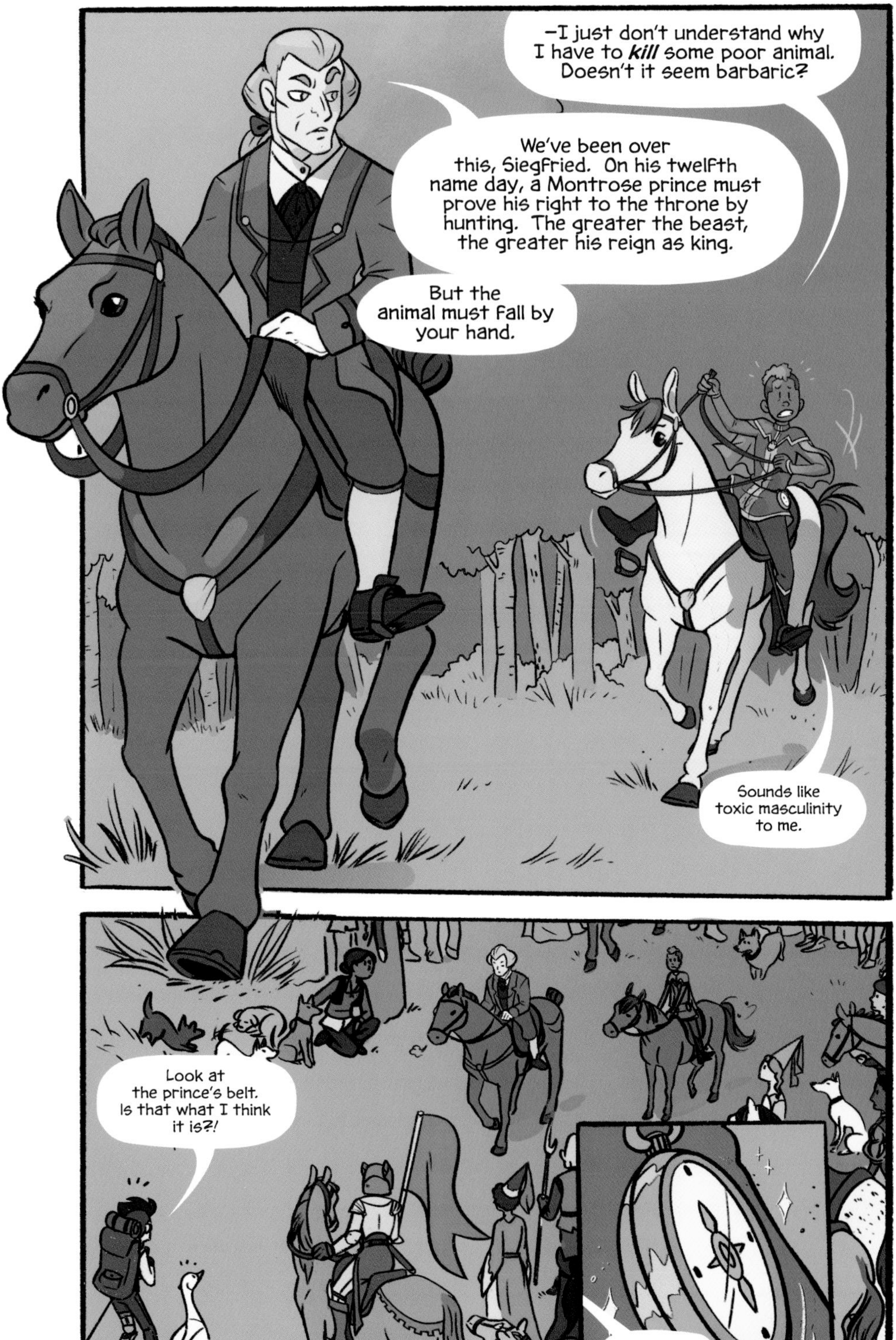
–I just don't understand why I have to ***kill*** some poor animal. Doesn't it seem barbaric?
We've been over this, Siegfried. On his twelfth name day, a Montrose prince must prove his right to the throne by hunting. The greater the beast, the greater his reign as king.
But the animal must fall by your hand.
Sounds like toxic masculinity to me.
Look at the prince's belt. Is that what I think it is?!
The magic compass!

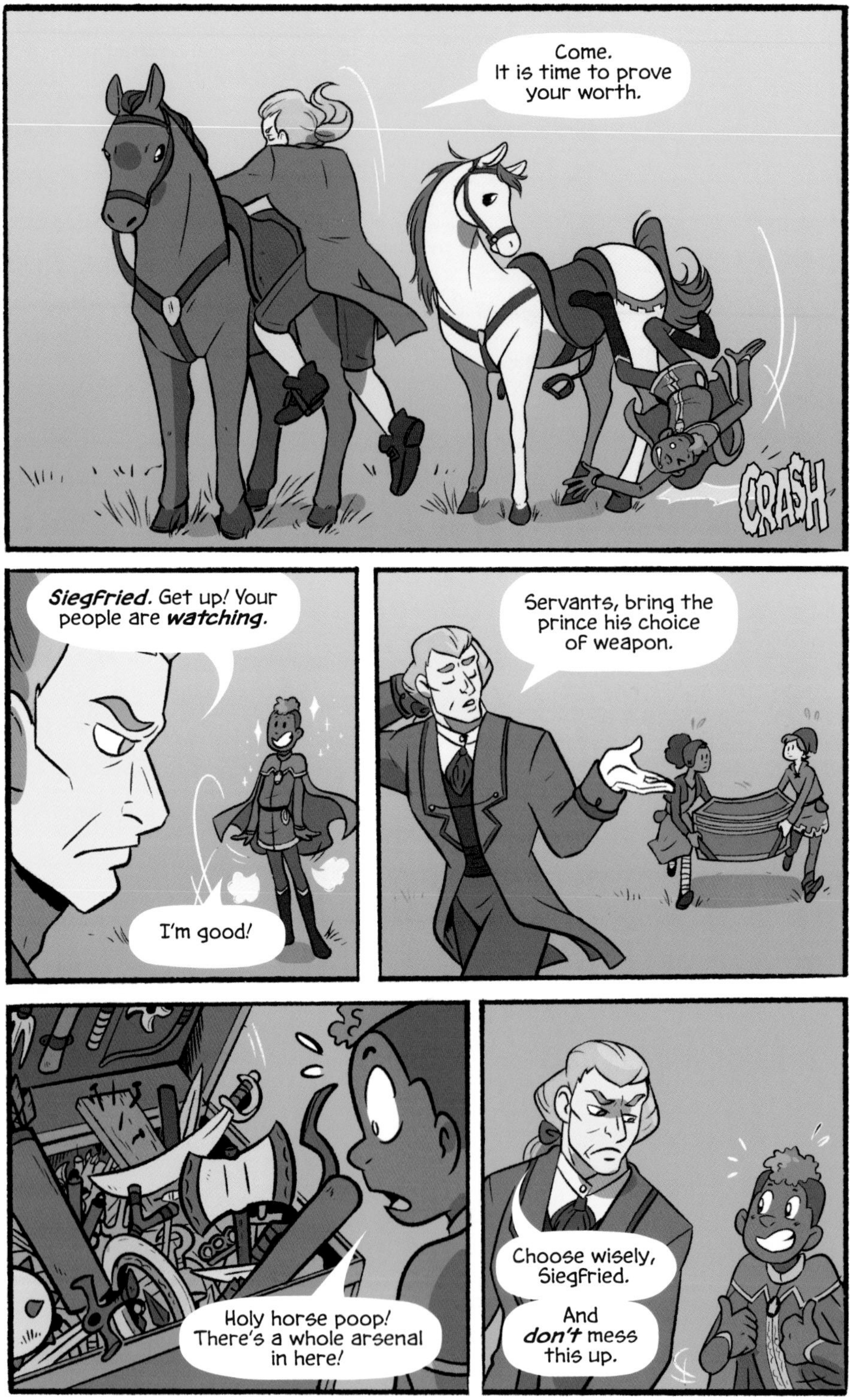

Come.
It is time to prove your worth.
CRASH
Siegfried. Get up! Your people are watching.
I'm good!
Servants, bring the prince his choice of weapon.
Holy horse poop! There's a whole arsenal in here!
Choose wisely, Siegfried.
And don't mess this up.

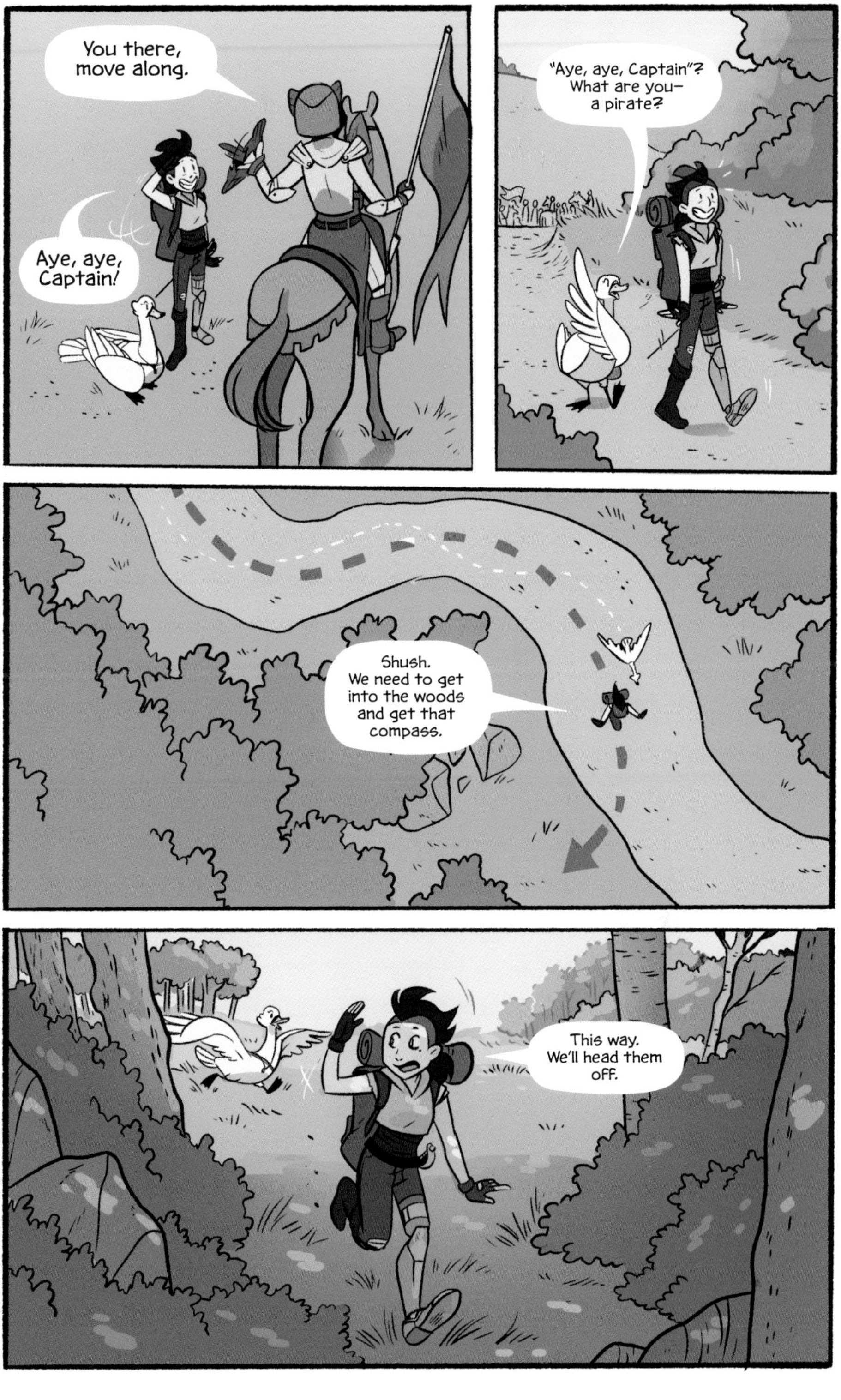
You there, move along.
Aye, aye, Captain!
"Aye, aye, Captain"? What are you– a pirate?
Shush. We need to get into the woods and get that compass.
This way. We'll head them off.

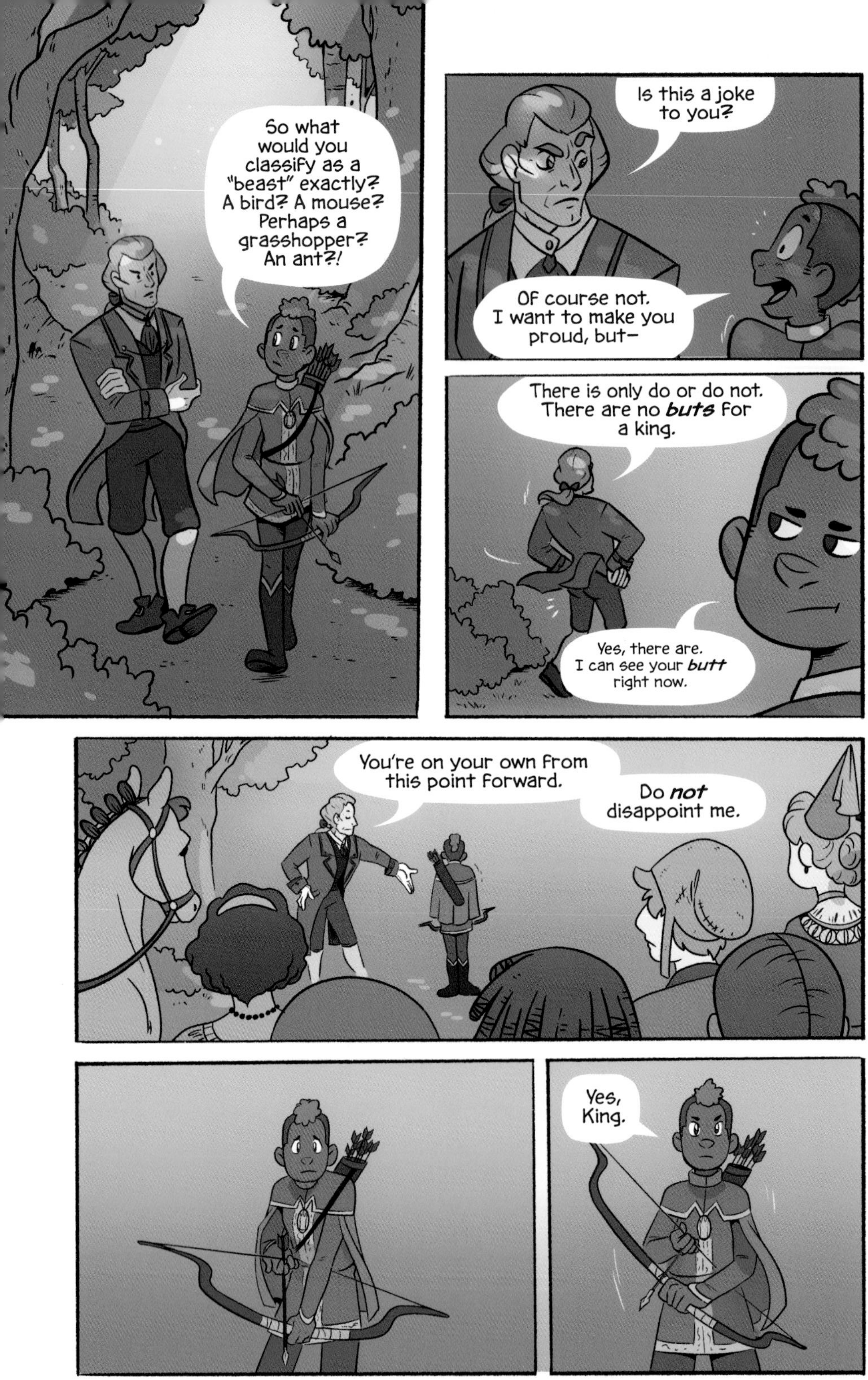

So what would you classify as a "beast" exactly? A bird? A mouse? Perhaps a grasshopper? An ant?!
Is this a joke to you?
Of course not. I want to make you proud, but—
There is only do or do not. There are no *buts* for a king.
Yes, there are. I can see your *butt* right now.
You're on your own from this point forward.
Do *not* disappoint me.
Yes, King.

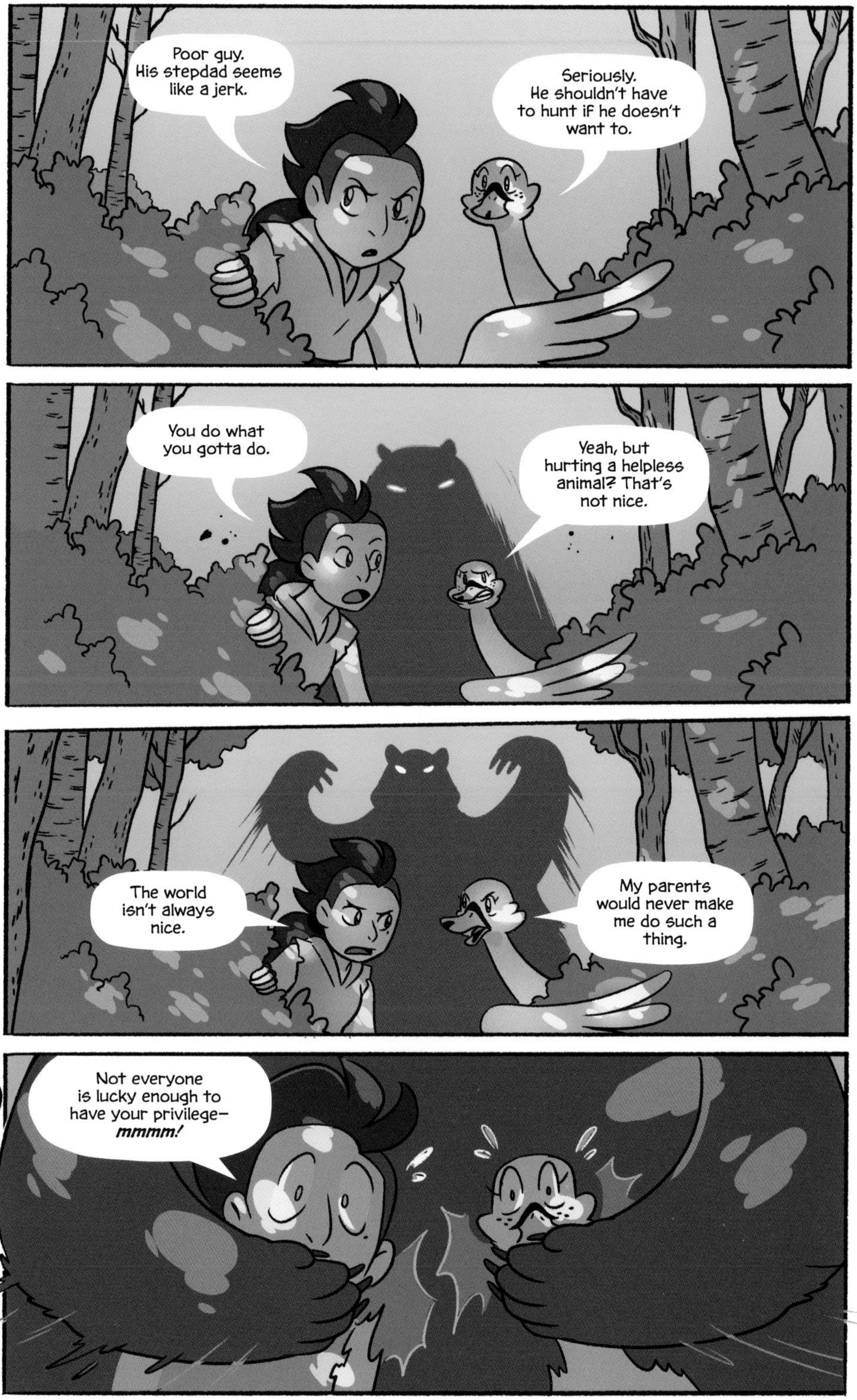
Poor guy.
His stepdad seems like a jerk.
Seriously.
He shouldn't have to hunt if he doesn't want to.
You do what you gotta do.
Yeah, but hurting a helpless animal? That's not nice.
The world isn't always nice.
My parents would never make me do such a thing.
Not everyone is lucky enough to have your privilege—*mmmm!*

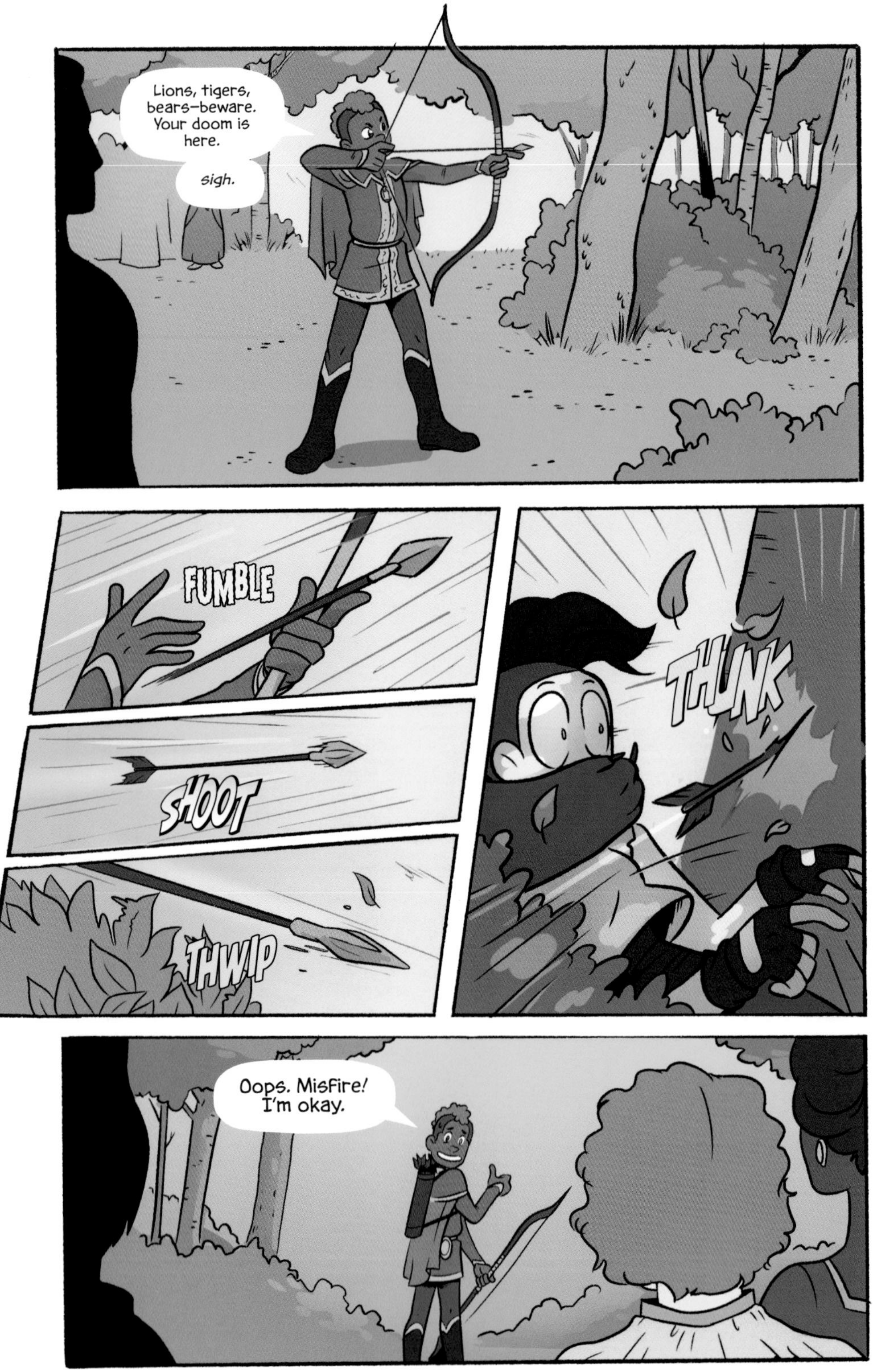
Lions, tigers, bears–beware. Your doom is here.
sigh.
FUMBLE
SHOOT
THWIP
THUNK
Oops. Misfire! I'm okay.

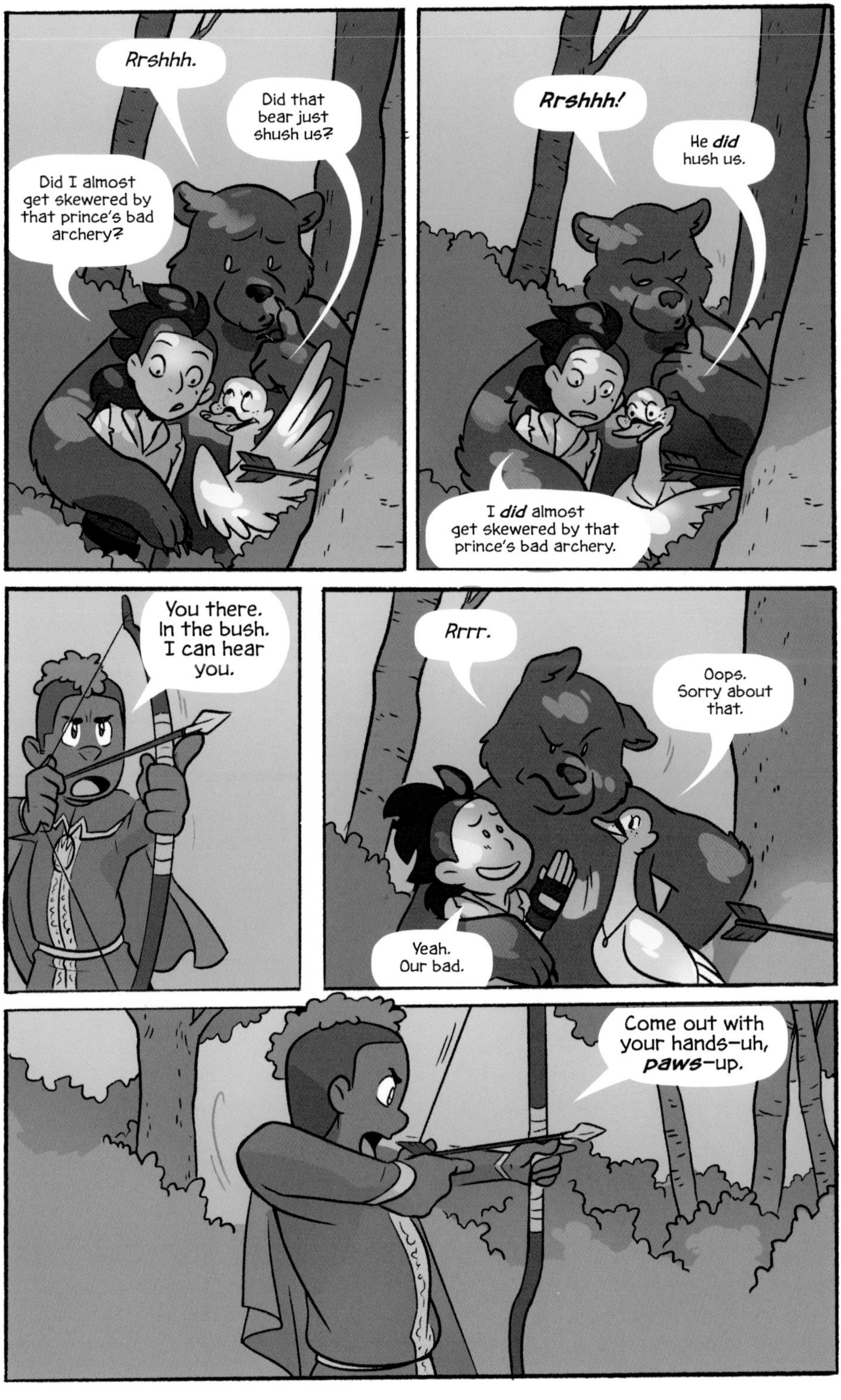
Rrshhh.
Did that bear just shush us?
Did I almost get skewered by that prince's bad archery?
Rrshhh!
He *did* hush us.
I *did* almost get skewered by that prince's bad archery.
You there. In the bush. I can hear you.
Rrrr.
Oops. Sorry about that.
Yeah. Our bad.
Come out with your hands—uh, ***paws***—up.

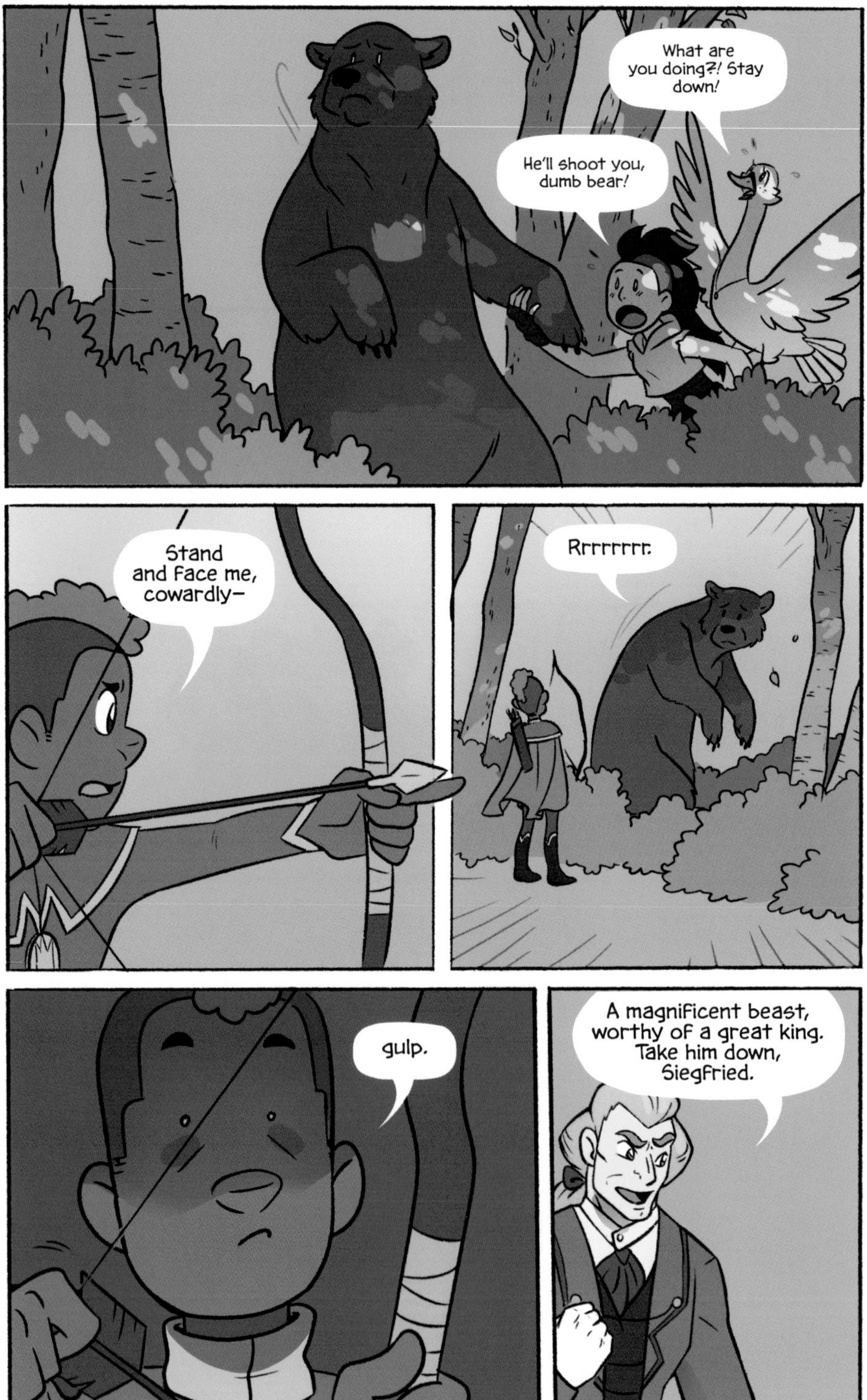
What are you doing?! Stay down!
He'll shoot you, dumb bear!
Stand and face me, cowardly—
Rrrrrrrr.
gulp.
A magnificent beast, worthy of a great king. Take him down, Siegfried.

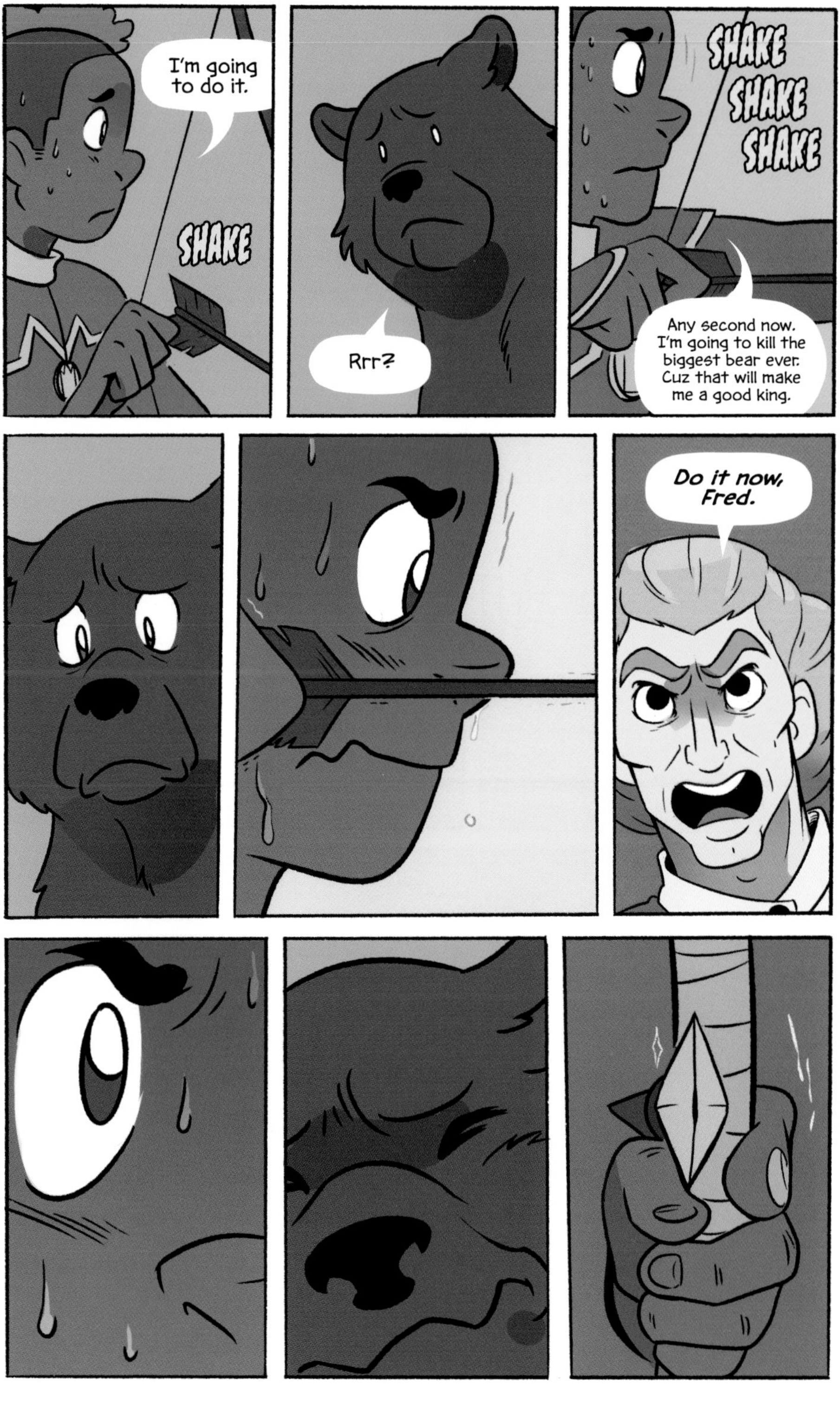
I'm going to do it.
SHAKE
Rrr?
SHAKE
SHAKE
SHAKE
Any second now. I'm going to kill the biggest bear ever. Cuz that will make me a good king.
Do it now, Fred.

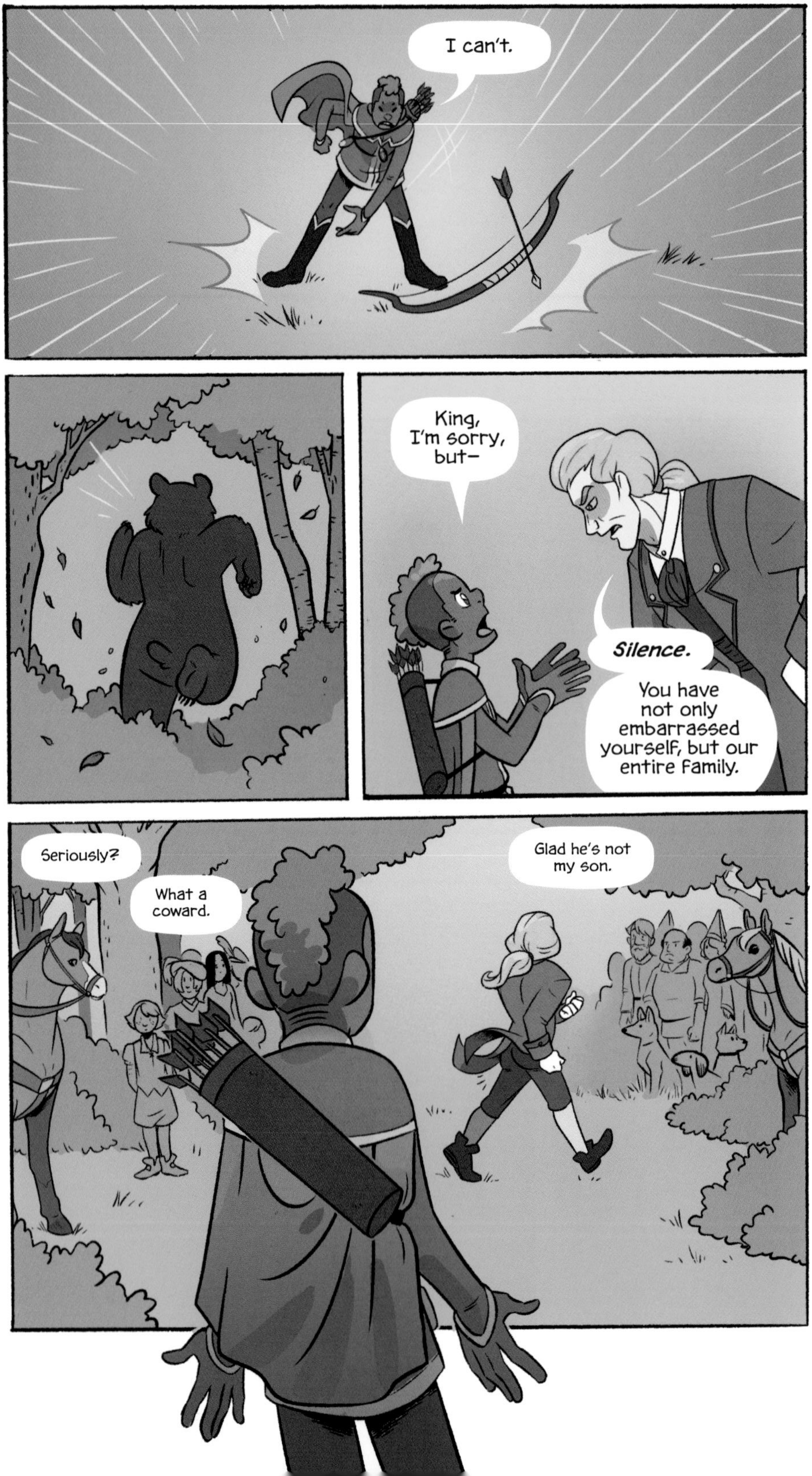
I can't.
King, I'm sorry, but–
Silence.
You have not only embarrassed yourself, but our entire family.
Seriously?
What a coward.
Glad he's not my son.

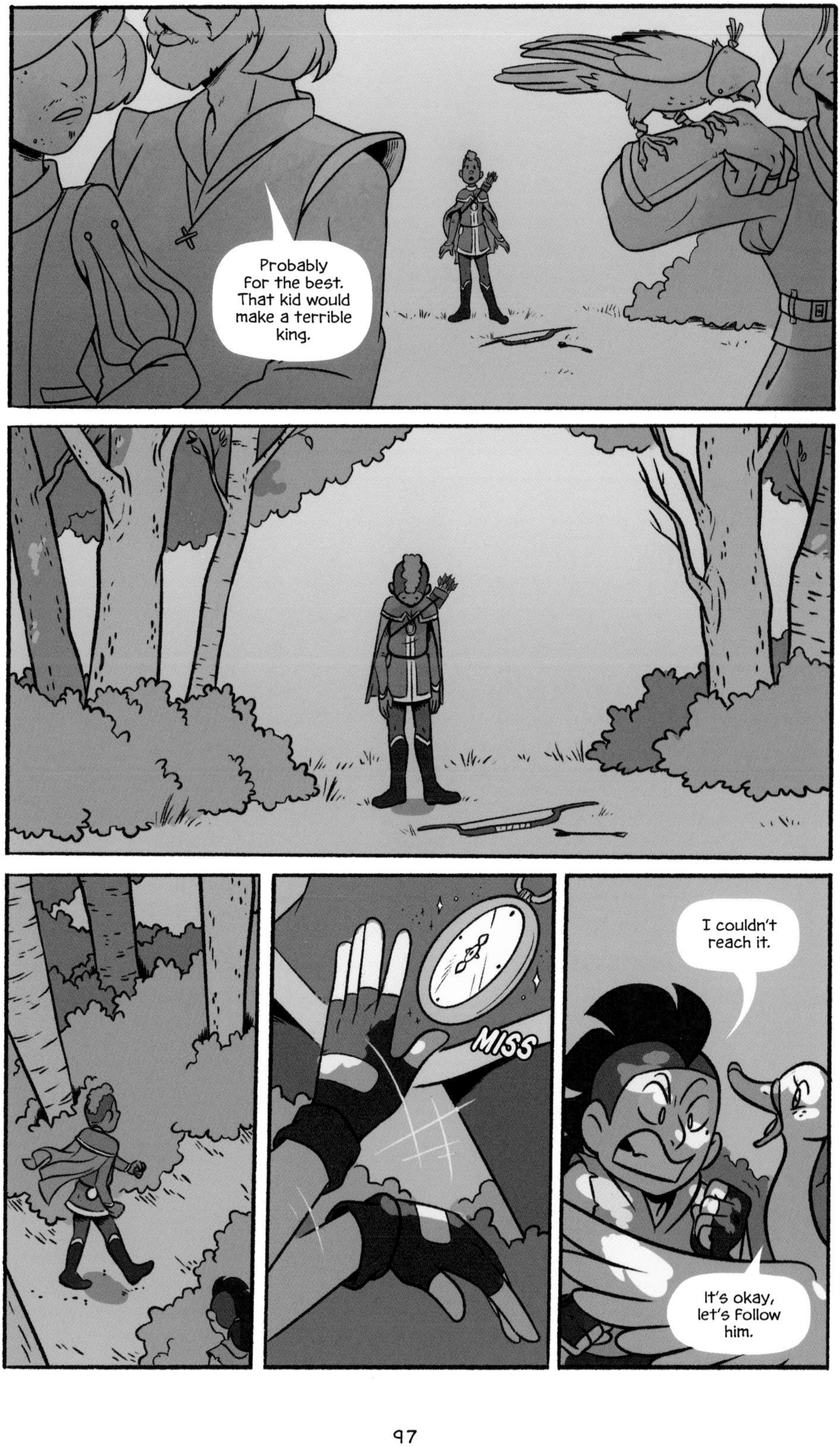
Probably for the best. That kid would make a terrible king.
MISS
I couldn't reach it.
It's okay, let's follow him.

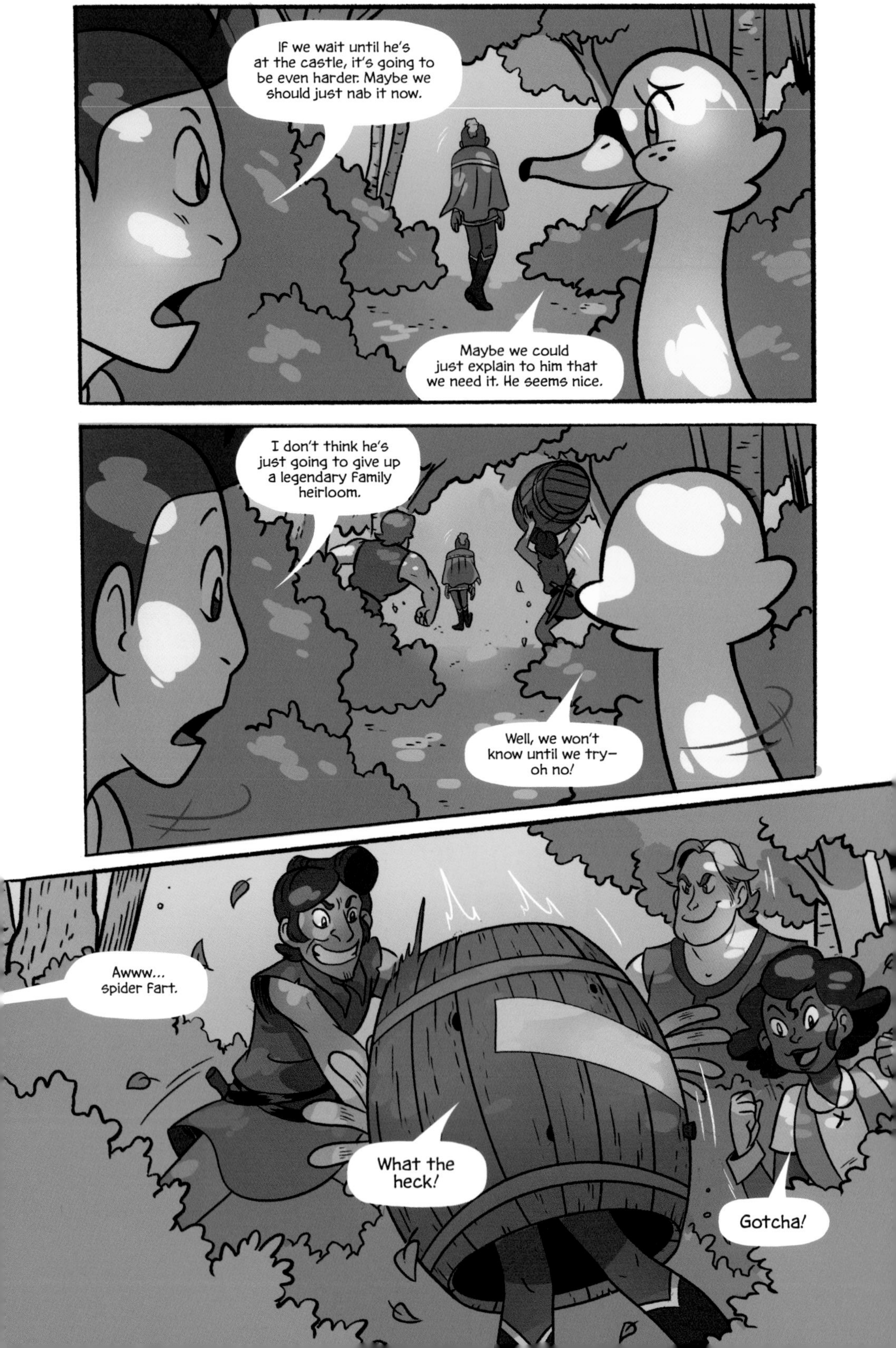
If we wait until he's at the castle, it's going to be even harder. Maybe we should just nab it now.
Maybe we could just explain to him that we need it. He seems nice.
I don't think he's just going to give up a legendary family heirloom.
Well, we won't know until we try—oh no!
Awww... spider fart.
What the heck!
Gotcha!

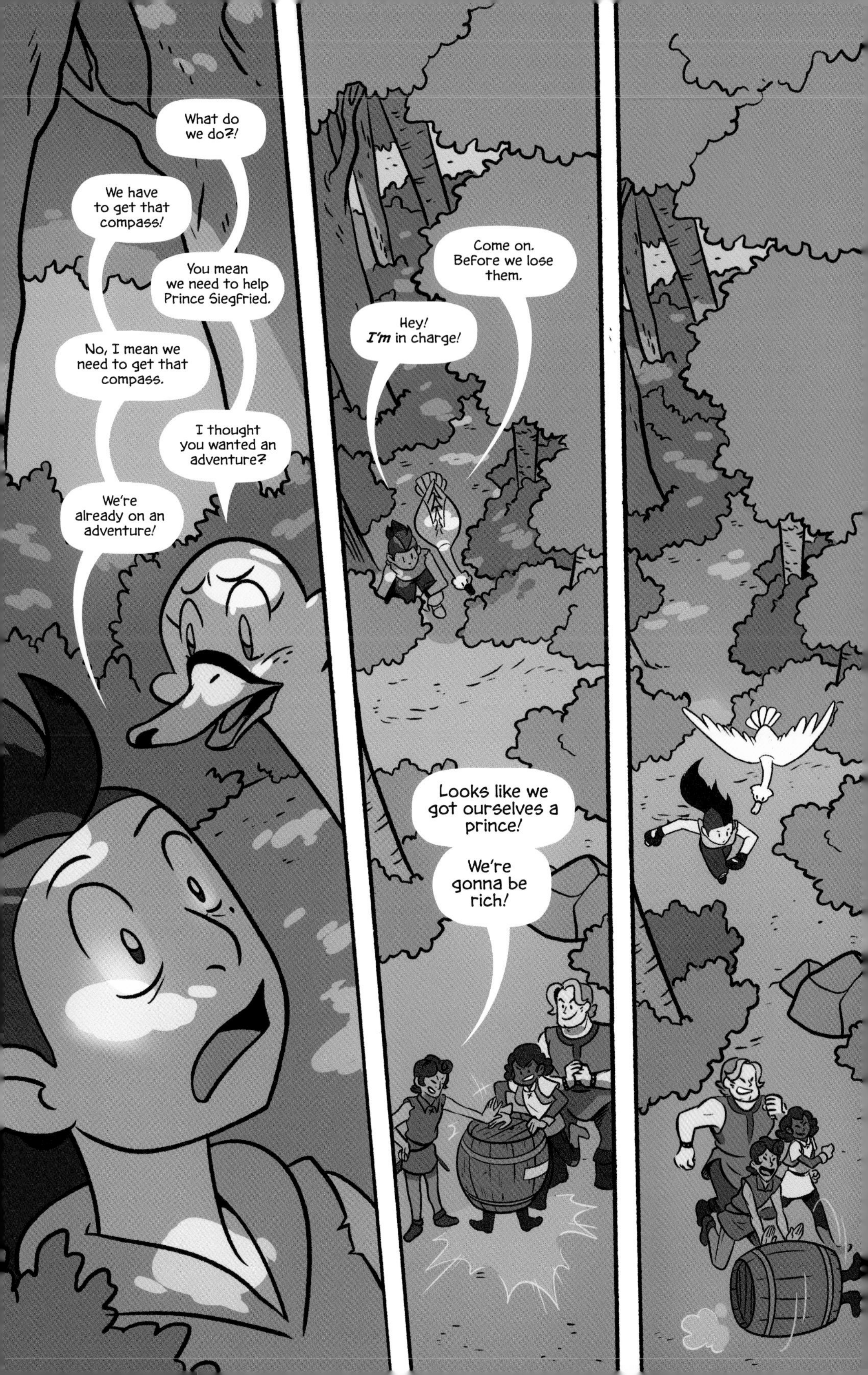
What do we do?!
We have to get that compass!
You mean we need to help Prince Siegfried.
No, I mean we need to get that compass.
I thought you wanted an adventure?
We're already on an adventure!
Come on. Before we lose them.
Hey! *I'm* in charge!
Looks like we got ourselves a prince!
We're gonna be rich!

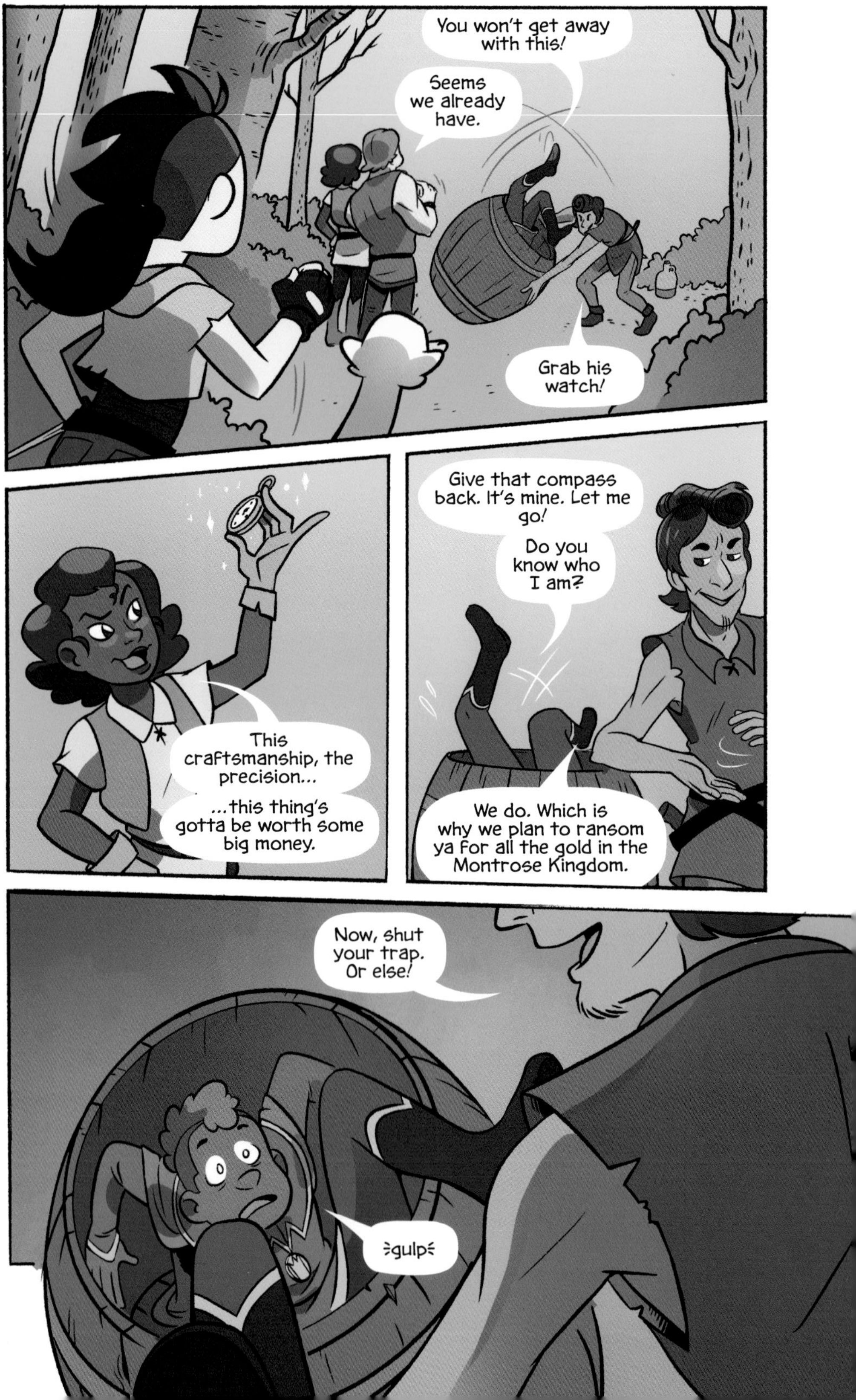
You won't get away with this!
Seems we already have.
Grab his watch!
This craftsmanship, the precision...
...this thing's gotta be worth some big money.
Give that compass back. It's mine. Let me go!
Do you know who I am?
We do. Which is why we plan to ransom ya for all the gold in the Montrose Kingdom.
Now, shut your trap. Or else!
≷gulp≶

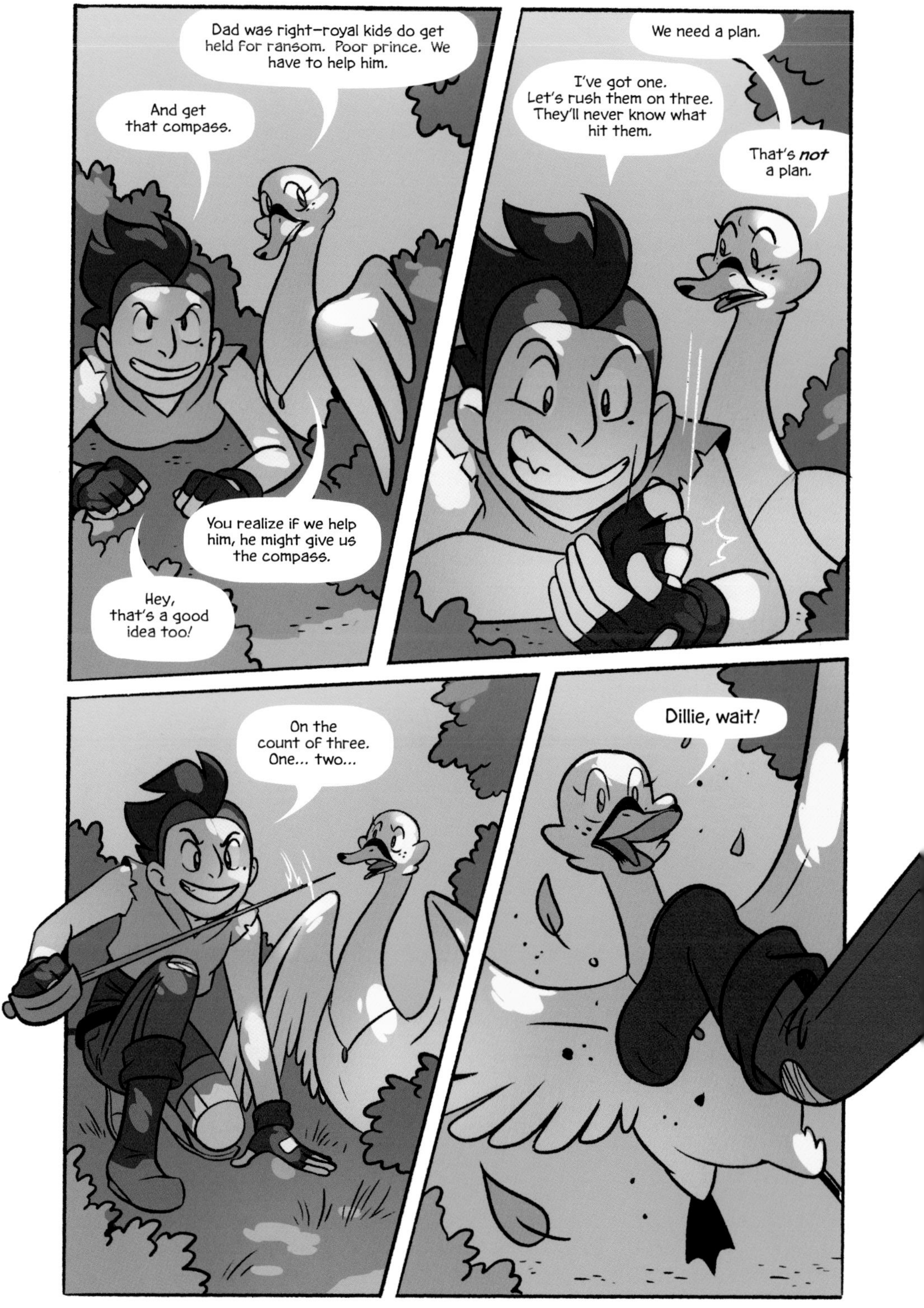
Dad was right—royal kids do get held for ransom. Poor prince. We have to help him.
And get that compass.
You realize if we help him, he might give us the compass.
Hey, that's a good idea too!
We need a plan.
I've got one. Let's rush them on three. They'll never know what hit them.
That's *not* a plan.
On the count of three. One... two...
Dillie, wait!

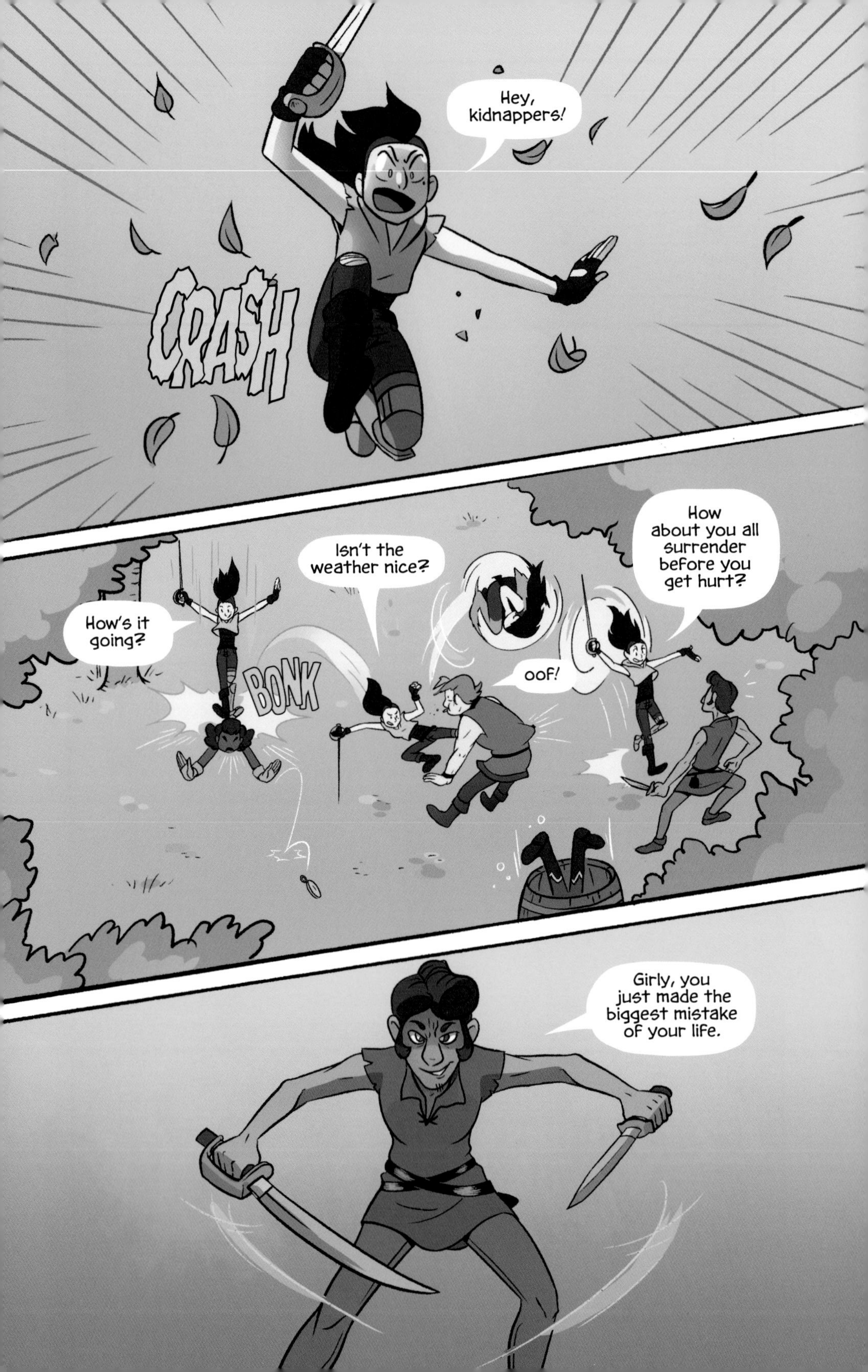
Hey, kidnappers!
CRASH
How's it going?
BONK
Isn't the weather nice?
oof!
How about you all surrender before you get hurt?
Girly, you just made the biggest mistake of your life.

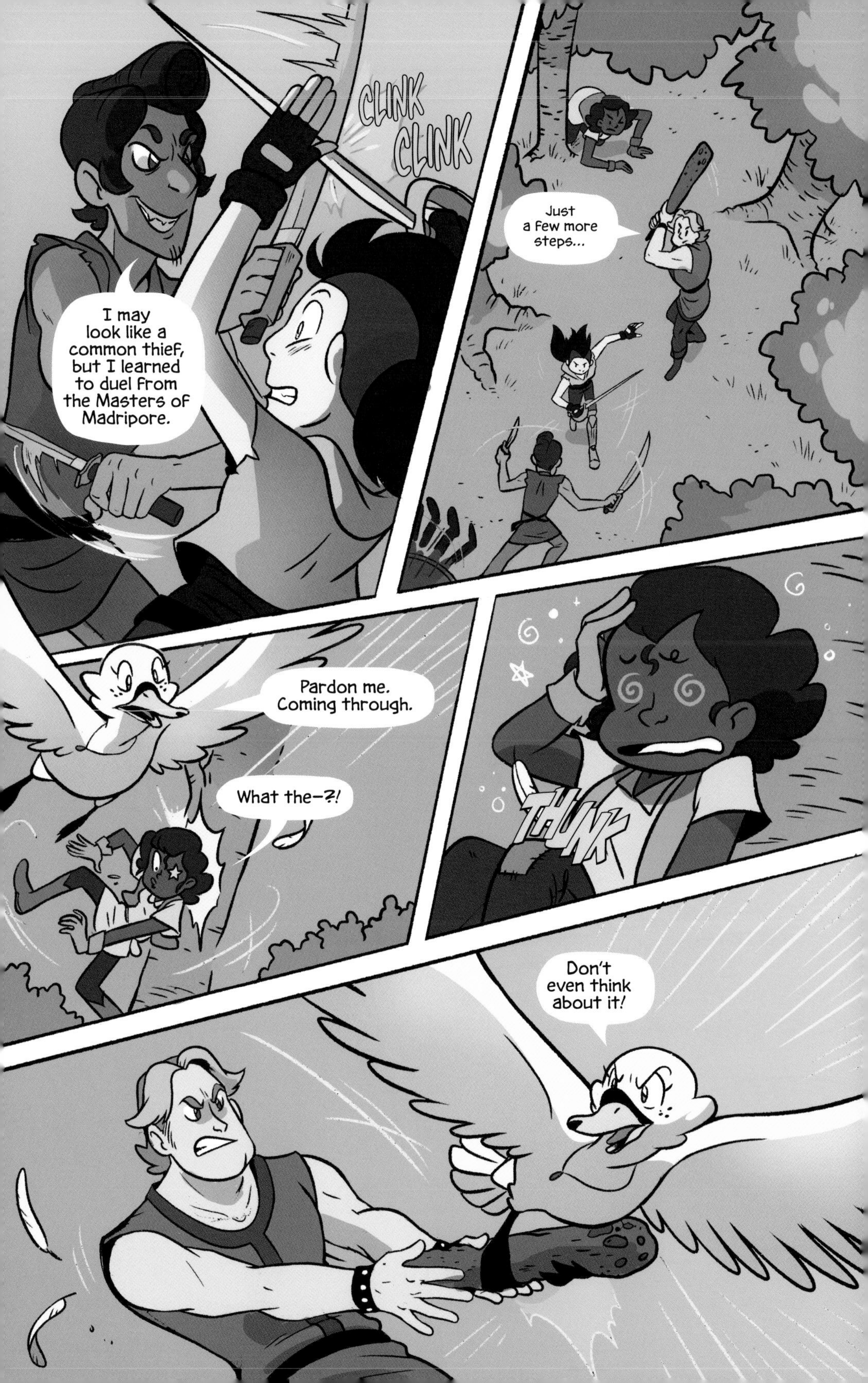
CLINK
CLINK
I may look like a common thief, but I learned to duel from the Masters of Madripore.
Just a few more steps...
Pardon me. Coming through.
What the–?!
THUNK
Don't even think about it!

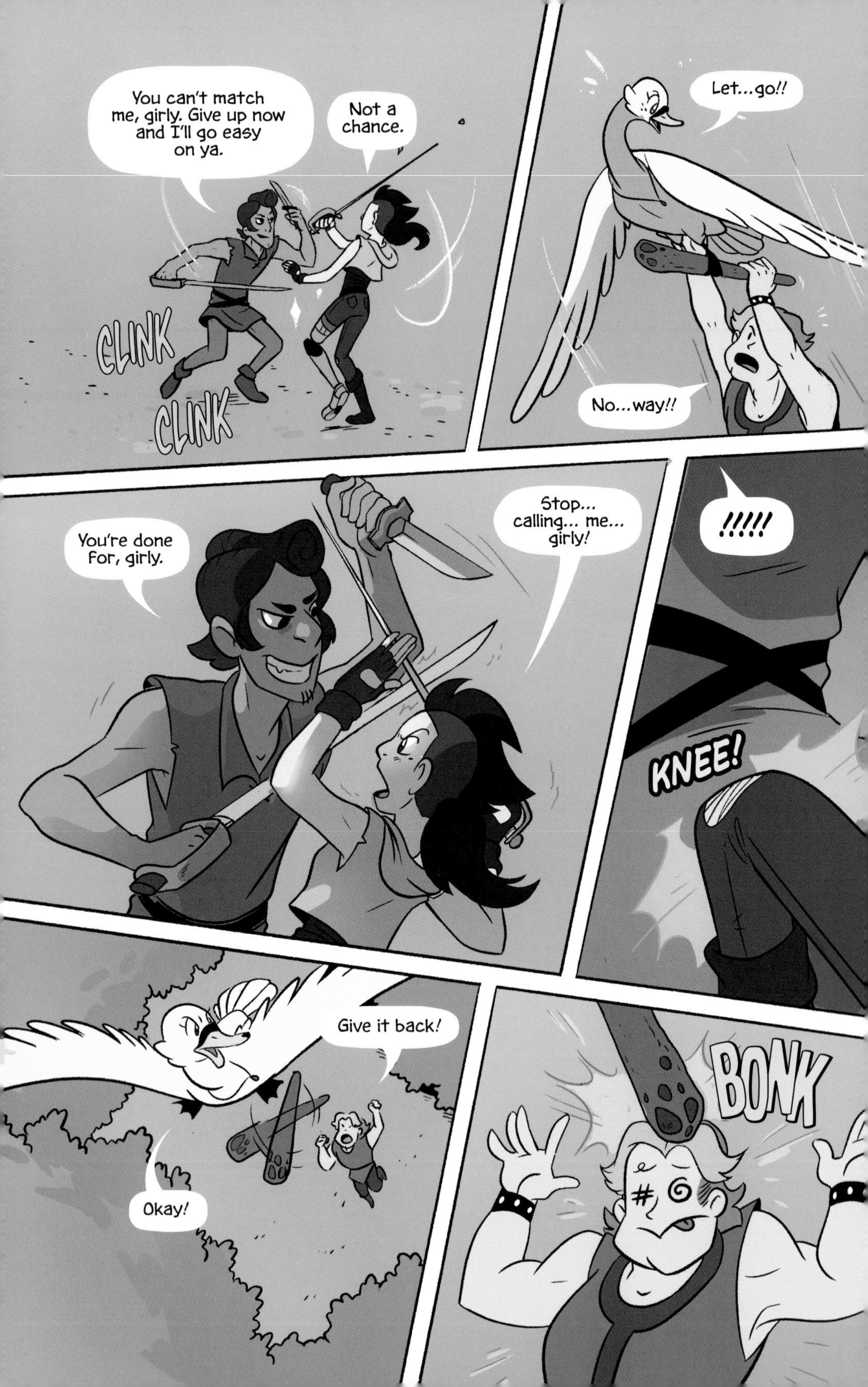
You can't match me, girly. Give up now and I'll go easy on ya.
Not a chance.
CLINK
CLINK
Let...go!!
No...way!!
You're done for, girly.
Stop... calling... me... girly!
!!!!!
KNEE!
Give it back!
Okay!
BONK

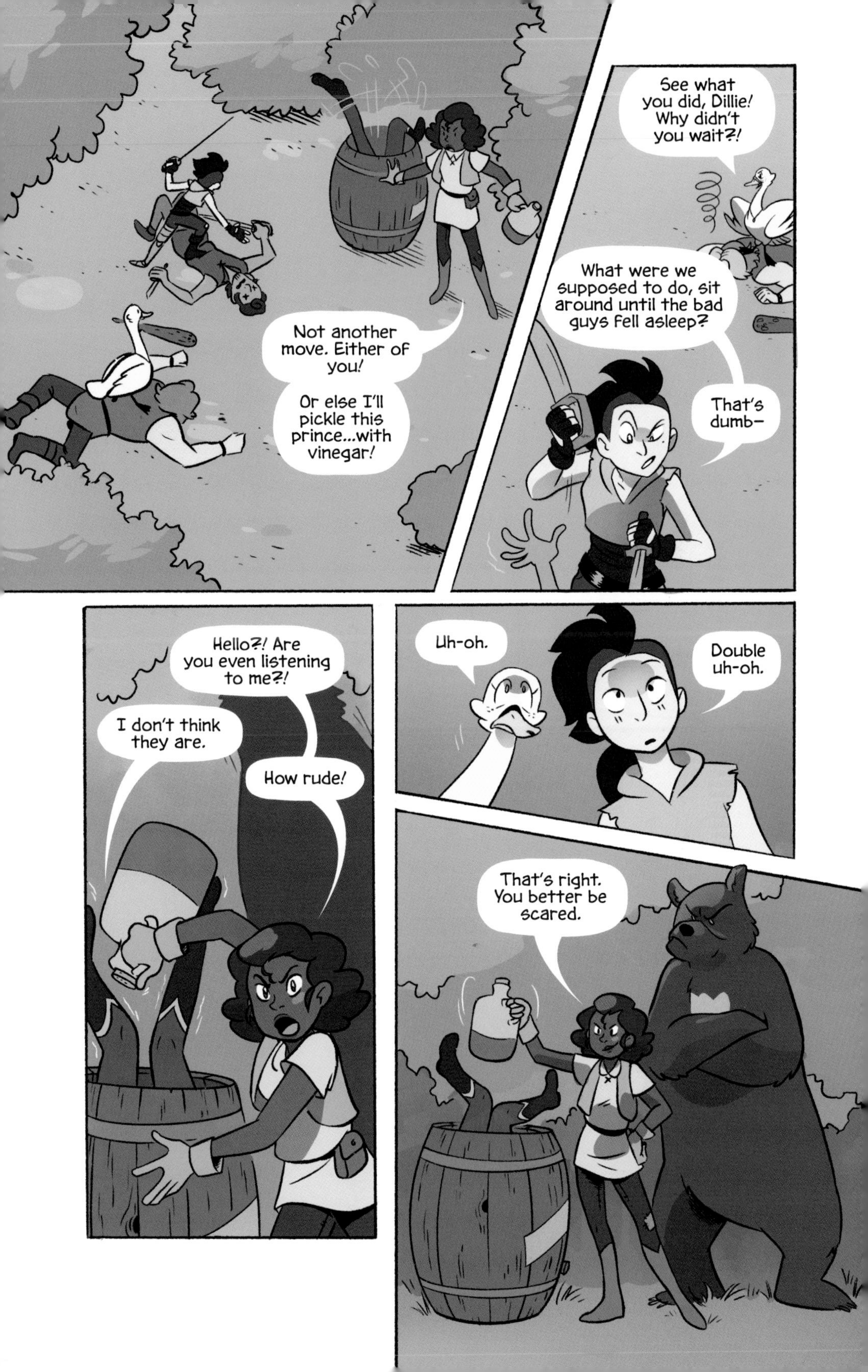
Not another move. Either of you!
Or else I'll pickle this prince...with vinegar!
See what you did, Dillie! Why didn't you wait?!
What were we supposed to do, sit around until the bad guys fell asleep?
That's dumb—
Hello?! Are you even listening to me?!
I don't think they are.
How rude!
Uh-oh.
Double uh-oh.
That's right. You better be scared.

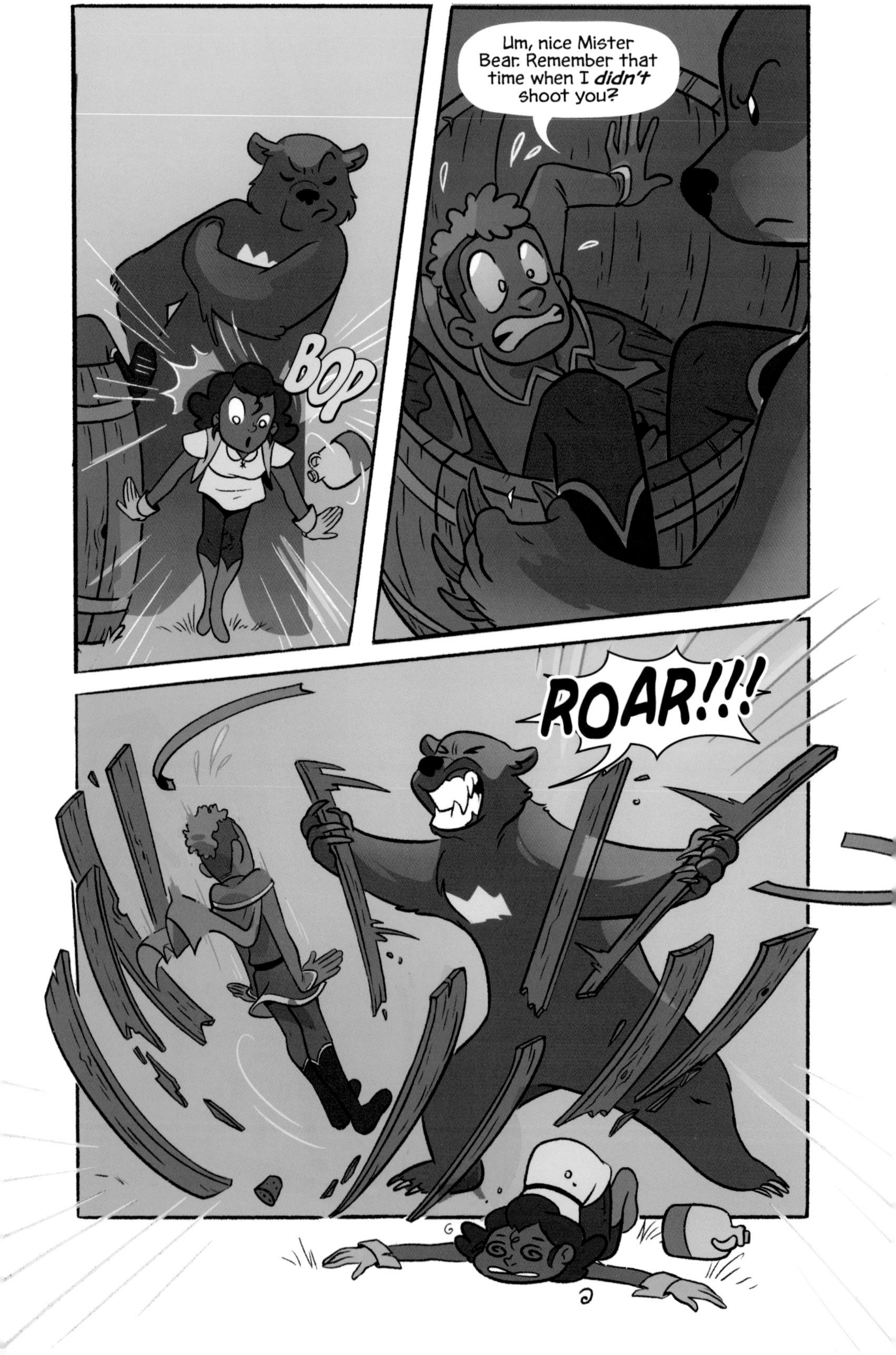
BOP
Um, nice Mister Bear. Remember that time when I *didn't* shoot you?
ROAR!!!

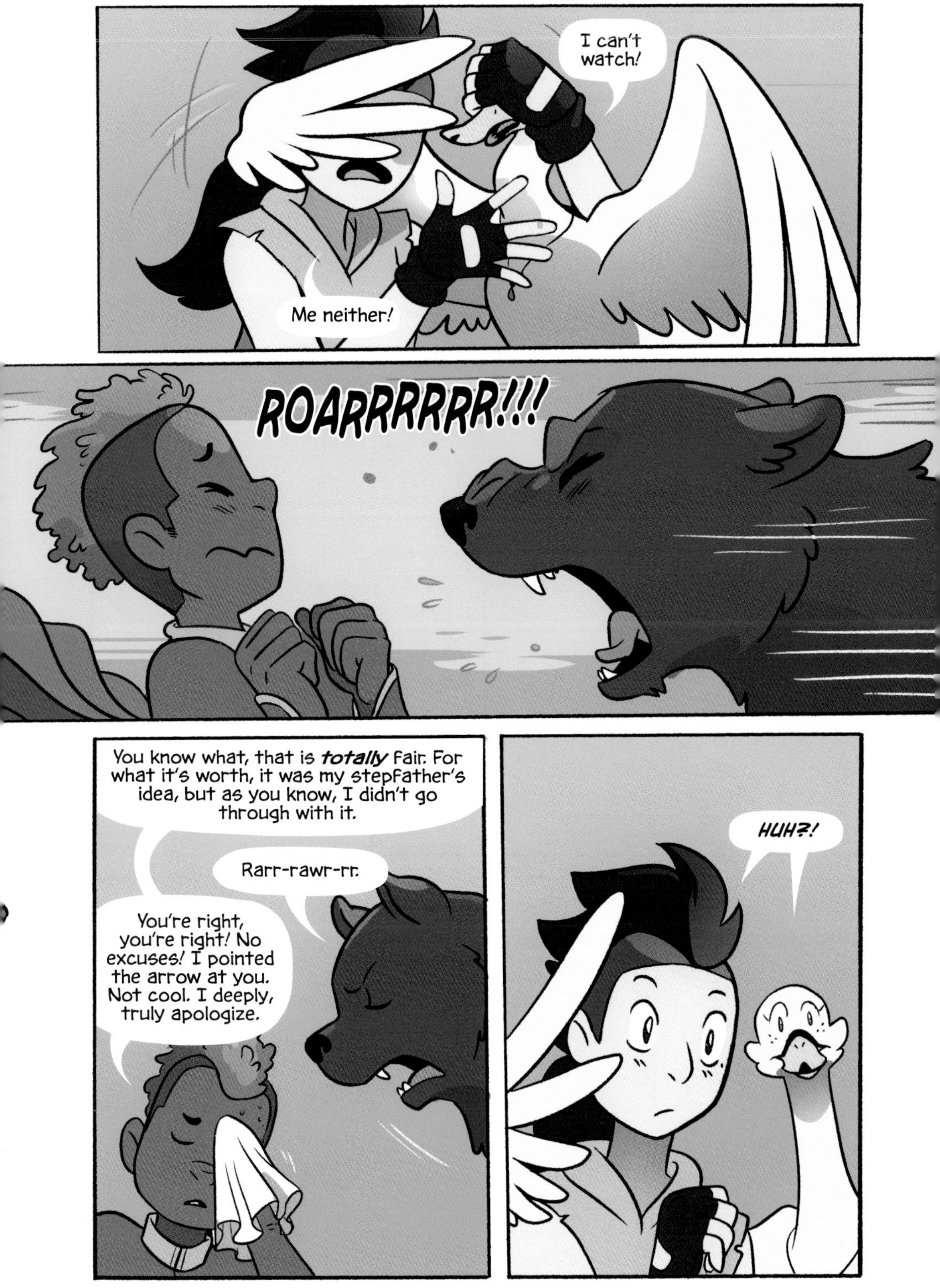
I can't watch!
Me neither!
ROARRRRRR!!!
You know what, that is *totally* fair. For what it's worth, it was my stepfather's idea, but as you know, I didn't go through with it.
Rarr-rawr-rr.
You're right, you're right! No excuses! I pointed the arrow at you. Not cool. I deeply, truly apologize.
HUH?!

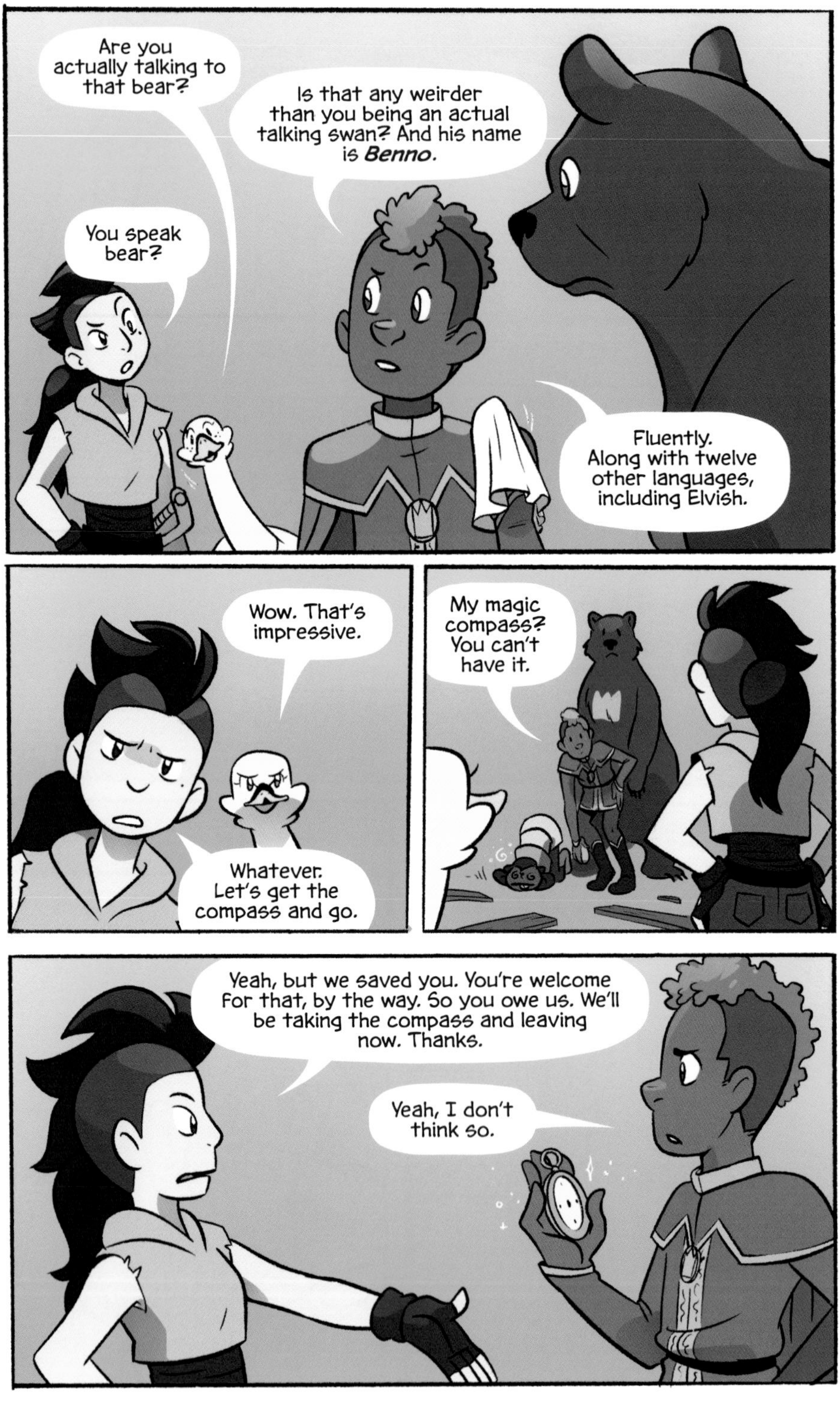
Are you actually talking to that bear?
Is that any weirder than you being an actual talking swan? And his name is *Benno*.
You speak bear?
Fluently. Along with twelve other languages, including Elvish.
Wow. That's impressive.
Whatever. Let's get the compass and go.
My magic compass? You can't have it.
Yeah, but we saved you. You're welcome for that, by the way. So you owe us. We'll be taking the compass and leaving now. Thanks.
Yeah, I don't think so.

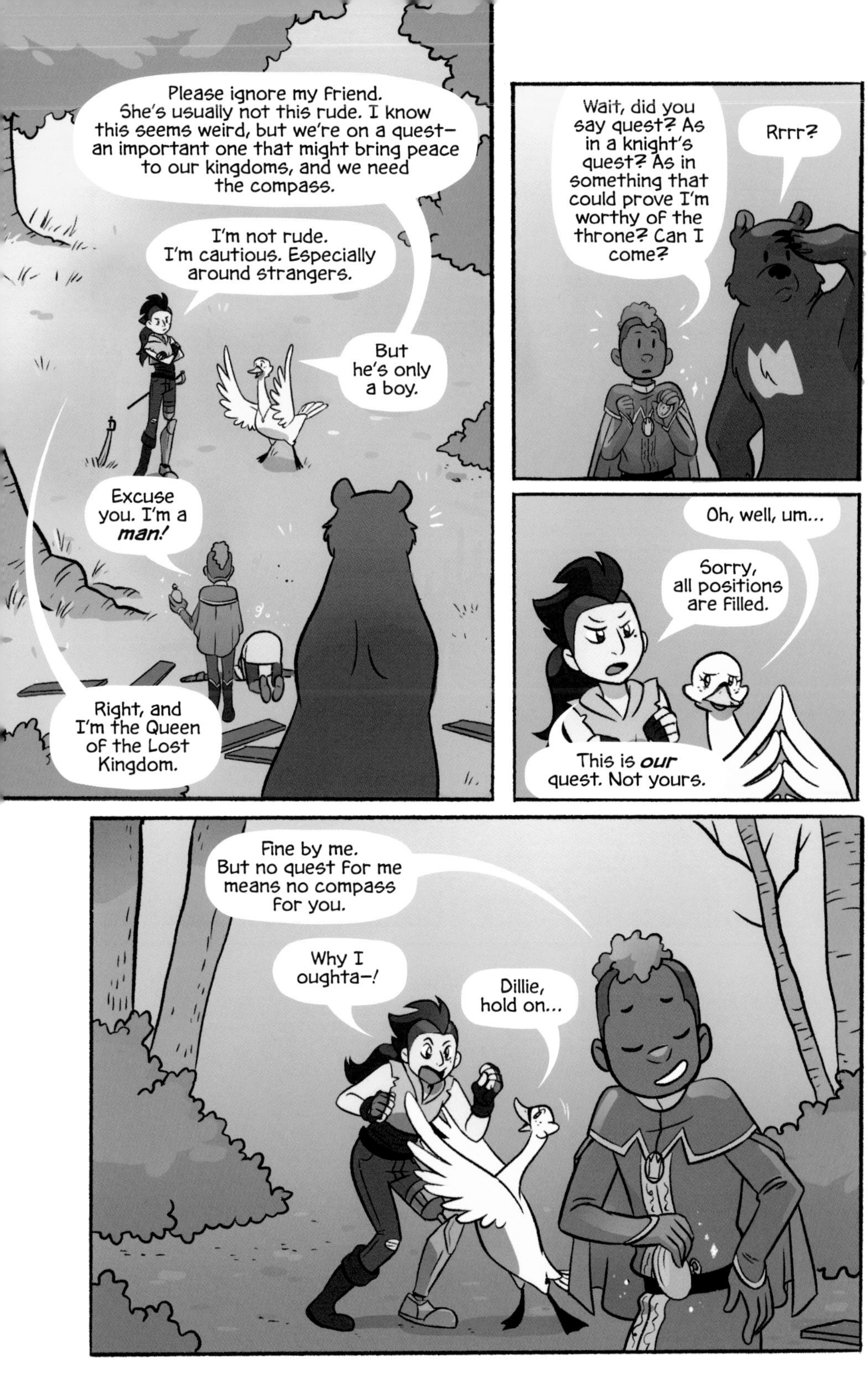
Please ignore my friend. She's usually not this rude. I know this seems weird, but we're on a quest— an important one that might bring peace to our kingdoms, and we need the compass.
I'm not rude. I'm cautious. Especially around strangers.
But he's only a boy.
Excuse you. I'm a *man!*
Right, and I'm the Queen of the Lost Kingdom.
Wait, did you say quest? As in a knight's quest? As in something that could prove I'm worthy of the throne? Can I come?
Rrrr?
Oh, well, um...
Sorry, all positions are filled.
This is *our* quest. Not yours.
Fine by me. But no quest for me means no compass for you.
Why I oughta—!
Dillie, hold on...

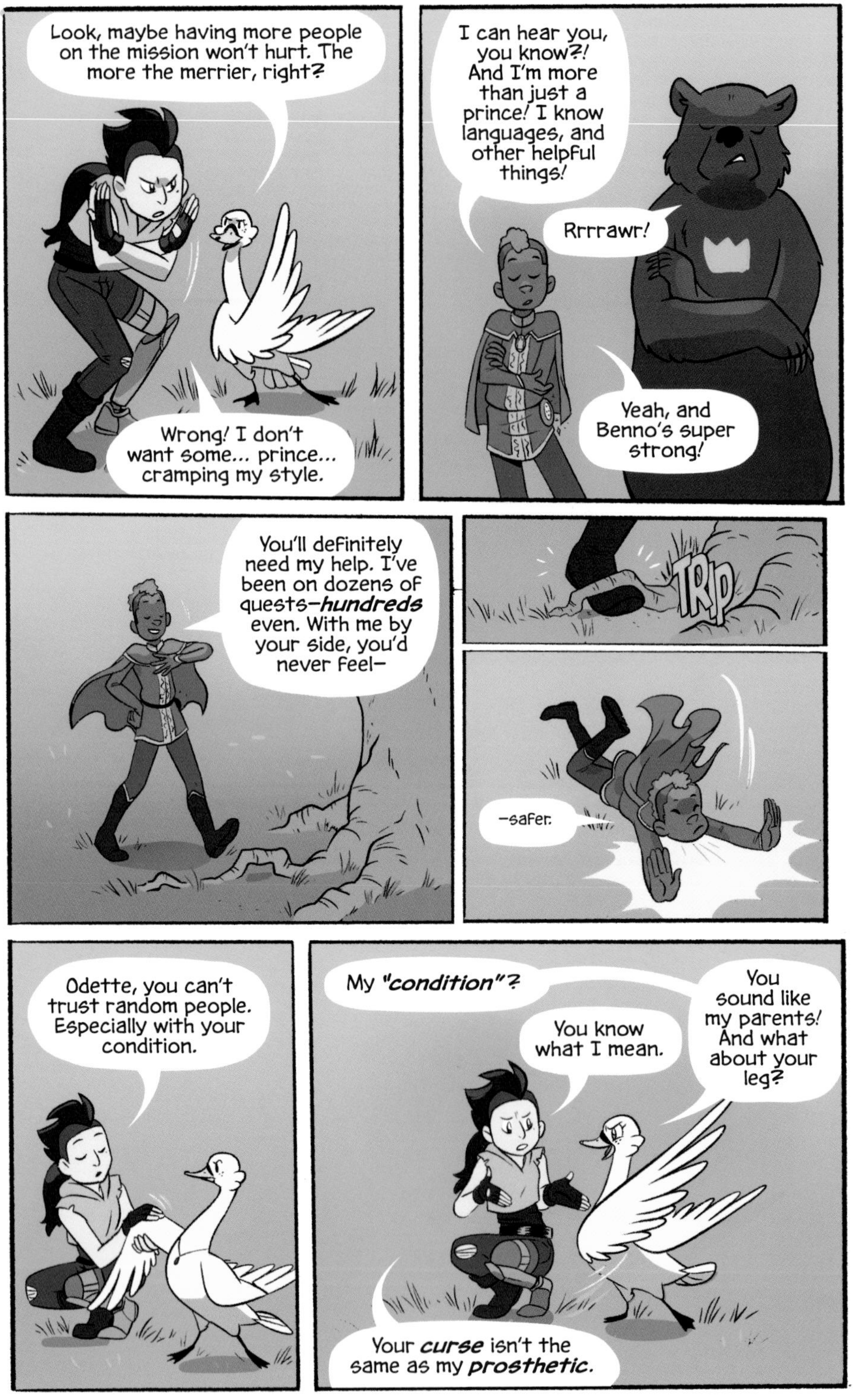
Look, maybe having more people on the mission won't hurt. The more the merrier, right?
Wrong! I don't want some... prince... cramping my style.
I can hear you, you know?! And I'm more than just a prince! I know languages, and other helpful things!
Rrrrawr!
Yeah, and Benno's super strong!
You'll definitely need my help. I've been on dozens of quests—*hundreds* even. With me by your side, you'd never feel—
TRIP
—safer.
Odette, you can't trust random people. Especially with your condition.
My *"condition"*?
You know what I mean.
You sound like my parents! And what about your leg?
Your *curse* isn't the same as my *prosthetic*.

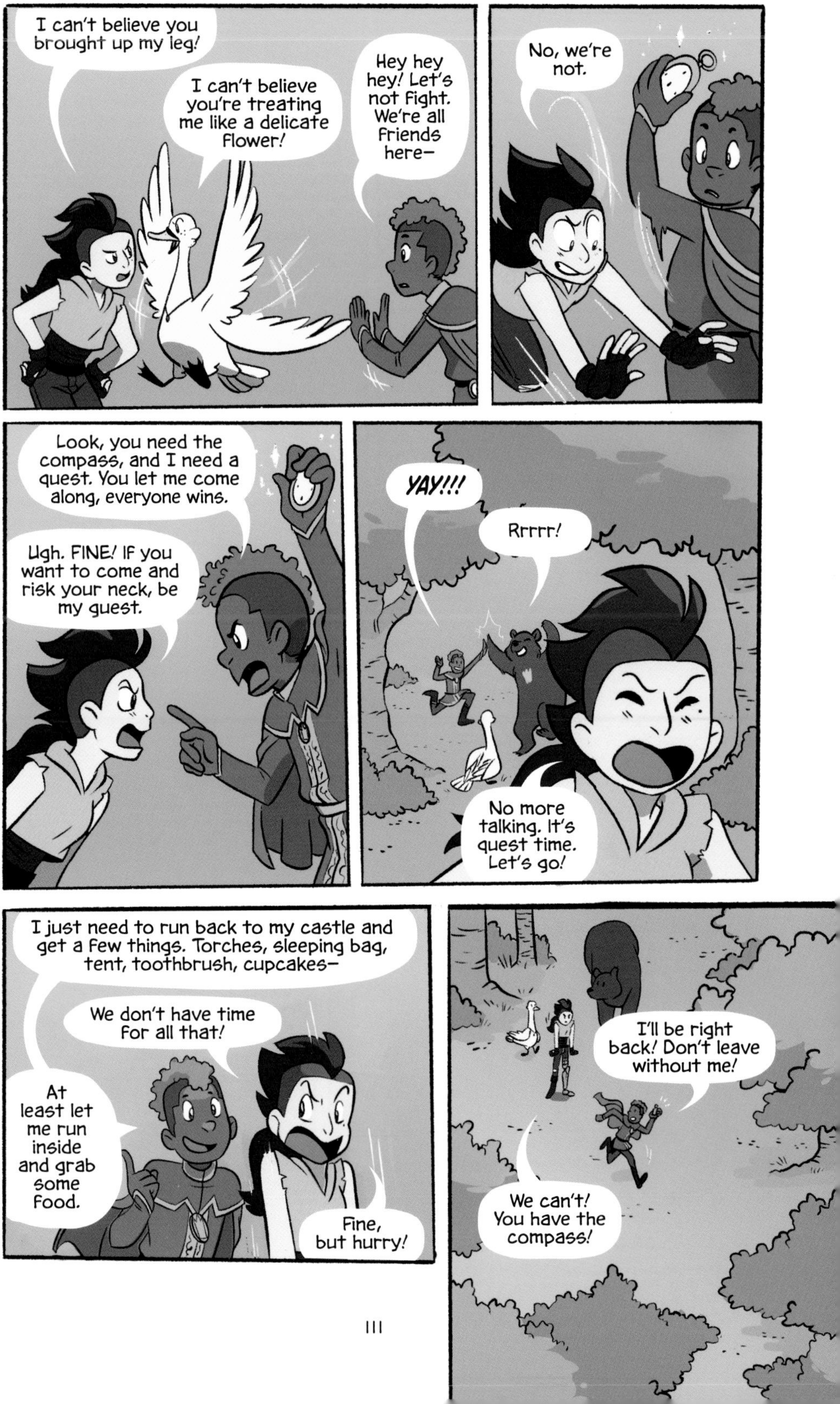
I can't believe you brought up my leg!
I can't believe you're treating me like a delicate flower!
Hey hey hey! Let's not fight. We're all friends here—
No, we're not.
Look, you need the compass, and I need a quest. You let me come along, everyone wins.
Ugh. FINE! If you want to come and risk your neck, be my guest.
YAY!!!
Rrrrr!
No more talking. It's quest time. Let's go!
I just need to run back to my castle and get a few things. Torches, sleeping bag, tent, toothbrush, cupcakes—
We don't have time for all that!
At least let me run inside and grab some food.
Fine, but hurry!
I'll be right back! Don't leave without me!
We can't! You have the compass!

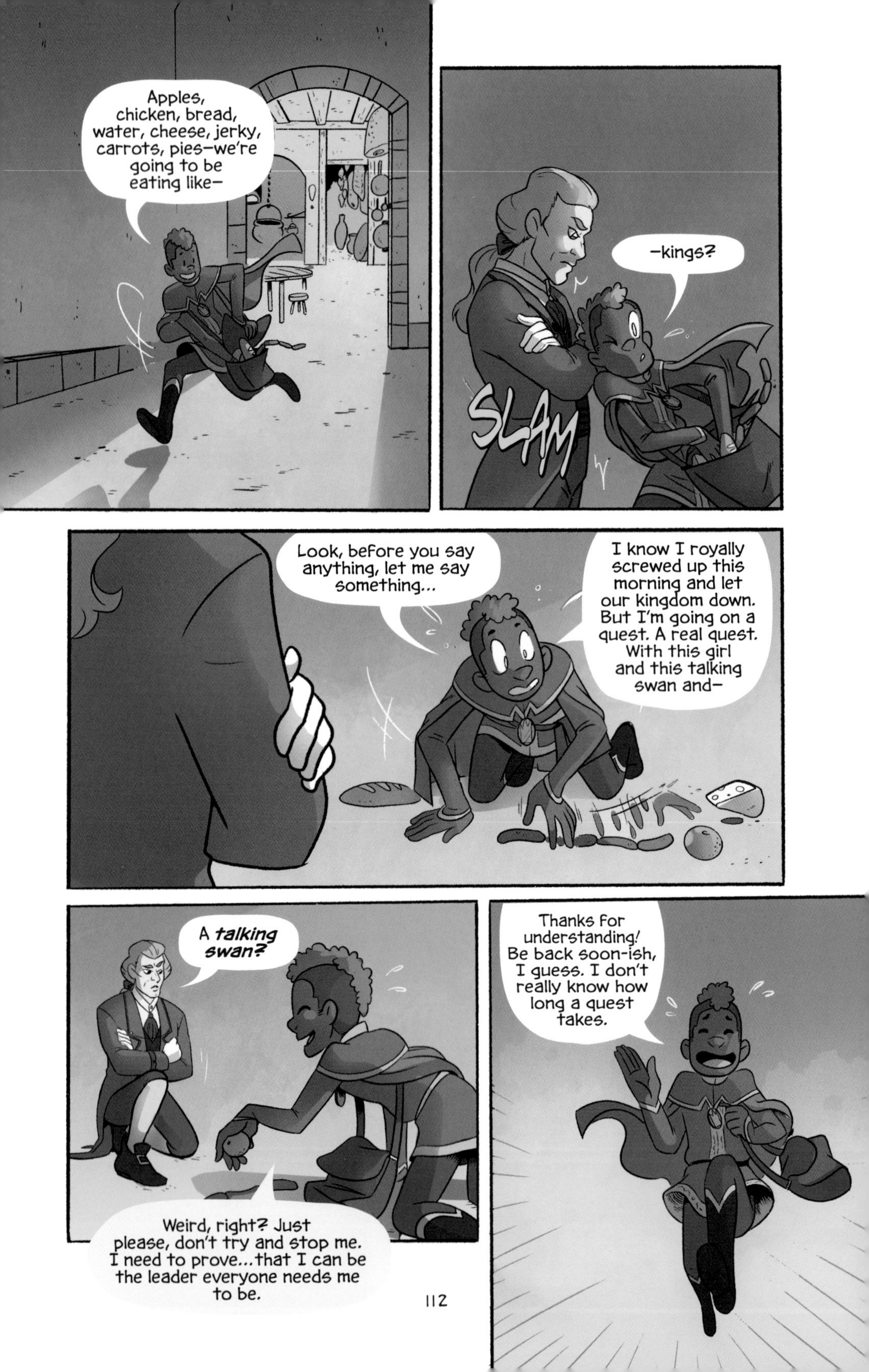
Apples, chicken, bread, water, cheese, jerky, carrots, pies—we're going to be eating like—
—kings?
SLAM
Look, before you say anything, let me say something...
I know I royally screwed up this morning and let our kingdom down. But I'm going on a quest. A real quest. With this girl and this talking swan and—
A *talking swan?*
Weird, right? Just please, don't try and stop me. I need to prove...that I can be the leader everyone needs me to be.
Thanks for understanding! Be back soon-ish, I guess. I don't really know how long a quest takes.

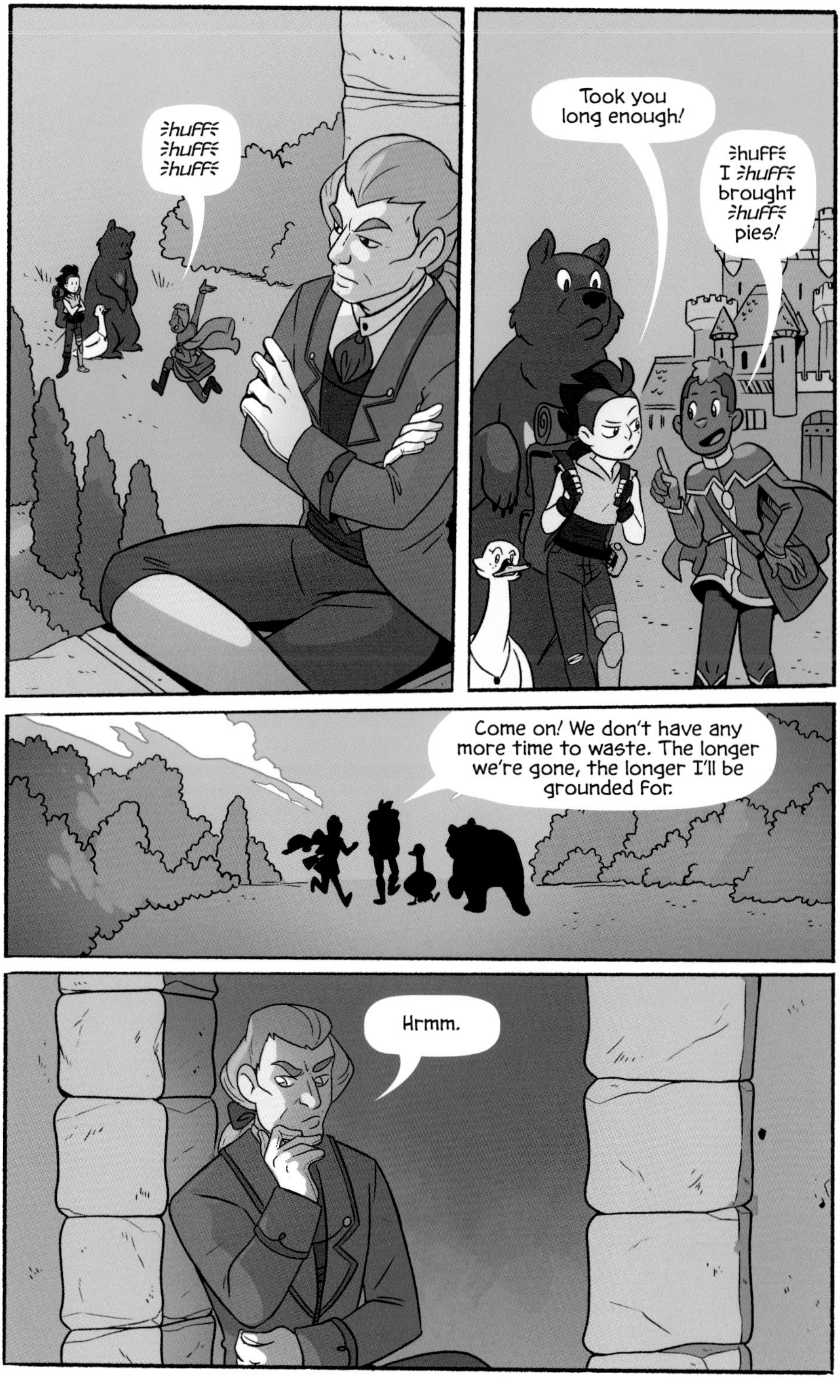

≑huff≑ ≑huff≑ ≑huff≑
Took you long enough!
≑huff≑ I ≑huff≑ brought ≑huff≑ pies!
Come on! We don't have any more time to waste. The longer we're gone, the longer I'll be grounded for.
Hrmm.

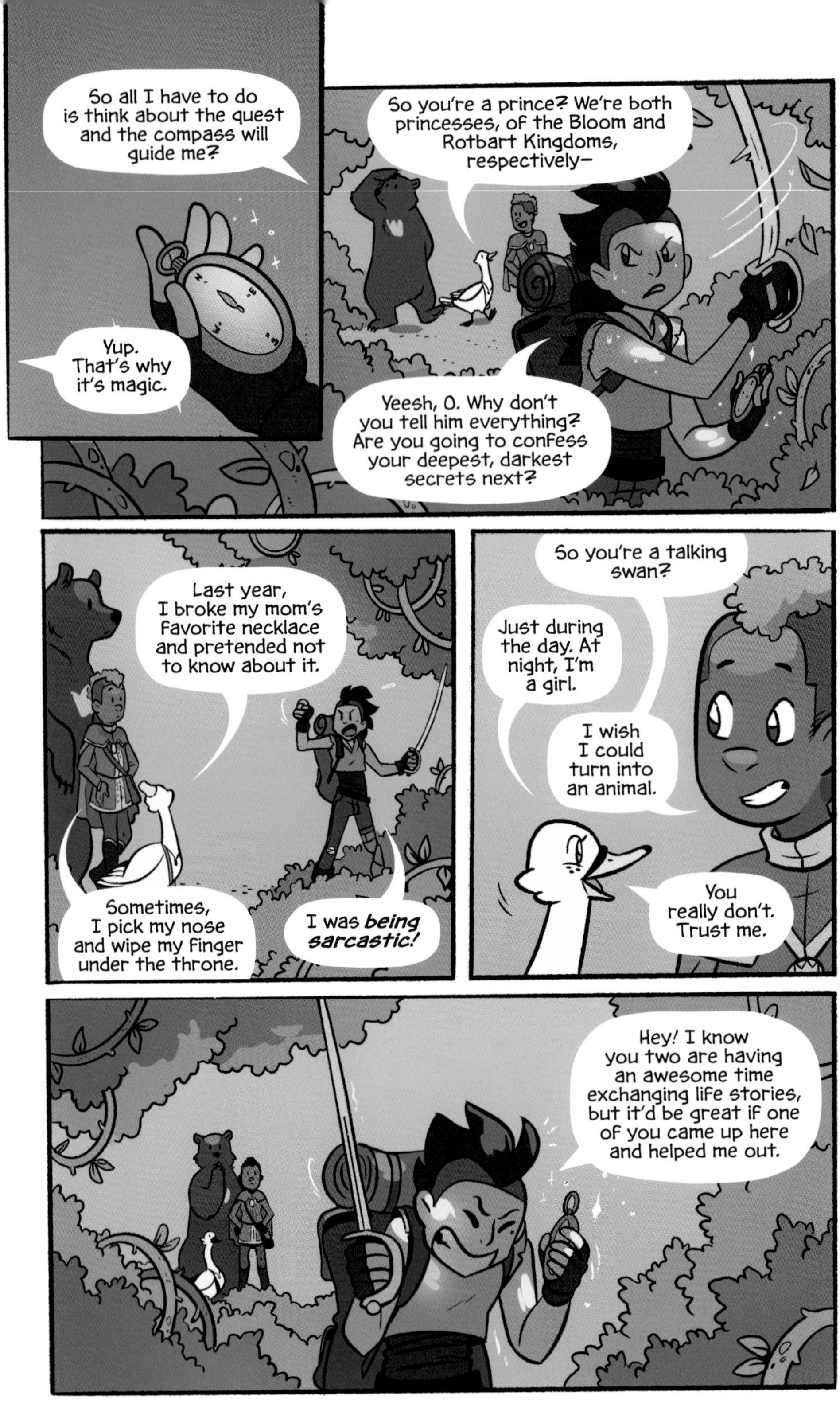
So all I have to do is think about the quest and the compass will guide me?
Yup. That's why it's magic.
So you're a prince? We're both princesses, of the Bloom and Rotbart Kingdoms, respectively—
Yeesh, O. Why don't you tell him everything? Are you going to confess your deepest, darkest secrets next?
Last year, I broke my mom's favorite necklace and pretended not to know about it.
Sometimes, I pick my nose and wipe my finger under the throne.
I was *being sarcastic!*
So you're a talking swan?
Just during the day. At night, I'm a girl.
I wish I could turn into an animal.
You really don't. Trust me.
Hey! I know you two are having an awesome time exchanging life stories, but it'd be great if one of you came up here and helped me out.

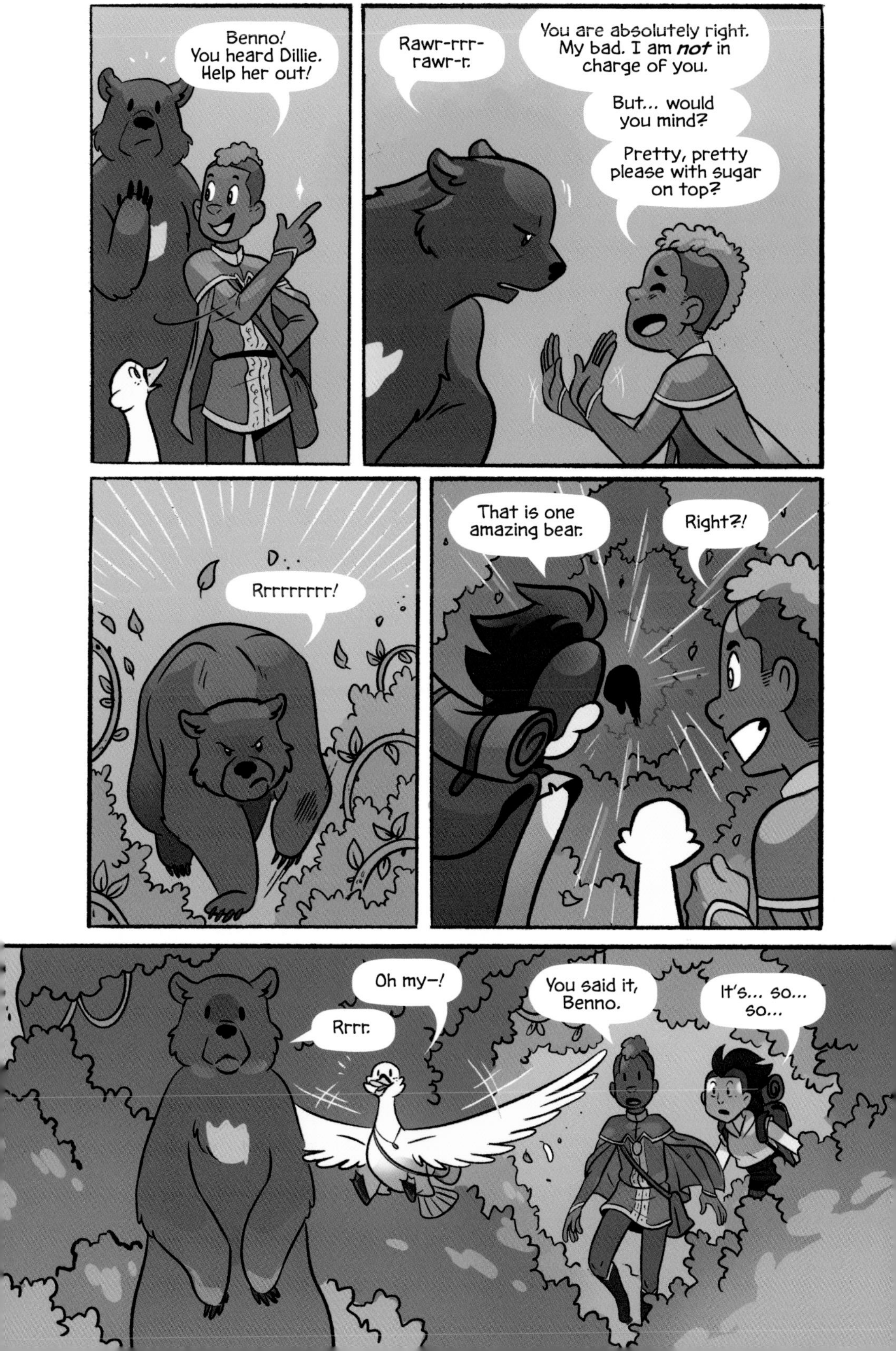
Benno! You heard Dillie. Help her out!
Rawr-rrr-rawr-r.
You are absolutely right. My bad. I am *not* in charge of you.
But... would you mind?
Pretty, pretty please with sugar on top?
Rrrrrrrrr!
That is one amazing bear.
Right?!
Oh my–!
Rrrr.
You said it, Benno.
It's... so... so...

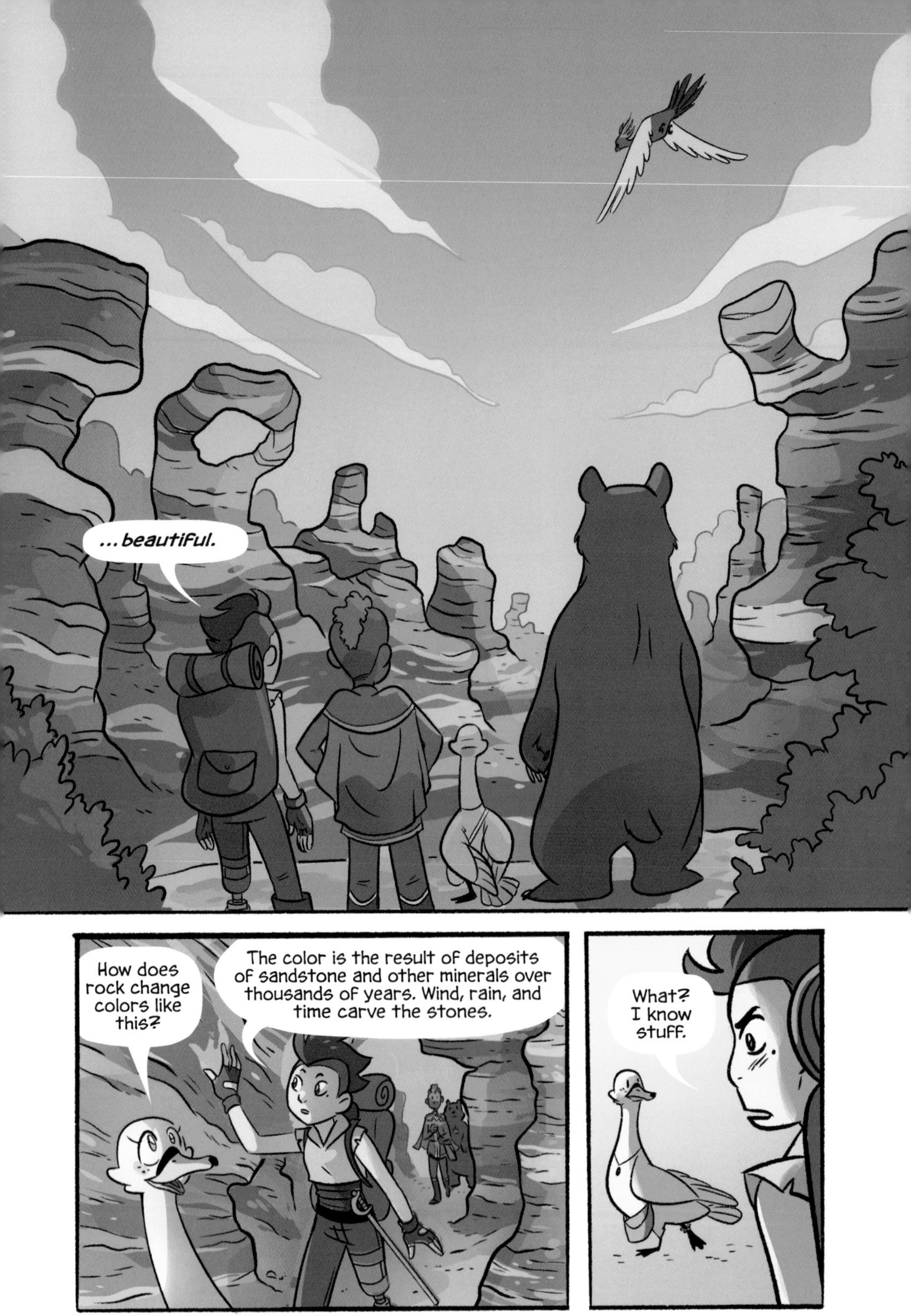
...beautiful.
How does rock change colors like this?
The color is the result of deposits of sandstone and other minerals over thousands of years. Wind, rain, and time carve the stones.
What? I know stuff.

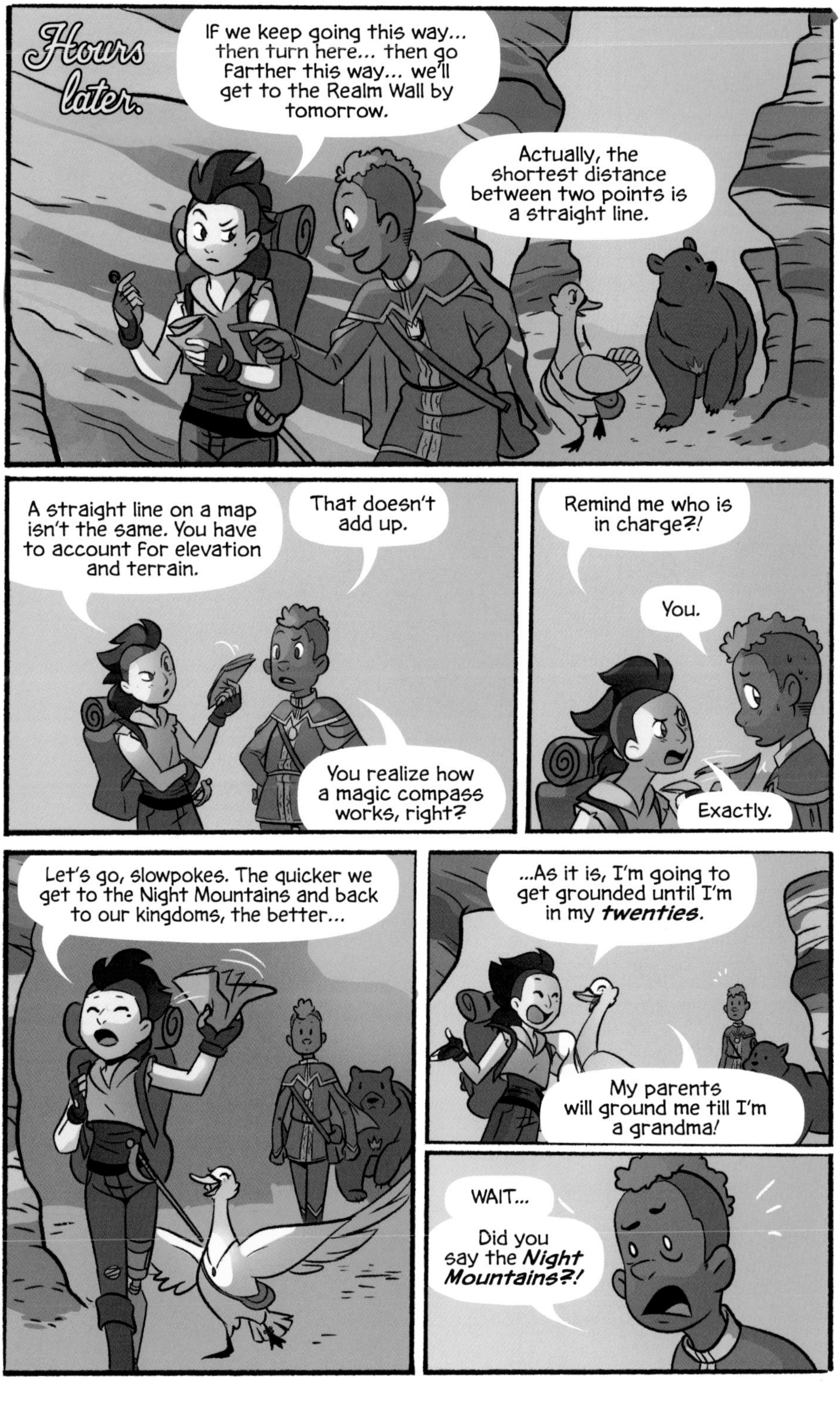
Hours later.
If we keep going this way... then turn here... then go farther this way... we'll get to the Realm Wall by tomorrow.
Actually, the shortest distance between two points is a straight line.
A straight line on a map isn't the same. You have to account for elevation and terrain.
That doesn't add up.
You realize how a magic compass works, right?
Remind me who is in charge?!
You.
Exactly.
Let's go, slowpokes. The quicker we get to the Night Mountains and back to our kingdoms, the better...
...As it is, I'm going to get grounded until I'm in my *twenties*.
My parents will ground me till I'm a grandma!
WAIT...
Did you say the *Night Mountains*?!

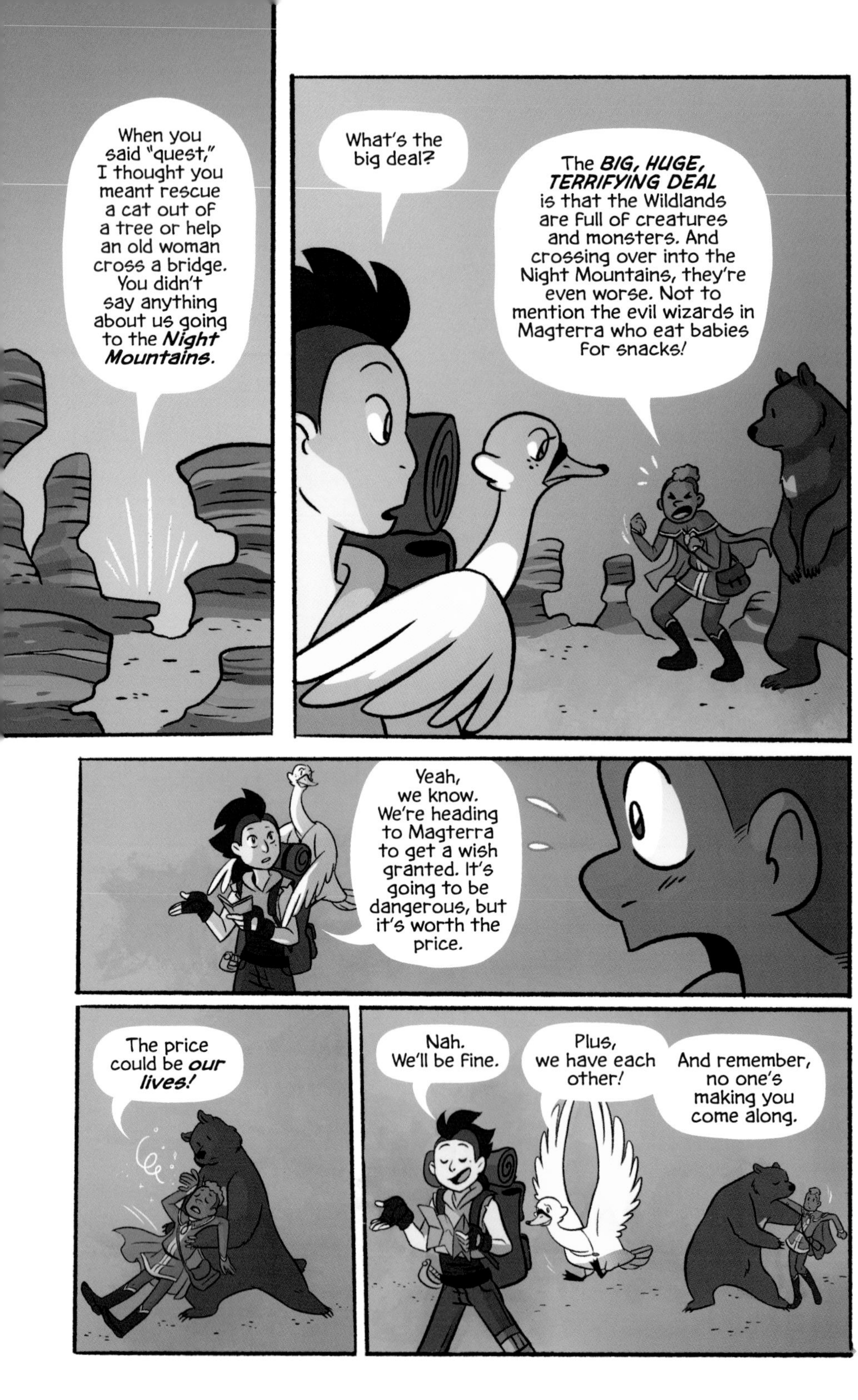

When you said "quest," I thought you meant rescue a cat out of a tree or help an old woman cross a bridge. You didn't say anything about us going to the *Night Mountains*.
What's the big deal?
The ***BIG, HUGE, TERRIFYING DEAL*** is that the Wildlands are full of creatures and monsters. And crossing over into the Night Mountains, they're even worse. Not to mention the evil wizards in Magterra who eat babies for snacks!
Yeah, we know. We're heading to Magterra to get a wish granted. It's going to be dangerous, but it's worth the price.
The price could be ***our lives!***
Nah. We'll be fine.
Plus, we have each other!
And remember, no one's making you come along.

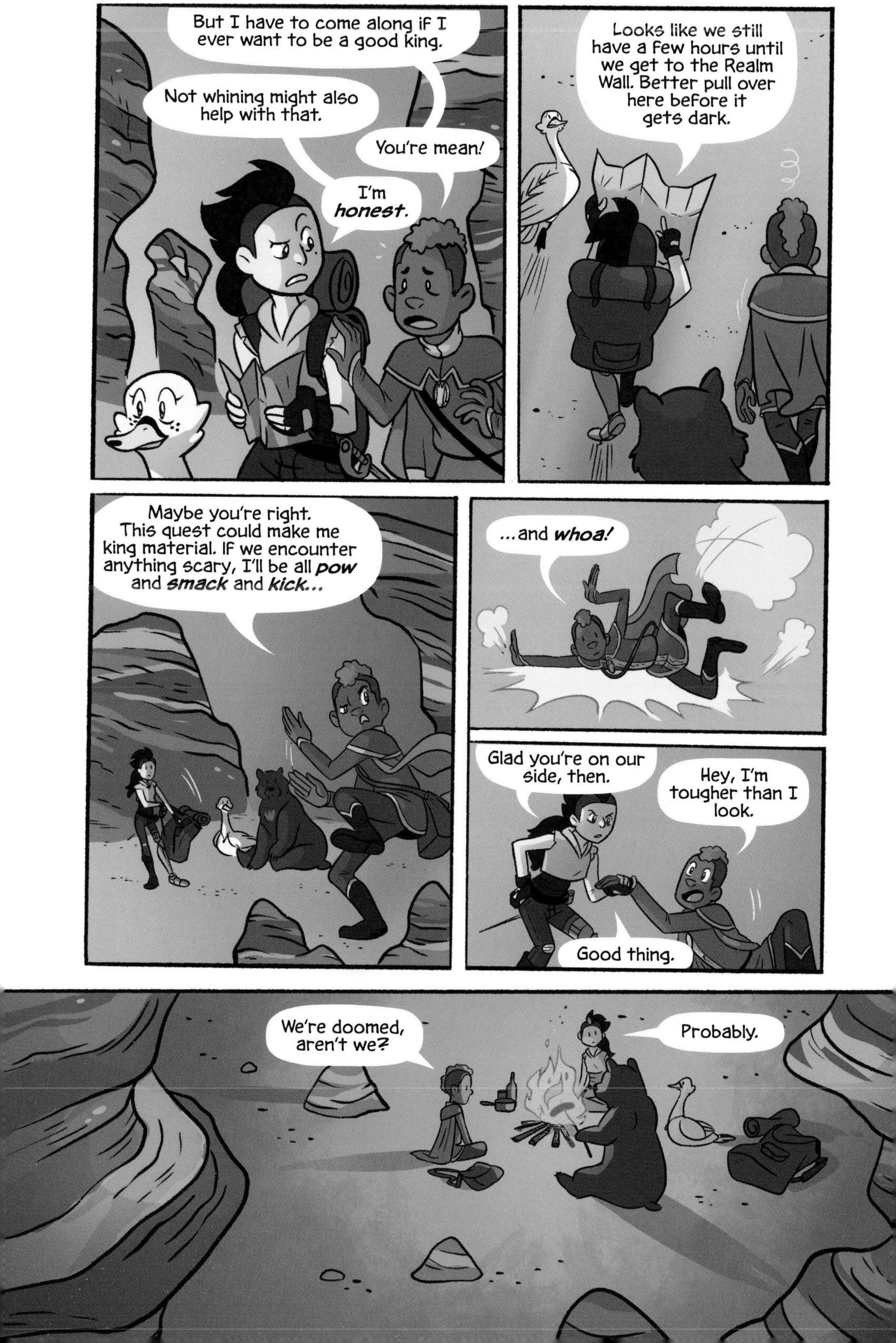

But I have to come along if I ever want to be a good king.
Not whining might also help with that.
You're mean!
I'm *honest*.
Looks like we still have a few hours until we get to the Realm Wall. Better pull over here before it gets dark.
Maybe you're right. This quest could make me king material. If we encounter anything scary, I'll be all *pow* and *smack* and *kick*...
...and *whoa!*
Glad you're on our side, then.
Hey, I'm tougher than I look.
Good thing.
We're doomed, aren't we?
Probably.

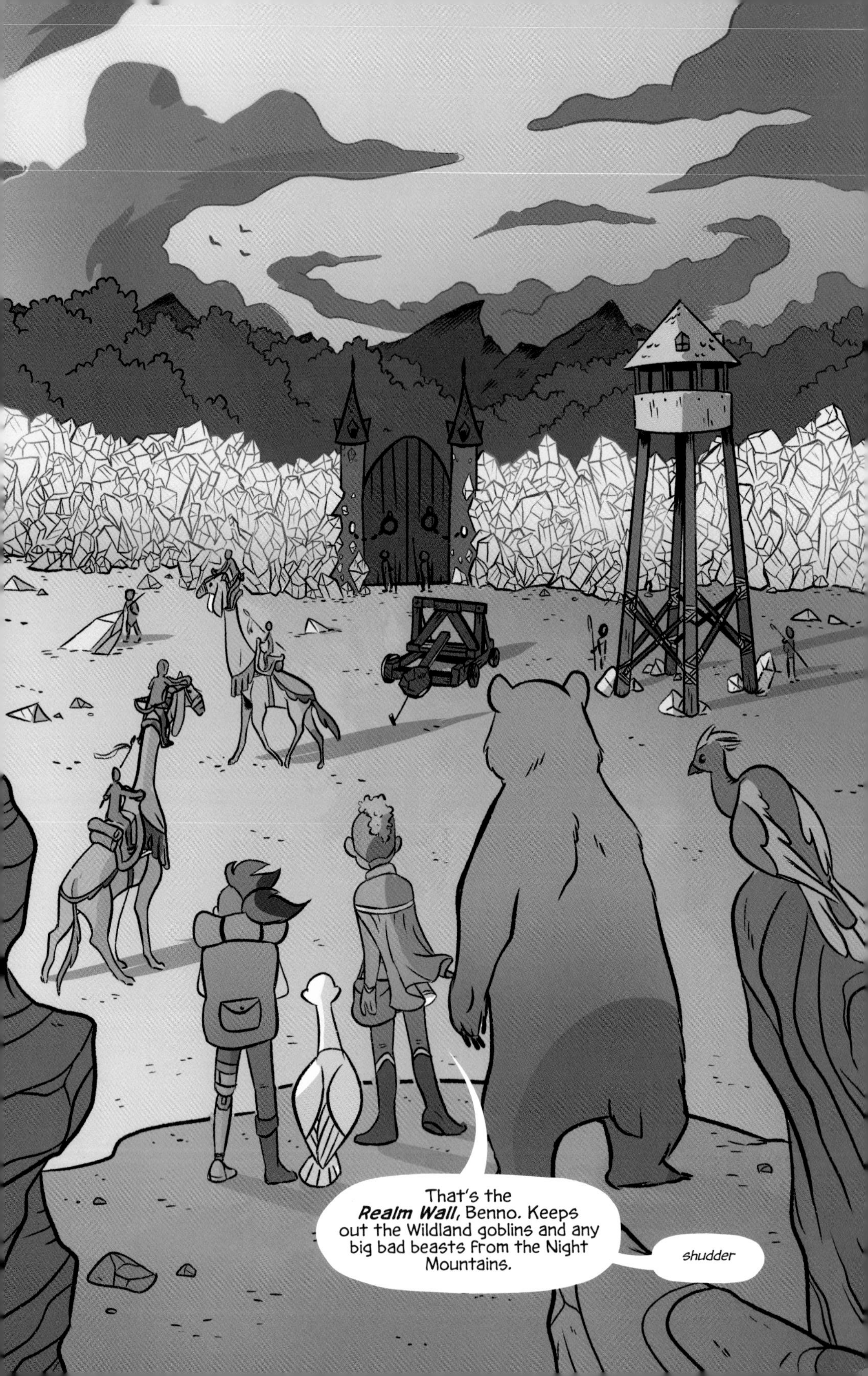
That's the
Realm Wall, Benno. Keeps
out the Wildland goblins and any
big bad beasts from the Night
Mountains.
shudder

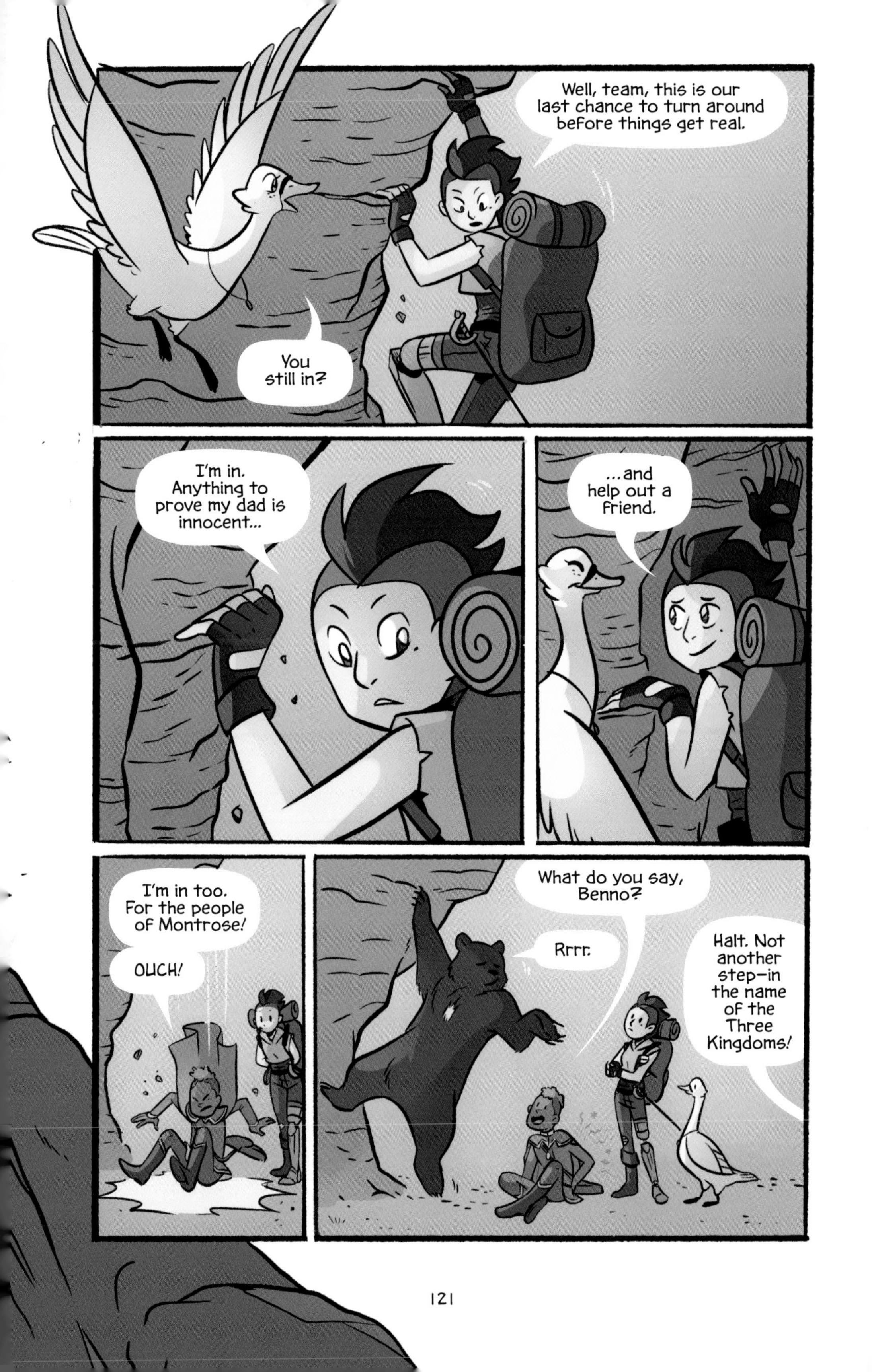
Well, team, this is our last chance to turn around before things get real.
You still in?
I'm in. Anything to prove my dad is innocent...
...and help out a friend.
I'm in too. For the people of Montrose!
OUCH!
What do you say, Benno?
Rrrr.
Halt. Not another step—in the name of the Three Kingdoms!

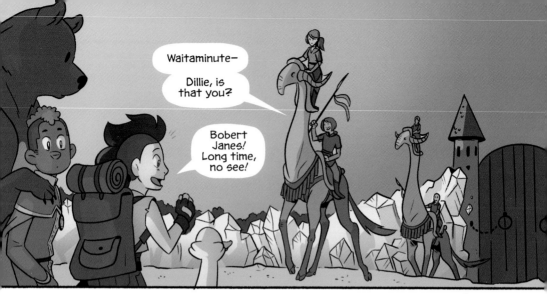

Waitaminute—

Dillie, is that you?

Bobert Janes! Long time, no see!

How long's it been?

Too long, soldier.

Knock off that salute stuff. You're the princess.

FISTBUMP

Barely. You know I'd rather be a knight off on an adventure.

Or are you *already* on an adventure? A little far from home, aren't you?

Who? Me? Nah. We were just, um, you know, on a stroll. Thought we might take a little walk outside the Realm Gate for a few.

Odile, you know it isn't safe for adults, let alone a wee bit like yourself.

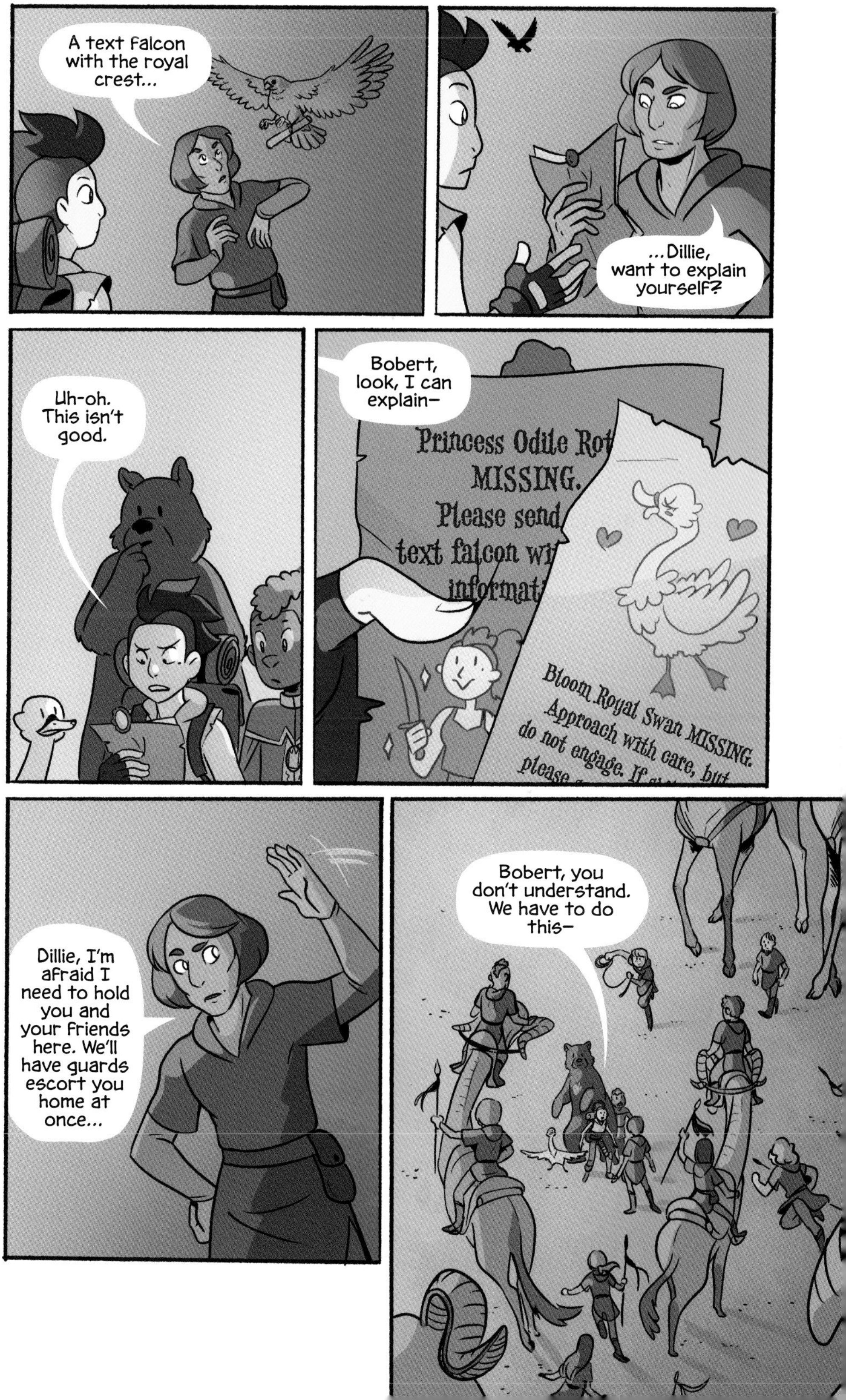
A text falcon with the royal crest...
...Dillie, want to explain yourself?
Uh-oh. This isn't good.
Bobert, look, I can explain–
Princess Odile Rot
MISSING.
Please send
text falcon wi
informati
Bloom Royal Swan MISSING.
Approach with care, but
do not engage.
Dillie, I'm afraid I need to hold you and your friends here. We'll have guards escort you home at once...
Bobert, you don't understand. We have to do this–

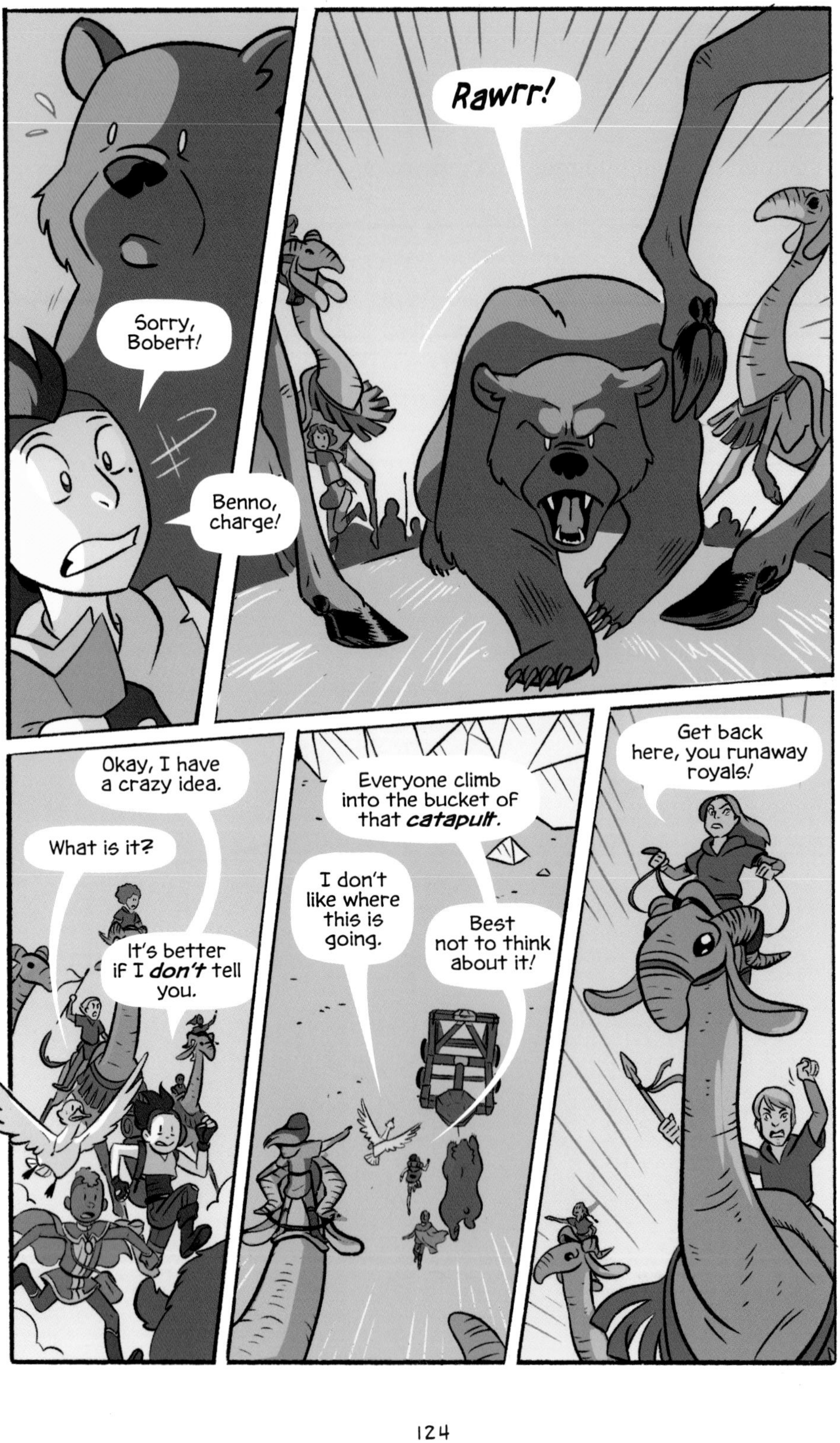
Sorry, Bobert!
Benno, charge!
Rawrr!
Okay, I have a crazy idea.
What is it?
It's better if I *don't* tell you.
Everyone climb into the bucket of that *catapult*.
I don't like where this is going.
Best not to think about it!
Get back here, you runaway royals!

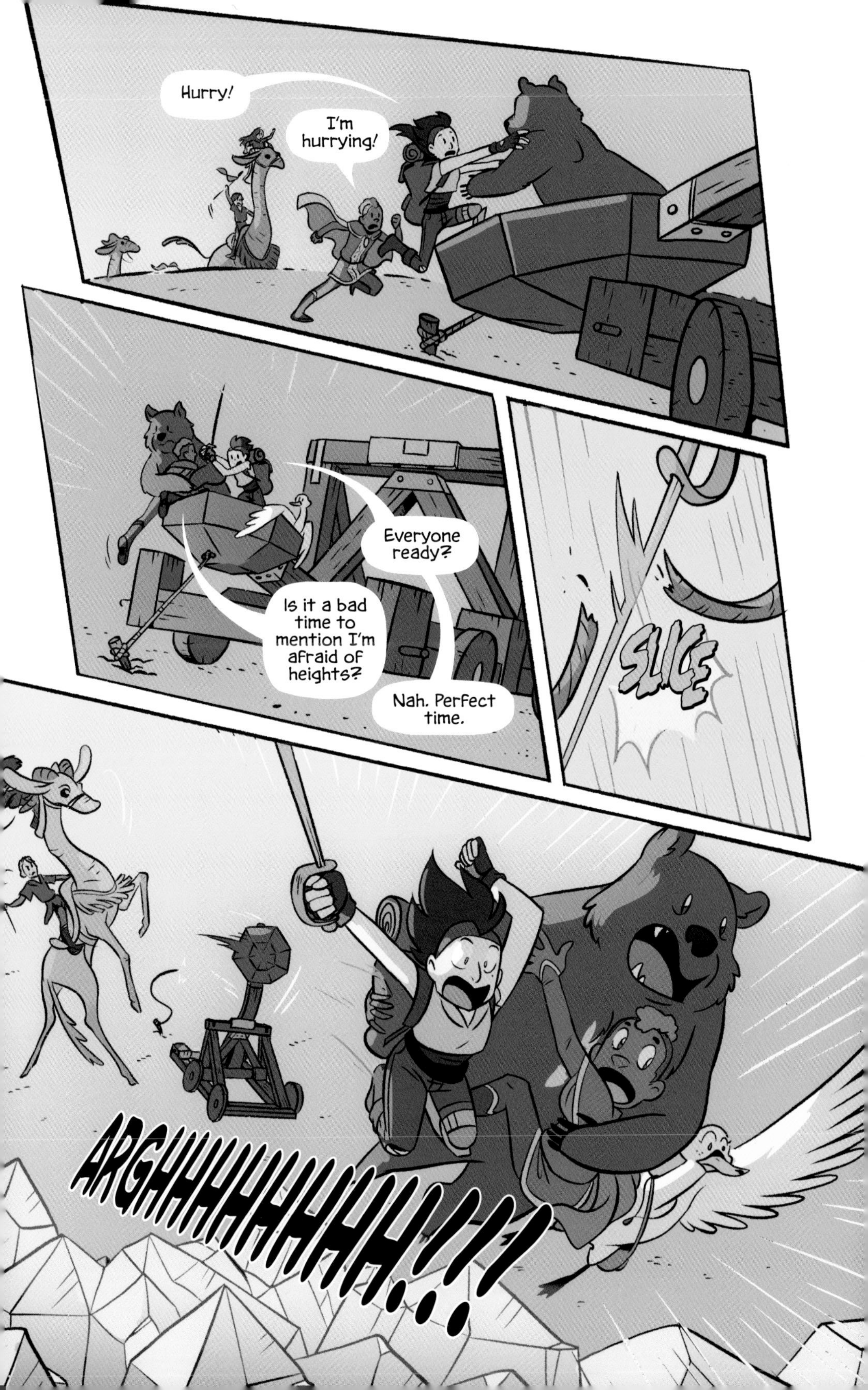

Hurry!
I'm hurrying!
Everyone ready?
Is it a bad time to mention I'm afraid of heights?
Nah. Perfect time.
SLICE
ARGHHHHHHH!!!!

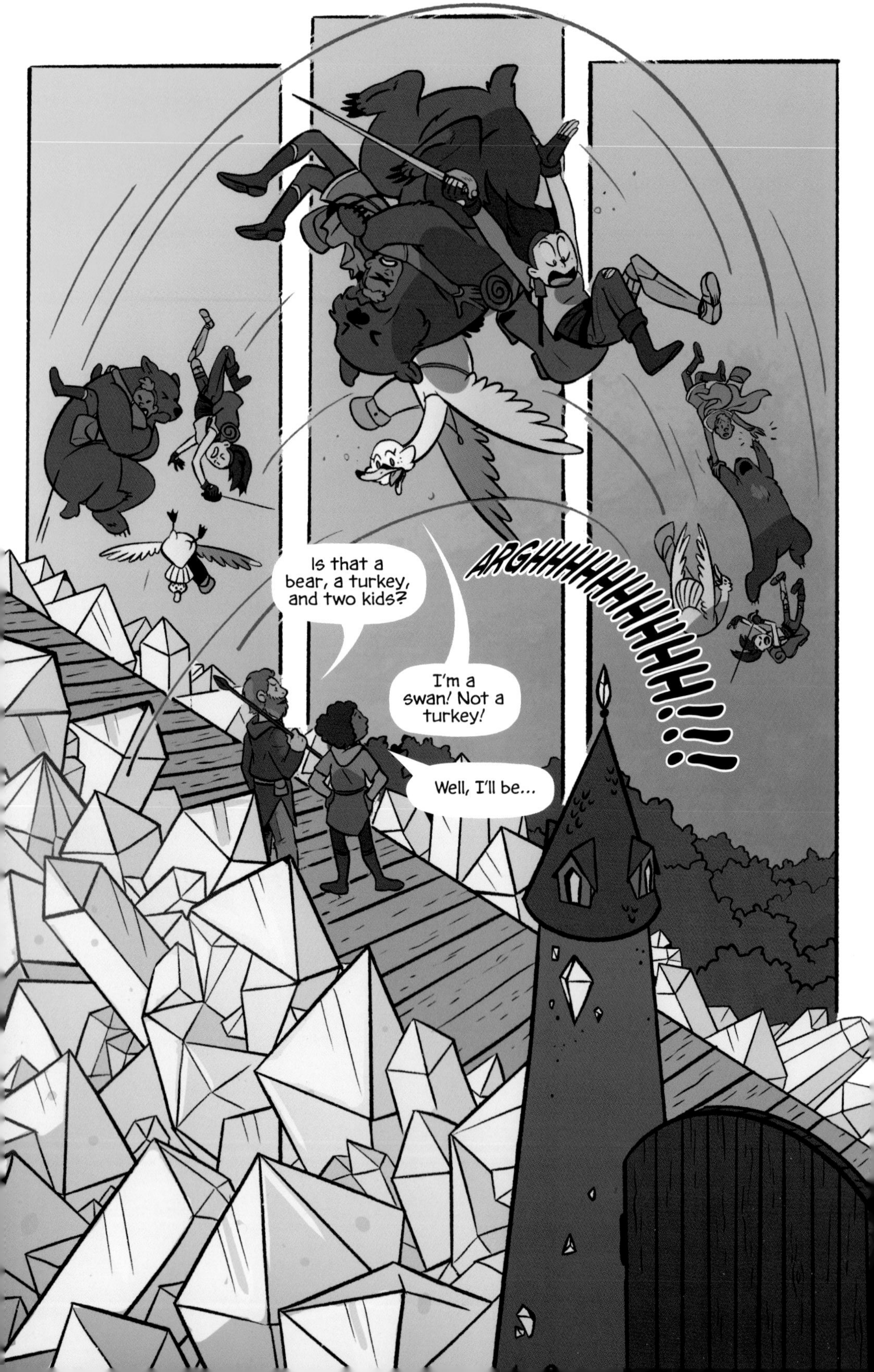

Is that a bear, a turkey, and two kids?
ARGHHHHHHHHHHHH!!!!
I'm a swan! Not a turkey!
Well, I'll be...

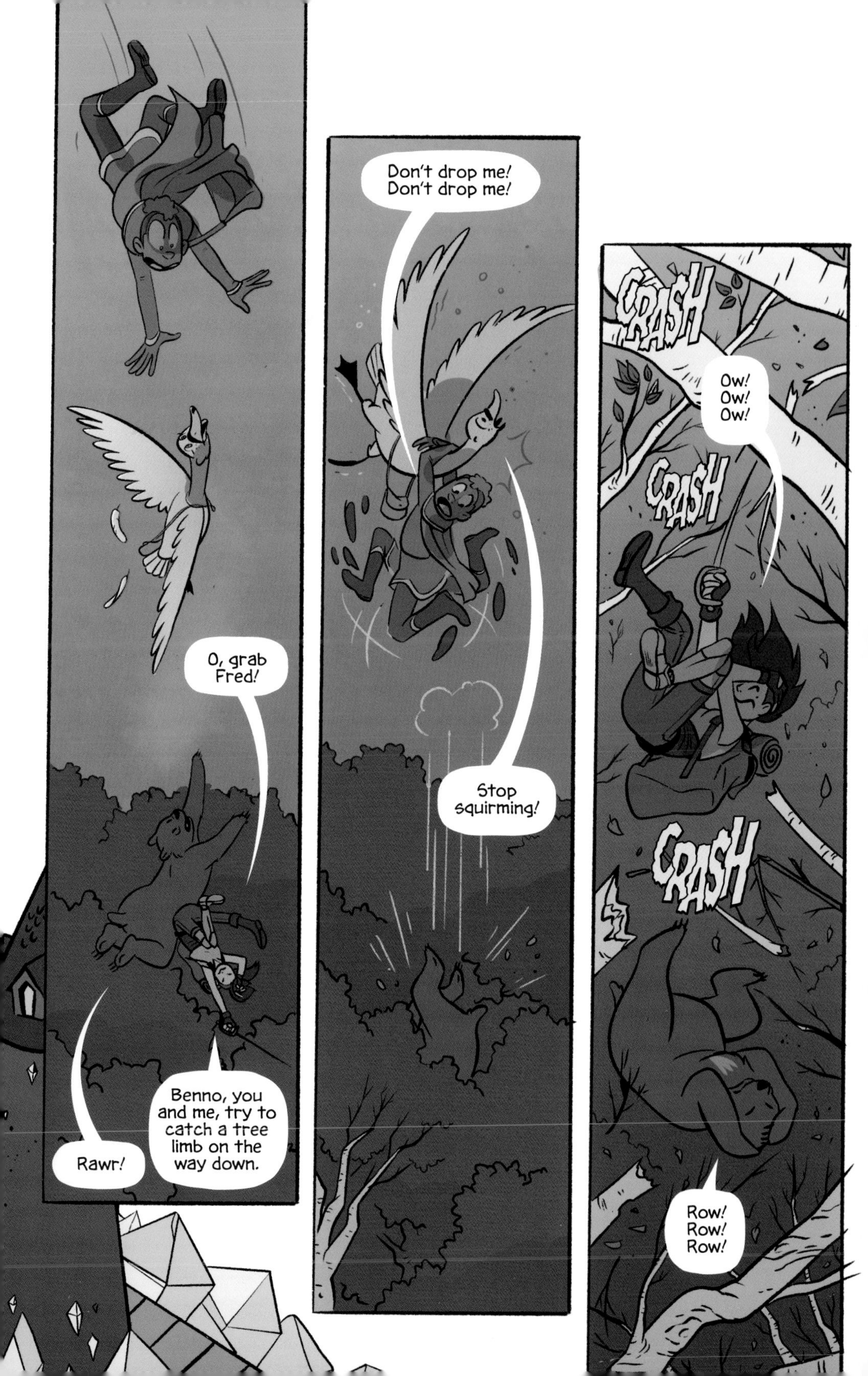
O, grab Fred!
Rawr!
Benno, you and me, try to catch a tree limb on the way down.
Don't drop me! Don't drop me!
Stop squirming!
CRASH
Ow! Ow! Ow!
CRASH
CRASH
Row! Row! Row!

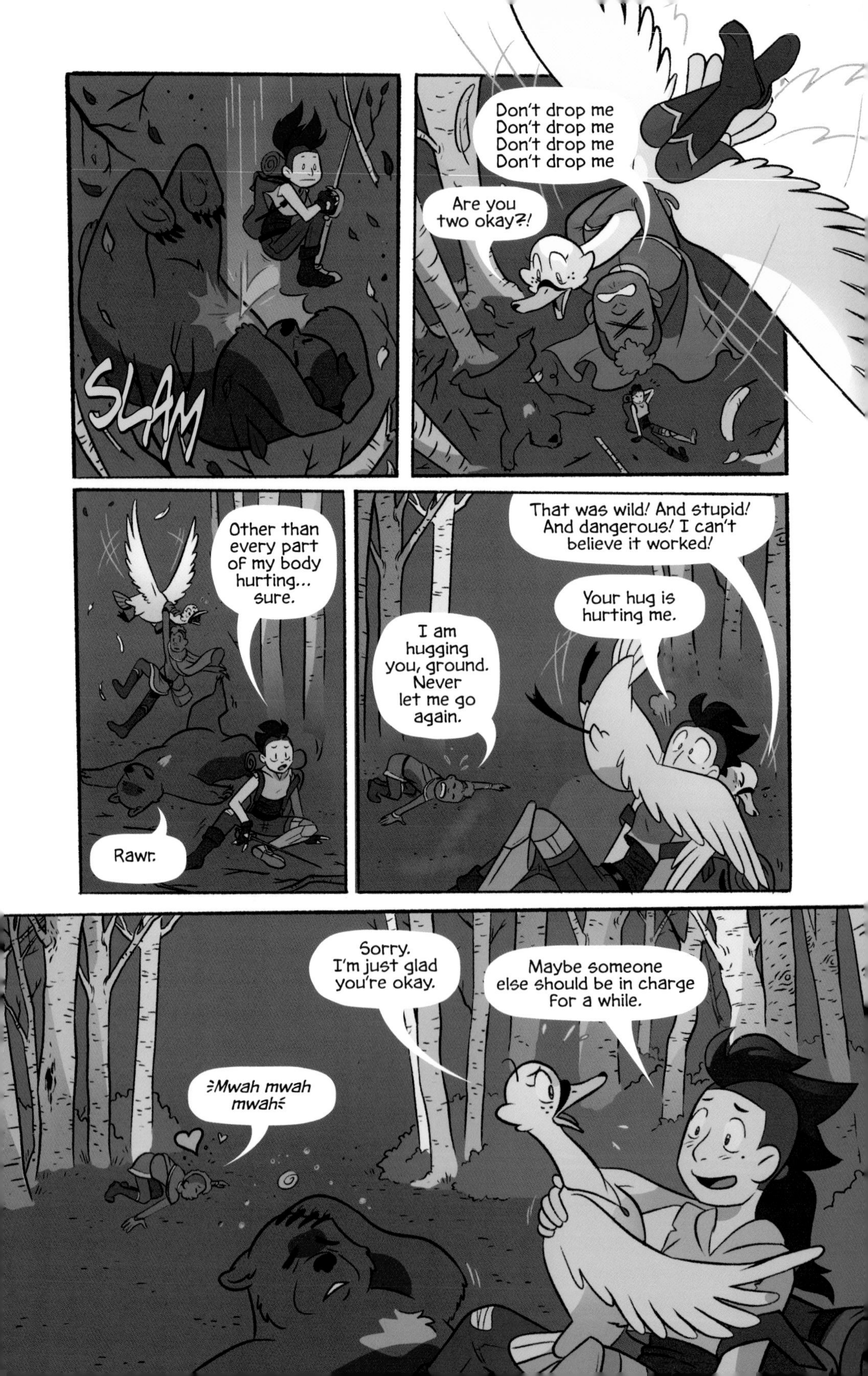
SLAM
Don't drop me Don't drop me Don't drop me Don't drop me
Are you two okay?!
Other than every part of my body hurting... sure.
Rawr.
That was wild! And stupid! And dangerous! I can't believe it worked!
Your hug is hurting me.
I am hugging you, ground. Never let me go again.
Sorry. I'm just glad you're okay.
Maybe someone else should be in charge for a while.
Mwah mwah mwah

I'll take the lead, then.

But we should probably hurry. Those guards won't be too far behind.

Could we hurry a little more slowly? I think I broke several ribs in that fall.

Benno, can you give her a paw?

Hey! No, I'm fine. I can walk.

You did put her in charge.

Exactly. And you are riding Benno until we make camp tonight.

You're our strongest fighter, and we need you rested in case we're attacked by anything.

You make a fair point. Plus, Benno does make an excellent steed. Just like the *nightmare donkey* I had when I was a little girl.

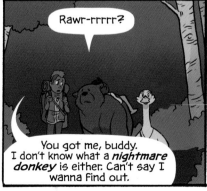

Rawr-rrrrr?

You got me, buddy. I don't know what a *nightmare donkey* is either. Can't say I wanna find out.

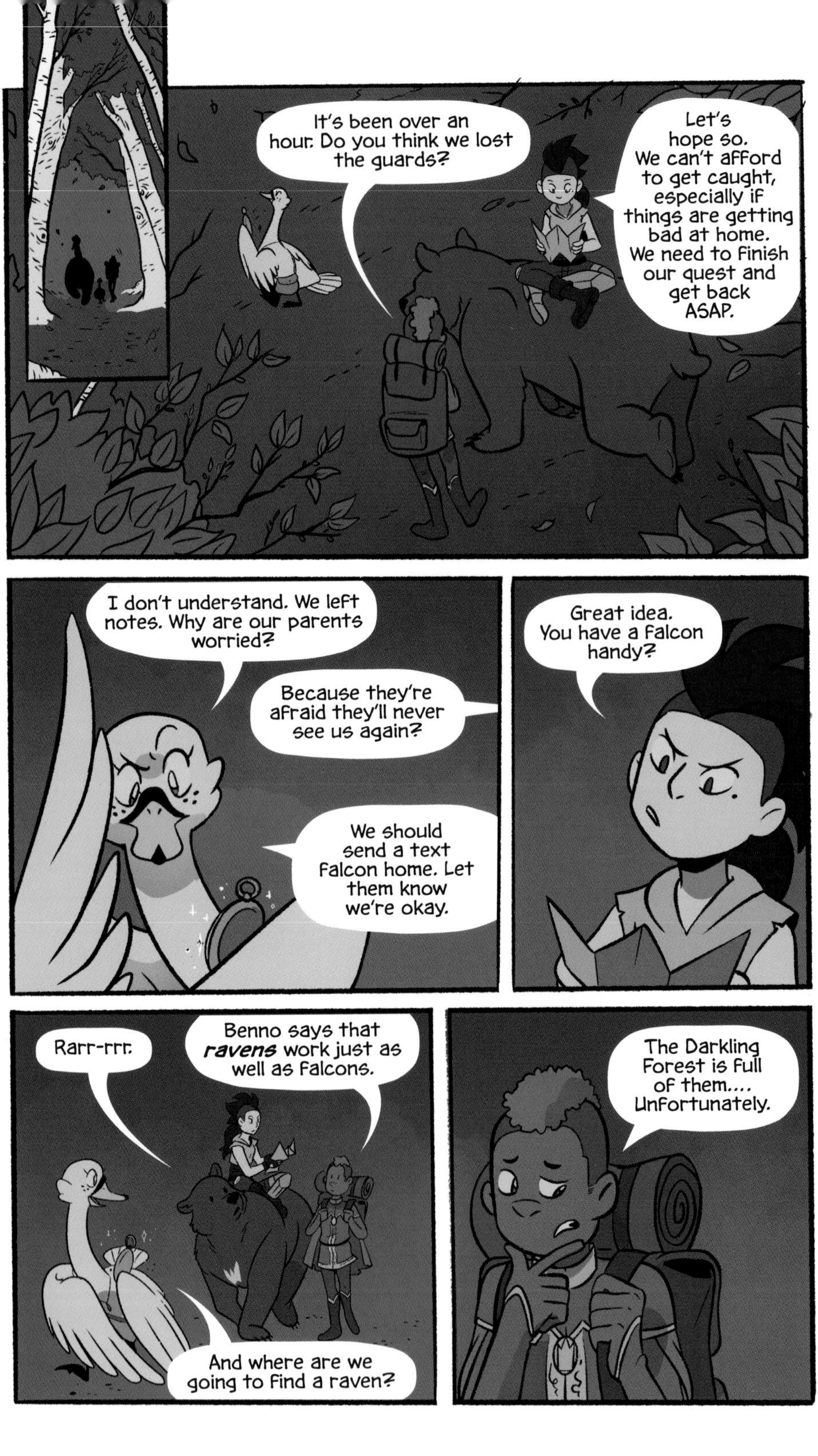
It's been over an hour. Do you think we lost the guards?
Let's hope so. We can't afford to get caught, especially if things are getting bad at home. We need to finish our quest and get back ASAP.
I don't understand. We left notes. Why are our parents worried?
Because they're afraid they'll never see us again?
We should send a text falcon home. Let them know we're okay.
Great idea. You have a falcon handy?
Rarr-rrr.
Benno says that *ravens* work just as well as falcons.
And where are we going to find a raven?
The Darkling Forest is full of them.... Unfortunately.

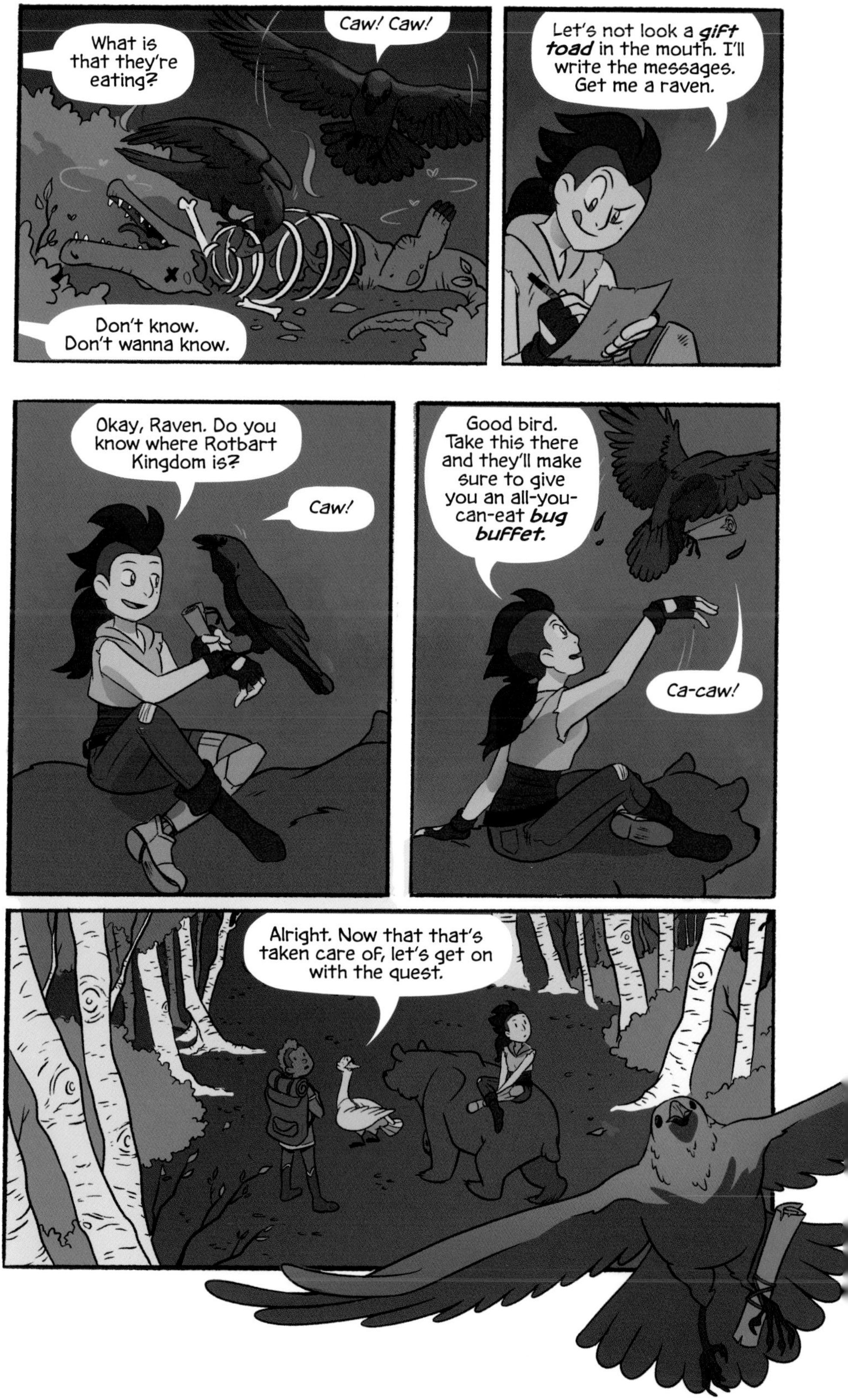

What is that they're eating?
Caw! Caw!
Don't know. Don't wanna know.
Let's not look a **gift toad** in the mouth. I'll write the messages. Get me a raven.
Okay, Raven. Do you know where Rotbart Kingdom is?
Caw!
Good bird. Take this there and they'll make sure to give you an all-you-can-eat **bug buffet.**
Ca-caw!
Alright. Now that that's taken care of, let's get on with the quest.

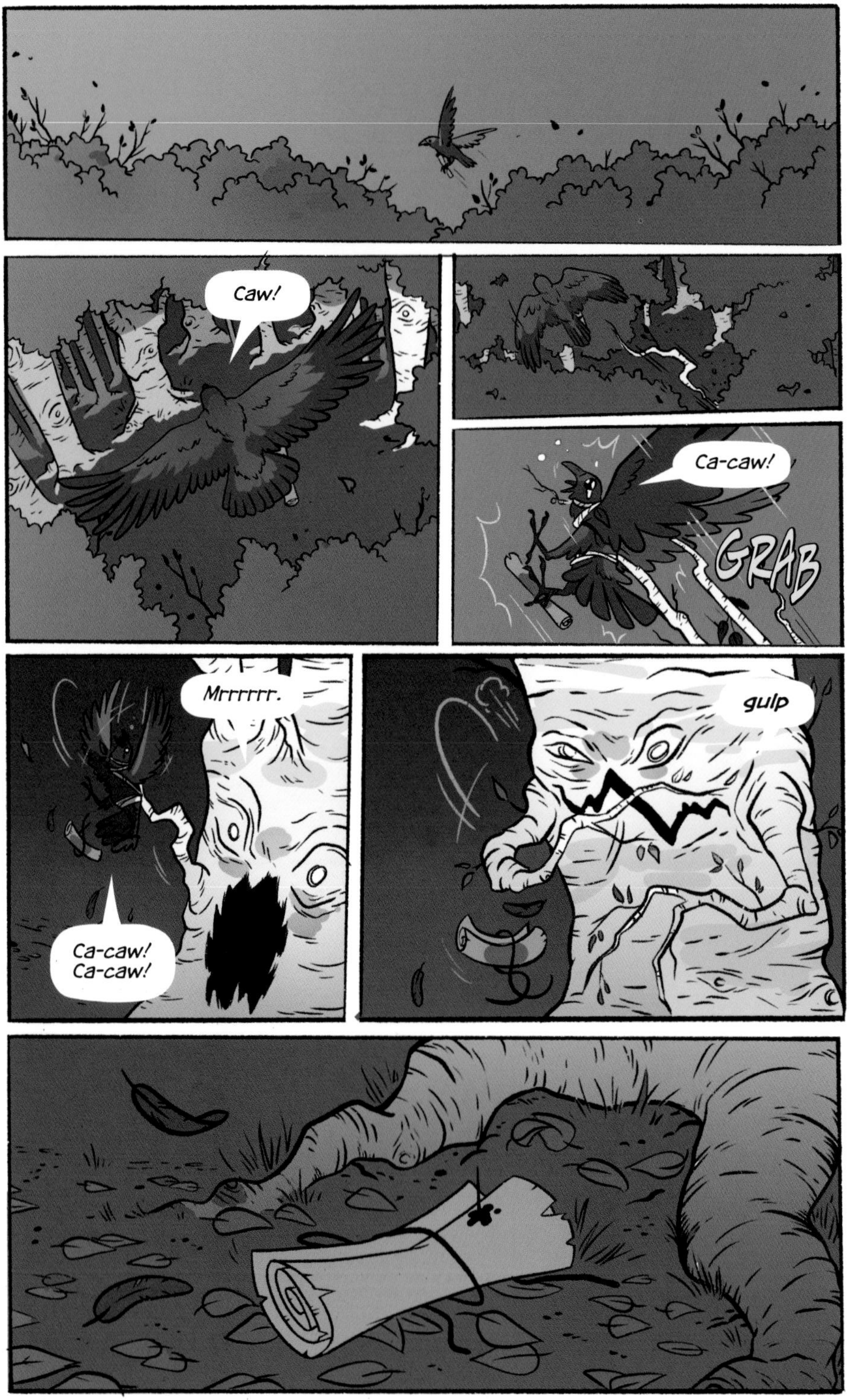
Caw!
Ca-caw!
GRAB
Mrrrrrr.
Ca-caw! Ca-caw!
gulp

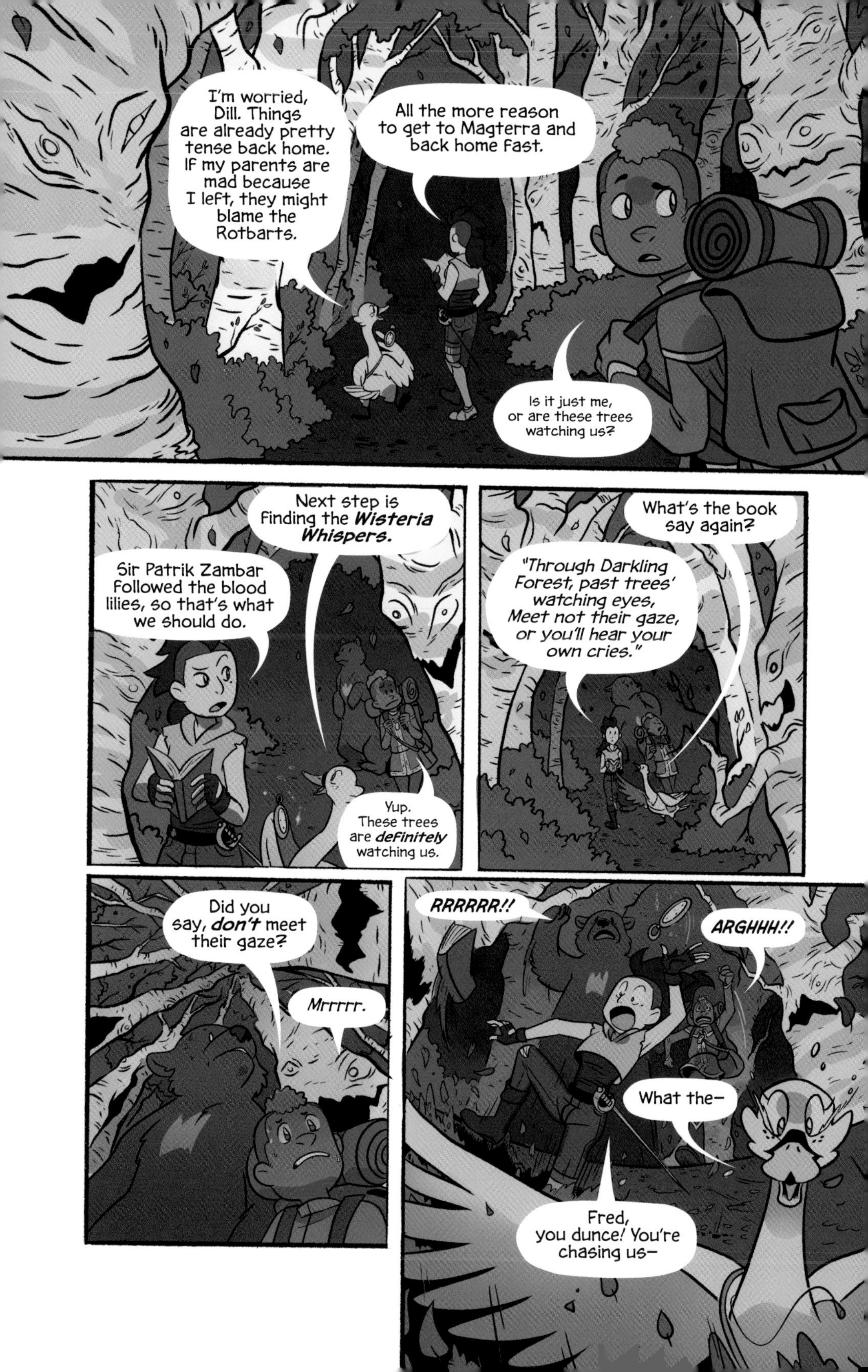

I'm worried, Dill. Things are already pretty tense back home. If my parents are mad because I left, they might blame the Rotbarts.
All the more reason to get to Magterra and back home fast.
Is it just me, or are these trees watching us?
Next step is finding the *Wisteria Whispers.*
Sir Patrik Zambar followed the blood lilies, so that's what we should do.
Yup. These trees are *definitely* watching us.
What's the book say again?
"Through Darkling Forest, past trees' watching eyes, Meet not their gaze, or you'll hear your own cries."
Did you say, *don't* meet their gaze?
Mrrrrr.
RRRRRR!!
ARGHHH!!
What the—
Fred, you dunce! You're chasing us—

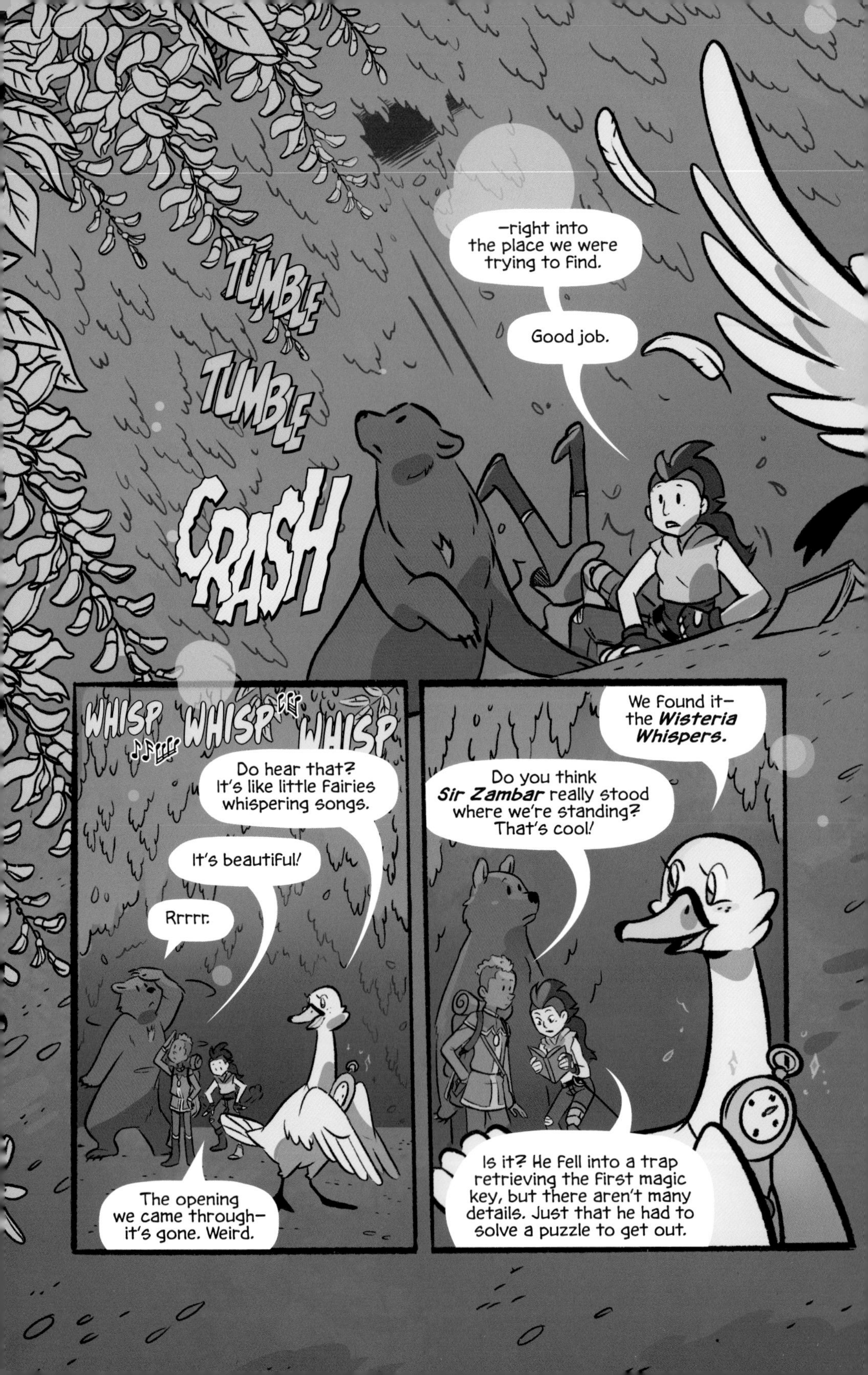

TUMBLE
TUMBLE
CRASH
–right into the place we were trying to find.
Good job.
WHISP WHISP WHISP
Do hear that? It's like little fairies whispering songs.
It's beautiful!
Rrrrr.
The opening we came through–it's gone. Weird.
We found it–the ***Wisteria Whispers.***
Do you think ***Sir Zambar*** really stood where we're standing? That's cool!
Is it? He fell into a trap retrieving the first magic key, but there aren't many details. Just that he had to solve a puzzle to get out.

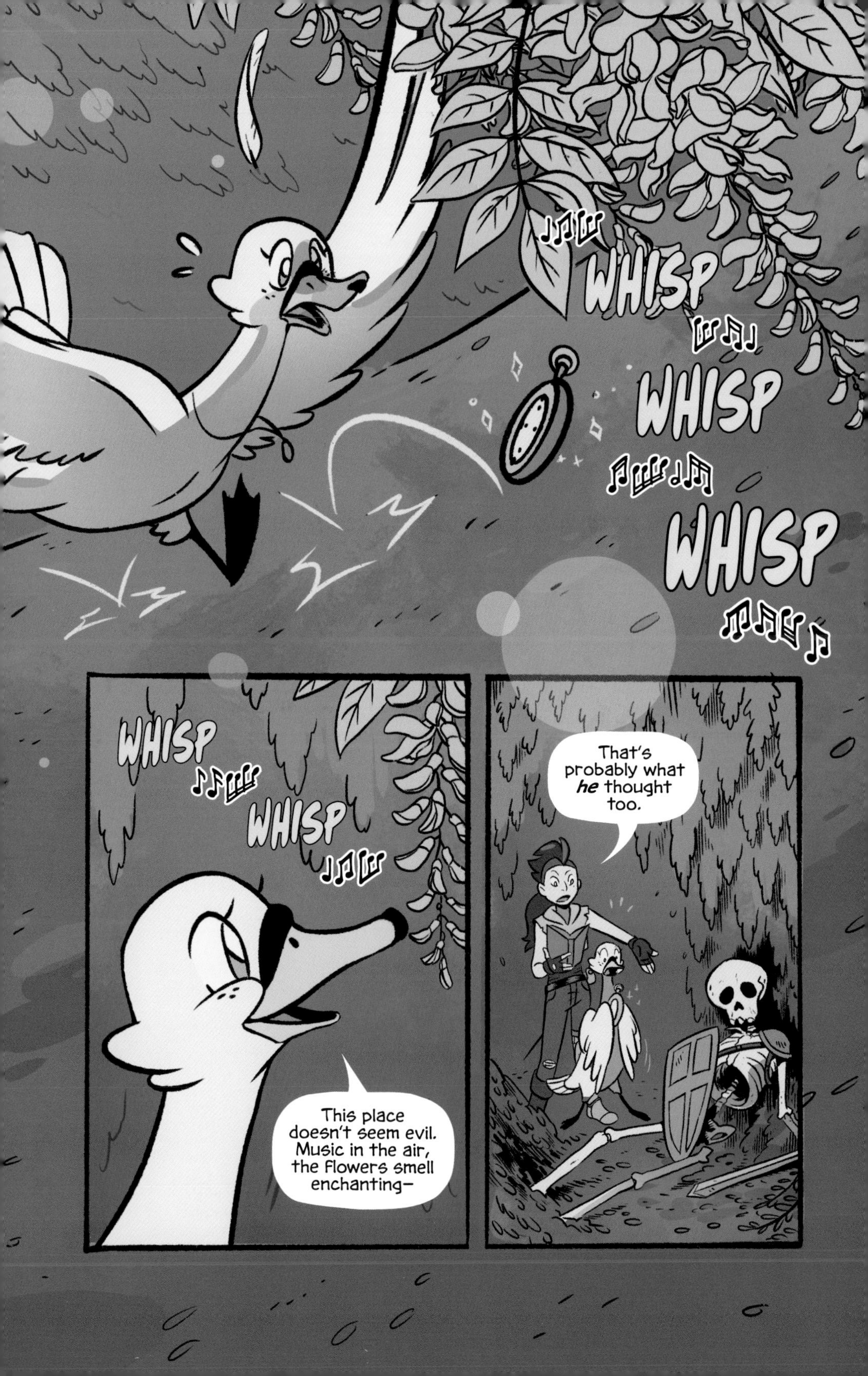
WHISP
WHISP
WHISP
WHISP
WHISP
This place doesn't seem evil. Music in the air, the flowers smell enchanting–
That's probably what *he* thought too.

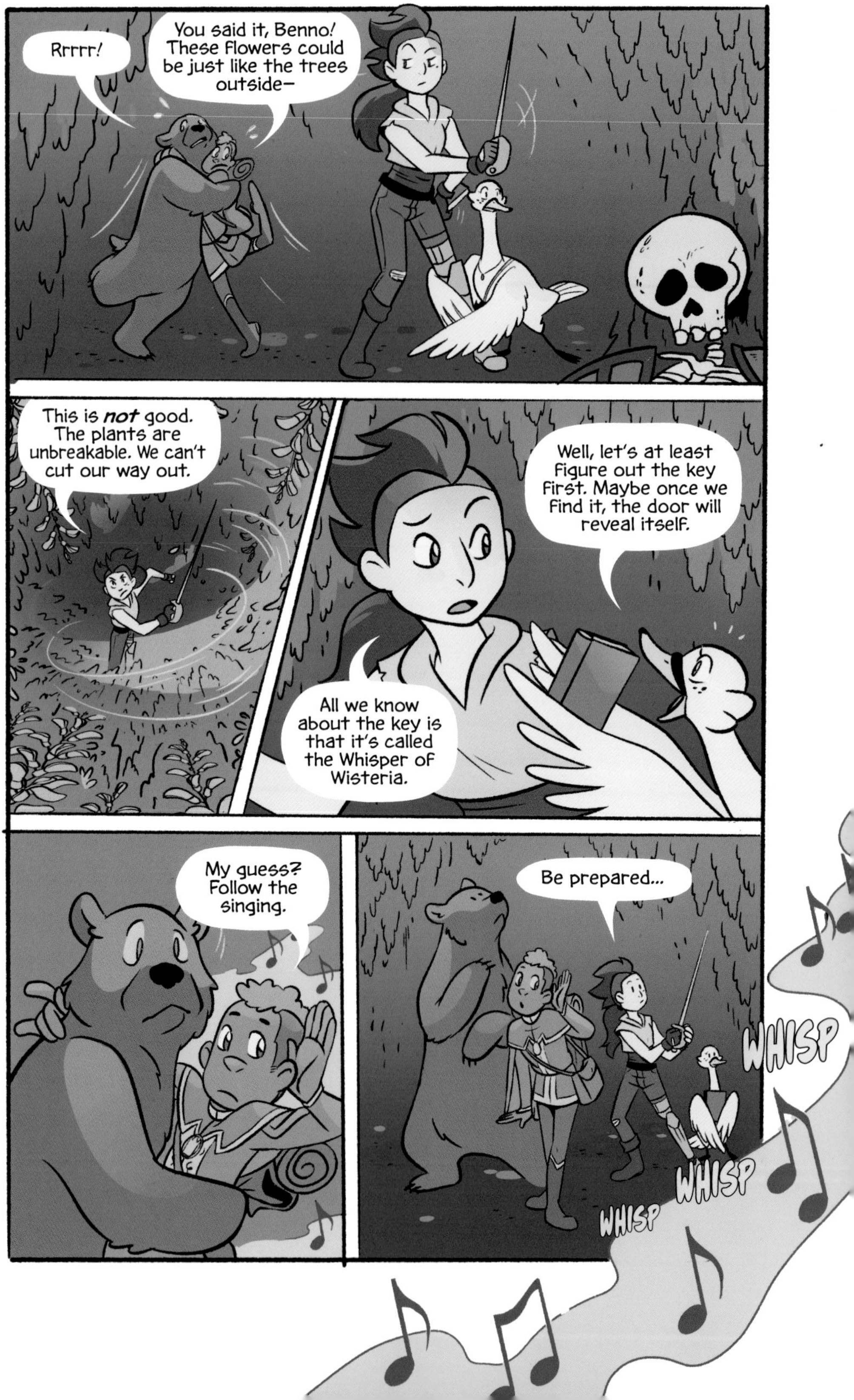
Rrrrr!
You said it, Benno! These flowers could be just like the trees outside—
This is *not* good. The plants are unbreakable. We can't cut our way out.
Well, let's at least figure out the key first. Maybe once we find it, the door will reveal itself.
All we know about the key is that it's called the Whisper of Wisteria.
My guess? Follow the singing.
Be prepared...
WHISP
WHISP
WHISP

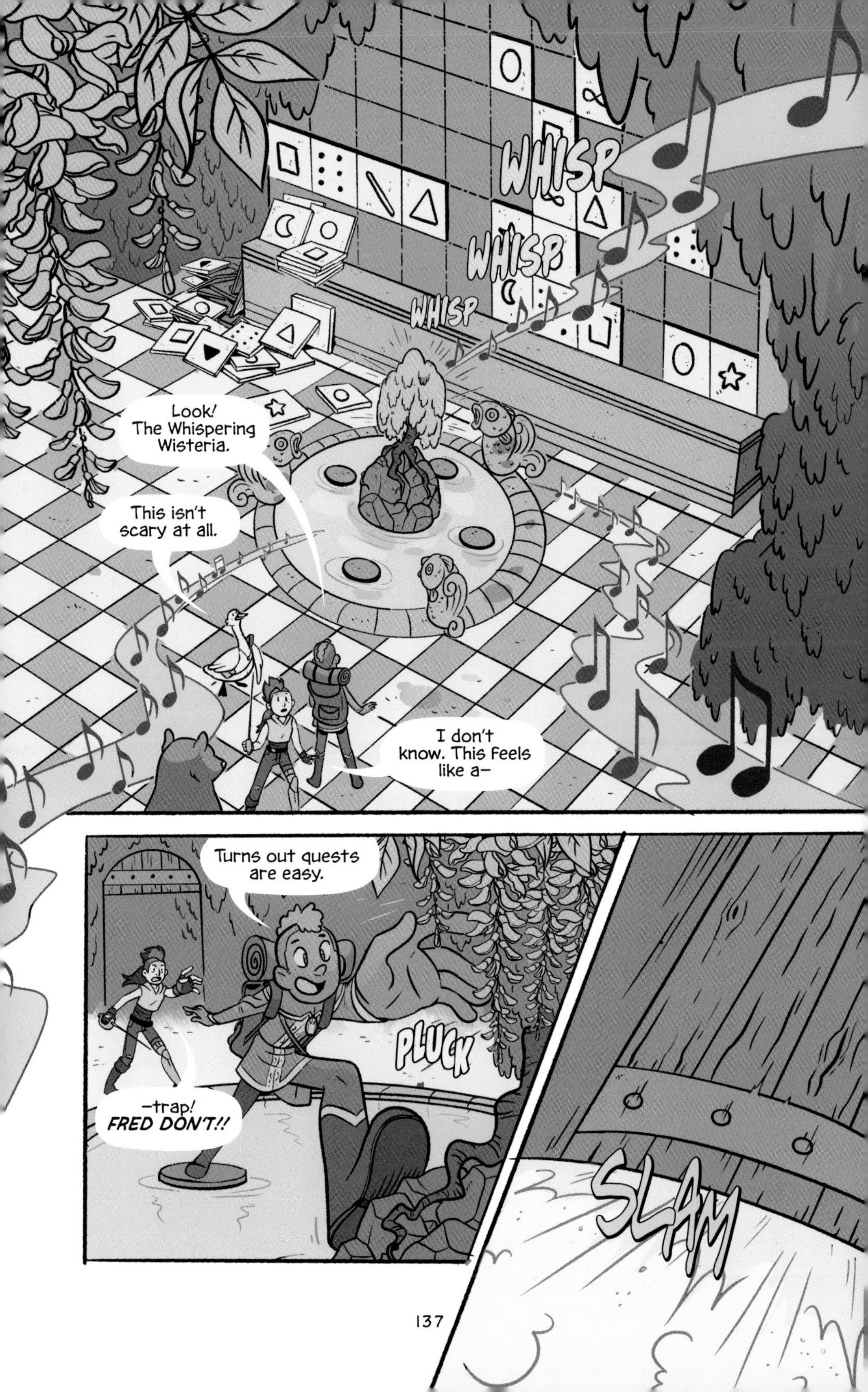
WHISP
WHISP
WHISP
Look! The Whispering Wisteria.
This isn't scary at all.
I don't know. This feels like a–
Turns out quests are easy.
PLUCK
–trap! FRED DON'T!!
SLAM

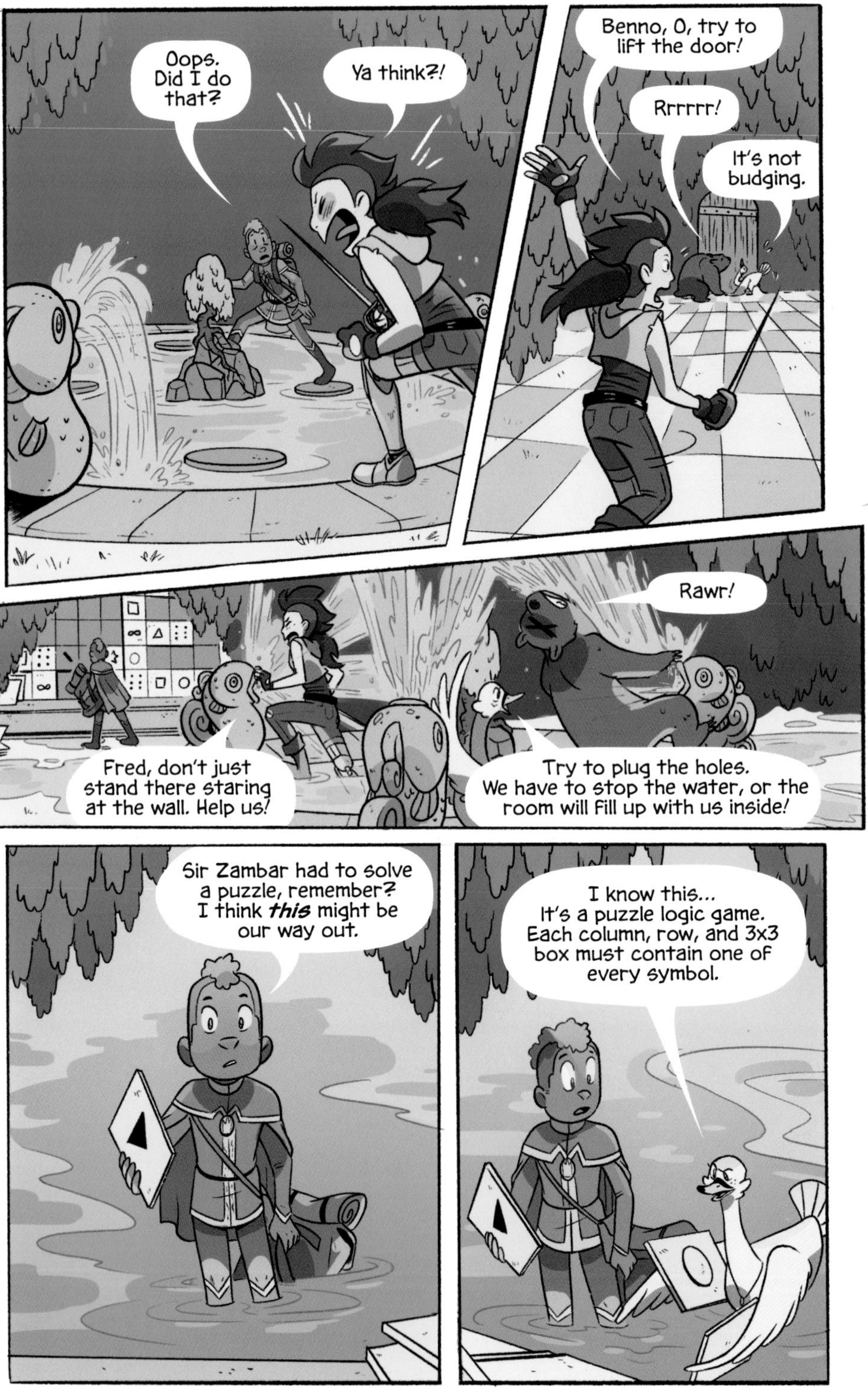
Oops. Did I do that?
Ya think?!
Benno, O, try to lift the door!
Rrrrrr!
It's not budging.
Rawr!
Fred, don't just stand there staring at the wall. Help us!
Try to plug the holes. We have to stop the water, or the room will fill up with us inside!
Sir Zambar had to solve a puzzle, remember? I think *this* might be our way out.
I know this... It's a puzzle logic game. Each column, row, and 3x3 box must contain one of every symbol.

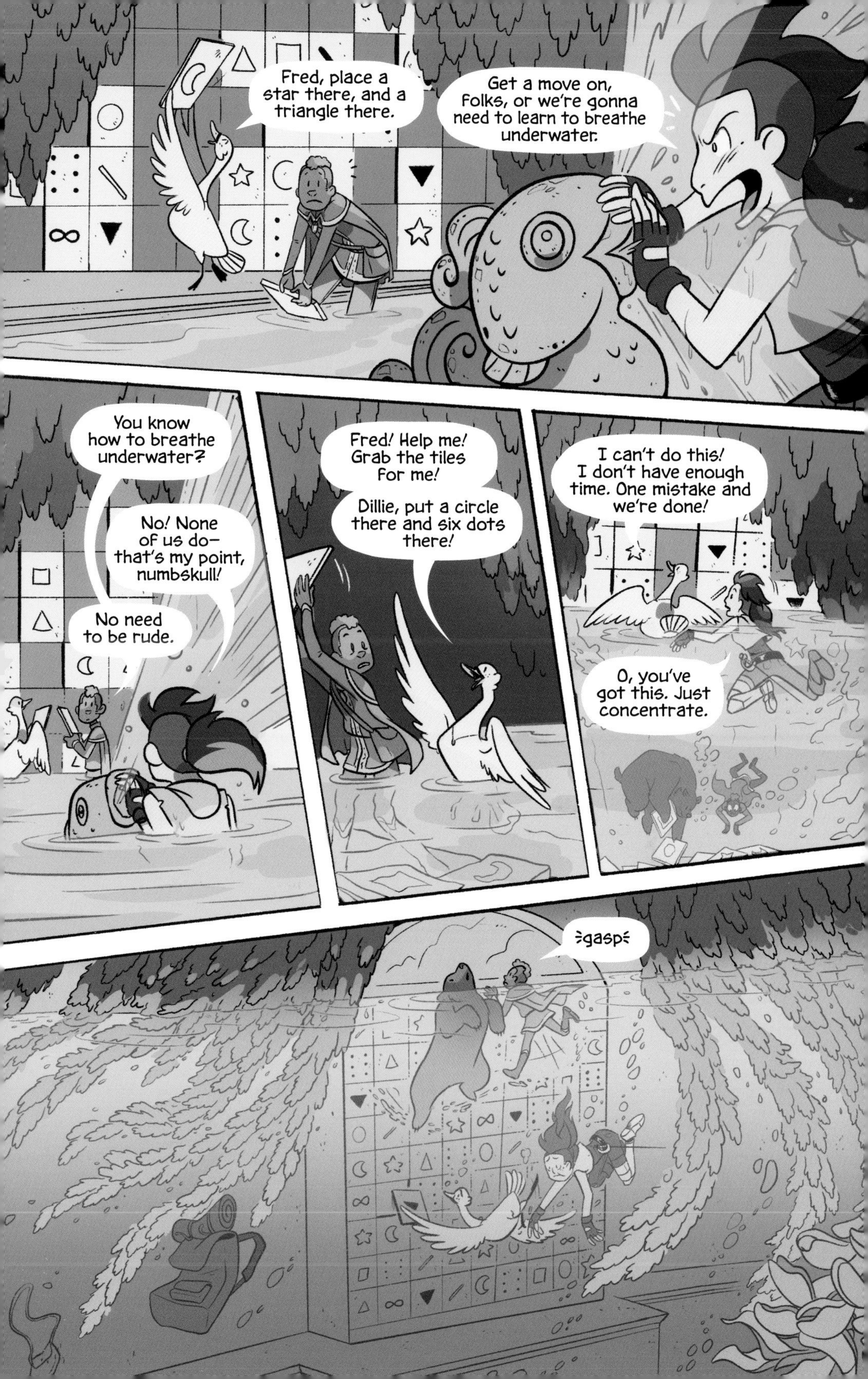
Fred, place a star there, and a triangle there.
Get a move on, folks, or we're gonna need to learn to breathe underwater.
You know how to breathe underwater?
No! None of us do— that's my point, numbskull!
No need to be rude.
Fred! Help me! Grab the tiles for me!
Dillie, put a circle there and six dots there!
I can't do this! I don't have enough time. One mistake and we're done!
O, you've got this. Just concentrate.
gasp

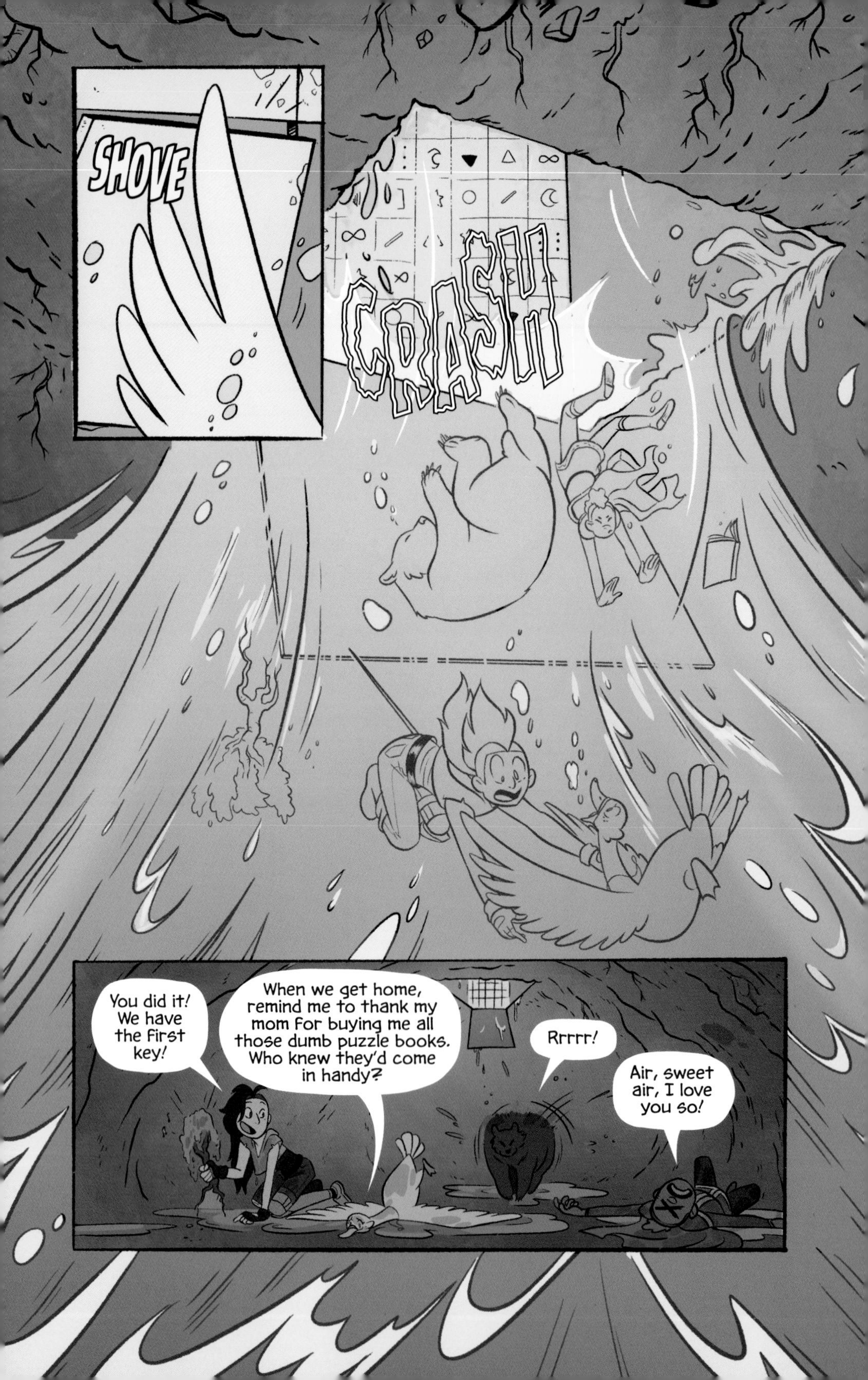
SHOVE
CRASH
You did it! We have the first key!
When we get home, remind me to thank my mom for buying me all those dumb puzzle books. Who knew they'd come in handy?
Rrrrr!
Air, sweet air, I love you so!

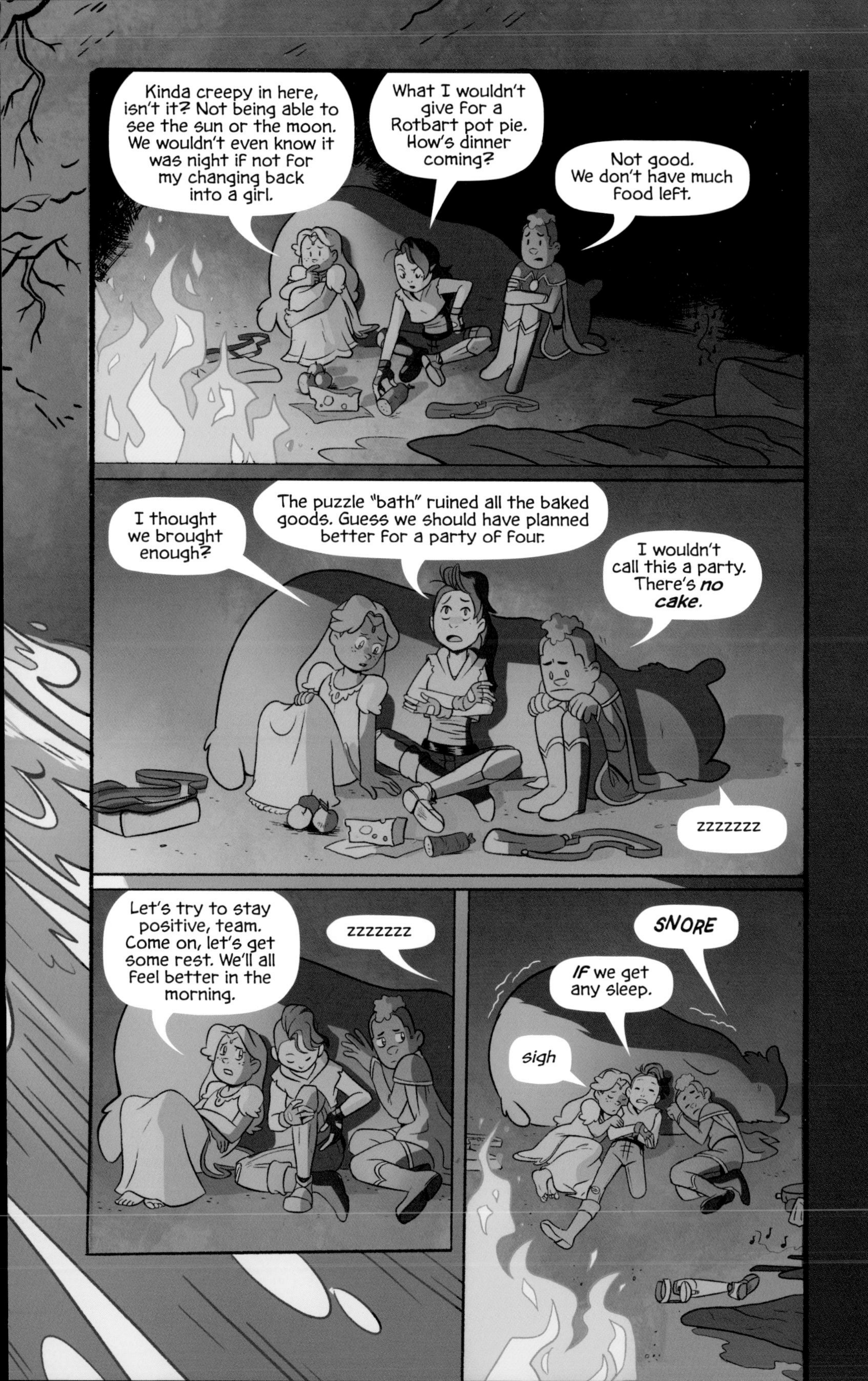

Kinda creepy in here, isn't it? Not being able to see the sun or the moon. We wouldn't even know it was night if not for my changing back into a girl.
What I wouldn't give for a Rotbart pot pie. How's dinner coming?
Not good. We don't have much food left.
I thought we brought enough?
The puzzle "bath" ruined all the baked goods. Guess we should have planned better for a party of four.
I wouldn't call this a party. There's ***no cake***.
zzzzzzz
Let's try to stay positive, team. Come on, let's get some rest. We'll all feel better in the morning.
zzzzzzz
SNORE
IF we get any sleep.
sigh

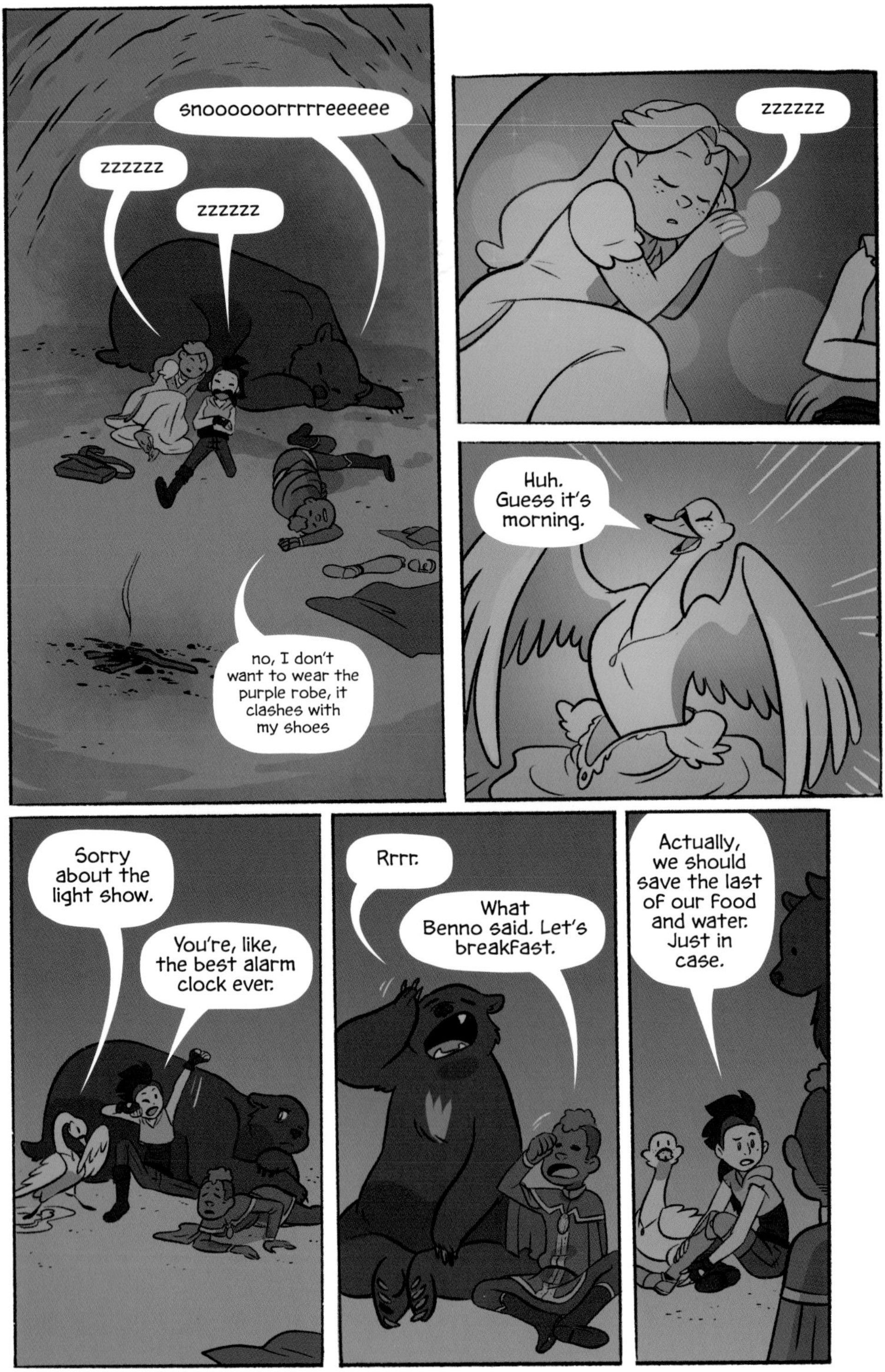
snoooooorrrrreeeeee
zzzzzz
zzzzzz
no, I don't want to wear the purple robe, it clashes with my shoes
zzzzzz
Huh. Guess it's morning.
Sorry about the light show.
You're, like, the best alarm clock ever.
Rrrr.
What Benno said. Let's breakfast.
Actually, we should save the last of our food and water. Just in case.

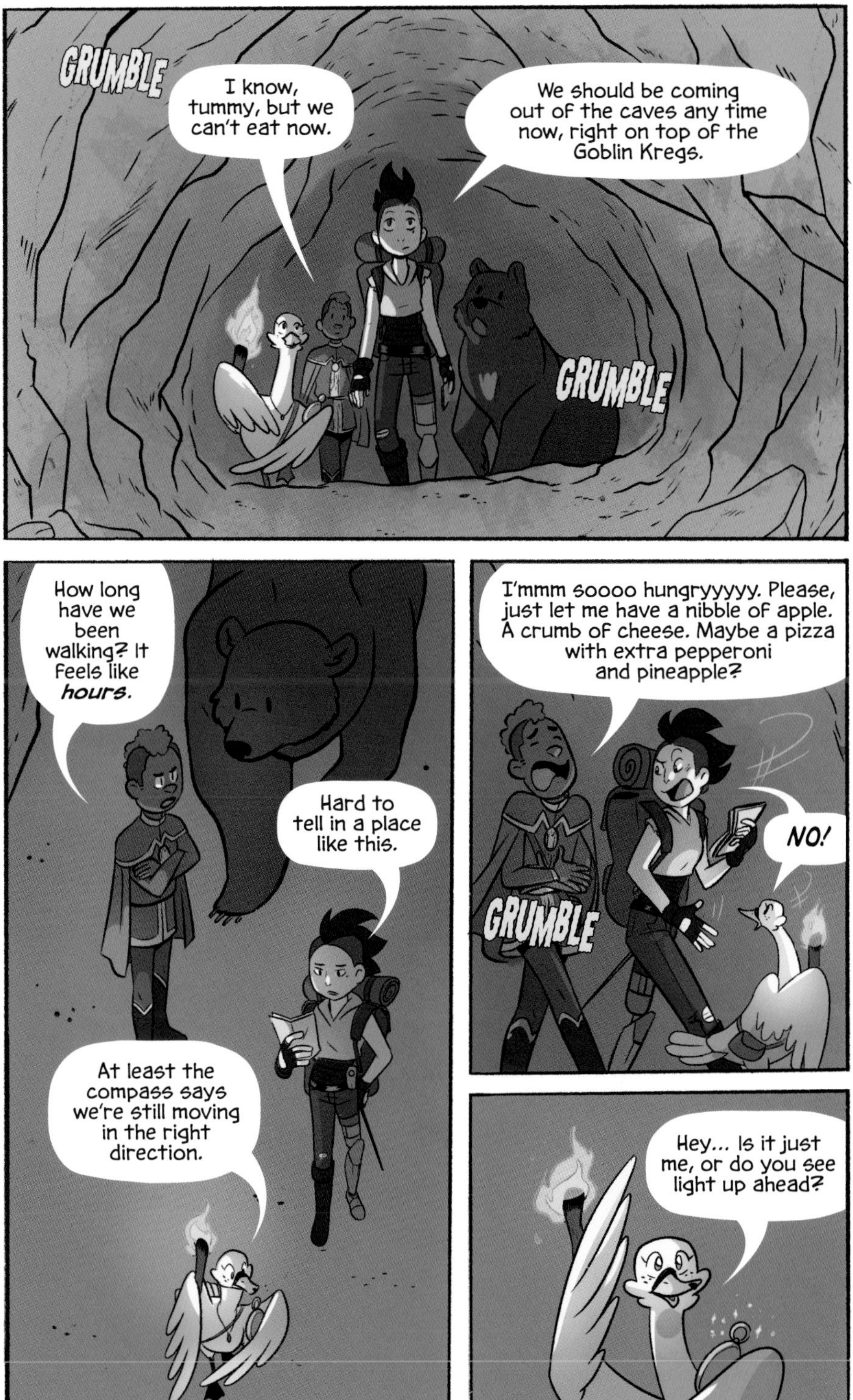
GRUMBLE
I know, tummy, but we can't eat now.
We should be coming out of the caves any time now, right on top of the Goblin Kregs.
GRUMBLE
How long have we been walking? It feels like *hours*.
Hard to tell in a place like this.
At least the compass says we're still moving in the right direction.
I'mmm soooo hungryyyyy. Please, just let me have a nibble of apple. A crumb of cheese. Maybe a pizza with extra pepperoni and pineapple?
NO!
GRUMBLE
Hey... Is it just me, or do you see light up ahead?

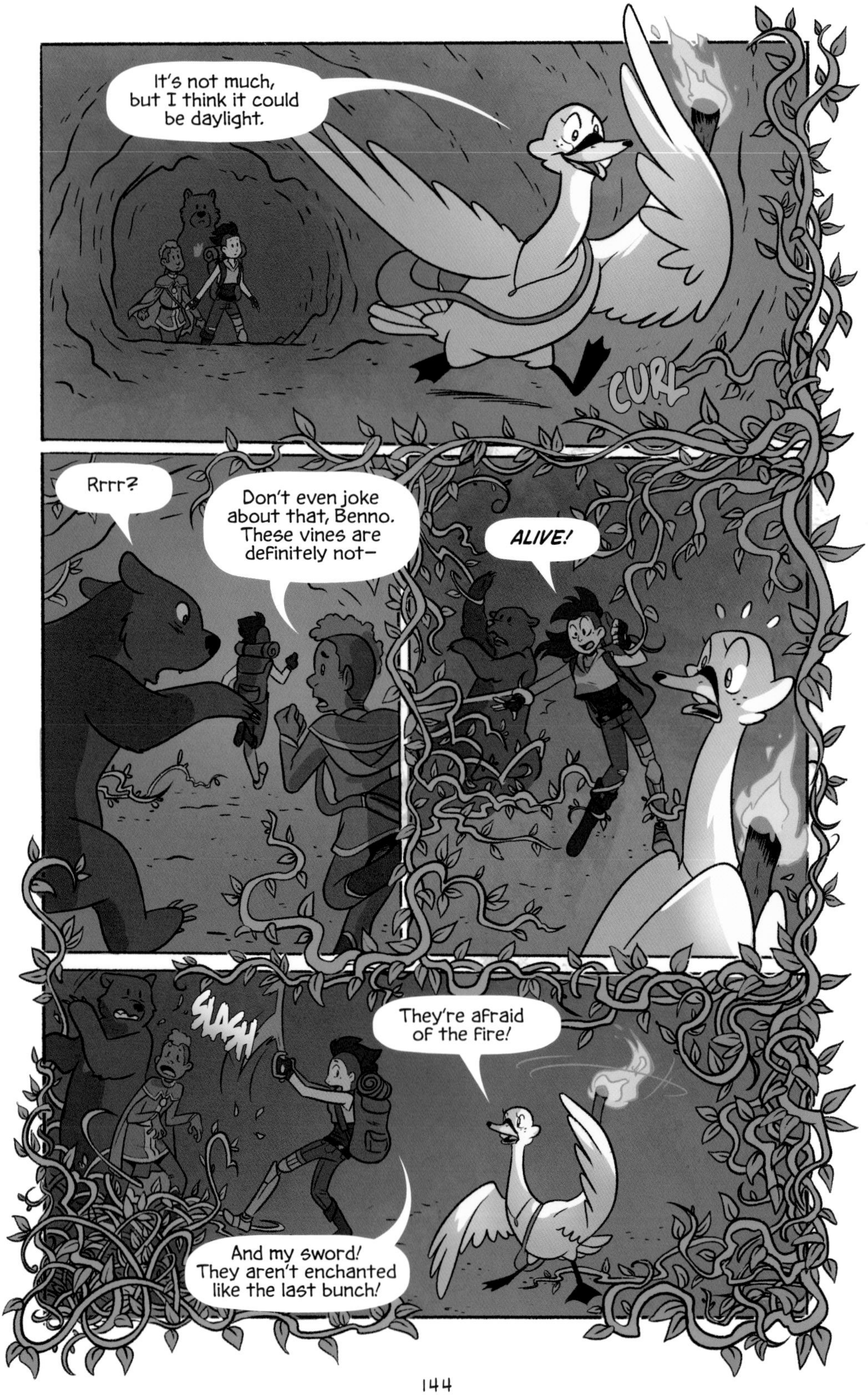
It's not much, but I think it could be daylight.
CURL
Rrrr?
Don't even joke about that, Benno. These vines are definitely not—
ALIVE!
SLASH
They're afraid of the fire!
And my sword! They aren't enchanted like the last bunch!

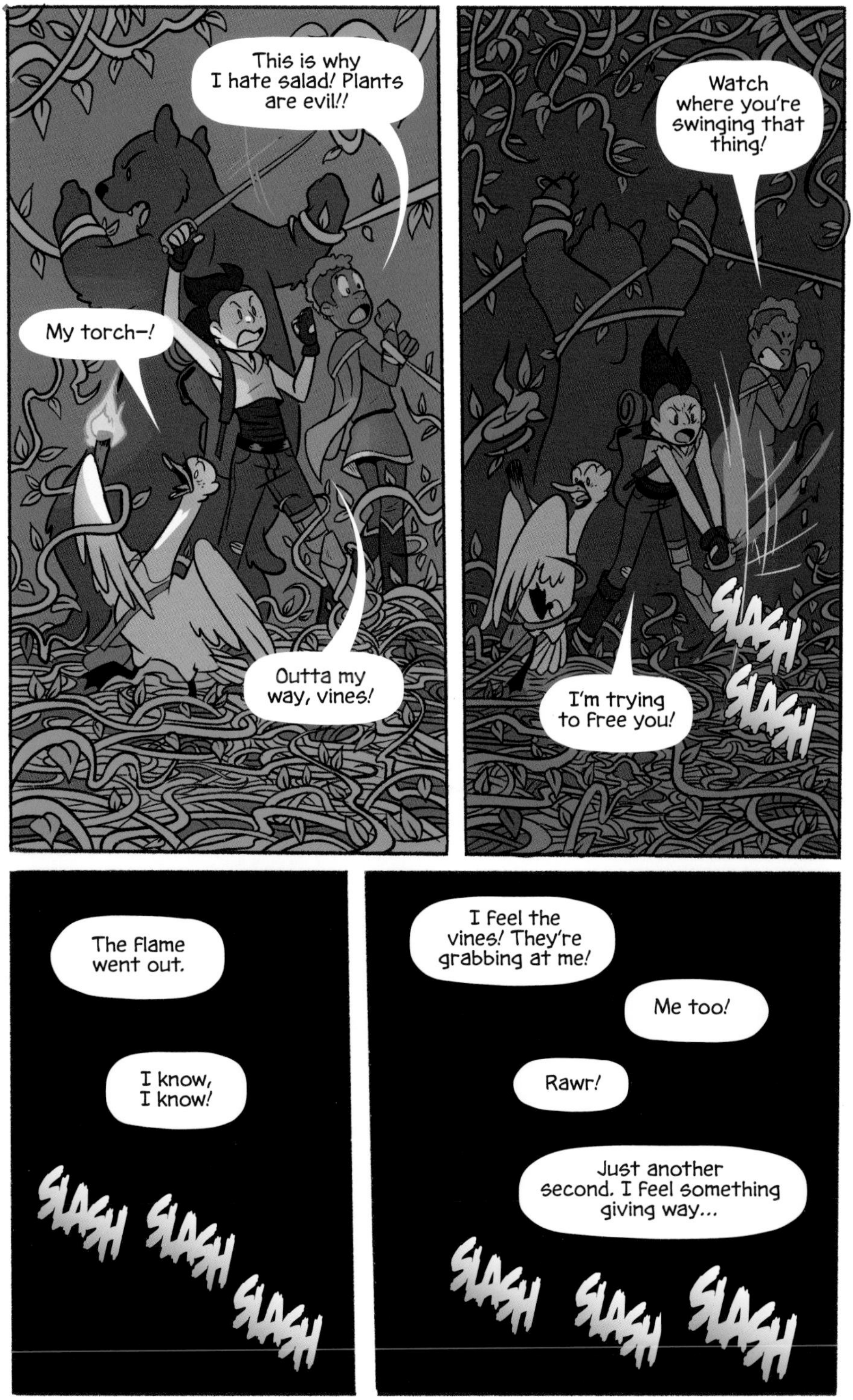
This is why I hate salad! Plants are evil!!
My torch—!
Outta my way, vines!
Watch where you're swinging that thing!
I'm trying to free you!
SLASH
SLASH
The flame went out.
I know, I know!
SLASH
SLASH
SLASH
I feel the vines! They're grabbing at me!
Me too!
Rawr!
Just another second. I feel something giving way...
SLASH
SLASH
SLASH

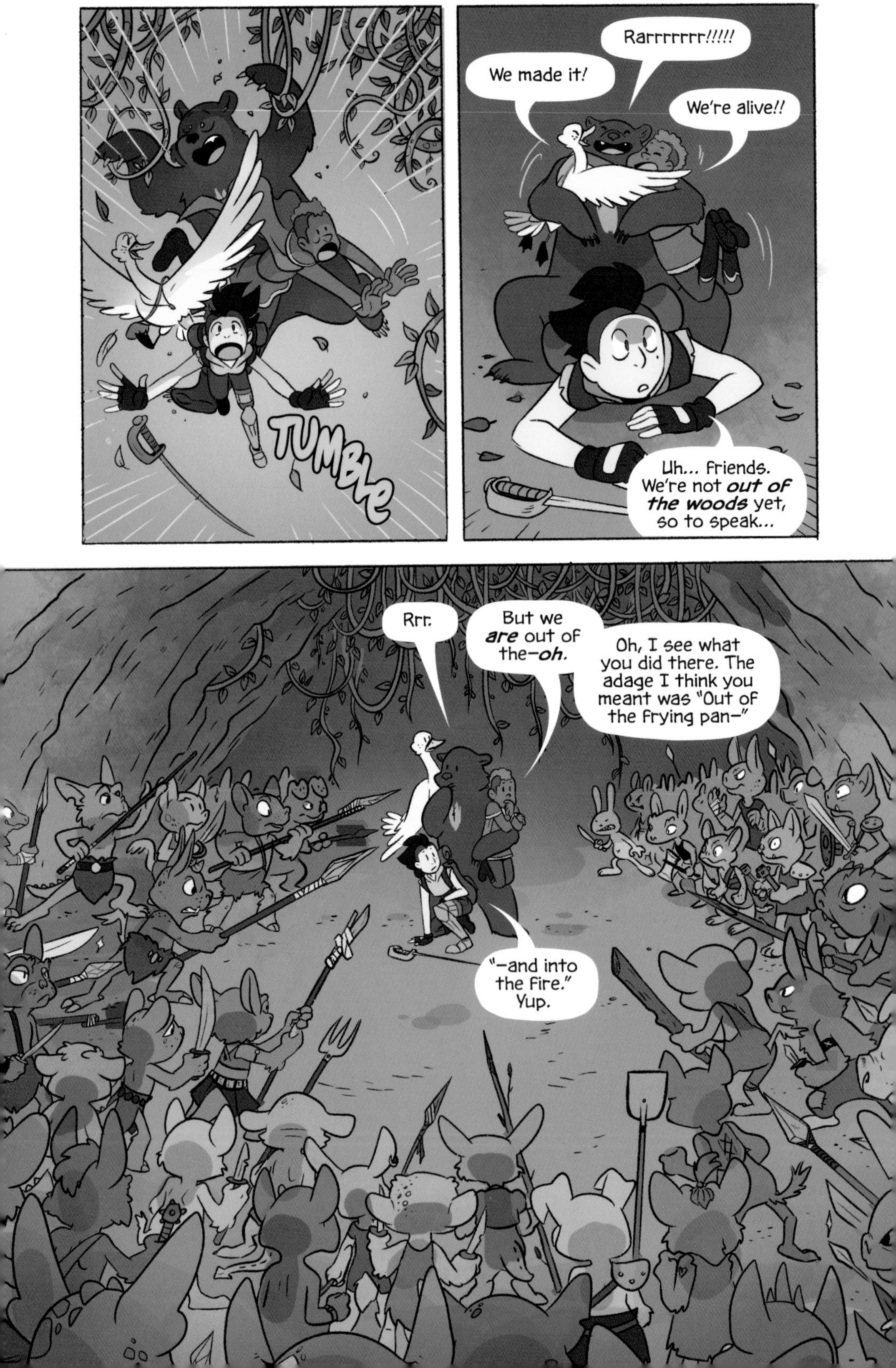
TUMBLE
We made it!
Rarrrrrrr!!!!!
We're alive!!
Uh... friends. We're not ***out of the woods*** yet, so to speak...
Rrr.
But we ***are*** out of the–***oh.***
Oh, I see what you did there. The adage I think you meant was "Out of the frying pan–"
"–and into the fire." Yup.

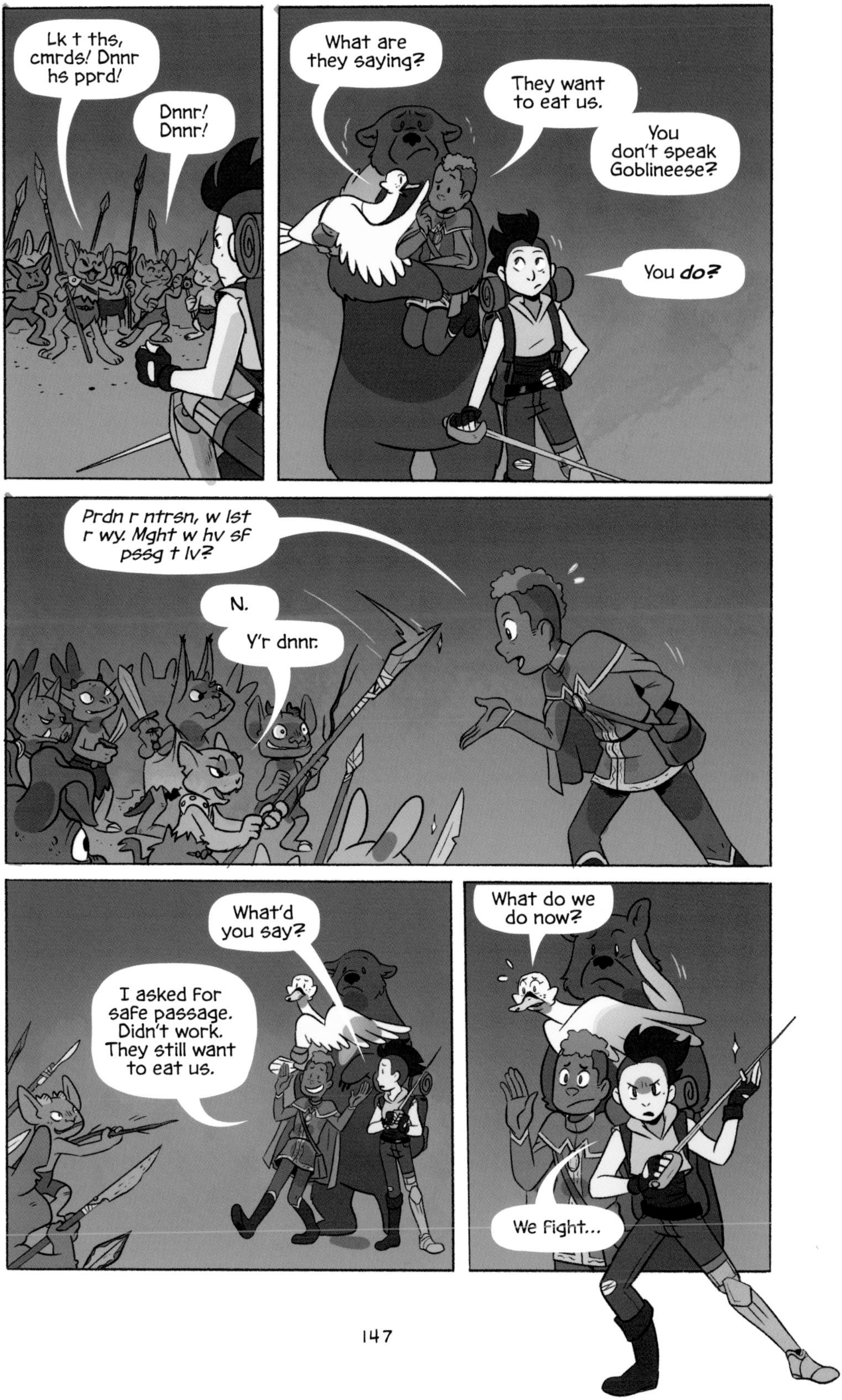
Lk t ths, cmrds! Dnnr hs pprd!
Dnnr! Dnnr!
What are they saying?
They want to eat us.
You don't speak Goblineese?
You *do*?
Prdn r ntrsn, w lst r wy. Mght w hv sf pssg t lv?
N.
Y'r dnnr.
What'd you say?
I asked for safe passage. Didn't work. They still want to eat us.
What do we do now?
We fight...

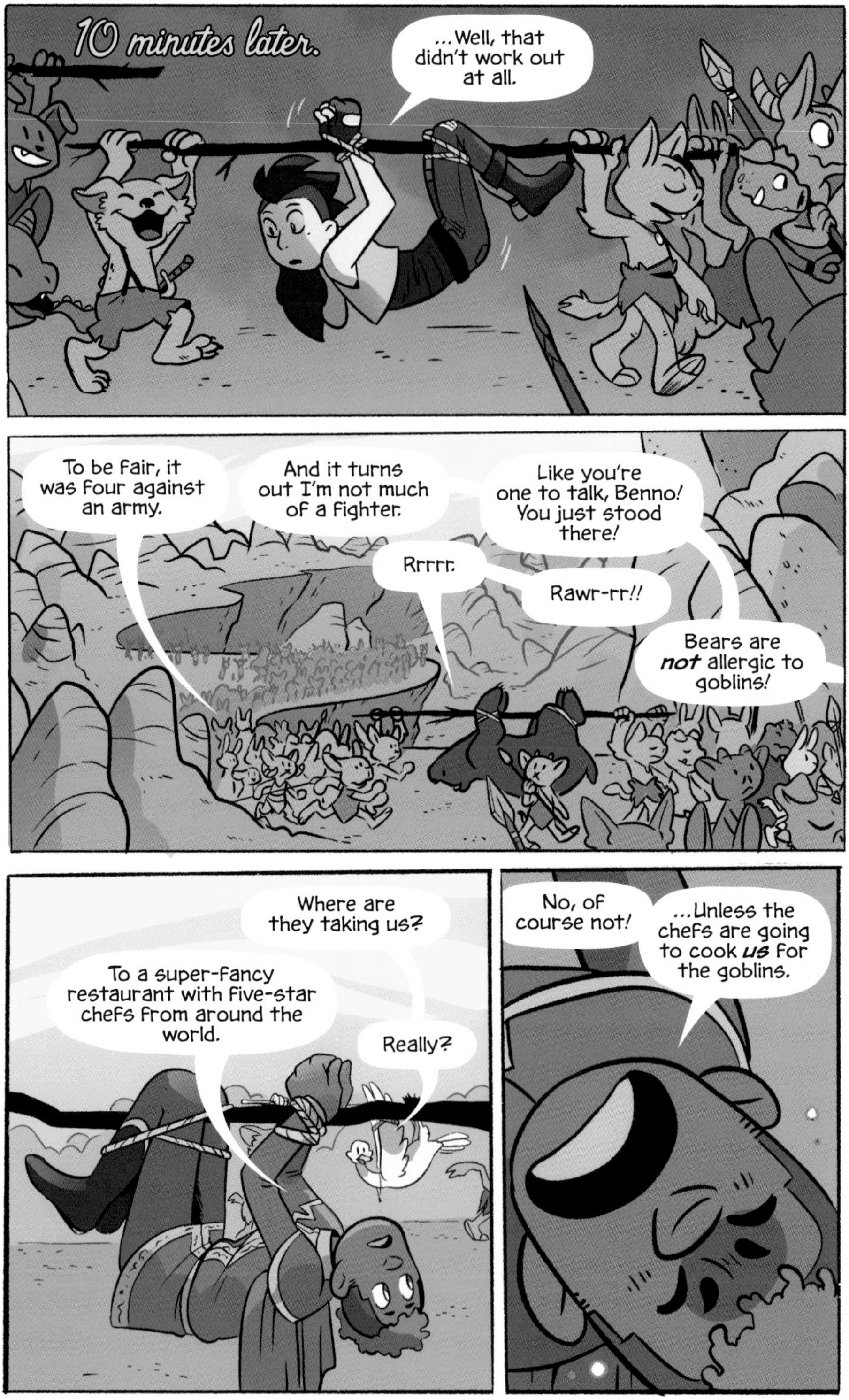

10 minutes later.
...Well, that didn't work out at all.
To be fair, it was four against an army.
And it turns out I'm not much of a fighter.
Like you're one to talk, Benno! You just stood there!
Rrrrr.
Rawr-rr!!
Bears are *not* allergic to goblins!
Where are they taking us?
To a super-fancy restaurant with five-star chefs from around the world.
Really?
No, of course not!
...Unless the chefs are going to cook *us* for the goblins.

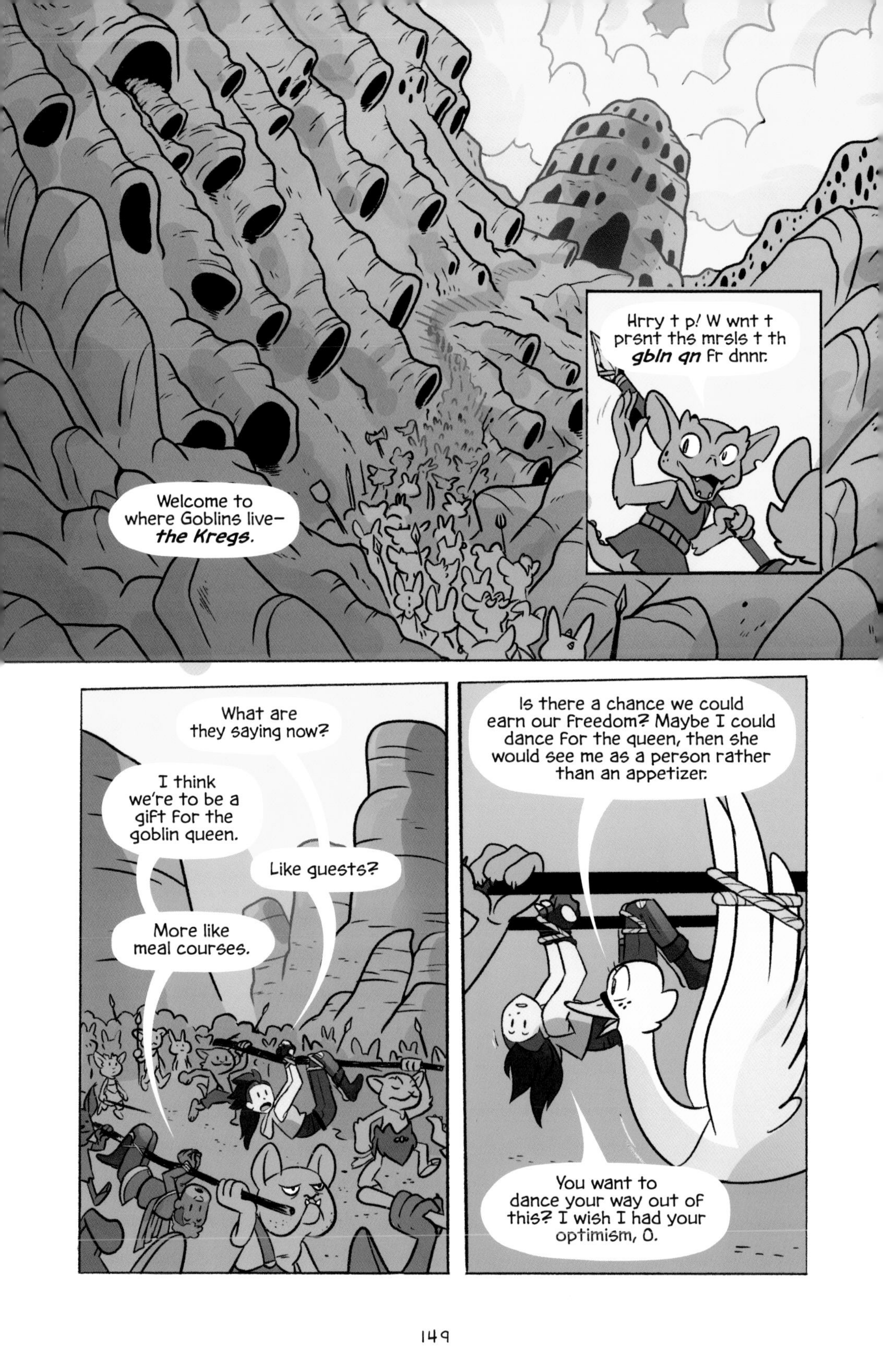
Welcome to where Goblins live— ***the Kregs.***
Hrry t p! W wnt t prsnt ths mrsls t th ***gbln qn*** fr dnnr.
What are they saying now?
I think we're to be a gift for the goblin queen.
Like guests?
More like meal courses.
Is there a chance we could earn our freedom? Maybe I could dance for the queen, then she would see me as a person rather than an appetizer.
You want to dance your way out of this? I wish I had your optimism, O.

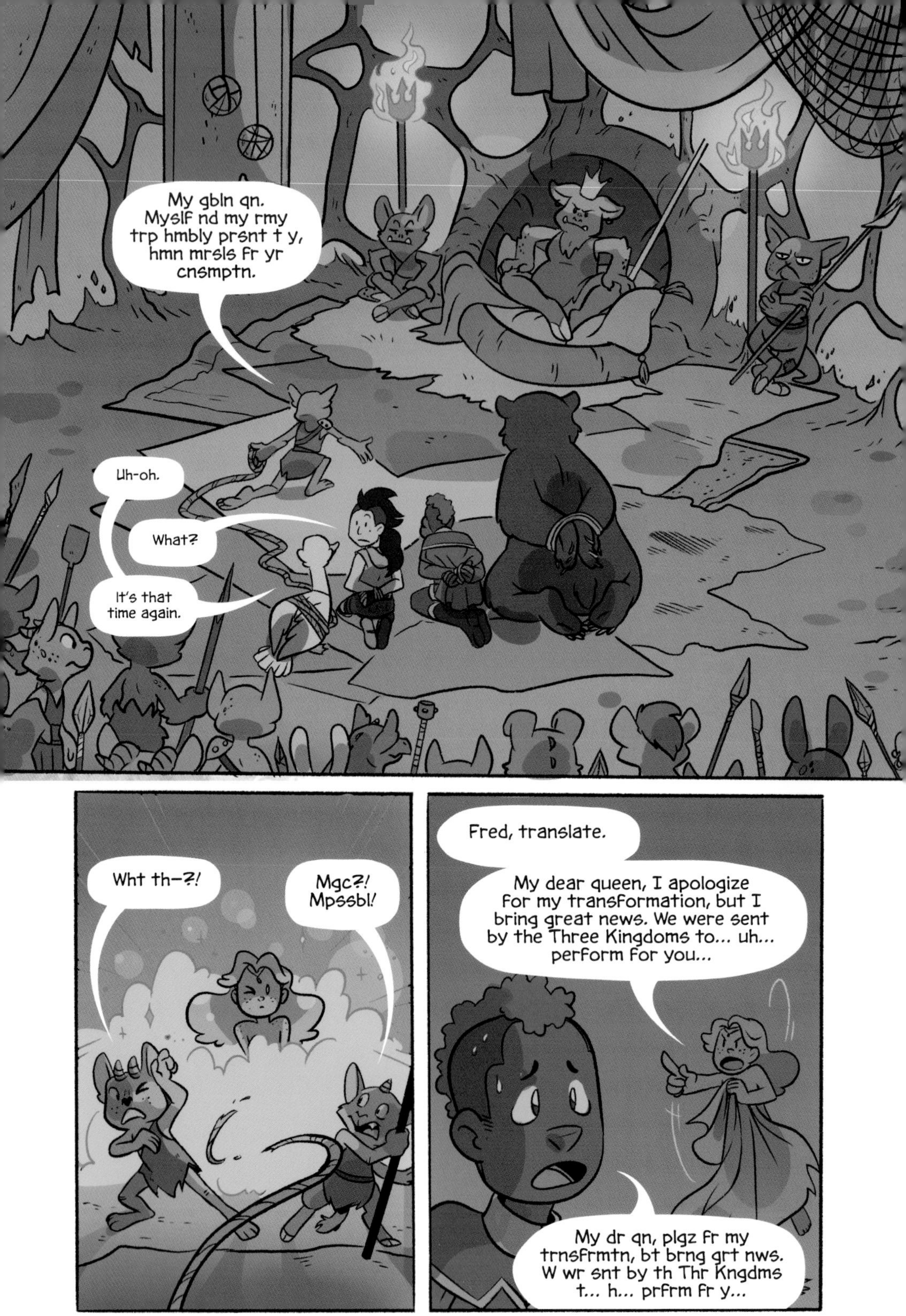
My gbln qn. Myslf nd my rmy trp hmbly prsnt t y, hmn mrsls fr yr cnsmptn.
Uh-oh.
What?
It's that time again.
Wht th—?!
Mgc?! Mpssbl!
Fred, translate.
My dear queen, I apologize for my transformation, but I bring great news. We were sent by the Three Kingdoms to... uh... perform for you...
My dr qn, plgz fr my trnsfrmtn, bt brng grt nws. W wr snt by th Thr Kngdms t... h... prfrm fr y...

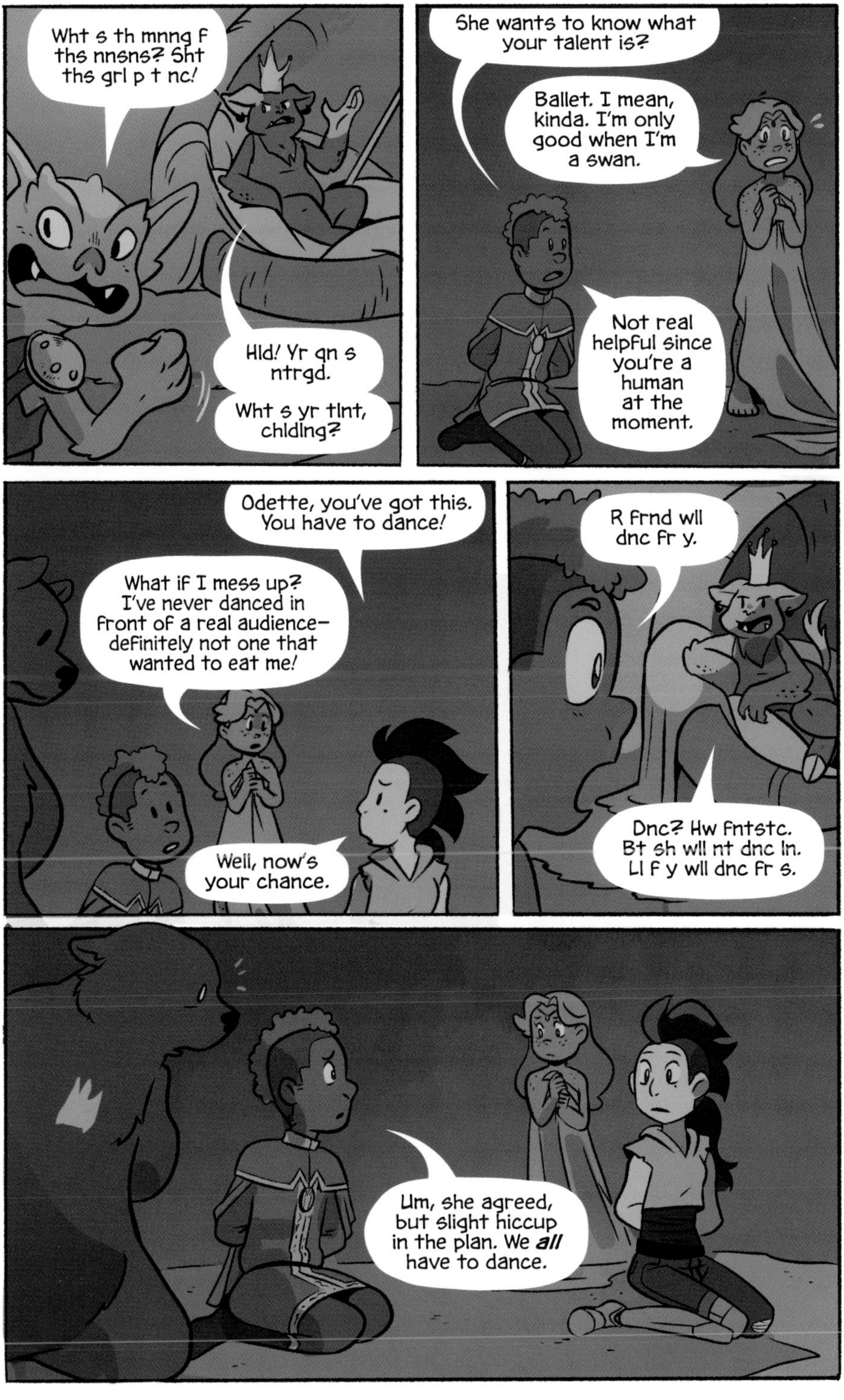
Wht s th mnng f ths nnsns? Sht ths grl p t nc!
Hld! Yr qn s ntrgd.
Wht s yr tlnt, chldng?
She wants to know what your talent is?
Ballet. I mean, kinda. I'm only good when I'm a swan.
Not real helpful since you're a human at the moment.
Odette, you've got this. You have to dance!
What if I mess up? I've never danced in front of a real audience—definitely not one that wanted to eat me!
Well, now's your chance.
R frnd wll dnc fr y.
Dnc? Hw fntstc. Bt sh wll nt dnc ln. Ll f y wll dnc fr s.
Um, she agreed, but slight hiccup in the plan. We ***all*** have to dance.

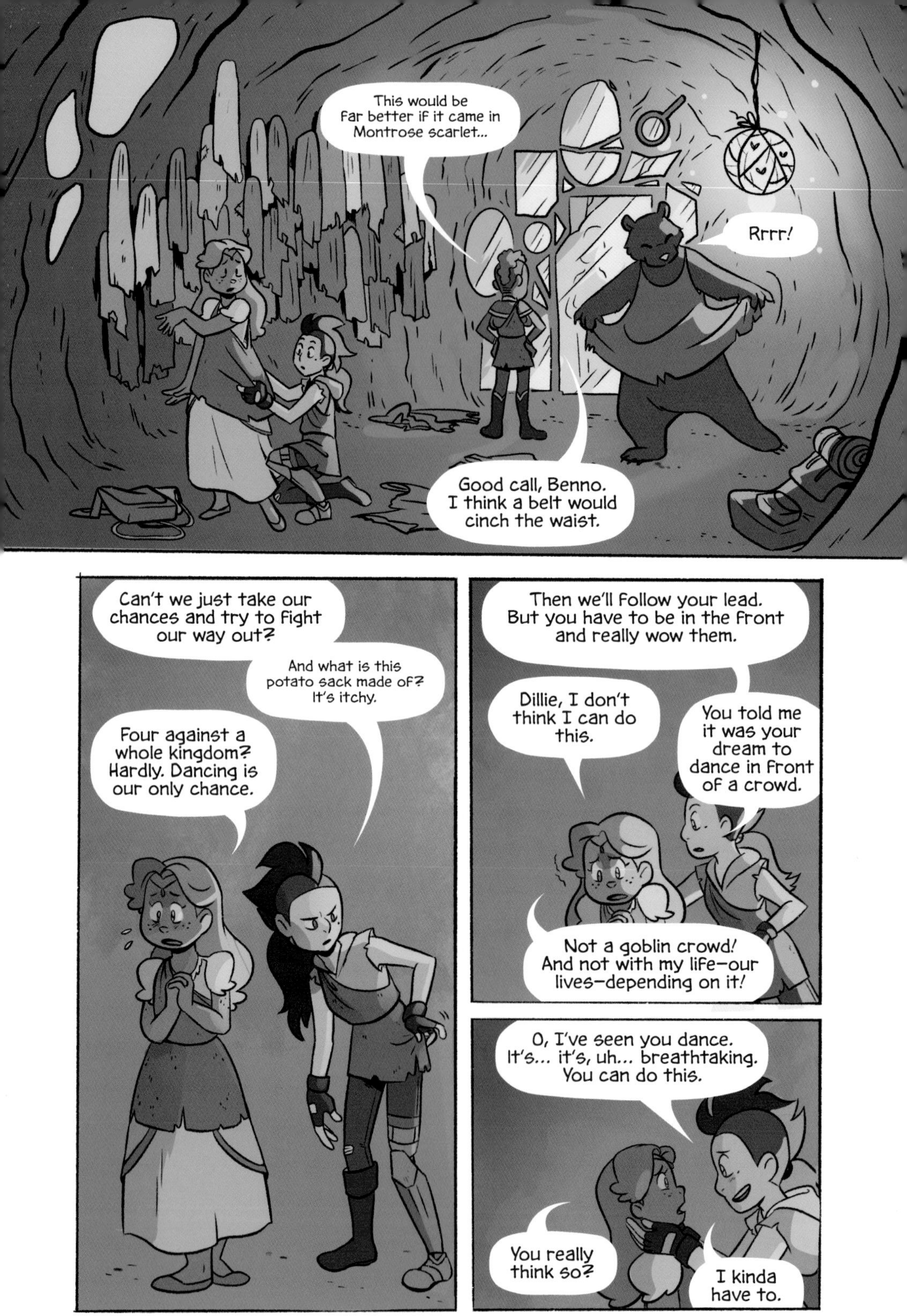
This would be far better if it came in Montrose scarlet...
Rrrr!
Good call, Benno. I think a belt would cinch the waist.
Can't we just take our chances and try to fight our way out?
And what is this potato sack made of? It's itchy.
Four against a whole kingdom? Hardly. Dancing is our only chance.
Then we'll follow your lead. But you have to be in the front and really wow them.
Dillie, I don't think I can do this.
You told me it was your dream to dance in front of a crowd.
Not a goblin crowd! And not with my life—our lives—depending on it!
O, I've seen you dance. It's... it's, uh... breathtaking. You can do this.
You really think so?
I kinda have to.

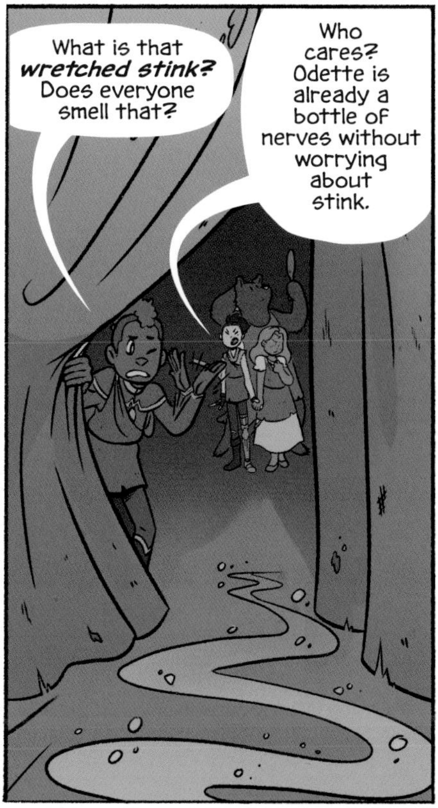
What is that *wretched stink?* Does everyone smell that?
Who cares? Odette is already a bottle of nerves without worrying about stink.

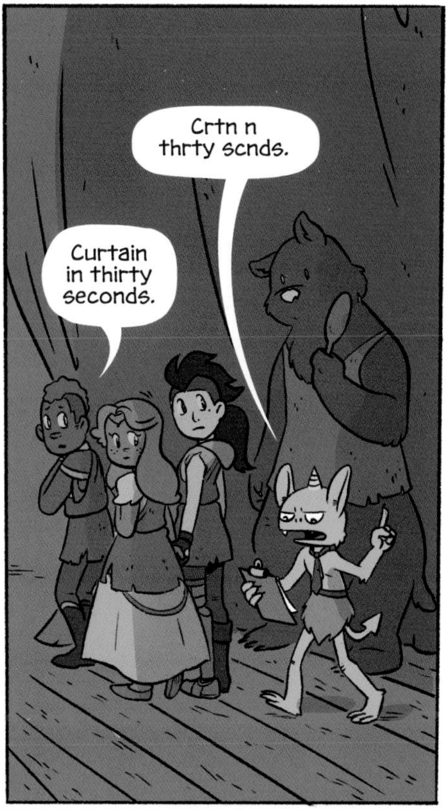
Crtn n thrty scnds.
Curtain in thirty seconds.

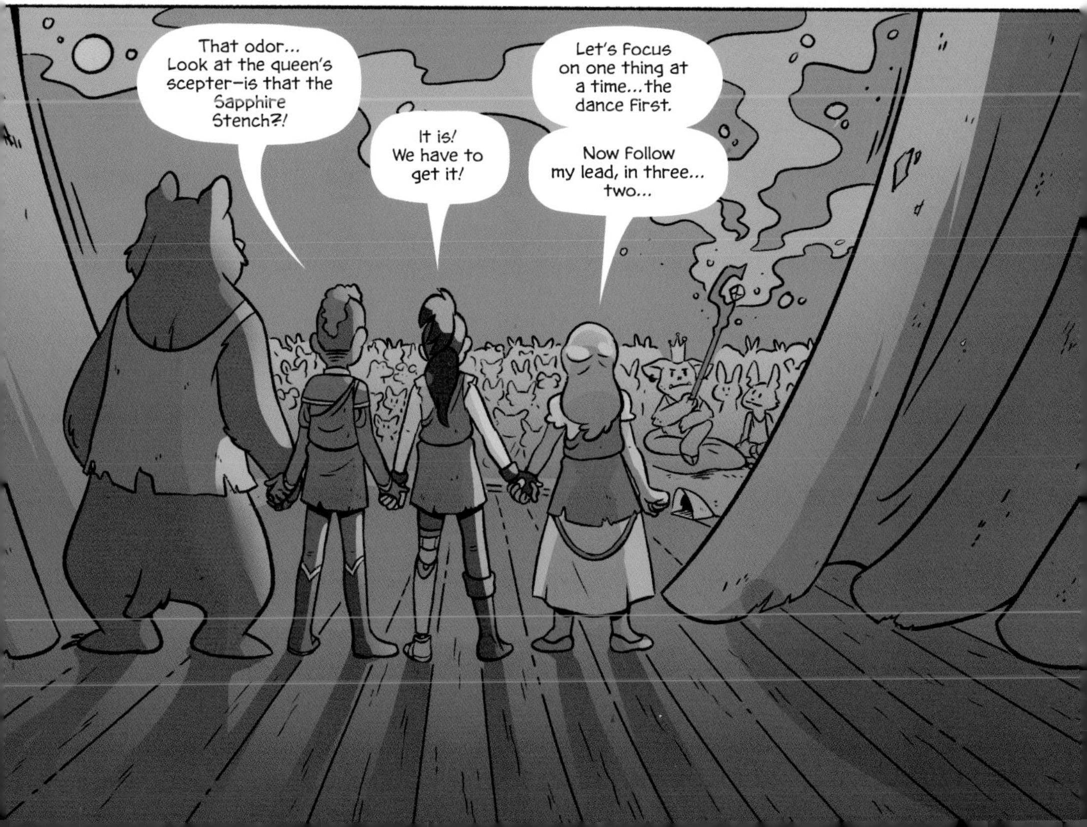
That odor... Look at the queen's scepter—is that the Sapphire Stench?!
It is! We have to get it!
Let's focus on one thing at a time...the dance first.
Now follow my lead, in three... two...

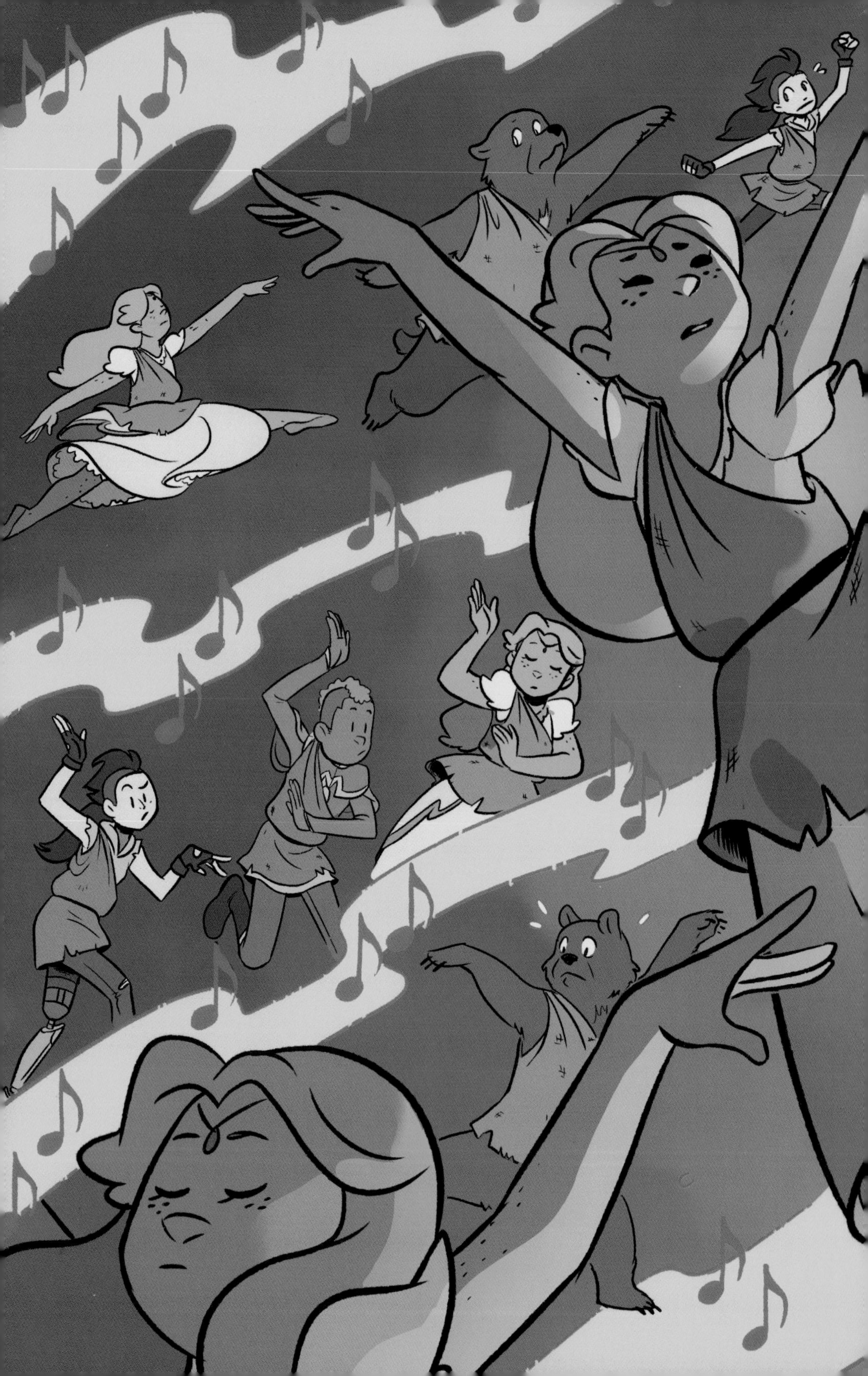

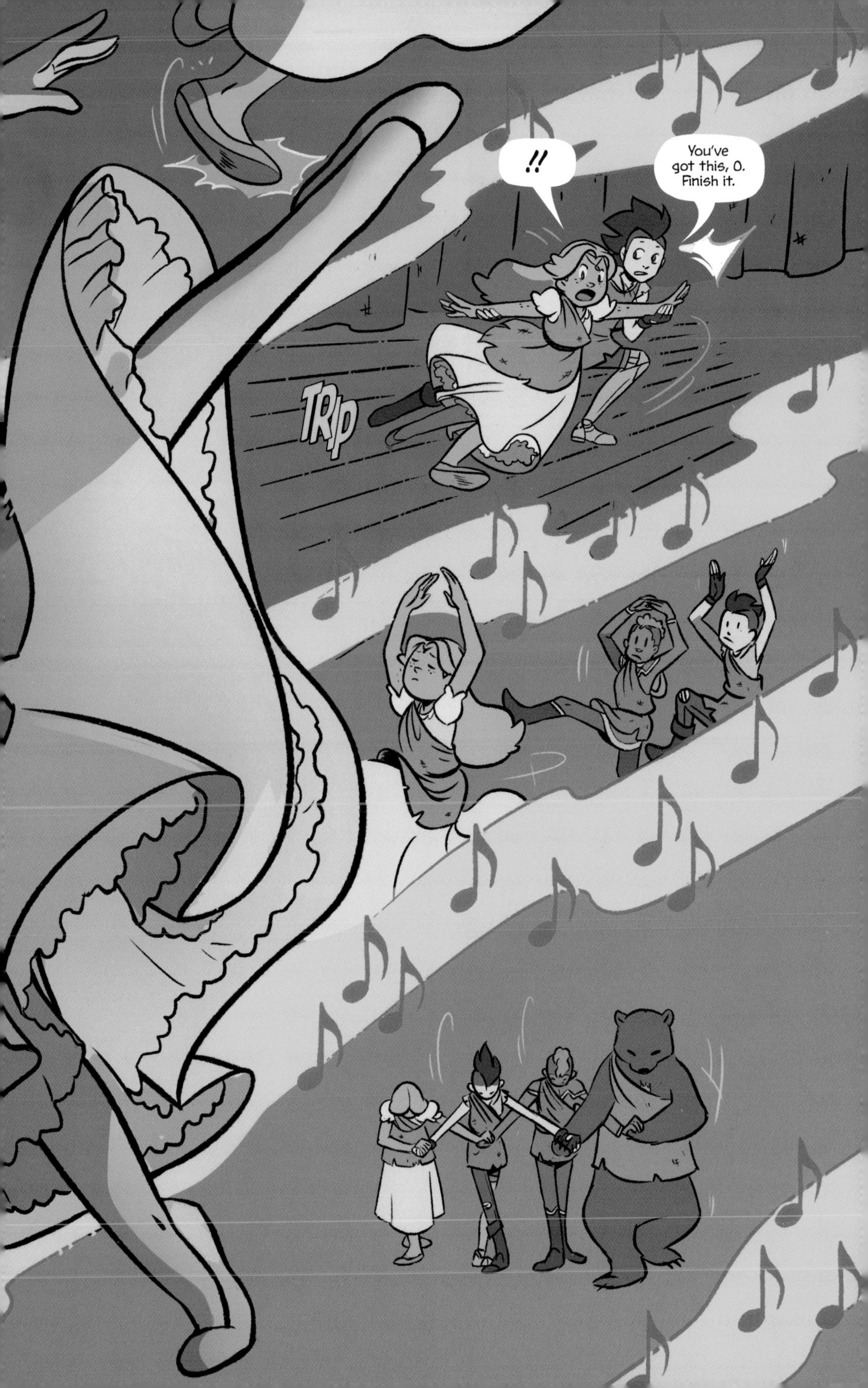
!!
You've got this, O. Finish it.
TRIP

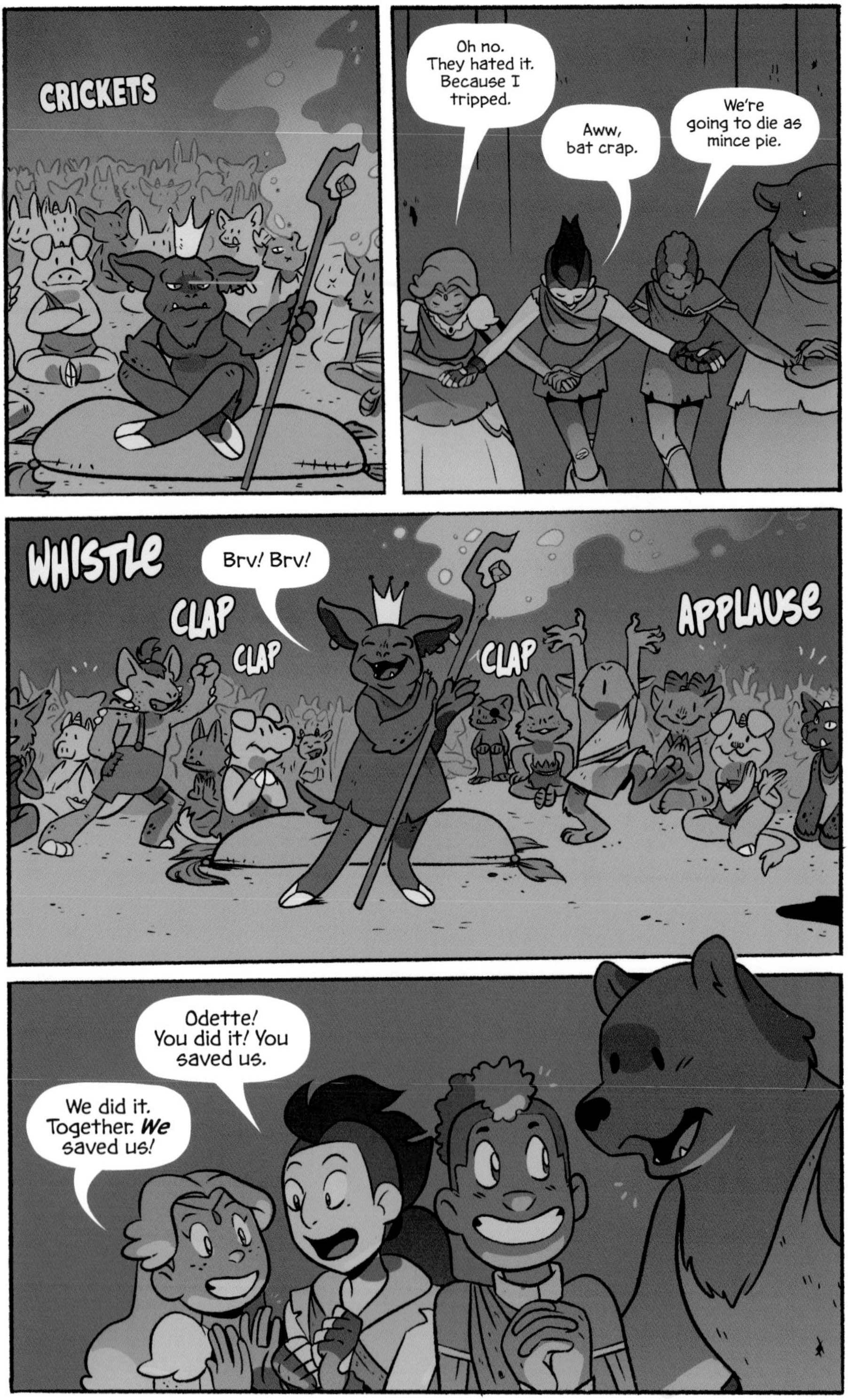
CRICKETS
Oh no. They hated it. Because I tripped.
Aww, bat crap.
We're going to die as mince pie.
WHISTLE
Brv! Brv!
CLAP
CLAP
CLAP
APPLAUSE
Odette! You did it! You saved us.
We did it. Together. *We* saved us!

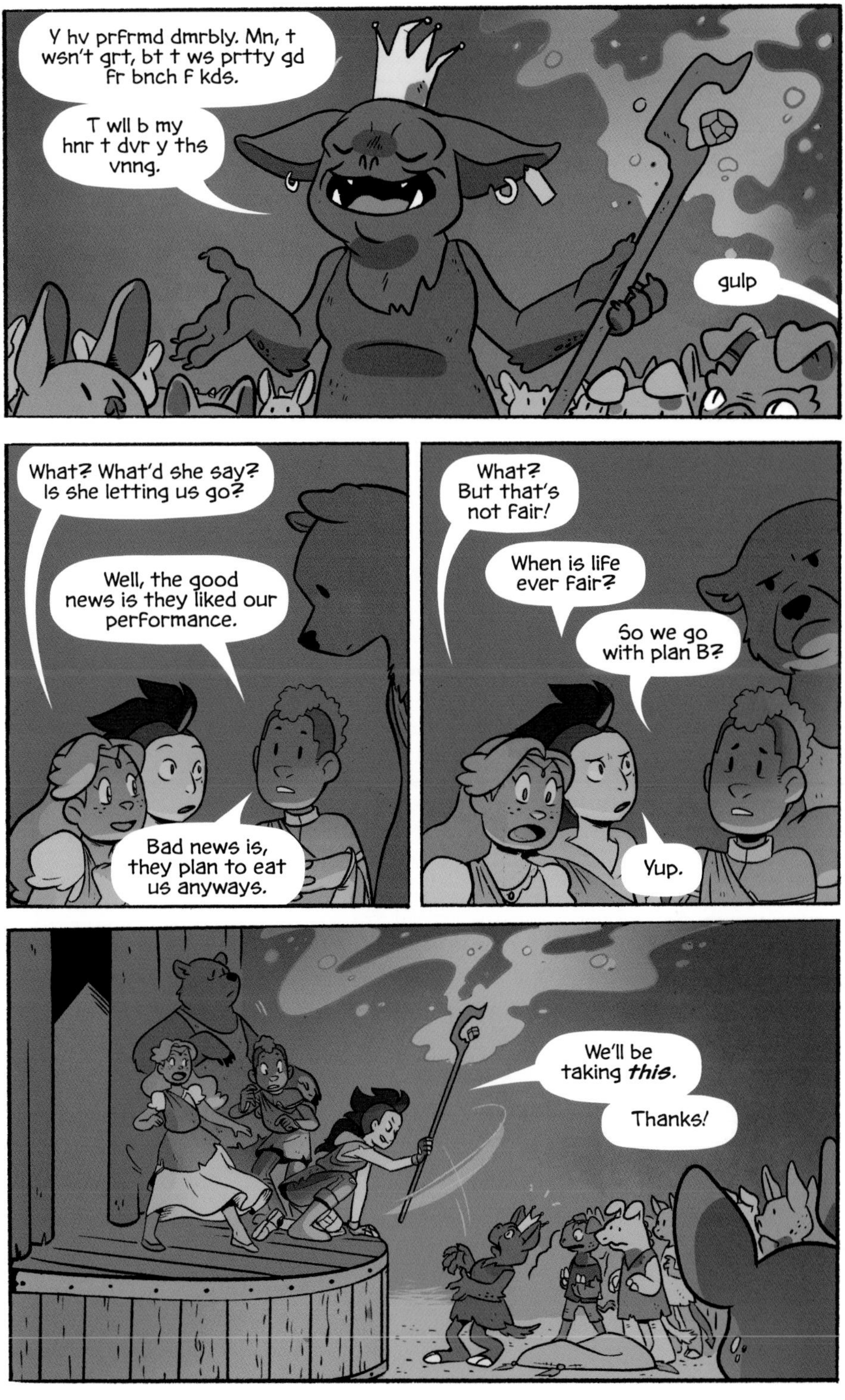
Y hv prfrmd dmrbly. Mn, t wsn't grt, bt t ws prtty gd fr bnch f kds.
T wll b my hnr t dvr y ths vnng.
gulp
What? What'd she say? Is she letting us go?
Well, the good news is they liked our performance.
Bad news is, they plan to eat us anyways.
What? But that's not fair!
When is life ever fair?
So we go with plan B?
Yup.
We'll be taking *this.*
Thanks!

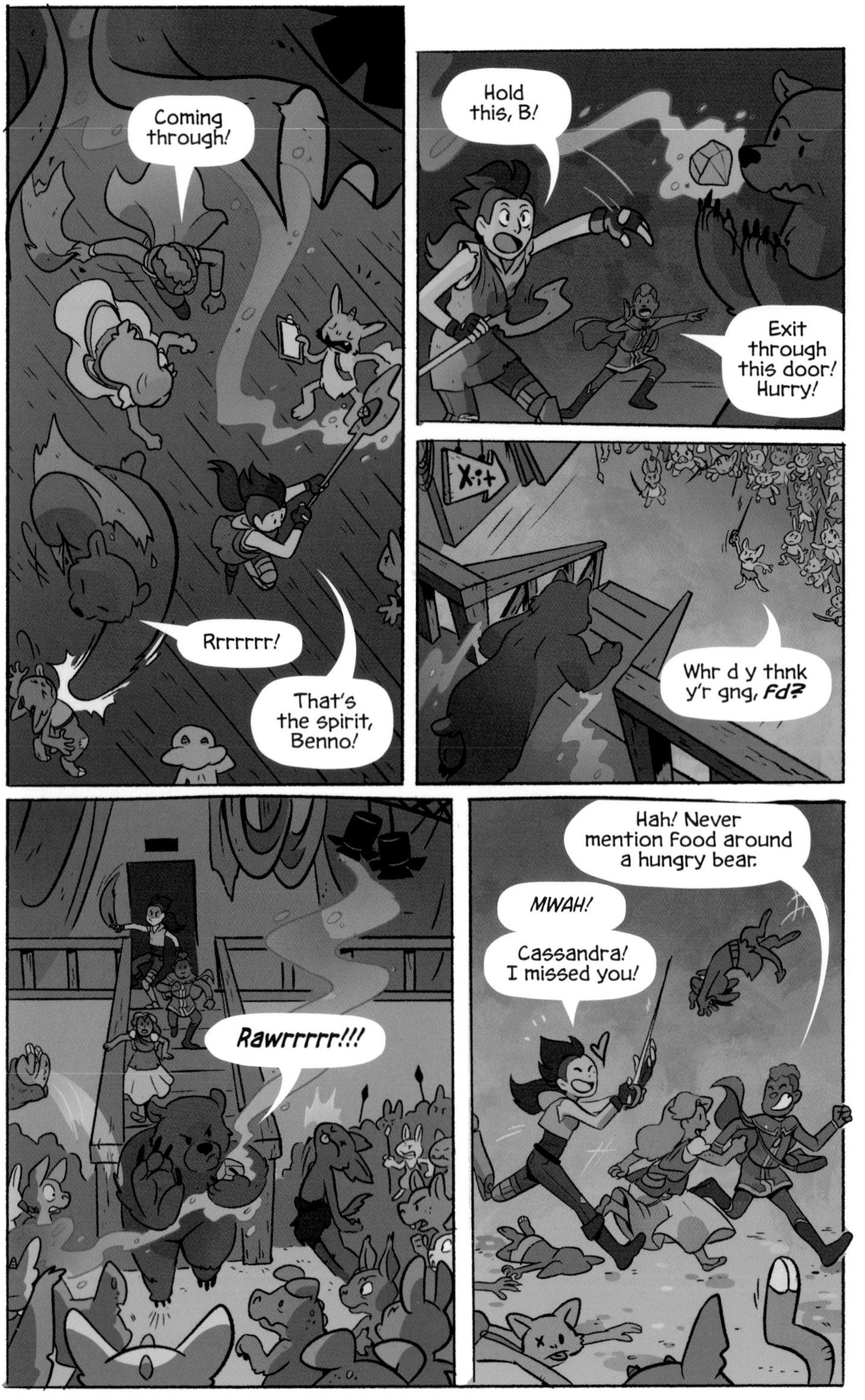
Coming through!
Rrrrrrr!
That's the spirit, Benno!
Hold this, B!
Exit through this door! Hurry!
X-it
Whr d y thnk y'r gng, Fd?
Rawrrrrr!!!
Hah! Never mention food around a hungry bear.
MWAH!
Cassandra! I missed you!

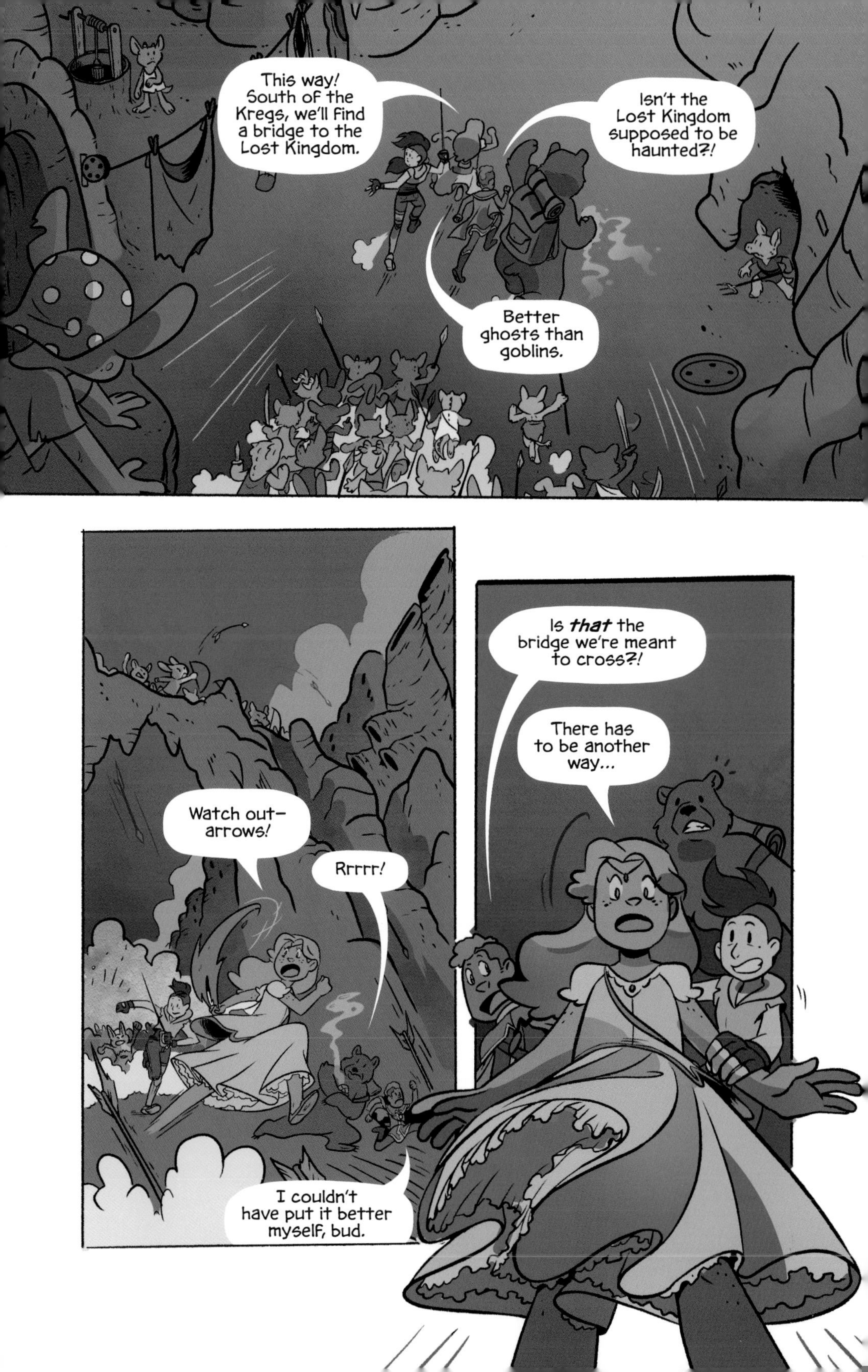
This way! South of the Kregs, we'll find a bridge to the Lost Kingdom.
Isn't the Lost Kingdom supposed to be haunted?!
Better ghosts than goblins.
Watch out–arrows!
Rrrrr!
I couldn't have put it better myself, bud.
Is *that* the bridge we're meant to cross?!
There has to be another way...

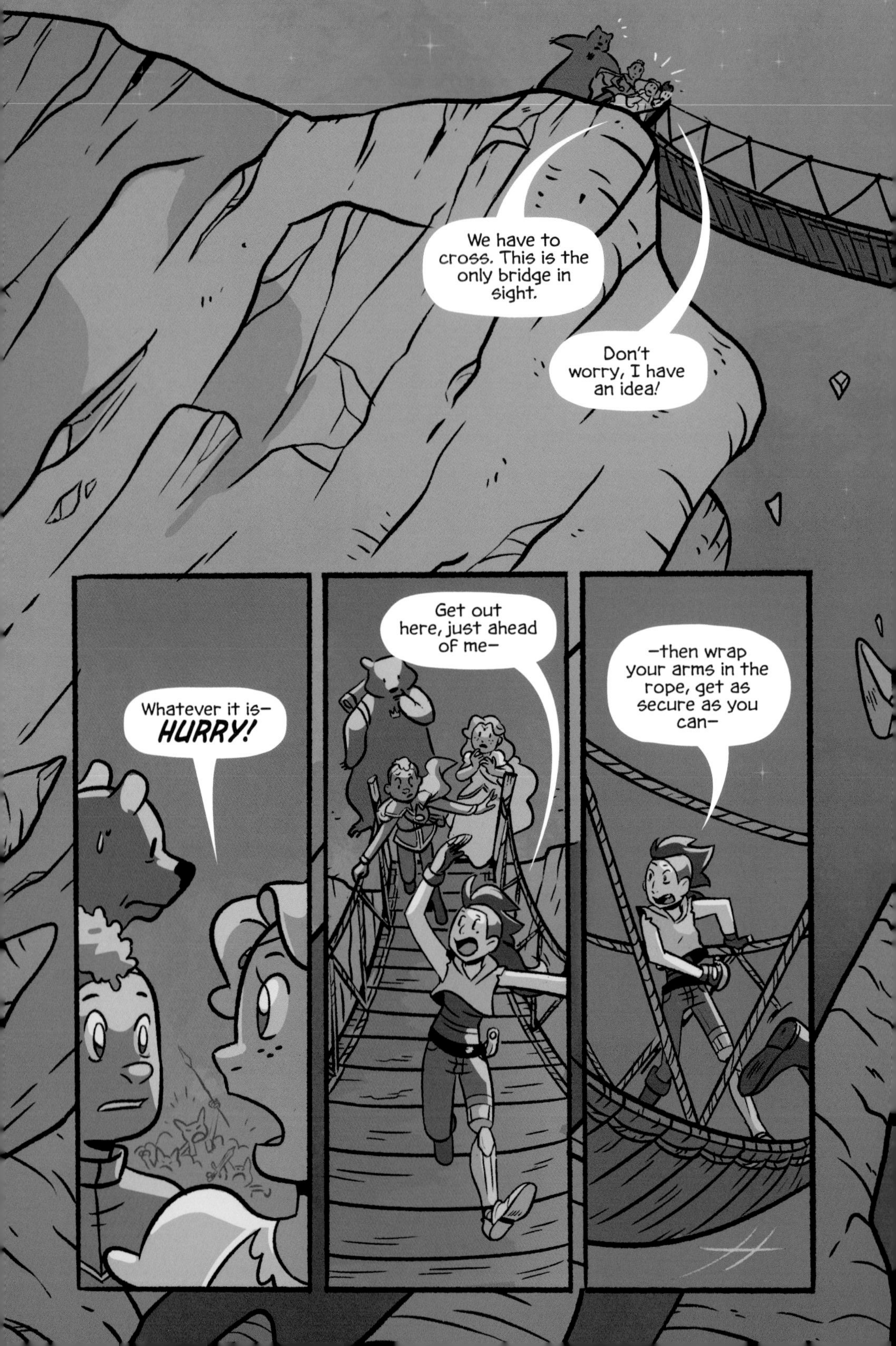
We have to cross. This is the only bridge in sight.
Don't worry, I have an idea!
Whatever it is— HURRY!
Get out here, just ahead of me—
—then wrap your arms in the rope, get as secure as you can—

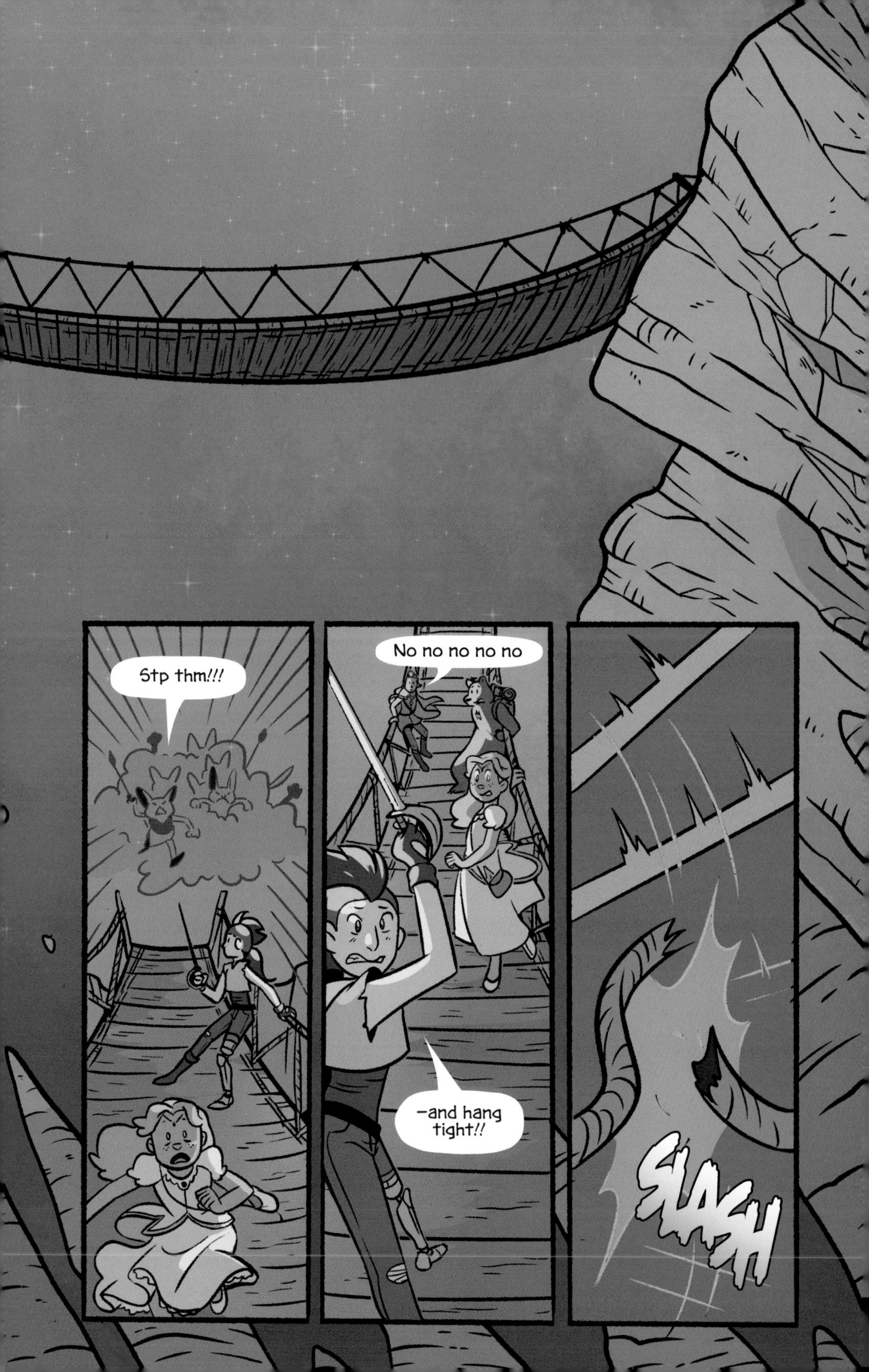
Stp thm!!!
No no no no no
-and hang tight!!
SLASH

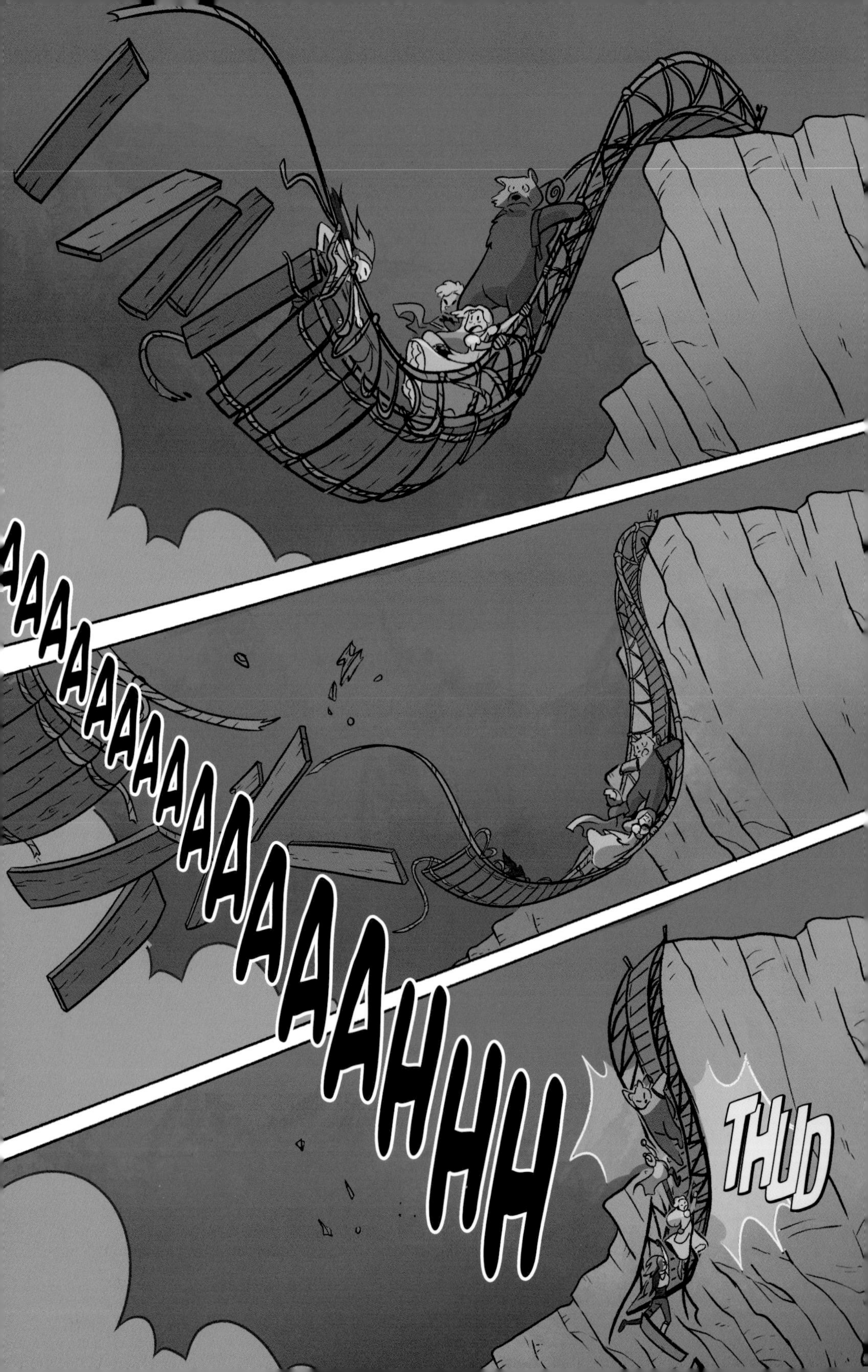
AAAAAAAAAAAAAAAAAHHHH
THUD

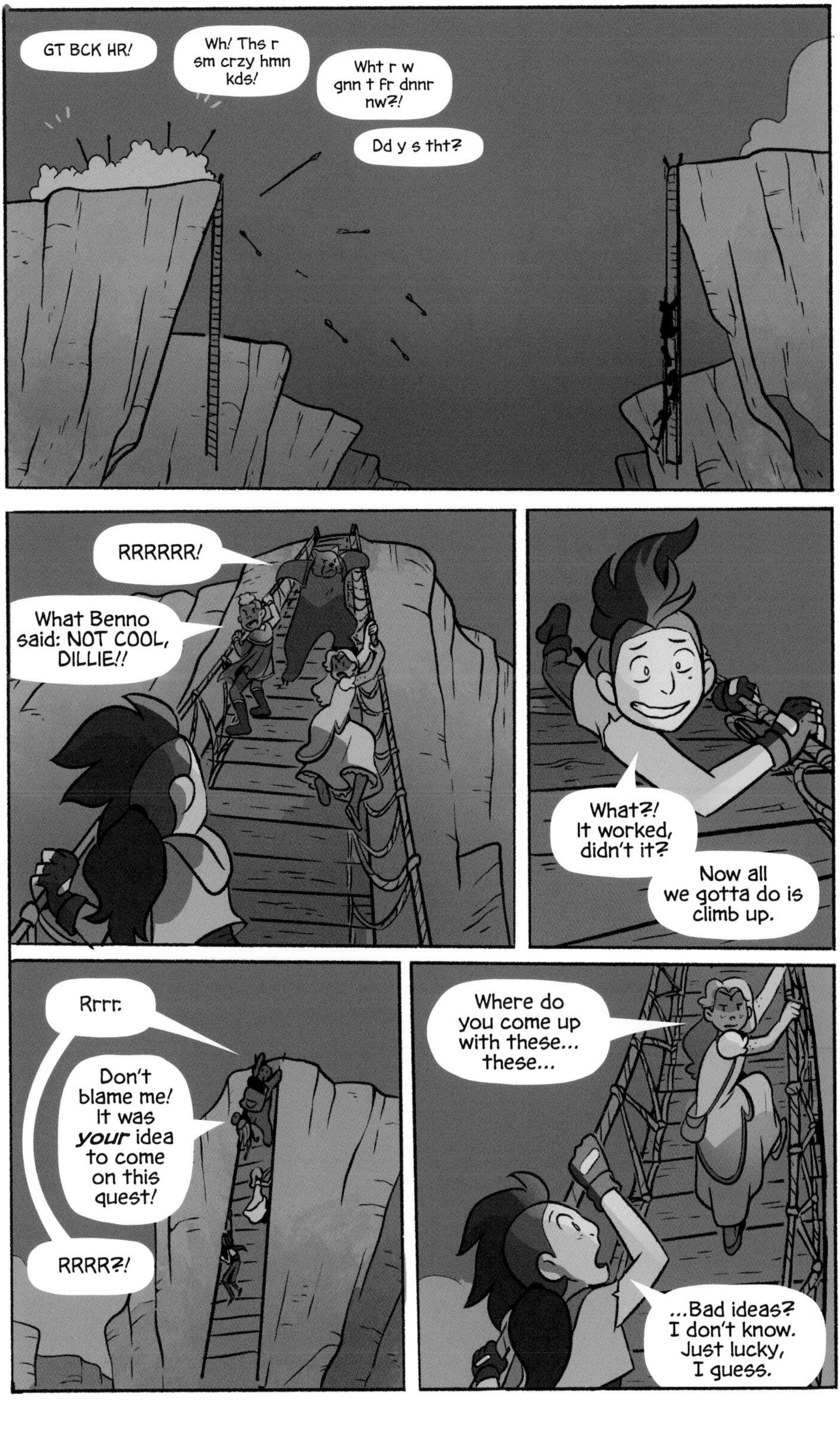
GT BCK HR!
Wh! Ths r sm crzy hmn kds!
Wht r w gnn t fr dnnr nw?!
Dd y s tht?
RRRRRR!
What Benno said: NOT COOL, DILLIE!!
What?! It worked, didn't it?
Now all we gotta do is climb up.
Rrrr.
Don't blame me! It was *your* idea to come on this quest!
RRRR?!
Where do you come up with these... these...
...Bad ideas? I don't know. Just lucky, I guess.

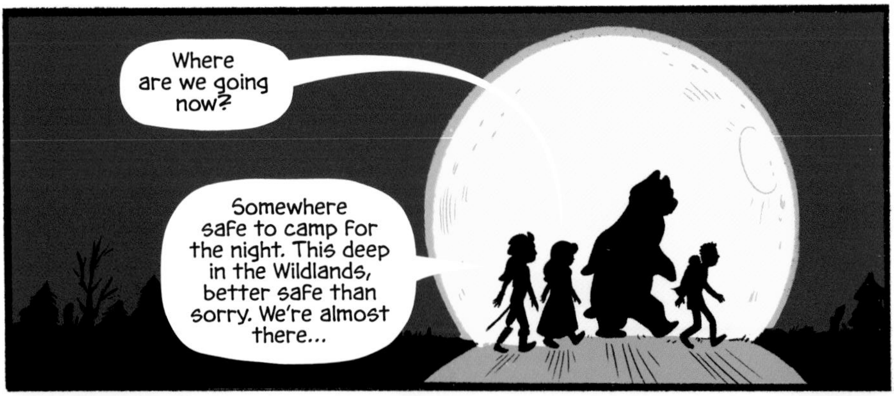
Where are we going now?
Somewhere safe to camp for the night. This deep in the Wildlands, better safe than sorry. We're almost there...

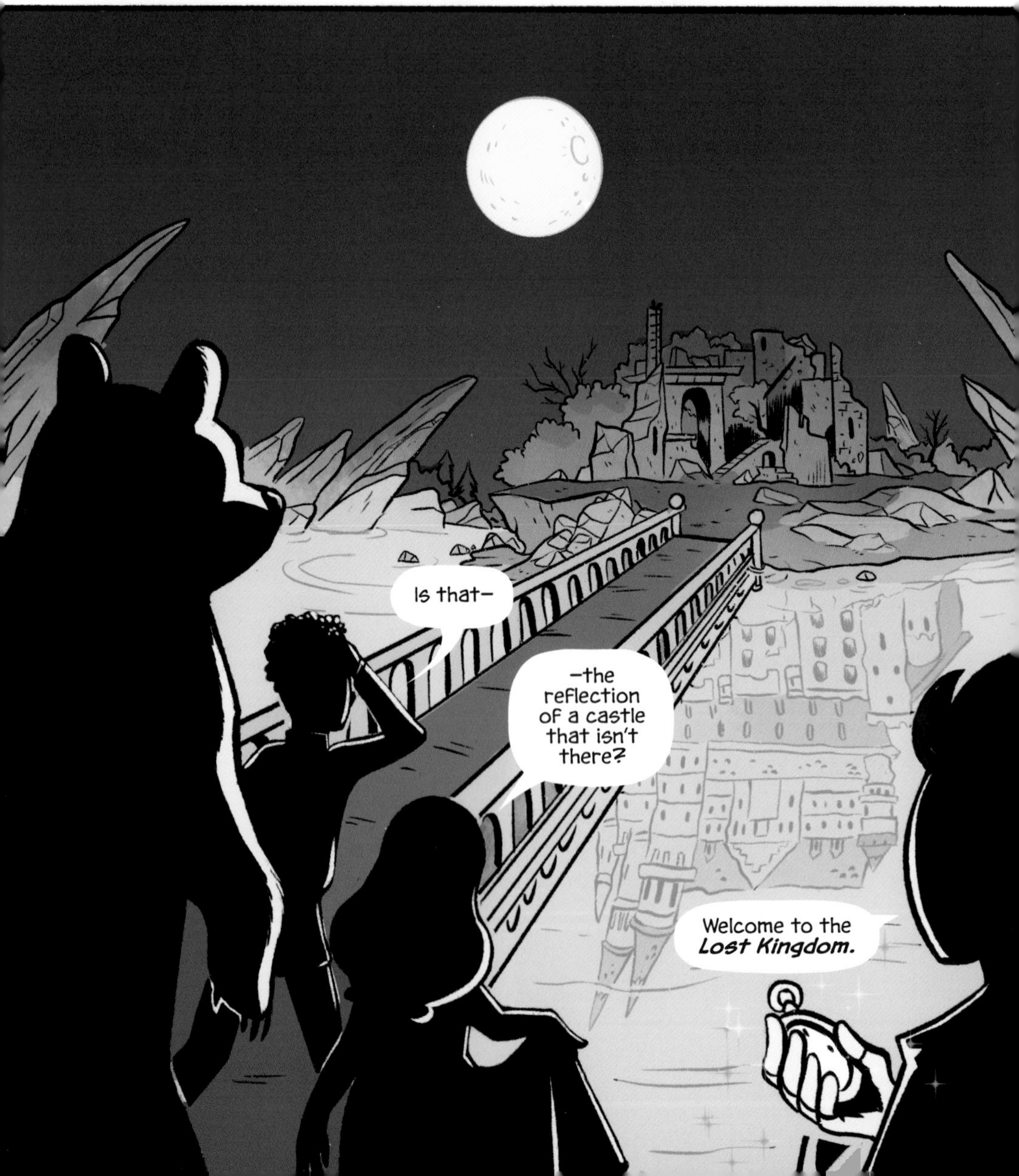
Is that–
–the reflection of a castle that isn't there?
Welcome to the *Lost Kingdom.*

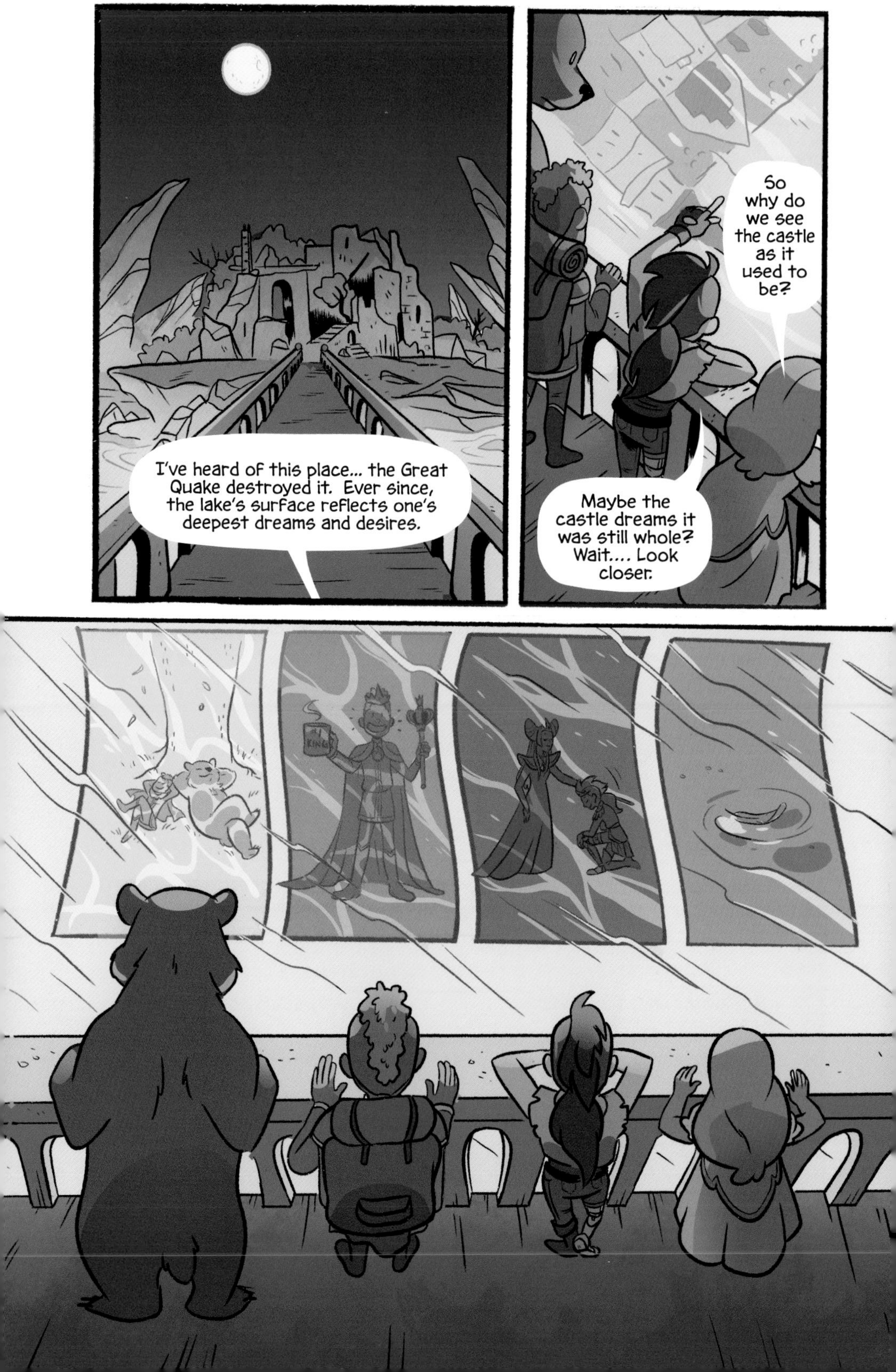
I've heard of this place... the Great Quake destroyed it. Ever since, the lake's surface reflects one's deepest dreams and desires.
So why do we see the castle as it used to be?
Maybe the castle dreams it was still whole? Wait.... Look closer.

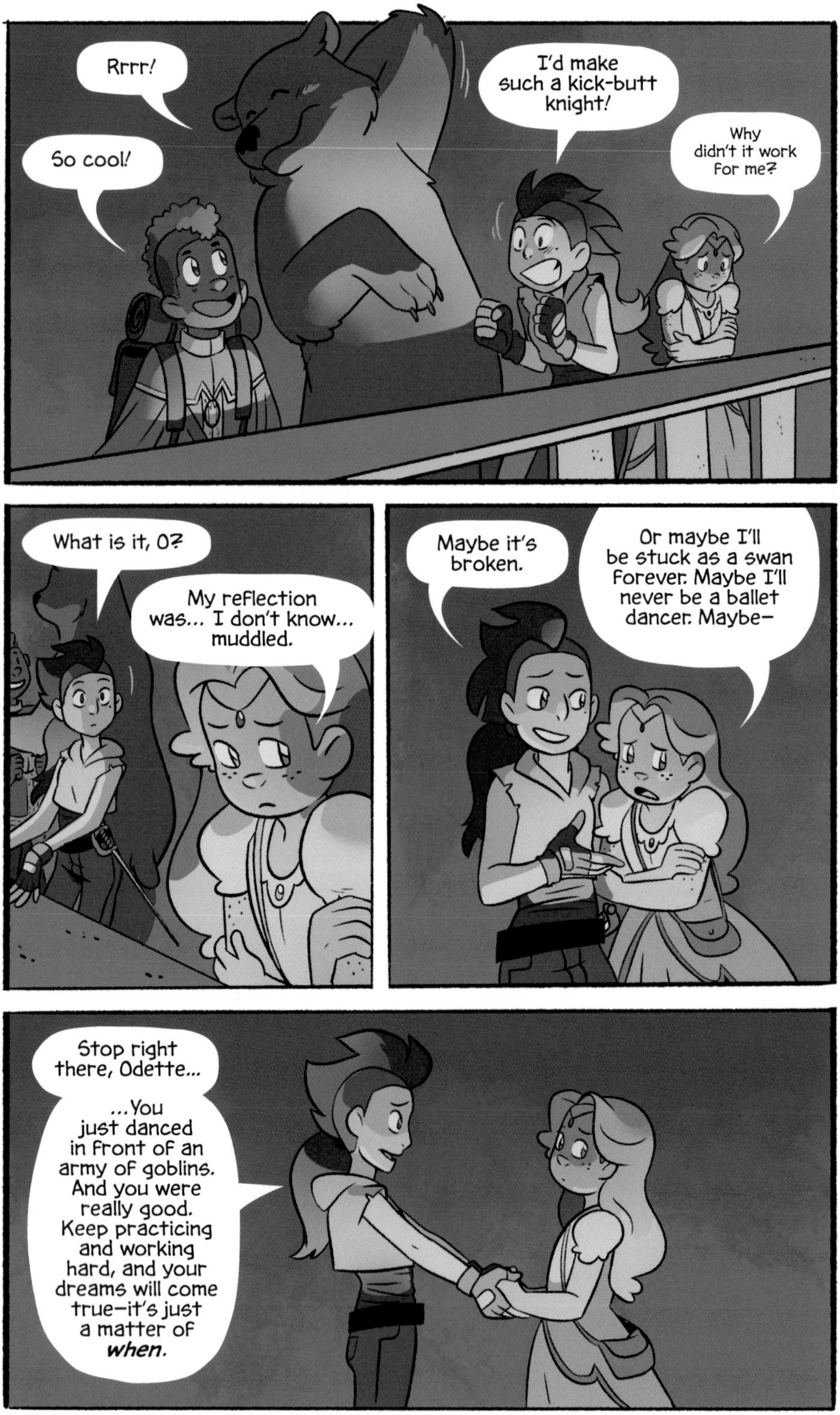
Rrrr!
So cool!
I'd make such a kick-butt knight!
Why didn't it work for me?
What is it, O?
My reflection was... I don't know... muddled.
Maybe it's broken.
Or maybe I'll be stuck as a swan forever. Maybe I'll never be a ballet dancer. Maybe—
Stop right there, Odette...
...You just danced in front of an army of goblins. And you were really good. Keep practicing and working hard, and your dreams will come true—it's just a matter of *when*.

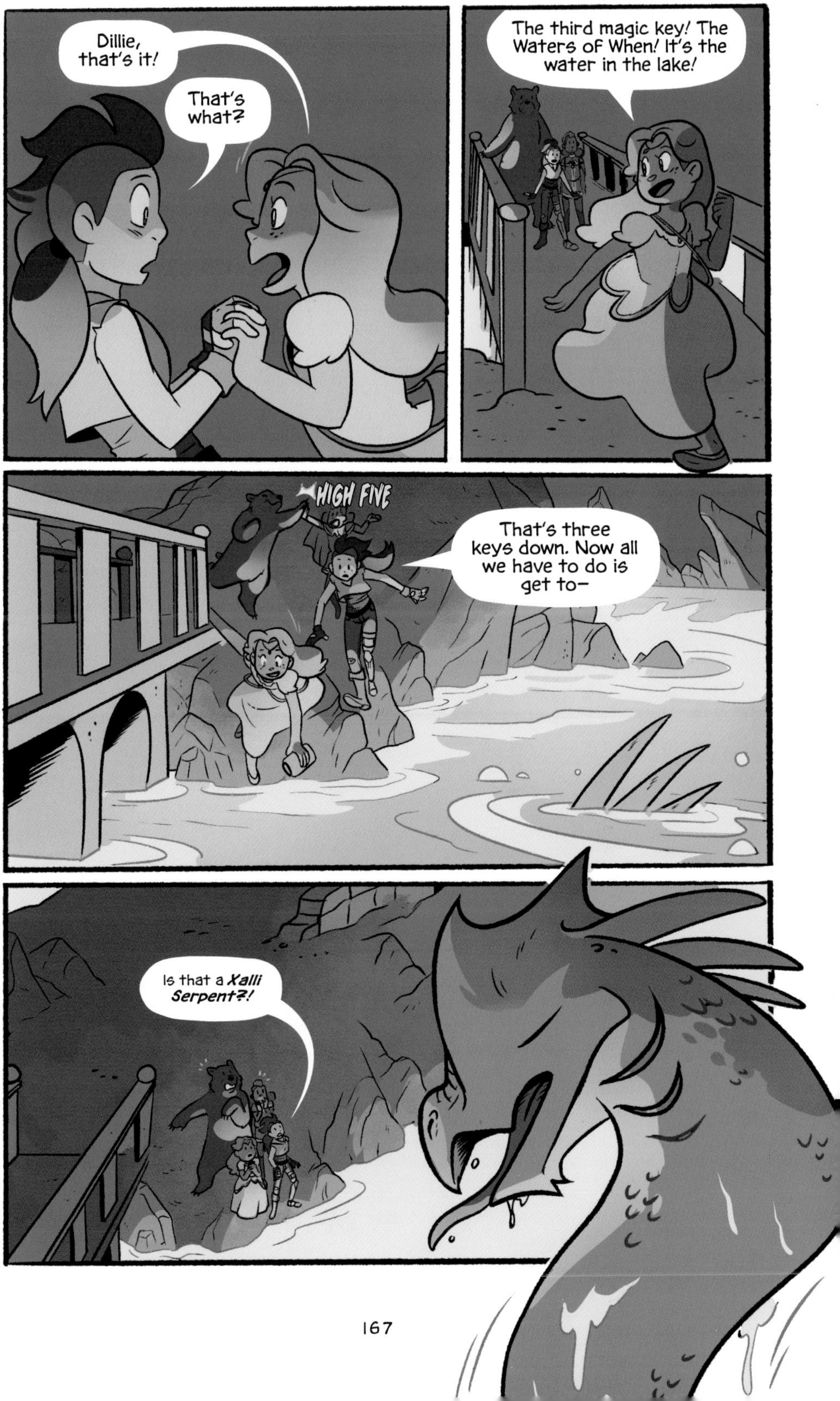
Dillie, that's it!
That's what?
The third magic key! The Waters of When! It's the water in the lake!
HIGH FIVE
That's three keys down. Now all we have to do is get to—
Is that a *Xalli Serpent*?!

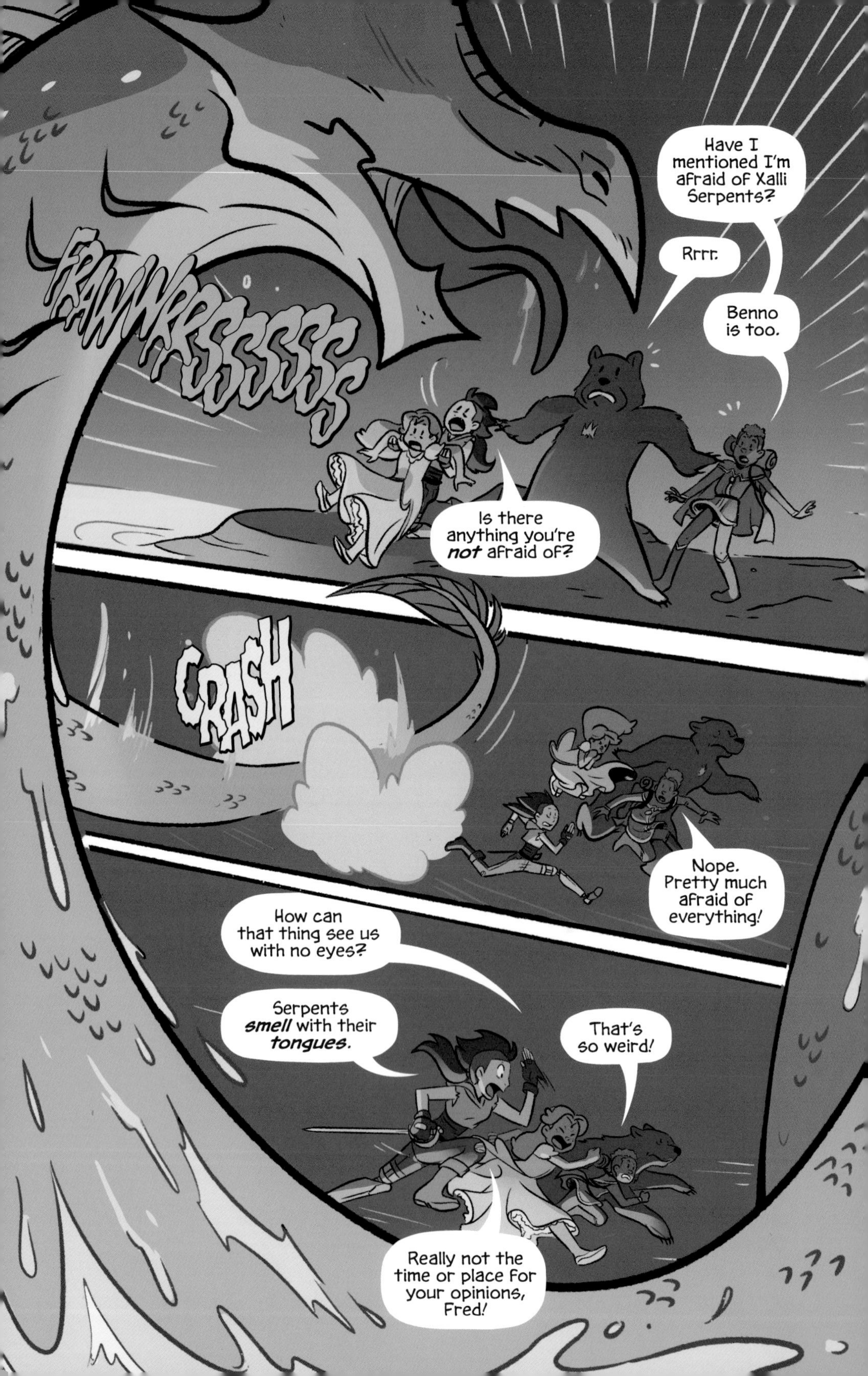
FRAWWRRSSSSSSS
Have I mentioned I'm afraid of Xalli Serpents?
Rrrr.
Benno is too.
Is there anything you're ***not*** afraid of?
CRASH
Nope. Pretty much afraid of everything!
How can that thing see us with no eyes?
Serpents ***smell*** with their ***tongues***.
That's so weird!
Really not the time or place for your opinions, Fred!

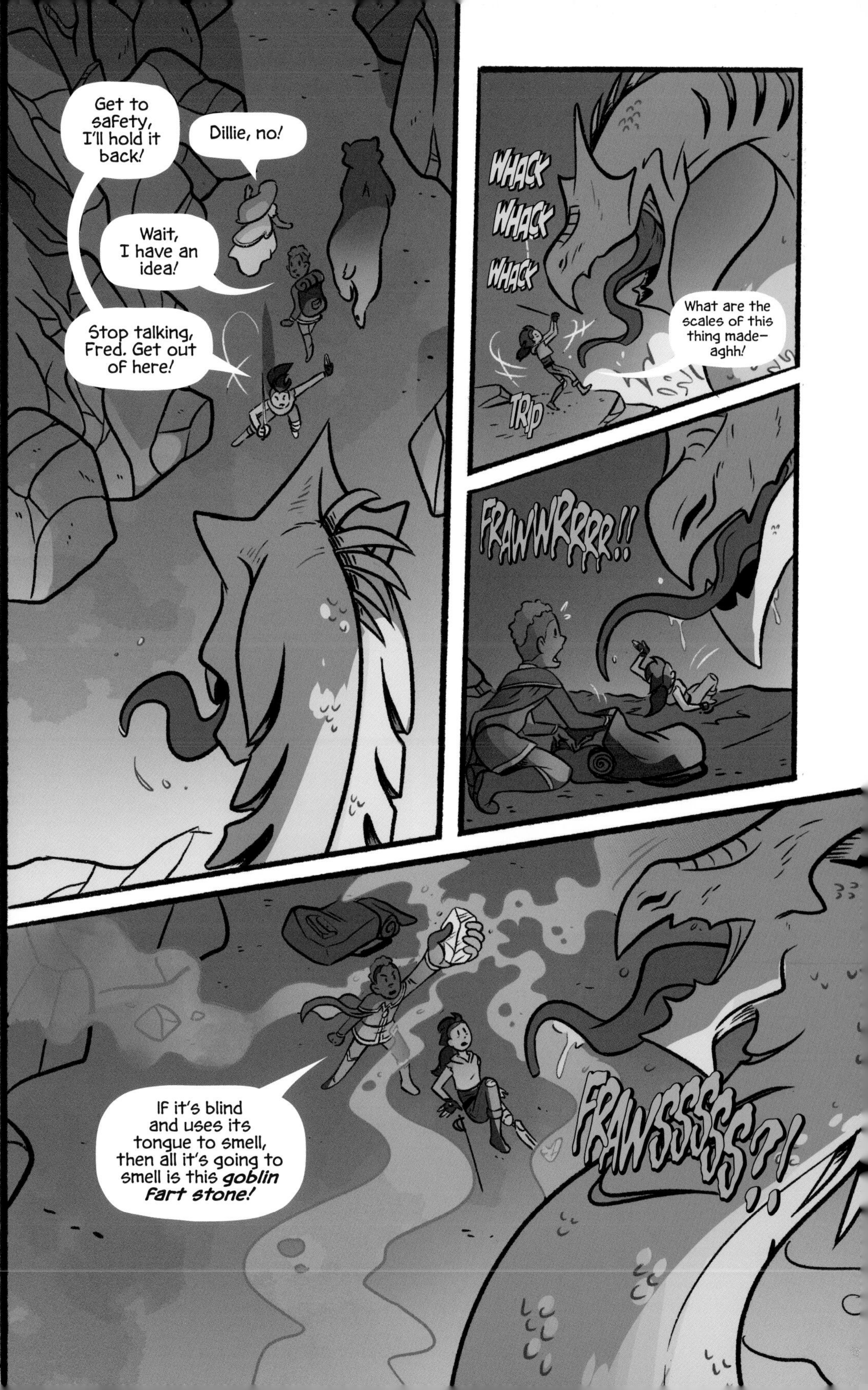

Get to safety, I'll hold it back!
Dillie, no!
Wait, I have an idea!
Stop talking, Fred. Get out of here!
WHACK
WHACK
WHACK
What are the scales of this thing made— aghh!
TRIP
FRAWWRRRR!!
If it's blind and uses its tongue to smell, then all it's going to smell is this *goblin fart stone!*
FRAWSSSSSS?!

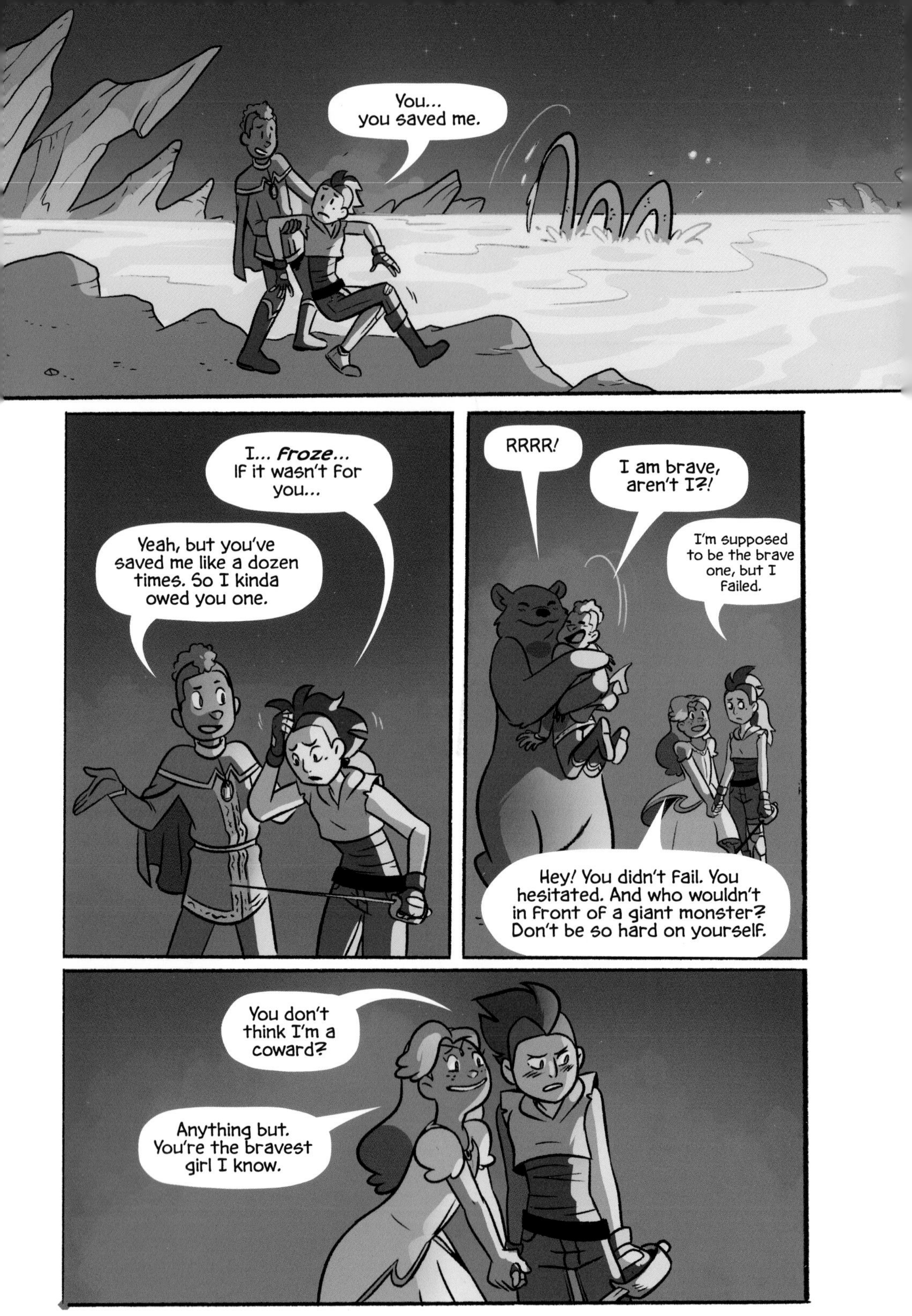
You...
you saved me.
I... *Froze*...
If it wasn't For
you...
Yeah, but you've
saved me like a dozen
times. So I kinda
owed you one.
RRRR!
I am brave,
aren't I?!
I'm supposed
to be the brave
one, but I
failed.
Hey! You didn't fail. You
hesitated. And who wouldn't
in front of a giant monster?
Don't be so hard on yourself.
You don't
think I'm a
coward?
Anything but.
You're the bravest
girl I know.

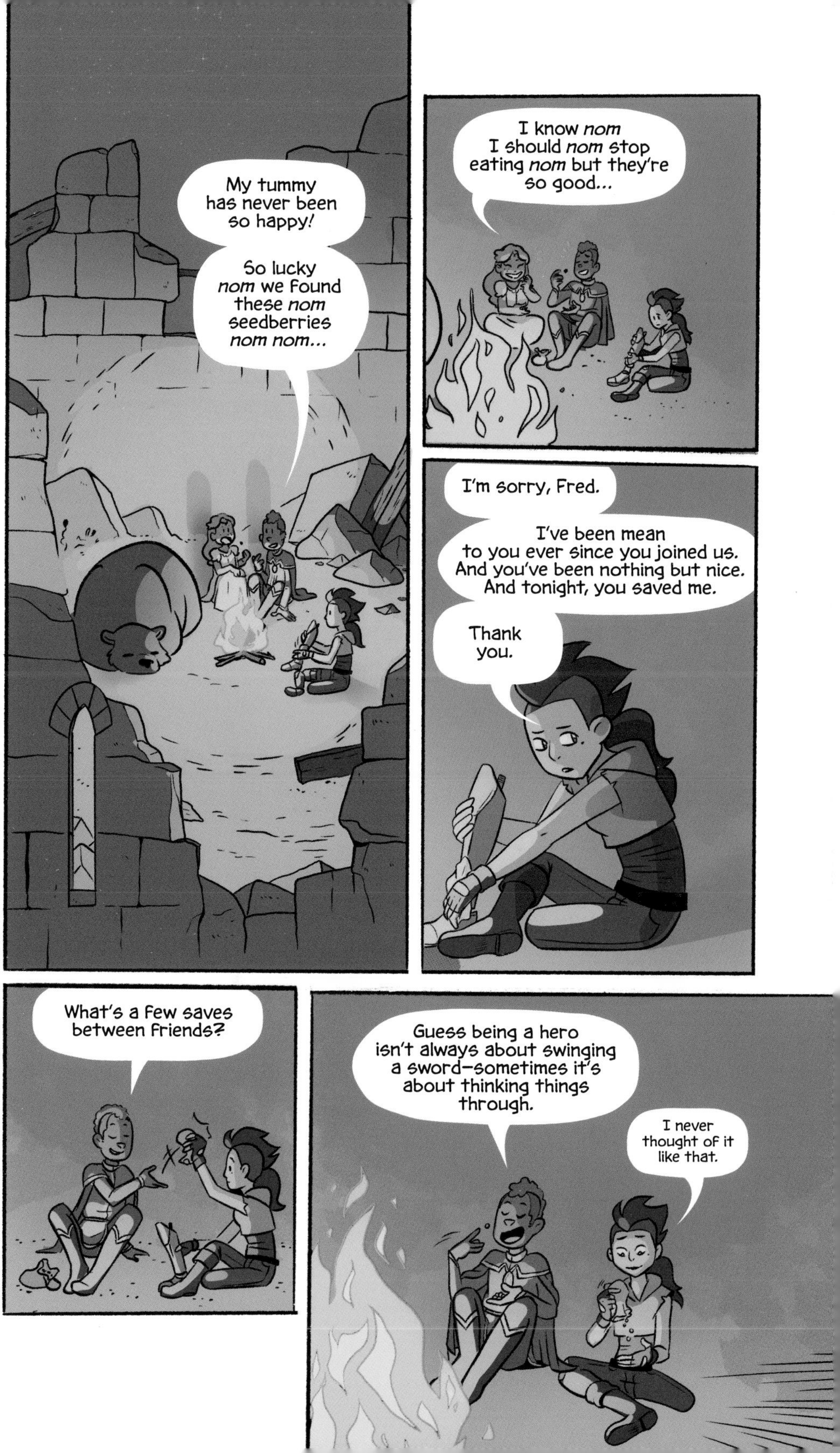
My tummy has never been so happy!
So lucky *nom* we found these *nom* seedberries *nom nom*...
I know *nom* I should *nom* stop eating *nom* but they're so good...
I'm sorry, Fred.
I've been mean to you ever since you joined us. And you've been nothing but nice. And tonight, you saved me.
Thank you.
What's a few saves between friends?
Guess being a hero isn't always about swinging a sword—sometimes it's about thinking things through.
I never thought of it like that.

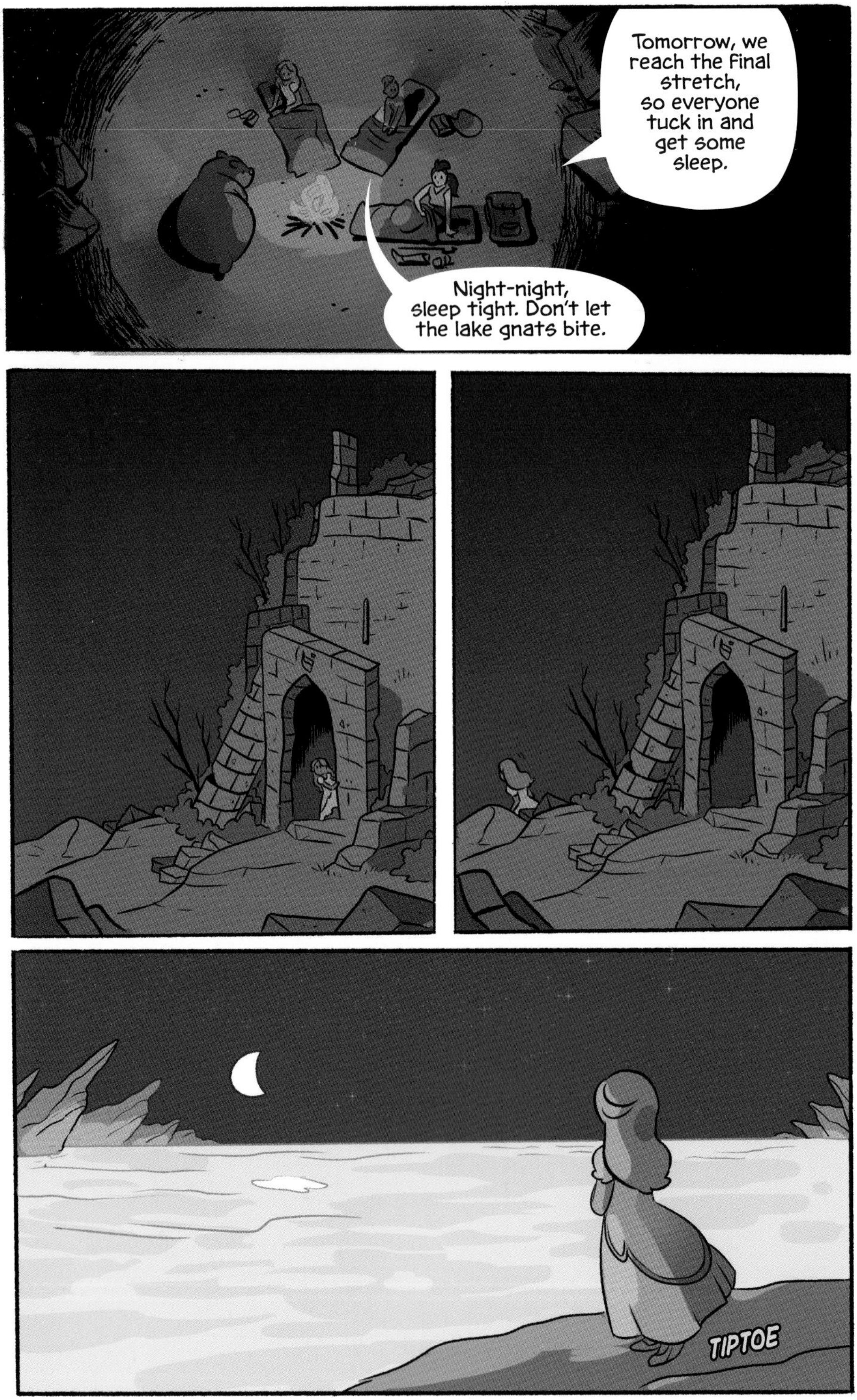
Tomorrow, we reach the final stretch, so everyone tuck in and get some sleep.
Night-night, sleep tight. Don't let the lake gnats bite.
TIPTOE

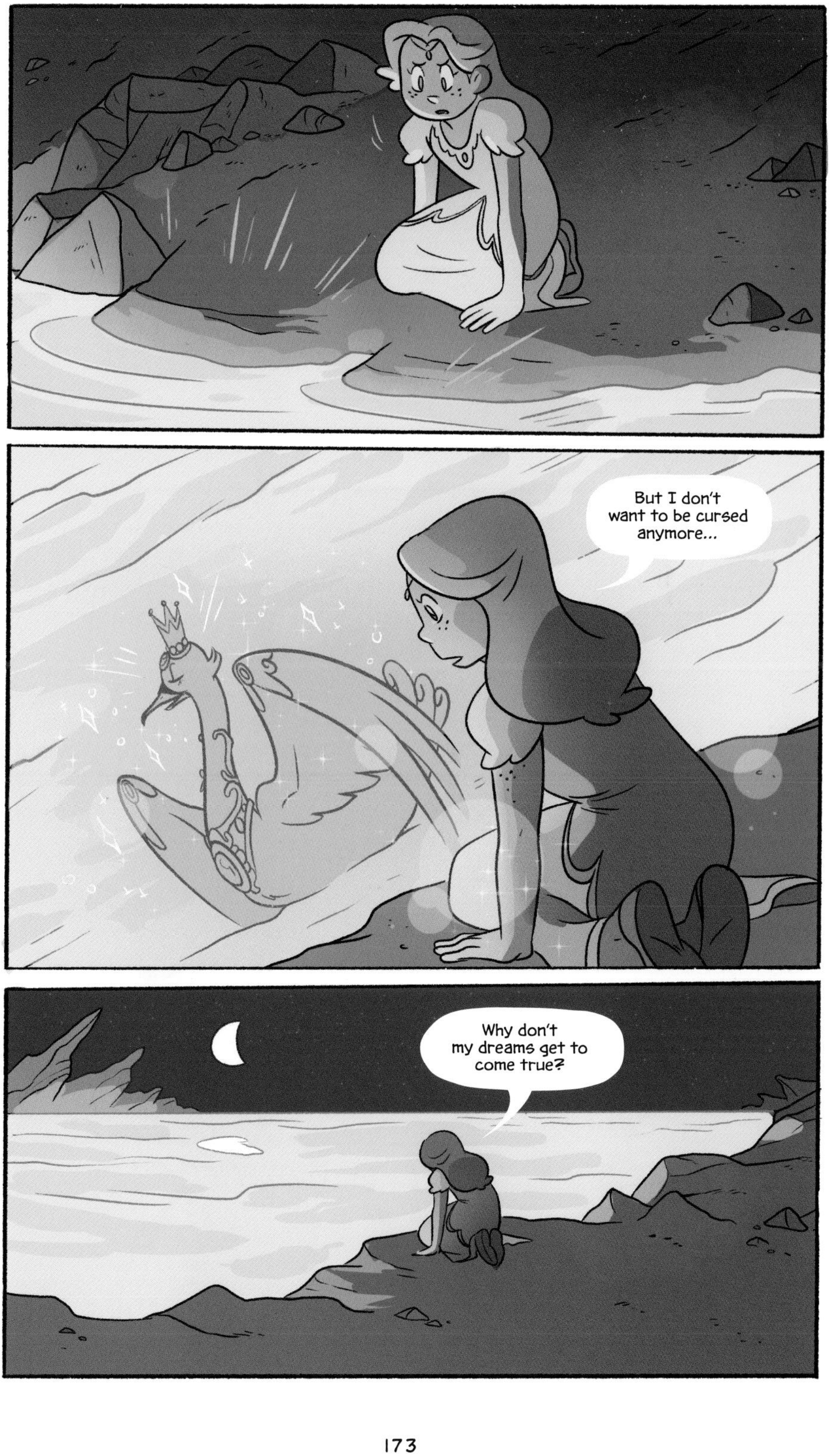
But I don't want to be cursed anymore...
Why don't my dreams get to come true?

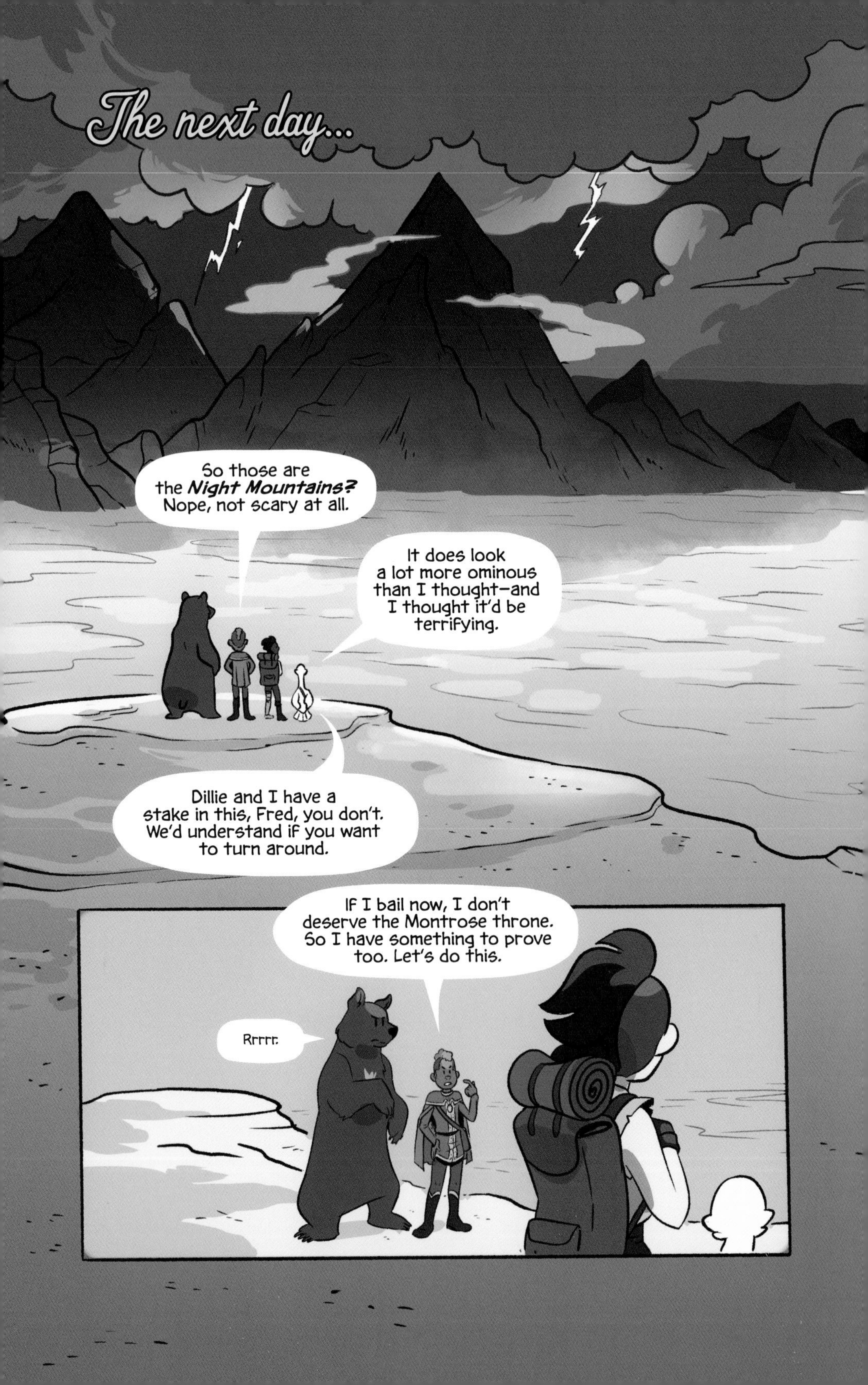
The next day...
So those are the Night Mountains? Nope, not scary at all.
It does look a lot more ominous than I thought—and I thought it'd be terrifying.
Dillie and I have a stake in this, Fred, you don't. We'd understand if you want to turn around.
If I bail now, I don't deserve the Montrose throne. So I have something to prove too. Let's do this.
Rrrrr.

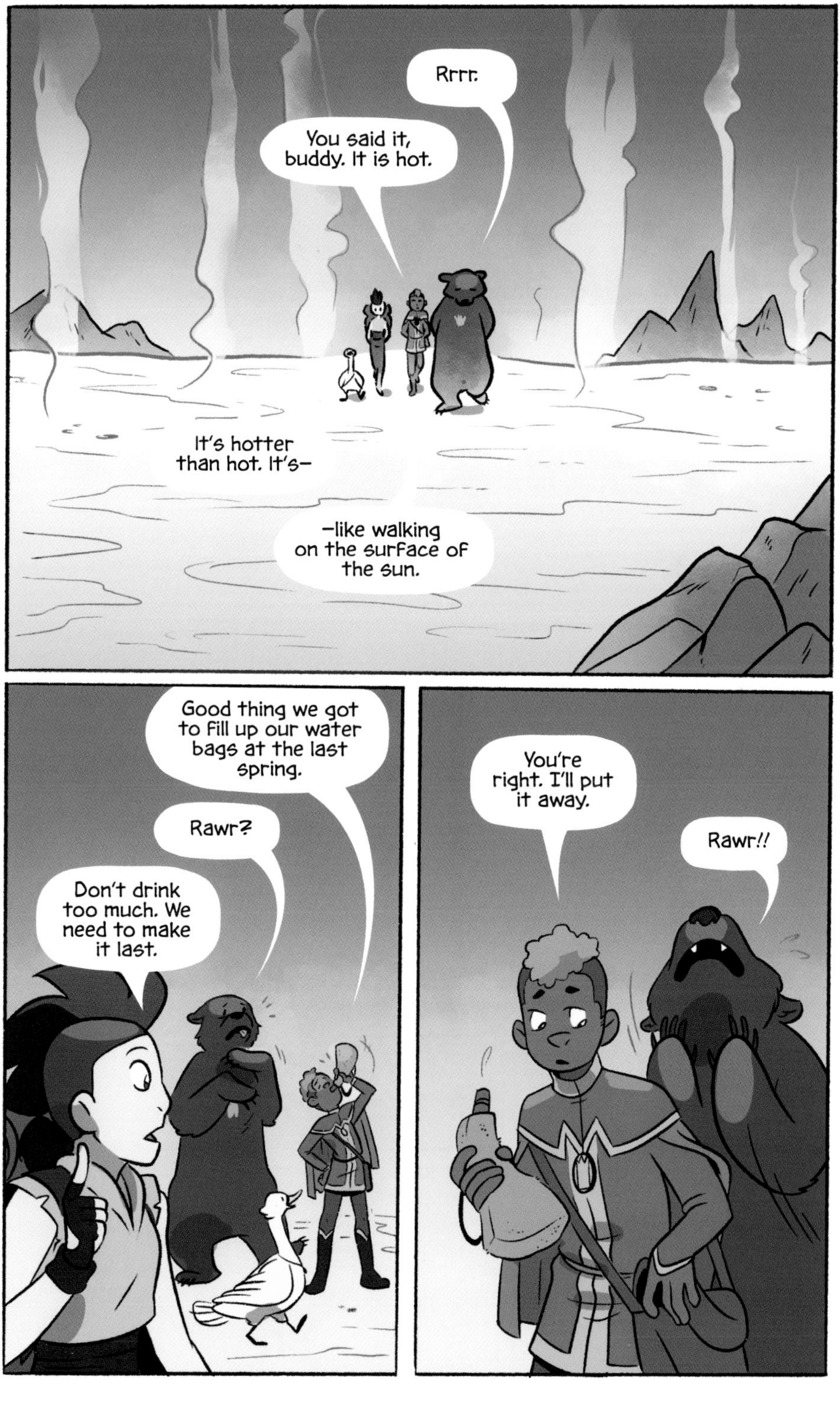

Rrrr.
You said it, buddy. It is hot.
It's hotter than hot. It's—
—like walking on the surface of the sun.
Good thing we got to fill up our water bags at the last spring.
Rawr?
Don't drink too much. We need to make it last.
You're right. I'll put it away.
Rawr!!

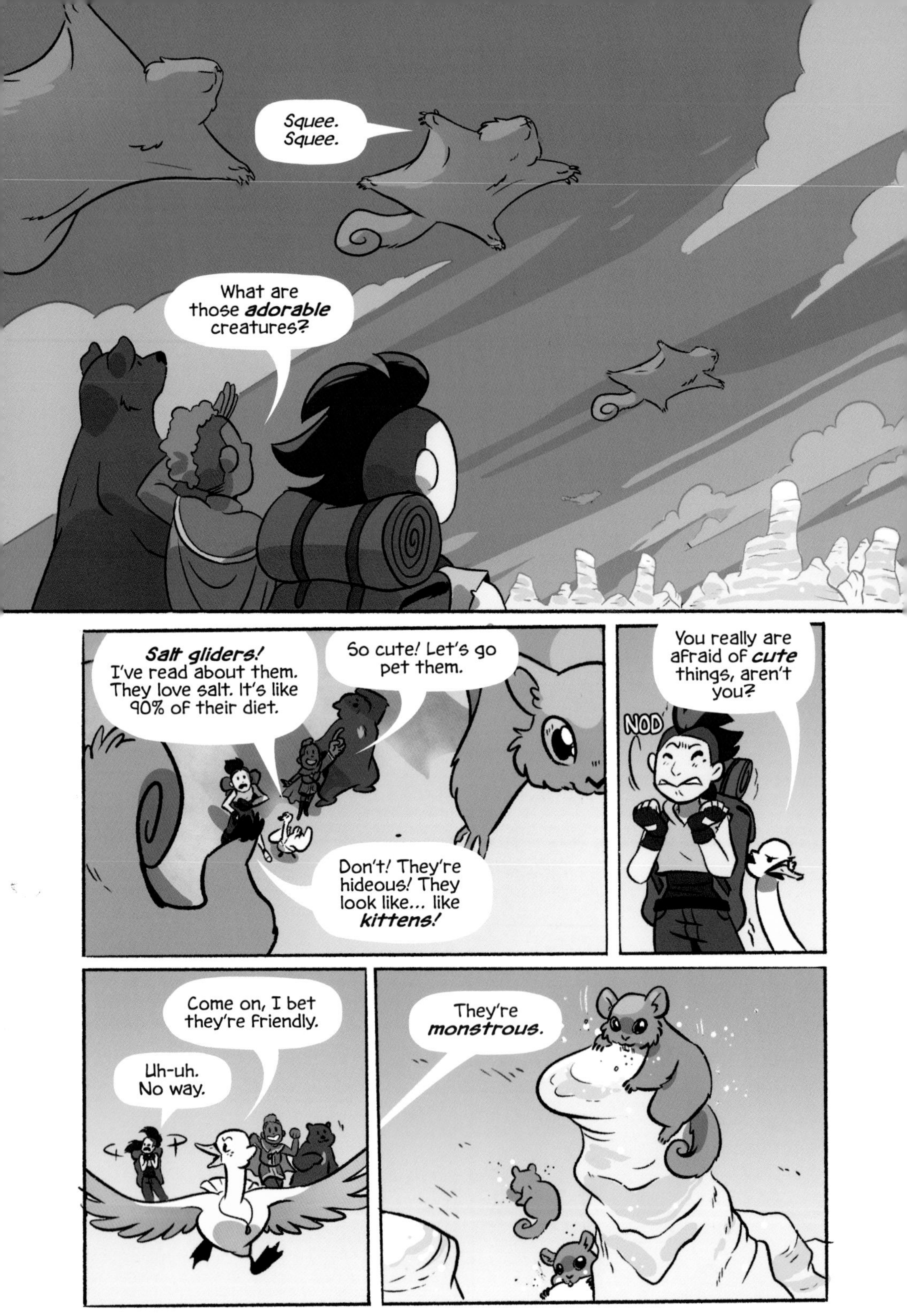
Squee.
Squee.
What are those *adorable* creatures?
Salt gliders! I've read about them. They love salt. It's like 90% of their diet.
So cute! Let's go pet them.
Don't! They're hideous! They look like... like *kittens!*
You really are afraid of *cute* things, aren't you?
NOD
Come on, I bet they're friendly.
Uh-uh. No way.
They're *monstrous.*

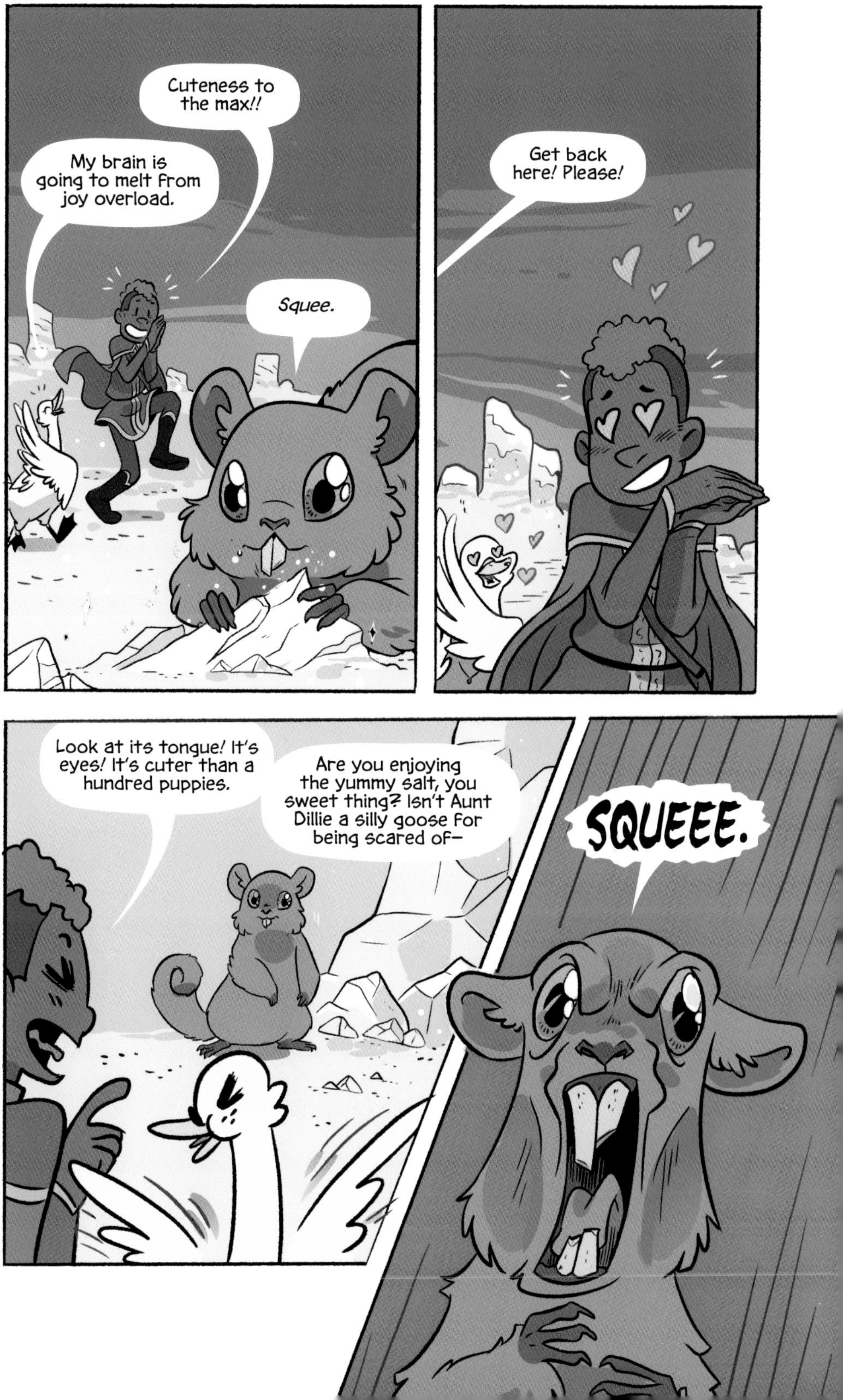

Cuteness to the max!!
My brain is going to melt from joy overload.
Squee.
Get back here! Please!
Look at its tongue! It's eyes! It's cuter than a hundred puppies.
Are you enjoying the yummy salt, you sweet thing? Isn't Aunt Dillie a silly goose for being scared of—
SQUEEE.

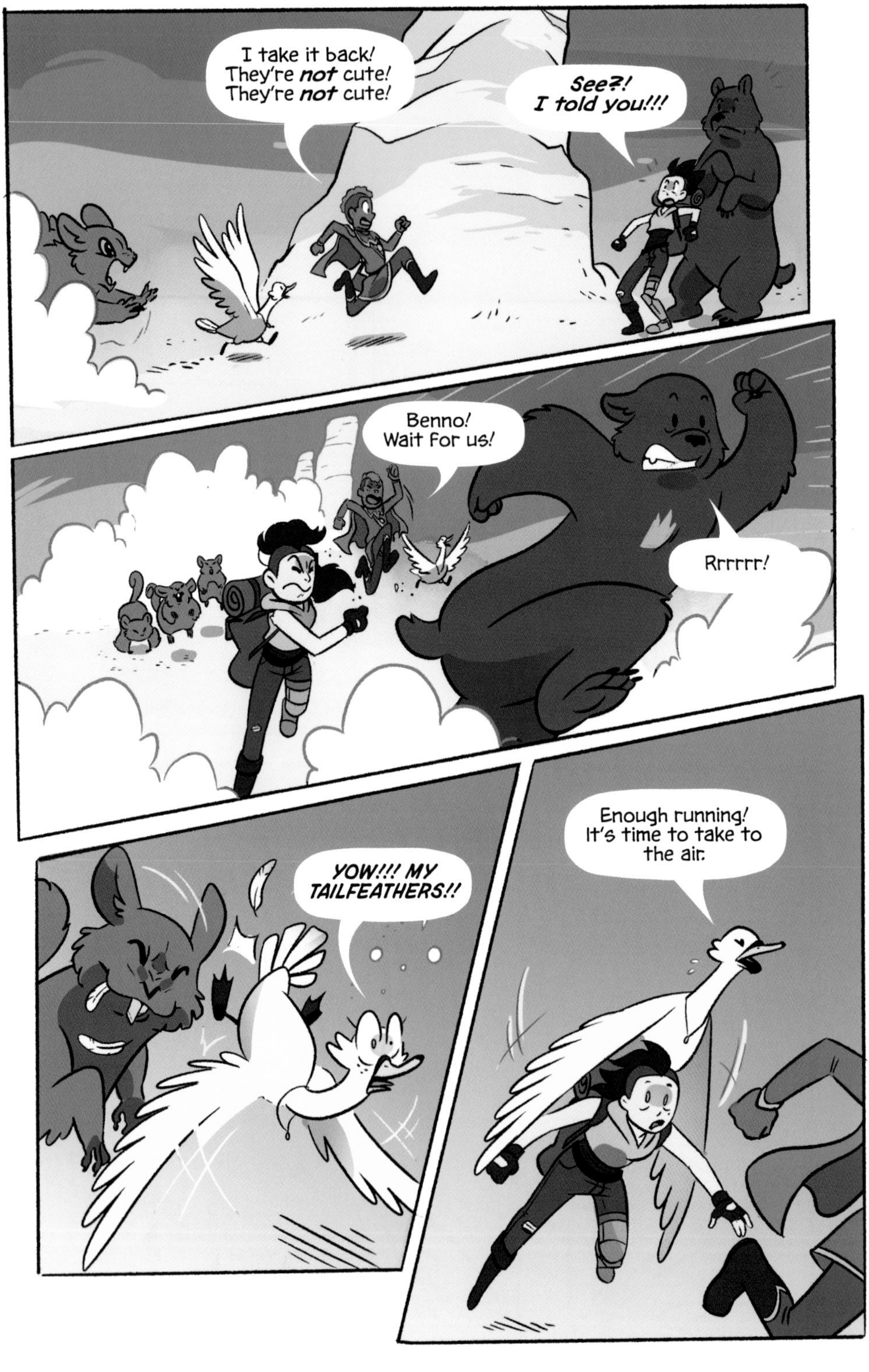
I take it back! They're ***not*** cute! They're ***not*** cute!
See?! I told you!!!
Benno! Wait for us!
Rrrrrr!
YOW!!! MY TAILFEATHERS!!
Enough running! It's time to take to the air.

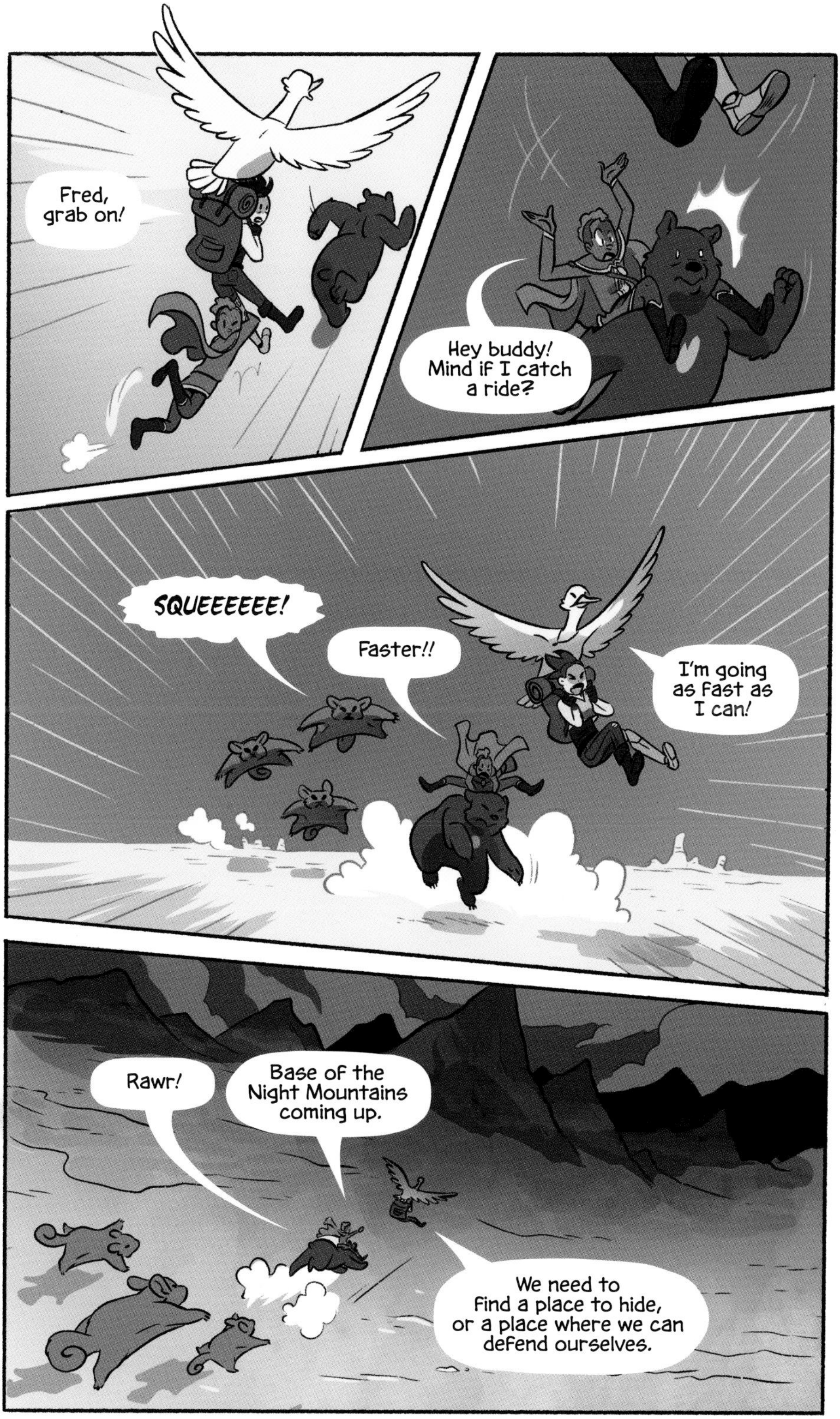
Fred, grab on!
Hey buddy! Mind if I catch a ride?
SQUEEEEEEE!
Faster!!
I'm going as fast as I can!
Rawr!
Base of the Night Mountains coming up.
We need to find a place to hide, or a place where we can defend ourselves.

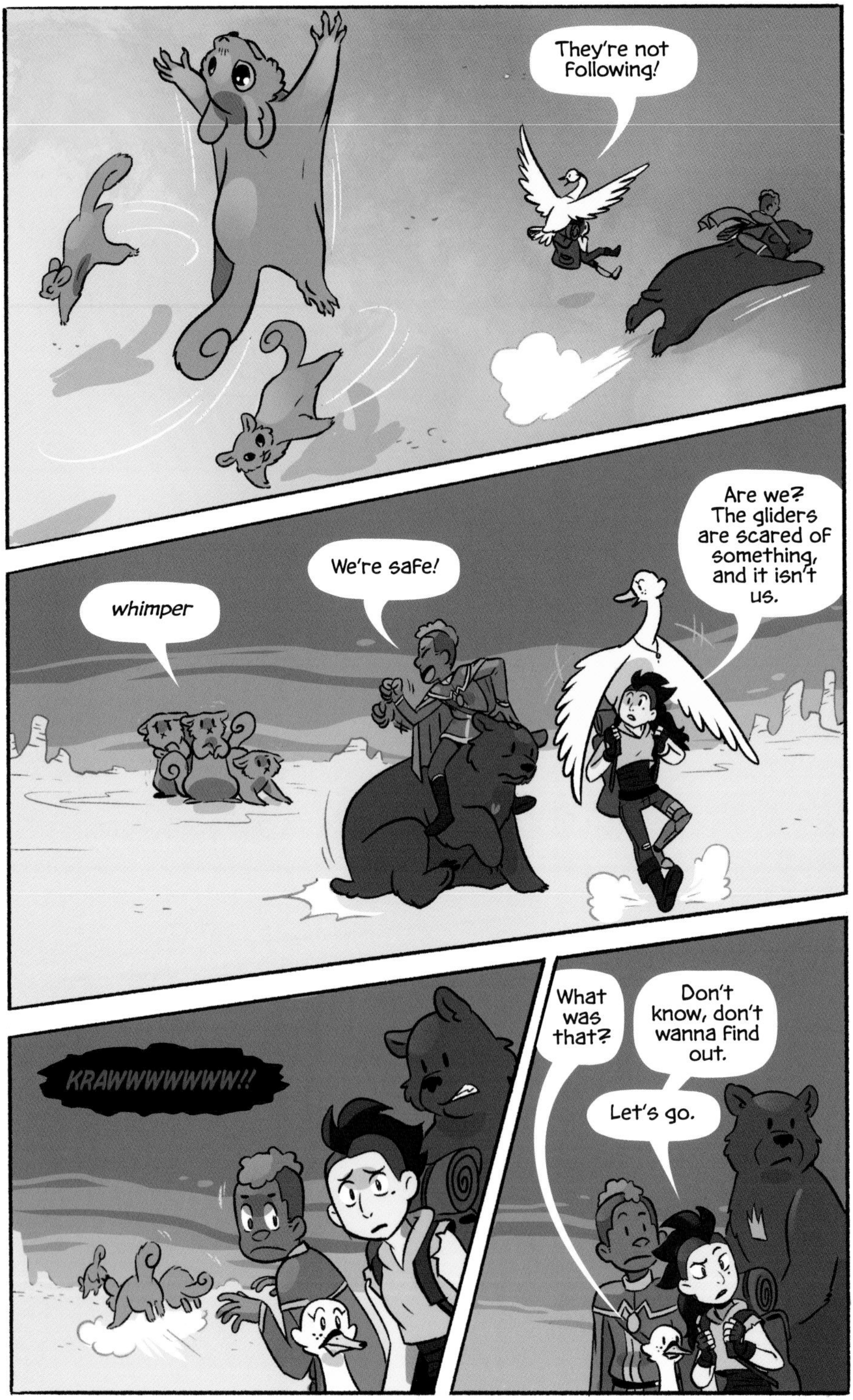
They're not following!
whimper
We're safe!
Are we? The gliders are scared of something, and it isn't us.
KRAWWWWWWW!!
What was that?
Don't know, don't wanna find out.
Let's go.

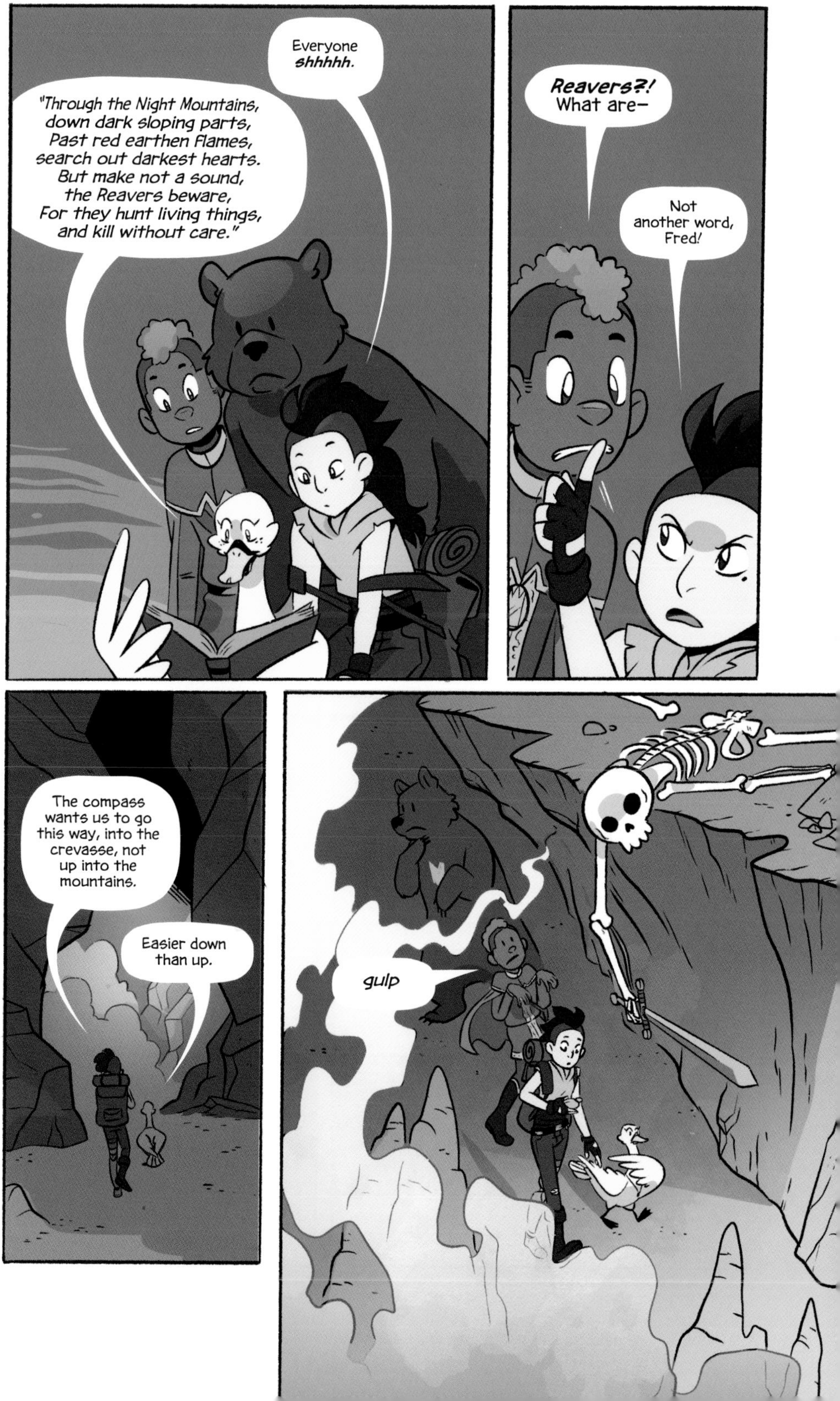
"Through the Night Mountains, down dark sloping parts, Past red earthen flames, search out darkest hearts. But make not a sound, the Reavers beware, For they hunt living things, and kill without care."
Everyone shhhhh.
Reavers?! What are–
Not another word, Fred!
The compass wants us to go this way, into the crevasse, not up into the mountains.
Easier down than up.
gulp

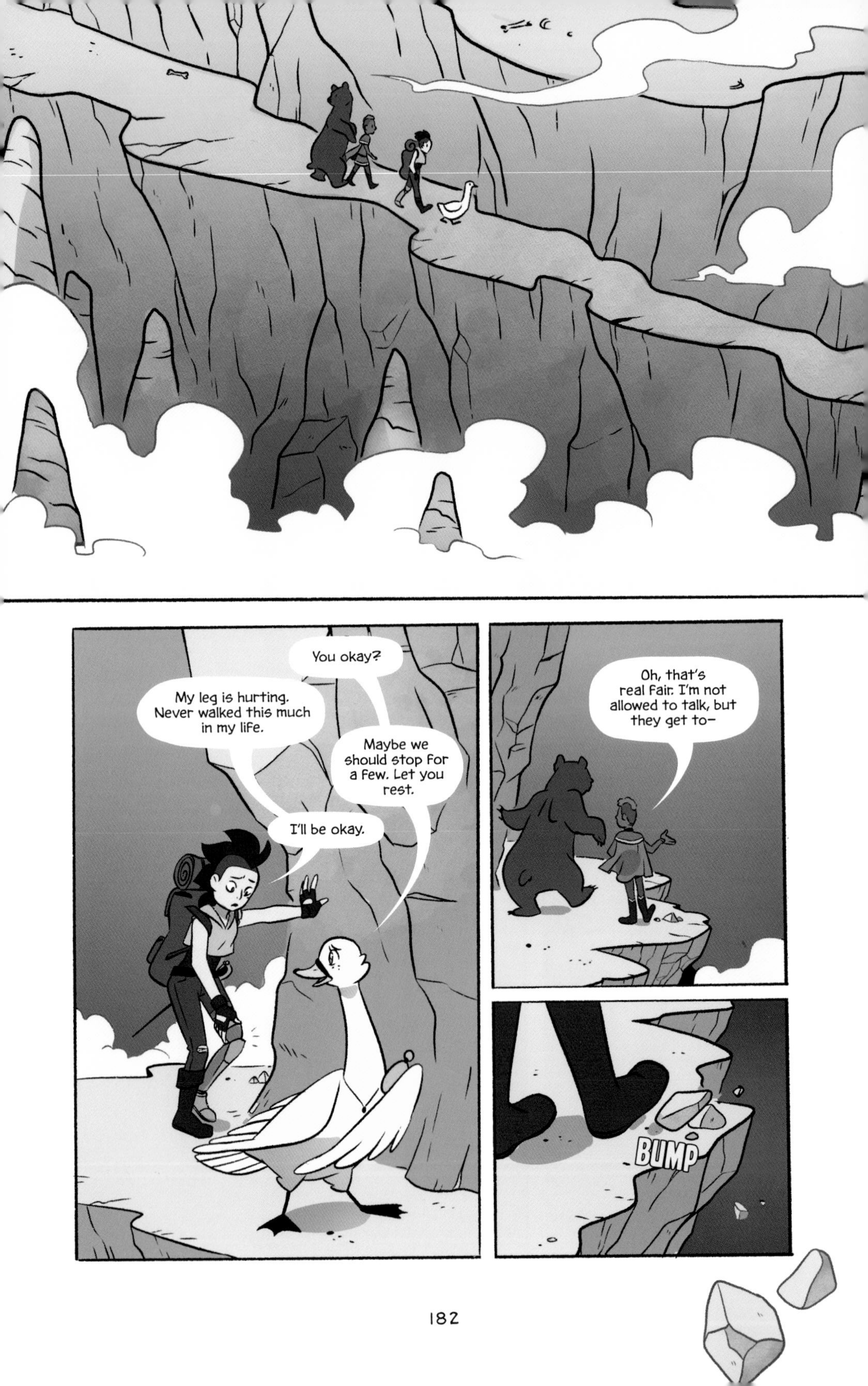
You okay?
My leg is hurting. Never walked this much in my life.
Maybe we should stop for a few. Let you rest.
I'll be okay.
Oh, that's real fair. I'm not allowed to talk, but they get to–
BUMP

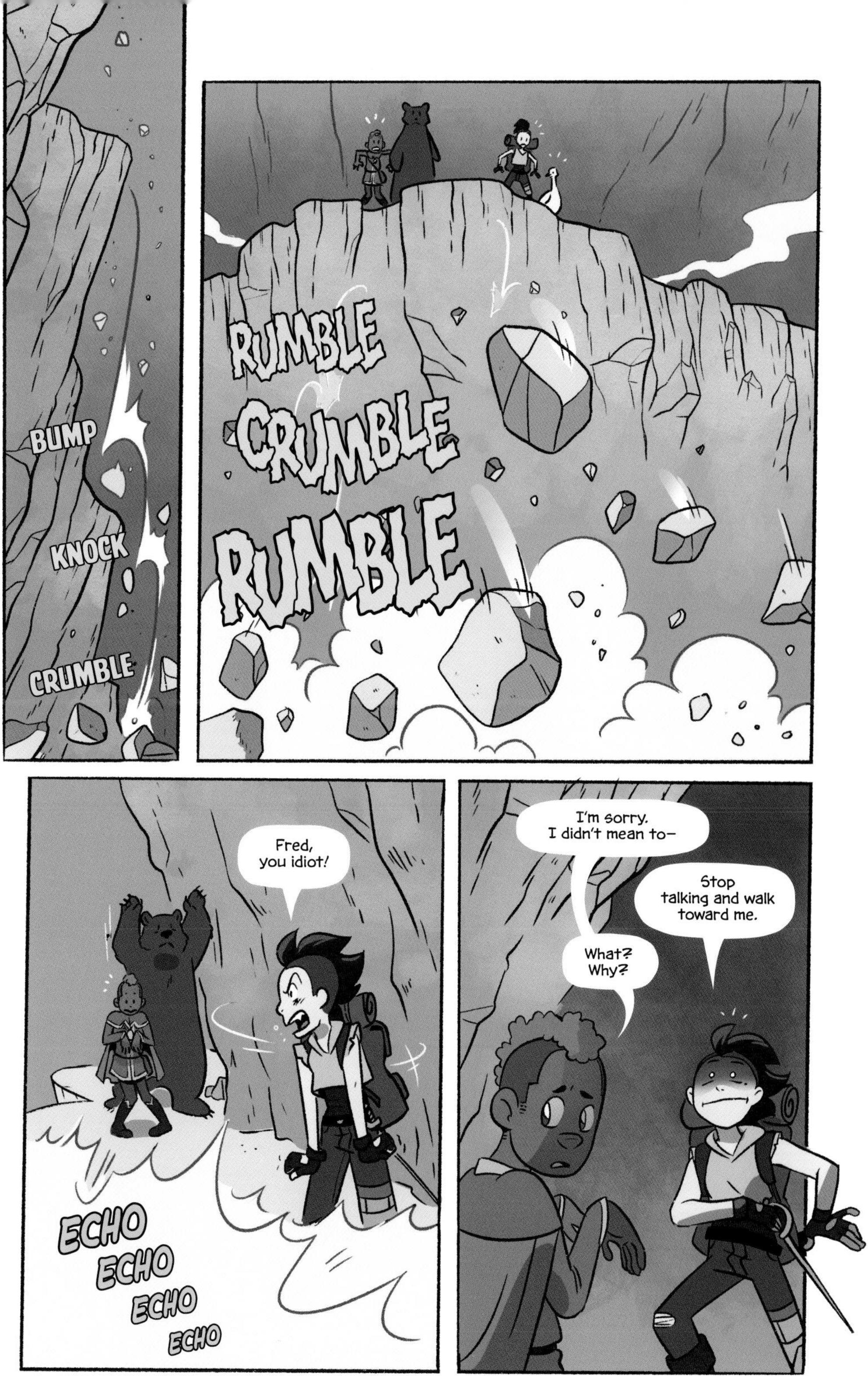
BUMP
KNOCK
CRUMBLE
RUMBLE
CRUMBLE
RUMBLE
Fred, you idiot!
ECHO
ECHO
ECHO
ECHO
I'm sorry. I didn't mean to—
What? Why?
Stop talking and walk toward me.

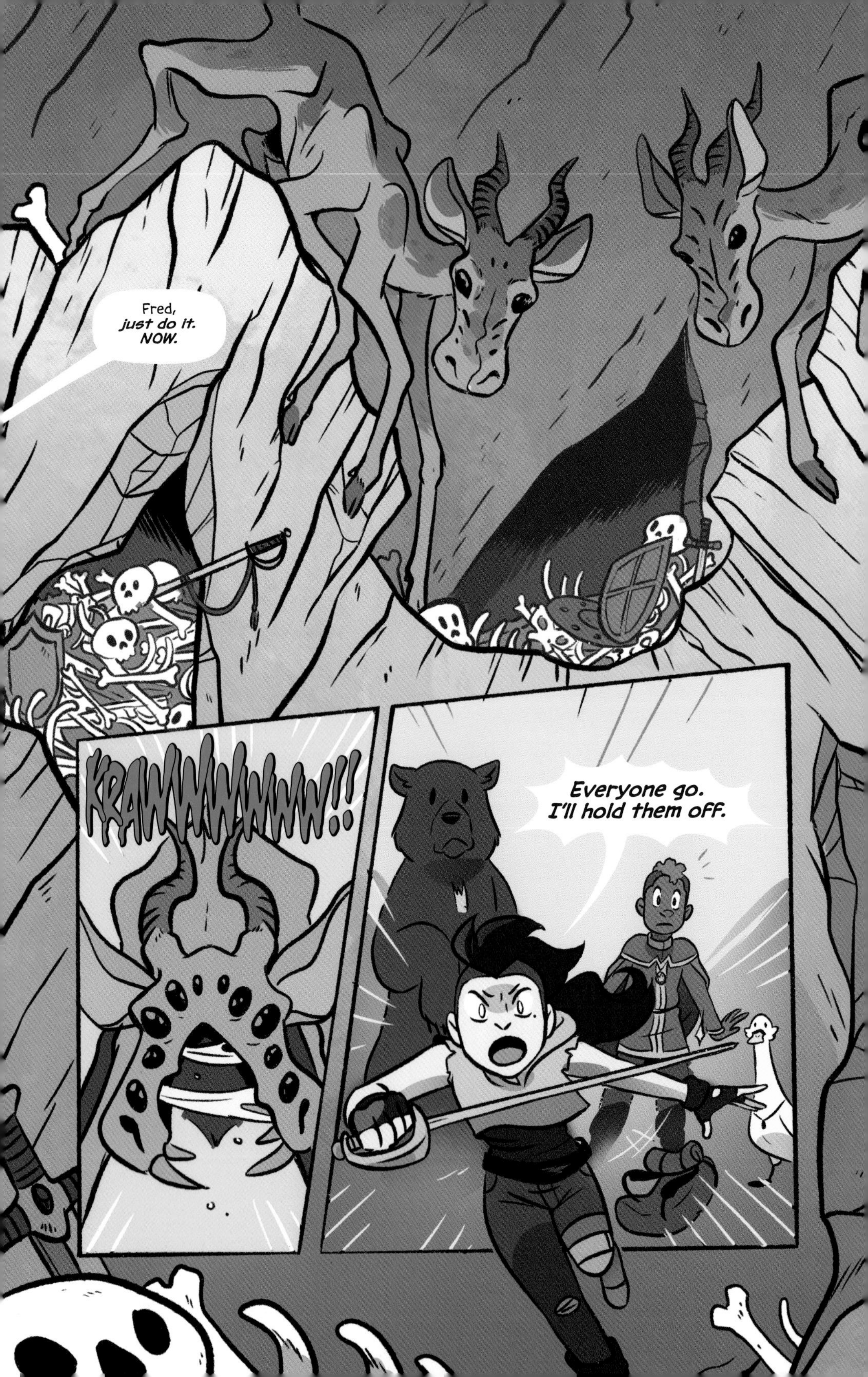
Fred,
just do it.
NOW.
KRAWWWWWWW!!
Everyone go.
I'll hold them off.

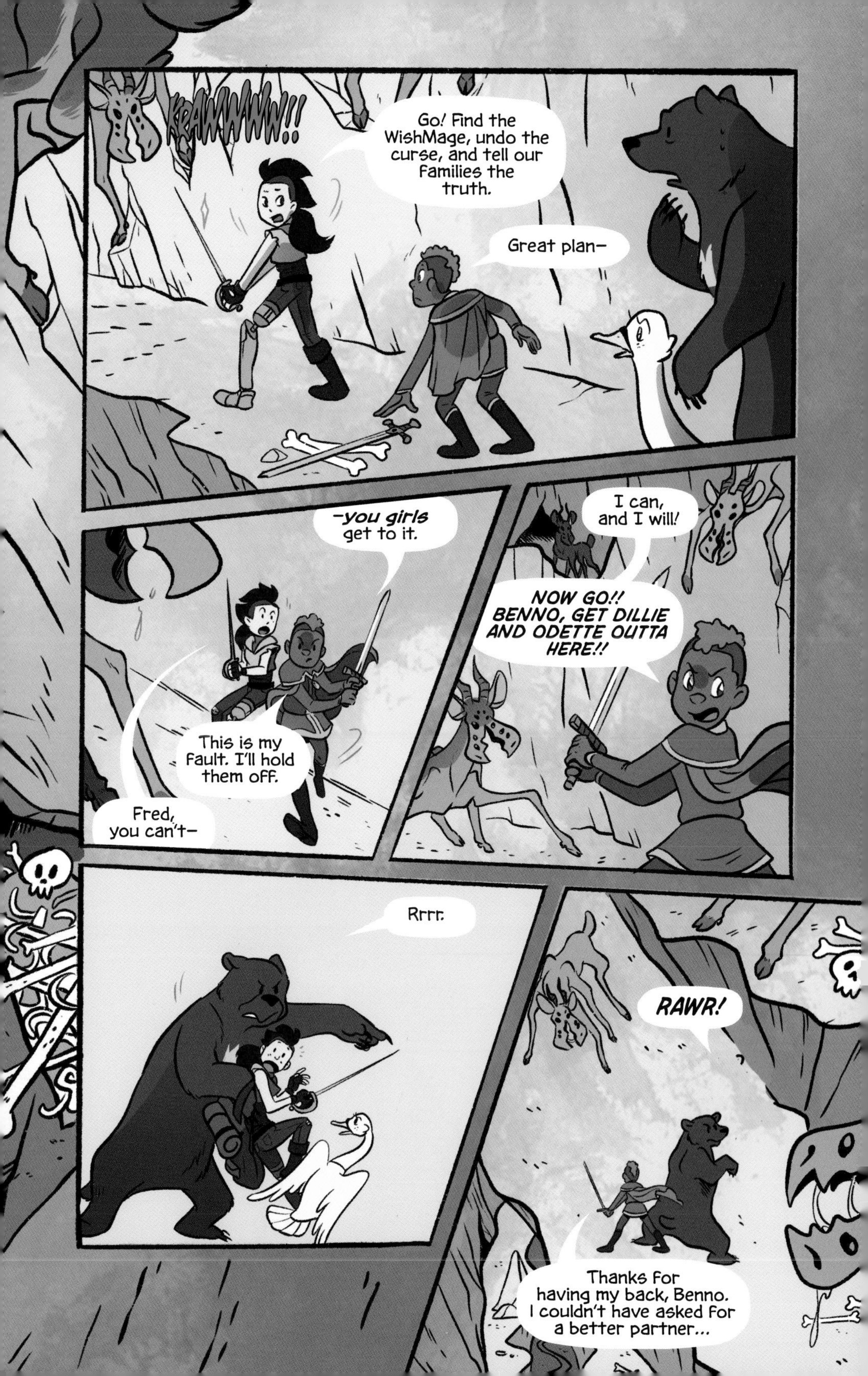
KRAWWWW!!
Go! Find the WishMage, undo the curse, and tell our families the truth.
Great plan–
–*you girls* get to it.
This is my fault. I'll hold them off.
Fred, you can't–
I can, and I will!
NOW GO!! BENNO, GET DILLIE AND ODETTE OUTTA HERE!!
Rrrr.
RAWR!
Thanks for having my back, Benno. I couldn't have asked for a better partner...

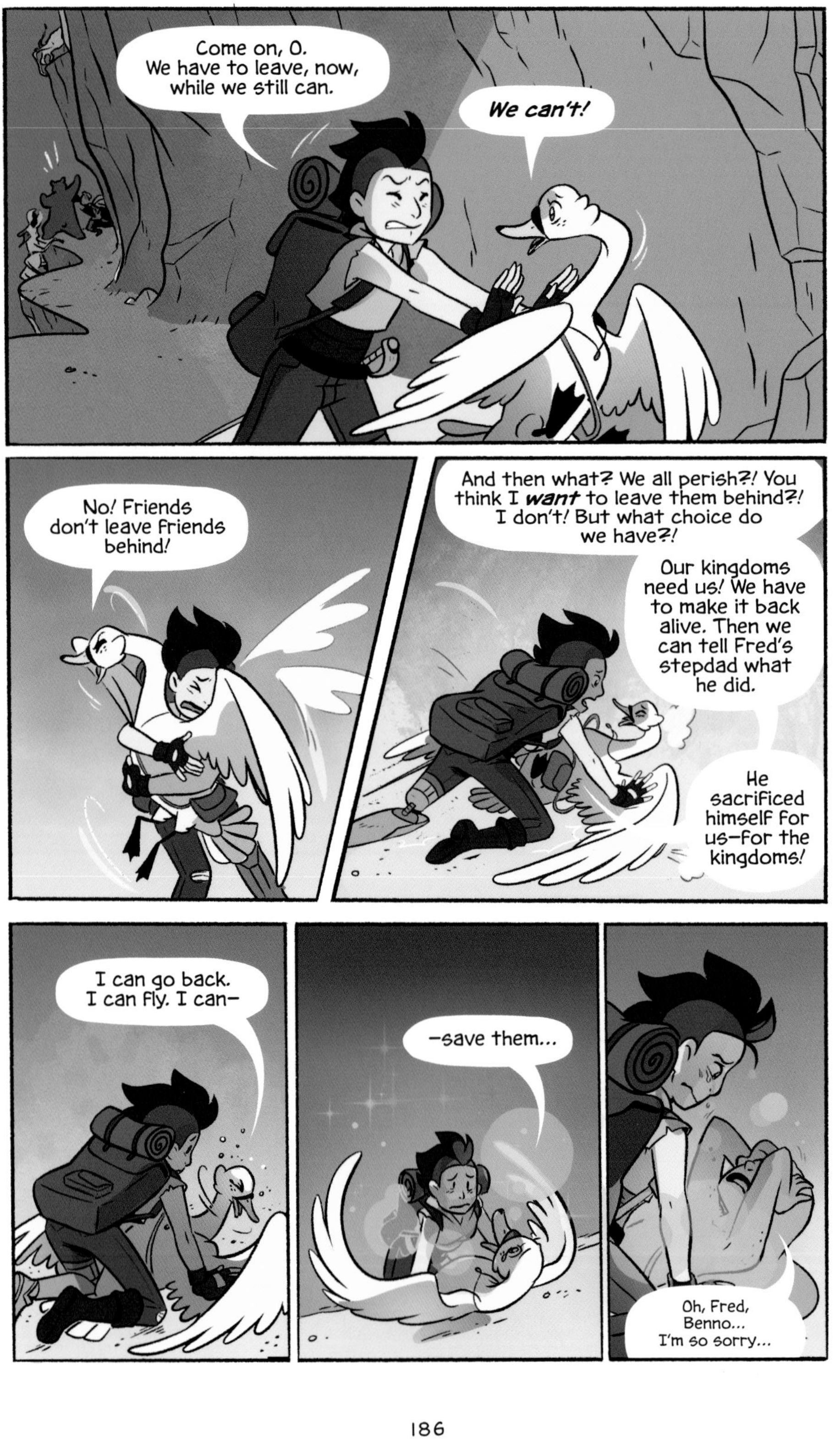
Come on, O. We have to leave, now, while we still can.
We can't!
No! Friends don't leave friends behind!
And then what? We all perish?! You think I *want* to leave them behind?! I don't! But what choice do we have?!
Our kingdoms need us! We have to make it back alive. Then we can tell Fred's stepdad what he did.
He sacrificed himself for us—for the kingdoms!
I can go back. I can fly. I can—
—save them...
Oh, Fred, Benno... I'm so sorry...

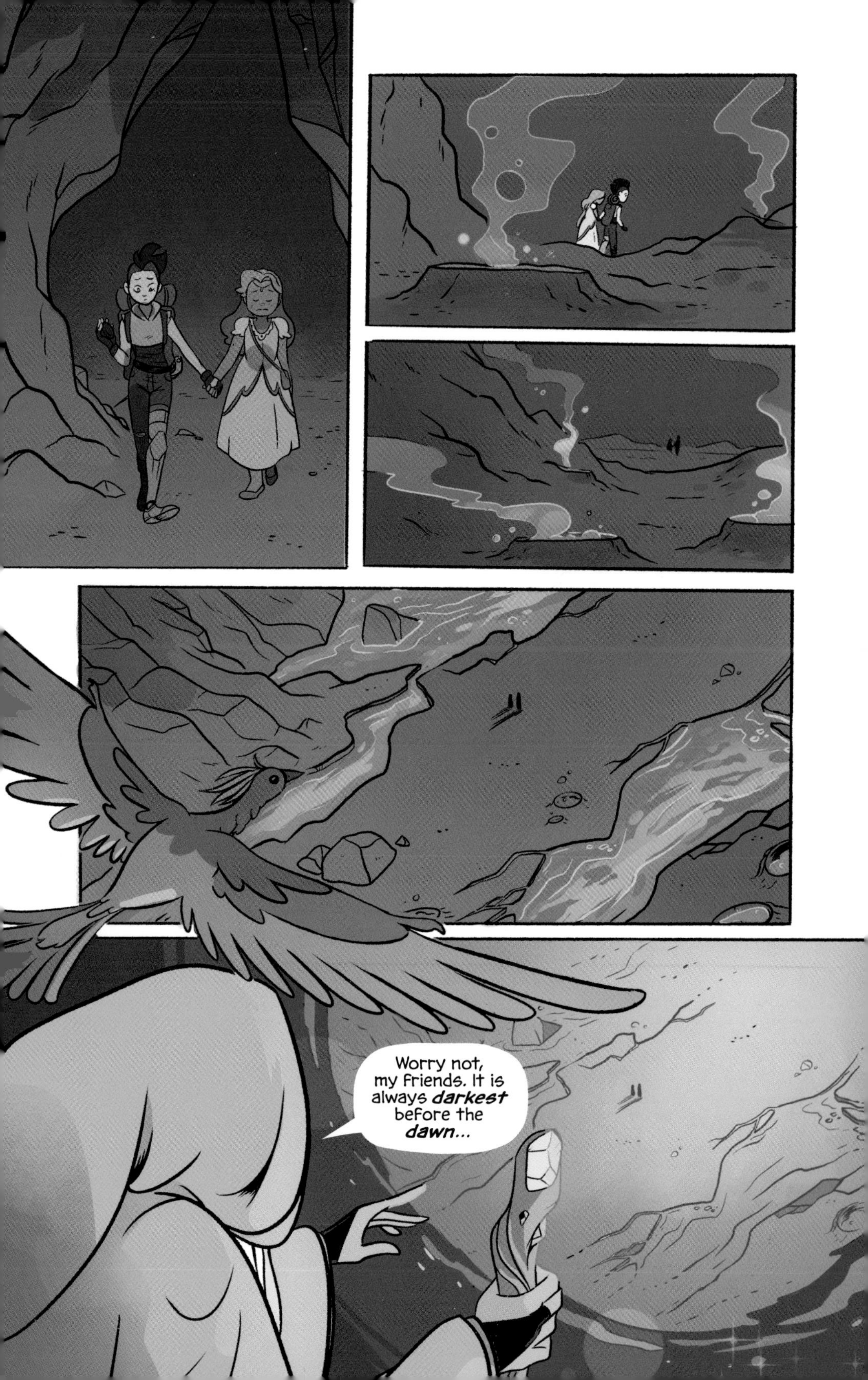
Worry not, my friends. It is always **darkest** before the **dawn**...

PART III

MONTROSE

SALT SAND FLATS

THE NIGHT
MOUNTAINS

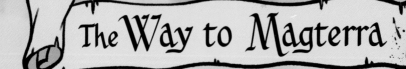

The Way to Magterra

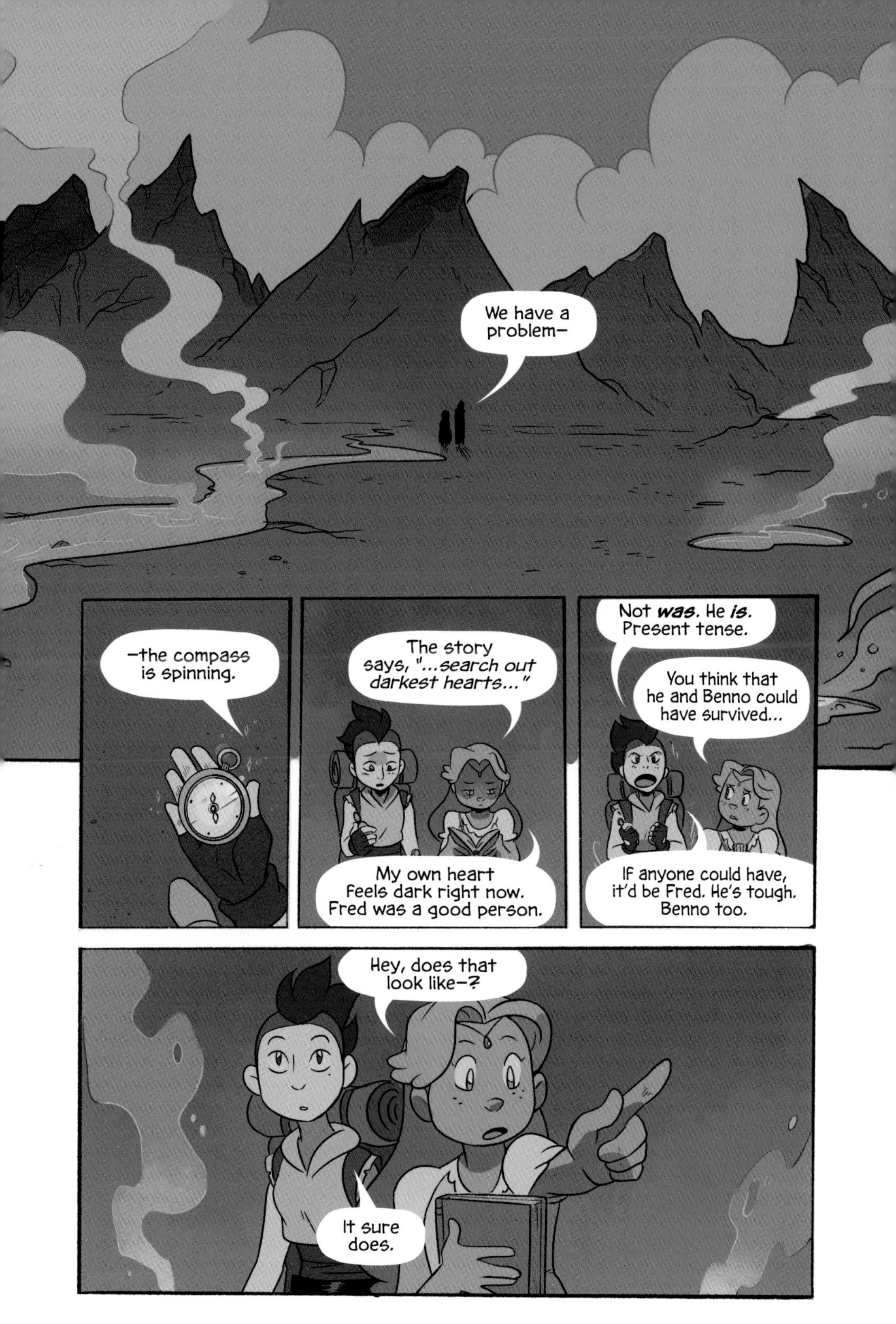
We have a problem—
—the compass is spinning.
The story says, "...search out darkest hearts..."
My own heart feels dark right now. Fred was a good person.
Not *was.* He *is.* Present tense.
You think that he and Benno could have survived...
If anyone could have, it'd be Fred. He's tough. Benno too.
Hey, does that look like—?
It sure does.

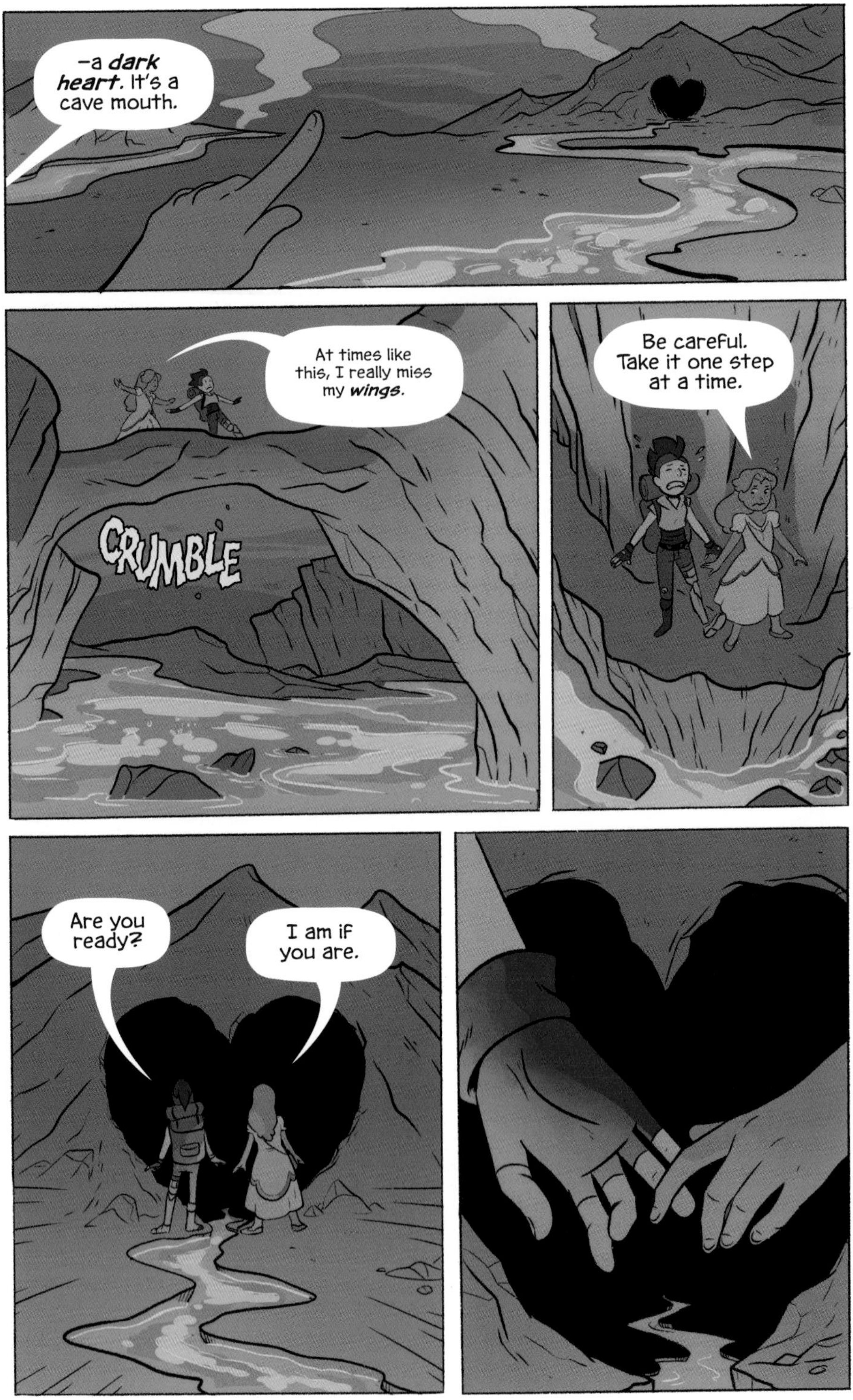
–a **dark heart**. It's a cave mouth.
At times like this, I really miss my **wings**.
CRUMBLE
Be careful. Take it one step at a time.
Are you ready?
I am if you are.

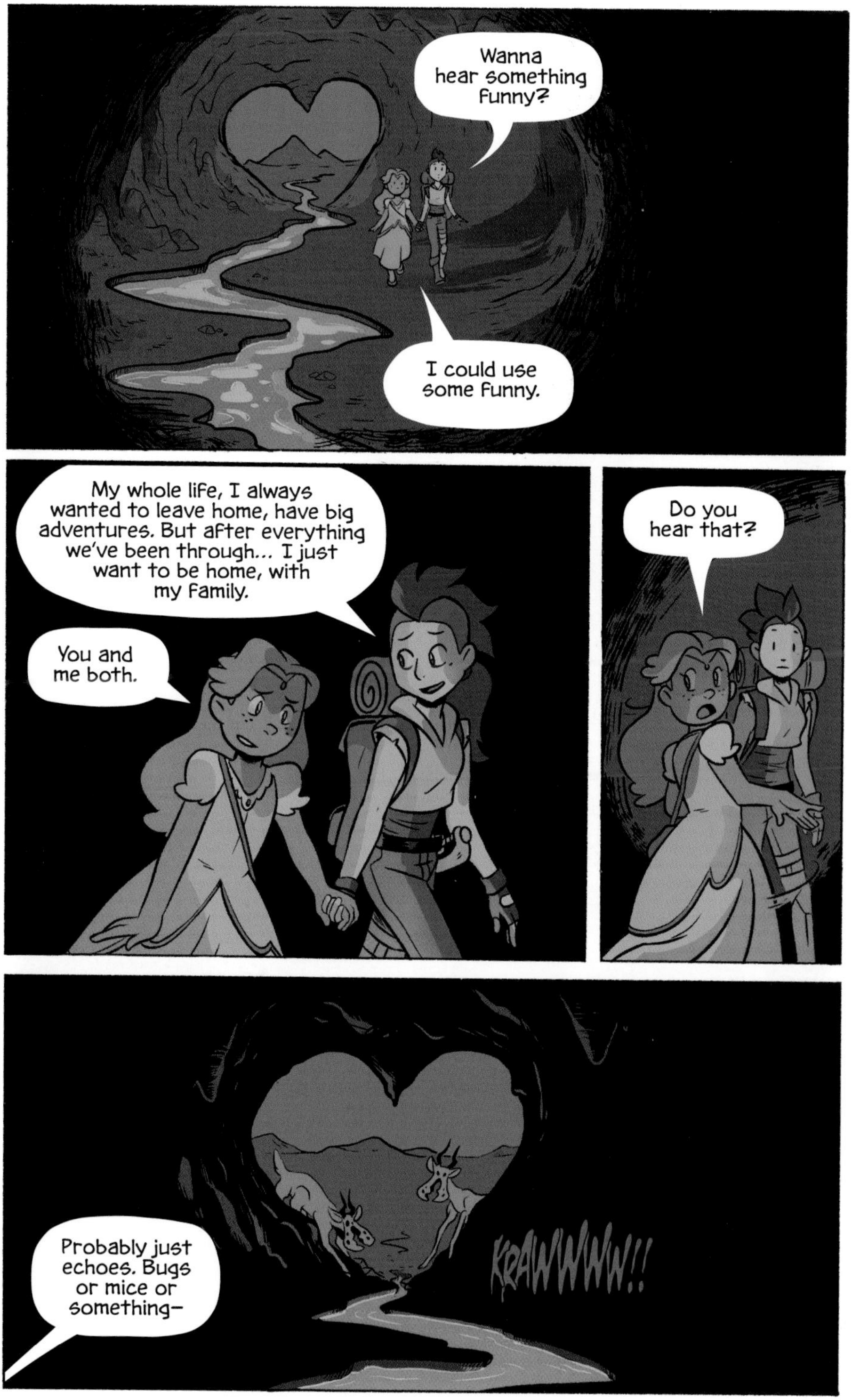
Wanna hear something funny?
I could use some funny.
My whole life, I always wanted to leave home, have big adventures. But after everything we've been through... I just want to be home, with my family.
You and me both.
Do you hear that?
Probably just echoes. Bugs or mice or something–
KRAWWWW!!

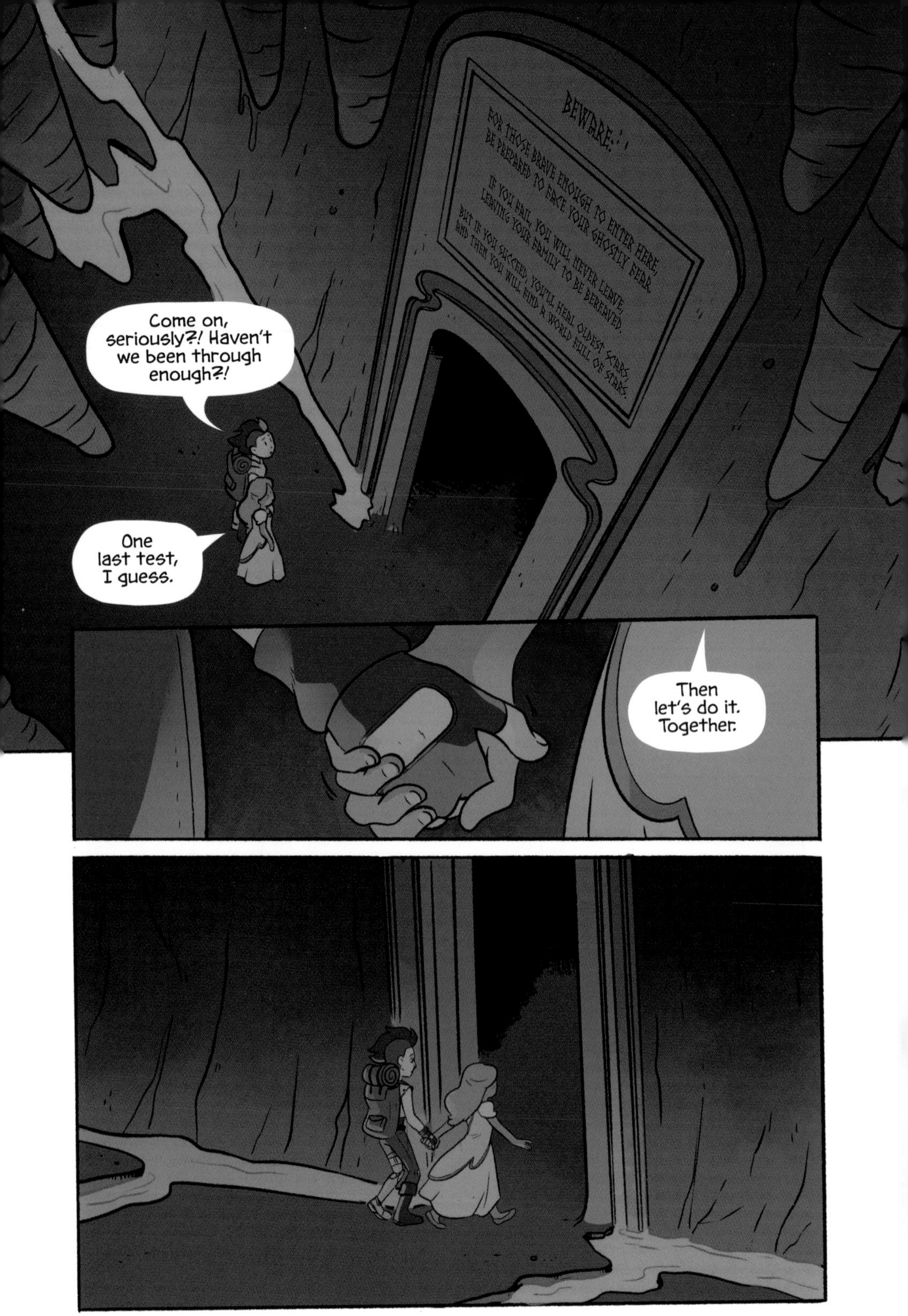
BEWARE:
FOR THOSE BRAVE ENOUGH TO ENTER HERE,
BE PREPARED TO FACE YOUR GHOSTLY FEAR.
IF YOU FAIL, YOU WILL NEVER LEAVE,
LEAVING YOUR FAMILY TO BE BEREAVED.
BUT IF YOU SUCCEED, YOU'LL HEAL OLDEST SCARS,
AND THEN YOU WILL FIND A WORLD FULL OF STARS.
Come on, seriously?! Haven't we been through enough?!
One last test, I guess.
Then let's do it. Together.

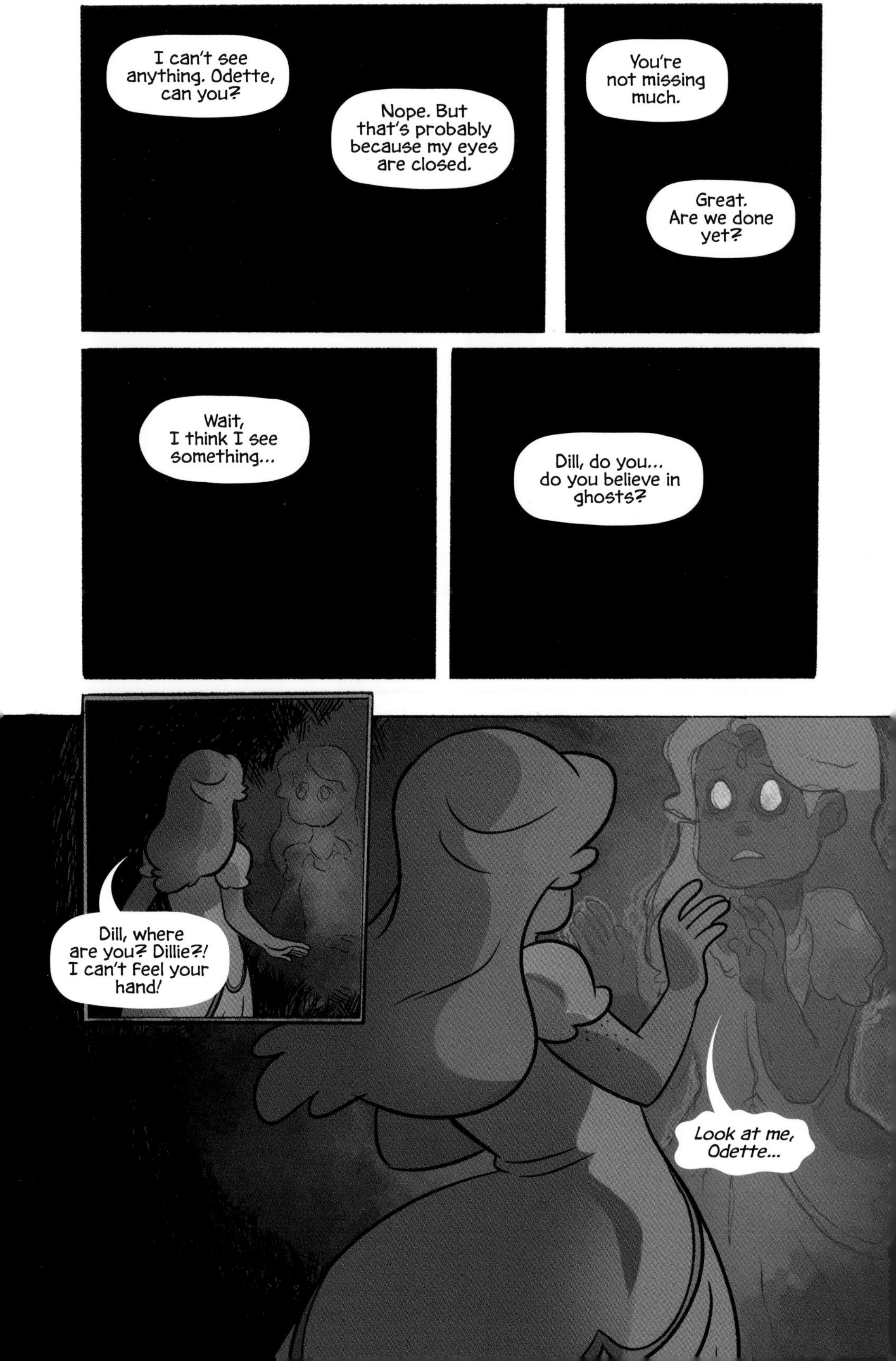
I can't see anything. Odette, can you?
Nope. But that's probably because my eyes are closed.
You're not missing much.
Great. Are we done yet?
Wait, I think I see something...
Dill, do you... do you believe in ghosts?
Dill, where are you? Dillie?! I can't feel your hand!
Look at me, Odette...

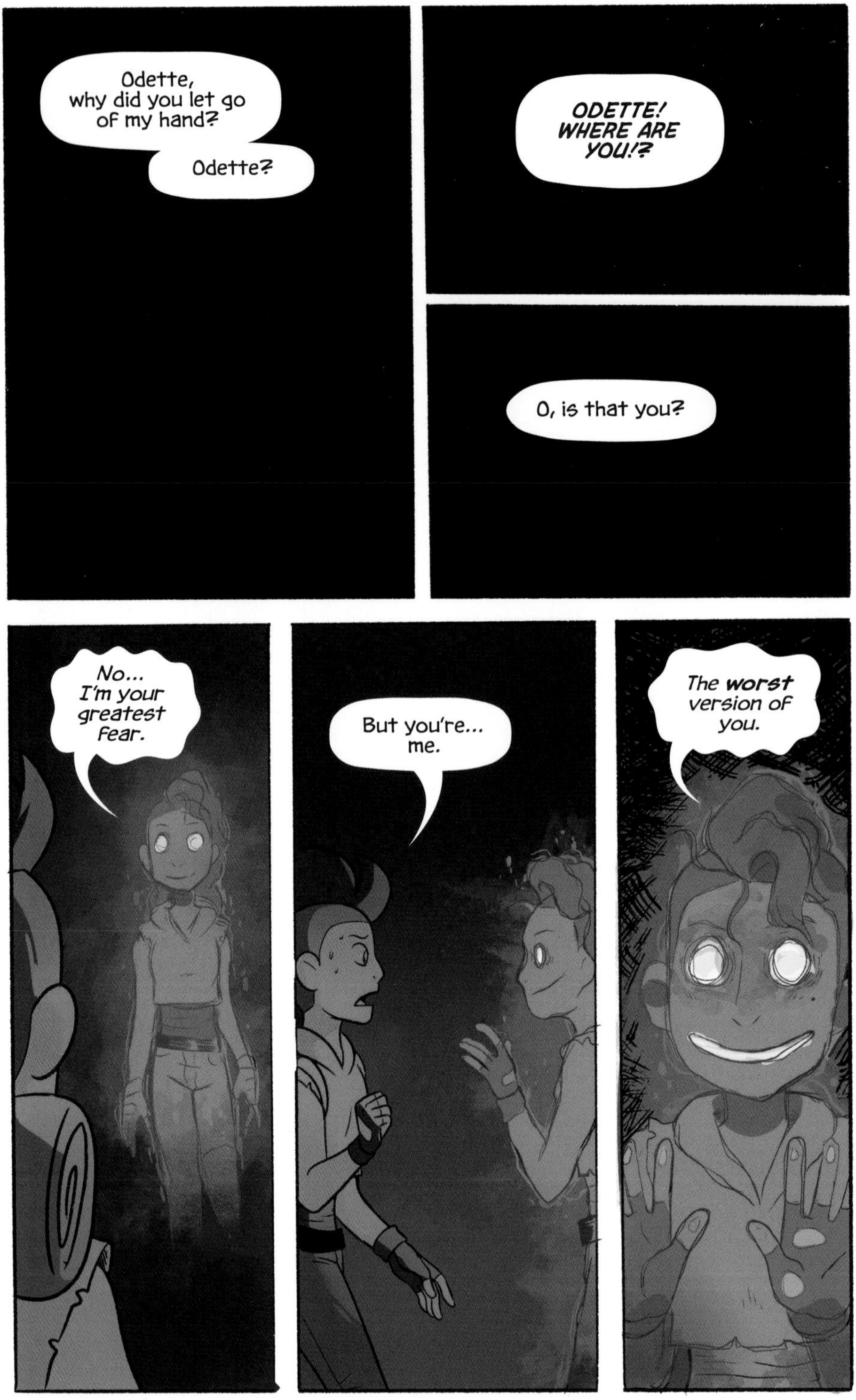
Odette, why did you let go of my hand?
Odette?
ODETTE! WHERE ARE YOU!?
O, is that you?
No... I'm your greatest fear.
But you're... me.
The **worst** version of you.

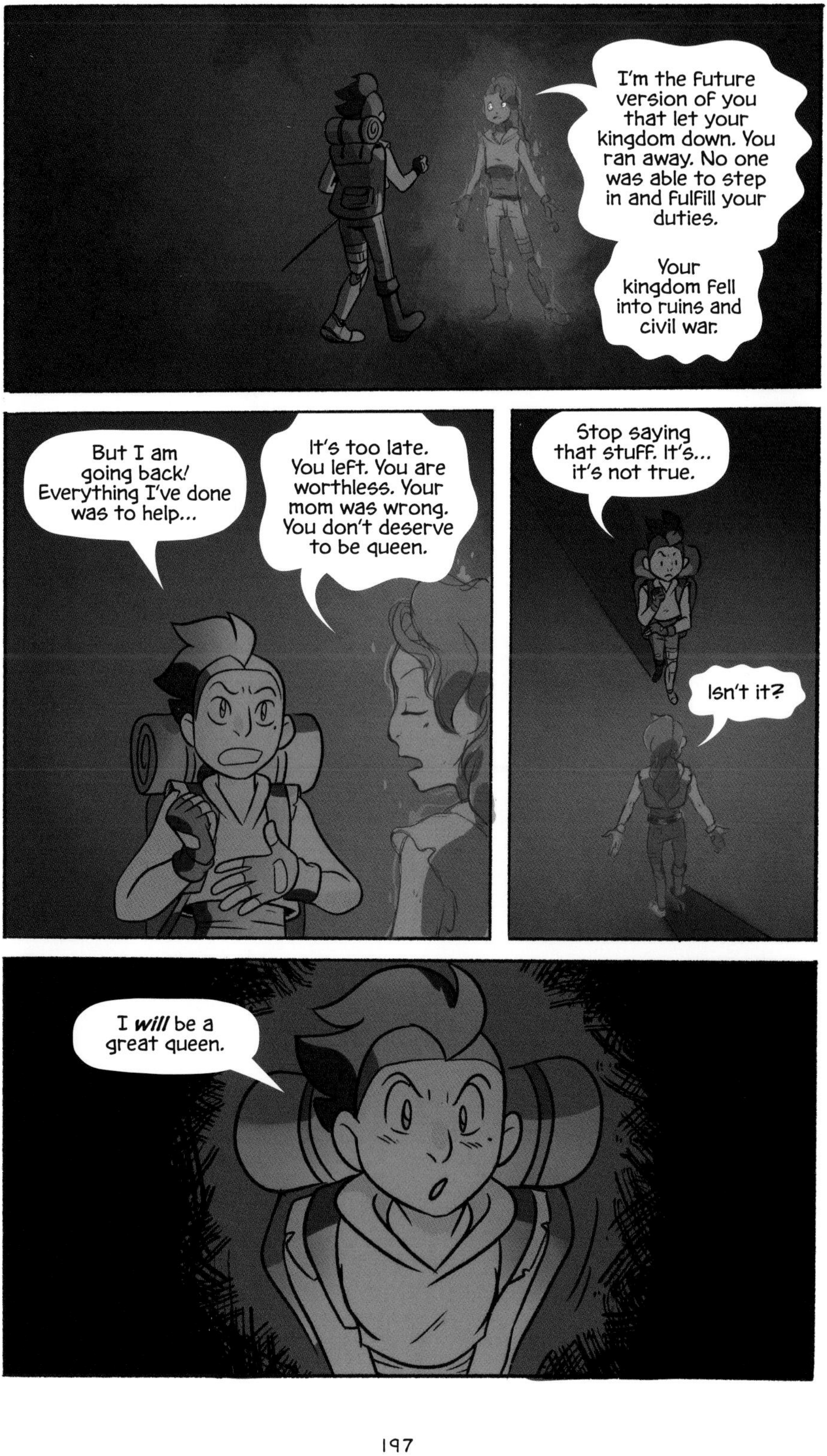
I'm the future version of you that let your kingdom down. You ran away. No one was able to step in and fulfill your duties.
Your kingdom fell into ruins and civil war.
But I am going back! Everything I've done was to help...
It's too late. You left. You are worthless. Your mom was wrong. You don't deserve to be queen.
Stop saying that stuff. It's... it's not true.
Isn't it?
I *will* be a great queen.

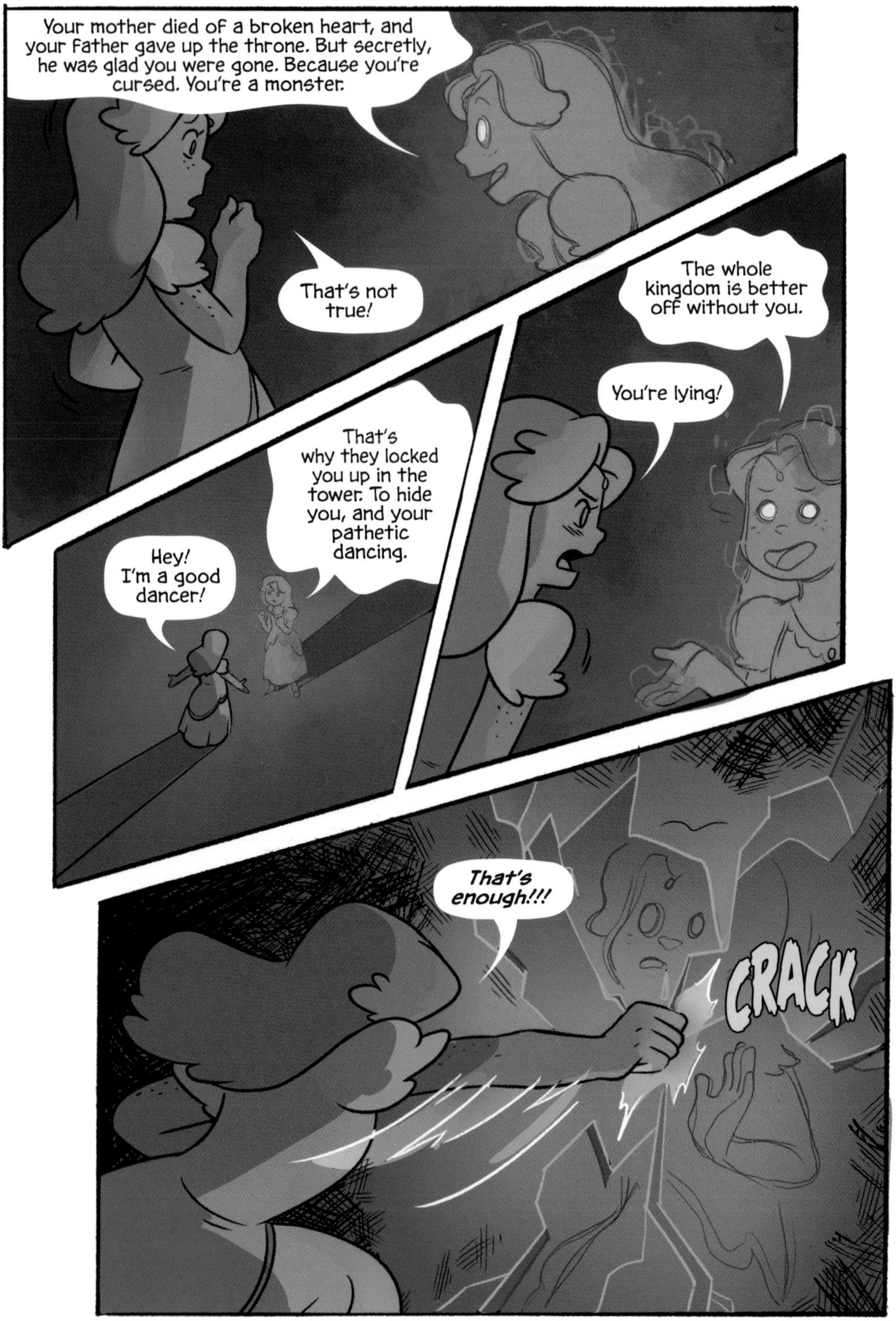
Your mother died of a broken heart, and your father gave up the throne. But secretly, he was glad you were gone. Because you're cursed. You're a monster.
That's not true!
The whole kingdom is better off without you.
You're lying!
That's why they locked you up in the tower. To hide you, and your pathetic dancing.
Hey! I'm a good dancer!
That's enough!!!
CRACK

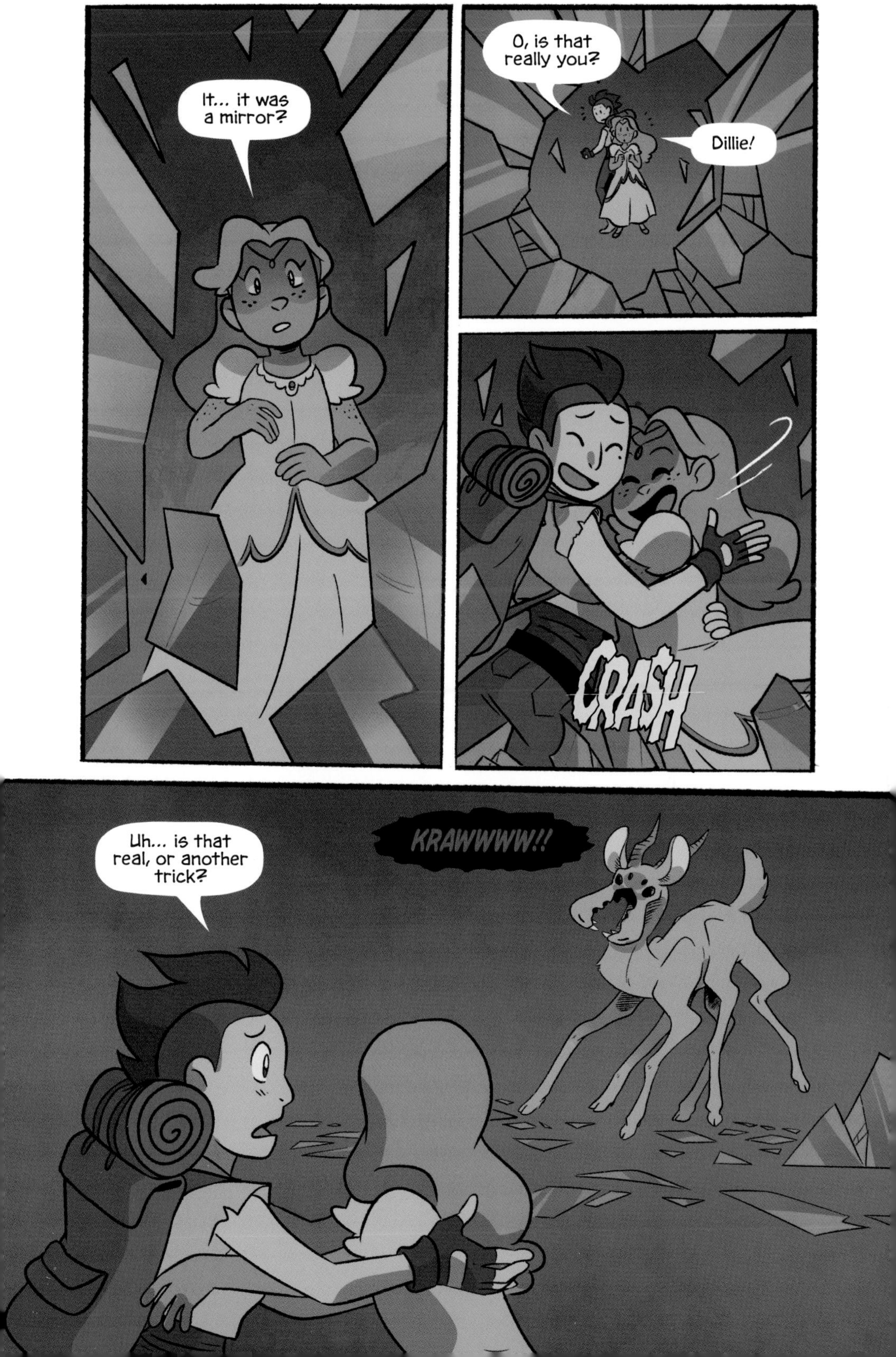
It... it was a mirror?
O, is that really you?
Dillie!
CRASH
Uh... is that real, or another trick?
KRAWWWW!!

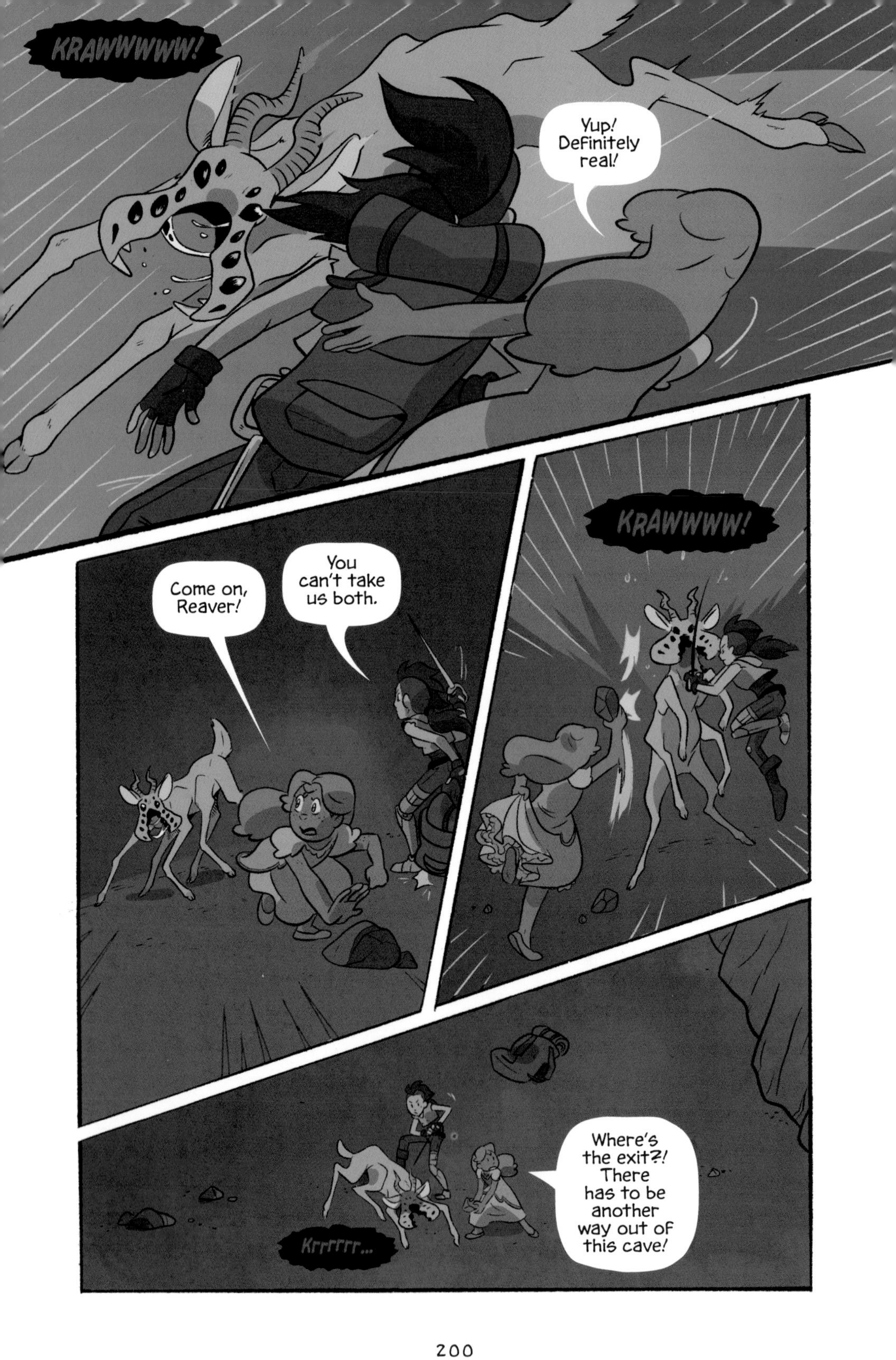
KRAWWWWW!
Yup! Definitely real!
Come on, Reaver!
You can't take us both.
KRAWWWW!
Where's the exit?! There has to be another way out of this cave!
Krrrrrr...

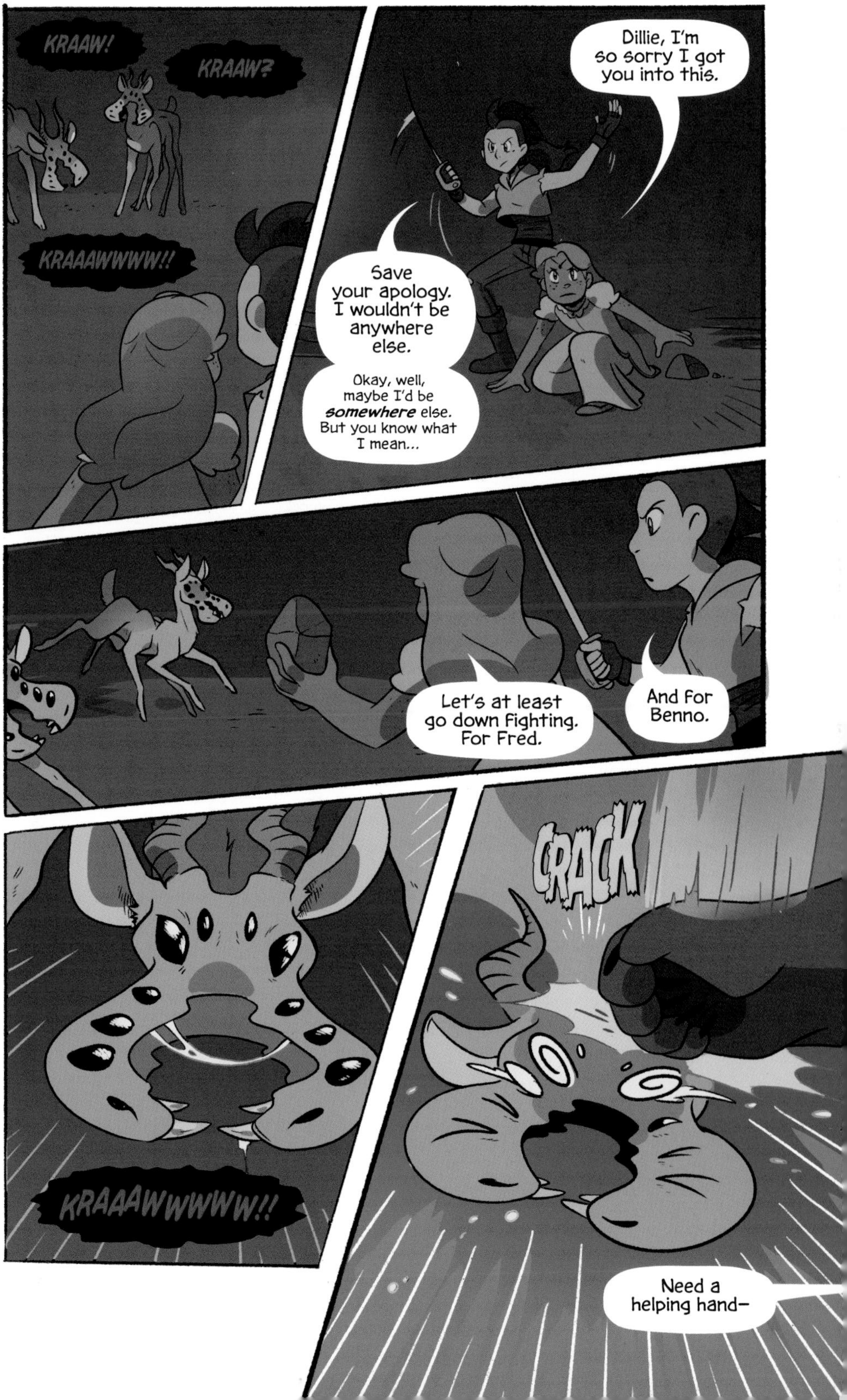
KRAAW!
KRAAW?
KRAAAWWWW!!
Dillie, I'm so sorry I got you into this.
Save your apology. I wouldn't be anywhere else.
Okay, well, maybe I'd be *somewhere* else. But you know what I mean...
Let's at least go down fighting. For Fred.
And for Benno.
KRAAAWWWWW!!
CRACK
Need a helping hand—

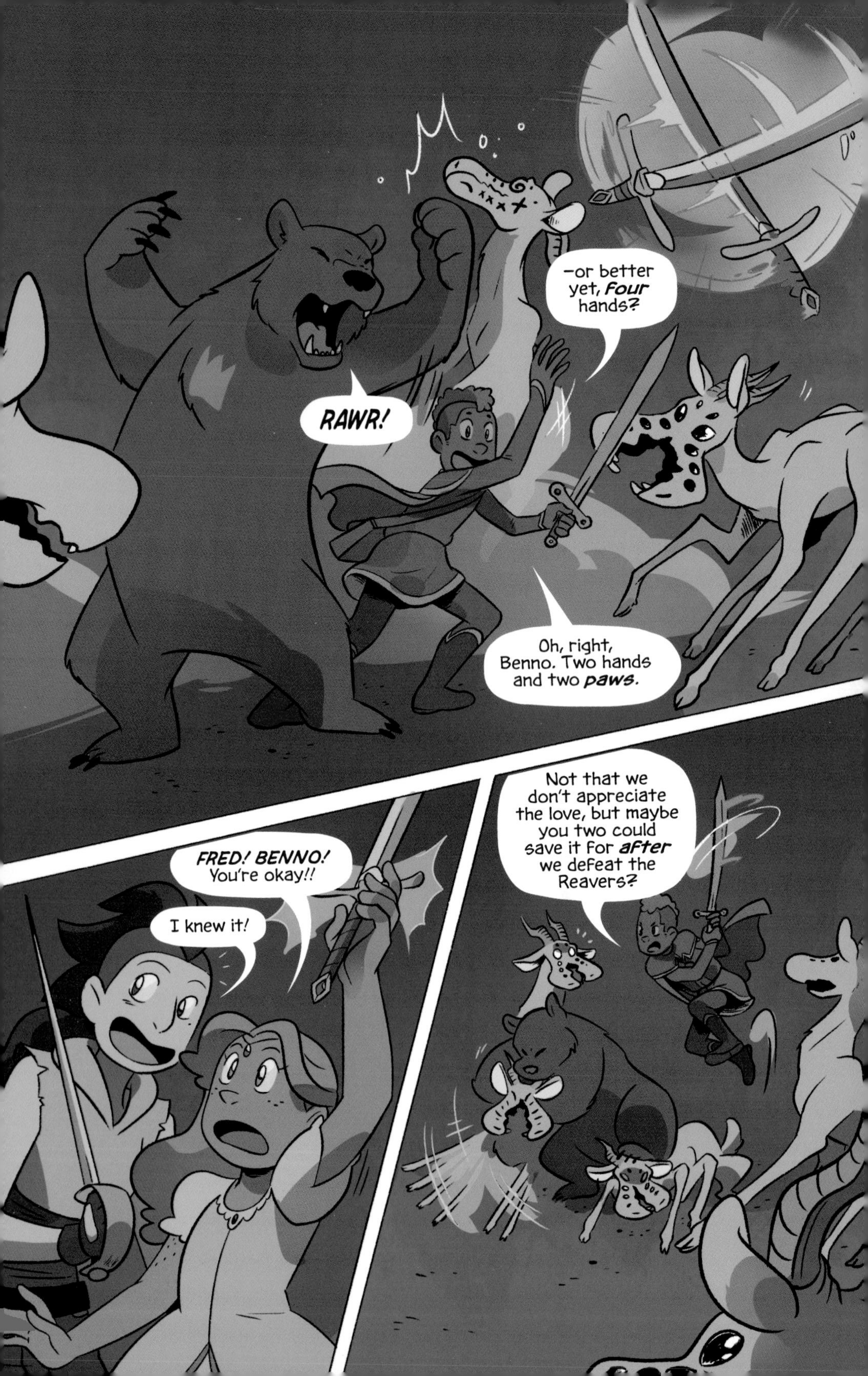
-or better yet, *four* hands?
RAWR!
Oh, right, Benno. Two hands and two *paws*.
FRED! BENNO! You're okay!!
I knew it!
Not that we don't appreciate the love, but maybe you two could save it for *after* we defeat the Reavers?

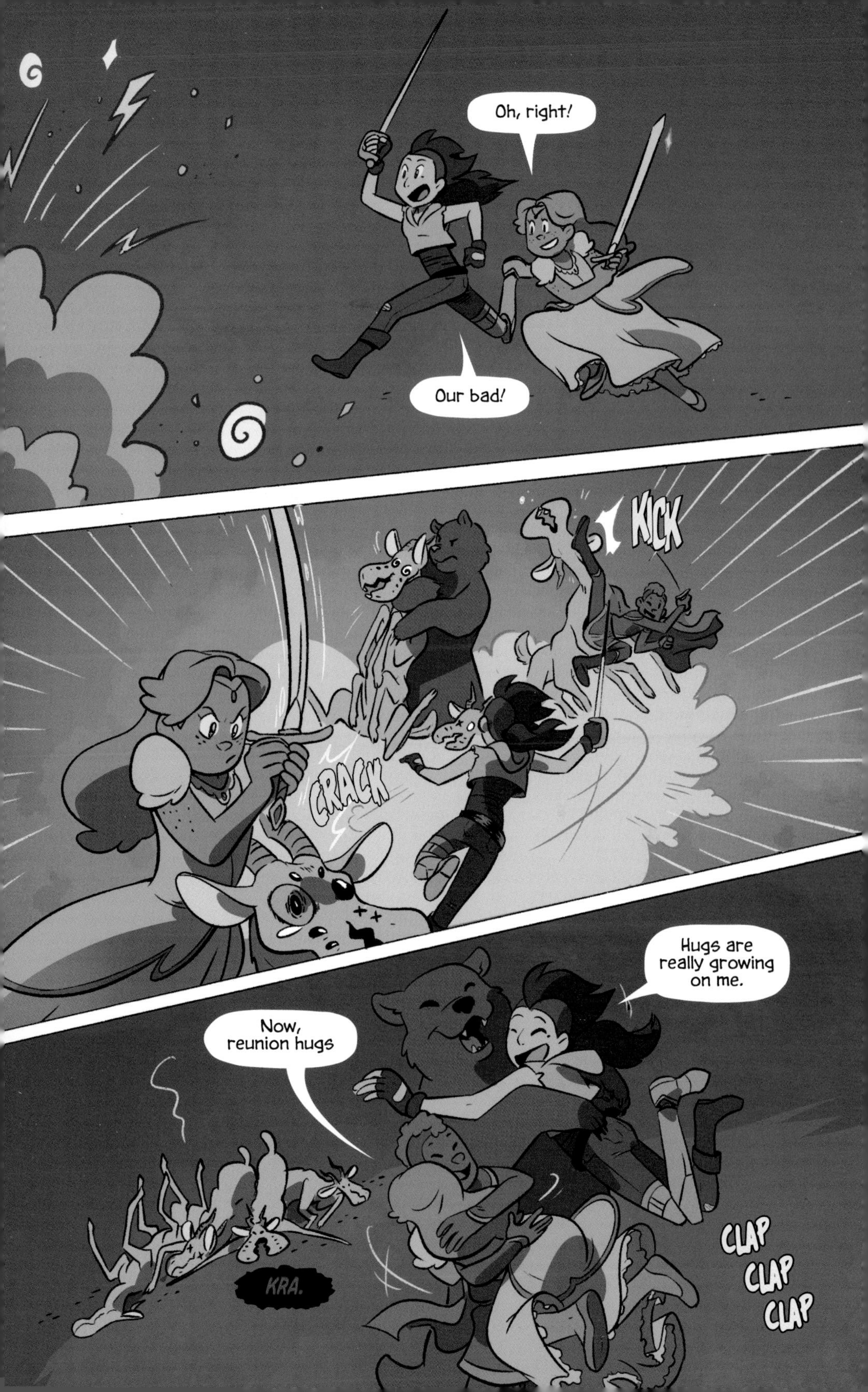
Oh, right!
Our bad!
KICK
CRACK
Now, reunion hugs
Hugs are really growing on me.
KRA.
CLAP
CLAP
CLAP

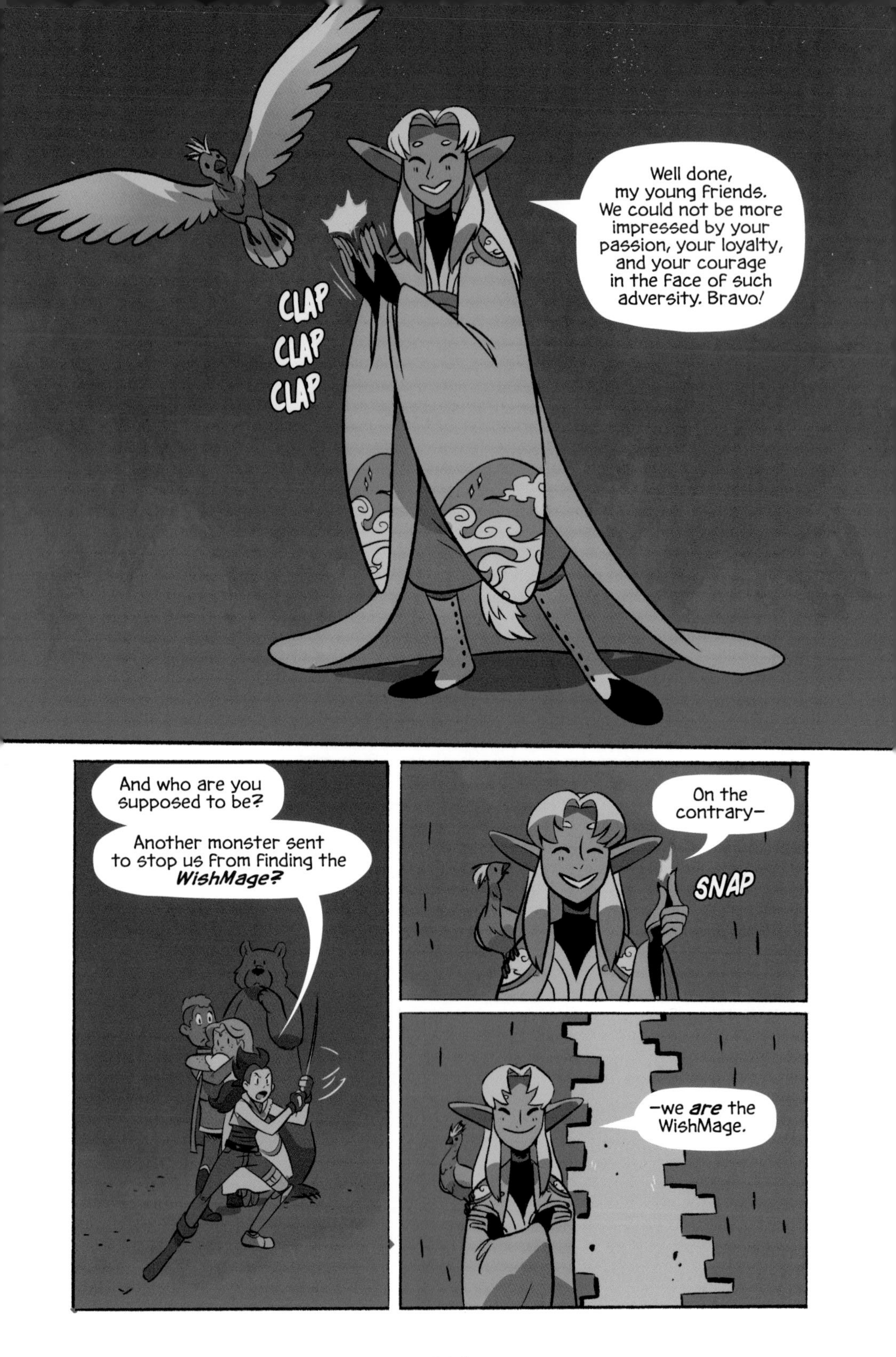
Well done, my young friends. We could not be more impressed by your passion, your loyalty, and your courage in the face of such adversity. Bravo!
CLAP CLAP CLAP
And who are you supposed to be?
Another monster sent to stop us from finding the *WishMage?*
On the contrary—
SNAP
—we *are* the WishMage.

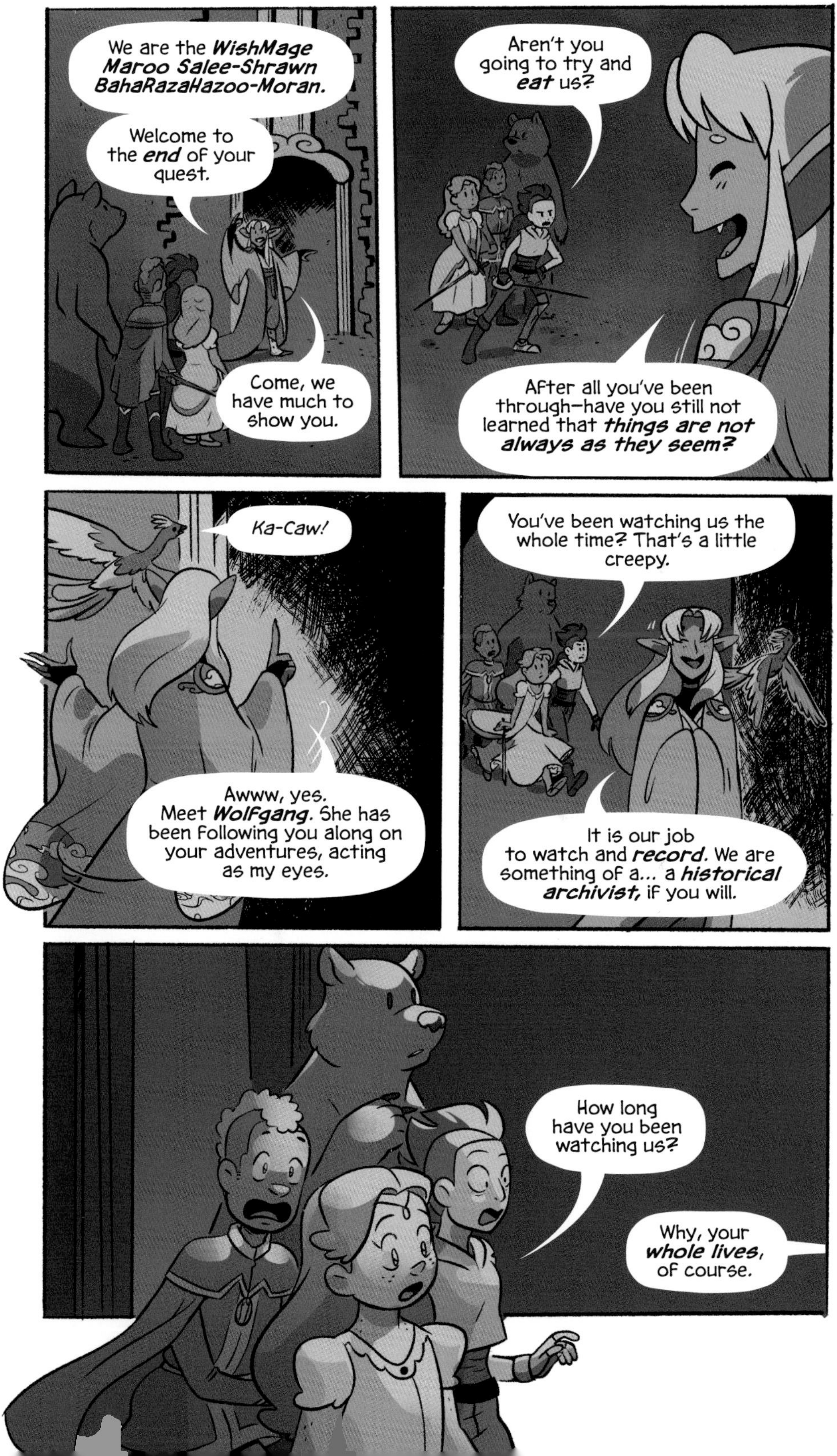
We are the *WishMage Maroo Salee-Shrawn BahaRazaHazoo-Moran.*
Welcome to the *end* of your quest.
Come, we have much to show you.
Aren't you going to try and *eat* us?
After all you've been through—have you still not learned that *things are not always as they seem?*
Ka-Caw!
Awww, yes. Meet *Wolfgang.* She has been following you along on your adventures, acting as my eyes.
You've been watching us the whole time? That's a little creepy.
It is our job to watch and *record.* We are something of a... a *historical archivist,* if you will.
How long have you been watching us?
Why, your *whole lives,* of course.

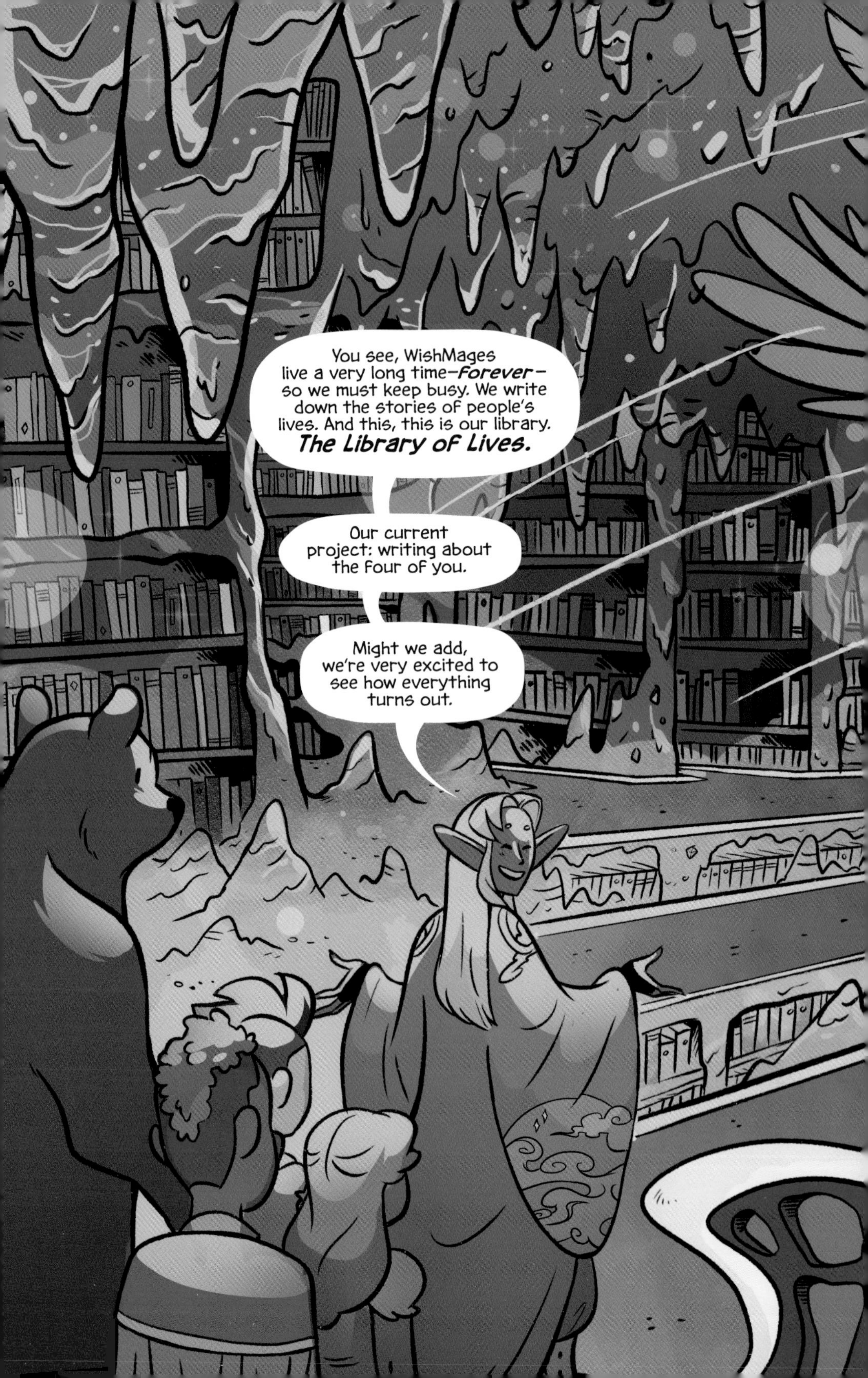
You see, WishMages live a very long time—*Forever*—so we must keep busy. We write down the stories of people's lives. And this, this is our library. ***The Library of Lives.***
Our current project: writing about the four of you.
Might we add, we're very excited to see how everything turns out.

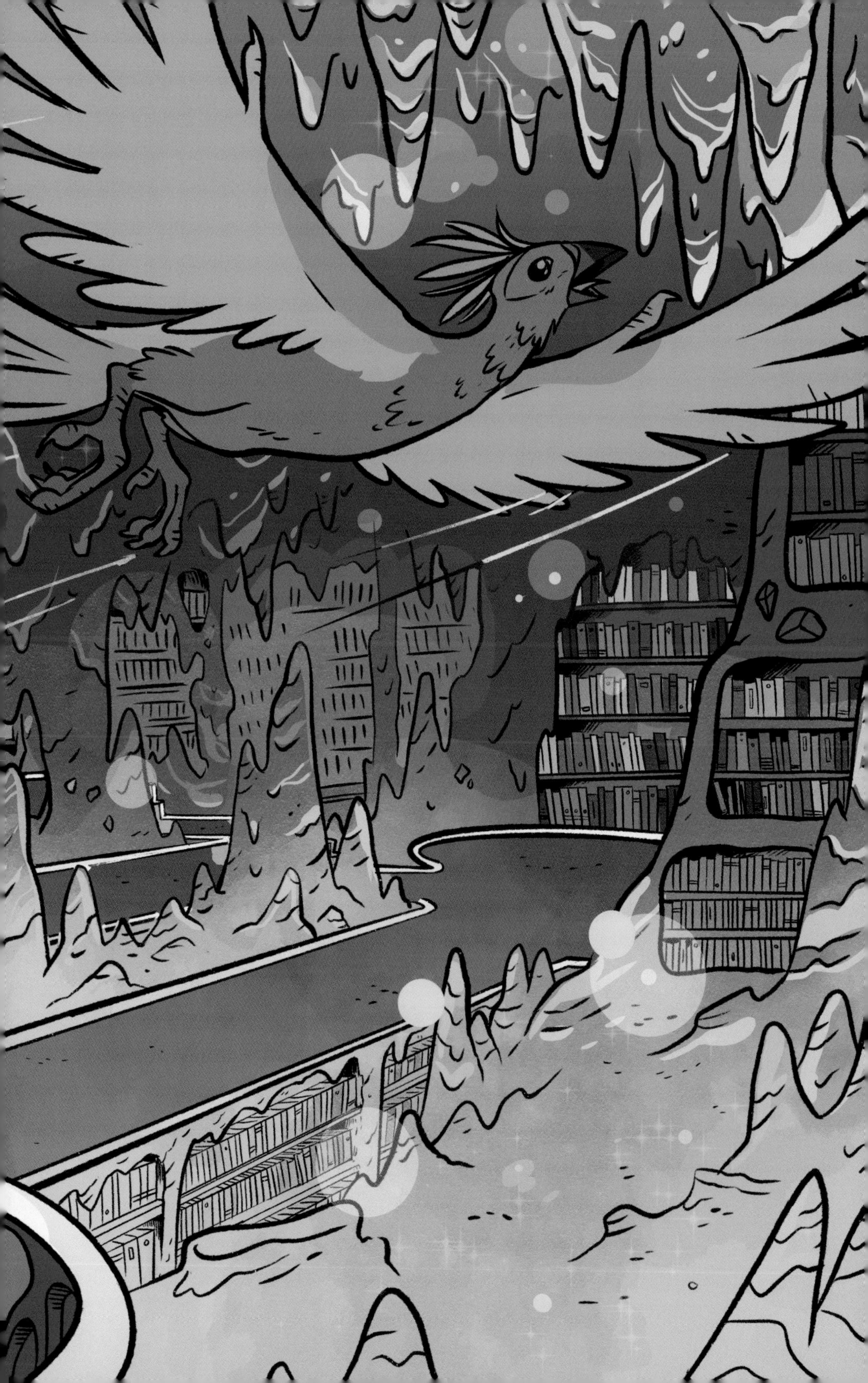

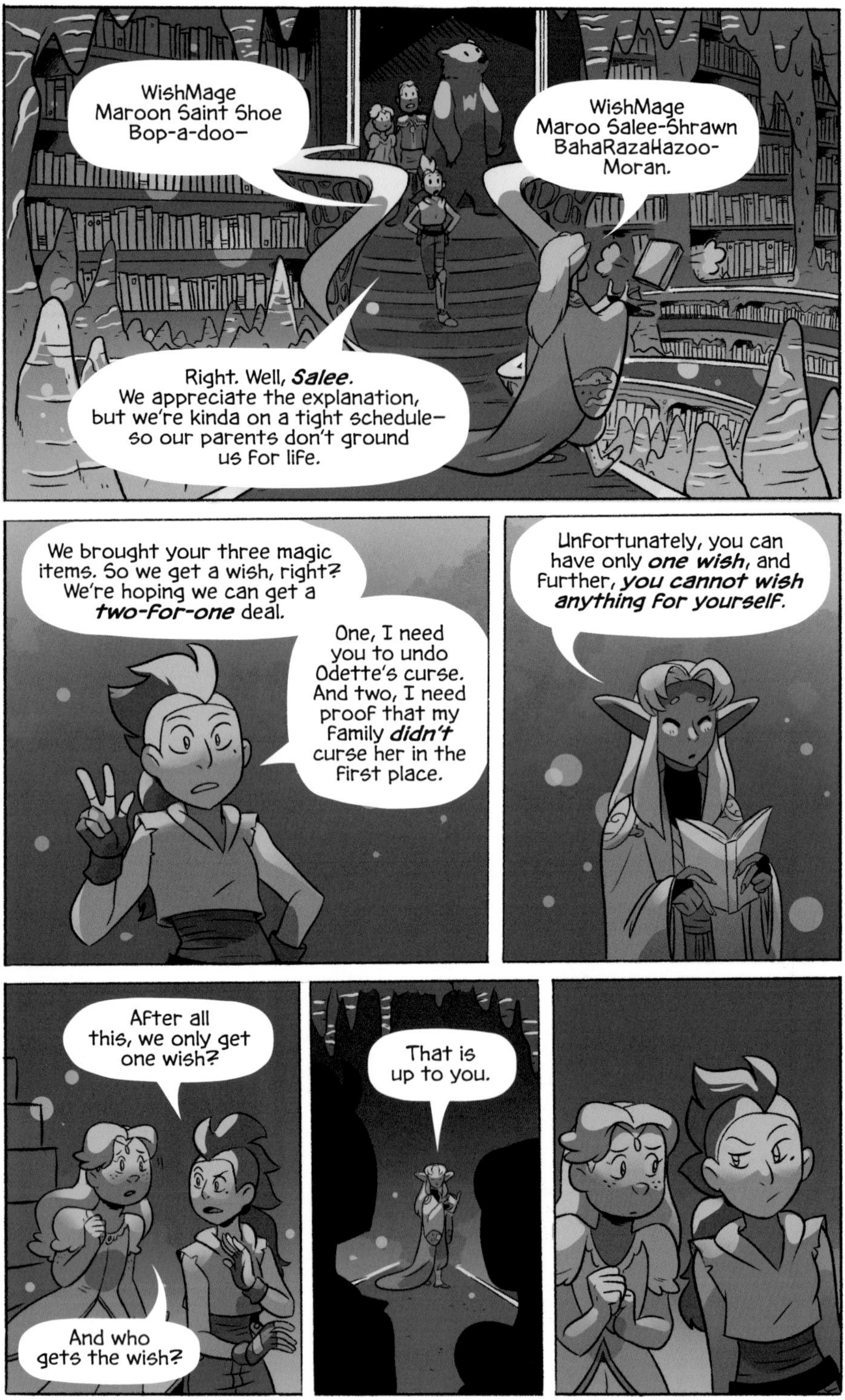
WishMage Maroon Saint Shoe Bop-a-doo–
WishMage Maroo Salee-Shrawn BahaRazaHazoo-Moran.
Right. Well, ***Salee.*** We appreciate the explanation, but we're kinda on a tight schedule– so our parents don't ground us for life.
We brought your three magic items. So we get a wish, right? We're hoping we can get a ***two-for-one*** deal.
One, I need you to undo Odette's curse. And two, I need proof that my family ***didn't*** curse her in the first place.
Unfortunately, you can have only ***one wish***, and further, ***you cannot wish anything for yourself.***
After all this, we only get one wish?
And who gets the wish?
That is up to you.

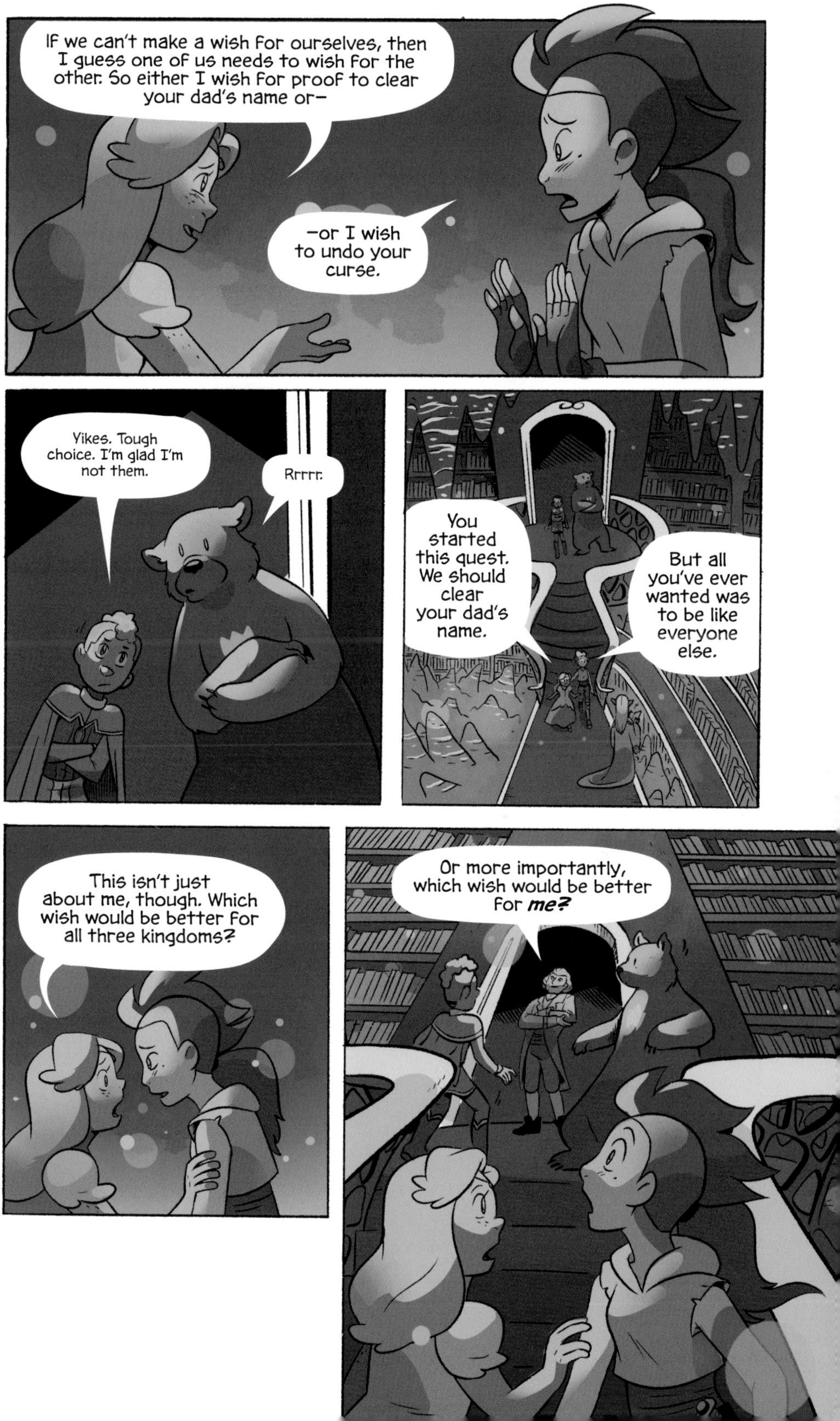
If we can't make a wish for ourselves, then I guess one of us needs to wish for the other. So either I wish for proof to clear your dad's name or–
–or I wish to undo your curse.
Yikes. Tough choice. I'm glad I'm not them.
Rrrrr.
You started this quest. We should clear your dad's name.
But all you've ever wanted was to be like everyone else.
This isn't just about me, though. Which wish would be better for all three kingdoms?
Or more importantly, which wish would be better for *me?*

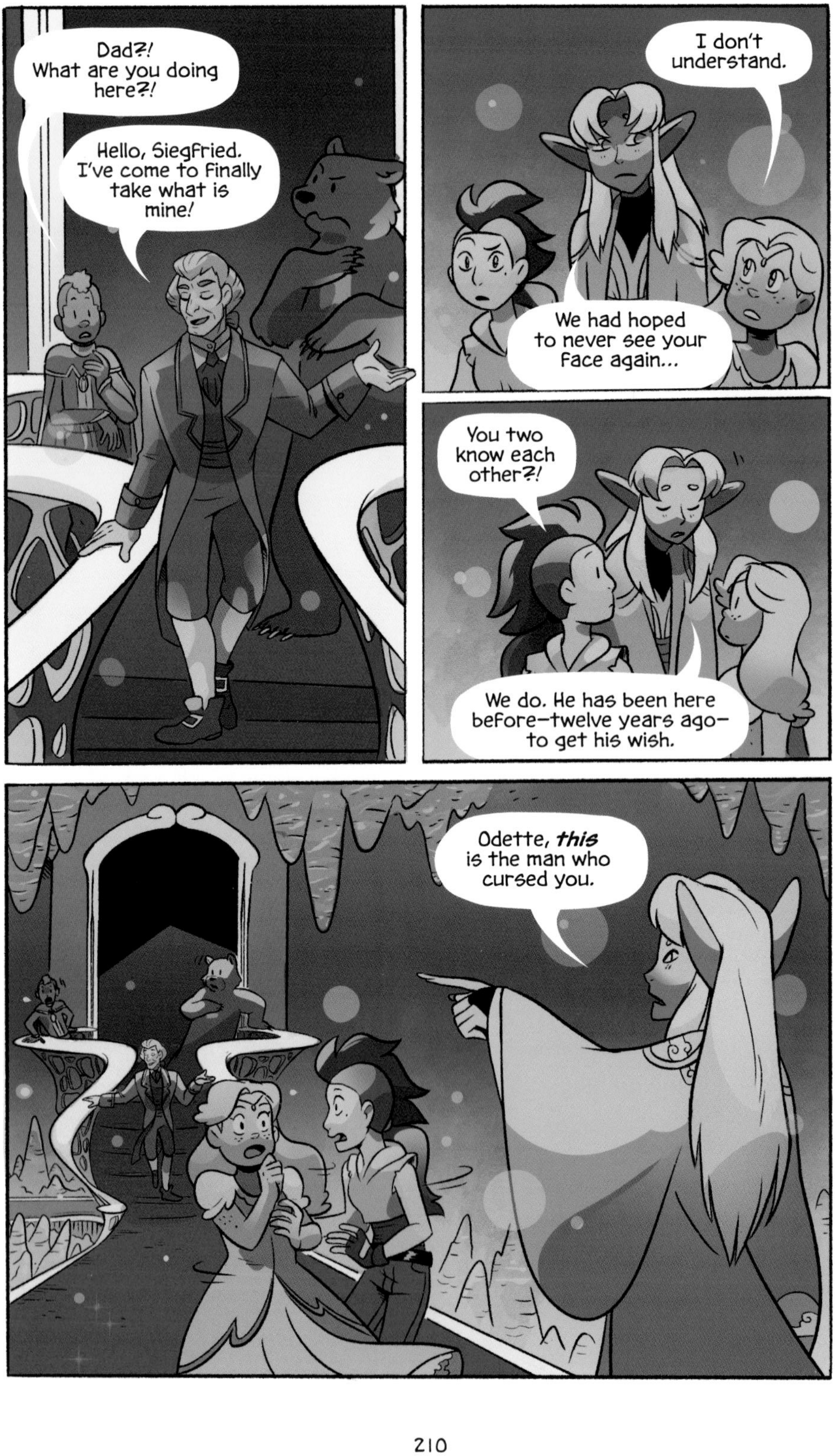

Dad?! What are you doing here?!
Hello, Siegfried. I've come to finally take what is mine!
I don't understand.
We had hoped to never see your face again...
You two know each other?!
We do. He has been here before—twelve years ago—to get his wish.
Odette, *this* is the man who cursed you.

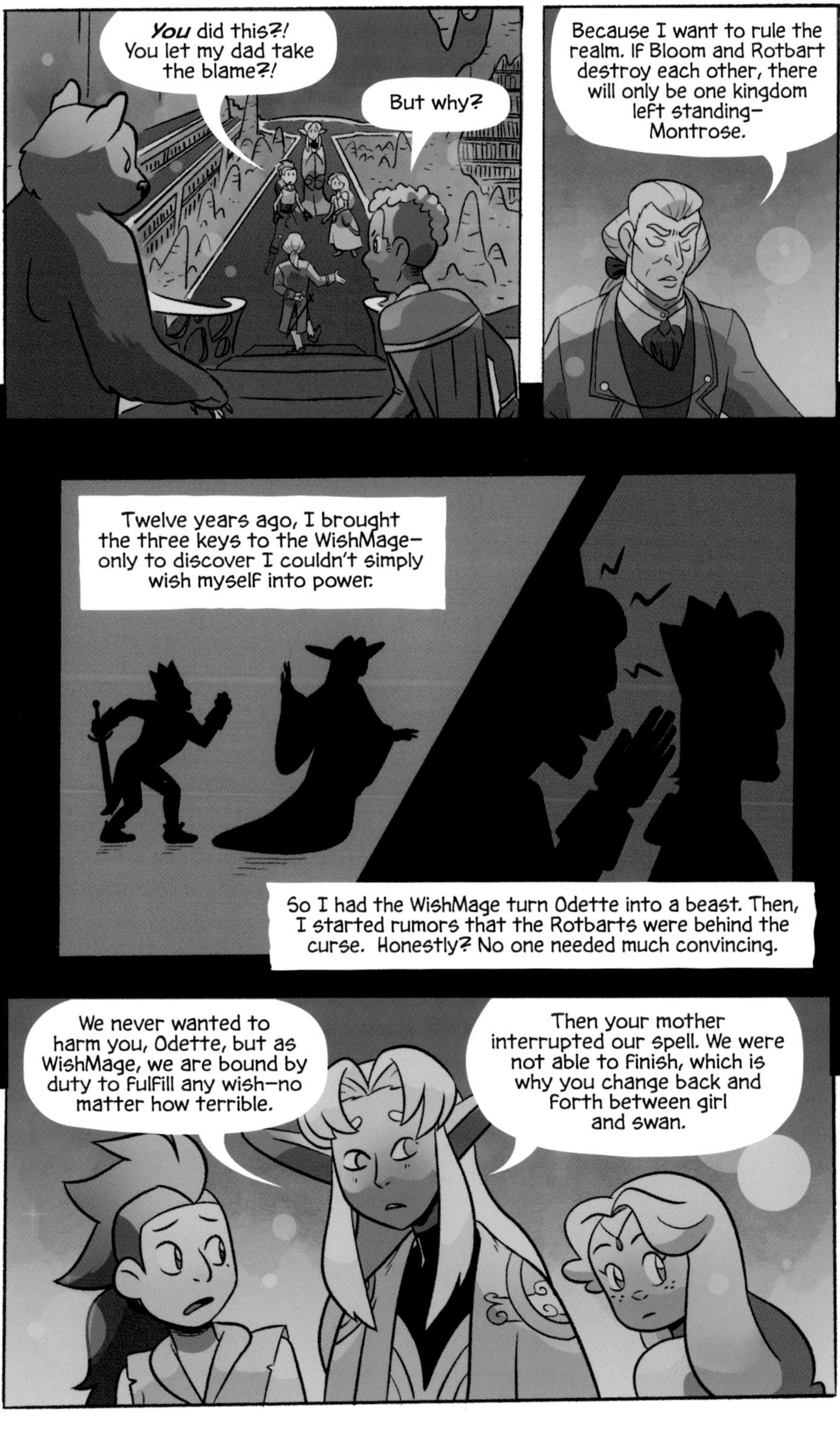
You did this?! You let my dad take the blame?!
But why?
Because I want to rule the realm. If Bloom and Rotbart destroy each other, there will only be one kingdom left standing— Montrose.
Twelve years ago, I brought the three keys to the WishMage— only to discover I couldn't simply wish myself into power.
So I had the WishMage turn Odette into a beast. Then, I started rumors that the Rotbarts were behind the curse. Honestly? No one needed much convincing.
We never wanted to harm you, Odette, but as WishMage, we are bound by duty to fulfill any wish—no matter how terrible.
Then your mother interrupted our spell. We were not able to finish, which is why you change back and forth between girl and swan.

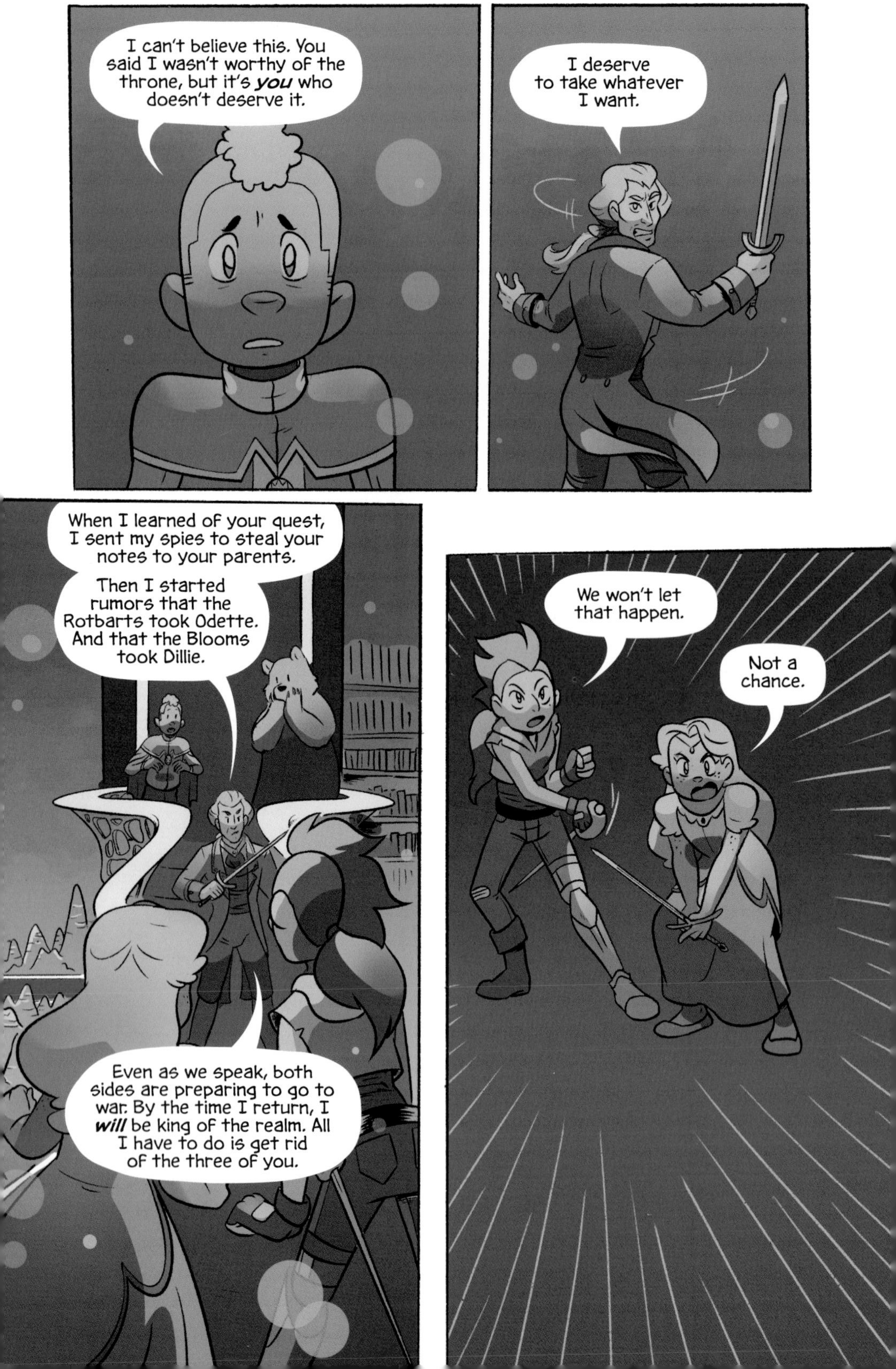

I can't believe this. You said I wasn't worthy of the throne, but it's ***you*** who doesn't deserve it.
I deserve to take whatever I want.
When I learned of your quest, I sent my spies to steal your notes to your parents.
Then I started rumors that the Rotbarts took Odette. And that the Blooms took Dillie.
Even as we speak, both sides are preparing to go to war. By the time I return, I ***will*** be king of the realm. All I have to do is get rid of the three of you.
We won't let that happen.
Not a chance.

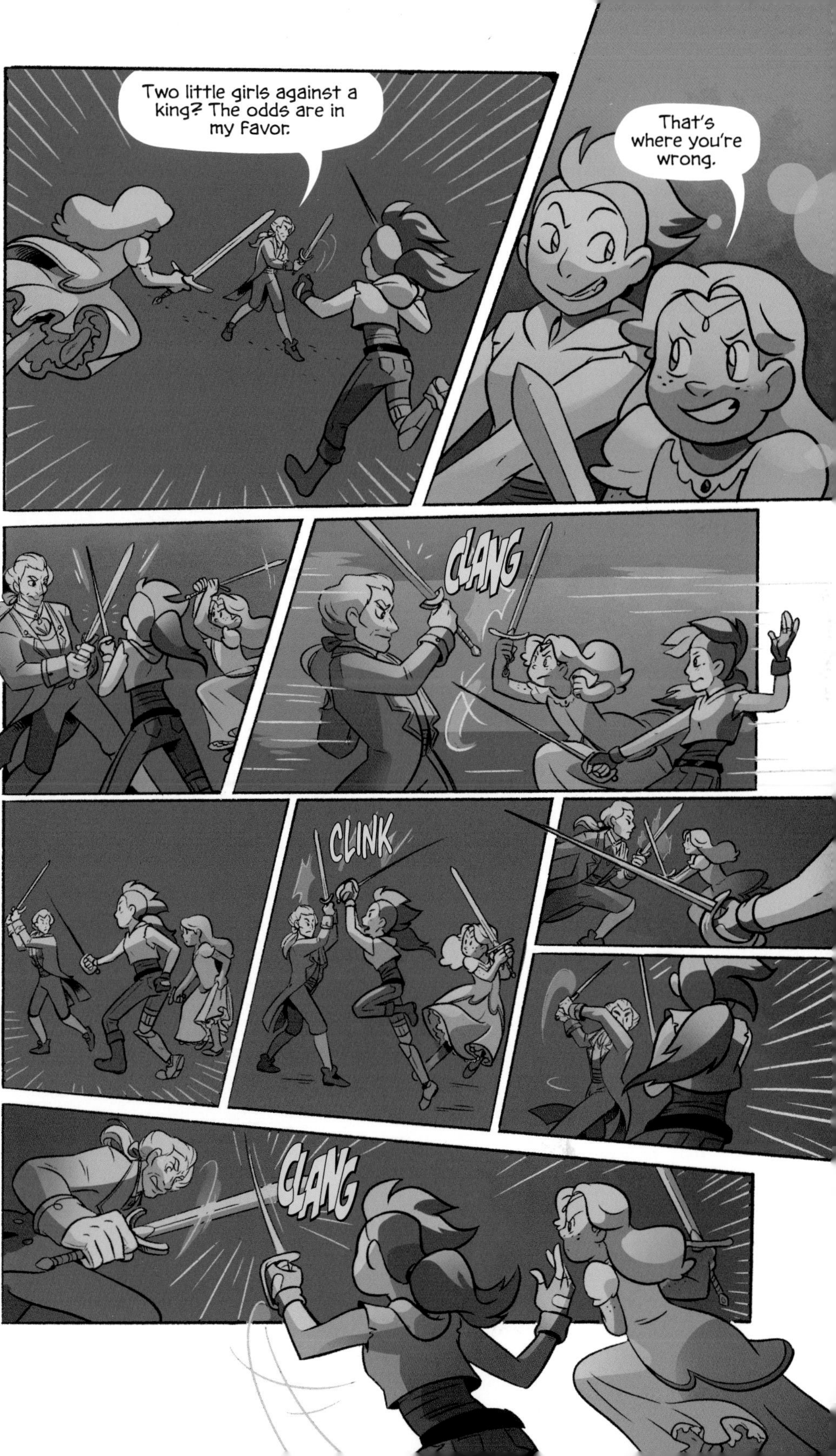
Two little girls against a king? The odds are in my favor.
That's where you're wrong.
CLANG
CLINK
CLANG

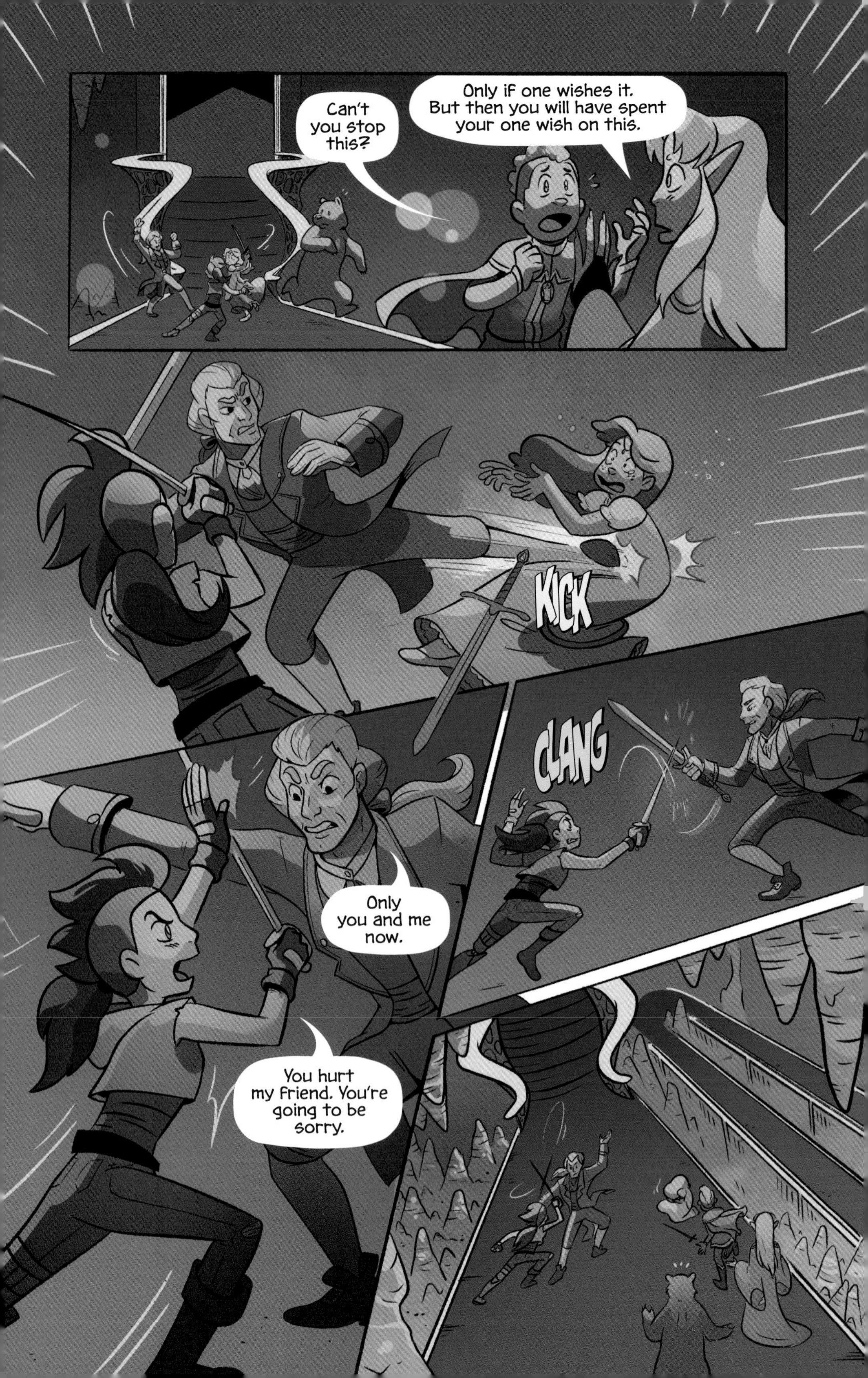
Can't you stop this?
Only if one wishes it. But then you will have spent your one wish on this.
KICK
CLANG
Only you and me now.
You hurt my friend. You're going to be sorry.

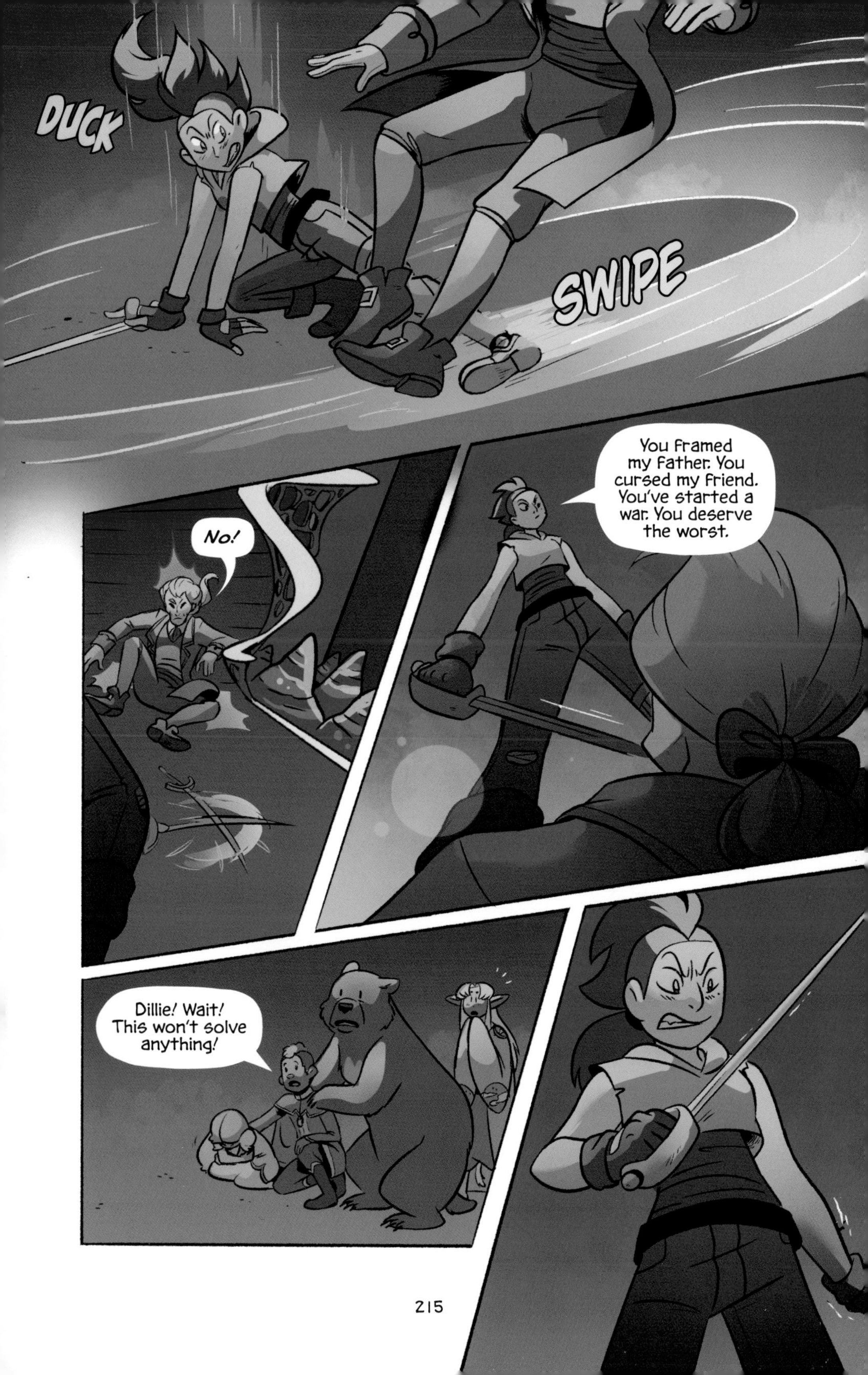

DUCK
SWIPE
No!
You framed my father. You cursed my friend. You've started a war. You deserve the worst.
Dillie! Wait! This won't solve anything!

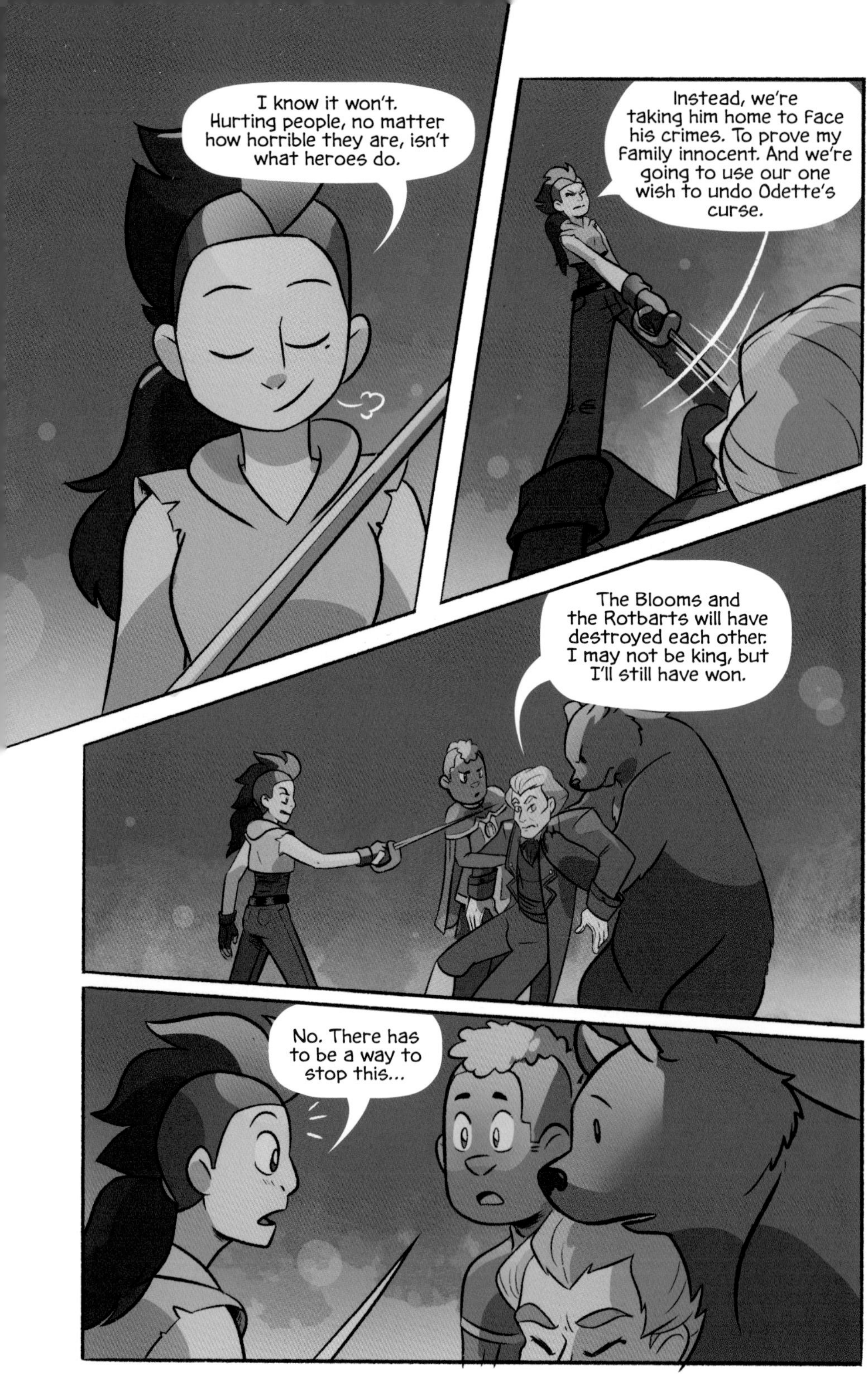
I know it won't. Hurting people, no matter how horrible they are, isn't what heroes do.
Instead, we're taking him home to face his crimes. To prove my family innocent. And we're going to use our one wish to undo Odette's curse.
The Blooms and the Rotbarts will have destroyed each other. I may not be king, but I'll still have won.
No. There has to be a way to stop this...

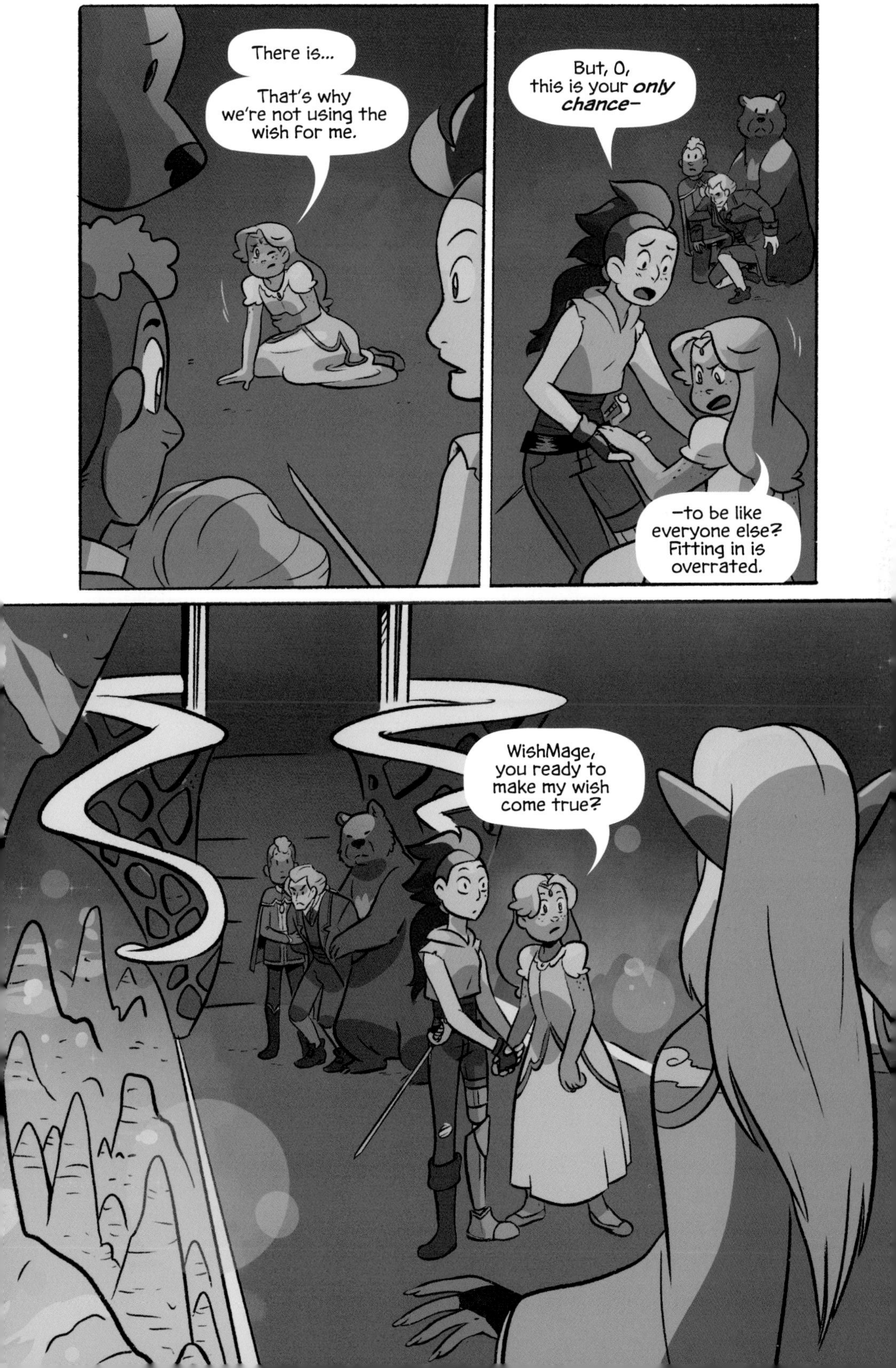
There is...
That's why we're not using the wish for me.
But, O, this is your *only chance*–
–to be like everyone else? Fitting in is overrated.
WishMage, you ready to make my wish come true?

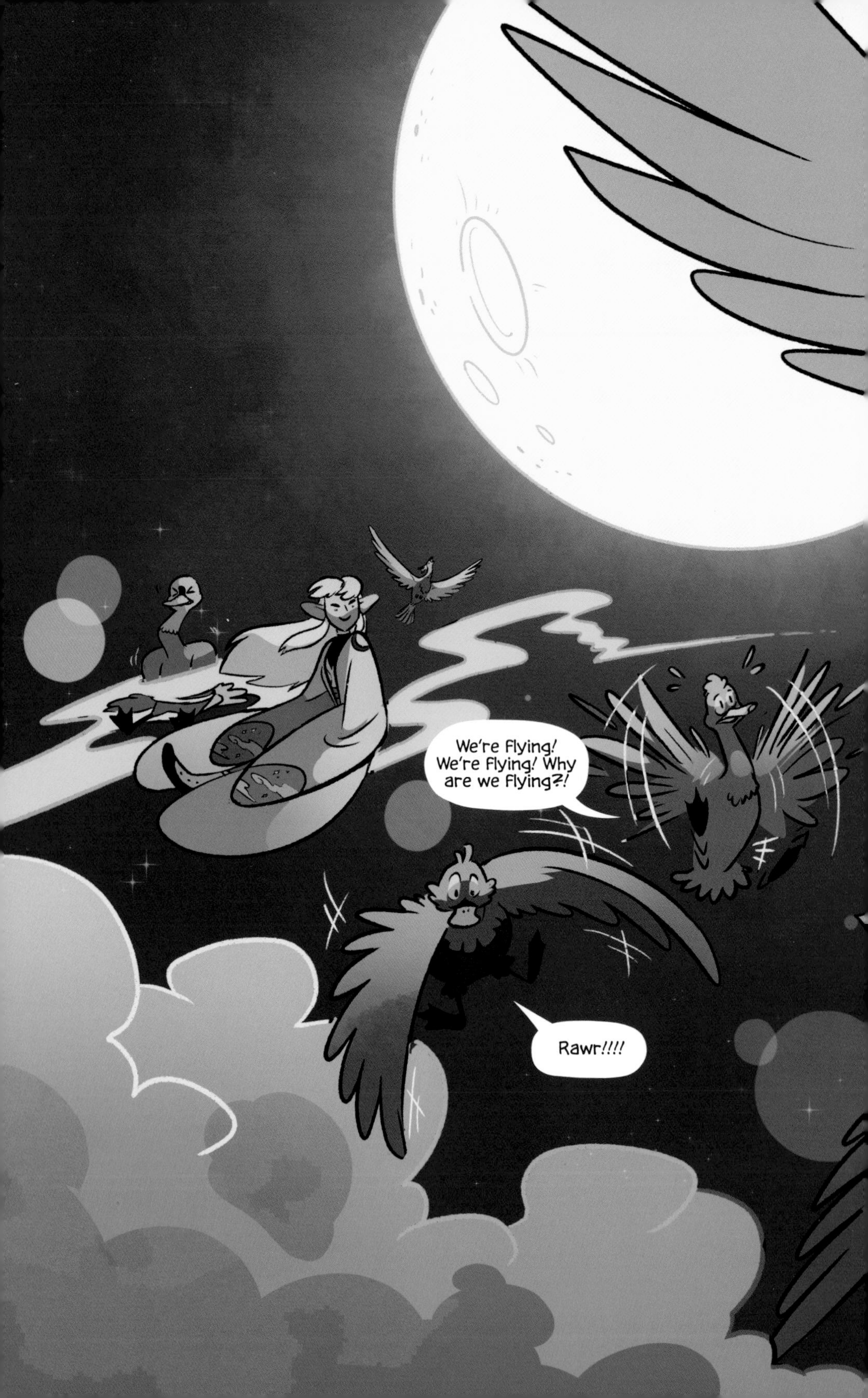
We're flying! We're flying! Why are we flying?!
Rawr!!!!

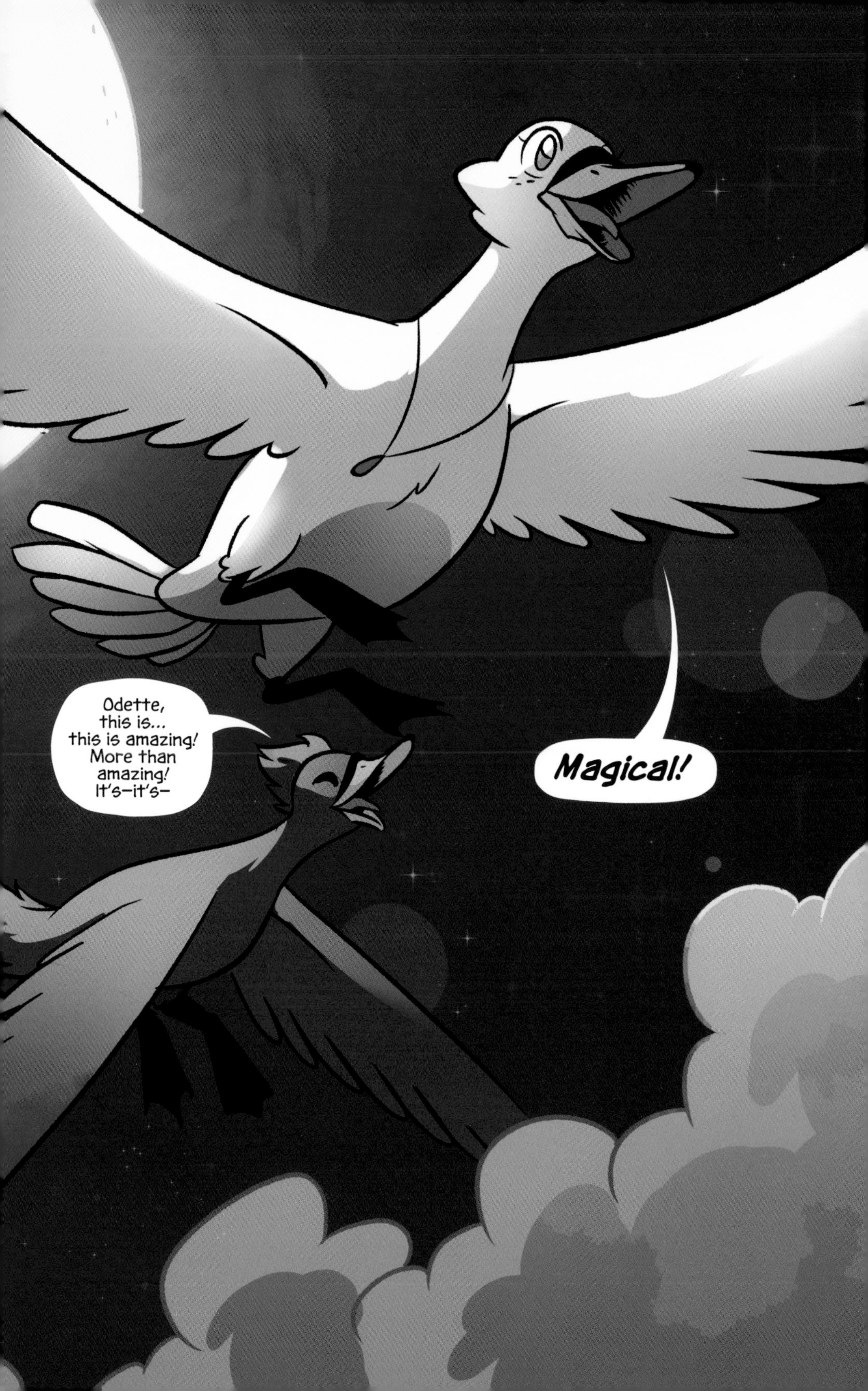
Odette, this is... this is amazing! More than amazing! It's–it's–
Magical!

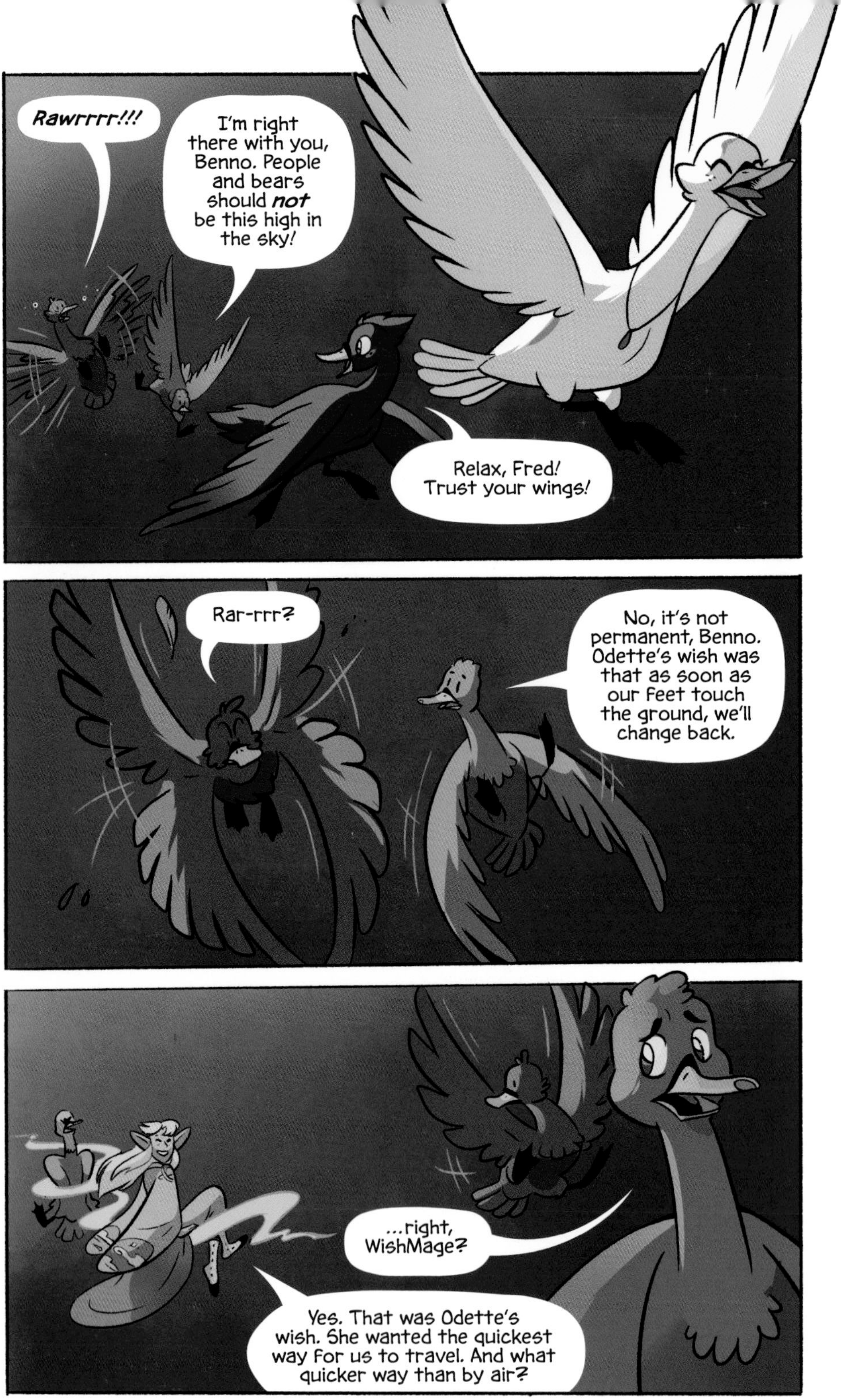
Rawrrrr!!!
I'm right there with you, Benno. People and bears should *not* be this high in the sky!
Relax, Fred! Trust your wings!
Rar-rrr?
No, it's not permanent, Benno. Odette's wish was that as soon as our feet touch the ground, we'll change back.
...right, WishMage?
Yes. That was Odette's wish. She wanted the quickest way for us to travel. And what quicker way than by air?

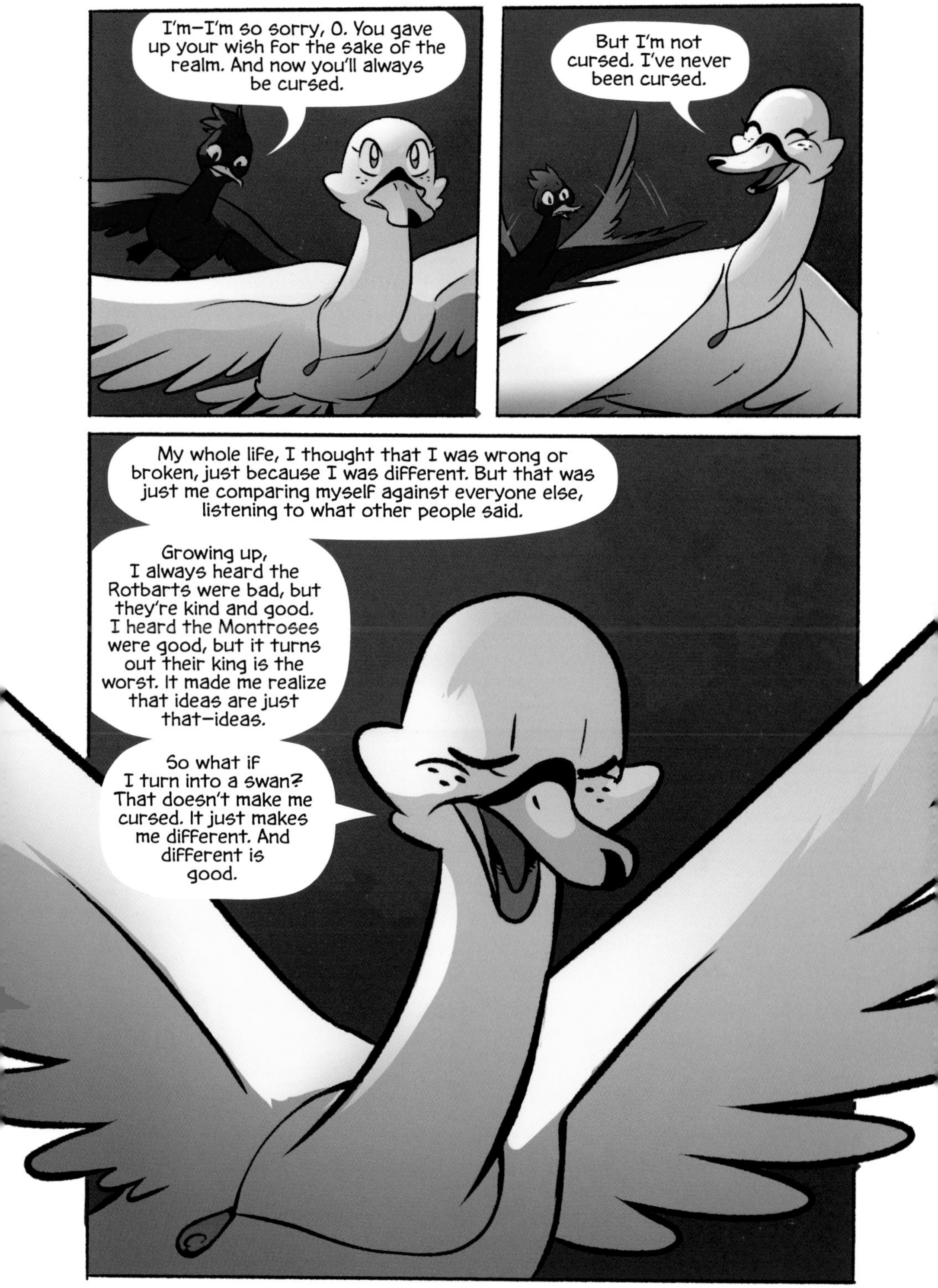
I'm—I'm so sorry, O. You gave up your wish for the sake of the realm. And now you'll always be cursed.
But I'm not cursed. I've never been cursed.
My whole life, I thought that I was wrong or broken, just because I was different. But that was just me comparing myself against everyone else, listening to what other people said.
Growing up, I always heard the Rotbarts were bad, but they're kind and good. I heard the Montroses were good, but it turns out their king is the worst. It made me realize that ideas are just that—ideas.
So what if I turn into a swan? That doesn't make me cursed. It just makes me different. And different is good.

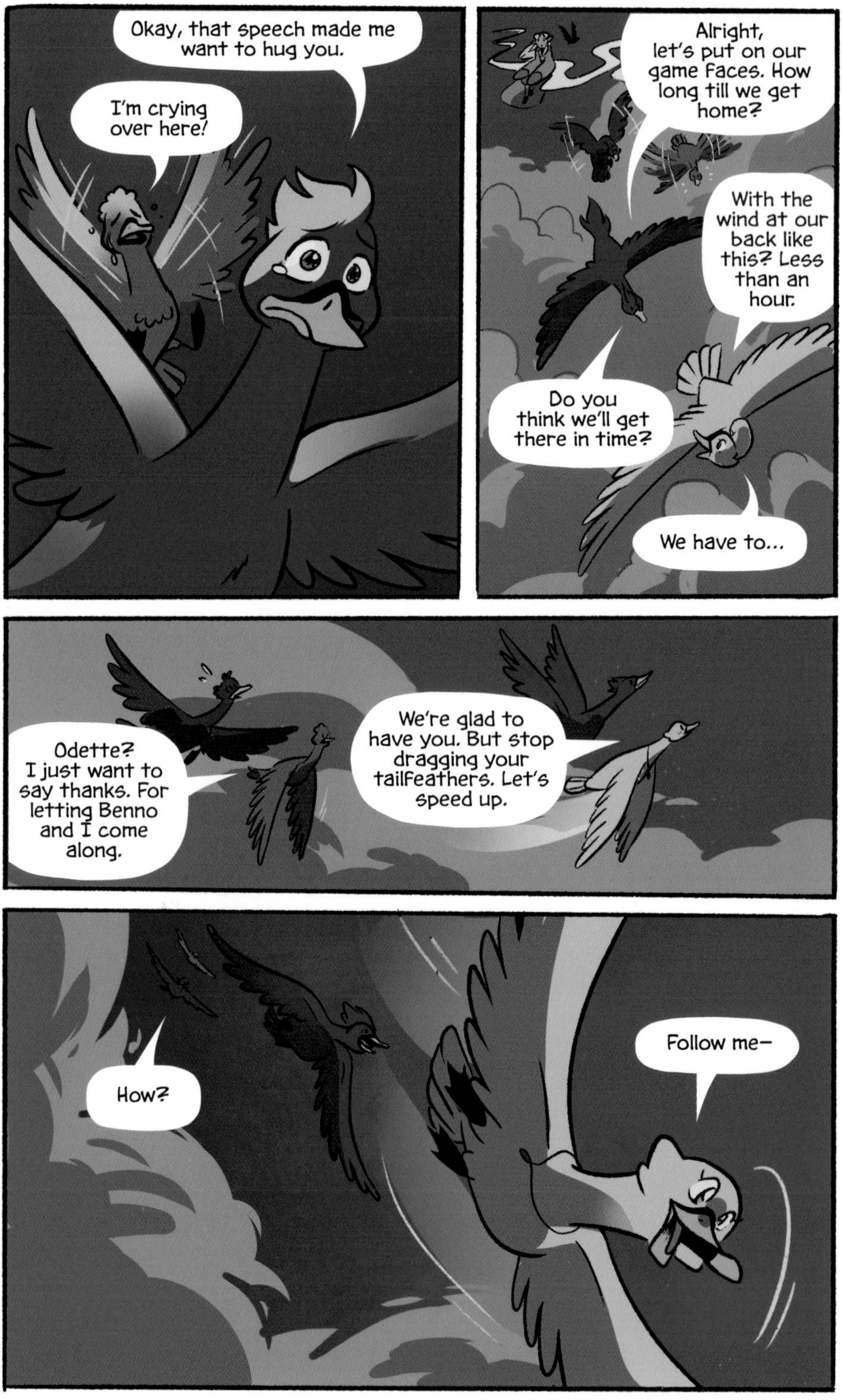
Okay, that speech made me want to hug you.
I'm crying over here!
Alright, let's put on our game faces. How long till we get home?
With the wind at our back like this? Less than an hour.
Do you think we'll get there in time?
We have to...
Odette? I just want to say thanks. For letting Benno and I come along.
We're glad to have you. But stop dragging your tailfeathers. Let's speed up.
How?
Follow me—

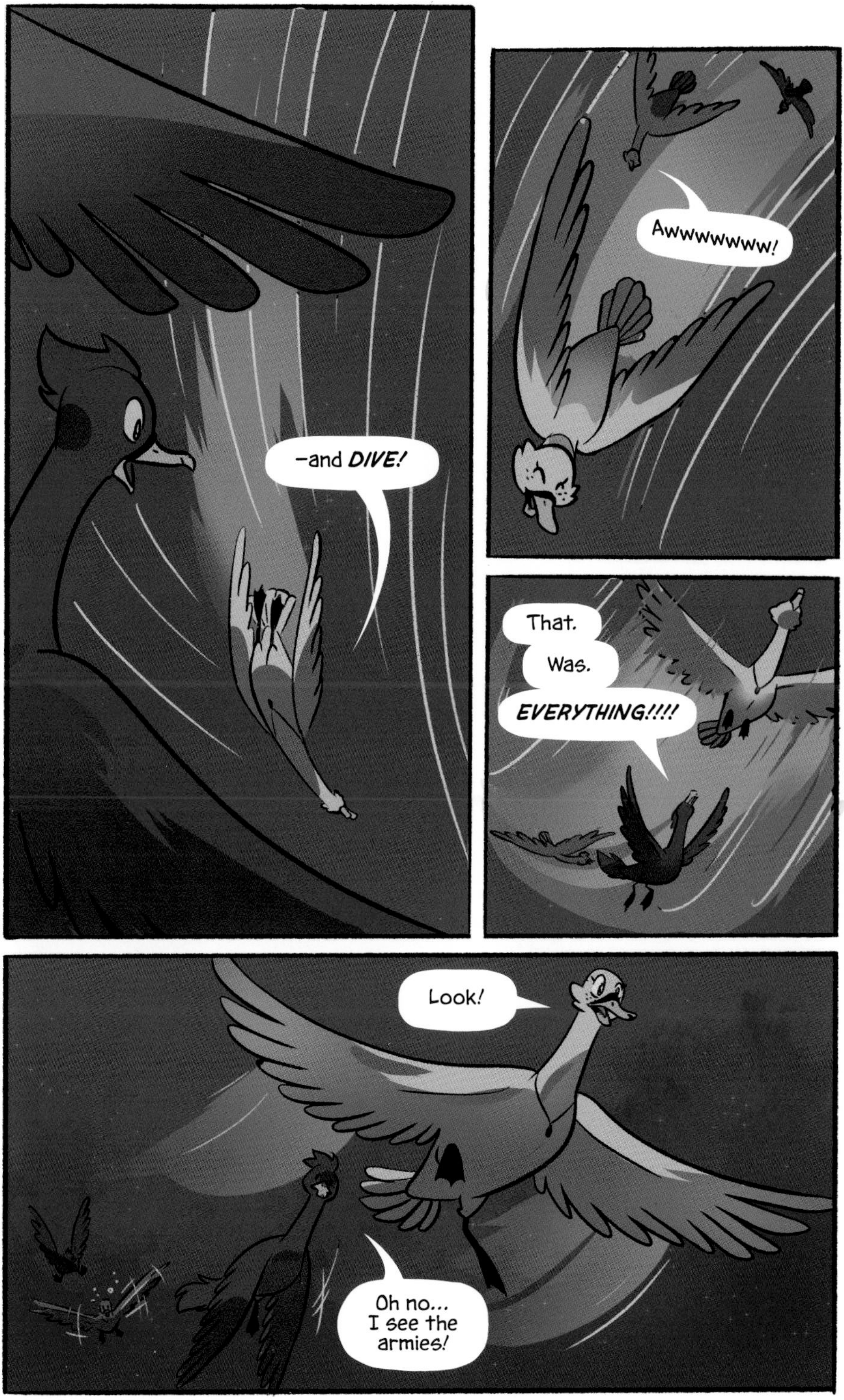
–and DIVE!
Awwwwwww!
That.
Was.
EVERYTHING!!!!
Look!
Oh no... I see the armies!

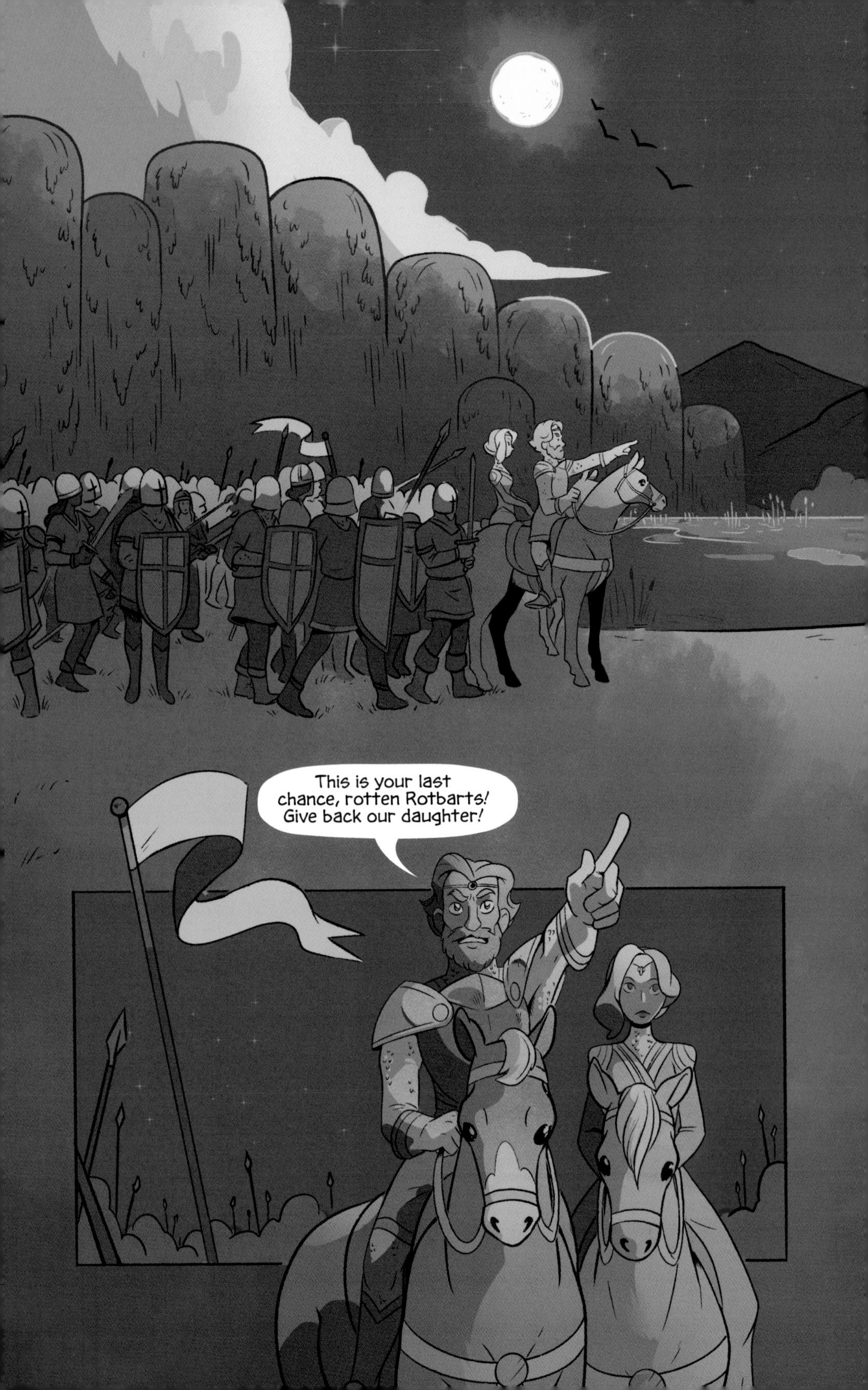
This is your last chance, rotten Rotbarts! Give back our daughter!

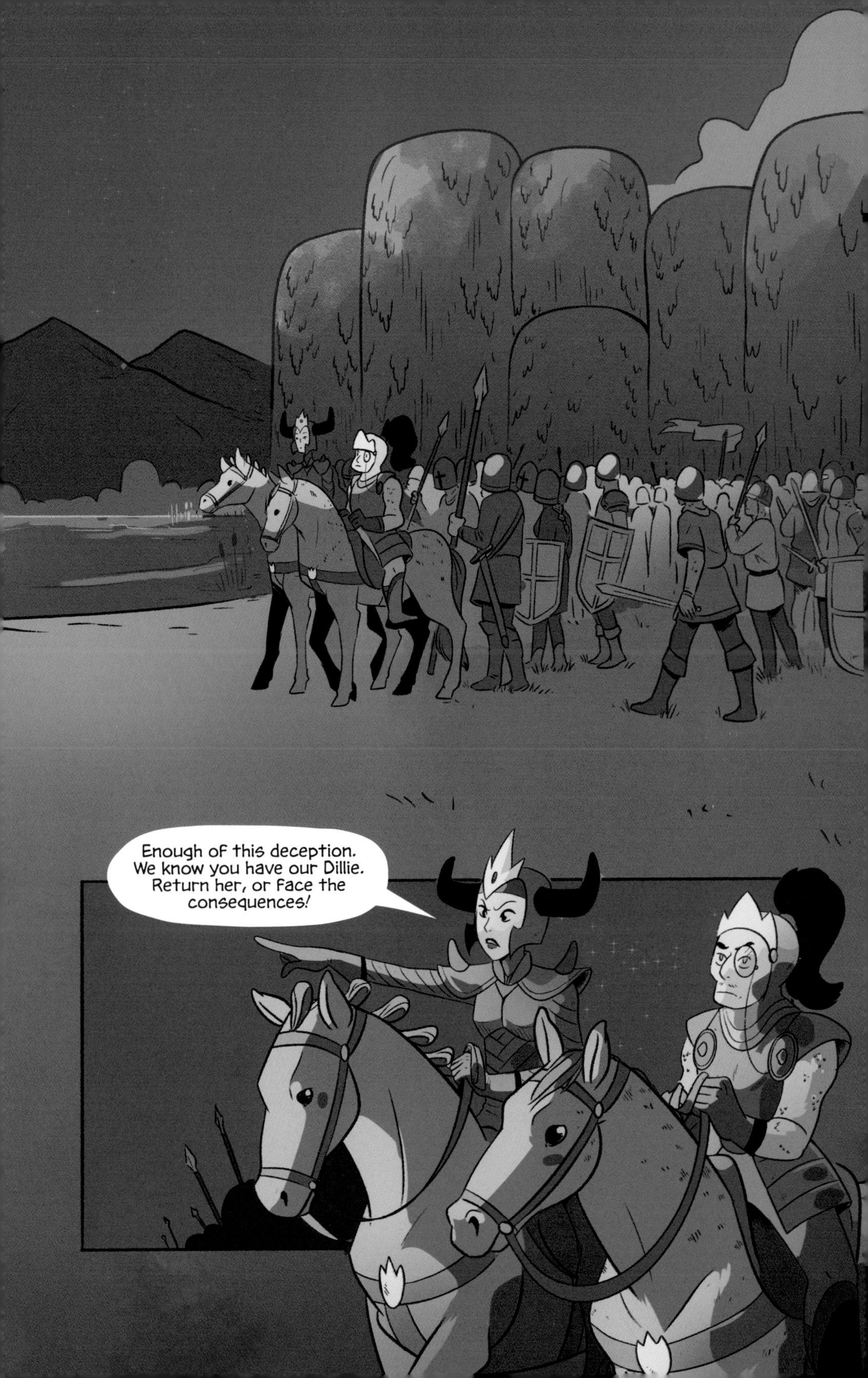
Enough of this deception. We know you have our Dillie. Return her, or face the consequences!

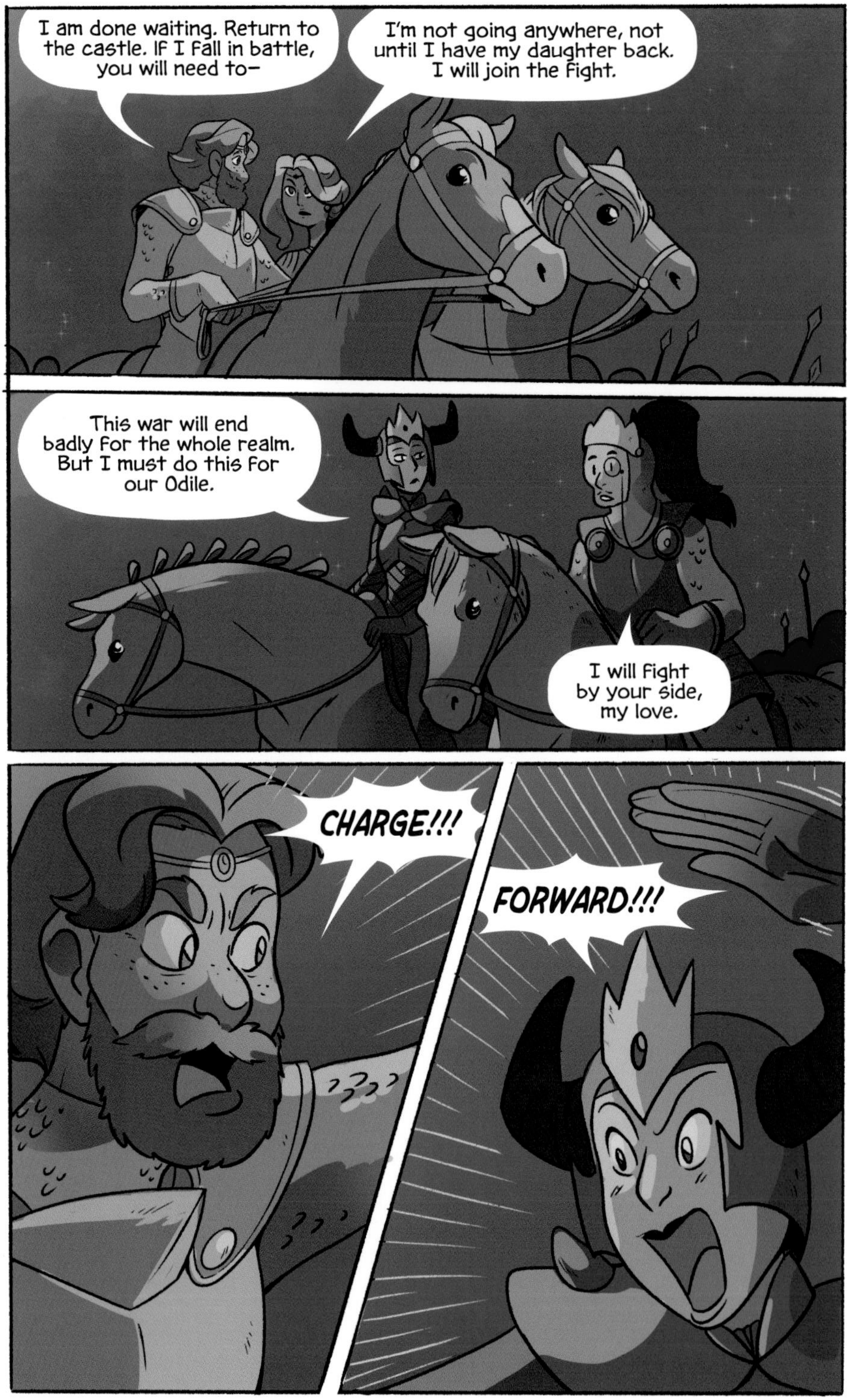
I am done waiting. Return to the castle. If I fall in battle, you will need to–
I'm not going anywhere, not until I have my daughter back. I will join the fight.
This war will end badly for the whole realm. But I must do this for our Odile.
I will fight by your side, my love.
CHARGE!!!
FORWARD!!!

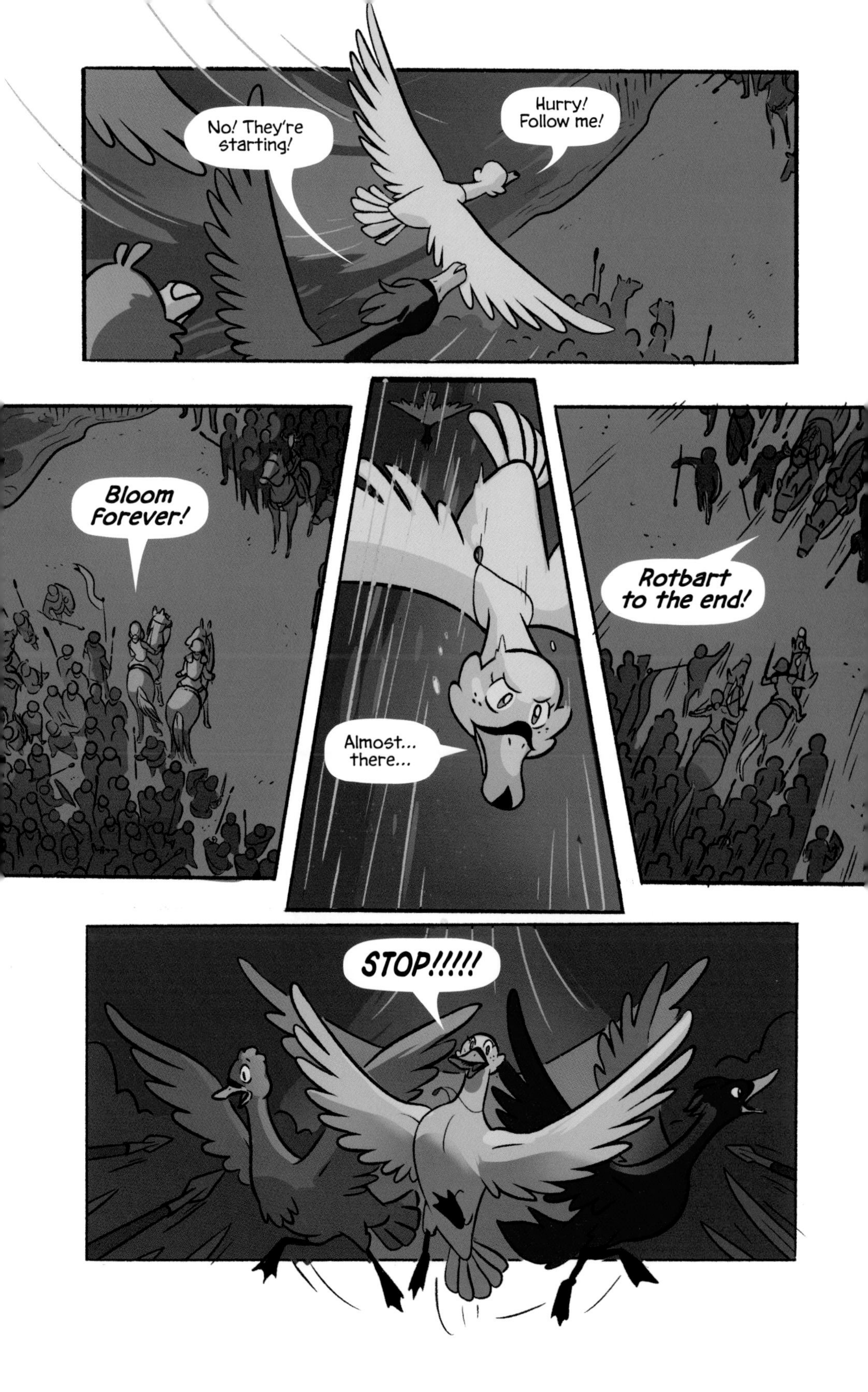
No! They're starting!
Hurry! Follow me!
Bloom forever!
Almost... there...
Rotbart to the end!
STOP!!!!!

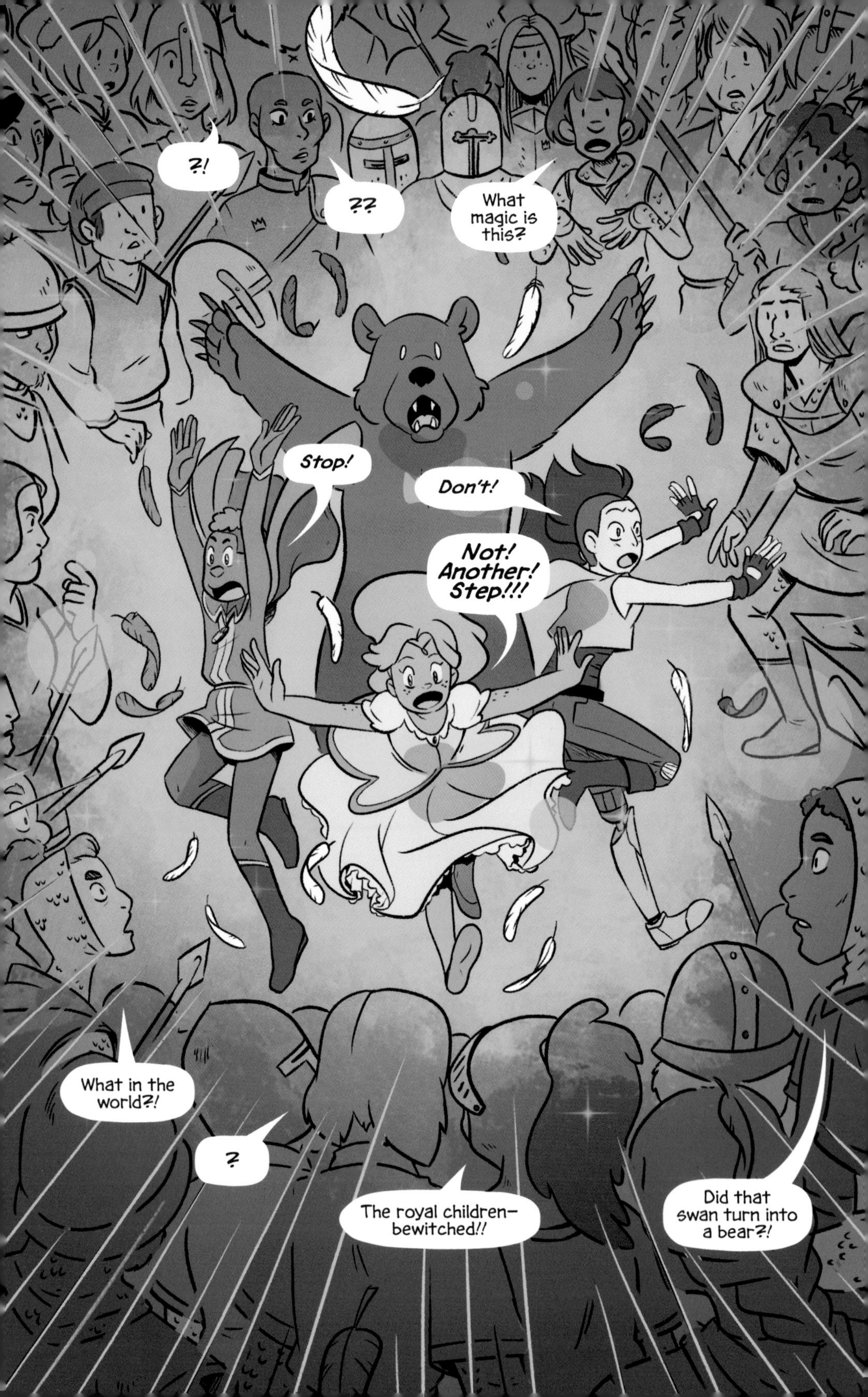
?!
??
What magic is this?
Stop!
Don't!
Not! Another! Step!!!
What in the world?!
?
The royal children—bewitched!!
Did that swan turn into a bear?!

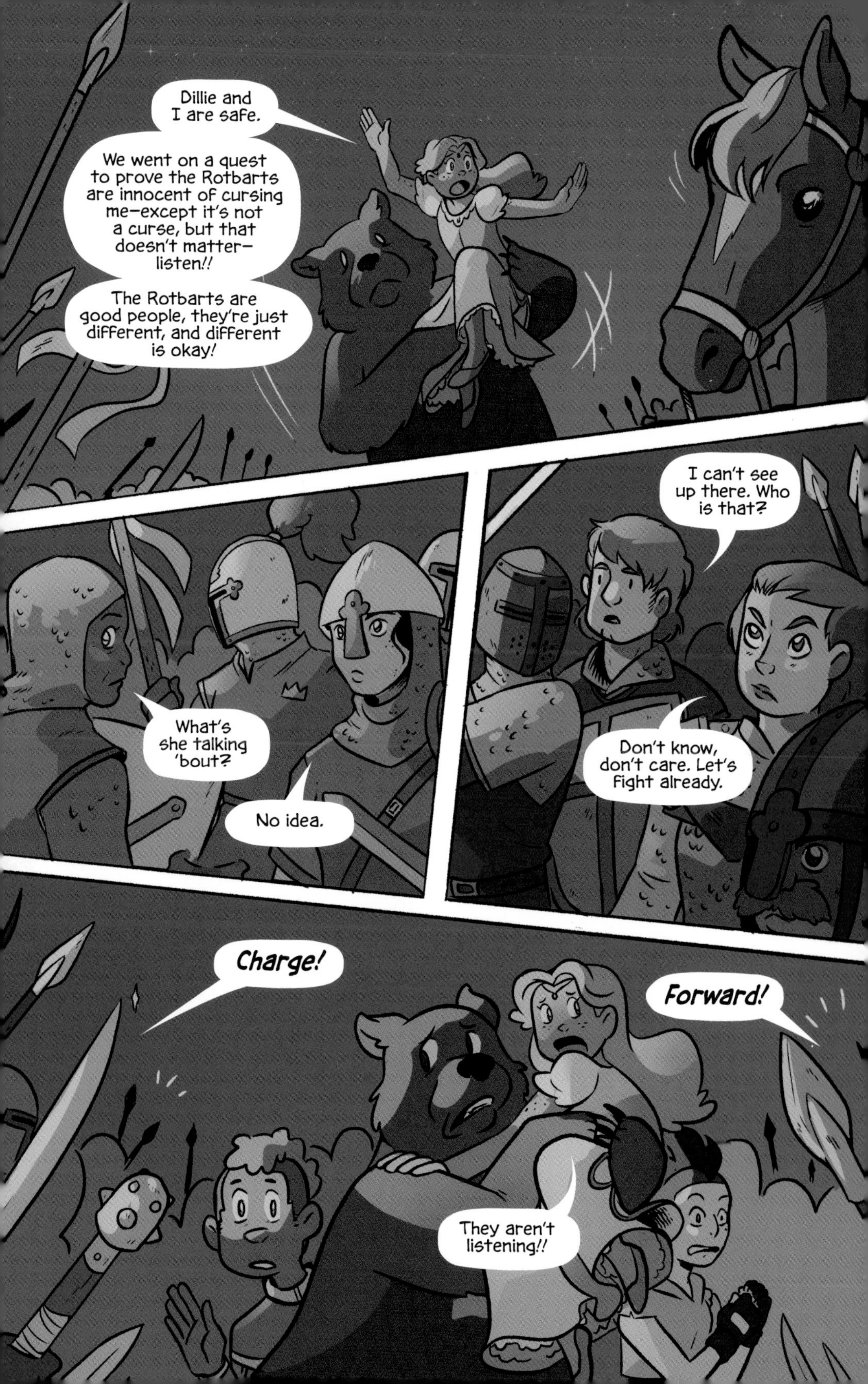
Dillie and I are safe.
We went on a quest to prove the Rotbarts are innocent of cursing me—except it's not a curse, but that doesn't matter—listen!!
The Rotbarts are good people, they're just different, and different is okay!
What's she talking 'bout?
No idea.
I can't see up there. Who is that?
Don't know, don't care. Let's fight already.
Charge!
Forward!
They aren't listening!!

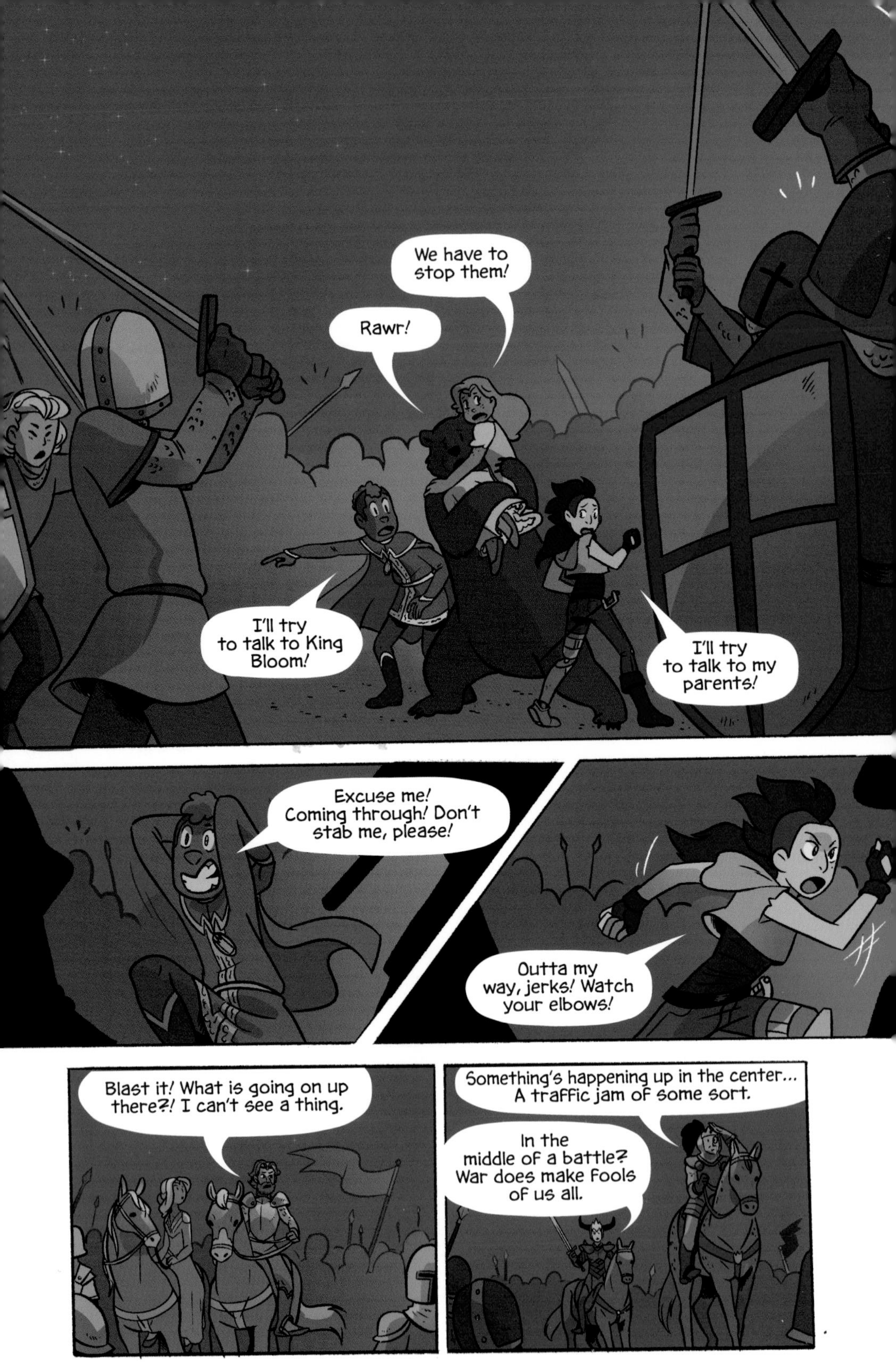
We have to stop them!
Rawr!
I'll try to talk to King Bloom!
I'll try to talk to my parents!
Excuse me! Coming through! Don't stab me, please!
Outta my way, jerks! Watch your elbows!
Blast it! What is going on up there?! I can't see a thing.
Something's happening up in the center... A traffic jam of some sort.
In the middle of a battle? War does make fools of us all.

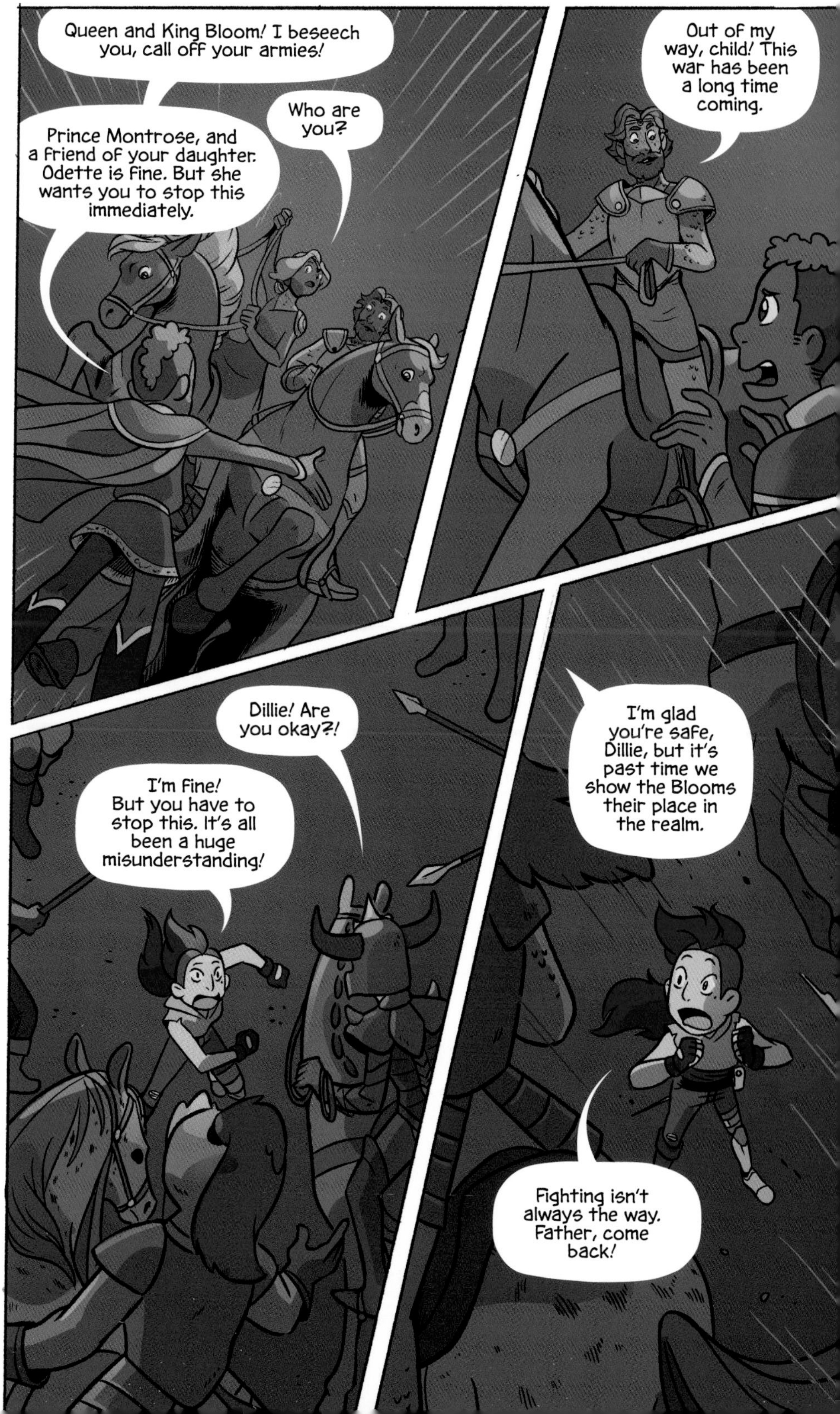
Queen and King Bloom! I beseech you, call off your armies!
Who are you?
Prince Montrose, and a friend of your daughter. Odette is fine. But she wants you to stop this immediately.
Out of my way, child! This war has been a long time coming.
Dillie! Are you okay?!
I'm fine! But you have to stop this. It's all been a huge misunderstanding!
I'm glad you're safe, Dillie, but it's past time we show the Blooms their place in the realm.
Fighting isn't always the way. Father, come back!

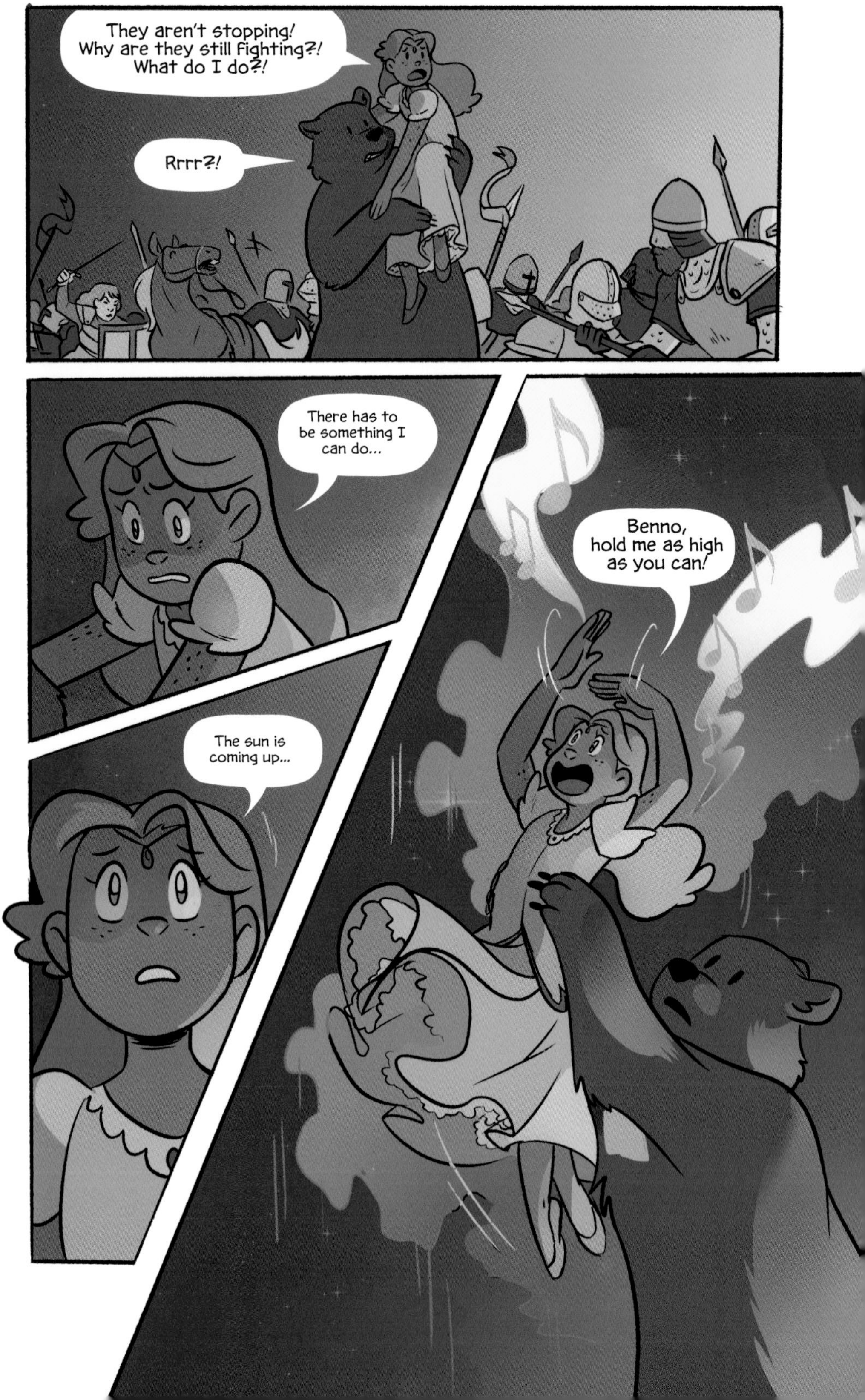
They aren't stopping! Why are they still fighting?! What do I do?!
Rrrr?!
There has to be something I can do...
The sun is coming up...
Benno, hold me as high as you can!

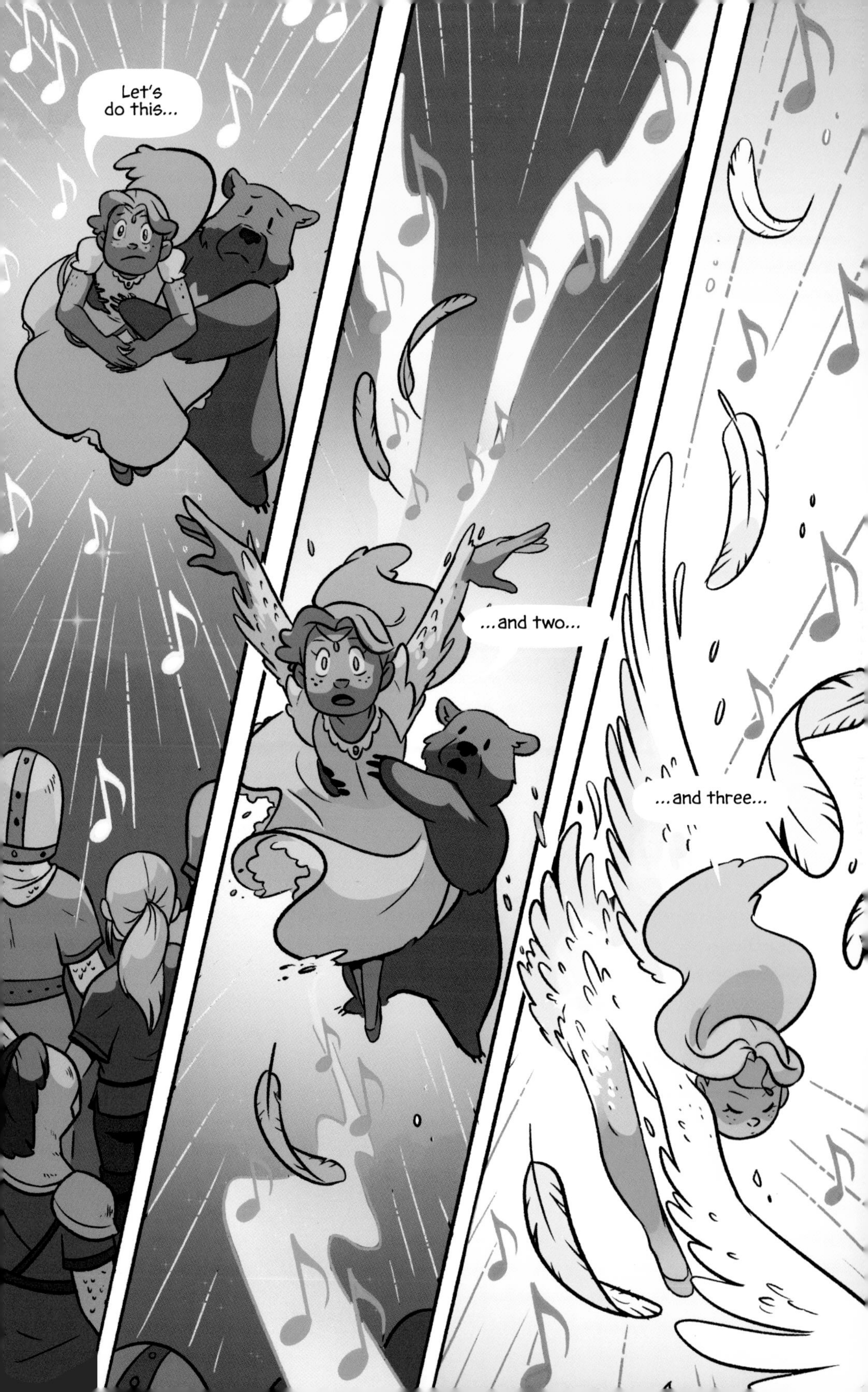
Let's do this...
...and two...
...and three...

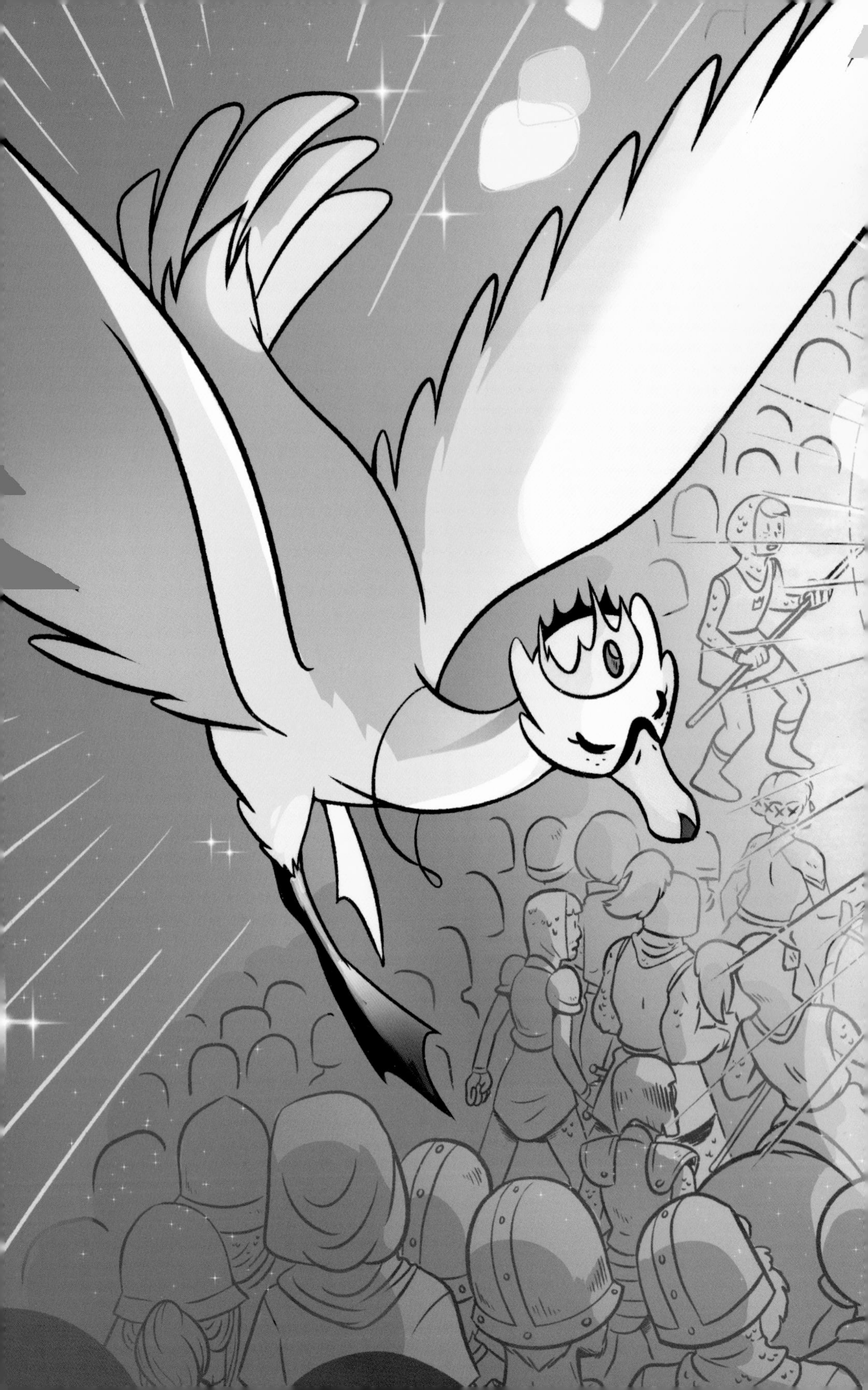

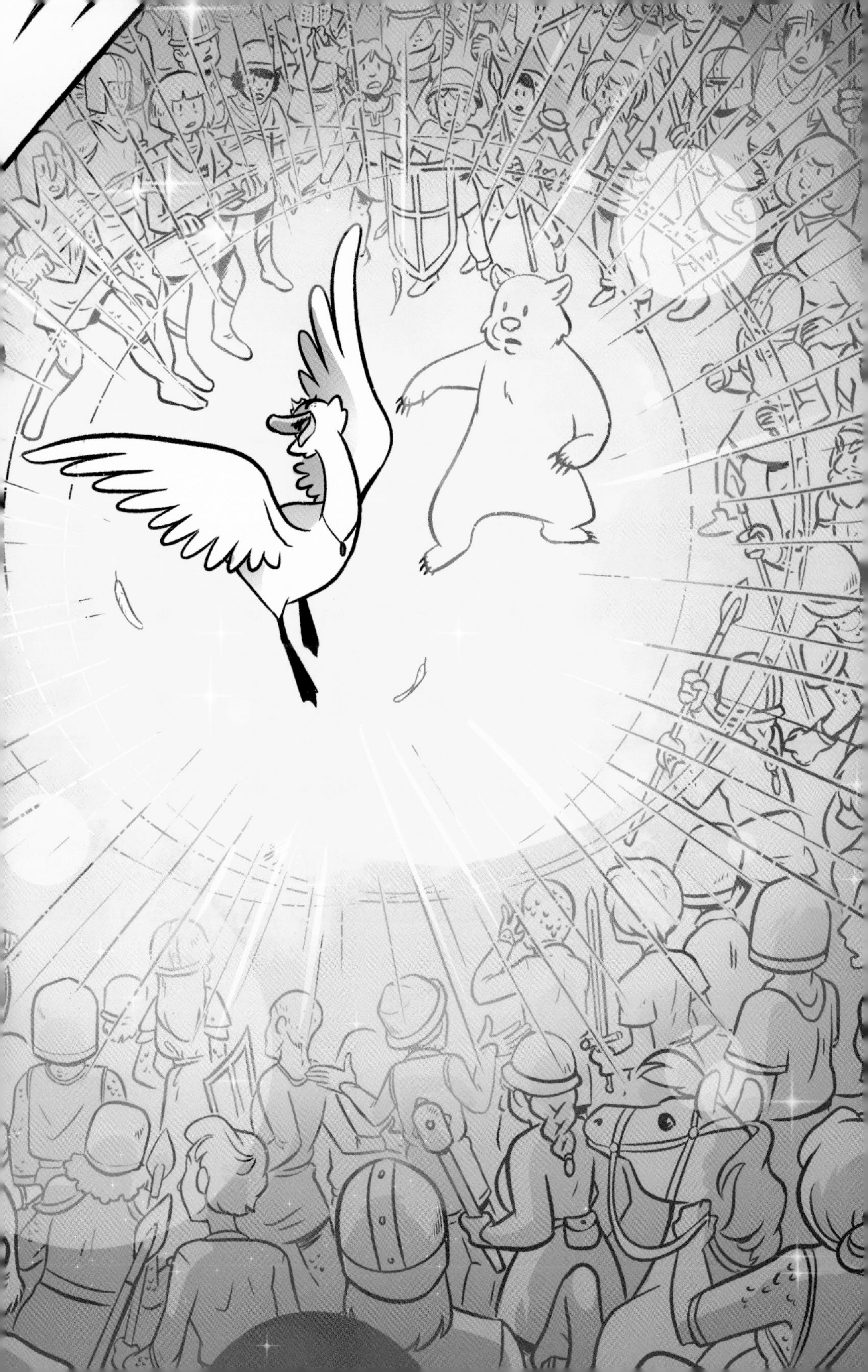

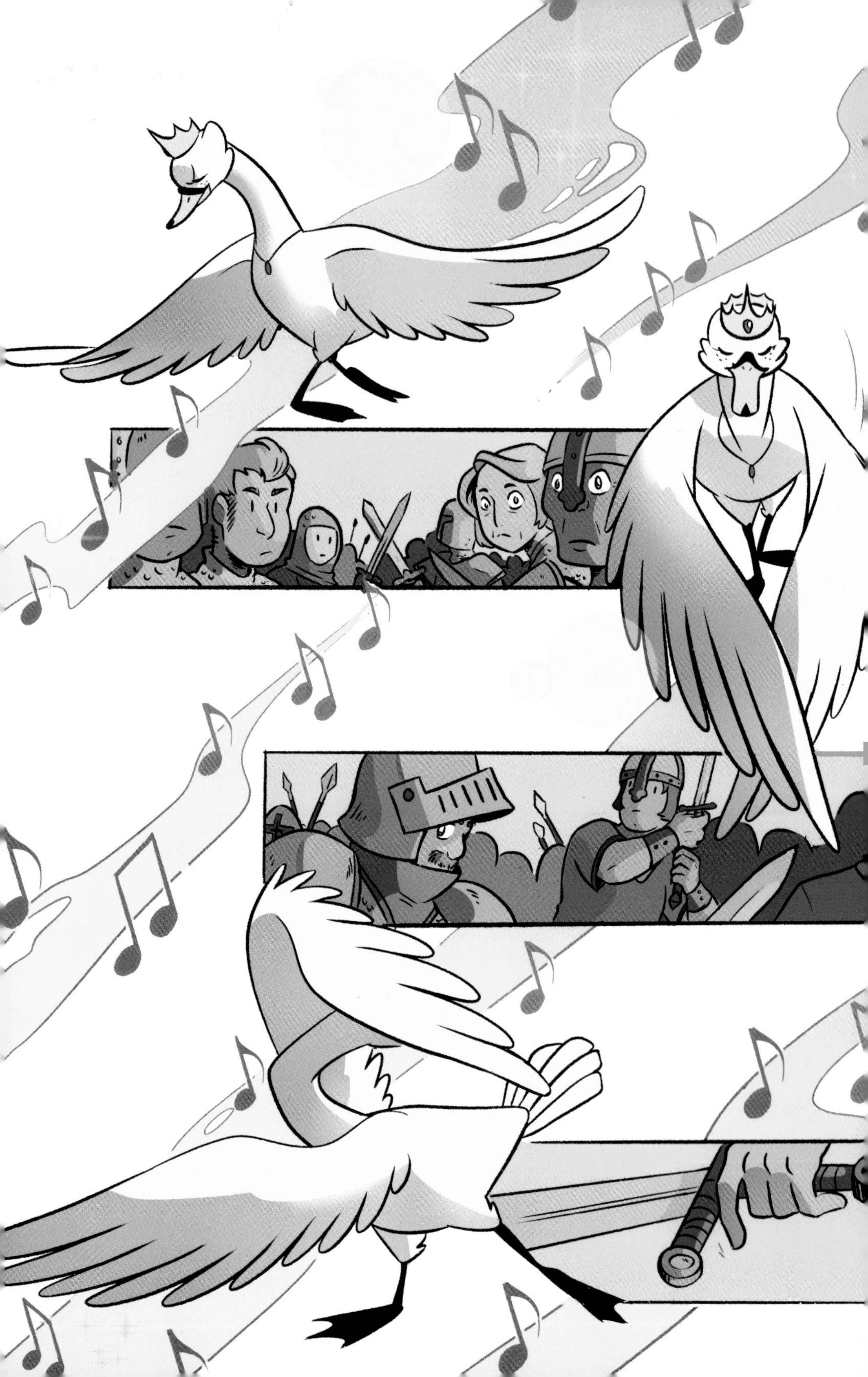

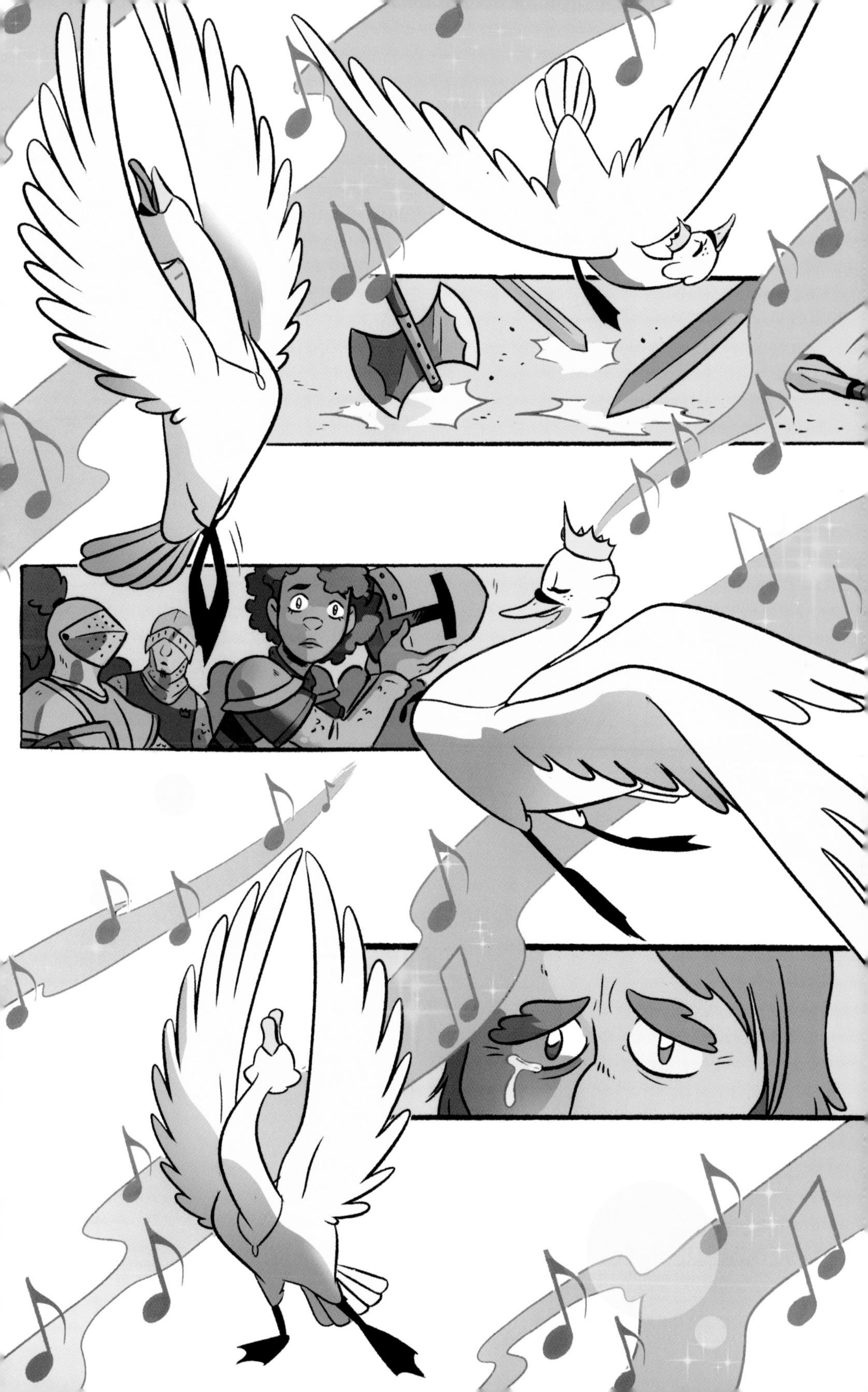

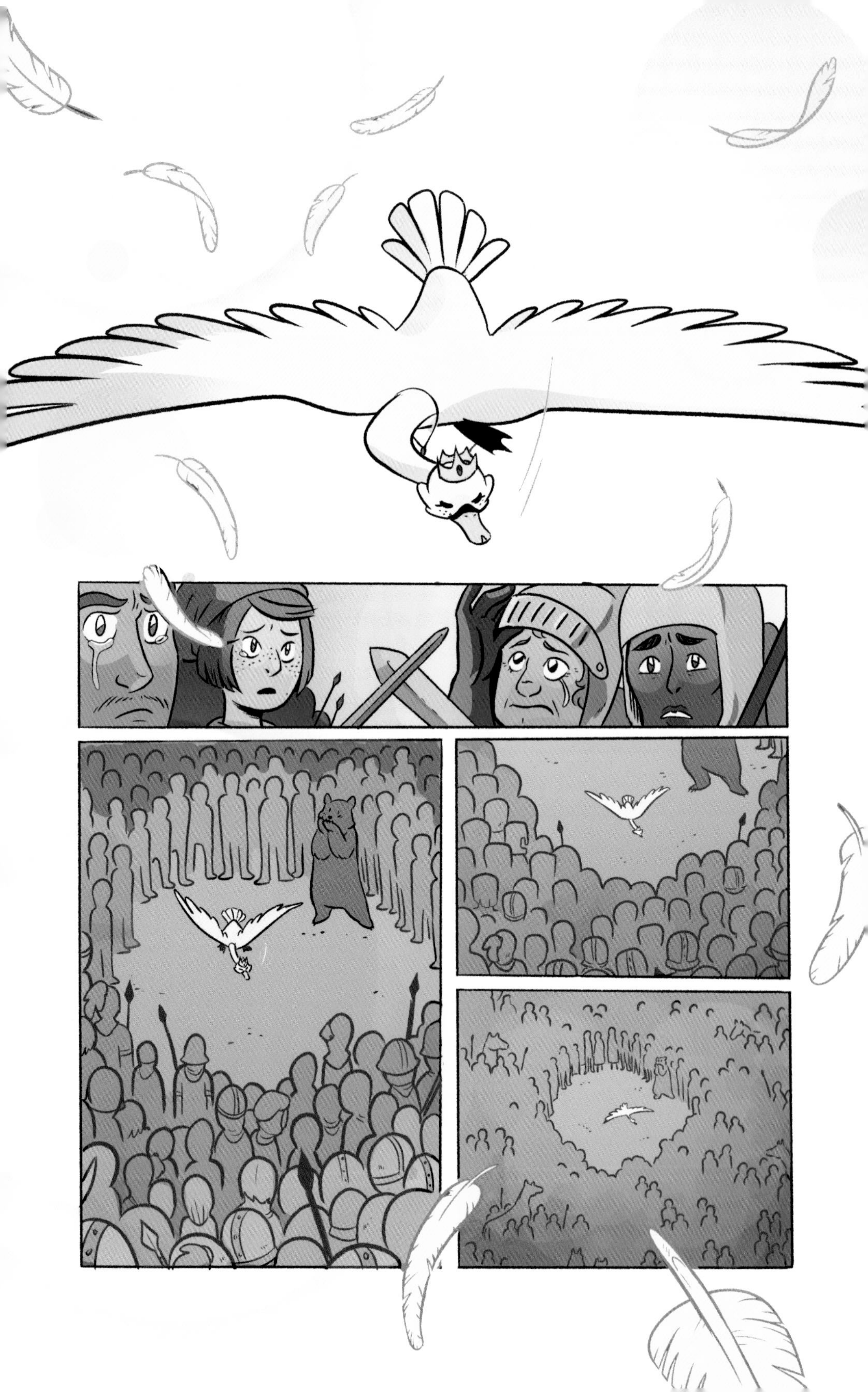

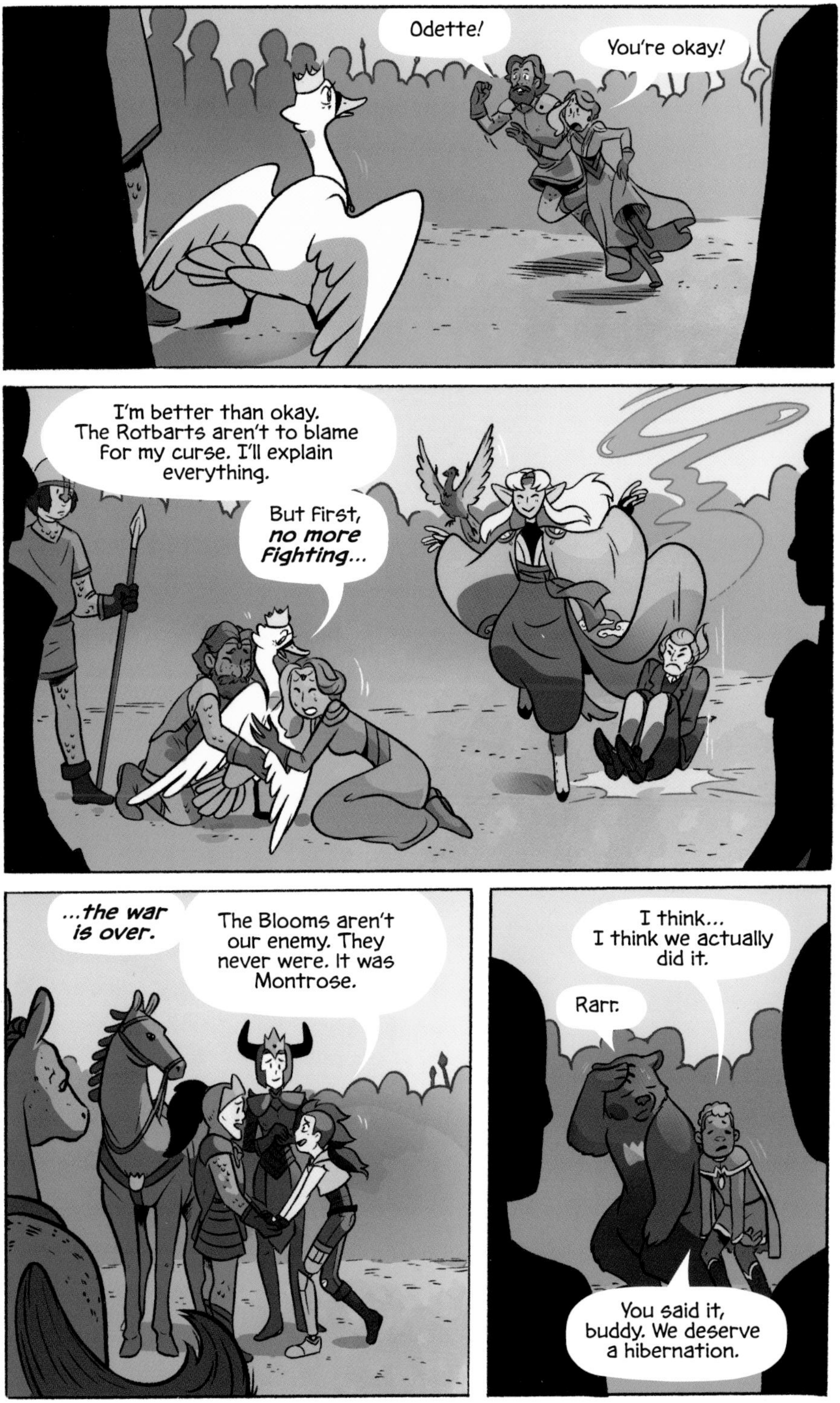
Odette!
You're okay!
I'm better than okay. The Rotbarts aren't to blame for my curse. I'll explain everything.
But first, *no more fighting...*
...the war is over.
The Blooms aren't our enemy. They never were. It was Montrose.
I think... I think we actually did it.
Rarr.
You said it, buddy. We deserve a hibernation.

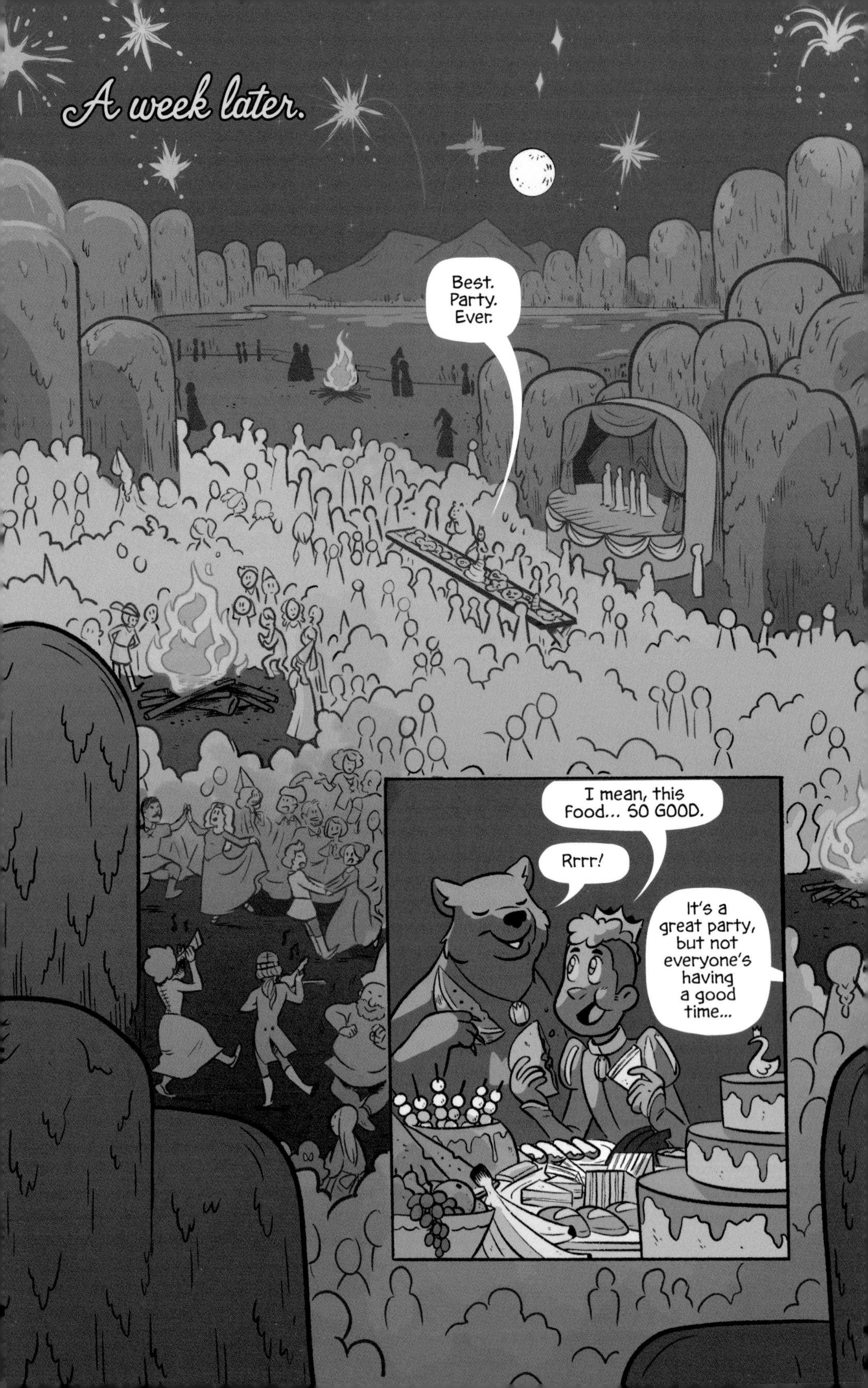
A week later.
Best. Party. Ever.
I mean, this food... SO GOOD.
Rrrr!
It's a great party, but not everyone's having a good time...

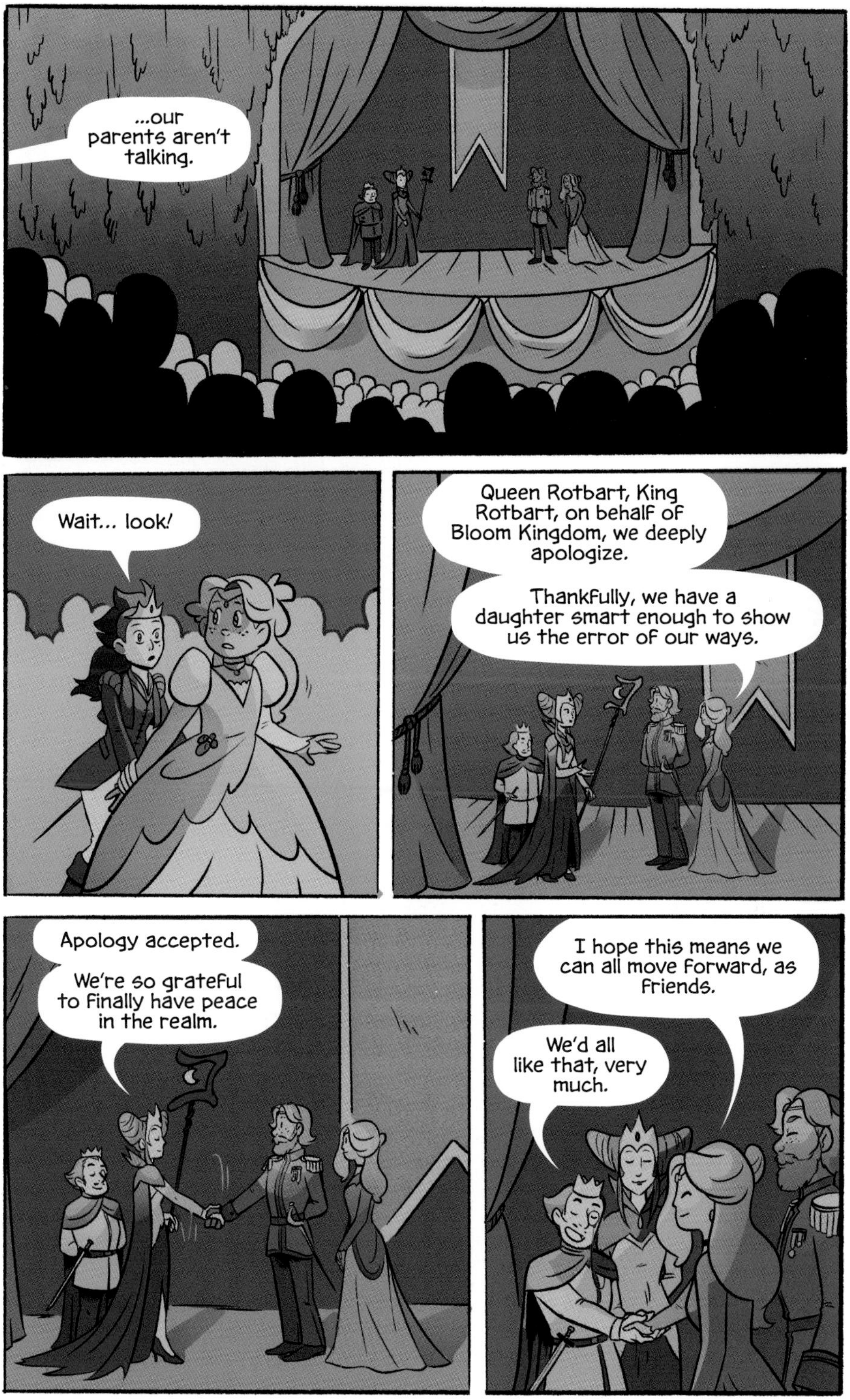
...our parents aren't talking.
Wait... look!
Queen Rotbart, King Rotbart, on behalf of Bloom Kingdom, we deeply apologize.
Thankfully, we have a daughter smart enough to show us the error of our ways.
Apology accepted.
We're so grateful to finally have peace in the realm.
I hope this means we can all move forward, as friends.
We'd all like that, very much.

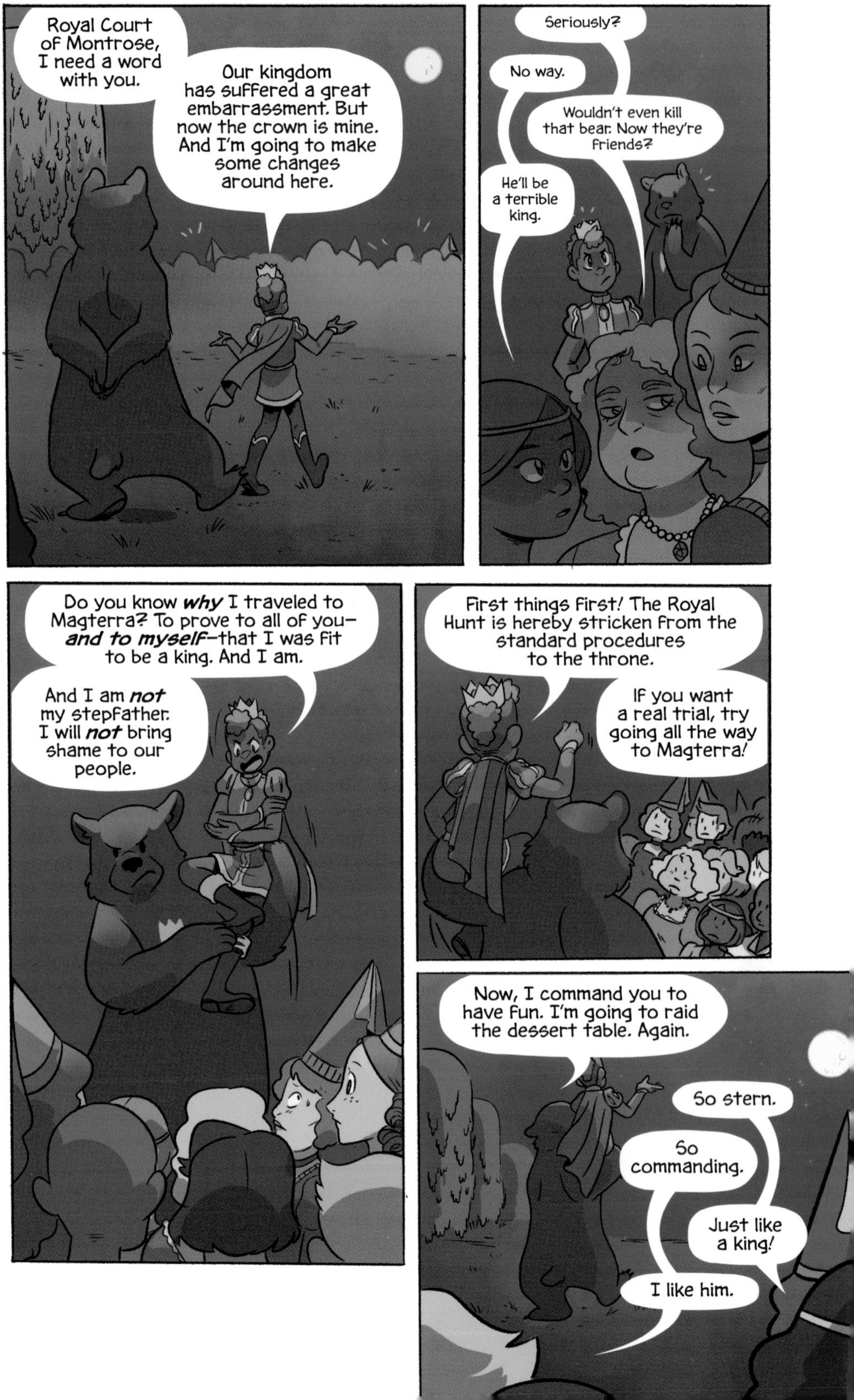
Royal Court of Montrose, I need a word with you.
Our kingdom has suffered a great embarrassment. But now the crown is mine. And I'm going to make some changes around here.
Seriously?
No way.
Wouldn't even kill that bear. Now they're friends?
He'll be a terrible king.
Do you know *why* I traveled to Magterra? To prove to all of you—*and to myself*—that I was fit to be a king. And I am.
And I am *not* my stepfather. I will *not* bring shame to our people.
First things first! The Royal Hunt is hereby stricken from the standard procedures to the throne.
If you want a real trial, try going all the way to Magterra!
Now, I command you to have fun. I'm going to raid the dessert table. Again.
So stern.
So commanding.
Just like a king!
I like him.

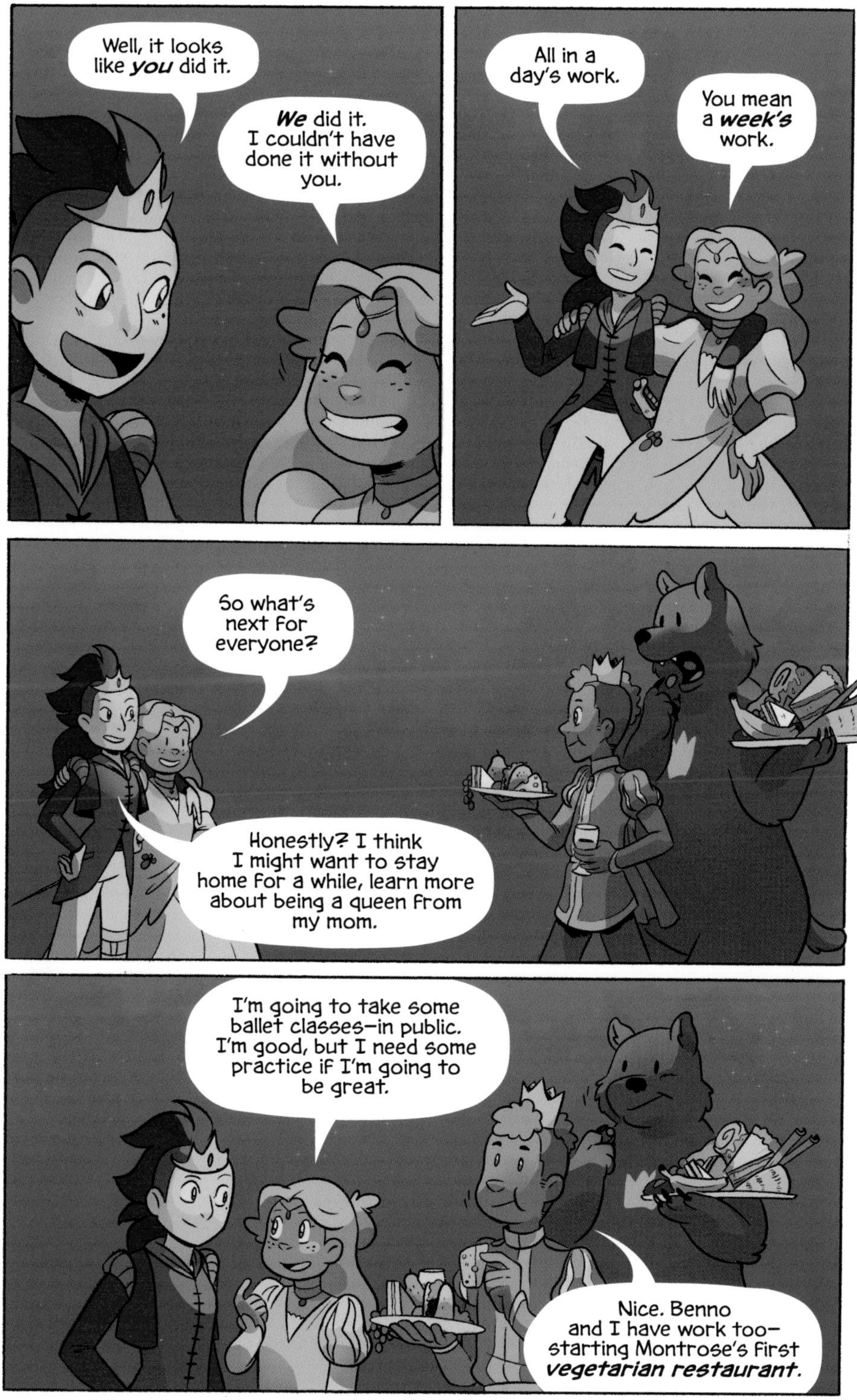
Well, it looks like *you* did it.
We did it. I couldn't have done it without you.
All in a day's work.
You mean a *week's* work.
So what's next for everyone?
Honestly? I think I might want to stay home for a while, learn more about being a queen from my mom.
I'm going to take some ballet classes—in public. I'm good, but I need some practice if I'm going to be great.
Nice. Benno and I have work too—starting Montrose's first *vegetarian restaurant*.

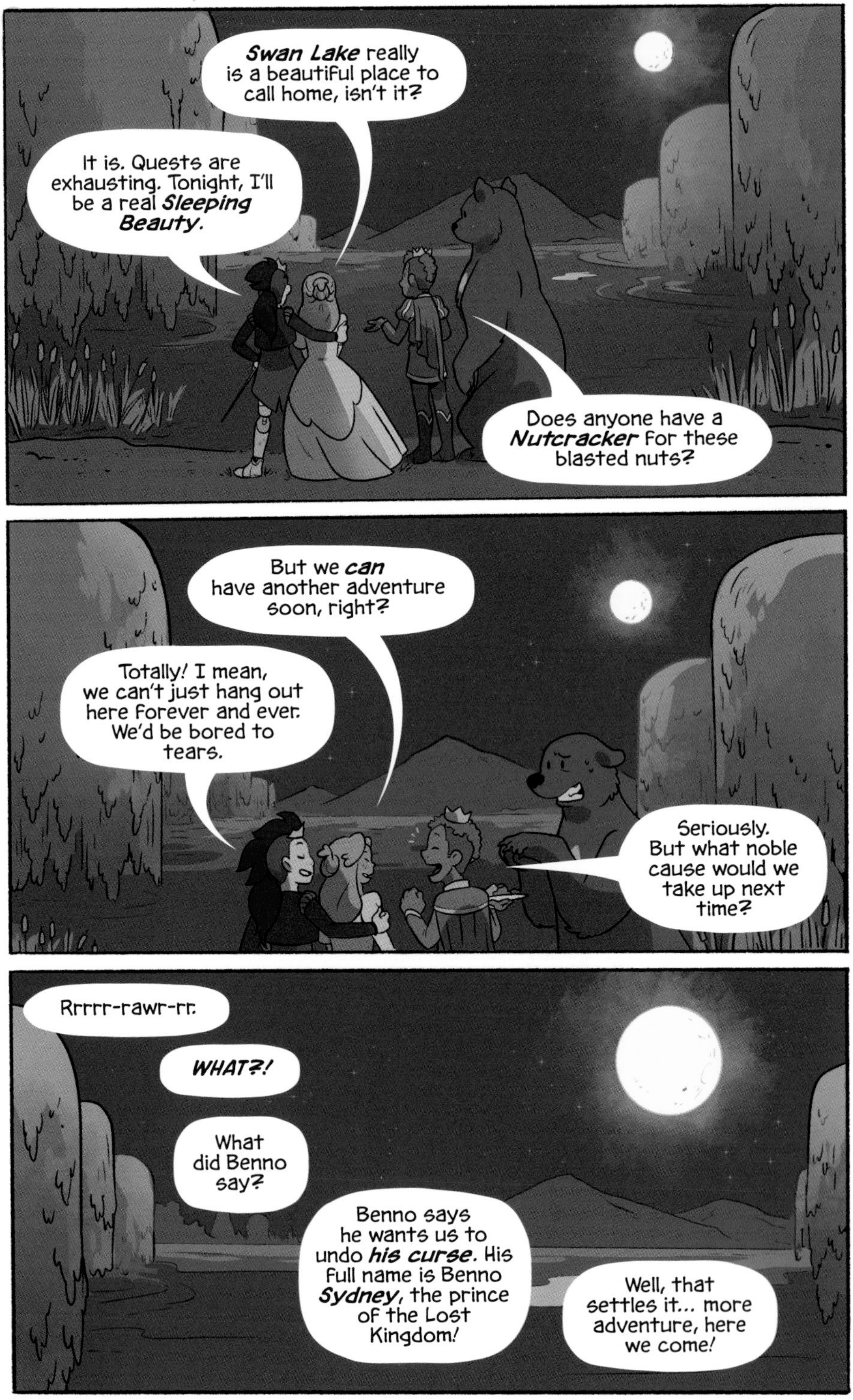

Swan Lake really is a beautiful place to call home, isn't it?
It is. Quests are exhausting. Tonight, I'll be a real Sleeping Beauty.
Does anyone have a Nutcracker for these blasted nuts?
But we can have another adventure soon, right?
Totally! I mean, we can't just hang out here forever and ever. We'd be bored to tears.
Seriously. But what noble cause would we take up next time?
Rrrrr-rawr-rr.
WHAT?!
What did Benno say?
Benno says he wants us to undo his curse. His full name is Benno Sydney, the prince of the Lost Kingdom!
Well, that settles it... more adventure, here we come!

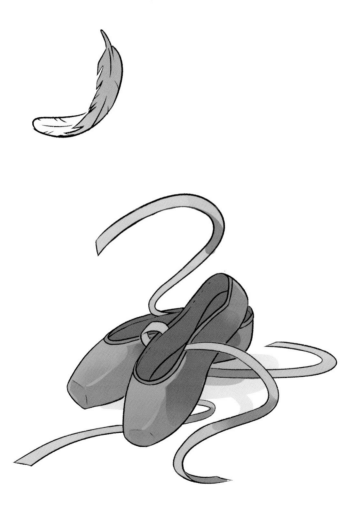

The End

Curses, Cowboys & Ballet

AUTHOR'S NOTE

I was a boy in Texas in the 1980s, and boys were supposed to be cowboys or army soldiers or astronauts. We were not supposed to be into ballet. But in first grade, Mrs. Hamm wheeled in a TV and a VCR and played us ***Swan Lake***, and I was mesmerized. It was the most beautiful and graceful thing I'd ever seen. And even cooler? Mrs. Hamm explained that it was a story about a princess turned into a swan by an evil sorcerer's curse. It sounded like my favorite cartoons: ***He-Man*** and ***Dungeons & Dragons***.

Of course, that weekend my mom's boyfriend found me dancing around the living room, trying to leap, and fly, and bounce on my tippy-toes, and—the hardest part—spin and spin and spin and spin (I'd later learn this was called a ***pirouette***). My mom's boyfriend took one look at me and sneered, "Quit acting like a dang sissy." I didn't know what a sissy was, but his tone suggested it wasn't a compliment.

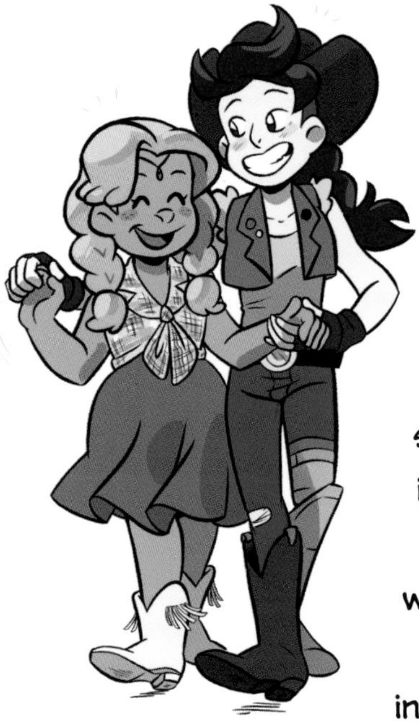

I honestly didn't understand what I'd done wrong. On Saturdays, I knew he and my mom dressed up in tight jeans, plaid shirts with pearl button snaps, and cowboy boots to go two-stepping. That was dancing. Why was cowboy dancing okay but ballet wasn't?

It was a different time, and I'd like to believe the world has come a long way. Maybe it has, maybe it hasn't. But what I do know now is that there's nothing wrong with a boy liking—even loving—ballet. It's a beautiful art form, as powerful an expression as painting or photography or writing a book or creating a graphic novel, like the one you now hold in your hands.

I kept dancing (not well, mind you), and anytime I was caught, I simply said I was playing *Spider-Man*, another hero of mine. It's funny that my mom's boyfriend considered that acceptable because if you've ever seen Peter Parker swinging around on a movie screen, then you know he's every bit as graceful and powerful as a ballet dancer.

As a writer, I wanted to create my own *Swan Lake*, a high-octane fantasy story that focused on friendship, adventure, and of course, a terrible curse. The result is this book, a love letter to my six-year-old self, to let him know he should keep dancing, keep having adventures, and never let anyone tell him that loving art is wrong.

-Rex Ogle
(aka Rey Terciero)
October 2020

A NOTE ABOUT THE ORIGINAL CREATOR

Born in 1840, **Pyotr Ilyich Tchaikovsky** was a Russian composer whose music, symphonies, and operas are

known all over the globe. He was probably best known in his own time for his orchestral composition of Shakespeare's ***Romeo & Juliet*** and the *1812 Overture,* which commemorated his country's successful defense against Napoleon's invading armies during the French Invasion of Russia three decades before Tchaikovsky's birth.

However, some would say his lasting legacy came in the form of three ballets: ***Sleeping Beauty, The Nutcracker,*** and ***Swan Lake.***

Tchaikovsky's ***Swan Lake*** was said to have been originally inspired by Russian and German folktales, including "The White Duck," collected by Alexander Afanasyev and "The Stolen Veil" by Johann Karl August Musäus, but went on to become its own tale. When

it debuted in 1877, it was considered a failure.

But, eventually, **Swan Lake** would grow to become one of the most popular ballets of all time. It is referenced in music, cartoons, movies, books, and even video games. It has also inspired dozens of retellings, re-imaginings, and re-inventions, including the one you've just read.

FOR MARK,
BEST FRIEND, PARTNER, AND MY HERO.
—REX

FOR MY GRANDMOTHER, BARBARA MINAKER.
PIANIST, POET, AND TEACHER.
—MEGAN

HarperAlley is an imprint of HarperCollins Publishers.
Swan Lake: Quest for the Kingdoms
Copyright © 2022 by Temple Hill Publishing LLC
All rights reserved. Manufactured in Bosnia and Herzegovina.
No part of this book may be used or reproduced in any manner
whatsoever without written permission except in the case of brief
quotations embodied in critical articles and reviews.
For information address HarperCollins Children's Books,
a division of HarperCollins Publishers,
195 Broadway, New York, NY 10007.
www.harperalley.com

Library of Congress Control Number: 2021941536
ISBN 978-0-06-294146-6 (paperback)
ISBN 978-0-06-294148-0 (hardcover)

Typography by Rob Steen
21 22 23 24 25   GPS   10 9 8 7 6 5 4 3 2 1
❖
First Edition